Summerwode

- BOOK FOUR OF THE WODE -

(Being a tale of Robin Hood (a.k.a. Robyn Hode)

J TULLOS HENNIG

Forest Path Books

SUMMERWODE

Published by
FOREST PATH BOOKS
Summerwode Copyright © 2017 by J Tullos Hennig. All rights reserved.

Forest Path Books publications may be purchased for educational, business, or sales/promotional use.
For information please email the publishers at:
info@forestpathbooks.com
or address:
Forest Path Books, LLC
P. O. Box 847, Stanwood, WA 98292 USA

Stay informed on our releases and news!
Join the reading group/newsletter at:
https://forestpathbooks.com/into-the-forest/

Interior and Cover design © 2021 Mahli (*bookdesignbymahli.com*)
Cover content is for illustrative purposes only, and any person depicted on the cover is a model.
Map illustration © 2017 by J Tullos Hennig
Pi Rho Runestones font © Peter Rempel (licensed for use)
First published in North America by DSP Publications, 2017

Library of Congress Cataloging: 2019918881
ISBNs:
978-1-951293-37-6 (hardcover)
978-1-951293-59-8 (trade paper)
978-1-951293-08-6 (e-book)

READERS LOVE THE BOOKS OF THE WODE!

"Hennig's Wode series continues to reinvent the legend of Robin Hood . . . Thick with conflict and intrigue, this retelling turns a well-known legend into a fresh, earthy tale of human passions twisted by politics and ancient powers."
—*Publishers Weekly*

"There's nothing quite so exciting as an author taking an overused traditional narrative and breathing full and rich life into it the way that Hennig does with her retelling of the Robin Hood/Green Man stories in her *Greenwode* series. I was smitten, right from the beginning."
—*Charles de Lint*

"Hennig expertly weaves the threads together in seductive, evocative prose that put me in the scene as few others have ever done . . . An enthralling transformation of folklore and legend into something wonderfully original from start to finish."
—*Susan R. Matthews*

"An intensely emotional, breathtaking version of the Robin Hood legend . . . Beautifully showcases the cultural and religious upheaval between peasant versus nobility, oppressed versus oppressors . . . Highly recommended."
—*Bella Online*

"A complex, meticulously researched, and vividly realised re-imagining of the Robin Hood myth, which depicts Robin and Guy as lovers instead of sworn enemies."
—*A Swimming Pool Library*

"I can't recommend this book highly enough. The prose is poetic, powerful, insightful. Hennig has a masterful command of weaponry and battle-speak, as well of wode magic. This is a soul-plumbing, life-changing experience."
—*Historical Novel Society Review*

"It felt like discovering a fine wine. There was incredible tension: romantic, character-driven, and plot-driven. This isn't a light sip of a read."
—*Queer SciFi*

"Given the author's innate ability to take classic lore and make it new again through works of fantasy, fans of other genres or literature in general are sure to enjoy these."
—*Amazing Stories Magazine*

"With *The Wode* books, Hennig weaves Welsh mythology into the classic tale and reimagines Robin Hood and Guy of Gisbourne as lovers and Maid Marian as Robin's sister–and all three entwined by magic and fate. The world-building is intricate, the language is gorgeous . . . and the characters are achingly flawed. It's the best Robin Hood retelling I've encountered."
—*Kathy Shin, Pages below the Vaulted Sky*

- BOOKS BY J TULLOS HENNIG -

The Books of the Wode
(Tales of Robin Hood, a.k.a. Robyn Hode)

Greenwode
Shirewode
Winterwode
Summerwode
Wyldingwode

To the readers--

Without whom those of us cursed/blessed to be storytellers would just be gibbering to the shadows on the wall.

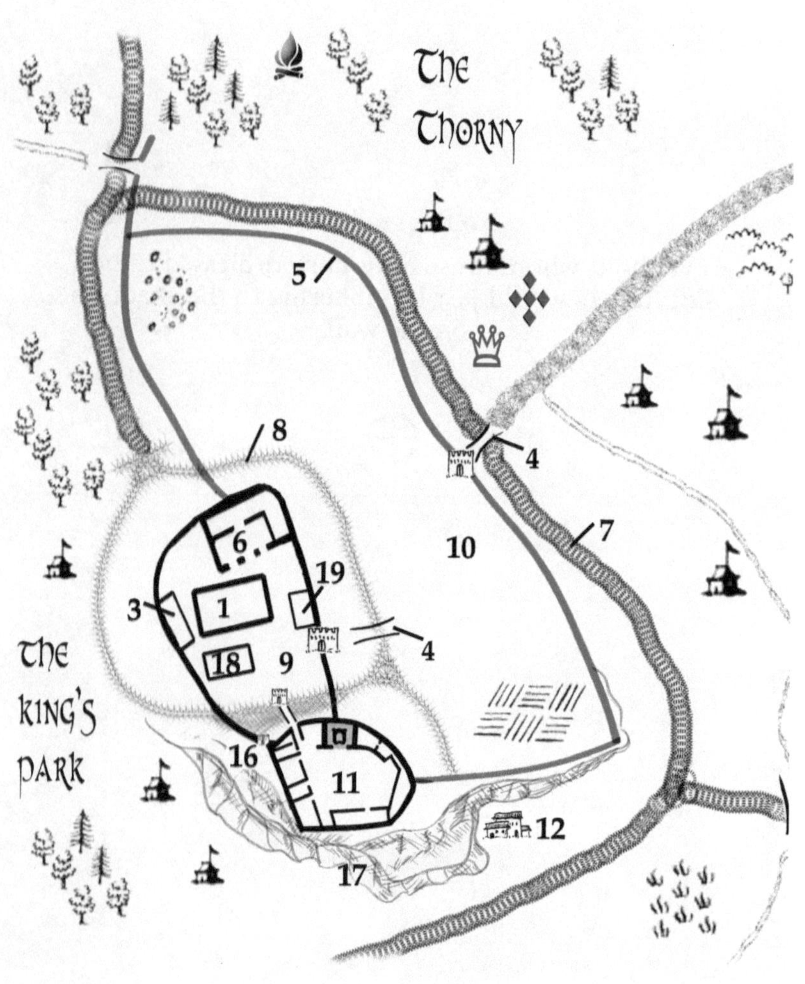

The Thorny
The King's Park
5
8
6
19
3
1
18
9
16
11
17
12
10
4
4
7

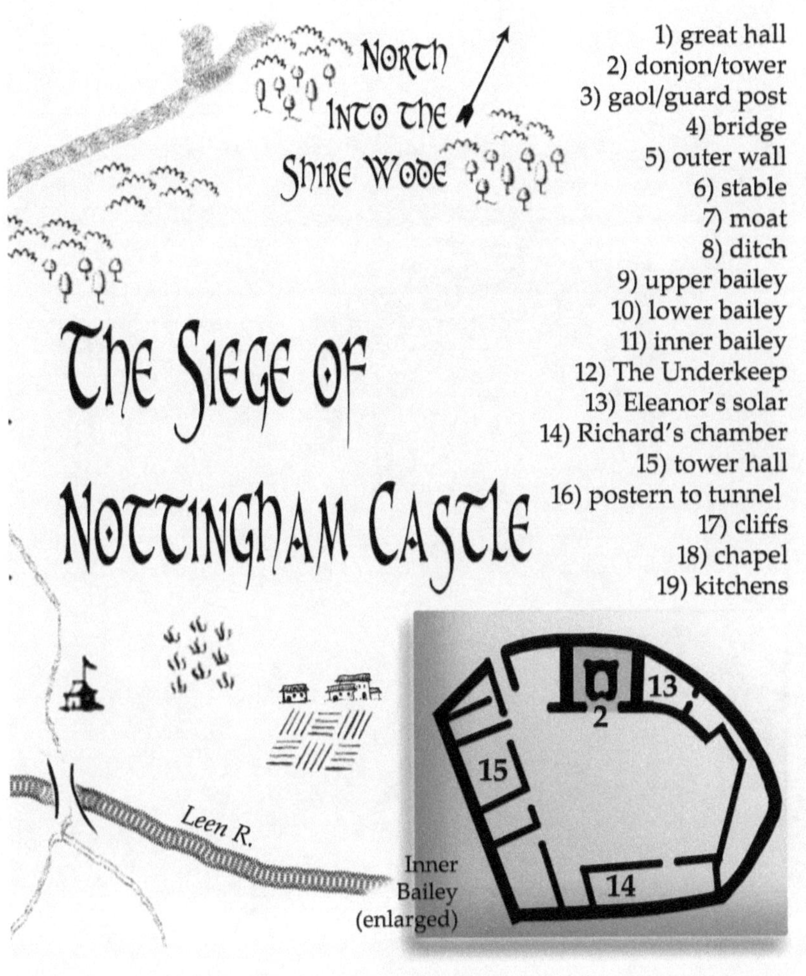

NORTH
INTO THE
SHIRE WODE
THE SIEGE OF
NOTTINGHAM CASTLE
Leen R.
1) great hall
2) donjon/tower
3) gaol/guard post
4) bridge
5) outer wall
6) stable
7) moat
8) ditch
9) upper bailey
10) lower bailey
11) inner bailey
12) The Underkeep
13) Eleanor's solar
14) Richard's chamber
15) tower hall
16) postern to tunnel
17) cliffs
18) chapel
19) kitchens
Inner Bailey (enlarged)
2
13
15
14

Summerwode

- PRELUDE -

Nottingham Castle
Waxing of Oimelc
(Feast of the Maiden), 1194 CE

Candles, everywhere.

Full dozens of them illuminated the east-facing solar, commingling with the roaring hearth to banish murk from stubborn corners. Nevertheless, shadows lingered. In alcoves they tarried, and from without the light-filled sanctuary, they crept over stone walls into the stair beyond, dispersed only by an inadequate spatter of gilt to mark comings and goings.

And when the candles thought to gutter, John, Count of Mortain and Lord of Gloucester, demanded more.

Nightmares lingered in Nottingham Castle.

He knew why. Comprehended the realities—all of them—as few others might. Still, he craved light even as he nursed its reminders. The possibilities. The impediments . . . aye, the impediments.

It had been a right bloody bastard of a fortnight.

One of his favourite castles invaded—not by storm and fire, but by a horde of savages who'd stolen his best piece in a crooked, desperate game. The hunt after, a failure. The removal from Blyth Castle to here in Nottingham, a dogged try at re-establishing what political ties he could, dispelling an enduring terror of spectres from a hellish Hallows . . .

And then, this.

He'd known it was coming. But, still.

John gave the fire a savage thrust with the iron poker. Sparks fled upward and flared, albeit cold, against the emerald adorning his left hand. The centre log collapsed with another burst of light. Spilled gold over the clenched parchment.

"My lord, I—"

"Count. You will address Us as Count John. Or my liege." Poker still in hand, John put his backside to the fire, contemplating both the hastily vacated bed and the figure to whom he spoke, standing shadowed by the post drapes. "For despite circumstance rendering Us low, We are nevertheless the latter. Yes?"

"Of course, my liege," the figure soothed. "I was merely—"

"Questioning me. And what else would you have me do? Just knuckle under whilst my brother beggars England? First his bedamned holy war, and now this!" Rage nearly choked him. He gave another savage poke at the fire, showering sparks. "God's *teeth*, but more than a king's ransom is worth! All for my mother's precious and shining idiot son!"

Over by the open door, Nottingham's newest castellan inched towards escape, gaze equally held by his liege lord and by the one still lurking in the shadows.

Bloody annoying, that.

"And always, your like in the midst of it! Riding in mid-night, upsetting everything, dragging me from my bed and scaring that poor maid so."

The castellan started to make excuse, realised the words were, again, not for him, and continued his steady creep.

"It took well over a se'nnight to cozen her from her shift, and now your dour manner and that bloody cross on your chest has no doubt set me back another!"

Silence. John gave a fleeting grin—he knew exactly with what weapons to pink his visitor—and rounded on his retreating castellan. "Murdac!"

The man froze in place, his broad, bewhiskered face nigh white with both fear and regret. He had nearly made the door.

John let him bask in both for a full intake of breath, then snapped, "Wine! Mulled hot and sweet!"

A flush this time, dark as the man's beard, and Murdac wheeled, making a grateful escape into the shadows.

It was humiliating, but John didn't envy him.

The candles glimmered, warm sanity, over the draperies and tapestries. John stretched a hand out towards one, flitting his fingers through, back and forth. "Of course, you and your like always are. In the midst of things."

"It is the way of our Order, my lord Count. It has, I would suggest, in its time served you well."

The shadowed acknowledgment was silk over steel, but conciliatory. As it should be. Along with his other titles, John was overlord of this bloody castle beneath their feet and regent of England—well, to be frank, his mother had been that for the past several years—but no matter. He was damned determined to be more. *Was* more.

"And as to my precipitous entry, I fear I'd little choice." A pale flicker in the shadows, the heavy shush of a cloak being flung back. A gesture towards the parchment clenched in John's fist. "Particularly once my agents delivered *that.*"

Rage swelled, humid heat, and John lurched forwards. In the next moment, dread choked the furious outburst, roiling in from the shadowy stones. John scooted back for the fire—for the light.

Had John been his father, he would have stomped and bellowed, rolled on the floor, and chewed the rushes. His brother Richard would have laughed, then led his mercenaries to burn a few towns in retribution. No fear in them . . . no imagination.

They'd no need for it. They'd never been the least of anything. They didn't know. Hadn't seen. Hadn't . . . Seen.

"My lord?" It was rigid with calm.

As if that calm were contagious, John turned, took a deep breath, and met the Templar's gaze.

"You must take care, my lord Count," Wymarec de Birkin counselled, low. "He is, after all, our king."

"'He is, after all, our king.'" Mockery curled upon John's lips. "Is he, then? Truly?"

The pale blue eyes shifted, uneasy.

"And what sort of king? Barren as his sodding marriage—taking, always taking! From the moment I stood on my own and reached for what was mine, he was set to take it. Or had it given to him as if by right! Even now . . . " Dropping his gaze to the parchment, John refused to unclench his stiff fingers. The emerald ring glittered, hand atremble.

Shadows in Nottingham. Ghosts in the Wode, and a power called from it to eclipse his own. And now, one line—just one line, set with ink and careful quill. One line, to inspire more dread.

Look to yourself—the Devil is loose.

No signature or felicitation. None was needed; John recognised France's hand. Lovely, treacherous Phillip had penned this himself.

Wymarec was frowning. Or was he? Damn Templars, anyway, they'd no fear of shadows—they captured and set them to their bidding with countenances of iron and ice.

"Master of England, eh?" John growled. "You, Master de Birkin, mouth promises of powers and unholy Kingships, yet all the while, you play Us with this game of yours!"

"It is no game, my lord. Surely—"

"Game. You bluff keenly as any dice peddler, claim to wield things which you do not yet possess, whilst my brother beggars the country, blind to any might save that of mace and chain, sword and cross. And wins. Whilst a wolfshead rides with demons, calls spirits down upon my people and my lands, takes my forest and my crown! And wins!" It was ramping up into a scream, and he didn't care. "He is mocking me, and you give him aid?"

"Not aid, my liege. A spy. Gisbourne will find what needs be known."

"So you say?" John snorted. "Unless you're keen to know the size of the wolfshead's prick, I doubt you'll gain much from your precious Sir Guy."

"A small price to pay, lying with animals," de Birkin insisted, albeit cautious, "if one can learn secrets thought long lost to us. Such a power, my liege! It still lingers in Nottingham Castle, whispering within every shadow of the stones beneath our feet."

The sentiment sank home with a barbed and poisoned crossbow bolt. John shivered, inched closer to the fire. Realised the parchment remained, clenched, in his fist. A talisman of ruin—or mayhap just of patience.

All he could hope for now was escape. Richard indeed had the devil's luck, always had. What was there for John to do but let his brother further plunder the kingdom? He could hardly stop him. Could do little but wait.

But the waiting? Interminable.

With a snarl, John threw the parchment into the hearth. It flared, brief brilliance to shame the tens of candles. Dread retreated, banished by scorn even as light chased shadow and nightmare into their corners. And suddenly John found himself laughing.

"My lord?" De Birkin looked puzzled.

"What a homecoming our lovely king shall have! A country drained of its resources, nothing more to give him. A brutal winter, poor hunting, meagre crops. And an eldritch power that Richard could never wield or understand, coiled in wait for him."

Upon the hearth the parchment roiled, curling into sullen embers. Still chuckling, John shook his head.

"The devil is indeed loose—in Sherwood Forest! And I daresay my dear, lumbering brother has no idea."

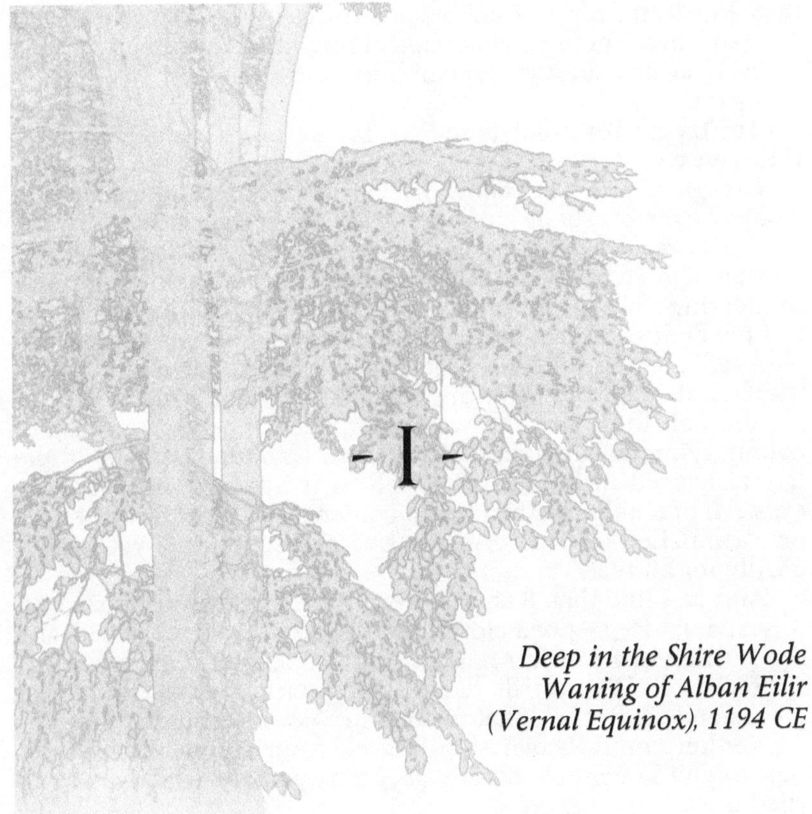

- I -

Deep in the Shire Wode
Waning of Alban Eilir
(Vernal Equinox), 1194 CE

"I can't."

"You mean you wain't."

"I mean exactly what I said."

Stubborn git. Robyn whirled on Gamelyn, angry-quick, and Gamelyn rocked back, almost tripping on a gorse. "You mean, you *wain't!*" Only a step more and Robyn was on him, nose to nose. Gamelyn's expression had an instant of shock—slight, to be sure, but there.

Good. It meant Robyn was getting to him.

"You're the one who won't. You're not even trying to understand." Aye, the mild control to Gamelyn's voice had a scratch around the edges, and his eyes more the giveaway, witching from soft juniper to a gilt-trimmed verdigris.

If only it were witchcraft. The beginnings of admission, or agreement, or capitulation to . . . well . . . everything. If only it weren't threatening to rain. Again. If only the sun would make some sort of appearance and dry the slippery ground beneath their booted feet. If only the bloody game weren't wily as hares— again—and they'd not tracked that hart halfway to Nottingham, then lost it. If only Robyn, brassed off at losing their first fresh meal in a brace of fortnights, hadn't brought all this up just to ram his head against another type of brass and stone.

Again.

"I'm trying to understand! You're the one's makin' precious little sense!"

Enough of this squabbling, the Horned Lord rumbled behind Robyn's eyes, his shade a resolute track upon their heels. *You and the Maid are too lenient. Put the Oak on his knees and keep him there.*

Gamelyn scowled—he'd heard—and twitched akin to a horse shuddering a biting fly from his withers. "I'm not making any sense? Is it my fault you seem incapable of using what brains you have?"

Aye, Robyn was definitely getting to him. Gamelyn only tossed the *bloody stupid peasant* die when he was that angry. Not to mention all those freckles were disappearing beneath a flush of colour vying for a match with his hair. Unbound, strands of the latter snagged in his beard . . . all of it bronzed against those eyes. All of it akin to metal left in winter rains—held frozen by his own runnelled-on rust of pride and protection . . . yet canny-deadly for all that.

And just like that, Robyn's own fury melted from brassed off to sexed up. He stepped closer, head cocked, eyebrows lifted, and lips curling in a smirk. An appreciative one—yet Gamelyn didn't appreciate it. His nostrils flared white, stark contrast to all that ginger-and-scarlet . . . that furious, he was, and couldn't hide it.

Neither could Robyn stop himself from saying, "Sweet Lady, but do you know how bloody gorgeous you are when you're all riled up?"

"God grant me patience!" It escaped—not without an accompanying eye roll—and one hard hand slapped against Robyn's chest, gave a shove that sent him sprawling.

Right, then. Mayhap a good rut wasn't in order, even though sometimes 'twere a bloody fine way to quit an argument.

The Horned Lord growled louder.

Not that you're helping! Robyn growled back, and started after.

Gamelyn stampeded across the small clearing before he lurched to a stop—and then Robyn wasn't sure but that sodden curtain of willow hadn't been the true reason.

Its own giveaway, that.

Gamelyn made a snatch at the lithe green branches before him, and they sent a shower over his boots. Indeed, the woodland hung heavy about them, scented and thick and nigh dripping—plumped not only with rain, but the beginnings of spring. With waiting. No longer time to hold back, or yearn after oaths gone conflicted and awry. It was long past any expectations that Summer should keep dragging his feet like he wished the frost would cover him . . . *again.*

Gamelyn half turned, opened his mouth, closed it again. Finally said, "You know the only reason they let me go."

They didn't let you go. They made you. That still lay between them, a hot brand neither would touch.

But Gamelyn wasn't the only one who could bite back words until his teeth bled. Revision was proper unnatural to Robyn, but he did it—several times over in his head—and settled for "Marion wants it. The Horned Lord, the Lady. It . . . it must be done."

"And you? What do you want? And me—what about what I want? Am I allowed an opinion in this?"

Bloody damn, what is he on about? Robyn sent the darting, inward query to god or goddess or forest spirits all woven with them into skeins of *tynged.* But there was nowt to be found in the foretelling or the fate. Merely ice and rust, a cairn carven deep and bound about with iron.

Aye, but his lovely Oakbrother had barriers like to none Robyn had ever known. Such times he wished Marion were here, to untangle the secret weave of metal and stone when Robyn himself couldn't broach it with fire. Maybe that was the problem. Robyn had always been the throwback, too much of his mother's Barrow blood rushing his veins.

Iron was murder to the fae, after all.

"Gamelyn." Robyn pitched it soft—light as his footfalls, coming after. "You're here, en't you? I even think most-times you want to be here."

"I *do* want—"

"Then come with me. To the caverns."

"Aren't you afraid of what I'll witness?" It was flat.

"How can you betray what's yours?"

Ah, and that went home, somehow. A bone-deep shudder along that rigid spine—and more, quivering its way through heart and mind.

Robyn scented it, marked it. Stole after. "Twill be all the more yours after I take you below. Me and John'll see to it, see you to rights. See you prepared for what comes of it."

The words were gentle, reasonable. But Gamelyn was no less a predator; he sensed the stalk beneath.

"You're willing to take me into the caverns and do this—"

"Initiation. Aye."

"And you're not worried about what I'll witness."

"It's what you'll See that matters. And that, you'll take nowhere."

"And you're sure of that."

"Never sure with you, pet, there's too much as you keep close when you needn't. But this I do know. You'll not be able t' speak of what comes, save to those as have rights to hear." Robyn put a hand to Gamelyn's face. More, Gamelyn let him. Robyn leaned closer. "You'll have no choice."

"I've little enough of that already." A grumble against Robyn's fingertips.

"Aye, He'll heel us 'til we drop," Robyn murmured back. "And if you wait for the drop, you'll have precious nowt to fight with. Nowt to keep yourself . . . whole."

He was going for blood with that; sure enough, Gamelyn's cheek twitched beneath Robyn's palm. His eyes met Robyn's. "Is it you, being such a bastard? Or the Horned Lord merely assuming his favourite role?"

Robyn started to speak; instead, the Horned Lord steamed through both their minds. *You say that as if you think there's a difference.*

"Robyn." Gamelyn's gaze didn't drop, and his next words were slow, weighted. "You don't understand. Mayhap your god is keeping things close as well."

Not half so much as you are. "I want to," Robyn insisted, his fingers softening to stroke the line, from temple to jaw, of fox-tinged beard. "And I want you to understand. I want you with me. I want to offer you what's yours. Your right. All of it. 'Tis . . . empty for me otherwise."

The stony eyes wavered and dropped, gilt veiling a sudden darkling spark, shadowing damp cheeks.

Robyn stole the moment and tipped his chin, kissed Gamelyn hard and long. Then closed his own eyes, tilted his forehead to rest against Gamelyn's, and said, silent, *See?*

No words, now, merely visions: blurring thisnow, and into then. . .

A young man flung naked and senseless upon an altar stone, black hair spidering over a blank face and breath misting upward into a cavern deep and warmed with fire, lit with torches. The young man lies upon furs, horns placed reverently at the head of his stone couch, runes scrawled dark over pale skin. There is a cord, shimmering and pulsing as if alive, an umbilical knotted around narrow hips. His eyes are black and thick with falling skies . . . and see nothing. Drugged.

To open the senses, Robyn whispers. *I endured it. Blooding and binding, quickening and going within. All who are* dryw *must endure. Aye, there's fear, and madness lurking. But I'll be there. I would watch over, as mine own did for me.*

An ancient All-Father hovers over the lad, twining the ends of the blood-cord through his fingers. Watching. And the lad's earthly sire bears the Horns as if a great weight, a sentinel sifting dreams so as to guard the vulnerable dreamer.

Sifting dreams. . . It echoes between them, back and forth and . . . sinks, somehow, between them. The reverberations linger, and in Gamelyn's spirit quivers a sudden, sick dread.

Robyn fights it, tangling his fingers in flax-fine hair, in strands of thought and will. *Please. Wain't you trust me, Brother?* He combs those strands smooth between them, breathes across fear and sets it shimmering into possibilities: *tynged* quivering into the black. *Summerlord, wilt tha take tha's crown?*

A flutter of thoughts into darkling shadows, brilliance bursting through high carven windows, setting in relief the dark places. Birds erupting upward, winging desperate towards light and freedom. One hesitates, stalling overhead. A hawk, eyes gleaming bright. Robyn mutters a charm into the still air and reaches out, as if luring it to the fist. Instead the hawk stoops, dives for the prey . . .

With a small groan, Gamelyn shoved away. Thought-strands frayed, burst, and scattered, instinctive sword-thrust across *tynged's* unfinished loom, then a severance of emotion to rival it. It punched the breath from Robyn, flung him back.

As swift as he'd retreated, Gamelyn lurched forwards and caught Robyn. Held him there, close but not, at arm's length with arms that nevertheless shook, wanting to pull away—or even closer.

"It isn't you I don't trust." It choked tight, but those eyes gave the lie: verdigris, swimming with rust and rain.

Then he loosed Robyn, and vanished behind the wet willow curtain.

✟

"See? Up this arm and 'crost th' shoulder."

"Bloody hell! And 'twere poisoned, you said?"

"Aye, stung like stoke from t' smith's forge," Much answered Will, flexing his scarred right arm, bared where he'd half shrugged aside his tunic.

Not that Marion minded that last. Around them, the rain pattered, off and on, but they were dry beneath a makeshift roof of laced-together tarpaulins. Food might be down to the barest of necessities in the back caves, but they were eating. The wood stocks had held through a brutal winter, even now fuelling the fire warming her toes. Better still, her hands were busy. John had carved her a small spindle, and her fingers had swiftly remembered their old skills—pull and drop, twirl and twist.

It left her eyes free to appreciate the fine bicep Much was displaying. She'd been a bit scornful when this game had started— really, scar comparison?—but it was proving to have some proper benefits.

One being that Will had taken quite a shine to Much. Which was inexplicable in too many ways, bearing in mind . . . well, how Marion had made it plain whose bed she preferred sharing, and how Will hadn't even sulked about it.

Maybe her mam had been wrong and men *could* change.

"Made me sick as a poisoned hound. Milor . . . Gamelyn," Much corrected with obvious effort, "he'd to suck out the poison."

"Aye, well, milord's likely good at *that*, en't he?" Will spun it out with a grin and a drawl.

Marion sighed and gave an unnecessary tweak to the wool-wound distaff stuck in the ground at her side. Mayhap "change" was overly optimistic.

Much wasn't amused. Arthur, however, barked a laugh, and David also chuckled, amidst sharpening a lot of knives against a whetstone. Ferret Tess opened one sleepy eye, then resumed her nap, curling tighter at David's nape. John and Gilbert paid no heed, each in his own world. The latter sat, cross-legged on several furs, humming under his breath and surrounded with the tools of fletching: wooden shafts, a glue pot, sinew, and a basket filled with not only grey goose quills, but peacock tail feathers. The former huddled, intent upon a small hunk of wood, another spindle taking shape beneath knife and nimble fingers. John wasn't satisfied by half with the one Marion now used.

Will, mayhap sensing that the quivering of Much's bared bicep signified less tension than an eagerness to answer the jab at his master, bent down and pulled up one legging. A jagged, shiny set of scars displayed across his calf. "Got these two years ago, nigh to Wakefield."

As diversion, it was reasonable enough. Much frowned, peered closer. "Nasty, those are. What did—"

"Teeth marks!" Will boasted. "Bloody big hound, too."

"Aye, a bloody big hound belonging to a pretty lass's bloody big, brassed-off husband!" Eyeing down the length of a half-fletched arrow, Gilbert proved he was paying some attention by further adding, "Great sod of a mastiff, actually, and treed Will over the river! If that branch hadn't broken and sent him swimming, we might be one member less in our band today."

"As I recall, Black Tom was th' jealous type." David was still chuckling.

"And Wakefield's smith," Arthur put in with an eager wave of both arms—one minus a hand, the other with palm spreading to emphasise his next words. "Big, hammer-handed feller as made two of our Charming William—and that en't easy."

Will smirked and stood taller, tossing his mane of fair hair.

"Mayhap you should show the scar 'crost your arse, then," Gilbert suggested, flashing a brilliant smile as Will puffed up—affront, this time.

"Aye," David agreed. "Where t' love of Gilly's life nailed you?"

"How can a woman I've not seen in months be the love of my life?" was Gilbert's plaint.

"By being absent?" David flipped one of the daggers and threw.

It sank point-first and unerring beside Gilbert, who snatched it up for inspection. He grinned thanks for the knife; for the comment, made a threat with his glue brush in the direction of David's nose.

"I've heard nowt of this." Marion's hands never ceased their slide and spin upon the skein. The wool was a gift from the Master of Temple Hirst to the Lady of the Shire Wode—dyed a grey to match her eyes, or so Gamelyn claimed when he'd brought it. He'd had little else to say of that brief trip a fortnight previous, with Robyn pacing a furrow until Gamelyn returned.

"The Saracen lass as helped Robyn escape Nottingham." David threw another dagger towards Marion. She didn't stop her spinning, merely nodded thanks as the sharpened blade sank into the earth about an inch from her booted toes. "The archer whose arrow Robyn split at the archery contest. Siham."

"I remember her. I wish I'd gotten to know her. But I didn't realise she darted Will's bum."

"Lucky shot!" Will protested.

"Lucky for you," Arthur pointed out, "she weren't aiming elsewhere."

Will grinned, diverted as Much started to shrug back into his tunic. "And that one?"

Much peered at him, the mildness returning to his face. "What one?"

Marion was beginning to realise Much was true Saxon: at his most placid when most annoyed. *Is it wrong*—her query was silent, for the Lady's ears alone—*to have a wee private wager on which arses are likely to be kicked come t' Maying?*

Your hopes make all challengers strong. Whoever is fit to wear the crown, will was the Lady's implacable reply.

"T' one down yer back, lad," Will pointed out.

Much's eyes went even more flat-mild. He shrugged and angled about, showing what Marion already knew to be there—as painful to contemplate as the old whip scars on Robyn's back.

Only these were the marks of hot iron.

Will's eyes popped and he gave an admiring whistle. "I said one, but . . . Sweet Lady, those must've proper hurt!"

Marion smirked to herself, kept working at the spindle. *Boys.*

"You fetched those over t' desert, then?" Will moved closer, looking them over.

Much nodded and started to speak.

"He's back." Rare as warm sun in November was speech from John. Everyone turned, found his carving stilled and his earth-brown eyes searching.

A soft, hooting whistle confirmed it a few breaths later. Further, John was right in that only one "he" came walking into camp. Robyn's long legs ate up the distance, but not with any eagerness. Black hair tumbled from the pulled-up hood to nigh cover his narrow, downcast face, longbow slung careless—listless—over broad, bony shoulders.

No Gamelyn. In fact, no game.

"No luck, then?" David's query might have been superfluous—but the concern was real. Despite winter's retreat, any meals on the hoof—or paw—had been less than cooperative. They were all proper tired of salted fish and bendy carrots.

It was never on to forget more starved this time of year than any.

But the look on Robyn's face worried Marion more.

"Out allockin' about 'stead of working, I'm thinking!" Will gave no chance for his jibe to twist cruel; he went over, snagged an arm in Robyn's. "There's hunting partners and playing partners, and how're ye t' do the first when you're all over the second? Silly sod."

A tiny quirk tried its luck with Robyn's mouth. At that moment, Marion wanted to snog Will stupid.

"You've a face like a soppy girl—and only one cure for that. Success."

Soppy . . . girl? Marion could have said a lot of things just then, but the return of a spark to Robyn's eyes made her hold her tongue, keep to her spinning.

And her mind set equally to spinning, wondering: what had happened with Gamelyn?

She wouldn't know soon. Will, arm still locked with Robyn's, was leading him in the opposite direction.

"We'll be back!" With the heedless abandon of younger days, Will caught midair the bow Arthur pitched. "This time, wi' sommat for our larder."

Breathtaking. Not only the forest humming with beginnings, wet and verdant, but all the past brace of fortnights. Literally taking his breath with days that had run together, one into the next—a lovely, uninterrupted peace. No more nightmares to plague slumber. Only waking dreams. Time. Healing. Content.

Bitter winter had finally melted into early spring, complete with birds singing in the chill morn and a lover's kisses upon his nape. His reappearance amongst the outlaw band had been rather anticlimactic. Thankfully. Gamelyn wouldn't say he'd been welcomed with open arms. But things had . . . changed.

Even, it seemed, Will Scathelock.

Arthur, of course, blew the way Scathelock's wind carried him, acknowledging the inevitability of Gamelyn's return with a rough, sardonic resignation. John had always sided with Gamelyn, sharing heart and body—and Robyn—in a gift of devotion and faith that still had the power to weaken Gamelyn's knees. And David and

Gilbert had been willing to camaraderie, once their original—and warranted, considering—misgivings had been broached.

Gilbert—once a minor lord's son and weaned on the sword—had even gone so far as to ask Gamelyn's instruction in the finer arts of swordplay.

Then Scathelock asked Much the same.

Gamelyn wasn't sure what to make of that. Scathelock had a peasant's knack with fine steel—mainly, none—but had taken to Much's lessons. And Much, too, despite the fact that he shared Marion's bed furs.

Respect for a mutual crofter's heritage had seemingly inured Scathelock to Much being That Templar's Lackey.

Not that it had changed Scathelock's mind about the Templar himself. And no matter pleasantries, Gamelyn didn't trust the man any farther than he could fling him, and knew that mistrust reciprocated. Nay, Scathelock was waiting. For what, Gamelyn wasn't sure.

He disliked ambiguity, particularly regarding this. There was too much at stake.

Putain de merde, mayhap Robyn was right and Gamelyn was too set on rending things nigh nonexistent with his insistence upon some understanding, however tiny. But one thing had been made quite clear: the outlaws loved Robyn, and since Robyn remained adamant as to keeping a vicious lion and claiming it a house cat? They'd shrug, smile indulgence—and all the while keep knife to hand, just in case.

Gamelyn appreciated that last in particular. Grasp this small bit of Eden as he might, he knew it was under sufferance. His Templar masters would, in due course, call the debt.

As will I, the Lady's voice rippled through him, a wave setting every nerve on edge. *For, fair one, with Us you have an accounting well in arrears.*

And that swerved his thoughts to Marion.

If Robyn's stubborn insistence demanded Gamelyn's presence, Marion's open affection was a slap and reminder to the outlaws: they were, one and all, deadly wolves. And if Robyn's fierce and dangerous passion netted Gamelyn skilfully as any fish, Marion's insistent trust whetted a boning knife, rendering useless any attempts at pride or detachment. It had done from the time a lord's son had come off his horse and been brought to a forester's cottage in Loxley, to fall in unlikely friendship with commoners.

And now, despite any discomfiting truths lurking in dark corners, Marion remained so at ease with their affection, as whole in her own skin as . . . well, as Robyn. Gamelyn couldn't parse that, either. His own feelings were altogether too complicated.

All the way around and back again, perceptions spinning a skein of possibilities in a matter of breaths.

For that lovely taken/held breath had to be exhaled and another drawn. Reality had to be acknowledged. Robyn became every sunrise more persistent—nay, insistent—as Marion had after the waning of winter's solstice.

Wain't you trust me, Brother? As if Robyn still lingered beside him. Beseeching him with that purling baritone of maddening-beautiful rhythm, oft as not swallowing consonants as wasteful yet unfolding vowels into sounds like *troos* and *brootha.*

Gamelyn closed his eyes. *It isn't you I don't trust.*

Summerlord, wilt tha take tha's crown?

I can't. Don't you see?

A root tripped him, body then mind, and after a small wheel of arms and balance, Gamelyn halted. Looked around. Realised he had come into the old Saxon place, a hillock due west of their new camp. Thynghowe was plied a wide and fearful berth by peasant and noble alike—the first from ha'nts, the latter from a certain outlaw and his followers. It was secure enough to satisfy any hardened soldier; moreover, Robyn insisted it was safe from . . . other things.

There was nothing here to resemble any fae or elder gods, no primordial otherworld banished or reburgeoning. The mound that had, in Saxon times, been cleared was now bounded by a thick grove of oak, the remaining spaces overtaken by birch and alder. Runners rooted at his feet; muted silvers and new greens sprang upward beneath the grey sky. It was but another reminder: spring had stolen in between those lovely, taken breaths. Beltane was approaching.

Beltane. The same rite into which he had, a handful of years ago— a lifetime ago—blindly brought about the destruction of everything that had mattered.

The rite towards which Robyn so wanted to prepare him, with an initiation meant to bring them all together . . .

Nay. More likely 'twould free the magic trammelled in his soul like an untrustworthy beast.

Such consideration. Such tangled and fearful webs you spin, merely to trap yourself.

Aye, and wherever he would go, the Lady would not be far away. Only this was not the winter-gentled Madonna whispering words of calm and healing in his ear. She walked the Wode, dark and lovely, Her black hair scented with desert roses, clad in all the hues of spring. She had Marion's curious, clever smile. She had Marion's eyes.

And—another oath, shattered at his feet—Gamelyn wanted Her more than he'd ever thought himself capable of desiring any woman.

The Rite winnows all hearts, my Oak. All truths. So, consider this. You pride yourself in your detachment, all those cool assessments and judgments. . . what if, in not acting, you bring about the very thing you fear?

What if I bring it about by acting?

What if, by all this fighting and denial and refusal of what you are meant to be, you snarl the threads of tynged past repair?

"*Tynged!*" He growled it into the dense foliage like a curse. "It's a lie, a dream . . . a way to convince ourselves of our own importance! Nothing's meant!"

So certain. Heavy with irony. *Yet here you are, speaking to Me as one with a destiny, a fate.*

Fate. Meaning. *Tynged.* A magical, parasitical mistletoe, its loving climb along oak bark to be snipped with a druid's ancient sickle and *used:* as Magician, as pawn, as Fool, as instrument, as . . . as . . . *the Destroyer of Worlds. . .* and a chuckle into the stillness, salt and rue. The only world he had ever truly desired, and Gamelyn could not look to any soft future without also seeing its destruction, with blood on his hands and the fires of every Hell he had ever known.

Never again. If he was to be a pawn for these . . . powers, he would not take a step without scrutinising it, testing it.

Yet nothing is meant. A deeper Voice this time: the Horned Lord taking irony and unfurling it into derision. *You cannot have it both ways, Oakbrother. Symbols do not have such luxuries.*

"Symbols!" Gamelyn twisted to lean against a birch. The swath of damp along his spine lent chill reality with which to fight dreams. "Of what?"

Of something greater. Of powers that refuse to die.

"Don't you mean that we die for you? That he—" It broke, and he gritted his teeth, finished it, silent—*dies for you.*

Everyone dies. Robyn's voice, soft and deep and weakening every resistance Gamelyn possessed. *We're born dying.* It went harsh, deeper. Less human. *Yet you refuse to See, to submit—*

"To your Immortal Will?" he snarled and shoved from the tree, started walking.

Not that distancing himself from the Voices could be so easily done.

To your own Sight. A tsk. *You need Me. You hate Me. Small wonder you fight Robyn so, for he is, in truth, Me.*

"He isn't. You aren't—"

I am given life by him. And you. Has all the guilt, the sin—the last a cold, derisive hiss—instilled in you by the empty stones of your Christ's followers. . . has it resurfaced, Oakbrother? And here I thought you had slaughtered it. Like you and your fellow monks slaughtered all those innocents in Acre.

Gamelyn's hand flicked to the dagger at his hip.

Quite a tally. And all in the name of a supposed god of love and a king who pretends to the sacring, asserting himself the choice and biddance of his god.

"One day"—a vicious snarl—"you will push too far."

I merely remind you of the services you did your desert god. No doubt you would do Me much less, having become an ineffective craven fearing shadows in the night.

Gamelyn swiped at a branch, felt leaves sting his palm, shallow cuts cooled with rain and new growth. Kept walking.

Kept his hand upon his dagger.

And now, when contentment seeks to warm that cold heart of yours, anger and regret can no longer hold those shadows at bay. A pause, almost musing. *I think, mayhap, you hate and fear yourself most of all. For you know the predator lying within. You know what you are capable of—*

He whirled, dagger in hand—as if he could kill a god!—but even before the futility of the strike, the Lady spoke again.

Enough. It was as close to a growl as Gamelyn had ever imagined. There was the unearthly, discomfiting feel of fingers riffling through his thoughts, of tangled threads being smoothed, combed. Gamelyn had the strange and no doubt irreverent image of Marion grabbing the Horned Lord by one tine and smacking his nose. Hard.

Take that, he thought, and laughed out loud.

You cannot hide behind Her skirts forever, Summerlord. A bare echo, it mingled with the sound of Gamelyn's mirth and lingered in the air, teasing him until it wisped into blessed silence.

Gamelyn took in air, released it and watched the exhaust rise, contemplating what a relief it was to hear nothing but his own breath. However did Robyn stand it, having this . . . this tug-of-war battering within his skull?

He turned, started back for the camp.

Halted as another sound infringed upon the peace. Something altogether familiar, yet seldom encountered in the past cache of fortnights.

Hoofbeats. Not a leisurely rate, and not just a few.

A great company of horse travelled the road a mile distant, pace reverberating through the treetops like thunder.

- II -

S ound was deceptive in the Wode, acutely so when spring bade
a lush—and early—sprawl over the landscape.

Nevertheless, Gamelyn followed it, waft and wobble, with the
precision of a hungry lion. Mayhap the deadliest of his skills had
been gained in desert heat and high, dry alpine, but he'd been bred
here, born here. He'd begun learning woodland lore before his
voice had broken, and from two of the best. Even the youths of
Alamut who had trained with him, hated and feared then respected
and honoured him, had realised that with their friendship and a
name: the fire-haired djinn of the forest.

Hariq aljini alshier al-ghaba. The liquid syllables sounded
strangely comfortable upon the Horned Lord's soft breath. No
taunt this time, but esteem. Gamelyn smiled, kept to the track.

The sounds were fading, though. Travelling at speed, so likely
the North Road. Merely a short sprint to reach it, but once there,
he'd no horse and they would leave him behind, unless . . .

Another burst, a two-beat rhythm carried on the damp breeze.
They'd slowed.

Gamelyn also paused, fingers trailing the new bracken. It
swayed, reaching for his hips. He cocked his head, intent.

Ah. Heading south.

Gamelyn leapt over the creepers of gorse to his left and
followed.

The deer paths were becoming overgrown—particularly for
someone of his height. Gamelyn spent as much time ducking and
dodging new branches as he did in forward progress. More

gratitude, accompanied by a surge of relief at what Marion's wortwife mastery of root and leaf had recaptured in him. What the Wode granted him, sap-heat in his veins and a power both exhilarating and terrifying, like riding into battle bridleless and bareback.

He owed Marion beyond any price. Owed Robyn beyond any sense of sanity. Owed them *both* more than evasions, and this dance around the truth of why he couldn't do as they wished.

If only that little ginger-haired lad hiding in a dark corner of his heart wasn't so adamant in his superstitions: *If you do tell? Give it voice? Make it real?*

"First there was the Word. And with the Word was made flesh. . ."

Not only Christian. The Heathen folk believed even more that utterances were power.

Gamelyn paused, misted breath roiling from pursuit to advance scout. The trees opened up ahead, brighter: the North Road, cutting a twisting clearance through the Shire Wode. Still plenty of cover, though, for a Templar turned outlaw. This time of year, the woodland remained persistent in its retaking the cleared ribbon of pounded-down soil. He trotted down a rise, leapt a small rill, and headed up the other side, to be rewarded with sight of the road. Taking refuge beside a thick tangle of hedge, Gamelyn made careful measure of the surround.

Nothing.

He let out a small huff, reached up to stroke the hilt of his sword—ensuring the shoulder scabbard's easy reach—then circumnavigated the hedge, hopped a rotted log, and strode onto the open sward.

Still nothing. The hoofbeats maintained their southward retreat.

With a frown, then a shrug, he followed.

Mayhap Scathelock were right. Hard enough to catch supper lately *without* distractions, and Gamelyn offered ones beyond any desire to shag him senseless.

The staghead oak was a rare—and auspicious—denizen amongst its kind. Likely lightning-struck at some time during its reign, it was aged and doughty, with plenty of new leaf cover, allowing two hunters to forgo stalk for the advantage of a natural stand. Better yet, the small clearing it guarded was edged to the south by a grove of silver birch and bracken, the latter bruised and the ground fresh with deer sign. Robyn stroked the old tree as gentle as he would little Tess. A fond blessing of breath, asking both permission and success, whispered past parted lips.

They'd stored their bows, strung and ready, in a makeshift hide tent. Sometimes there was no choice, wet or dry, but . . . well. Nowt louder than a sodden bowstring loosed. Tufts of otter fur only silenced so much. Thankfully, this sort of weather made the deer less spooky, what with the rain slackened into thick mist. The does would be tucking up, either guarding early fawns or growing heavy with them—fair enough, with orphans being made every day as 'twere. The bucks were most likely the ones a-wander in little bachelors' herds, browsing on new spring shoots.

Any outward conversation was sparse, nigh silent. The wait turned long, each of them taking turns at a light doze, yet Robyn didn't allow himself to contemplate another failed hunt. Will was right: the deer would come. Had been coming, from the look of this glade, for several days, and the forage still plentiful. Besides, just being here gave comfort beyond measure. The broad warmth of Will, hunkered down shoulder to shoulder, made fond reminder of seasons past as foresters' sons. Robyn's da had often sent them out on culls, once they'd left off fooling about and set more to proving themselves. Robyn had the best marksmanship, and Will, even before his balls dropped, had possessed the brawn to wrestle any carcass onto the sumpter mule . . .

"Arthur's told me sommat I think you should know."

The murmur broke silent reverie, not so much because of sound but because of tone. Head turned so his cheek nearly rested against Robyn's shoulder, Will sounded . . . hesitant? Defiant? Smug?

All those and more.

Robyn slid a wary gaze sideways.

Will's amber eyes were downcast, his cheeks misted with wet. "Y'know the wool as Marion is spinning?"

Wool. Well, that was harmless. Robyn chided himself for being so tetchy, let his gaze roam the clearing once more, and nodded.

"It's fine stuff. Me da used to say the better wool grew up t' North."

"John's mam would have at you ower that," Robyn teased. There was a goodly wool trade in the Peak District, and John's family had been shepherds for the lord at Peveril.

"Well, but there's no arguing wool from up North is different."

Robyn yawned. "Aye. And?"

"And." Will took in a long breath, as if girding himself for confession. "Well, it's northern wool."

"Y' keep saying."

"It's only . . . David knows how—*where*—it came from. And it en't from where your poncy ginger paramour said."

Doziness wicked itself away. "Will—"

"Nay, Rob, hear me out. Please. I swear by t' Horns you need t' let me finish." Not an oath taken lightly, and earnest, the plea.

Of course, it always was.

Encouraged by Robyn's silence, Will turned. Barely a leaf stirred as he reached out, put a broad hand upon the nearest of Robyn's crossed knees. "See, Arthur were out 'n' about a fortnight ago, checking snares."

A fortnight? Aye, and Robyn was proper sure where *this* was going . . .

"He'd set 'em up quite a ways out—you know what hunting's been like—and ended up passing nigh t' Lodge."

Most of the denizens hereabout had a bitey sense of humour; no question but *t' Lodge* was a nip at the ginormous, fat, and fancy manor adjacent to Clipstone, complete with not only a great hall and gatehouse, but dovecot, stables, rabbit warrens, and a bloody big fish pond. The old King Henry had built it, enclosed a prime swathe and proclaimed it untouchable Royal Forest, turfing out a great lot of people in the doing. The villagers couldn't so much as hunt a bunny or gather acorns on the fifteen hundred odd acres of land that had once been theirs to roam.

Supposedly King Henry had given the nigh-a-castle to his youngest son as a hunting retreat, which was why Robyn had told his band more than the once to stay clear of the place. No telling when his Royal Arse-Pain-ness might show up again. No matter that Gamelyn insisted Count John had left the country. Plenty of guards bided there, and Robyn would make book those guards had specific instructions regarding a notorious pack of outlaws. Count John wasn't about to forgive them for humiliating him at Nottingham.

"Minding his own business, nowt but, and . . . um." A pause, then lower. "He saw Gisb . . . well, *him*. At the Lodge. And he weren't alone."

And how long had Will sat here, gathering his nerve for this particular subject? Because bloody *damn*, but by now he should know better!

"Saw Gamelyn." Flat.

Will was too intent on what he was saying to heed. "Aye. Talking to some woman."

"And this has sod-all to do wit' wool?" Robyn made the tired start, then frowned as something rustled over by the birches.

"The woman got the wool from another visitor that Arthur saw earlier." Will slid an equal frown Robyn's way. "It was a Templar. T' Lodge is some kind of meeting place for 'em! So Gisb . . . Well. He didn't fetch it from no pedlar, did—!"

Robyn cupped a quick hand over Will's mouth. As a protest started against his fingers, Robyn tapped at his own ear, inclined his head to the birch thicket.

This time they both heard it. Another faint rustle, then a telltale *blat*. A damp shudder, a *shuss* of hide against bracken, and the slip-stop of cloven hooves against soggy roots and earth.

Anger melted into the moment, tickling at anticipation as Robyn lipped the fletchings brushing his cheek—as usual, he'd a trio of broadhead arrows knotted into his hair. He leaned, oh-so-silent, to slide first Will's, then his own bow from under makeshift cover.

Five deer meandered into view, brockets in their second or third year. Just as the velveted spikes burgeoning upon their skulls were scarce representation of the lethal antlers slowly forming, the little bachelor group gave no indication of the bad temper that would divide their ranks come autumn. Nibbling at the new green, their coats plump and glossy-brown against the silvered mottling of the birch trunks, the brockets seemed placid as fawns beneath the soft rainfall.

And prosperous, certainly more so than two outlaws lean from short rations. By their Lady, but Robyn was bloody tired of bloody salted fish!

As he and Will put careful arrows at nock, the largest of the brockets reared up on the gnarled trunk of an oak. Will nodded his claim. Well enough, Robyn would take the one stepping into his sights; not only supper, but for the larder.

The yew bows uttered a mild creak, complaining like any old granddad with the damp. The large buck swung his head around, eyes wide and ears pitched. Neither Will nor Robyn waited for him to bolt, but loosed their arrows. One of the brockets leapt in the air and fell. Will rumbled a foul curse as his target sprang sideways off the tree and crashed to earth, but rolled up to flee. A second arrow sang, then a third, which finally downed him.

The last sight of the remaining brockets was their flagged tails, as they escaped with a thrash-crush of foliage.

"Since when do y' need three arrows for one deer?" Robyn swung down from the tree. Sniping, and no more did he care.

"He heard the damned bows!" Will defended, leaping after. He rolled as he landed, regained his feet, and darted over to ensure the last shot had done its work.

Robyn's quarry, by the thicket, was still twitching. He crouched by the brocket, gentled him with soft hands and breath—invocation, then gratitude, then mercy with the skinning dagger at his belt. Drawled, "So. You're saying things weren't what they seemed at first glance. Fancy that."

Will straddled his own kill—well away from the possibility of a final kick—giving honour to the slain with a smoothing hand and soft hex-breath. He threw a puzzled frown Robyn's way. "Eh?"

"I were just remarking on how you're bloody set t' queer sights on some things." Robyn bent, tapped at the deer's open eye with one finger, murmured, "Aye, you're gone, lad. Good journey to you."

"Robyn, are you off wit' fae again? Queer sights? You saw, t' buck spooked—"

"I en't after deer!" Working on two rows in one day, Robyn was. Mayhap he should take his temper back to camp, see if anyone else needed kicking. Like Arthur. "You said Arthur followed Gamelyn."

"Arthur weren't meaning to follow nowt, I tell you. And that en't the point."

"What *is* the point? Other than you're bloody set on—"

"You're acting like I'm one as is sneaking off and doing what he oughtn't!"

"And you're actin' as if I weren't knowing where Gamelyn went!" That set Will back on his heels.

"Do you *really* think I'm such a daft sod, Will?" Robyn snorted. "Mayhap I am. You had me all cozened, you and that best-mates act with Much—"

"It weren't no act! I *like* the man."

Robyn raised his eyebrows, gave purposeful prod. "Should I be jealous?"

Will rolled his eyes. "*Rob—*"

Another prod, harder. "Y' know, if you're thinking on sleeping with Much, you'll be shoving Marion out t' way."

No reaction—at least not the one Robyn was expecting. Instead, a tiny—and canny—smirk twitched at Will's lip. "Aye, well, summer's coming."

Eyes narrowing, Robyn started to speak.

Before he could, Will's grin widened and he gave a shrug. Once again the uncomplicated companion of green summers past, he toed the carcass at his feet. "See, you only ever needed summon keeping your sights on a proper hunt. We've more meat than we figured, now. Let's parcel and take 'em home. Or"—another impudent smile—"are y' feeling too dainty wit' all those late nights, and we need to hang 'em and fetch help?"

Clipstone.

They'd ridden to *Clipstone*.

Robyn and the others called it the Old King's Lodge. It was indeed that but also more—an area Gamelyn knew well for his own reasons. A hunting eyrie was maintained here, with an attached dovecote, and the servant who minded that dovecote was sworn, mind and soul, to the Templars. Sarah, placid as the birds she tended, safeguarded whatever messages came via human or avian messenger from Temple Hirst. It had been Sarah who'd confirmed the rumours of Count John's flight from England. And Sarah who had passed to Gamelyn the singular communication from his Master within the past several fortnights, complete with cryptic warnings towards political matters, and a bundle of fine wool in pointed acknowledgment of the Feast of the Maiden.

There had been no further messages, which had rendered Gamelyn both grateful and apprehensive.

He shrugged his cloak closer and settled into the thick stand of trees north of the side entry, watching the small group of horsemen milling about. Most had dismounted, the captain chatting up Clipstone's seneschal—another friend to the Templars, who didn't seem concerned by the sudden descent of Pontefract upon his doorstep.

And they were Pontefract's. The saffron cloaks and the purple lion sketched upon the captain's shield—athwart the saddle of the horse he handed to a servant—testified to that.

Why were Baron de Lacy's men making camp at a royal site?

The hairs on Gamelyn's nape shivered. He frowned and twitched his cloak even closer, stilled midshrug. Stiffened.

Parting the saffron and brown of the soldiers like Moses commanding the Red Sea, a tall, grey figure strode into view. At his heels were two men clad in dark kit, their only adornment a formidable sword and a telltale, tiny cross breasting their cloaks. Their leader's close-cropped head was bared despite the drizzle of rain, eyes keen over the small outer courtyard. He flung aside his plain cloak to reveal an ivory tabard emblazoned with a scarlet cross.

Of chance happenstance, surely this ranked amongst the most bizarre. A jongleur would be hard put to credit it as anything save the most fanciful of contrivances. But here they were—and likely this was no chance.

Standing, Gamelyn raked back his own hood and walked from concealment towards the gathered horsemen. Voices rose—he'd been spotted. Accompanying that, the scatter of booted feet, the scuff of steel freeing from leather and chainmail rasping cloth—all the sounds of well-armed men preparing for a possible enemy.

Gamelyn ignored them with a deliberate stride for the white-clad Templar. The Templar turned, saw him. A hint of surprise, and what might have been a twinkle in steely blue eyes, then a sharp mutter of command. Its message was plain. The surrounding soldiers, albeit reluctant, reseated their weapons and allowed Gamelyn's approach.

"Ah." Hubert de Gisborough, Commander of Temple Hirst, inspected his *Confanonier* fore and aft and clearly found him lacking. "How . . . fortunate you should join us, Brother."

"Events have moved much swifter apace than any could have foreseen." Hubert's long-legged, bold gait always had the power to carry Gamelyn along with it—this time it led through a small inner bailey and into Clipstone's main hall.

Meanwhile, Hubert's Templar companions—both well-known to Gamelyn—split their duties: the squire to see to the horses; the sergeant taking up residence at the door. This was to be a private audience. Pontefract's men lingered in the courtyard. Waiting for others, no doubt. Gamelyn had encroached upon some sort of meeting.

Not that Hubert seemed ruffled or resentful of the intrusion. His boots clipped a steady measure over the stone floor, laid an echo against the bare far wall and the dais crouched there. The latter lay unburdened by so much as a wooden bowl. The great hall of Clipstone might be built comfortable, but it sat chill: a demesne without its monarch, pretend or legitimate. Silent and obedient, Gamelyn followed over to the hearth—a round, blackened pit in the hall's middle, where a fire leapt and crackled with fresh-kindled vigour. Upon one edge of the hearth's perimeter perched a ragbag of rough-spun resembling more a tattered, grubby sheep than any man. But a bundle of splits lay piled between two horny, filthy—and human—feet. Concerned solely that the smoke should curl upward and out a narrow set of unshuttered upper windows, the villein paid them no heed, waited with mute and tedious patience for a proper moment to further his charge.

Hubert's close-cropped hair gleamed like well-tended steel, backlit by the fresh blaze. Little else was visible; nonetheless, Gamelyn could discern a wry eyebrow cocked his direction the closer he came.

With an abrupt, loud sniff, Hubert untucked a pouch from his belt and pitched it over. "Don't those outlaws feed you? You're too thin."

Gamelyn snatched the pouch midair, opened it to find an assortment of dried fruits and nuts. Only then did he realise he was, indeed, hungry. And chilled. "It's spring," he replied with a shrug.

Hubert snorted acknowledgment as Gamelyn popped a delicacy in his mouth. One of the benefits of having regular shipments of supplies to outfit strongholds in the Holy Land: those ships oft returned bearing marvellous things. Like apricots. Bliss.

"You're a distinct shade of blue as well. Come, by the fire." Hubert made room for Gamelyn with a flick of his cloak.

The flames danced, inviting. The old villein didn't so much as flinch. For long moments they remained in silent comfort.

Hubert reached out, tapped fingers against Gamelyn's cheek. "I say, you're thin, but by God you're fit!" Quiet before, the deep voice resonated through the hall with unbridled approval. "And healing strong, I see. Mayhap I should send all my invalids for a stint of, ah, rough living in Sherwood."

Gamelyn's own satisfaction let loose in a broad smile as Hubert clasped his shoulder, gave it a fond shake.

"But tell me, lad, how came you here? Were you looking for a message? I have tried to not disrupt your time—there was healing to be done, in various ways."

"I was . . . hunting. With Robyn." It was strange, to admit such a thing aloud to his Master—but this was not the same, to take game for food and not for sport. His own culpability surprised him—after all, how many other tenets of the Rule had he bent, stretched, or broken? And at his Master's behest?

Hubert was, of course, serene. "Ah. Does the wolf of Sherwood wait, then, out of sight?"

Gamelyn shook his head, a sudden and barren thought sinking him: what if Hubert kept him here, and that ungainly parting the last?

Only if you allow it. The Lady, unlike her Consort, seemed quite comfortable lingering in walls of Church-consecrated stone. *You are born to wield your power, not subsume it in unthinking obedience, however it may comfort you.*

Hubert peered at him, frowning. Gamelyn cast his gaze down, away. Such evasion brought his gaze to the crouched villein. No longer an impenetrable blank of dingy rags and matted locks, the old man contemplated the two nobles in his realm, thick brows drawn almost in . . . puzzlement?

The moment Gamelyn's eyes met his, however, the villein turned back to his fire with a sullen hunch.

"Nay," Gamelyn answered, soft, his eyes upon the villein. "Robyn Hode is to green Wode gone."

The ancient intonation was purposeful. Rag-clad shoulders twitched, went stiff, hunched further. The villein took a split of wood from between his bare toes and leaned over the great open hearth to arrange it upon the blaze. Nevertheless his eyes flickered towards Gamelyn again—Gamelyn knew, for he saw the glint of them beneath a lock of grey-wool hair.

"*Qu'est-ce qui se passe?*" Hubert's query was low, for his *Confanonier's* ears alone. Uncertain.

What is happening? I'm not so certain myself, Master. Who am I, here? Tell me, I beg you, who I am.

Ambiguity washed in, merely to be drawn away by a relentless tide of artifice.

Gamelyn snagged another apricot and several nuts from the linen bag, tossed it back to Hubert. "All progresses to plan, Commander. I am your ambassador, no more, trusted by both and neither. As it should be." Hubert frowned, his blue eyes piercing nigh to bone, so Gamelyn pursued an alternative subject. "What brings you here? You said events were moving apace?"

And Hubert, bless him unto eternity, gave and followed the

evasion just as swift. "King Richard should land upon our southern shores any day now."

"It is no rumour, then. He is free."

"Indeed, and the powers are gathering, vying for position."

"Which is why Pontefract's men are with you."

"He is due later today, with Durham. Huntingdon and Chester will likely not be far after, though from a different direction. Their men already bide at Nottingham."

"A baron, a bishop, and two earls," Gamelyn murmured. "This is no small assembly being prepared."

"The word has been given, with the King's seal upon it: his most noble brother, Count John, is hereby disseised of his English possessions. Those castles that persist in holding in his name are to be taken, if not by parley, then by force. Marlborough and Lancaster are being dealt with, and Mount St. Michael has surrendered to the inevitable. Rumour has it the commander there dropped dead of fright in the north transept when he heard of the King's release."

"Reputation has its advantages."

Hubert's lip twitched. "There is, ah, also another matter, closer to home. Two other castles resist, unshaken by threats and altogether defiant beneath the beginnings of siege. One is Nottingham. The other"—blue-grey eyes fastened to green and held—"is Blyth."

Gamelyn blinked midchew.

"If you had not arrived so fortunately, I was preparing to come find you. After all," Hubert angled closer, "mightn't one whose childhood knowledge of Blyth Castle retrieved a Queen and thus ensured a king's ransom?—ah, mightn't that one prove useful against said fortress?"

Another wide-eyed blink; Gamelyn couldn't help it.

"My lord Commander?" A question from the door, hurried and a bit breathless.

Hubert nodded, and the squire sprinted into the hall.

"My lord Commander. My lord *Confanonier*," the squire gave rushed acknowledgment of his lord's favoured lieutenant. "My lord of Huntingdon has arrived. And my lord the Bishop of Durham has been sighted, riding with my lord of Pontefract."

"*Bon!* Well ahead of time!" Hubert dismissed the squire with another nod, grasped Gamelyn's arm when he also thought to heed the dismissal. "*J'aimerais que tu restes.*" And when Gamelyn tensed, something within him resisting the request, wanting dismissal—*escape*—Hubert sensed it and repeated, in Anglic, "I would prefer you stay. You are used to the company of the exalted, and I would have my faithful *Confanonier* at my side for this."

Tell me who I am.

It seemed Hubert had just done so. Odd, though—the only protest within Gamelyn was his own. The Lady remained silent, satisfied and . . . *approving*. Complicit, for some reason, in this scheme of Temple and Church and Crown.

That, plus the deep-hewn glint of affection in Hubert's gaze, set Gamelyn back into reflection, commingling self-possession and disquiet.

"So we're to go up tica's hill," Gamelyn murmured. His fingers stung, cold. He held them to the fire.

It came lumbering on four legs through the gloaming and over the rise girdling the old Saxon meeting-howe. Lumped and laden, it might have been some ferocious and legendary malformed bear's spirit, or mayhap a fell and demon-shackled 'Ob 'Oss straight from stories told to keep children from wandering the Wode o' nights.

Yet no one in camp so much as reached for a weapon.

Marion leapt to her feet, spindle and spinning chasing altogether close to the fire. She didn't notice. Fisting warm skirts up to her knees, she ran to greet her brother and Will, laughing.

"Sweet Lady!" David sang out. "But will you look at the pair of you? Bring on the supper!"

Gilbert was even more demonstrative, starting an impromptu jig around the hearth's edge. This woke Much, who'd been dozing. A strike of his hand outward and he'd grabbed Gilbert's ankle, sent him tumbling sideways. Unfortunately for Much, Gilbert landed right atop him. Arthur howled with laughter.

"Ah, for . . . quit allockin' about and come help!" Robyn gave a stumble—somewhat feigned, Marion was sure—beneath carry pole and sacks. "'Tis bloody *heavy*, this lot!"

"That's more than one deer." Marion crossed her arms, trying to look fierce and failing, she knew, miserably. Her stomach had already started up a plaintive rumble at the thought of fresh meat roasting on a good fire. "Why didn't you send for help?"

"Will insisted," Robyn complained. "I'm thinking he pined after looking t' proper hero."

Not just Will. Both of them had the smug, giddy look that had surely been on Man the Hunter's face since their ancient ancestors had roamed with stone spears and brought food to cavern hearths.

Well, they deserved it. Marion kissed her brother's cheek right atop a dried smear of blood, gave Will the same service, then grabbed one of the leathern sacks and swung it over one shoulder.

Not without an "Oof!" It *was* bloody heavy. "Well done, you!" Marion acknowledged, pretending her own stagger.

Much strode up with a grin—he'd disentangled himself from Gilbert—to take Robyn's end of the pole. Arthur was right behind, easing Will's end, all the while Will boasting, "Two of 'em, mind."

"We'll eat fine for a stretch," Gilbert agreed. "And plenty to take to . . . whose turn for the portion, Marion?"

"Matlock." Marion unloaded, smiling at David. He and John were clearing a large stone to one side of their camp—surrounded by new grass and perfect for further rendering the meat. "You can take it come t' morn, see your gramma and your boy."

The nod and tilt of David's face told of a pleasure past any smile. It quivered silent outrage in Marion's heart. There was no excuse that David shouldn't be with his family. Aye, there were those as were so dangerous they needed to be locked away or, better yet, sent back to the otherworlds, to start over and mayhap be kinder in another form. But all David had tried to do was feed a family sick with starvation. In thisnow, that often meant taking what the lords wouldn't let you earn.

In her mam's time, outlaws had been forbidden the Shire Wode's ancient covenant. Now outlaws were the last bastion to uphold the hallowed ways of Horned Lord and Lady Huntress, using heath and cunning to help their own survive hard times.

Marion rubbed her hands on a thick-new patch of grass, picked up her scattered spinning, then went to see about warming some water. The light might be fading, but 'twas plain Robyn and Will were filthy with blood and mud.

"Blidworth's a need as well," Robyn said, shrugging his carryalls beside the stone. "A fever's gone through there of late. Fresh meat would do them good."

"If you can get past the priest." Gilbert unloaded his own burden next to Robyn's. "Brother Aelred's been replaced by Uptight Pillock What-sis, remember?"

"You'll leave it nigh t' *dryw* stane, then." Robyn grinned.

"*I'll* leave it?"

Robyn smirked, blew him a kiss. Marion brought a large bucket of rainwater—gathered from the overhead tarpaulins—over to the fire. As she poured it into an empty cauldron, she saw her brother pass Much, hesitate and turn back, leaning close with a murmured question. Much listened, then shook his head, frowning. Contagious, that frown; Robyn caught it and turned away.

And as she set the cauldron over the coals, Marion summoned up *Gamelyn. He en't returned, yet.*

"I'm off for a wash." Robyn started off opposite the way he and Will had come in, waving a grimy hand in the air.

"I guess since you and Will did the skinning and breaking, we'll let you!" Gilbert called after.

"That's right fair of you, lad," Robyn allowed, with a hint of a grin. "Comin', Will?"

"Too cold for me," Will declared. "I'm for waiting on that lovely hot water Marion's brewing."

Robyn snorted and disappeared into the darkening trees.

Marion saw the water well started and Will minding it. She set up a spit for what meat the others were busy portioning—she'd offered many a time, and been every time refused. The chore hierarchy was quite fixed in her brother's band; those who couldn't do in one fashion were expected to make up in other areas, and no whinging. Marion and David both did most of the cooking, so they rarely had to process the game. Indeed, David had disappeared into the small cavern that based their present camp—going through stores, no doubt, for seasoning.

So Marion dusted off her hands and went after her brother.

- III -

"**L**et us be to business right away!" The voice filled Clipstone's great hall: Norman French, without the slightest hint of quaver or aged rasp. But then, Hugh de Puiset's unwillingness to resign to any dotage was well-known. Indeed, he marched into Clipstone's great hall with a pace that belied holding Durham's bishopric for well over forty years. "Some wine, mayhap, and quick introductions . . . you. Boy. Leave us."

Gamelyn's comprehension came belated: the Bishop spoke to him. A scant patience for niceties with those considered underlings was part of Durham's legendary repertoire. The scruffy, ginger-haired young sergeant was plainly little more than Commander Hubert's baseborn and uppity underling.

"I think not. You have your attendants." Hubert gestured to the monk in Durham's wake, as well as the two young men with their own masters: Pontefract and Huntingdon. "I too would have my Brother's participation in these matters."

A small snort escaped the Bishop.

"Let neither his youth nor manner of dress fool you." Hubert's serene insistence could, Gamelyn was sure, erode stone. "He bears the honour of *Confanonier* to my Preceptory."

"Then you are welcome, Brother *Confanonier*," Durham conceded, with a rather frosty bow and an extension of one beringed hand. Just as impassive, Gamelyn bent and touched his lips to the proffered ring.

"Hirst isn't *that* far from Durham, Hugh. Surely you've managed to hear of the skill with which Sir Guy de Gisbourne upholds his place as the Commander's personal guard?" This from Pontefract's lord, coming forwards with a small bow for Hubert. With a rather-cheeky grin to Durham's frown, de Lacy tendered another bow, the smile lingering. "It is a pleasure to see you again, Sir Guy."

The name tickled Gamelyn's nape, both comfort and goad. *Tell me who I am. Here.*

It seemed de Lacy just had.

"The pleasure is mine, my lord Baron." Gamelyn returned the bow, unable to help a swift glance in Hubert's direction.

But Hubert was greeting David of Huntingdon with a graceful bow, the picture of impervious—and effortless—civility. "Good day, my lord Earl. I hear your royal brother is riding from Scotland."

"William always has gotten on with Richard." A respectful inclination of silvered head, and a careful shrug of burgundy-clad shoulders, yet Huntingdon's gaze lingered upon Gamelyn. "Please to meet Roger's man, Geoffrey, and Brother Lucias over there with Hugh, and of course my seneschal, Raymond . . . faiths, but where has the man scarpered the now?" A quick scan of the hall gave no answer, so Huntingdon's dark eyes returned to Gamelyn, this time openly curious. "*Your* man seems altogether . . . familiar, Commander."

"I've no doubt he is, my lord. My *Confanonier* came to us bearing the name of Gamelyn Boundys."

"Boundys." Huntingdon's gaze strafed Gamelyn, intent, and his frown deepened. Small wonder, since a freckled, copper-haired youth's only resemblance to a tall and broad-shouldered man with an incongruous Templar's cape thrown over rough clothes was said hair and freckles. Gamelyn had been born at Huntingdon, had in fact done homage to Earl David at the age of nine, upon his father's enfeoffment with the honour of Tickhill and the castle known as Blyth. Of course, not long afterward had the King sold the honour—and Sir Ian's allegiance, did he want to keep his fee— to Roger de Lacy. Supposedly Huntingdon had encouraged Sir Ian's decision, sanguine with his vassal's gain, if not de Lacy's.

"Ian Boundys de Blyth," de Lacy prompted, with an air suggesting Huntingdon's memory was failing him. "His youngest."

"Ian's lad a Templar!" Huntingdon marvelled, not without a halfhearted glower at de Lacy—one remarkably well humoured, considering.

Well, players upon such a powerful field had to realise the capricious favour of kings . . . and the repercussions of inconsistent loyalties.

De Lacy merely loosed another offhand grin in Gamelyn's direction. Gamelyn returned a brief, courteous nod: acknowledgment, but one leery of full trust. By nature, Roger de Lacy remained an ebullient sort, true—yet it was also true Gamelyn had been involved with the death of de Lacy's sister. Granted, the Abbess

Elisabeth had shot Gamelyn in the back, and de Lacy maintained the same sort of consciousness about his chivalric position as any who'd fought and bought their way into it. Or mayhap Pontefract's baron considered his sister unworthy of lament, not unlike Gamelyn with his own sadistic swine of an elder brother.

"Old name, Gamelyn." Huntingdon stepped closer, arms crossed and head tilted. "I'm sorry to see you've left it behind."

I haven't. It's only. . . only that it's. . . complicated.

"Did you know your mother gave it to you, before you were born? 'My little Gamelyn' she'd say, with a pat to her belly and a teasing wrinkle of nose to your father. He was, of course, a good twenty years her senior, and they'd not thought to have another child as the time passed after your middle brother's birth. Though she said she liked the sound of the name, she also liked to tease him . . . ah, but Cousin Marjory was a lovely lass. Even more redheaded than you, if not so serious"—this with a charming smile—"always laughing. Her death broke your father's heart, I fear. But as we often do, he found ease in her children. Particularly the one most like her." It seemed impossible, but the smile widened. "Aye, lad, we're family. Should the need ever arise, you've only to come and bespeak a place at my hall."

Gamelyn found himself smiling back, broad and genuine. No wonder Huntingdon was so powerful. He'd a gift few men possessed by nature: artless and undeniable magnetism.

"If the family reunion is over, might we attend to business?" Durham was clambering up the dais, where his acolyte was sweeping clean the table board. "Where are the . . . ah, excellent!" This as the young man clad in Huntingdon's colours reappeared with a trio of servants in tow. The latter bore several platters and a steaming cauldron. "Christ *Jesus,* but you read my mind. I was ready to do battle for a good draught of warmed wine. This Godforsaken forest holds the chill like wet braies. What of Chester, David? Does he come?"

"Ranulf stays in Nottingham." With one last smile in Gamelyn's direction, Huntingdon angled towards the Bishop. "He's staging our men. I will relay our strategies to him. It would have been unwise for both of us to venture here, however brief. And you know Ranulf. He always has preferred action to talk."

A brief, sardonic smirk flitted across Durham's face, fading as he snapped, "Nay, girl, not on the dais. We've our own need of it!"

The serving girl changed her course as if she'd no idea of landing her platters upon the main table. Instead she hopped down, giving a jerk of her head that had one lad relinquishing his half of the cauldron to scamper for a narrow side door.

The old villein tending the fire had backed into the shadows, Gamelyn noted, nigh invisible.

"Nottingham is proving difficult," continued Huntingdon. "Not just the redoubt, but in the just-as-formidable stubbornness of its keepers."

"Tickhill's keepers are proving no less intractable," Durham grunted, pulling a large roll from the folds of his vair-lined cloak.

Brother Lucias hurried to assist; he was immediately distracted in a dithering search for suitable weights to hold down the tight-curled skin. It was a smirking de Lacy who snatched several empty cups from the serving girl as she passed, and tossed them to his own seneschal with a gesture towards the dais.

"Well, at least word has it Lancaster has seen reason and surrendered," Huntingdon offered.

"Excellent! Of course," Durham scoffed, "southerners have no fortitude."

"I would say they are . . . hmm . . . less obstinate?" Huntingdon flashed his charming smile.

"If by that you mean we're more pigheaded here in the North"—de Lacy drawled his flattened hint of Yorkshire just that much more—"aye, say 't and be damned!"

Gamelyn hid a smile beneath a smooth of his moustache.

"Come now, Pontefract. I say nothing without thinking it through."

De Lacy let out a laugh as broad as himself. "Come now, Huntingdon, you're as northern-bred as any of us. More, mayhap?"

A *scree* of wood against stone announced trestles and another board being dragged through the side door. The lass at the hearth left off stirring the cauldron and scurried to help.

With a long-suffering sigh, Durham turned his attention from both the meanderings of unprepared peasantry and the jibes of nobility. "King Richard would prefer we make quick dispatch of these small rebellions—he has other matters to occupy his mind at present."

Gamelyn found it hard to fathom that the overlord responsible for the butchery of Acre found any excuse for battle repellent. Though 'twas all too true: a stint in prison could change many an outlook.

"Such as his brother." Durham eyed his companions, but without rancour. He knew most there had treated with Count John—and he also knew why.

"And France," de Lacy added.

"Those two matters are well within our king's talents to sort," Huntingdon pointed out. "But of present relevance, no less and mayhap all the more, is reengaging the hearts of a nation beleaguered by wars and ransom." The dialect of his birth crept into his mellow voice, as if it too bided uncertain. "He's no' likely to come up the North Road meek and quiet."

"Queen Eleanor is just as unlikely to allow it," Durham furthered.

The sideboard made ready, the youngest lass gave a last, perfunctory swipe as the eldest of the trio plunked down her platters. One overflowed with a large spread of salted fish suitable for Lenten repast— Gamelyn couldn't help an inward groan—but there was also a bowl of steaming pottage, fresh-baked manchet loaves in honour of Clipstone's distinguished guests, and a sizeable platter of honeyed cakes. His stomach, primed from the dried apricots, gave a plaintive burble. The elder of the lasses glanced his way, a grin trying to tip her lip—she'd heard. From a steaming pitcher, she began pouring into a clutch of pewter goblets.

None of the others paid the slightest attention to Gamelyn's overeager appetite. Huntingdon and de Lacy were already at the table, inspecting the parchment as the stewards finished securing it. Durham was speaking with Hubert.

"I understand the Master of England is detailing Temples Hirst and Bruer to assist with taking Tickhill."

"Yes, my lord Bishop. Master de Birkin is, of course, on his way to Temple London for the King's expected arrival. He sent orders detailing not only the Brethren of Bruer, but Hirst. My Under-Marshal has orders to join Bruer at the old church of All Hallows, and see things well in readiness." Hubert looked over and beckoned to Gamelyn, who joined him at the massive board.

What waited there was a surprise. He'd expected notes and plans, but not a full-out map. They were hard to come by here, and most wildly inaccurate, based more on theological interpretations than any charted reality. This one depicted the honours of Tickhill and Nottingham with a veracity Gamelyn hadn't seen since the maps of Outremer . . . and those drawn by Saracen cartographers.

The notations here and there, however, were Latin, not Arabic or any similar abjadic script.

"Quite a decent sort of sketch, eh?" De Lacy sidled close. He'd noticed Gamelyn's curiosity. "My own time in Outremer was necessarily brief, but it left me with some notable resources. A few Saracens joined my service—one of which, I believe, you know by pure chance from those wretched doings at Nottingham."

"*Siham* drew this?"

De Lacy's eyebrows lifted at the name, and Gamelyn realised his error. 'Twas highly unlikely de Lacy knew his prize Saracen archer had acquaintance with not only a Templar, but a band of outlaws . . . through chance entanglement to be sure, but before any "wretched doings at Nottingham." He covered his gaffe by reaching for the wine the servant girl held out to him.

The girl's hands lingered upon the goblet as Gamelyn took it, and her curtsey, too, delayed just that much more than necessary. "Lord." It was barely above a whisper. The girl's cheeks were flushed as her brown eyes met his.

"Aye," de Lacy was saying. "Siham's father was a battle comrade. I agreed to see to her favourable dispensation. A good husband is out of the question, of course, but I'd lose a valuable asset in the giving. My archer not only has a bow arm that takes a notorious outlaw to best, but a scripting skill a monk would be hard pressed to match."

The serving girl retreated to fetch more goblets for the others. De Lacy watched her go, intent, then gave an abrupt smile and tipped his goblet to Gamelyn in salute.

"Serving *you* first," he murmured. "Well done. You could have that one tonight, did you crook your smallest fing—" A stutter and frown, as if only then had de Lacy remembered he was speaking to a Templar.

Gamelyn acknowledged the gaffe with a shrug and tip of his own goblet. The assumption rankled for reasons well beyond any vows . . . or outward expression, amongst these men. It didn't prevent his following the girl with his eyes. More from bewilderment than any fancy, to be sure . . . *Lord?*

"Infernal methods, but practical. We'll put them to God's use." Durham jabbed two fingers at the sketched plan of Blyth, then slid them over to the one of Nottingham, more detailed. "Where is Ranulf gathering, David?"

"My men have met Ranulf's *here*." Huntingdon traced a line along the river winding just south of the castle. "We plan to secure the outer bailey first. The mill and the lower town are already taken. Relatively easy and bloodless—only a few soldiers needed to be positioned there—but alas, taking the surround was never the true difficulty."

Gamelyn exchanged a glance with Hubert. Nottingham's sheer cliff-face redoubt made "difficulty" an understatement.

"The outer bailey is the only sane approach." Durham nodded agreement. "You'll waste good men trying the Rock."

"If my brother still bided there . . . but alas." De Lacy's gaze touched Gamelyn's again, a momentary frown, then tilted his head upward, eyes fastening to the huge, curved beams of the ceiling. Recollecting his thoughts. "He held to his choices for too long."

"An easy thing to do in such times," Huntingdon agreed.

Gamelyn's attention wandered from the parchment replica of Nottingham to that of Blyth. His fingers itched to correct it. Siham obviously possessed only the barest knowledge, and that likely filled in by de Lacy and Durham. Neither of whom knew it as well as Gamelyn did . . .

Hubert was watching; his mouth twitched as if he read the thought.

"Engines," Durham suggested.

"For Nottingham they'll need to be substantial. And the engineer capable of such feats is in London, preparing for the King's arrival."

"Aye, and because of that arrival, we've no time to starve Tickhill out. I've already brought an engineer from York. Rest assured they"— another intemperate jab of fingers at the sketch—"will think twice when we start constructing a *petraria*."

A siege engine would reduce Blyth's walls to rubble. An inchoate sound of protest started in Gamelyn's throat—and unfortunately didn't halt there.

Worse, the others heard. Durham's jaundiced gaze slid sideways, eyebrows drawing thunderous at such impertinence. The stewards mirrored their lords' reactions: Huntingdon surprised and de Lacy curious.

Gamelyn cursed—silent this time, nothing given on his face. The reflex had been foolish. The castle's fate was not within his rights to protest.

"My lord Bishop." Hubert intercepted Durham's affront. "Forgive my *Confanonier*, and kindly remember his father was lord of that selfsame keep upon which you think to wreak havoc."

"And has some grounds for dissent, as he proved his right to the castle's honour through trial by battle," de Lacy added, considering the spread map with crossed arms. He had, after all, been present at Nottingham the day Gamelyn had defeated his treacherous elder brother Johan—not only for his freedom, and Robyn's, but to reclaim his name right. "He's also the one who obtained the Queen's release this past winter."

Durham's eyebrows kept up their fierce dance, but now expressed less ire and more insistent query.

"I'd capable assistance," Gamelyn demurred.

Query dissolved into an incredulous snort. "Capable?" Durham repeated. "I'd say so, if rumour is true and the man who assisted you was the same who so 'capably' assisted me from my purse two springs ago upon a trip to London! I avoid Sherwood like plague, and I'm not the only one. How did it come to pass that one of Hirst's brethren can summon Robyn Hood?"

Gamelyn said the only thing he reasonably could. "We were . . . um . . . children together?"

Silence. Then Durham laughed, a rolling chuckle that echoed through the hall.

"I told you, Hugh," de Lacy drawled and extended a hand, palm up. "Told you that one of Hirst's own was privy to the wolfshead's trust. Pay up."

"Anon." Still chuckling, Durham waved de Lacy's demand aside.

"No weaselling from this, now. I know you men of God. My dear little brother the prior is the most acquisitive and tight-fisted devil south of the shire's border."

"Settle your wager over supper," Huntingdon suggested, tossing a casual grin towards the Templars. "I'll bear witness. For now, there are plans to be made."

Hip-deep in the riverlet, sideways to her approach, he kept splashing and scooping and showing no sign he'd heard—until she was halfway to the bank where he'd dropped his clothes. "You're noisy as a browsing cow, woman!"

Marion didn't alter her gait, not one whit. "And you can reckon it's a-purpose, *man*. Save me from spooking you into running lost and bare-arsed through the Wode! 'Tis still a sight cold, nights."

Robyn snorted through a palmful of water, let it trickle through his fingers, then dove. He surfaced upstream, sleek-wet and lean as an otter.

Marion shivered and lowered herself to her haunches, forearms wrapped about her knees. Robyn watched her, grinned, then lurched from the water and started over, shrivelled and shivering and dripping *wet*.

And too late for Marion to do anything but warn, "Nay, don't you dar—!" It rose into a shriek as he did dare, bent over her, and shook like a rangy, wet dog.

She rolled out from under, clawing up a chunk of loam to throw at him. "Give ower, you pillock, t' water's bloody *cold!*"

The damp earth hit Robyn square between the eyes, and he yipped. Slinging wet ringlets from his face, he rubbed at the bridge of his nose with a look of vast offense.

"Serves you right. Silly sod," she grumbled as he pulled a soft leather split from his bag and began to dry off. "Our water'll be hot, soon enough, but you *want* t' swim in spring melt. Mam allus said you'd outgrow it."

"I hope not. Gets the heart pumping, right enough, and the skin stinging."

She rose, snatched the cloth, and snapped it at Robyn's arse. Another yip as he danced sideways. After a chary look, Robyn consented to her approach—this time, to rub his back dry.

"Did you chase Gamelyn away, then?" Lightly said, it wasn't lightly meant.

Nor did it fool her brother. Sloe eyes slid to hers, touched, then glanced away. "That one chases himself right proper wit'out me." It was a growl.

"He wain't, then."

"He's all mixed up in his bloody head. Again. He *thinks* too much."

"Allus has, allus will, pet," Marion soothed both with voice and the cloth at his nape, wicking wet from black curls. "'Tis part of what we love in him."

"Mm. More like part of what makes me addled!" Robyn snorted. "Still, he's addled up all the worse. And this?" A shrug beneath her hands, and pale skin drawing up in gooseflesh—but not from chill. "This bides . . . different. I've seen him confused, sure enough. Mixed up and mashed about, torn 'twixt heart and head and duty bound t' his hell and back. But now? It's *fear* what lights those pretty green eyes."

"The ritual's no light matter, Hob-Robyn—"

"There's no denying that."

"—particularly for the likes of him."

"The likes of him, aye. Sommun as has faced down those night-mares, and what he survived in Saracen lands?" Robyn gave a tiny huff and shrugged, pulled away. "I've oft wondered if there's owt left he does fear—and that's worrisome enough without . . . *this.*"

Her brother's deep baritone could fill the Wode or whisper akin to a lullaby; now it curled soft, bewildered. *Apprehensive.* A tiny shiver licked up Marion's spine. When had this happened? They had spent the last fortnights in a long and lovely thaw, heeding only the forest's breath and their own.

Aye, and she'd not been paying nigh enough attention, giddy with her own new-made lover. In her defence, Much was enough to fill a woman, heart *and* body. A tiny, appreciative grin quirked at her lip. Still, any tension between Robyn and Gamelyn—it had been growing, she conceded that now—she'd shrugged away as merely the newest feint and parry of normal swordplay, another sidestep in a dance of attraction between two wilful and rather arsy men.

"There's sommat more plaguing him than just the ritual, then," she reflected, slow.

A snatch at the pile of clothes on the turf, and Robyn began shrugging into them. Dark eyes met hers, open-earnest. "I'm think-ing t' like, aye. It's akin to a whisper, soft but there beneath every step he takes, cold and like to bend as well-forged metal." A snort. "That's nowt new, is it? But this is different. He en't that lad crippled by fear of his god."

"By what the Church says of his god."

"'Tis the same in the end. Aye? Our gods have the forms we give 'em—the life we breathe is theirs, from otherworlds to this-world. The White Christ was surely a just and holy man from what our mam said, here to make sacrifice for wrongs done in his god's name." Another snort, Robyn shaking his head and looking out into the forest. "Aye, and *that* were so well done. Instead his people took t' squabbling ower who mattered most to him, and who knew best what he'd said." He turned back to Marion, reached out, and fingered a cinnabar curl behind her ear. It was gentle as his next words, as the kiss he laid to her cheek and the forehead against hers. "And whilst the Christ walked equal with women, his bloody-minded followers do nowt but make 'em into virgins or whores, all the while respectin' neither. Why d'you think I take such care with you, pet? I know *they* wain't."

Tears burned behind her eyes. The two of them remained there, foreheads touching, silent comfort for long moments. Robyn kissed her other cheek, turned away, and took up the rest of his clothes.

"I See the warp and weft, twining through and past me," he muttered, almost angry. "We've been safe enough in winter's grasp, but the Church wain't rest 'til they plough us under or scythe us down. We've two choices: submit or keep fighting. And there's nowt of submission left in me."

The words both chilled and warmed. Marion folded the damp hide over one arm without truly seeing it.

"I wain't fret ower what'll come of't; I've no fear of my *tynged*. But . . . he *does*. And he holds it so close that none can so much as make a guess to why. It's senseless!"

Robyn was right, their Summerlord had upon him a dread too powerful for words . . . but he was wrong too. It made an odd sort of sense.

"He doesn't know who he is," Marion whispered, nigh to herself, but Robyn heard. Turned, his frown curious and disquieted both. "'Tis what Much said to me, not so long ago." A sudden tremor flinched her spine . . . not only Much's admission, but Gamelyn's own. First by Barrow Mere. Then after a clandestine meeting in Worksop Abbey that had nearly gone terribly wrong. Both times hesitant and unwilling, circumstance forcing even that and only in private, to Marion, as if open admittance were a weakness not to be borne.

"Mari?"

"He thinks he's a . . . snake with two heads." At Robyn's confusion, she clarified, "Gamelyn."

"Mm. If only one would swallow the other," Robyn quipped without much humour. "Like that great wyrm old Cernun once drew for me in t' caverns, swallowing its own tail. Mayhap our lovely Oak'd be twice as wise, rather than denying everything 'twould make him whole."

"But to his people, serpents are temptation."

"'His people.' Aye, that nigh explains it."

"Nay, it wain't, because now *we're* his people!"

"We are. And sometimes, Mari, I think he might even believe it."

"Hob-*Robyn!*"

"Fancy I'd find Guy of Gisbourne oft easier to bide with than the lad I fell heart ower heels for." Robyn stepped into his breeches, squirming as damp skin foiled worn leathers. "Gamelyn's a different sort altogether, en't he?"

"Gamelyn has allus belonged here. Gisbourne . . . that one . . ."

"Careful, pet, else you'll start sounding like our Charming William."

As shots went, it flew square. And painful. Marion flushed. "I en't talking like t' Will, and you know what I'm meaning. Gisbourne died. Upon the Solstice."

"Did he, then? And here I thought t' Summerlord were *born* in winter's tide."

The words settled in her stomach, chill combat against the flush settling, angry, in her cheeks. Marion stubbornly chose the latter. "Hob-Robyn, are you *trying* to start a row?"

Robyn paused, shook his head, and went on tying his breeches. "You're one as said two heads, Mari, pet. You and Gamelyn both, refusing to look at it square and plain. Way I see it, Gisbourne is the one as kept our Gamelyn alive."

More chill, and Marion had no idea how to answer that.

Robyn milked the remaining wet from his curls and shook them. From across the waterway, something rustled, then creaked. Marion gave a tiny start. Robyn reacted with a breathtaking speed that suggested a gaggle of shire-reeve guards had stampeded the little clearing. Dropping to a crouch, he'd daggers snatched and ready in each hand before Marion had so much as let out her startled breath.

More rustles. Robyn crisscrossed his knives, scraped them together. Muttered something that sounded altogether kin to an iron charm.

A family of otters burst into view, sliding and tumbling along the opposite bank, leaping for the water rowdy as lads in for a bit of fun after harvest.

With a self-deprecating snort, Robyn twirled his blades, one and then the other, into the earth. Still crouched, he watched the otters sport, diving and fetching in the shallows until they reached the deeper parts, where they slid underwater and disappeared.

Marion came up behind to rest her hands upon his bare shoulders. She gave the thick, damp hair a questioning tug.

"There's spirits aplenty in our Wode o' late," he said, as if in apology. "I hear things that I think en't there . . . and sometimes they en't. But then?" Nostrils flaring, Robyn lifted his head, profile sharp but his murmur soft into the trees. "Sometimes they are." He regained the shortest blade, gave it an idle toss-and-twirl. "En't so bad here, at the Howe. Our da's people roped this valley with spells and prayers 'gainst the likes of 'em. Cold iron and All-Father lore stays t' fae, but . . . "

"Fae." It was nigh whispered, Marion half fearing to so much as summon the sound.

"Aye." Robyn met her eyes. "They're watching. More and more they're trying t' bounds, crossing over into thisnow. At the Mere. In the Hermit's caverns. Even, from what you told me, in the Templar places." As Robyn rose and turned to her, the dagger twined itself with milt-berried mistletoe even as antlers ghosted at his brow and his eyes glittered: sudden, eldritch gold. "Dos' tha hear, Maiden? Dos' tha *remember?*"

Marion did. The recollections of the past winter were scant but unforgettable:

Her brother sleeping in their camp yet present upon the banks of Barrow Mere as well, his shade clothed as the Horned Lord, with fireflies gilding His antlers, mimicking the reflected eyes of tens of creatures behind . . . creatures who vanished when Gamelyn, as much accident as deep-set knowing, had drawn iron: his sword.

The Hermit's caverns, where John and Robyn had been snowed in for over a fortnight by any normal reckoning . . . save that within those caverns, a mere three days had passed.

At Temple Hirst, where a fierce well of barely leashed powers lay in wait—yet where a dark Lady of the otherworld took a Virgin Maid's due and waited for Motherhood.

A breath, vibrating thisworld and into others. A rustle in the woodland, waking wet to dry itself at the embers kindling within her brother's gaze. Fear of, and longing for, something not quite there. Something not quite . . . human.

"Aye, Mari." Robyn was following her, easy as breathing. "The magic is rousing, turning in its sleep. Dreaming itself awake."

Every sense knew it for truth, spun it with gossamer strands that wrapped her own spirit tighter within the Lady's will. All those skeins, unravelling from Her fingers: to coax Summer's Knight into the flames and the green, to weave a timeless, crystalline pattern for Her dark and wilding Winterlord to dance.

Indeed, you have spent long enough rejoicing in homely things and a skilled lover's touch. The Lady's presence was soft as a sigh, but inexorable. *There are other needs to tend, Maiden.*

What must we do?

Weave the fates, even as they transform upon Our fingertips. We cannot always ken the steps. Particularly as your pwca brother calls the Dance.

Robyn seemed oblivious, girding the smallest dagger snug at his left calf. It still seemed so . . . peculiar how her brother, the forest magic overflowing his lanky frame, should so revere yet so scarcely hear Her. Whereas Gamelyn, who denied and jessed his talent like a recalcitrant haggard, felt Her beguile his every step.

"Gamelyn talks of choices like a nobleman, but there en't much choice to be had anymore." Mayhap Robyn needn't always hear the Lady, running tandem with his sister's thoughts as he oft did. "Our land needs us—*all* of us—heart-whole and wielding what power's left. Just by being here, the three of us together, we're giving cause for t' old magics to rear up into thisworld. Willed or nay." He bent, took up the dagger that had been Gamelyn's, ran a light thumb down the length of the gleaming blade. Slid it home in its sheath.

"We've called, Mari. In intent *and* innocence. An' they're answering."

-IV-

"**D**e Furnival's hip-deep in it, I'll warrant. He's thick with Count John."

Well, and Roger de Lacy had his own reasons to slight de Furnival. Gamelyn exchanged a quick glance over the map with Hubert, whose eyebrows were drawing together. Historically the seat of powerful lords—first Saxon Waltheof, then Normans de Busli and Lovetot—the honour known as Hallamshire oft held most of Sheffield and the southwestern borders of Yorkshire to the eastmost bounds of Tickhill, with holdings nigh to Conisbrough and down into Worksop. De Furnival had gained those with his recent marriage to the heir of de Busli and Lovetot . . . though, in the wake of foreign Angevin wars and ransom, his lady's inheritance had been winnowed and bought, piecemeal, by lords with more ready tender.

Such as de Lacy.

No doubt John had offered return of those rights in exchange for fealty.

"De Furnival is young and has realised his errors. He came to me for advice, and I gave it." Huntingdon's reminder voiced itself soft, but no less pointed. A slight, telltale flush worked its way up de Lacy's neck. He said nothing—in truth could not, since Huntingdon's own rights ran deep; his grandmother had, after all, been Waltheorf's daughter.

Aye, this was proving, as Robyn might have said, *more fun than a sack of brassed-off badgers.* Gamelyn kept his hands at his back, even when an injudicious tilt of head threatened to let fall most of his forelock into his eyes. He merely raised his chin, willed it to stay, and laced his fingers together. He was but an observer, considering the landed shenanigans at play.

Yet . . .

He *wanted* to wade in, as if it was his due. Part and parcel of his most egregious failing, yet just as Lionheart was returning to what was his, so Gamelyn felt the longing . . . the *pride*. . . and one nigh heated as any physical hunger. His father had been a good man, a competent warden of Blyth; he'd both succeeded and failed in bequeathing such things to his sons. Was it any surprise the longing also remained, handed down and inculcated? His own place, his own right. One Gamelyn had earned not by accident of birth, but reputation and blood and war.

Legacy to a home, long thought gone. A *haven*.

The tiny fancy, hitherto unuttered, dived away in panic as soon as it surfaced.

"—advice was truly heeded, David, for he brought men to the siege. They were needed, 'struth. The castellan has proven mule-headed. Won't listen to reason. A bloody waste, for Tickhill should have been easy, and now it looks as though we'll have to take it down in pieces."

No, not pieces! something protested, deep-set, in Gamelyn. As if *it* had the right. And as if right wasn't ultimately a slippery and pernicious concept. Richard might be by grace of God King of England, yet it was his punitive skills that convinced these proud, powerful men to bend beneath said right. Undeniable magnetism, the churning wake of a fearsome reputation in battle, and a family rumoured to be spawned of the devil himself was what sent vassals scurrying down the feudal chain to indulge in their own strangely muscular flex of "rights": a parcelling-out of territory sure as a stream of piss aimed at one's leg.

And *putain de merde*, not only prideful, but seditious as ever he'd accused of Robyn. A grin made its try for Gamelyn's lip, failed as the talk wove about him. More assurances of punitive action, with the possibilities of fire and stone delivering them, and his nape hairs were beginning to stand on end.

Home. *Mine.*

The feeling was stark—and bewildering.

"If Nottingham proves to last against you, our men will be of help," Durham was saying. "So Tickhill must be swiftly broken."

"Why must you 'break' Tickhill at all?"

Almost as one, the Bishop, the Baron, and the Earl swung around to stare at Gamelyn. They couldn't believe he'd spoken, much less what he had said. Gamelyn couldn't quite believe it himself.

"They will not bend, so they must break, young man!" Durham snapped. "Good Lord, Hubert, I thought you said this man was an experienced soldier, had been with you to the Holy Land!"

"He was in Outremer at my side for over three years," Hubert put in, deceptively mild.

"Then he should know better!"

"I know what comes of sieges, my lord Bishop," Gamelyn retorted . . . *and bloody hell,* but what was wrong with him?

Shut t' bloody fuck up, Gamelyn, Robyn teased from memory.

I'm trying! he spat back.

Trying, truly, to recapture Guy. Guy would have seethed—if at all—in sullen privacy. Would have kept his mouth shut, his thoughts in shadow, and his heart stone-cold. Guy was the defrocked Templar, the assassin whose sins held no power over him, whilst Gamelyn . . .

Gamelyn, the Lady suddenly breathed across his neck, *belongs to Us.*

He shivered, nearly ducked to let Her fingers flit that stray, wanting-to-fall bit of forelock into his eyes. Instead he tossed it farther back, bade Her silent.

All in a heartbeat, and the lift of chin provoking Durham to rally despite an underling's challenge. "You know sieges, do you?"

"He was at Acre." Hubert, again. "And Jaffa. And rode at my side upon the march to take Jerusalem."

Huntingdon's eyebrows rose. De Lacy looked down, grumbled a sigh. Durham blinked, but persisted, "Therefore, you comprehend what comes of siege, however ugly. We have demanded answer, given every opportunity for Tickhill to surrender upon order of the rightful King."

Aye, he will answer Us. The Horned Lord's hiss was muted, yet insistent. *His Church will ken your power—Our power—'ere this is done.*

Oh God, not *now.* "And, my lord Bishop, why should Tickhill believe you?"

Durham blinked again. *Because I'm the sodding Bishop of Durham, that's why!* flashed in his eyes; his mouth was too taken aback to shape any answer.

Whilst Gamelyn's mouth kept running on despite those level gazes, and he still couldn't so much as . . . *shut the bloody fuck up.* "Count John received the honour of Tickhill *from* King Richard."

"But not the castle. Not Blyth."

"Indeed, my lord, but the Count has spent his time ensuring the loyalty of the castle and its demesne over the past several years, as my lord of Pontefract well knows. Several years, my lord Bishop, of a king powerless in gaol, of a country beggaring itself to free him whilst regents come and go and make a precarious situation into pure chaos. Small blame to Blyth if they found a powerful lodestone in Count John and followed it. Small blame to anyone, in such times."

The words pinked them; from the two stewards' puffed-up

affront, to Huntingdon's silvery upraised brows, to de Lacy's shoulders thrown back, to Durham still gaping not unlike a landed fish, and Hubert . . .

There was a faint twinkle to Hubert's eye.

The latter was what finally, *finally* caused Gamelyn's mouth to snap shut, all the while thinking, *Bloody sodding Hell, but you have been around Robyn too long!*

It was then the quirk chased across Hubert's mouth. Once more he inserted, smooth as well-churned butter, "My *Confanonier* has been long at the wars and in the wild. In consequence, our tenets of silence are oft overawed by brutal necessity."

Ears heating from the slight reproof, Gamelyn nevertheless did not lower his gaze. Or unclasp his hands from behind his back—even when the bit of forelock that had been threatening to fall did, spilling across his face.

"And as prideful as any Templar born, I see!" Durham finally spoke—though it was more a snort.

"Prideful, mayhap." Huntingdon's look towards Gamelyn was altogether close, intent. "But nonetheless sensible."

"Sensible! Cheeky, more like!" Durham glared.

Gamelyn met it with every ounce of bland courtesy he could summon.

"Mayhap Sir Ian's son acquired his father's canny head for tactics as well as his mother's looks," Huntingdon insisted. "Mayhap it is why you insisted upon his presence, Commander? A man who grew up in the castle's walls might well see a way to ensure its surrender—one that others cannot. And if that man is also the same who enabled Queen Eleanor's escape—from beneath the nose of her youngest son, mind you . . . ?"

With an abrupt bark of laughter, Durham shoved back from the map, still peering at Gamelyn. "Well, Sir Ian of Blyth's son the Templar. You might have made your way in and out the once all unawares, but you'll not find yourself so easily skulking into a castle buttressed and held against attack. Unless your brain"—a drawl, scathing—"is bold as your tongue."

Gamelyn slid a fleeting glance towards his Master. Hubert's eyes were fairly alight. The old fox had been waiting for just this moment.

The Lady was, for a mercy, silent.

Holding his Master's gaze, Gamelyn took a deep breath, then let it out before speaking to the others. "At the very least, my lords, I know several who can make up any lack I possess, and mayhap know the castle even better than I."

"Not Templars. I assume"—Durham's tone was resigned—"you mean these outlaws of yours."

Gamelyn tucked a smirk into one cheek. "Aye, my lord Bishop. One of Robyn Hood's men was a stable lad at Blyth from a very young age. My paxman too was bound there as guard. What places I don't know, they do. We can find a way."

De Lacy spoke into waiting silence. "I have my own information. Another reason why this young Templar might be our damage-proof way into Blyth's walls . . . and without relying upon outlaw scum, I might add."

Gamelyn slid a chary glance to de Lacy, standing at the table's end. The favour wasn't returned. De Lacy's expression, intent upon Durham, would have been well at home on a mousing cat.

"The man Count John left to hold the castle is one who, until a few months ago, was my own steward." De Lacy crossed powerful arms, still focused upon Durham. "When I was pondering—as were we all!—the most politic way to heed a royal request of support—"

"A support that had already rid us of bloody Longchamps," Durham muttered.

A fleeting smirk from de Lacy, but he continued. "Aye, and this steward of mine acted as my intermediary to Count John. Former steward, I should say. His defection was a surprise at the time. Both grateful and loyal, he possessed scant initiative—or so I thought— to change allegiance once given." Only then did his gaze flit to Gamelyn and hold, challenge and—mayhap—a slight.

Gamelyn refused to let so much as mild puzzlement quirk his brow.

De Lacy hadn't quite the same mastery over his own emotions. He frowned and continued, still peering at Gamelyn, "As you said, Brother Guy: Who can blame a man who grasps the lodestone of royal favour in troublesome times? Otho Boundys de Blyth has always been altogether prone to the literal."

The name snuck in and heeled with a sharp nip. *Otho.*

Thankfully, Gamelyn still couldn't react. Wouldn't, insecure in this place, with these people.

Huntingdon did it for him. "You mean, 'tis Ian's second son who holds the castle *against* us?"

Hubert slid his gaze sideways and held to Gamelyn's. He hadn't known either.

"Aye." De Lacy seemed a bit put out that his words provoked no reaction. His next ones were directed at Gamelyn. "The Count wooed Otho with promises of hereditary holdings—all quite legitimate, mind you, as your eldest brother . . . ah . . . died without issue. As to the youngest, who won the right to his own claim through trial by battle on Nottingham's bailey, then disap- peared into Sherwood, mortally wounded?" A shrug. "Of such things are jongleurs' tales made. Most believe Gamelyn Boundys never returned from the Holy Land. Including his middle brother."

"Go it!" Marion crowed and thumped one fist into her palm. "*Take him, then!*"

Another clank-clash, then a scrape, then a heavy *whup!* of steel sculpting air. A glittering arc reflected against the firelight as Gilbert twisted in a lithe whirl of disengagement and circled his opponent.

Will was sweating. This time he didn't make the mistake of wiping it from his eyes, merely tossed his head to one side, moisture flying.

"Watch it, lads!" Arthur coaxed.

Will grinned, then lunged.

Gilbert danced aside and smacked the flat of his blade on Will's arse . . . only to yelp as Will spun and whacked the blade nigh from his grip. Another lunge followed, and Gilbert leapt over the fire in retreat.

"A Gilly!" David sang out as Arthur whooped his delight.

"That's more like it!" Marion cheered.

"An' who're you rooting for, then?" Robyn nudged her with a grin.

"Does it matter?"

"It might, should that lovely lad you're tupping decide to get in on t' game."

Marion wrinkled her nose at him, and Robyn grinned wider. By his lights, it had been just this short of brilliant to come back from too much thinking after a bath to this little bit of entertainment.

"Not bad for a 'ham-fisted peasant,' eh?" Will growled at Gilbert, who blew him a kiss from across the fire.

"I'm a peasant," Much drawled from the sidelines and waggled his fingers. "See, no ham fists. You use 'em proper, and they'll loosen up."

"But 'twere better?" Will's query was just this side of plaintive, and Robyn couldn't help his loud snort. Will scowled. "Belt up, you!"

"Aw, Scathelock, but for such a handsome, shaggable beast, you're a proper bairn."

Marion was giggling. Good.

"Aye, and this from one who *is* a ham-fisted peasant when it comes to a sword!" Will retorted.

"Are y' after practicing, or back-talking Himself?" Much put in. "Or are you wanting *me* to pick up a sword?"

Robyn smirked. It was a proper threat, no question. Will had come along well, but he was still struggling to stand down Gilbert. Against Much . . . well.

Marion exchanged the smirk with him, nudged him back.

"Give me a bit more o' this practice," Will boasted. "Come summer, I'll give you a right thrashing."

Much snorted, but his eyes lit with that lazy, dangerous glint.
"You and two more like you."

A frown wanted to twitch at Robyn's brow, smoothed away as
John came up beside him, slipping a hand into his and leaning his
brown head against Robyn's shoulder.

And was forgotten as David tipped the lid from the cauldron.
The roasted-spice scent of cooking venison wafted outward as he
sang out, triumphant, "Supper!"

The pool is wide and black, a shimmer of half light stretching out,
lapping gently against his bare toes. The other side beckons, thick
with undergrowth, heavy with trees in first leaf. A wet fog
meanders, hanging upon this limb, that bush, plastering his hair
to his skull and leaving a velvety scrim upon bare limbs.

*Come, Oakbrother. Leave by the iron and bells. Be dancing with us.
Be swimming beside us.*

Alarm thrills up and down his spine—has he heard these voices
before? Has he not?—but no matter; he wants to obey. Of their
own accord, his hands set aside sword and dagger, a foolish
concession. He tells himself it is safe enough, the voices are merely
the hum and whir of fireflies. They are the only light in the glade,
fits and starts illuminating hanks of mist, darting about him as he
disrobes, skimming reflections upon the opaque mirror that is
Barrow Mere. The moon is dark behind the clouds, the stars
obscured . . .

Nay, not the only light. His instincts are true; *something*, though
he knows not what, lurks in Barrow Mere. A passage in the
underbrush, a promise of adversity. Ghost-trails upon the water,
gleaming. Voices and dancing shadows. Eyes regard him, winking-
wet, reflecting the fireflies dancing in the murk.

Watching.

He angles down, naked but for the cord about his hips—
Templar's measure, Templar's oath—and palms the discarded
dagger. It is the one Robyn wears, but in this place . . .
thisnow . . . it has returned to his hand for some purpose. The
fireflies cluster about it, curious lights upon sharp steel.

Gamelyn sends them scattering with a twirl of the dagger, then
utters several sounds all breathy and laced together. Not Frankish,
not Latin, not Arabic, nor any of the myriad tongues he garnered
in the Holy Land. This is a language he does not truly know.

But the eyes know it. They go out. A whirl and *whuff* of breath
brings wild eddies to the mist. As if summoned, sharp tines rise
from the mists of the opposite bank, the god-man abandoning His
cloak of shadows, eyes glowing like a beast faced by torches. The

fireflies abandon Gamelyn for their master, cutting swathes of gilt against ivory skull and horns. And the light . . . expands.

Lean and pale, the god-man spreads his arms. Breathes. The horns burst from tawny to green: holly twined with mistletoe and ivy, acorns and oak. A staff seems to grow from one outstretched palm; it blossoms into spring leaves in the time it takes the god-man to breathe twice. From behind Him the sun begins to rise, light misting further the glade, spreading farther, and farther, letting summering into the land.

And the forest begins to dance.

Gamelyn cannot so much as join them; he is fixed in place by the Seeing, how it spirals out from the god-man . . . from himself . . . *tynged's* loom spinning them into one source.

Into such fair welcome, She enters: rising sinuous from the Mere, gleaming dark-wet beneath tendrils of cinnabar hair. The Lady spreads Her arms, and in their embrace is illuminated a scene of golden peace and plenty. Blessings made with games of fire and strength. Dances winding the year's wheel through mist and rain, snowfall and bare branches, into warm sun and clear night, leaf-fall and renewal.

Until games are no longer enough.

The change is subtle: first the shadows. Creeping in, absolute, they banish all between. The eyes, one by one, wink out. Fierce winds blow a conflagration of flames through the forest. The Horned figure's immense rack dips, green withering, skull-face stark from beneath. His cloak falls, turns to ash, sprinkles in a gust of chill wind to scatter the Mere's surface.

Winter-borne . . . the skull remains, shivers, then begins to rise: the figure cowled beneath the bare horn-crown, carrying bow and arrow instead of staff. There is fire behind Him, eyes glinting in the blaze blown upon the wind and spreading through the green—but it does not burn. It illuminates, gilt and green, the Wheel's turning.

Rebirth, the Hooded god-man whispers. *The reason. . . the truth. . . of Sacrifice.*

That voice is wildfire; one that will wreck, wound, and wend shivers down his spine. And in truth, upon the opposite bank does wildfire wait, personified. It blazes in the sloe gaze of a man become Hooded archer become avatar of a woodland spirit. It leaps and glimmers upon the pitch-wrapped tip of a nocked arrow. Bow canted horizontally before him, as long as he is tall—and the archer is, indeed, tall—it is half at nock, with arrow-tip aflame.

A flash of teeth beneath the cowl, and the archer raises then bends the bow. Aims for Gamelyn's heart, flames licking at the arrow shaft. Looses. Gamelyn does not so much as flinch.

The arrow strikes him through the heart, burning. It is agony. It is . . .

Welcome.

Falling from his hand, the quillion dagger buries itself halfway into the soft, fecund earth.

Guy of Gisbourne died on Samhain, beheaded by Robyn Hode. He did not go easily. The Lady's voice, tickling his ear.

"Nothin' should go easy, pet." And it is impossible, but Robyn is with him, placing a hand upon the fire-wound, sending agony into a different, sweeter pain. "Not you. Not me. But we must go, aye?"

Not you. Not yet, the Lady murmurs against Gamelyn's nape . . . only She is Marion—just as impossible as Robyn's presence. Cradling him, surrounding him with the scent of desert roses whilst he lies dying. Clad in all the greens of summer, horn-crown gleaming sharp upon her cinnabar head, his Maiden sings to him a song old when they were children:

> *"Sumer is icumin in*
> *Lhude sing, cuccu*
> *Groeþ sed, and bloweþ med*
> *And springeþ Wode new*
> *Sing! Cuccu. . ."*

It has to be a dream. Has to be . . .

Dream? Or nightmare? Robyn leans forwards, kisses his fore-head. *'Tis all they are, Guy. Haven't you already lived enough of your hell in thisworld?*

Stop calling him Guy! Marion says. *Guy is dead.*

Is he? Gamelyn's own voice, a memory quiet yet slurried with threat. *Is he, really?*

Nay, says Robyn, and over one bare, sinewy shoulder, Gamelyn can see another dream/vision/nightmare: the Horned Lord across the Mere. And whilst the Lady wears His crown, He wears a wreath of mistletoe and oak.

Make of him dryw, *Hooded One. Only with the magic will he survive. And he must survive, for we will need him, when the time comes.*

Then it is mine to make the sacrifice. Robyn stands, clad only in sky and shadows and long curls of ebon hair, then pulls from the earth the lovely filigreed dagger—once Gamelyn's—that now never leaves his side.

Holds it out to Gamelyn. Smiles.

Says, *Take it, Oakbrother. Take me* . . .

Gamelyn bolted upright, both hands over his mouth. The shout castrated itself into a whimper, buzzing against his palms, fizzling into the barest of echoes against dark stone walls.

Slowly, reality crept back. He wasn't at Barrow Mere, wandering where he didn't belong in nightmares come to life. Nay, 'twas Clipstone's great hall, where he lay on a rush-padded cloak, with his Master and his Templar Brethren close. Taking in a long breath, Gamelyn closed his eyes, looked again just to be sure. Aye, six gathered, weapons to hand, lying beside the fire. Gamelyn could have reached out and touched Hubert's shoulder.

All of them were still sleeping, thank God.

Gamelyn put first one hand to the pallet beneath him, then another, propping himself, panting. Firelit embers spilt orange light across his splayed hands. For a sparse heartbeat, it darkened, resembled blood.

Gritting his teeth, Gamelyn shook his head, stared into the fire for long moments, then shut his eyes. Even the brilliant remnants ghosting his lids didn't obscure the play of it, over and over again, a foul mummer's dance with but one ending: betrayal. One last arrow shot into the sweet green Wode, then the dagger laid across the pale throat.

Sometimes Robyn lay in his arms willing. Others he struggled. But always, the same inexorable end: sacrifice wrought with the lovely gilt-and-glimmer knife, lovers/rivals in the long dance of myth become life, and Winter's blood upon Summer's hands.

"It is what you are meant to do, were born to do, within this little Dance in which we've found ourselves."

The nightmares had returned.

Gamelyn lurched up and stumbled from the hall.

It took some time to regain control. The flagstones swallowed his steps. The wall bordering the inner bailey had escorted him thrice around. Gamelyn made it four, breath wafting thick behind him as he stalked, nigh soundless beneath a diamond-and-ebon sky and burrowed into his cloak. Incense clung there, musky-sweet reminder of the peace only a few hours hence, spent with his Brethren in observance of Evensong.

Once it had been all he wanted: the peace of prayer, the waft of frankincense, a library full of parchments. Fate—*tynged*—had decided otherwise, and faith? It had given way, inevitably, to reason and his own intelligence: damnably complicated, truth was not some unfaltering star a naïve and devout boy had pursued, and the portals of knowledge oft held fast by corruptible, fallible *men*.

There were many mansions in a Father's house . . . and a Mother's.

The latter waited, as always, a soft-thick presence beyond the walls of Clipstone: the Wode beckoned with Her own, darker peace. Gamelyn wanted to turn away, instead found himself taking in that calm with long, slow draughts of misted green, heady in its own fashion as any frankincense.

As if in answer, the breeze quickened over the courtyard, teasing at his hair and rustling the heavy boughs beyond. Gamelyn tensed, as if nightmares could become flesh.

For they could. He no longer doubted that.

Silence broke itself with a soft, mournful call. He started, then grimaced as another scratch and flutter rippled into a wave of rustles and coos from the top story of the building a stone's throw away. No more than the dovecote, settling in for the evening.

Gamelyn ran a hand over his face, found it damp with sweat, cursed beneath his breath.

He needed a smoke. Or a stalk. Or to mete out an arse-kicking to some deserving sod. He was keen as a good blade for the siege; if nothing else, 'twould set his head back on its axis.

Mayhap Hubert had a bit of the hashish lying about, to dull the edge until then.

Was it too much, he asked, silent into the waiting forest, *to hope the dreams gone?*

Is it too much, She answered, grave, *to hope you would stay where you belong?*

And where is that, Lady?

Silence, as deep within as without.

So. This is punishment, then.

Only a Fool cloaked in church resin would sass a goddess and imagine it penance.

The Voice wafted away as if on the breeze, replaced by the sound of approaching steps. Gamelyn stiffened for a bare moment, let out the breath he only then realised he was holding. The tread was nigh familiar as his own heartbeat.

"It is discomfiting, *non?*" Hubert murmured as he stalked over, an aged panther who'd lost none of his predatory grace. "To be confined within walls after sleeping beneath sky and bough."

Gamelyn turned a hesitant gaze, found those eyes upon him— and no less mindful than his own. Then he saw what Hubert held: a pewter goblet. Steam rose from it and wafted upon the night air, touching Gamelyn's nostrils with spice and ferment.

Not the hashish, but nonetheless a kind offering. He accepted it, drank deep. The mulled wine spread warmth from chilled toes to bared head.

Hubert was peering at the sky above the night-black trees. "A successful assembly. We have more options coming out than we did going in. And, my Brother, your grasp of tactics has but improved. I think this outlaw and his . . . *insurgeré?* Yes, this, ah, sense of insurrection has added an irregular sheen to your already considerable arsenal."

"*Werran,*" Gamelyn murmured.

"Eh?"

"*Werran.*" Louder this time, but not so as to disturb the surrounding quiet. "A Saxon word. It means to bring confusion."

"Ah. How apropos. Considering." Delicate, the phrasing. Reluctant to pry too far.

"A word Marion would use . . ." Gamelyn began, only to warble away, baffled by the sudden tangle of his tongue and the warmth brushing his cheeks. Hubert knew Marion, knew she was part of the outlaws Gamelyn had been ordered to accompany—

Infiltrate, a snide inner voice reminded. *Spy upon—*

—and what she represented to the Old Faith, so why should he fear to speak her name in the company of his Master, as if Marion represented some broken vow? Thank God the Lady had retreated, with the moon's rising. She would merely encourage such fascination.

Hubert watched Gamelyn flail in an inexplicable mire for a few heartbeats, and those overloud to his ears. A singular, throaty plaint wafted from the dovecote. From somewhere within the Wode's shadows, another answered.

And another grateful oath whispered upon Gamelyn's lips as Hubert did not pursue the silence. "You quite impressed my lord the Bishop."

Gamelyn shrugged. "Not that it matters."

"Ah, but it does. Durham is a powerful man. Our lord King thinks to flex his wings over the midlands and the North, but in truth? Between Durham and Richard's bastard brother—Bishop and Archbishop—*they* rule Yorkshire, albeit uneasily." A small *tsk.* "Hugh de Puiset is not an easy man to impress. To have him on your side in this little game can only serve us to the good."

Game. Everywhere I turn, the game draws closer, beckoning. And I've no wish to play.

A low, derisive snort, and the glint of tines against dark woodland. *If only Our Lady had an ardent lover for every time you were so certain. She'd no need of you, would She?*

Bugger off.

I should think that more reflects your *tastes, my Oak.* A chuckle wafted through the trees; the Horned Lord was Amused. *Ivy twines within your more-pleasant dreams, yet ever your fiercest passions long for the tangle and scratch of Holly. How confusing it must be for you. . . or mayhap not. You merely, O serpent, have twofold lusts to companion your twofold—*a pause, then a purr—*appendages.*

"I like it not that de Lacy was able to surprise us," Hubert said, thankfully unaware of any silent back-and-forth. "A congenial sort, *non?* But clever, and playing his own game."

Don't We all?

You would know, Gamelyn retorted inward even as he shrugged outward agreement.

"Pontefract thought his toss a winning one, to be sure. He wants something from you." Curious, the words, but unsurprised. Hubert turned his gaze upon the wall and the forest beyond, repeated, soft, "Most believe Gamelyn Boundys never returned from the Holy Land." The words scratched at the surface of control, looking to expose the whirl of anger, dread, and confusion that lay beneath. Blue-grey eyes turned to Gamelyn, gauging. Piercing. "I thought so myself, for some time."

"Mayhap"—slow, cautious—"he hasn't."

"Only mayhap?"

"I fear so." The admission made control easier, somehow. It helped that any sense of revelation was subsiding, seeping into different wisps of thought.

Yet none were pleasant—or unambiguous.

"Have no fear, my *Confanonier*. This . . . *amour fraternel?* It could prove useful. To us even more than de Lacy." Hubert's rich voice held firm, but allowed a soft etch about its edges.

Brotherly love. Gamelyn's mouth gave a sideways, sardonic tic. Aye, Hubert knew.

"In this peculiar instance, de Lacy is correct. Such a connection is as valuable as others you, ah, possess."

"I am a Templar, my Master. I possess nothing."

Hubert snorted fit to rival the Horned Lord. Concurrence, or reproach . . . or both, which Gamelyn considered most likely.

From the dovecote came another plaint. The wild bird answered.

"Our Master is upon necessary business, though he plans to meet with us at All Hallows Church. He will, no doubt, expect your, ah, *possession* of useful information." This time Hubert's tone dipped severe—a warning—even as he kept peering into the trees.

Wymarec de Birkin, Master Preceptor of all England's Templars, had dispatched Brother Guy to learn the Wode's secrets. It was no small disobedience, but likely a sin worthy of expulsion, to not accede to Robyn's persistence. A smile twitching at his lip—it held absolutely no humour—Gamelyn once more closed his eyes. Heard the dream-voice . . .

It is what you are meant to do, were born to do, within this little Dance in which we've found ourselves.

Shuddered, and drew his cloak closer.

Hubert misunderstood his reaction—or else, pretended to. "Of course, this newest development must not dissuade what course originally set itself within that clever brain of yours. Your paxman . . . ah, considering the circumstance, I will petition our Master Procurator to shorten Much's time of banishment. Until then, 'twill be easy to look the other way should he accompany you to siege." A smile, albeit small.

Relief filled Gamelyn. Granted, Much had found another occupation in courting Marion—and enjoying it—but he missed his former life, fretting like a warhorse tied whilst his companions galloped into battle. Gamelyn understood that all too well.

"And this other outlaw, this, ah, Little John?" Hubert continued, peering at him. It almost seemed . . . wary. "*Oui*, I understand these companions will prove adequate to the need, but if you bring the man himself, then Master Wymarec will be well pleased. And not only because wild Robyn can aid the cause to which we have been set."

Adequate to the need. Adequate to the danger. Aye, Much would help, but . . .

With Otho in residence, was there need for the outlaws to be endangered? Was this what the nightmare was trying to express?

"Of course"—Hubert had turned, watching Gamelyn close as if he guessed the rebellious timbre of his thoughts—"there will be sanctuary assured for any who choose to aid us. I myself will uphold it, with the Rule of the Temple."

And what of our Master, Master?

Wymarec de Birkin no doubt longed to see Robyn brought before the Templars, spoil of a war to which Gamelyn had grudgingly been committed.

Letting his own gaze wander to the trees, Gamelyn kept silence—further insubordination though it surely was. One likely unavoidable when consorting with a lot of Pagan rebels.

Too much had changed in a season's turning. *He* had changed.

The Temple is Gisbourne's place, he'd told Marion in the midst of winter's turning. *Gamelyn never lived there.*

Guy de Gisbourne belonged to the Templars, soul and body, questionable heart and predator's instincts.

Gamelyn—idealistic, curious Gamelyn—was *werran*.

Again, the captive dove sent a question into the night. Again came the answer, clearer: *Brother, here I am.*

"Ah, but Sherwood Forest is a dark place. Truly, none but those of the *dryw* would find such depths comforting." Hubert crossed his arms. "Finish the wine, clear your head, then come back inside. Sleep well, then join us for morning observances."

"I should return. We parted uneasily, and Robyn should be troub . . . " Gamelyn trailed off, realising the careless trust—the *confession*—in the words.

But then, Hubert already perceived so much. Did it matter?

Mayhap, the Horned Lord rumbled. *Should your Hubert stand in Our way—*

He will not.

Yet if he does—

Then I will not.

"I think, my *Confanonier*, Sherwood is indeed good for you." Hubert's voice was soft. "She cracks that carapace of yours quite adequately, eh?"

She. Hubert knew. Altogether more than Gamelyn lay easily with.

"If one considers such a thing 'good.'"

"*C'est ça.* If we do not occasionally crack and bend, we break. It is a knowledge that comes with age. When one is but . . . almost one-and-twenty, *non?*"—Hubert questioned Gamelyn's age with a tilt of eyebrow, which Gamelyn confirmed with a tiny nod—"one is loath to believe we are, in the end, very brittle creatures."

"I do realise that, you must know." Wry.

"You might realise it"—Hubert's return was just as wry—"but you're young enough to still not *believe* it. Not as I must."

"And if the . . . bending does not take?"

The wild bird called to its caged brother yet again. There was, this time, no return trill from the dovecote. Gamelyn found his eyes returning to the forest.

"It is a difficult thing, *non?* To bend something which is set so resolute."

"Mayhap impossible, without breaking."

Silence. The wild bird spoke, several times—*Where are you?*—and Gamelyn had the sudden, almost desperate need to compel an answer.

"Sometimes," Hubert murmured, his grey eyes altogether piercing, "the breaking must come. If we wish to rest. Or to be *whole.*"

Gamelyn closed his eyes.

Stillness was a strange and welcome peace. Only the sounds of night's breath rustled the new leaves, the thin scorch of hearth smoke trailing up and out, losing itself into the undeniable, green-dark *presence* beyond. The doves had gone silent.

No doubt they realised the impossibility of their situation.

"Guy. *Gamelyn.* Will he come?"

"I . . . " Gamelyn swallowed, hard, and looked away. "I know not."

- Entr'acte -

Even shielded in the best and most binding of silks and spells, the thing vibrated, this close to the Pagan folly.

He could see the latter, a long hill ridge of new green and old sere that dwarfed even the keep within which he stood. The top level of Peveril Castle's tower contained a spacious hall, lime washed bright-white and embellished with a dusty ochre blush that, the castle's seneschal had assured, nigh matched the heather when it bloomed. It was also bedecked with a wealth of colourful tapestries. At the north end, a massive window was newly unshuttered to greet warmer weather . . . and the magnificent view of Mam Tor.

Wymarec de Birkin whispered another cadence, further subdued the thing in its satchel at his side, and wondered how much longer he was to be kept waiting.

Before the seneschal had left, he'd vowed that the Templar's paxman would be seen to and the horses given some fodder for the wait . . . which could be a while, he confided, for his master's schedule had become, well, more erratic of late. Indeed, the seneschal had ended up confiding more than he should, including the fact that Pontefract's master still suffered the nightmares of the damned. The seneschal's intentions had been good; he obviously hoped the Templar's holy prayers could help his stricken master.

No mundane prayers could vanquish the effects of what had Hunted, Wild through Nottingham the previous autumn. Neither within the haunted walls of the castle, nor the people haunted by them.

And even the highest of magicks, wielded by a Master who had time upon time proven his superiority against the Elder Elementals . . . *gah!* They were failing him, somehow. Unable to tame spells conjured by a *boy*.

The thing quivered again, as if the thought of its maker stirred it to some fit of . . . something. Wymarec had tried to break its secrets, to no avail. Had waited, patient, for the possibility of answers.

He had waited overlong, for too many things. It was past time to set a few more in motion.

A scuff and scrape sounded at the entry, then a voice. "What do you want, Templar?" Curt, bare of civility.

Wymarec turned and delivered a graceful bow. "In actuality, I think I might have something *you* want, my lord."

Eyes puffy with too much drink and too little sleep, clothes rumpled and only perfunctorily brushed, the former Sheriff of Nottingham looked like something warmed over and served for several days running.

"I doubt that. Your kind has given me nothing but trouble."

"You speak of Nottingham, I assume?"

"Of course I speak of Nottingham. What else could I possibly mean?" Voice rising to echo against the hall, de Lisle meandered the rest of the way in. The seneschal had been on his heels, lurking, and scooted for a table against the far wall. The wine earlier offered Wymarec still sat there upon its tray; quickly, the seneschal poured for his master.

"You were the one who hired one of my Templars to rid you of a wolfshead, my lord. How is that the fault of the Order?"

"Things are never simple, my lord. With your Order, or the chaos of a country without a king. There were plots within plots from the moment you sent Guy de Gisbourne to my gates, and well you know it. Thomas!" he snapped at the seneschal, "Fetch the Templar some more wine."

Thomas hastily obeyed . . . but nay. This wouldn't do, not at all.

"I am the Master Preceptor of all England, my lord. Have the Hood's spells robbed you of all courtesy, as well as your wits?"

De Lisle jerked and spun about, eyes narrowing upon Wymarec. After a moment's study, he raised the goblet, said, with slight rancour, "My pardon, Master Preceptor. To what do I owe the, ah, *honour* of a visit from such an . . . exalted personage?"

"What if I could give you rest? Sleep, without dreams?"

Ah, Wymarec had him with that. The dark eyes widened, and de Lisle turned away, rubbing one hand at his nape. "You churchmen, all alike in your admonishments! Pray to God for salvation and forgiveness, and all will be well! My brother the prior says the same . . . yet I note that he, too, still has his share of nightmares."

"It will not be immediate, the cure of which I speak. But with luck it will be lasting."

De Lisle took a large gulp of the wine and, shaking his head, walked over to the window.

Wymarec followed. "That place. The Tor. It is my understanding the Old Religion still holds sway there."

A snort into the goblet. "Do you think to call Crusade upon a barren hill, then?"

"Some of my Order would, no doubt. Blind stupidity, to destroy something without knowing it. Any power can be understood, controlled. Made to serve the greater one."

"Well, there's little way of making that place serve anything." De Lisle peered sideways at him. Curiosity piqued, no doubt—he was an intelligent man, if spoiled by authority. Undisciplined. A cynic, to boot. "Hill and caverns both, there's none in their right mind will go there. When I first took the place, I would threaten . . . aye, and I would, the lash and stocks and anything else to hand. But the people would take beatings rather than settle anywhere near, or even use the land at certain times. Particularly during the waning moon; the villeins would let wolves take the sheep before they'd so much as round them up! It's been worse these past several years, since—"

"Since your sister led her own crusade against a lot of Pagans there."

"She should have killed them all! If she had, she'd still be alive, I would still be Sheriff, and Robyn Hood, curse him, would be *dead.* I scoffed at her zeal, but she was right. Witches, all of them, and they should *all* be captured and hanged. Or burnt!"

"Burning is no solution." Wymarec could not help a slight shudder—it had been long ago, the fire that had marked him, yet its scars lingered. "Such things have a habit of rising from the ash, like the firebird of the east."

De Lisle took another drink. "Why are you *here*, Templar?"

"As I said. I would offer you some modicum of peace."

"Why would you do that?"

"Oh, make no mistake, you are but one player in the game. Unlike some, however, you are—shall we say—motivated? Your castle bides on the edge of a very powerful place. A place my Order desires to bring beneath its control."

Again, he had him. De Lisle's wine consumption had slowed, and the glance he hazarded Wymarec's direction was thoughtful, considering.

"If you can be of assistance?" Wymarec gestured out the window. "Give me what knowledge you're able to find, here on the verge."

"And what sort of knowledge would that be? I've little wish to explore superstitions, after all."

"Superstition! I take it, then, 'twas superstition that ran rampant through Nottingham?"

De Lisle scowled but gave his own shudder and glanced away.

"You see, as you come nigh to the powers, you shall know them. They have marked you. But I can aid you. Give you the means of respite, ways to help combat the worst. These uncanny *things* can be . . . dissuaded, with proper inducement. In exchange, you will be my eyes and ears over"—he gestured, again, towards Mam Tor—"*that.*"

De Lisle was silent for long moments. Then, "You must do me the honour of staying to sup. I would like to hear more."

Wymarec nodded. As de Lisle turned away, giving his seneschal orders for the evening, Wymarec patted the pouch at his side, almost fondly.

Mayhap the wait would not be so long, after all.

"So far, he has failed us," he whispered to the Pagan artefact. "But you and I will succeed, shan't we? Force the issue. Make progress, unlike our obstinate Brother Guy."

- V -

He'd a little over a se'nnight, by any reckoning.

Gamelyn groomed Falcon with a slow and thorough care that had the young warhorse leaning into the stiff brush. His hands gave an occasional tremor—wine or nightmare, either was possible—but Gamelyn refused to entertain it further. Instead, his mind sped far ahead with other matters—ones more easily pondered—no less a machine being prepared for battle, cranked and tensioned.

Siege engines. Blyth besieged. Much. John.

Robyn.

Blyth.

Otho.

Gamelyn smacked the brush against the wooden comb in his other hand, pulled it through. Dust spattered, caught the beginnings of dawn filtering in through high windows and the open east door. Falcon snatched a bite of leftover hay. Down the row of stalls, the other horses dozed or picked at their own forage. The stables were, before morning feed and the bells of Matins, almost meditative, with the soothe of mindless labour and the vagrant solitudes of thought.

Displeased with the break in his massage, Falcon rolled air through his nostrils. When Gamelyn continued to peer into midair, the horse shifted his haunches sideways, nudging Gamelyn into the wall.

"You . . . *sod.*" Gamelyn snorted a soft chuckle and rolled his knuckles over Falcon's ribs. The horse was too well trained to ignore the pressure; he did, however, turn his head and peer at Gamelyn, reproach and plea.

"All right, then, be still." Still smiling, Gamelyn resumed his motions. A few strokes in, however, the smile faded.

So far his horse had dredged from him more sentiment than his remaining brother.

He wasn't sure what he felt about that. Or if, indeed, he felt anything. Surely he should feel *something?*

After all, Otho hadn't been Johan, hadn't spent upon Gamelyn's hide years of brutal umbrage against a father's love and a mother's death.

But neither had Otho stood in Johan's way.

So, something remained after all: unspent resentment. Gamelyn paused, gave wry consideration to the dust on his hands and the resultant gleam of Falcon's bay hide.

What he didn't want to consider was what that resentment signified. Instead, Gamelyn reattended to his grooming, long strokes beneath the black mane. Falcon stretched his neck, upper lip twitching, clearly in whatever paradise lay reserved for horses. Gamelyn's smile widened, then faded.

Had Otho been in residence when they had stolen in and taken Queen Eleanor?

Not that it mattered. What mattered was how, as Hubert had put it, a filial connection should prove of some usefulness. What mattered were results: a swift conclusion, with minimal casualties and Blyth Castle undamaged.

Durham had agreed upon more time: three days before he gave the order to begin construction. Depending upon the skill and swiftness of his people, the *petraria* could possibly be operational within another four. It needn't be huge to tackle Blyth. She had been built before the great siege engines had begun their dispersal westward. The motte—*tica's hill*, the common folk called it, a name that had altered itself, as such things did, and adhered to the surrounding honour and the tourney fields just past the fens as *Tickhill*—was the highest point amidst acres of flat grazing, marsh bottoms, and scant rises here and there. One could see any army coming for miles, but only the moat and the thick walls, beginning to crumble on one side, actually protected the castle.

Gamelyn brushed harder. He had a se'nnight. He also had his gear and his stallion, brought from Hirst. No subtlety there: Gamelyn was to attend the siege a Templar whether accompanied by outlaw escort or no. Little hardship . . . save on his heart. And, of course, *that* was all too well accustomed to being set asunder.

He took in a fierce breath, blasted it out like a challenged buck.

Falcon gave a feathery grunt, almost a query: *What's on, mate?* The other horses answered, a run of whickers from stall to stall.

With another indulgent smile, Gamelyn began running the

comb through Falcon's thick black tail. "Soon we'll be off," he promised the stallion as his thoughts skittered and tilted more pleasant.He missed Robyn. Craved a coax of that quick-wild grin. Wanted the presence of quicksilver and brass, some reassurance that maybe, just maybe, there could be an outcome for them that didn't involve dream/threats of *tynged* traced in fire and blood.

Not that he was prepared to openly admit that latter.

Seven days and seven nights had, supposedly, seen Creation. Surely it was time enough to persuade an outlaw. Even if Gamelyn wasn't yet sure of what.

Falcon started and gave a loud snort, eyes gleaming in the dim. It echoed, loud, into the stable, was answered just as energetically by the other horses, all more than willing to take their mate's assurances that a good spook might be in order.

"Ssh," Gamelyn told the horse. "All right then, don't start a row. I'll finish brushing, you greedy—"

"Milord?" A hiss from the dark.

Gamelyn stiffened and swivelled, dropping the comb in the straw. His hand stayed open, seeming lax, but all it would take was a quick twist to drop a shiv from bracer to palm.

Movement, from the shadows across the barn aisle and towards the next stall. Gamelyn cocked his head, frowned as a small dip of tangle-twisted grey caught the light. A bow, of sorts.

It was the barefoot ragbag of a villein who'd tended the hearth.

And *putain de merde*, but the man had come up quiet as a dog fox after pullets. Falcon snorted again and shifted in the ties. Gamelyn put a soothing hand to his rump. No use letting the man be kicked into the next fortnight . . . not yet, anyway.

The villein nodded, with a self-satisfied flash of teeth. "Aye, and th' like don't startle easy, do 'ee?"

"I can't afford to," Gamelyn said. "What do you want?"

"Yer help. 'Tis trouble in the Wode."

Gamelyn tensed. The man sounded as if he were from the south, yet pronounced that last as only the Pagans did. "Who sent you?"

"None sent nawthin'. I've a charcoal kiln up Rufford way. 'Tis my people payin' the price of relying on damned monks, wit'—"

"I'm a monk," Gamelyn interrupted, terse.

"Nay, milord, truly not." Another flash in the dim; another smile, with only a few gaps. Mayhap the man was younger than he looked.

Mayhap Gamelyn would nonetheless scrub the stable floor with him, did he not state his business. "Do you want to banter or tell me about this trouble?"

"Aye, and girl wanted to tell 'ee." A snort. "An' more, I reckon. I tells her nay, 'tain't like 't used t' be. Folks be talking, like, do she swell up with a ginger-haired bairn."

You could have that one tonight, did you choose. . .

Gamelyn was beginning to suspect that neither he nor de Lacy kenned the half of it. Heat rose in his cheeks, mixing with annoyance, neither of which he'd any business indulging.

The charcoal burner was oblivious to any discomfort, staring down the stable aisle. "Aye, 'twas honour when me mam was of the Heath, but now? Nawthin' but wide eyes and pruny-pursed lips and pointin' fingers, wit' 'ee calling a Wode-gotten bairn 'sin'"—it hissed bitter, leaving no doubt as to the man's opinion—"and not knowing 'ee from any other lord who takes all and leaves nawthin.'"

The words wound down, choked all fierce and into silence. It twisted Gamelyn's own discomposure sideways, gave him a curious chance to speak. "So you . . . know me, then." *Know what? How?*

The whites of the man's eyes glinted beneath twisted and knotted grey. "Me mam's ways ain't forgotten, not whilst I draws breath. Of course I knows 'ee, milord, and heard it said: 'ee were hunting with wild Robyn, to green Wode gone. I knew, as I heard. Knew 'ee'd help. Told girl— me granddaughter, see?—that we'd ask. She fancies 'ee, and would have done 'ee honour. But more'n any early blessing matters this: fambly's in a muddle t'ward Rufford Abbey, sure as—"

"Rufford Abbey, then." Gamelyn still wasn't altogether comfortable addressing the serving girl's notions of "doing honour"; he fastened, curt, upon something more manageable. "You said trouble. Why not go to Robyn, then? Why come to me?"

"Scarlet, en't 'ee? Scarlet Knight as serves Woman, who saved Dark Man Himself in Nottingham and runs with such folk. 'Ee much as said so in hall. I knows who'll help His own, do they beg Hood's justice."

The Scarlet Knight. A waft of desert roses accompanied the Lady's murmur, and Gamelyn shivered. *No doubt such a man could do suitable honour to a willing lass.*

I believe I've shattered enough vows in your honour, Gamelyn retorted.

Not as yet, you haven't.

He clenched both teeth and fists, bid Her silent. With a soft chuckle, She faded.

Gamelyn leaned against Falcon, crossed his arms, and peered at the charcoal burner.

"Tell me," he said, "of Rufford."

Rain had begun to patter the thatch overhead, dense and familiar-soft. Another rhythm: Falcon dug a halfhearted front hoof into the straw, his normal anticipation upon saddling. Even the charcoal burner's tale contained a quiet and expectant cadence. Yet Gamelyn was growing more and more agitated.

His hands, steady upon the leather billets, gave no hint of his anger. He wasn't even sure why he was so angry. It was common enough: a small cotholding turned out to enable more afforestation within a lord's demesne.

"Headin' fer Wellow, granddaughter said they were." The charcoal burner fell quiet, sucking on a tooth.

Aye, all too common. And the results even more predictable. Rufford Abbey was likely the only home the villeins had ever known. Left to their own devices, they'd wander like cote-bred partridges, fit quarry for predators both four- and two-legged. And they'd find precious little help where they were heading. No village could afford to take on more mouths to feed, not after the bitter winter they'd just endured.

A bitter winter, indeed. Where Summer, in his turn, walked the halls of the otherworld.

Not the Lady. She had gone quiet, but unfortunately the Horned Lord had risen in Her place. His presence was a hot gust, gaining in fractious strength with Gamelyn's own mien.

It is time, Oakbrother, to show your horns and your challenge. Time to give evidence of that journey upon which the night mare took you. Time to act *upon what you are.*

What do you think I'm doing, damn you? Your people need—

Our people, O Knight. Your Holly lord once fell beneath death's grip as Summer rose; he came back stronger, brimming over with the magic, whilst you . . . A growl. You fled, Oakbrother. Did not even think to wrest him back or find him. Abandoned him—Us!—for the punitive sands of your desert god, choosing the cloak of betrayer rather than stay to meet your tynged.

I had what choices you left me!

False or true, you made them, aye. And still you cling to them. Cripple the acuity won in Winter's depths—

Acuity? Of what?

—and use denial as a flayed-hide shield.

I'm not Robyn!

Nay, you are not, but there's the sharpest edge. You have the ability within you to be his true counterpart, his worthy rival.

I am not his rival! I cannot be! A stag's blast of defiance. There's no magic in my veins, to usurp a wildwood King! I will not!

The west-facing stable doors burst open with a chill and violent howl. Hay and dust went soaring through the long stable and out the far end. The horses yanked at their ties with a slip-scuttle of hoofs. Falcon reared, snatching the rein from Gamelyn's grip, and lunged against the front boards of his stall. The villein gave a yip and ducked into the next stall, empty save for a barn cat that yowled and fled up into the rafters.

The damp gust ripped at Gamelyn's cloak and hair, yet he'd not so much as flinched. Instead his gaze hung, as if fascinated, upon the flung-open doors. They shuddered and creaked in the wind's aftermath, swinging to and fro.

No magic, so you say, the Horned Lord growled. *Yet your anger can fill Us to call the winds.*

Gamelyn's hands seized upon the saddle cloth. "I did . . . nothing." It was a whisper.

It was also a mistake. The villein peeked over the boards of his hiding place, gave the ambiguous reply, "Uh-uh-aye, milord."

The Horned Lord didn't give the slightest appearance of capitulation. *So certain. So. . . intransigent.*

Your vocabulary is improving, Gamelyn sniped.

Mayhap it is the company I am forced to keep.

The villein was still staring, eyes white-wide, fingers clenched tight upon wood. As tight as Gamelyn's own grip upon the saddle cloth.

And the doors, whining soft upon their hinges, back and forth. Back and forth . . .

"Secure those doors," Gamelyn ordered, terse.

Eyes still wide, the villein obeyed.

And did Gamelyn take his gaze from the man's progress, look down, surely the new-donned scarlet upon his breast would be lurching with the force of his heart.

He refused to look. Swallowing the spastic lump of breath and alarm, he shook his head and attended to his gear. Another torment, nothing more. Some random game the god was playing, another lie to shake him from his own sensibilities.

I admit to a wish to see you on your knees. The Horned Lord rustled the hay in Falcon's manger, whispered the stallion to calm. His breath along Gamelyn's nape, however, was anything but soothing. *But I do not lie.*

You are the father *of lies!*

A *tsk,* and the sudden there/not there weight of antlers resting upon Gamelyn's shoulders. It roused him worse than the Lady's touch, left him empty and wanting and all a-quiver.

Surely you can do better than prattle ill-made ravenings, and those stolen from your desert god's less-educated zealots.

Fury was, as ever, salvation, its heat replacing alarm and desire.

And outwardly noticeable, from the hesitant scuff of the villein's bare feet as he approached.

It was a relief to Gamelyn's nerves to turn to the man, snap, "I'll ride for Rufford. You will go north from here."

The man halted, tatters swaying. "Into Shire Wode?"

"How else will you find Robyn Hode?" Deliberate, the use of the old intonation.

"Milord!"

Gamelyn shrugged and led Falcon past the man, through the latched-open doors and into the grey dawn . . . not, however, without a lift of chin and grit of teeth. The stallion, pacified by the Horned Lord's animal touch, had his mind on other things; he snuffed the crisp air and snorted, hoofs ringing against hard-packed earth as he began to dance in place. Unwilling to sour the horse's good spirits, Gamelyn bound his own ire tight, checked the girths once more.

The villein halted in the stable door, still less than eager. "Milord." The chide was faint but there. "How 'n hell will I *find* 'ee?"

"Just head north towards Thynghowe." Gamelyn swung up and swayed in the saddle as Falcon gave a tiny hop sideways, eager for the road. "They'll find you, believe me."

They were on the Rufford Road, all right, more towards the vill of Ollerton than east and Wellow. A small and bewildered group, carrying upon their backs what meagre belongings they possessed.

And who, at present, looked to be in serious danger of having those belongings taken. They were surrounded—gathered, really, clumped biddable as sheep herded to the slaughter pens—by five ragged men, each of whom held a nasty dagger.

Nasty, indeed. Gamelyn had halted some distance away, concealed by both the misty patter of rainfall and a small outcropping of hawthorn, but he could see well enough. Those blades would snap like dried twigs did they encounter any true obstacle, yet might kill someone merely from the amount of filth and rust they had acquired. Their wielders looked no better, thin and unkempt, ill-suited for anything other than stealing a bare pittance from browbeaten serfs. The fatal flaw in Gamelyn's view: they'd no weapons other than the foul daggers.

Desperate, certainly. Outlaws, mayhap, but there were few outlaws who dared roam Robyn's territory—and those who'd had the guts to ply their trade in the Shire Wode ended said attempt with their skulls adorning the Hunter's Oak. This winter's hardships had brought out a different kind of rogue, living off the easy pickings of their own kind.

Gamelyn smirked. A warm-up for Tickhill's upcoming mêlée would fair suit his temper.

It suited Falcon as well. The stallion pranced, eager for a gallop; Gamelyn bade him walk, making appeasement with seat and hands and voice: *Soon, I promise.* The sword Hubert had offered—with a sour glance of reproach that any man of Hirst Preceptory should wander without one—stayed in its scabbard athwart Gamelyn's shoulders, upholding biddance.

Unlikely he should need it, anyway. For the rogues? Well, they weren't. Sodding useless, more like. Even with the rain starting to come down harder, not a one saw an armed man a-horse until he was nearly upon them. At that, it was one of the Rufford villeins—a young boy—who did espy him.

Cried, "Milord!" and started to run.

Gamelyn had a glimpse of dark hair and darker eyes in a thin, pale face before the lad was grabbed by a fair-haired lass. She nigh yanked the boy from his threadbare braies. They both slipped on the muddy road and nearly fell. The boy thought to protest, but the lass gathered and shushed him, shooting Gamelyn a captious gaze. Resentment, fear, and hope made a fair mix with the rain upon her dirty face.

It arrested both thought and action; a brief incapacity spurred by a wrench, deep in Gamelyn's belly. Incomprehensible. Nigh debilitating.

Just as swift as his senses had telescoped inward, they seemed to expand outward . . . and too much, *too much*. An assault, really: not merely the lad and lass, but the abrupt and audible whispers of wind and tree, the cling within his nostrils of churned mud and rancid sweat, the tang of rust upon the neglected daggers. Gauzy, fraying-smooth strands of *something* trying to plait a pattern in an entire surfeit of countenances fastened upon Gamelyn. They shone, not only with the wet, but a mix of hope, fear . . .

And hostility.

This lay particularly amongst the knife-wielding thieves. The familiar, welcome brace of it struck Gamelyn back to necessary distance. To his purpose.

It was Guy de Gisbourne—weapon, assassin, and right arm of Hubert de Gisborough of Temple Hirst—who turned a stony gaze upon the enemy. Waiting.

An elder man begged, faint, "Please, milord!"

"Shut your face!" One of the thieves brandished a blade chipped like a weak tooth. Nevertheless, the man shrank back. Two more thieves flanked the first. Like to starving dogs eyeing meat and bone, they'd enough menace to once more gather the Rufford villeins into a knot.

"And you, man!" Chipped Blade ordered. "Pass on by!"

"Nay." Gamelyn rubbed his rein hand up and down Falcon's crest, soothing. For now. "I think not."

That got their attention. One of them, a young man with sandy hair and beard, eyed Gamelyn. Undoubtedly the leader, but with more brass and balls than sense. He didn't perceive the silent menace waiting, saw only the horse and tack, the cloak—plain, but finer than any he'd likely seen of late—and the likelihood of more booty than a small lot of serfs could ever hope to provide. "May happens this 'un wants to contribute, eh?"

Chipped Blade grinned. One of the thieves guarding the villeins hawked and spat. Another let out a braying laugh. The villeins knotted tighter, though it hardly seemed possible. Gamelyn didn't even entertain the idea that they would spring to assistance—he knew better. Unfortunate, but a reality: sheep rarely donned the cloak of a wolf. Or even a deer.

No matter; they would only get in his way.

"Better my contribution be in the form of some good sense." A scarlet mist was wafting—weaving—behind his eyes, urging completion. Gamelyn restrained it even as he quieted Falcon, kept his chide soft. "Walk away. Whilst you still can."

The leader snorted. "The day I let some rich sod stupid enough t' come prancin' in by his lonesome and tell me what's what? That's when I'll be laughing at auld Horny in Hell!"

Keeping up the soothing knead at Falcon's mane, Gamelyn dropped his free hand to his thigh. Moreover, the thief let him.

Gamelyn smiled. It wasn't the least bit affable.

Another of the thieves, a shaggy pate of grizzled hair nigh hiding his eyes, crept up behind his leader to tug at his tunic, muttering what was likely caution. The leader shrugged him off, instead crossing negligent arms over his long and ultimately friable dagger.

"Off your horse, man." A demand, nothing less.

Gamelyn kept smiling. Shook his head, slowly.

This seemed to startle the leader. Beside him Shaggy Pate, wielding his blade more as protective artefact than any weapon, hissed more cautions. Again, the leader shrugged him away.

"You arrogant bastard." And damned if the leader didn't swagger towards Gamelyn. He really *was* a bloody daft pillock. "Don't you know where you are?"

Better than you, I'll warrant, you stupid sod. But Gamelyn kept his silence.

Which the leader, of course, misread. "*Sherwood,* you clot. You're in Sherwood, where no man comes wit'out risking his life or, at t' least, his livelihood."

"He's the devil, he is, milord!" One of the Rufford women, heedless. "Says he's Robyn Hood hisself!"

A laugh nigh burst itself from Gamelyn's chest.

In the same moment, Chipped Blade cursed, turned on the woman, and shoved her into the dirt. With a wail she tottered into the fair-haired lass. The dark-eyed boy growled and started forwards. Another of the thieves swung his staff, sent the lad sailing backwards with a blow to the head just as the leader, face flaming, leapt towards Gamelyn.

But Gamelyn wasn't there. Falcon lunged, slipped on the wet footing, and dug in. He bowled over both the leader and Chipped Blade, charging after the man who'd raised his hand to the young serfs. People went scattering, shrieks echoing through the forest. Falcon snorted, hot on his quarry's heels. Flinging his cloak back,

Gamelyn laughed again and loosed the rein, let the stallion blow and strike and chase the thief across the road and into a stand of brambles.

Gamelyn caught the staff as it went flying.

Behind him, the leader was bellowing orders. Before any of the thieves could obey, possibly regroup, Gamelyn checked Falcon and spun him on his muscular bay haunches. A smile still playing across his mouth, he tapped the staff on the ground and twirled it thrice, bringing it to a halt against his rib cage: challenge in a makeshift lance, albeit a too-short one.

Any actual fire to action was guttering. The thieves no longer beheld a chance to get their own back from some rain-soaked uppity nobleman, but a warrior knight astride a fire-eyed beast, and that straight from some jongleur's tale of war and siege.

Falcon felt the energy of it and reared, gave a tiny hop in the air, and danced sideways, quivering between Gamelyn's knees, asking: *Again? Now? Come* on, *then!* Gamelyn answered with instinctive shifts of weight, light fingers, and the occasional murmur: *Wait. Soon.*

The horse sighed and stood, champing the bits. Gamelyn leaned on the pommel—carefully; the slightest shift in weight would be eager excuse to charge, and he didn't want that.

Not yet, anyway.

"Well, fancy that." His lover's favourite expression curled, sardonic, from Gamelyn's lips. "So *you're* Robyn Hood?" He smiled, and the odd gauze weaving itself behind his vision went blood-dark. "Liar."

"What did you call me?" the leader blustered, trying to regain control.

"I believe you heard me." All too courteous, and as the man puffed up like an angry—and foolish—goose, Gamelyn continued. "I've some acquaintance with Robyn Hood, you see. You look nothing like him, man."

Several of the villeins had begun a loose semicircle behind their tormentors. The dark-eyed boy was amongst those few, a bruise beginning to blossom high on one cheek. The lass was next to him, thin shoulders squared and mouth set. The boy met Gamelyn's gaze with a quick, irrepressible smile. Only then did Gamelyn comprehend the violence of his emotions, and what had eluded him until just this moment.

Unbidden, strands of thought . . . forms . . . other*whens*. . . wove themselves behind his sight, yet more textures of mayhap and perchance. He wobbled in his saddle.

Aye, the Horned Lord muttered, soft power, *had you never ridden in Loxley Chase, followed another strand of* tynged*'s weaving, might you have met leman and lady both, dirty and defiant, upon some roadside amble?*

"*Take* th' noble-bred bastard!" the leader bellowed.

Gamelyn legged Falcon up into the bridle and sat down. The stallion shot from his crouch as if by longbow.

More shouts and curses, echoing in the trees. One of the thieves went down beneath Falcon's hoofs. Several well-aimed spins of the staff-*cum*-lance sent first one sailing backwards—a burst of blood where his nose had been—then another sinking to the muddy ground, puking his guts.

And bloody damn, but Shaggy Pate *could* throw that knife. Falcon let a squeal of pain as the dagger raked his shoulder. Gamelyn growled a foul and angry curse, dropped the rein, twisted his left wrist. He let the shiv settle into his palm merely long enough for the throw.

Shaggy Pate fell, the shiv buried in his windpipe.

Falcon was slipping again, careless and going short on his sliced shoulder. Gamelyn swung off, unsheathing his sword in the same motion.

With a quick *chirrup*, he ordered Falcon from the action's centre; the horse, obedient, whirled away.

There were only two left, after all. The leader and the staff wielder . . . *ex*-staff wielder, whose threadbare clothes were more so from the bramble patch.

Gamelyn swung the sword, a heavy *whup* and glint against the wet air, and tapped the staff on the ground. Lifted it, once again a mock lance. It was too much for the staff wielder's nerves. He bolted.

Gamelyn let him, eyeing the leader. That one's nerves were strung in a different place—and not one sane or sensible.

Sure enough, the leader came for him. And was more skilled with that friable knife than Gamelyn would have credited. He managed to get in several blows, all of which Gamelyn blocked with the staff.

"This is Robyn Hood's place!" the leader burst out. "You've no say here, *nobleman!*"

With a tilt and slash of the staff, Gamelyn cracked a bone-shattering blow to the man's knife arm. The leader howled and the knife went flying, to splinter on a nearby cluster of rock.

Holding his arm close, backing away—still, the man wouldn't shut *up*. "We're not him, but he'll come! The noise you've made, in his forest . . . he'll see to you, right enough!"

Gamelyn followed. "Believe me, I sincerely hope he does."

"He doesn't let just anyone pass through Sherwood!" The leader stumbled, fell on his haunches, started a frantic, backwards scramble.

"It's called the *Shire Wode*, you grotty imbecile."

And the broadsword sliced downward with a dull gleam and a wet rip of flesh and bone.

Silence. The cry of a bird, some distance away, and the rain pattering upon earth and trees.

Gamelyn flung the wet forelock from his eyes, bent to wipe his sword on a bracken fern next to the leader's body. He then turned, looking for Falcon. Best tend to him quickly, before whatever had lain festering upon that rusty knife started its inroads upon his stallion's shoulder.

Movement shook the silence and broke through the shock of the watching, strangled-tight knot of villeins. Milling and confusion ensued; everyone began talking at once and—some weeping, some praying—they flocked towards Gamelyn, surrounded him. The youngsters crept up to him with wide, wary eyes, as if uncertain he wouldn't turn on them with his bloodied sword. The adults were more direct. They approached him with hands clasped or reaching, fervent in their gratitude. Several plainly recognised the scarlet cross on his tunic; one even fell on her knees and grabbed the hem of it, babbling about angels and deliverances.

Not the first time, encountering the like. The Templars had liberated several besieged towns in Outremer, and oft-violent expressions of gratitude, overwhelming to a newly belted knight, still unnerved.

Now, however, Gamelyn comprehended how to best direct it. "We'll have you all safe, never fear. Stand aside, now. Let me pass. I need to see to my horse."

"Bless you, milord, but me wife be seeing t' him. She knows this and that," the eldest of the men said, gesturing to the road's edge.

Sure enough, an elder woman was beside Falcon. No more the fiery weapon of a warhorse, he stood quiet and soft-eyed as any aged sumpter, letting a heavily pregnant young woman hold his rein and stroke his nose.

"Bless you, milord, bless you," another woman kept repeating, hanging on to Gamelyn's sleeve.

"What're we gonter do wit' those?" Staring at the dead bodies, the young lad had no little fascination in his dark eyes.

Another was with him, slightly older. "Peter, hush!"

"Leave them to the wolves." Gamelyn shrugged free of the woman clinging to his arm. "All of you, gather your things. We're going."

"Milord." A middle-aged man—there were only two males in the group, Gamelyn noted—dogged his heels. "Where are we going, milord?"

"To shelter." He kept walking. "To find Robyn Hood."

"More wolves!" The middle-aged man fell back, and the woman who'd clung to Gamelyn's sleeve grabbed his, shushing him.

"Surely y' wain't take us to th' likes of Robyn Hood, milord?" she protested.

Gamelyn didn't answer, gaining Falcon's side and inspecting

the eldest woman's handiwork. She'd a bag over one shoulder that he well recognised from Marion's wortwife doings, and was mixing a paste in one palm. She didn't cease her work but gave a courteous nod and dipped the knee. The pregnant lass also curtseyed, adding a shy half smile. Falcon turned, still quiet, to lip Gamelyn's tunic.

"I knowed they weren't Robyn!" another lad was insisting to any who would listen. "I knowed they couldn't be."

"Robyn's a devil!" the hanger-on insisted and crossed herself.

"Milord, you're a man of God, one o' those Templars, en't ye? How can you lead us t—"

"Robyn will help us." The pregnant lass slid a scornful gaze towards the hanger-on. "Grandsire said."

"And so *I* say." Gamelyn turned, eyed them all. Beneath the pressure of his gaze, they quieted, fidgeting. "All of you heed me. Gather what you can. We're going."

And not long after that, on a small cart path heading north, they were found by Robyn Hood.

- VI -

"Has Rufford Abbey lost what sense they have left?" Gamelyn snapped. "Turfing these people out midday, with the light so short?"

"The old man told Gilbert they were supposed to go to Wellow." It had been a simple question, nowt more, about what Gamelyn had in mind for these people—and no idea Robyn would unfetter a mad lion with the simple question. Propping a foot against the tree's trunk, Robyn furthered, quizzical-quiet, "And they did go, but Wellow—"

"Turfed them out too!"

"They hadn't means—"

"Of *course* they hadn't! Because it's sodding *spring!* Are those *merdaille* churchmen that bloody daft? Or just that bloody-minded?" Voice and body still tense, Gamelyn paced back and forth beneath the boughs of the guardian larch as if single-handedly taking out five of the Motherless scum hadn't been near enough. Of course—Robyn smirked— it wouldn't be, would it? And no more 'n the cheeky Motherless sods deserved, using his reputation to rob *villeins*.

Those villeins seemed unaware of the low back-and-forth taking place a stone's throw from the fire they'd gathered around. Well, the sun had only just decided to peek from behind the clouds, at that. David and Gilbert were helping them shed the worst of their wet gear. Their numb response suggested they'd equally accept cruelty and kindness.

Villeins at his fire, runaways who'd left a clod-clumsy trail even the daftest soldier could track. Runaway *Christian* villeins, from the way most of them had crossed themselves when Robyn, Marion, Will, Arthur, and Much had slid from the trees into their path. One had gone so far as to mutter prayers against witchcraft, no matter Marion's patient explanation as to why they'd known where to find the villeins: mostly from the telltale scatter of carrion birds in their wake.

The latter was no surprise, Robyn considered, his smirk fading as he contemplated the man pacing a furrow beneath the larch, but the horse had been. The sword, gleaming and plain. The tabard, crisp and black with its crimson cross. And the sudden weft of *tynged* behind Robyn's gaze, shimmering blood-dark.

Unlike the seated villeins, the outlaws were quite aware of Robyn and Gamelyn's exchange. Whilst adding more ale to the cauldron of stewing pottage, Marion kept sliding a frown their way. Much was likely to set himself on fire, he was paying that much attention to his master's outburst and that little to stoking the hearth. The remainder of the outlaws, amidst seeing to the displaced villeins, were starting to stare. They'd certainly never seen Gamelyn go on like this. Robyn had to admit he'd rarely had the dubious pleasure himself.

Taking a deep breath, he leaned his head back against the tree and said, skyward and muted, "Aye, well. When they find their serfs have gone missing—"

"*Sod* that! They gave up any rights!"

"Gamelyn." Robyn reached out, grabbed one dark-clad arm to halt the tense pace . . . and nearly obeyed the impulse to duck; the look Gamelyn threw him was that furious. "Coom by, pet." It was soothing. Reasonable. "You know damn well those monks en't about t' see it that way. All the bloody-minded abbot will ken is how a croft of serfs bound to his service disappeared into the forest. And law will be on that abbot's side."

Tossing the russet forelock from his eyes, Gamelyn looked to shrug away Robyn's hand. Robyn merely gripped tighter, kept peering at him. Gamelyn threw him a wild look, transferred that to the listless villeins.

"*Gamelyn.*" Still soft, but edged. "I need that clever brain of yours thinking *clear* on this. We've to figure this 'un careful. If we don't find a place for these people—and within their lord's demesne, mind—you know what'll happen."

"Outlawed," Gamelyn snarled.

"Aye, outlaws all. And *we* canna take 'em in. They'd not last a fortnight. Wit'out mentioning only a daft fool'd ken we could hide a village's worth of folk in our Wode!"

David had left off aiding the villeins to have a quiet—and intense, it seemed—conversation with Will and Arthur by the store cavern. Gilbert had, with John's help, set to charm and cheer the youngsters. There were a lot of children, considering there only seemed to be two women of breeding age, and neither of the men overtly territorial, as their kind tended to be.

Gamelyn was muttering to himself. Robyn started to speak again, but fell silent as David shook his head and Will threw up his hands. As he turned Robyn's way, David's expression tendered a plea.

With a sidelong glance at Gamelyn—who didn't seem to notice—Robyn ambled over to the cavern. "Trouble?"

"This lot!" Will wasn't bothering to hide his annoyance. "Look at 'em, Robyn!"

Robyn was. But what did that have to do with anything?

"Giving us a berth as if we've pox. Eyeing up Marion as if she were some drab. Stumbling through our Wode noisy as browsing cattle, crossing 'emselves every time you so much as twitch an eyebrow . . . gah! I'll warrant they'd as lief curse us as accept our help."

"That doesn't mean we shouldn't give it, Will," David retorted. "And th' old charcoal burner Gamelyn sent—he's one of us, had the proper signs, the blessings."

"Neither should that Templar've sent *anyone* near here, giving away our place!"

"Aye." Just past Will, Arthur was leaning against the half-high entry. "It means changing camp, you know that." A sigh. "I *like* Thynghowe."

It wasn't just the prospects of shifting camp. Things were changing with every step and every word, *tynged* tangling and knotting into the black, tens of imperceptible possibilities. Robyn watched Gamelyn, who seemed to feel Robyn's gaze upon him. A chance meeting of gazes, and for the longest heartbeat of Robyn's life, he Saw it, coiled in Gamelyn's eyes: an unyielding reflection of frayed and shadowy tendrils behind verdigris. Or mayhap not so unyielding: it flickered, and they chased away.

"What were he supposed to do, then?" Robyn asked. "Send the man away, despite him being of our people, wit' rights of coming to us for help?"

"Are *these* our people? Truly?" Arthur asked.

Will continued the protest. "And your ginger paramour'd no rights to risk a good place—"

"We were like to leave camp soon, anyway." Temporising, Robyn watched the "ginger paramour" not watch him.

"But Robyn, for him t' just *give* it away, and on a bad bet like this lot!"

"Gamelyn gave nowt away 'tweren't his to give, Scathelock." The round glare and heavy growl rendered the same response that had, of late, come from saying "Scathelock" in just that fashion. Will looked away and hunched his shoulders: a sullen, nose-smacked hound.

It settled in Robyn's stomach, burning. He leaned closer to Will. "Listen. I hear you about these folk. They're chancy, right enough, and we'll be careful. Aye?"

Will's eyes cleared as he slid them to Robyn, saw he was serious. "Aye, Rob."

"I'll fetch the venison, then." David, plainly satisfied, turned and ducked into the cavern's entry.

Arthur suddenly snorted. "I'll wager Gilly could find a willing tup in a nunnery."

Gilbert was making a resolute attempt to woo a little lass who was buried in her mother's skirts, just as resolute upon resistance. The young and gravid mother, however, was open to be charmed, as were the two other lasses, creeping closer. They weren't old enough to be doing much more than thinking about it, but plainly were, one freckled-fair and one with brown hair hanging in two thick ropes down her back.

"Those two 're too young for his tastes, and the mam's too fertile." Robyn grinned. "Our Gilly en't keen on lasting consequences."

Will snorted, but it was grudging. Arthur gave a good-natured slap at the back of his head.

"Robyn's right, Will. 'Tis the right thing t' do. No matter their beliefs, these 'uns 've suffered from the Church's doings much as any of us."

"Aye, well, they're here, en't they? T' little ones need meat, right enough, as does the breeding lass." Will signalled capitulation with a nudge to Robyn's shoulder. It didn't stop him shooting Gamelyn what was just this side of a glare as he followed Arthur to the other side of camp.

Not that Gamelyn noticed, staring off into the trees and stewing more than the cookpot.

Marion had left off the latter and was making herself comfortable between Gilbert and John. Several of the children were watching her, big-eyed. Several of the adults were doing likewise, only with censure.

Aye, and if that middle-aged man opened his yap once more about "women acting above themselves" like he had on the way here, Robyn would shut it for him. He debated doing it anyway, but decided to go back over to Gamelyn, poke at him instead.

Gamelyn didn't give him the chance—and proved he was paying some attention, after all. "What was Scathelock on about this time? The usual?"

The usual being Gamelyn, of course. "Nay. He's proper worried about these folk, and I wain't blame him there. They en't our people." Robyn kept on as Gamelyn drew breath for another irritated reply. "And I en't blaming you either. What else were there to do? They've suffered from the Church, and you'd full right to offer our help. Time for us to move on, any road. Our visitors just means it'll be quicker than planned."

Again Gamelyn thought to speak, instead shrugged understanding.

"For the now, we've venison hanging in the cool below to give everyone a good meal—save for Matlock's share. David'll set that aside. Two brockets Will and I took yester's even." He peered at Gamelyn. "You never did tell me what you were doing ower Rufford way."

The green eyes slid to meet Robyn's, wary, and chased away. "On my way home."

"And that would be?" There was a jab in it, keen on the edges even though the point proved dull.

Once again, Gamelyn started to speak, then didn't, patently uncertain of . . . what?

Quicksilver as the question, Robyn shook it off, like a horse shuddering its withers to repel a biting fly. "Later," he promised, walking back to the fire. "Later you'll tell me, and we'll have this out proper."

But when he looked back, Gamelyn hadn't moved, arms crossed, gaze fastened away and into the trees.

"As Green Hob came about the oak tree, you'd never ken what he found there. A proper strangeness, it were."

The younger boys gave a gasp. The two girls, fair and dark, leaned forwards.

"A young lord lay sleeping against the roots and beneath the budding leaves. And my, but this young lord were gold as Hob were dark, brilliant as the sunlight and *warm*. . . aye, that were odd! There was no fire nearby. Only a fur mantle wrapped him. But the stranger bided as flushed-warm as if he'd lain by a hearth all night."

The sun was beginning to dip behind the trees. Warm and well-fed, the youngsters were already rapt, but even the rest of Marion's audience was softening, bit by bit, as the story wound itself.

"So Hob crept closer, with all the cunning of his Wodewose kin . . . " Marion paused. "Aye, and do any of you know what a Wodewose is?"

"A wild one," the pregnant lass answered, soft, in the resultant silence 'round the fire. "A spirit as much woodland as flesh."

The other adults crossed themselves, and the eldest man forked an evil eye. Marion wanted to sigh out loud.

There were eleven of them, all told, and mostly female. Despite this, it had been the eldest man, Owain, who'd made subdued introductions all 'round as they'd sat to sup, and he'd mumbled the names so, Marion still had no idea who was who. Owain's wife sat next to him, and their middle-aged daughter past her; the latter was somehow attached to the surly man close to her own age, though Marion didn't think it marriage. The two lads were the lee side of ten years old, and the youngest likely brother to the fair-haired lass; Marion recognised an elder sister's protectiveness. Four more lasses completed the tally: the one with dark braids seemed several years the elder of the fair-haired one, with the wee one beside Marion the youngest, sister to the little one snugged in his dam's gravid belly . . . and *she* wasn't that much older than the two sisters despite having one walking—and teething, from the tot's fussing.

The pregnant lass needed to find a roof soon. She looked altogether close to her time, and Marion wagered few of her outlaw companions would be of much use did the bairn decide to come in their midst.

One of the children gave a tiny noise of protest; Marion realised she'd been silent too long with her pondering. It was no way to tell a story.

"Well. The lad's warmth put a powerful curiosity upon Hob, for Hob is drawn to mystery like bees to summer flowers. Not only that, but winter had been *so long,* y'see, so Hob fancied the light and the warmth of this strange young lord. He crept closer, reached out"—Marion extended a hand over their own fire—"and gave a sharp tug at the young lord's ear. But the young lord was deep asleep."

The little teether had been soothed with a finger's worth of Arthur's whisky on her gums, and turned brave enough to steal from her mam's side. A small, cold hand crept into Marion's, and she smoothed the tousled mop of sandy, child-fine hair. Once— and it seemed not that long ago—she had entertained the most homely of expectations: those of a freewoman's eldest daughter raised up to her place and power; mother and mistress of her hearth; cunning-woman to her community.

"Does he ever wake?" This from the younger lad. The eldest woman shushed him. Aye, these folk were fair different from the villages Marion knew, where stories were dreamed and shared about the fire.

It was her first chance, in truth, to tell stories. Such an honour was usually left to the village wise ones.

"Not right away," Marion answered. "But Hob, well . . . " A shrug, and a glance over the seated villeins' heads to see Robyn propped against Will, who was leaning against a tree. "He's persist-ent, en't he?"

Will snorted. Robyn grinned.

Persistence, aye, and Marion had her own. This was her home now. Her place to keep the hearth, and tell stories to keep it alive.

Already those stories were fading; this was one these Church-cowed villeins had never heard.

"And tricksy, is Hob," Marion continued, stroking the little girl's hair. "He en't about to follow rules."

No rules for outlaws with a price on their head, for a wortwife with her cunning talents twisted into charges of witchcraft by the abbey that once had been both shelter and gaol. No rules, and her own hearth, and *freedom*. . . but it was not without its price. The homely, commonplace existence Marion of Loxley had expected could never be, not for Marion of the Shire Wode.

No thatched roof on a cob cottage, with beams to hang herbs to dry and to keep field produce safe from mice. No wooden ark to store their hard-earned grain and upon which to knead out the loaves. No place of honour upon fertile ground for a village wortwife and her man and the children that would surely come, mayhap a little boy like Rob—if not quite so unruly—and, if the Lady truly blessed, a daughter to train up as wortwife even as her own mam had done.

Such things are not impossible, Maiden, merely different. The Lady's voice was fading with the sun, an insistent merge and sink into Marion's own consciousness. Unnerving, on the edge of uncomfortable. She had never felt Her presence in this fashion before . . . but mayhap not unexpected. The moon was rising full, after all, and the sun's path moving towards the Marriage and the Summering. *You are the fertile ground, the fruit and the vine. You are a free woman, the first in too long to roam Our Wode wild, to claim and tame the King Stag with an entire forest as your hunting ground and bower.*

"Plenty of room to raise a passel of fawns to sing the Lord and Lady's name," Marion murmured back, and in her hand, the child's twitched. Wide eyes slid her way, wary fascination, and Marion bent down to place a kiss atop the little girl's head. There was a whiff, sweet and also stale, of dust, light sweat, and smoke; she closed her eyes, breathed it in.

Anadl. . . tynged. . .

And the story began to wend its own path upon her tongue: Hob waking the young lord with a kiss and crowning him with mistletoe, showing him the ways of the woodland and the songs of the beasts. And, of course, the lovely-wild Maiden, enchanted by Hob with frosted pools tund snowflakes like gems, longing for summer's return.

The children were captivated, and the elders leaning in despite themselves.

She told the battle of blood and heat, light and longing, inevitable as Winter's retreat beneath Summer's warmth and Summer's covering by frost. Yet in her telling, Hob and the fair lord and the Maid all danced together at the Maying and the feasting, for the

Wheel was always turning, and both Winter and Summer would, each in their turn, fall and rise again.

Marion finished the story into a silence of held breath and crackling hearth, feeling the heart warmth of a tale that moved people to wonder in its wake.

"You told that well as Mam ever did," Robyn said into the silence that followed.

"Aye," Will seconded, very soft, and the other outlaws agreed, murmurs and whispers.

Movement from across the fire; Marion looked up and saw Much shift where he sat beside Gamelyn, a broad-proud smile on his lips. Gamelyn was pale, his eyes a-glitter, and when Marion cocked her head, questioning, he lowered his gaze.

"You have a mam?" The eldest lad broke the moment, leaning forwards so his nose almost brushed the fire. His gaze clung, avid, to Robyn.

Robyn's eyebrows disappeared into his inky forelock. He started to speak, was cut off by the younger lad.

"Me mam says Robyn Hood's a devil, wit'out mam or da."

Several of the adults looked fit to faint on the spot.

"Aye!" This from the fair-haired lass. "He kidnaps wee ones, and—"

"Hangs up skulls on t' devil's tree—"

"Like t' tree the young lord slept under—"

"Wain't go t' chapel—"

"And 'is touch *burns*, like iron pulled from smith's forge—"

Just as quick as the outburst had risen, it was stifled: by admonishing hisses, a swat or tap or, in one case, a quick clap of parental fingers over a child's mouth.

Marion's grasp of it was just as sudden. The raw apprehension on the villeins' faces, flickering chancy as the firelight, reminded her: there were darker side effects to her brother's reputation.

And Robyn, still standing on the edges of that firelight, John to one side and Will the other, arms crossed over his chest and hair in his face. As if willing to let it stand.

The bold lad persisted, "Are you, then? A devil?"

"M-my lord," the eldest, Owain, stammered. "Forgive 'im. The boy en't—"

"'Tis repeatin' women's foolishness, he is!" the other man interjected. "Nowt but."

"*Women's* foolishness?" Much rocked forwards angrily.

"He means nowt, lord—" The woman seated next to the surly man protested, albeit feeble.

"We en't yer lords!" Arthur growled.

"Where I were raised"—Much's soft comment was no less a growl—"we were taught better than t' be arsy wit' a woman at her own hearth."

"'Twould be no chore to take you back out t' forest path and leave you there," Will pointed out.

"'Twould be no chore to tell Brother Giles where a lot of outlaws bide—uh!"

This as Will dragged the surly villein up and nigh over the fire by the scruff of his worn tunic, growled, "Are you drunk or just daft, man?"

"The priest warns us," the woman nigh to Surly's age protested, "that sure enough such things are—"

"*Priest!*" A soft tenor grating into a harsh growl; Gamelyn had stayed well on the outskirts and busied himself with a broody cleaning of his sword once he'd eaten . . . until now. "One of Rufford Abbey, no doubt? The same so-holy brethren who turned you out to starve?"

The villagers didn't seem reassured by sense. The little girl was nigh burrowing her way into Marion's lap. Marion gave another soothing stroke to dusty hair and tilted her head to peer at Gamelyn. He fairly vibrated with affront. It was puzzling . . . troubling. He'd seen worse in the past few years, surely. They *all* had.

Again she found herself wondering where he'd been. Clipstone, again? Or Hirst itself, to come back dressed in Templar garb, riding a warhorse and avoiding Robyn's gaze?

"We meant no offense, milord," Owain soothed, with a stern look at the surly man.

Who wriggled from Will's hold, grumbling apologies. Will didn't seem best pleased that Gamelyn had prompted them.

Robyn advanced, his pace steady-slow. As one, the villeins all angled back, wide-eyed.

"Robyn." Marion made the warning mild. *Don't make it worse.*

He tossed her a quick grin—it worried as much as it becalmed—whilst lowering to his haunches nigh to the two lads. Another surprise, that; since his voice had broken, her brother had been wary of small children. Yet, still silent, Robyn held out one bow-hardened hand.

The second lad reared back from the gesture as if expecting a blow. The first one, however, ducked clear of another fearful grab from his mam and shinnied forwards on his knees. He reached out and grabbed Robyn's hand. Tight.

Robyn gave a tiny yip. The boy flinched, loosed him. But Robyn was laughing, shaking his hand and inspecting his fingers one by one. "Hoy, but if you en't a grip like a blacksmith, lad!" His grin invited everyone to join in.

The lad already was. A close, quick inspection of his own palm had revealed no diabolical burns, merely confirmed that he'd just survived—and bested—a handshake with the notorious Robyn Hood.

Chubby fingers clutched tighter to the kirtles bunched over

Marion's left knee. With a giggle, the little girl moved closer, eyes wide towards Robyn. Marion smiled, fingers unable to resist another stroke through the straggly, fine hair.

The lad put out his hand again. Robyn grinned—a boyish, cheeky expression that had, to Marion's memory, melted even an angry heart set on boxing his ears for whatever trouble he'd mixed in—and reached back.

"See? I en't about to burn no one . . . hoy, careful, lad!" Another small yip. "If you break me fingers, how 'm I to push a longbow?"

The boy's dirty face was glowing with pleasure—and pride. The second lad, emboldened, scuttered forwards. Grin widening, Robyn took his hand as well.

"Speaking of bows . . . John! Gilbert!" Robyn sang out. "Mayhap we should take this lot for a bit of archery practice, aye? Care for a try, pet?"

This last to the fair-haired lass, who stared, disbelieving. Robyn flashed a broader smile—and that expression, too, Marion knew well. It changed his features so completely, from warning predator to winsome—and devastatingly handsome—man. Disarmed, the lass stood and started after.

She was halted by a yank at her skirts. "Sit down, he en't talking t' *you!*" her mam fussed. "No girl's likely to use a bow."

"Happens I were talking to her, and happens *a girl* does!" Robyn snorted. "Me sister's one of t' finest shots here! Right, lads?"

Agreement all 'round, setting bright the fair-haired lass's expression.

"Mayhap Marion should show you all, aye? Come on, sister, and let 'em see!"

Marion grinned. "I will, at that."

And this time the lass followed despite her mother's chiding hiss.

Robyn ignored the latter, catching his bow as Gilbert tossed it to him. John grabbed a full quiver and disappeared into the cavern, likely to find a bow young arms could pull.

"Is that Little John, then?" one of the boys asked his sister as they ran to catch up. "I thought he was s'posed to be . . . well . . . a giant!"

"Then why would they call him *Little* John?" she shot back.

Robyn threw a wink over one shoulder at Marion, and she chuckled, rising from her seat and trying to convince the tiny girl-child to let go—not an easy task.

"What has he been drinkin'?" Will snorted and extended a hand to Marion. "Aye, but then he's John and Gilly at his back, and the bairns 're all older than weans. 'Tis the wee ones as make him run skairt . . . Hullo, pet," he addressed the little girl, still clutching to Marion even as Will helped her rise. "Mayhap you should chase after and tree our bold Hob-Robyn."

The child shook her head and clung to Marion tighter.

"Is he Hob, truly?" The dark-haired lass was curious, though conscious enough of her maturity to not play at archery practice.

"Of course he is," Will said, easily enough. "But it don't follow he's *allus* wicked. Now that 'un over there"—he dipped his head towards Gamelyn, who was saying something to Much but all the while watching after Robyn and the youngsters—"*he's* proper chancy, right enough."

Marion slid a glance Will's direction, a promise of damage when he least expected it.

After several attempts to coax her child to let loose of Marion, the pregnant lass gave it up, hauled to her feet, and came over. She prised the toddler free, quirking Marion a shy, half-apologetic smile.

"Is he the one who fights the Hob, then?" the dark-haired lass persisted. "To marry the Maid?"

"I'm sure he'd like to think so," Will answered, smooth as beaten cream. "But things as worth winning are worth fightin' for. Any as wants to take a maid has to win her first." This with a charming smile that set the lass's cheeks to a pretty flush.

Marion kept watching him; he seemed oblivious.

"Ssst!" the lass's mother interrupted. "Those old tales en't real, girl. Come sit by me. Now." *And quit twitching your skirts at that outlaw* was the unspoken chide, plain as plain. Indeed, just this edge of ripe and willing, the lass did as bidden, but not without a sidelong—and telltale—glance at first Will, then Gamelyn.

You also like 'em fair-haired and muscled, then? Hiding the wish to smile behind her hand, Marion spoke instead to the girl's mother, serious-soft. "Old tales can be the most real of all, dame."

"Marion!" Robyn yipped. "You coming, or what?"

"Just now!" Marion called back.

The pregnant woman gave Marion another shy smile. The elder couple echoed it, albeit muted.

It was all ignored by Surly, who was busy shovelling up another share of pottage.

That one would bear watching.

When the setting sun made archery practice not only difficult but dangerous, Robyn called a halt. The fair-haired girl actually had the best eye of all the young ones, come to that, and he made sure she knew it.

"Making little rebels?" Marion murmured as he passed by, and Robyn grinned, tugged at her coif.

Not long after, he bid a good evening to his guests, making it plain he would be away hunting for the remainder of the night.

Not before, however, a word; first with John, then with Will and Much . . . then with Tess, who noticed Robyn was going somewhere, clambered down from David's shoulder, and loped over to climb Robyn's leg. The little ferret ended up victorious, nestled into Robyn's hair as he approached Gamelyn.

Considering everything, Robyn was proper upskelled when Gamelyn looked up from over-polishing his sword and actually agreed to accompany Robyn.

So, with such companionship as it was—Gamelyn still stewing over sommat dark and tangled—Robyn walked a goodly distance from camp before doubling back. Again, Gamelyn didn't protest, just went along as if he'd known this was Robyn's plan all along. Mayhap he had, at that. They both made silent work of clambering up a tree just on the outskirts of camp. The massive oak gave plenty of cover, as well as a good view of their guests bedding down by the fire.

Will was already gone—also "hunting"—and Much with him. To all intents and purposes, the only ones left to defend the camp were a woman and several men who didn't seem up for a good fight, with the one left on night watch minus an arm, at that.

Then Arthur started to snore.

The surly villein had already settled himself on the outskirts of his people; it was little surprise to see him rouse. After waiting a bit longer—making sure—the fellow made careful progress to stand.

Bloody quiet, the man was, one had to give him that much. He took two furs, as well as a full ale skin and another bag—the same one John had noted earlier, wherein the man had squirreled enough food to last him several days at least.

"Well," Gamelyn whispered, "when one lies with thieves . . . "

Robyn smirked, elbowed Gamelyn as the villein crept away and vanished into the dark. "Brave, to wander t' Wode at night."

"Or merely stupid."

Another pile of sleeping furs shifted, and John emerged from apparent slumber. The glint of his eyes tracked the fellow's wake. Then, quiet as ferret Tess, he rose and followed.

Robyn's smile broadened. Did the villein innocently lose himself whilst going for a piss, John was to bring him back just as innocently. Did the villein do what Robyn suspected and head for Rufford Abbey, to buy his way back into the croft with a band of notorious wolfsheads as barter?

Perched next to him on a lovely, broad burl—a chair, almost, formed where limb and trunk met—Gamelyn watched the silent departures with the keen, detached gaze of predator tracking prey. He'd more than once claimed John—quick and quiet, deadly with knife or bow—was proficient an assassin as any Saracen from Alamut. But if John *could* be one, this one was. *Notorious Templar assassin,* Robyn thought, and smiled.

Then Gamelyn murmured, as if to himself, "If I'd Blyth, they'd have a place."

And if *that* didn't send every sense Robyn possessed from warming, lusty thrill to ice-laden chill.

He opened his mouth as if to speak. Still looking off into the trees, Gamelyn spoke first.

"We saw a burned village," he ventured, barely audible. Cryptic, aye, yet also nigh to conversational.

Robyn waited for the rest of it. Surely there was more. But after he'd waited a good two dozen of his own heartbeats, he shifted on the branch and prompted, just as muted, "Burned? On t' way here?"

"It was when we took Queen Eleanor to Temple Hirst. Marion, Much, and I." Gamelyn had transferred his gaze from their visitor's departure to his own fingers, twitching where they rested atop his knees. "I don't remember a great deal about that journey, what with the wound." A shrug of shoulders, as if "the wound" hadn't nearly done him in for a second time. A splinter of bone, Marion had said, from where an old and vengeful enemy had shot him in the back with a crossbow bolt.

That bloody Abbess had managed to nearly dispatch all three of them, one way or another. Robyn hoped she was biding her time in the otherworlds by roasting in the Christians' peculiar and tortuous contrivance of hell.

Yet Marion hadn't mentioned any village.

"What village?"

Gamelyn didn't answer. His head was lowered, forelock covering all but the fine-sculpted arch of nose.

Robyn reached out, smoothed back the fall of russet-gilt. Persisted, "What village?"

"One scarcely on the map. I wasn't exactly . . . sharp for most of that journey, as I said, but that happenstance was rather memorable. Its people weren't as lucky as these in our midst, believe me."

The moon passed from behind a thin cloud, set a scrim of ghost-silver over Gamelyn's face. Robyn leaned closer, thought to warm the sudden pallor with a kiss. Instead Gamelyn turned to him, and the glimmer in those eyes gave Robyn pause.

And for a span of frantic heartbeats, he saw—nay, Saw—the curve of horn gleaming, felt the summering heat of anger, a blast of breath.

"Lord," he whispered, willing the promise with his own. *Take it to you. Be it.*

"Don't call me that." Gamelyn turned away, the spell broken, misunderstanding purposeful—or mayhap not. "I'm quite serious, you tosser. I keep remembering what the Queen said to me as we passed that village."

Again he fell silent, in seeming contemplation of nowt more than his hands twined upon his upthrust knees.

Robyn was not of a mind to ask what Queen Eleanor had said. He was all too afraid he knew.

Yet this time Gamelyn continued, resolute. "She said, 'Mayhap, my lord Templar, you will do better, when King Richard returns and you are rewarded for all you have done.'" Again, he looked down and again, the length of ginger-gilt covered his face. "I cannot forget the words. For I . . . dreamt them."

Robyn blinked, angled back on the limb. Unexpected. Not the dreaming, but the admittance.

Gamelyn met his gaze. "Aye. Before it ever happened, I dreamt of it."

This time Robyn did lean forwards, to kiss Gamelyn's temple. Lingering there, he whispered, "Aye, well. Summer is *made* of soft dreams."

"If only." Sharp and short, unwilling to that much admittance.

Another pause, Robyn just as unwilling to retreat. *Tell me*, he bade, *tell me all. I can take it, hold it for you, help you bear the weight of it.* All the while, kept silent to the wait, breathing in the light, musky salt of sweat, the tang of smoke, the sweet, dried moss they'd padded beneath their bed furs.

The incense of a chapel, faint but there.

Where were you? Robyn wanted to say, but he knew. Aye, he knew.

Gamelyn leaned back against the tree trunk, rested his head with a tilt, eyes still holding to Robyn's. Still the scrim of moonlight there . . . and also, a fire behind. "If the castle were mine, once again. If the pardon were made, for you, and Marion, and the men."

"A lot of sodding ifs t' my mind." Robyn looked away, one hand seeking steadying purchase on the oak's rough bark. The other gave an absent caress to Tess, curled up for a short kip in his flung-back hood.

Queen Eleanor had indeed promised. For her rescue from a youngest son's perfidy and imprisonment, she would see her rescuers repaid in kind: Blyth returned to its disseised youngest son and the outlaws given royal pardon. Robyn had let it drift from his mind, frankly, never imagining it would come to fruit. It still likely wouldn't, with nobles being . . . well, nobles.

He should have known Gamelyn wouldn't forget.

Robyn wished *he* could forget that crowded pub in Worksop and its impromptu meeting with a royal trouvère who needed their help to free a queen. More, he wished away the remembered intensity behind Gamelyn's juniper-green eyes as he'd held a queen's golden signet ring in his palm and contemplated the stakes.

"I could go to Rufford Abbey, arrange for release of the villeins."

Robyn swung back around to Gamelyn, frowning.

Gamelyn was looking over their camp, as if he'd never ventured into what-ifs or the chancy nature of royal promises. "There's time. It wouldn't take all that much from your purse, Robyn Hood, and likely a better bargain than promising some nearby village enough tithe in victuals to make up for the extra mouths."

Time? Time for what? Still frowning, Robyn went along. "You'll go to Rufford—"

"A Templar will go to Rufford and see them round to our way of thinking. I've more than a bit of coercion, bribery, and cold bastardishness to spend on their like."

The thought was appealing. Amusing. Yet Robyn kept frowning as Gamelyn once more turned to him, face impassive save for the tiny possibility of a smirk lingering in one corner of his mouth.

"I can get more horses."

"At t' Lodge." It was flat. "T' go with Falcon, and your sword and tabard, aye?"

Nostrils flaring, Gamelyn conceded. "We'll need a cart. And permission to relocate the villeins. All I'll need is some silver."

"And Much."

"Of course."

"Mayhap I should spare meself the silver, have you fetch that from t' Lodge as well."

Gamelyn snorted and rolled his eyes. The smirk, however, kept teasing at his lip.

Robyn turned, contemplating his campsite and the sleeping villagers. Sucking in a tiny breath, he held it, teasing the magic from it like wool upon carding paddles. Loosed it, deliberate-slow, and half-shuttered his eyes, contemplating the strands that spun outward upon it. He needed the magic in thisnow. It wasn't a difficult decision, which dilemma to chase, but he felt upskelled, out of place with the manner of it.

And sure enough, there were numerous tendrils roping unseen into the black, enough to worry after and most of them bearing the particular scarlet shades of Gamelyn's *tynged*. But the rest held, vibrating true along the path he'd chosen to Seek.

"Aye, well. You'll have to take up Much wit' me sister; she's all too used to him warming her furs o'nights. But as to the rest?" Robyn shrugged, let his mouth describe an agreeable curve. "Makes sense t' me."

And what if I didn't agree, O Templar? What then?

The smirk broadened to a smile, albeit a quick one. With an equally brisk nod, Gamelyn started to climb down.

"Much is in the elm across," Robyn offered.

Gamelyn flicked him a long-suffering look. "I know."

Robyn snorted and watched him descend, fade like a pale-haired ghost into the trees. Sobering, he pulled his knees to his chest, wrapped his arms snug, and pondered the vagaries of Templars—this Templar—more, he was sure, than he cared to.

- VII -

"I en't surprised Walter's gone. He said he'd likely head south, find the odd job here and there, God willin'. Been sayin' it t' while, even before Abbot made us move on."

Marion nodded, slid a desperate gaze over the sun-drenched clearing to where David was keeling his wooden ladle through a second kettle of porridge. Midmorning, and surely he was ready to give up the cooking . . . but nay. No rescue there.

On Marion's shoulder, Tess nosed her ear, put her muzzle on daintily crossed paws, and continued to glare at their companion.

Who, unfortunately, kept talking. "Weren't bound to the abbey, leastways. Not like the rest of us. Eh, starving on what Abbot allowed were what made my James up and leave. He weren't bound, neither."

With a shift against the old downed tree trunk she oft used as seat, Marion gave a frustrated twitch at her spinning. No fault of the spindle; nay, she'd taken it up in sheer self-defence. Even as Arthur had done, off to take his turn at watch, and Gilbert, to check the snares. Much and Gamelyn had also escaped, off to the Lodge just before dawn. Will and Robyn were crouched beside a coppiced elm, overly intent upon their game of knucklebones. Keeping their distance.

Marion envied them. So far, and without asking a single question, she'd been informed that the woman who'd descended upon her was named Emma, that she'd seen thirty-eight summers, still had most of her teeth and, most importantly to Emma's mind, had been married for fifteen years to the brother of the man who'd exited last night. Not that she'd seen her husband in ten of those years. But she seemed as numbly unconcerned over the whereabouts of said husband as the brother-in-law, eyeing up Marion and the outlaw camp with a patent disapproval she didn't quite dare voice.

Unfortunately that didn't stop Emma from voicing other things. Or all the while eyeing up Marion like she were some sort of fae or witch, complete with baleful familiar perched on one shoulder.

"It wain't bite, will it?"

Marion ignored the question. Tess yawned, tongue curling and lips drawing back from shiny-sharp teeth.

The rest of the villeins were hunched in a small group—save the young ones circling David and the nutty smells wafting from his kettle like crows edging a battlefield.

"Where's milord the Templar gone?" Emma didn't wait for an answer. "Mayhap he'll find our Walter."

More like your sodding Walter found John's dagger in his throat. John had returned with the dawn; before burrowing into his furs for some sleep, he'd given Robyn a nod that suggested a new skull could be hung on the Hunter's Oak. The clot had turned on his own family in hope of some silver! And he'd been welcomed at Marion's hearth, accepted their food and drink!

Hearth law was sacred. Those who broke it . . . well.

"Robyn Hood's yer brother, en't he? My brother Tom married *that*'un"—a jerk of her head towards the pregnant woman—"for all the good it did 'im. Just a passel of brats, her swelling up with another one and him only buried just after Twelfth Night."

"I hardly see how it's her fault he left her pregnant and a widow—!'" The moment Marion said it, she was furious with herself for responding to such idiocy, clamped her lips over the rest: *Yours didn't even do you the grace of dying once he bred you; he just ran off. Not that I blame him.*

Emma nodded as if she agreed, but her words were venomous.

"Yeh sound like me ma, full of old nonsense. Not that it's surprising, wit' yeh surrounded by all these men, like."

Aye, and t' first chance to talk to another woman, woman to woman, since. . . Sweet Lady, how long has it been? And all this bag o' bile wants to talk about is . . . men!

There were so many other things to talk about. Better things. More interesting things. More important things, like making sure these ignorant villagers dug a proper latrine.

Of course, Marion *was* surrounded by men. Lived with a lot of them. Was damned sure at this point in time that she preferred their company to any sniping, whining, poor excuse for a woman.

"Brother or nay, everyone knows Robyn Hood has a woman in his band. Yeh'll find no respectable man'll have yeh, t' now."

Mayhap I en't wanting a "respectable man." Faith, but I must've been out of my mind, longin' for a proper home and hearth in your world!

An injudicious jerk of the spindle sent it scuttering sideways; Marion ducked to retrieve it before it spun off the withy mat at her feet, was foiled by a tug at her sleeve.

"I'd take it kindly should yeh warn those skivers off me girls."

Marion stiffened in affront, not only from the words, but Emma's tweak at her sleeve.

With a jerk of her head towards where her two daughters, porridge bowls in hand, kept inching closer to the game of knucklebones, Emma whined, "They're good, chaste girls, baptised proper. The youngest is more boy than proper girl, but the eldest? She's old enough to think on nowt but sinnin'. Don't need her head turned by a bunch of wild—"

"Get away, woman!" Sharp, the voice. As Marion twitched free, turning back to retrieve her spindle—it had gone into the dirt, curse it!— the grandmother was already there, snatching it up before it rolled farther.

"Go prattle t' sommun as *wants* to listen to yer nonsense. Iffen ye can find 'em." And when Emma hesitated, peering at Marion for rescue—as if she would!—the old woman repeated, "G'wan, I say! Go help t' man feed t' bairns!"

Emma went, muttering beneath her breath all the way.

Nodding in satisfaction, the old woman rose with rescued spindle in hand, slow, but with more vigour than Emma's draggy steps towards the cauldron. She brushed the tiny bits of dirt and leaf litter from the wool with gentle, exploratory fingers. Her hands were marked with the sinews and calluses of hard work, roped shallow with veins and age. The hands Marion would no doubt have in her own time. The hands her mother had begun to have, before she was murdered by the Church.

"Her like gives a good Christian wife a bad name . . . This is nice work, lass." The old woman brought the nearly spun thread up to her cheek, smoothed it there. "Me old eyes en't seeing so well, but hands know the work they've done. I do a fair job meself, if I do say so—I knows goodly spun thread. And first-rate wool."

As unasked as Emma, she settled on the tree trunk beside Marion, picking the bits of dirt and bark from the wool-wrapped spindle before handing it over. Marion took it with a smile of thanks. The woman bent, ran inspecting fingers over the tight-woven mat of withies beneath Marion's green and brown skirts. "Did'ja weave that 'un too?"

Marion nodded.

"Proper tight, this. I nivver had no true talent for baskets or mats, but I've done a share, though me hands en't so strong t' now." With a last caress to the mat, the woman straightened, looking to where Emma, declining to assist David, instead snatched her wayward eldest's arm and began dragging her back to where old Owain and the pregnant woman sat.

From the stolid resignation on the face of, well, everyone there, the harangue was familiar—and disregarded.

A sound solution, Marion decided. David didn't need that sort of help, anyway.

"By m' troth, that young 'un me boy married has more in her head than me eldest. Emma's plain useless. I'm Agnes, by t' by."

Of all the things Emma had droned on about, none of them had contained the names of her female companions.

"I prayed for help," Agnes continued. "Those thieves were set to do t' worst, and I prayed as I never had done, but I nivver thought God would send one of his own t' save the likes of us. Like some . . . scarlet angel, milord were, swooping in with his sword and all that hair like fire!" This with an appealing, half-apologetic grin towards Marion's curls, only partly covered by her woollen wrap. Agnes also had quite a few teeth left; it must run in the family. "Oh, my. Is 't himself?"

But nay, it was Gilbert ambling back into camp, toting a few snared coneys. He gave a tilt of his head to the group playing knucklebones, then headed over to the cauldron, where David was still scooping up portions for the youngsters. David served up both a hearty helping and a smile for Gilbert's efforts—but the smile didn't quite reach his eyes. Instead they followed the children. Thinking, no doubt, on his own family, mostly gone.

A long road from where your childhood walked, Maiden—of peasantry, true, but still free and of the Heath, from a lineage of wise and worthy women. Before you spins out the proof of what hopelessness begets, the endless thread of tynged for those powerless against thisworld's affronts.

Each of the youngsters slunk away with bowls cradled close; despite second helpings, they plainly feared someone might take away their bounty at any moment.

In such straits, what could be gratitude twists into resentment, wisdom into willing blindness, love to hate. Fear ever breeds more enmity than kinship. Your words will only touch those willing to hear them. So take care with expectation, and be strong in what sacrifices you must make.

The Lady's words burrowed deep, burning.

"I were surprised, mind you, that one of God's warrior monks would bring us t' an outlaw camp." Agnes gave a shrug. "But there en't many who en't heard of Robyn Hood's grace with folk in trouble. And his justice when sommun betrays him. *I* en't ungrateful enough to judge where mercy comes from."

"Not many who follow the Christ would say so." Despite the Lady's warning, Marion couldn't bite back her retort.

"Well, I hope milord Templar comes back anon, so we can thank him." Agnes looked troubled by her benefactor's desertion.

Marion reached out, patted her hand. "Gamelyn will return, soon enough. He's gone to find a place for you."

The rest of the villeins had clumped together, the children with noses buried in their bowls. Agnes eyed them, but her mind was on other things.

"Mm. Christ were all of mercy, though from what the priests say, his Holy Father weren't so loving, like. Me ma bided t' Heathen ways, Maiden." The soft stress made it the honorific it was—and that insight surprised Marion. "I've no doubt 'twere Aelwyn's family—me son's widow—what sent word to Robyn Hood. They were of t' Heath also, though Aelwyn were baptised when she married my boy."

Marion found herself wondering if that had been the price of acceptance, and if the girl regretted it. "Gamelyn said her grandfather came to him, asking for help."

"T' old charcoal burner, aye. His heart were in the right place. But ways are changin'. People long for simpler things, an easier path. Eh, I've seen it in me own bairns, the longing fer hope that en't bought in blood."

"Then they'll search a long while. Weren't it t' White Christ who died for his people's sins? Only now 'tis the lives and hearts of others, from the Holy Land to here, that those who say they follow the Christ would suborn or destroy. 'Tis Christians who bathe in t' blood of any who'd challenge 'em. Your hope—any hope you'd care to speak of—is bought in blood." Marion realised her hands were shaking upon the thread, forcibly stilled them, and met Agnes's gaze.

It was troubled. Unsure. It gave leave to say more.

"What of t' Mother's sacrifice, Agnes? What of t' Magdalene's? Wise and holy women given no rights or place in the Church. Precious little do we hear of them, of their blood and flesh, of what *they* gave to their god. A King's life en't his from the moment his god touches him—but what of those who love a god's son?"

Her words faltered, the truth of them, again, burning deep. Her eyes went to Robyn, who'd left off knucklebones. Leaning on a staff, standing on one leg with the other propped against his calf, he was in earnest conversation with Gilbert.

Aye, Maiden. You begin to understand.

As if Her words had called him, Robyn's gaze slid to meet Marion's. He smiled, beckoned her over.

She gave a slight shake of head. *Soon enough.*

"'Tis God's will," Agnes murmured. Tthe words were uneasy, almost rote. "This world is full of evil things, to make us cherish the next."

Marion took a deep breath, held it in her lungs for a moment, cleansing-magic. Felt the Lady's presence fill her, strong and sure.

"Thisworld has always been hard. It always will be. That en't 'evil,' and fighting it en't 'righteous.' It just is. Thislife tests us, aye, for ones to come. Mayhap that should make it *more* meaningful."

Agnes's eyes had widened—with trepidation, aye, but also with glimmers of comprehension.

"To walk thisworld and see no beauty or life, find nowt but sin and evil in it, to rend and despoil and claim our fine land is nowt more than sommat to use up? *That's* a sin. Or to be ready to just . . . give ower, let owt happen because we believe another life'll cosset us and give us what *we* think is owed us? Well, *that's* taking a god's name and worth in vain. Any god's son would weep, to find his life sold for so little."

Agnes looked down.

"The Church turfed you out," Marion persisted. "That en't righteous, or a plan of any god. You just got in the way of greedy men. Their like cares more about profit and power than anyone's souls. T' White Christ would've turfed *them* out! Mayhap your scarlet 'angel' brought you here to remind you of some truths."

"Mistress?"

Robyn's timing was usually better than this. Agnes's expression suggested she'd begun to listen. The exasperated look Marion turned on her brother melted away, however, upon sight of the two lads heeling close behind. They still cradled their licked-clean bowls, goggling at Robyn almost as eager as they had David's ladle.

"There's still no sight of your son, Mistress," Robyn said, courteous. One eyebrow did a questioning dance as he glanced at Marion: *All right, then?*

Marion shrugged, made a small gesture to the two lads. The resulting expression on Robyn's face made a comical mix from amusement and dismay.

"He en't my son, but Emma's brother-in-law. She said 'twere likely he'd headed off on his own." Agnes met Robyn's eyes calmly enough, but also made a furtive sketch of the cross against her breast. She seemed surprised Robyn had come to her with the news.

Warming his horn-hard, bare feet by the fire, her husband looked . . . offended.

Agnes's mother might have been Heathen, but Agnes and her man were a long way from it. To speak of family matters to any but that family's eldest female was something Robyn wouldn't have even considered. To Marion, with her past several years cloistered in a nunnery and deaf to her birthright, it was but another proof of the Lady's warning.

They had done the right thing in aiding these folk. But it was all they could do. No matter their guardian angel of a god-touched Templar; no matter Robyn walked amongst them and proved himself as much man as woodland spirit; no matter how Marion did her best to persuade what ones were willing to listen. The villeins were grateful, surely . . . but how long before it soured?

"When will Gamelyn be back?" Marion asked.

Robyn's eyebrows once more gave a curious dance. "Likely not until evening." Then to Agnes, "We hope he'll have good news, dame, and a place for you. It's like to be a fair journey, but we'll not send you on empty-handed."

Agnes nodded with some dignity, but her eyes flickered to her husband's as she spoke. "This is sommat you should speak to me man about, milord."

Again, the eyebrows, and Robyn's glance at Marion a query. She nodded, with a slight jerk of head indicated the grandfather.

With a curious shrug of bony, broad shoulders, Robyn ambled over to the fire.

Agnes watched him go. Murmured, "Some things is past any understanding or help. Past even t' wicked cunning of old gods."

Marion frowned.

With a shake of her head, Agnes held out a hand. "Forgive me, Maiden. I meant to ask what might be done to repay yer kindness, not question your right to believe as you must in yer own place. See, some villages and kirks might see t' honouring old ways as well as new . . . well. It weren't encouraged nigh Rufford."

Nestling her spindle into her lap, Marion covered the old woman's hands with her own. "You'd be one of a few who'd give me that much right. There is no debt owed. Save . . . " She hesitated, unsure as to whether or no she should voice it. But there was no dissent within, be it goddess-heart or Marion's own.

It was Agnes's turn to frown, then make as if to speak.

Marion forestalled it and squeezed the woman's hands. "We'd welcome you and your people t' Maying. If you're able, come back to the old places, see the Bel-fires one last time."

Trepidation still lurked in the elder woman's face, yet it was not so obstinate this time.

The quick trip to Clipstone had gone much as expected. Hubert tended as humanitarian after his own fashion as had the original Templars. Founder de Payens and his comrades had, after all, first banded as armed protection for pilgrims to the Holy Land.

In gratifying approval of Gamelyn's impromptu rescue—and despite readying to ride for Tickhill—Hubert requisitioned a few more horses, a cart, and kit for Gamelyn's use. He put his own seal upon Gamelyn's index finger, promised to deliver the news to Temple Bruer's Commander—also due at Tickhill—regarding his new villeins, and tendered the Order's blessing.

Not without a reminder of the looming deadline.

The trip to Rufford, on the other hand, was anything but gratifying, at least as far as Gamelyn was concerned. It didn't take as much silver as Robyn had feared, nor did it need the amount of cold bastardishness and coercion Gamelyn wanted—truly *wanted*—to summon.

Instead his appearance, flanked by Much, sent the Abbot of Rufford into quite a dither. Enough of one, in fact, that said Abbot aired a few concerns he never should have done without fully checking Gamelyn's credentials. The Abbot merely assumed him to be from Temple Bruer, come to see about the funds due—nay, overdue. Which in turn made the Abbot all the more susceptible to a suggestion that Temple Bruer would take, in lieu of arrears, the family of villeins Rufford Abbey had so wantonly and irresponsibly turfed out after a hard winter.

"Aye, well, that were too easy," Much lamented once they were mounted and the palfreys ambling at a good clip away from the arched gates of Rufford Abbey. "Bloody sods deserved a round of arse-kickin'."

Gamelyn agreed. Even the fear in the Abbot's eyes at two brawny Templars descending on his doorstep hadn't satisfied the sense of outrage. Even if Gamelyn wasn't sure exactly why he was so outraged.

If Blyth were mine. . .

But it wasn't.

If it were. . .

His own manor, made right again. Where he would have influence that mattered, in this time and place—to mould Blyth into a fair place . . . a haven . . . a *home.* One where they could live and love, their *own place. . .*

We have our own place, the Horned Lord growled all sudden, then wafted and shifted, inevitably, into the familiar. *We have a home.* You *have a home.* Once more He spoke in Robyn's voice, and it shivered Gamelyn to bone. *We have* Our forest. *And you would prison Us in stones and call it fair?*

Nay, Gamelyn argued, *I would make a place where pardoned outlaws could claim a home for their families without being maimed or murdered at the whim of corrupt sheriffs or Church edict! Where my lover could come freely to my bed—*

A snort, overriding. *It was My impression he did that now.*

Only in the Wode. And even there, some would wish it otherwise.

Every wolf must make his place. You learnt that in the parched land of your desert god. Such a powerful god, for all that he does not belong here. He woos My people away, promises them paradise yet wields control with a hell of shame.

Whilst you promise Hell at every turn! Every vision. Every dream!

To promise hell, one must sanction it. Low. Angry. *The only hell truly extant in thisnow, in My forest, is that which* you *bring, lordling.*

Is that so? It is in Your *forest, Horned Lord, where I am destined to betray my own! Where at any time our Winterlord could be taken and his head exchanged for a handful of silver!*

A laugh. *They have to catch Us first. As to the rest. . . so sure, you are, of your* tynged, *my lord.*

I'm sure of nothing, including my own heartbeat, in thisnow. Running the words together as the Heathen did, Gamelyn heard the Lady's resultant croon of satisfaction but did not let it sway him. Persisted. *If Blyth were mine—*

If! Contemptuous.

If Blyth were mine, Gamelyn insisted, fierce, *then our Archer could once again ride free. He could be that forester a brutal fate denied him. Our Maiden could fulfil the longing—I've seen it in her eyes even if you have not!—for her own home, her own hearth, her own people depending upon her skill, and the proof of it in the jangle of keys at her girdle.*

And, it whispered, behind barriers forged so tight even gods could not broach, *with the means, in these stones all mine to me, could I not find my own* tynged *and foul this loom of fate and betrayal upon which you would spin me?*

It took Gamelyn, shook him with no more mercy than a terrier would a rat. An answer, mayhap, to every question he had asked of late. He kept it silent. Buried.

Ah! But he says "our." At long last. Ever does My Summerlord long for his Eden. The Lady's voice held none of the mockery of Her consort; it was serious—pensive, even—and roused in him the same heat as She who flitted through the woodland like a ebony dryad, who had but a moon's passage ago freely trailed Gamelyn through the halls of Temple Hirst, longing and spirit and promise. *It is a goodly thought, to regain what is yours. In such a place, in Summer's rightful realm, We can but cultivate Our power. A Sacred Marriage in truth, an art of commingling both subtle and essential. The Templars spin their webs with a covert necessity thisworld more and more demands, and they understand how all wisdom is its own form of truth.*

The unerring accuracy of Her statement shook him even further. Gamelyn murmured, wry, "Ah, but what is truth?"

"Milord?" Much ventured, muted.

The words—his own and Much's—burst the bubble of delusion and otherworldly communication both, leaving Gamelyn abruptly foul-tempered. *Foolish,* he chided himself, *gormless pillock, to hope for such things! Have you learnt nothing?*

"Milord." It was sharper. Much leaned over and snatched at Falcon. The stallion had taken advantage of his rider's lapse of concentration and veered into a patch of sunny spring grass. "Methinks you ought to worry less on truths and instead ask Himself t' teach you how best to be away wit' spirits yet still ken what your body's about."

Gamelyn peered over at Much, then started laughing.

Much grinned and tossed him the rein.

Robyn woke mid-night, limbs wrapped around a familiar pillow; made of hard muscles and worn woollens, it had him sweated too warm, with fire-flax strands tangled in the curls of his beard. In his mouth, too.

"'Tis a good thing John was on watch," Gamelyn murmured. "Anyone could have snuck into camp and lain beside you."

"Nay." Robyn snuggled down. "Not just anyone." Then, "You missed supper."

"Marion set some aside for us."

"She knew likely you'd both be back before dawn. Much told her." *Whilst you said nowt. As usual.*

A pause, as if Gamelyn had heard unspoken as well. "And you?"

"And me what?"

"Did you know I'd be back?"

"You"—Robyn took the cords of Gamelyn's neck between his teeth in a warning nip—"ask too many bloody questions."

The frame against his softened—just for a heart's beat—then twisted. The kiss was thorough, not gentle, fire with a taste of ash upon its edges. From there, more fire: a suckle then nip of the throat Robyn willingly offered, sword-hard hands pinning him, a thigh firm across his own and, against his hip, a knot to rival the stones of Mam Tor.

Panting breaths trapped beneath a molten tent of furs; Gamelyn exhausting more humid heat down Robyn's breastbone. The pinch of fingers, of teeth—again, not gentle, not teasing, not lingering. Too swift, yet not *enough,* and that fire-flax hair now knotted in Robyn's fingers, snagging on bow-hardened calluses. The fierce pace flared and nigh finished him even before Gamelyn yanked Robyn's braies down to his thighs and did finish it: more heat, more teeth and tongue and rough-delicious hands.

No chance to so much as reciprocate, but Robyn realised as they lay there, heaving against the heavy sear of spent breaths, that it was unnecessary. The proof lay, heavy and sticky-wet, against his calf.

Robyn rolled to his haunches and flung the concealing furs aside, sucking in cool, fresh air. The lights behind his eyes subsided to a small fizz and dazzle. Everyone was still asleep— including their guests. David was snoring even more loudly than usual—likely because Tess was draped over collarbones and throat like a ferret necklet—and if the others weren't out, they were at least giving a polite impression of it. John was a sentinel by the fire. His brown eyes slid Robyn's way, gleaming soft beneath a dark forelock. A quick smile, then a return of attention to his hands, busy, of course, with carving knife and wood.

Robyn's own hands were still twined tight in russet hair. Gamelyn had folded half in Robyn's lap, beard prickling at his bared belly.

Softening his grip, Robyn began combing the snarls with his

fingers, as gentle now as earlier fierce. "So," he murmured. "Where were you, then?"

A ripple of surprise went through Robyn as Gamelyn half rose, forgoing concealment to snake a firm arm around his waist. "No worries," Gamelyn murmured against Robyn's shoulder. "That lot wouldn't hear a mangonel loose." True enough, but the brusque indifference seemed strangely contrary to the prior outburst of righteousness.

Aye, well, his Oak were nowt if not contrary. "So. Where were you?"

Gamelyn gave a tiny shiver. "You know where I was."

"Aye, well. You have me there."

"I think"—slow, barely audible—"I'd have you anywhere."

"Mm. Seems to me that en't quite so." It barely travelled past their tangled furs. "When there's nowt between us but breath and skin . . . aye, you're all mine then. But when you're acting t' monk, there's precious little shifts you."

Gamelyn was silent. Then, against the fur tracing Robyn's jawline, "Hubert has ordered my return."

Robyn should have known it was coming. Should have been prepared for the force of it, a mailed blow no matter it being dressed in the calm silk of Gamelyn's voice. Gritting his teeth, Robyn took that blow with the expectant composure of his conquered race. Asked, just as calm, "When?"

"Three days." Gamelyn's composure was even more considerable: ice, after all that fire. "Blyth has been put to siege."

"*What?*"

It burst from Robyn louder than he'd intended. Arthur's snore broke its rhythm for a moment. John threw them a querying look, and over against the cavern mouth, Marion murmured a sleepy sort of question. Much muttered something back.

Thankfully, none else stirred.

In a deft combination of roll and tug, Gamelyn pulled Robyn to lie against him, atop and along. Said, into unruly black, "Blyth is still being held in Count John's name, despite King Richard ordering his brother's lands seized."

"Hm. So that's why."

Gamelyn tensed beneath him, ever so slight. "Why?"

"Gilly and Arthur both have complained as how our roads 've been occupied this last se'nnight." Robyn muttered it against Gamelyn's chest, breath setting ginger-gilt fur a-shiver and that inexplicable tension, slow and just as curious, to loosen. "T' lads, they're spoilin' for some action, what with people starting to dare our territory. So. Herself the Queen delivered her parcel."

"It would seem so. Richard is on his way to England."

"And your lot has been ordered to assist."

"No doubt a secure England suits the Grandmaster's purpose."

"Secure!" Robyn snorted. "Better to my mind, whats'mever spirits bide in the sea take that great, grasping sod of a Christian king for their own before he so much as steps foot in our land. Will the man even see what his ransom's cost?"

Not that it mattered to *their* like. What was left would do nowt but trickle from between grasping fingers into more pitiless laws, hard work, and hungry bairns.

The sudden gleam to Gamelyn's eyes, scrutinising oh-so-careful, broke Robyn's ire into friable, insecure pieces. He didn't fancy that look, nay, not in the least.

"So." Once again, and oh-so-careful. "What else?"

"Else?"

"There's allus sommat else, pet."

Aye, and Gamelyn's face resulted in no little entertainment when he thought he was being so sly and distant, yet was called on the giveaways of it sticking out all over, plain as a brassed-off hedgehog. A flicker of those green eyes beneath Robyn's own, a quiver of mouth and eyebrows . . . then nowt, slick-smooth as butter.

Aye, and does your Hubert know you so well, then?

Gamelyn tugged Robyn's forelock over his eyes. "I've seen less predatory gazes upon a hunting lion."

Robyn didn't need sight to consider evasion. "What else, then? Because it seems you're off to fight another battle at Hubert's side, an' all for a Motherless sod as don't deserve so much as a drop of your blood. Summerlord."

A huff. Then, "Blyth's recent and unrelenting castellan is Otho."

"*Otho?*" A sudden squeak, it echoed through the clearing.

"Bloody *damn,*" Will growled, heedless with sleep, "if you're after going at each other, least be *quiet* about it!"

A mirthful snort from Marion, and a gleam of Much's teeth in the dim. John was grinning, too, and shaking his head. Their visitors didn't so much as stir.

"Aye, my brother Otho." A thread of humour tickled Gamelyn's voice into new warmth. "Do you see, now, why my presence might be an asset?"

"Some days," Robyn grumbled, "I see both more 'n lessen I like, wit' you."

Once again, pectoral muscles and breastbone shivered beneath Robyn's hands in a catch of breath, and Gamelyn's face gave that slight tic before juniper-green glittered into stone.

And some days never enough. Where are You tonight, O Horned One? Robyn thought mutinously. *Could use a sight of help about now.*

But the Horned Lord's presence lay deep within and between them, silent. Sated.

"Your brother, then. And a job dirty enough doing that the Templars want their prize assassin amidst." Robyn leaned closer, reached to trail a thumb along Gamelyn's lower lip. "So. Is there more you en't told me? Say, sommat as has you bent on rutting me stupid before you'd give owt a mention?"

"Obviously not stupid enough." The whispered thread of humour had slithered sideways, rueful—and purposeful. "Though I well know you find altogether too much joy in hiding that canny brain of yours beneath a dirty, ragged exterior—"

"Dirty? I bathed yesterday!"

"Mm." Gamelyn breathed him in. "I know." And then the tosser murmured something in Arabic, which yet again set Robyn's *other* brain lurching and quivering, all too hopeful.

"You're just hopin' another good rut'll make me soft."

A clever-cruel smile. "Well, part of you, anyway."

This was going all crossways. Usually Robyn was the one to coax with well-salted insinuation. "And what else?"

A pause, another intake of breath, this one slow and deep. The trees rustled about them; the wind was picking up, as if timed with Gamelyn's agitation.

Summerlord, Robyn thought, and wanted to speak to it; instead he repeated, low and between their bodies as if they were the only ones extant here and now, "What else?"

Still, the pause. Then, "Hubert needs me, Robyn."

Even when nowt else made sense, this much was unambiguous: Gamelyn honoured Hubert, loved him no less than Robyn had the old man who'd borne the weight of the god's horns before him. As Cernun had been magus and mentor, so was Hubert.

Still the breath seeped from Robyn, unsure, and the words he formed in its wake were as evasive as ever Gamelyn practiced. "So. Much'll go wit' you, then."

"Not this time. When I leave for Blyth, Much is the only one who isn't outlaw. He's already agreed to accompany you and see the villeins safe to Temple Bruer." A huff, steaming upward to wisp upon the chilly breeze. Green eyes followed, with more contemplation, and the faint whisper, "I'm running out of time."

"Running out of time?"

Gamelyn's nostrils flared. He paused, giving careful consideration to his next words. "I was given a se'nnight to report to the siege. And you're full of questions tonight."

More than you with answers. Slow, feeling his way, Robyn clenched fists upon Gamelyn's chest, leaned his black-scruffed chin against them. "But there's no doubt but Much'll come after you when he's able. So I'm wondering what me sister'll say to 't."

"Marion understands. She's lying with a soldier."

"As am I."

Gamelyn's gaze flitted up to Robyn's.

"Only as I see 't"—still slow, almost ponderous—"she wain't agree with you goin' alone."

"Surely you're not suggesting to let Marion occupy a siege."

"Nor would I, not with their like." Robyn watched Gamelyn like Tess at a hare's burrow. "So nay, not Marion, or even Much. I think 'twould be best did I go with you."

Gamelyn's eyes went wide-white against the sullen firelight. "*What?*"

Robyn reached out, gave ginger-gilt hair a tug. "You heard me."

And was sent rolling sideways as Gamelyn lurched up. And nearly kept going too; flung the furs aside, crouched . . .

Self-possession regained hold just in time. Gamelyn lowered himself back to his haunches, pulled the furs back into place, and spent time fussing with them, drawing that well-oiled cloak of composure and snugging it proper tight.

Robyn gave it another hard tweak. "You asked me to come before. To Blyth."

Silence.

"You were proper keen of my help, then. And for now, as I recall, your Master Hubert has more'n once offered vouchsafe, should I meet wit' him."

"To *treat* with him!" It was a hiss. "Not to a sodding *siege!*"

Choking off, fierce anger and . . . Ah, there it was! The faintest glimmer: candour, oozing from the cracks.

Fear. And something else, flitting from scrutiny the more Robyn bent his senses to it. Gamelyn raised his face to the sky, nostrils flaring. He knew Robyn was watching, had to, couldn't help *but* know.

Yet . . .

Once Robyn had seen a thief dragged onto Sheffield's common. They'd tied the poor sod spread-eagled between two draught horses, and whilst the horses had been blinkered, they were jumpy in the traces, knowing 'twas more than a plough they were about to pull. Unfortunately, a horse's instincts encouraged flight, so when they'd felt the whip on their haunches, they'd . . . fled.

He'd been barely six, had managed to escape the market confines and his sister's hawk eyes, been nosing about where he shouldn't.

Strangely enough, he remembered nowt of his mam's scolding but one half-muttered oath: *You canna un-see such things, not ever.* Eluned had been right—with one difference. 'Twasn't sight Robyn remembered the most, but *sound.*

And now, as he Saw Gamelyn's *tynged* flutter, then fray-sway all precarious in a darkling wind, Robyn fancied he heard the inevitable, eerie-sharp forerunners to the crack and shatter of bone: the stretch and rip of muscle and tendon.

The two horses in opposing and panicked flight? The Templars. The Wode.

Robyn wasn't about to force any choice. About now, he wasn't sure he'd fancy the outcome.

Gamelyn finally spoke, his voice nigh bloodless, contained. "Hob-Robyn, trus . . . " The old name came all too easily, but not the rest.

I do trust you, Robyn tried to say, yet could not. *Even if you wain't trust yourself.*

Gamelyn spoke again, softer. "I know what I'm doing. It's well worth the risk."

It en't worth this. En't worth you going back to them, lackey and servant when you are what you are here, with me! I don't ken this, never have. What man can hold to their kind of love and still feel ours?

Too bloody overmuch lay between them, unspoken. Robyn felt his head was like to burst with it. "Worth the risk to you, but not to me?"

"You're *outlaw,* in case you've forgotten."

"And you're Templar, following the orders of your master who told you to spy on a pack of Heathen wolfsheads."

A snort. "And those wolfsheads aren't likely to let you—"

"There's no *let me* to 't. We have each other, aye, but we also have our own heart, and there's no rule t' my band as says we need betray ourselves in bein' true to each other."

"And when your heart betrays them?"

"There's *no* betrayal, wain't you see?"

Gamelyn's eyes flickered again, but this time he peered at Robyn cool as the Trent in January.

Challenge me, will you? Robyn thought, and spoke the first thing that came to his tongue. "Leastways, did you bring me, that other master of yours'll likely piss 'imself with glee."

Gamelyn's eyes went flatter still. Aye, and with this one, the mask was as much giveaway as any mirror.

A soft growl purled in Robyn's throat—himself or the Horned Lord, there was no difference in the twist and spin of this, only in the sudden *knowing* of a rightful tide.

"Not to mention, Marion's insistent as to how t' man has sommat as belongs to me."

Another flicker, thick gilt and verdigris. Gamelyn closed his eyes, shook his head, and looked into the trees.

Aye, he does. Have sommat as belongs to me. Yet Robyn wasn't thinking of the Arrow that had slain one bitter enemy and now bided in the hands of another sort entirely.

The forest rarely lay silent, but it seemed near enough to it despite the wind once again picking up, swallowing whispers to toss them skyward on a *shuss* of new-broad leaves. Wood creaked and, from the depths of green-black, an owl made plaintive query.

It was rendering of a moment: *Who? Who are you?*

"So?" Robyn insisted.

"So." It was weary. Gamelyn's eyes were still closed. "You aren't. Going."

"I think I am, pet. Because you en't going alone. Not into *this.*"

- VIII -

It's worth the risk.

Risks . . . aye, those were foremost in his mind. He'd thought of little else, truly, beneath the smaller concerns and preparations.

Considered the ring upon his hand—Master's ring, Templar's claim—a weight as sure as the chainmail upon his torso and one nigh forgotten over the past fortnights. Also contemplated the accompanying weight of isolation draping his shoulders, its symbol a plain, black-and-scarlet tabard. Mused at the meaning of that isolation, the oddity that he should so much as feel it. Kept himself, along with Much and John, busy with the horses, checking breeching and traces, girths and keepers. Made cool inventory of how the rest of the outlaws also made industry into statement: they wouldn't be here after the villeins left, should any think to babble of the camp's whereabouts. Pondered tenacity, and Robyn— the same, actually, in these moments of preparation—and how the villeins also watched Robyn, apprehension giving way beneath an awed and chary fascination. Agreed, albeit with misgivings, as old Owain touched at his tunic sleeve and made timid query: could the holy brother give him a blessing? Noticed with a wry smile how the young girls and the pregnant woman kept following Marion, and how the two boys kept a tail on Robyn: a dawning of insurgency's daring. Brooded as he himself oversaw the horses and carts, as the villeins were provisioned and prepared— enough to see them able for a journey longer than most of them had ever taken: thirty-odd miles eastward to Temple Bruer.

You en't going alone. Not into this.

As Owain crossed himself, kissed Gamelyn's hand, and retreated towards the other side of the cart, Marion was giving another sort of blessing to the pregnant lass, hands clasped, and one so subtle the others wouldn't ken. As if he'd spoken her name aloud, Marion looked up, met Gamelyn's eyes. It was intimate and silent—and knowing. Another claim, with fetters of both rose and thorn.

At least if Robyn was so bloody insistent upon coming with Gamelyn, Marion was well out of it for now. Marion, and the others.

A council of wolfsheads had convened with the dawn, well away from the hearth and their visitors at breakfast. Gamelyn had taken up his normal post of leaning against a tree and being as invisible as possible. Not that it had mattered; the discussion stayed mostly a tight, tactile affair between Robyn and Will Scathelock, with many a resentful look flung Gamelyn-ward, couched in Scathelock's curled lip and narrowed amber eyes.

Speaking of tenacity . . .

Scathelock hadn't been the only one to protest. Yet Robyn, damn his black eyes, had possessed a firm answer to every objection. Any hope Gamelyn might have held upon the outlaws convincing Robyn to stay had been dashed and, in relative short order, accord reached. John would accompany them. Both he and Robyn would keep their heads down. Robyn in particular would merely play the hireling peasant archer and stay away from those few who'd know him by sight. Which, Gamelyn hoped, meant he'd stay away from the castle itself.

Traitor, a small voice niggled. *Your Master asked this much of you: to bring Robyn, obtain his assistance and company. Hubert himself guaranteed safety for any outlaw.*

Furiously, Gamelyn ordered it silent—all the while praying to whatever gods would listen that Robyn would do as he'd promised.

Much would lead the villeins' cavalcade to Temple Bruer. He carried a letter penned this morn upon a sheaf of Marion's precious hoard of parchment and sealed with Hubert's ring, as well as a pouch of silver covering Rufford's tax arrears. Marion, Scathelock, Arthur, Gilbert, and David would accompany him. They would all foregather north of Blyth within the se'nnight, did all go well.

From there, things weren't so easy. Gamelyn kept seeing . . . *things:* hints of Sight and sound at the corners of his vision, a full fabric of possibilities fluttering on the wind, misted scarlet and ebon. It was akin to a blood spatter filming one's eyes.

Wasn't it bad enough the nightmares had returned? Did he have to . . . to dream awake, as well?

"Milord?" Then, softer, "Gamelyn?"

The familiar voice brought him back from such musings. On the other side of the sumpter, broad-long fingers busy with the harness, Much met Gamelyn's eyes and jerked his head sideways.

It was John who approached, still dusted with hay from the horses' breakfast, several nut-brown tangles falling over eyes filled with too many things. He'd two more bridles draped over one shoulder, and Falcon's rein; the stallion followed, snuffling at John's hair and meek as the sumpter. As Gamelyn took the rein, John's fingers brushed his—another claim—before he turned away and went to bridle the others.

Gamelyn sucked in a small, silent breath, busied himself with checking girths. Falcon turned, lipped his sleeve. With an absent push at the horse's cheek, Gamelyn murmured, "I've nothing for you now."

"He's a lovely fellow." Silent as a bitch fox, Marion also had come over, was patting the furry bay rump.

Gamelyn nodded, checking over the rest of the tack. "Hubert brought him along."

"He knew he could count on you." It was soft, accepting. "He trusts you. Just as we do."

Don't trust me. You can't afford it. He can't.

Nay, he wouldn't think on that. "Can't you talk Robyn out of this?"

"I haven't the right to talk Robyn out of this. None of us do. He *loves* you, y'fool, wain't you see that?"

Startled, Gamelyn met Marion's gaze; she pinned it, held.

"You're so set upon this path, doubting or damned, I think you sometimes forget. And if you think either of us'll let you walk away now, without a fight?" She shook her cinnabar head. "Well, you're underestimating us worse than ever you underestimate yourself."

"Aye," Much murmured, ostensibly to the harness.

Marion peered at Much, smiled. He returned it with a satisfied nod. With a chirrup he led the sumpter, with empty cart jouncing and rattling behind, to where the supplies waited all bundled in sacks and barrels. Marion watched him go. Yet before Gamelyn could move away, she turned back to him and placed a staying hand upon the scarlet cross.

Gamelyn found himself abruptly tongue-tied, for no good reason other than she was peering at him, *touching* him, moving even closer as the Lady whispered into his ears:

Ah, the sun has burnt Me!

A flush tinted Marion's cheeks, all the coppers and pinks of desert roses. She'd heard. Gilt lashes lowering on those cheeks—and a hint of clever smile upon her lips—she traced the Templar's cross with her finger: benediction, and warning.

"I don't ken how you keep on like this, all to yourself and t' back of your hand to any—including ones who'd love you—as foils your way." Her voice bided uncharacteristically quiet, no hint of anger or even chide. "But I think, sometimes, I understand why."

Would you mind explaining it to me, then? was the first, wry thought that came to him, followed on its heels by *Oh God, I hope you truly don't.*

For something in him kenned this was merely the first inexorable step across thin and treacherous ice.

Grey eyes slid upward and met his, as if she'd heard. "A path and promise for us all, wit' Herself whispering it into *tynged's* black. She wants this. Wants to walk free in both stone hall and woodland bower, deep cavern and mere and hallowed transept. Wants allworlds moulded into one. Wants . . . " Her voice slipped, cracked just a little. Her fingers clenched against his tabard with a *squeak-shuss* of tight-woven woollen.

Then she slid that hand upward, curled it about his nape, and pulled him close. Kissed him.

Roses, heady in his nostrils and soft against his mouth. A caress of lips, then damp nap of tongue. His mouth opened and the breath seized, startled, in his lungs. He shivered . . . nay, the *world* shivered, unravelling Sight and sound into formless gilt and grey, tremoring a heartbeat that was not his but echoed his, as her breath filled his mouth and whispered, "Ah, but the sun has burnt me."

She pulled back, eyes a-glimmer with a goddess's moonsilver presence. One last flare, then a shift and fade back to storm-grey. It was Marion who smirked up at him, slid an equally cheeky glance towards Much. And damned if *he* didn't look entirely too pleased for someone whose lover had just tongue-bussed another man.

With one last stroke of fingers to Gamelyn's jaw, Marion turned and walked away. Her head was high, daring any—including the outlaws she rejoined—to utter so much as a sigh.

Scathelock had a face like thunder. Arthur wasn't much better. David seemed more worried than anything. Gilbert's eyebrows were rising into his curly forelock, respect *and* surprise. John was leaning against the tree where Gamelyn and Robyn had lain only last night, scratching Tess where she lay draped over David's shoulder. John's eyes gleamed, a satisfaction mimicking the half smile tugging at his lips.

The villeins were agog. The children were giggling, and that one woman—Emma—was shooting Marion a look fit to poison her. But it wasn't truly any of those Gamelyn saw; only Robyn, beside John. A soft gravity claimed Robyn's expression, a . . . was that hesitation Gamelyn saw? Or was it Gamelyn's own discomfiture, his mouth stung sweet and his ears fair a-hum?

Robyn merely smiled, sloe eyes tinged with silver, and Gamelyn saw the antlered shadow limning his black curls.

But 'twas Scathelock who had the final word.

Just as they were readying to leave—the outlaw escorts, the

villeins, the cart—he came close. Seemingly meandering towards the cart, Scathelock made a slight detour and shoved hard into Gamelyn. It was not friendly, no more than the smirk that crossed Scathelock's lips as Gamelyn gave a small totter sideways and checked an equally reactionary grab for a blade.

"Clumsy of me." The apology was anything but, and Scathelock's next mutter proved it further. "Nigh clumsy as you, actin' the monk and snogging *our* lass. Or to feign you en't willing t' have Robyn follow you 'crost shire into more trouble than we can fetch him free of."

Normally such comments were water runnelling off a diving duck.

Instead it pinked Gamelyn in a soft place he'd not known he possessed. "If you can think of a way to keep him here short of breaking his legs," he growled back, "kindly advise me of it."

"Bollocks t' that!" Scathelock snorted.

Gamelyn rolled his eyes and started away.

A snatch at his arm stayed him, yanked him close with a grip like to iron. "Iffen you walk him into a trap?" Scathelock hissed against his ear. "Templar or no, there'll be nowhere to hide. Nowt to save you."

Gamelyn slewed his gaze sideways, met Scathelock's. Held. "If so? I'll hand you the sword myself."

"Off you go, love." The murmur was quiet beside Gamelyn: Robyn to John, who rode pillion on the flea-bitten grey rouncey with his arms snugged at Robyn's waist.

A frown touched John's face. He angled his head against Robyn's back. Shelter from the reality . . . or mayhap just from the rain.

The latter had greeted them—and refused to let up—as they took the North Road; in fact, it fell all the more as they halted, steaming their breath as well as their cloaks and the horses' rumps. Hanks of ground vapor puffed and swirled upward from hoofs to stirrups as Falcon danced in place. Gamelyn ran a firm palm down the horse's crest, added a few soothing tugs to the black mane. The air had changed, and not altogether because of the rain. Falcon was as unfamiliar with the atmosphere of encroaching battle as the two riding beside Gamelyn . . . and sure enough, Robyn reached back to give a like tug of John's wet forelock.

The rain would either remain or blow through, but the tense bite in the air would increase—after all, they weren't yet there and thankfully, Robyn and John had agreed to not *be* there. Blyth Castle lay a good mile's gallop from where they'd stopped. The trees were thinning into a wider verge and, within a well-loosed arrow's flight, a fecund expanse of grazing was broken by one of the larger hills within the castle's demesne. At its crest, shrouded in mists, arose a dark rectangle of wood, thatch, and stone.

Both Robyn and John were peering at it, gazes just as made of stone.

But then, All Hallows Church was its own mystery. It had been ancient when the Bastard had conquered. Robyn claimed it had one time been a place of the *wicce* and cunning folk—the Old Religion—and remained as another holy site subjugated to the jealous avarice of newer gods. Gamelyn had his own memories of the place: first a youthful curiosity, followed by equally youthful dismay and an accompanying fascination, both unseemly and undeniable, once he'd discovered the Pagan associations not so deep into that past. No matter; All Hallows had settled in, aptly named, unperturbed. Would likely remain forever, a calm eye within whatever storm descended.

It was here the Templars had a supporter in the priest who tended to Dadsley's parish, and here they had made a peripheral siege camp. So it only made sense here was where Gamelyn was to receive his orders from the Under-Marshal.

Beyond that, he wasn't sure what to do.

Our pwca *has led you into a dance you cannot help but follow,* the Lady whispered. *Do you trust him?*

It's not—

Do you trust him? Implacable.

Gamelyn slid his eyes to take in Robyn, who was still peering up the hill towards the ancient walls of the church, frowning. John gestured, rapid and mostly hidden by Robyn's left arm. Robyn was nodding, somewhat slow and . . . curious, almost. He tilted his head, murmured something that disappeared into his cowl. John shook his head. Robyn spoke again; this time John's negation was less. Almost . . . resigned.

"Robyn?" As Robyn didn't so much as flick a glance his way, Gamelyn skimmed a boot heel across Falcon's left side. Eager for movement, the horse nearly sidestepped into his companion; a quick close of rein and opposite leg deterred him. Barely. Falcon resumed his prance.

"Robyn. John? Is everything all right?"

Robyn didn't respond. John's gaze flickered his way, fastened upon Robyn, fingers busy. This time Gamelyn saw, read: *Are you sure?*

Robyn nodded.

John sighed, all the while frowning at the hill—through it, actually—with head cocked as if he heard something. It wasn't pleasant, from his expression.

Then he grimaced, leaned forwards to brush a kiss against Robyn's damp cheek, and flung one leg over the horse's rump.

"Wait," Gamelyn said. "What are you doing?"

Neither answered, but John uttered a tiny yip as he hit the ground.

Another grimace, this time as he gave a cautious bend of knees. Robyn's laugh rose into the wet morn, albeit rueful.

"Aye, pet, a pity we should be arse-sore as the poorest villein. Been too long since we've had a hard ride. Save"—he slid a wink and grin Gamelyn's way—"with milord, mayhap."

John chuckled and put a light hand to Gamelyn's calf. An answering grin wanted to tweak at Gamelyn's lip as he peered down but died a-borning at the hard light glimmering behind peat-brown eyes.

"What," he asked again, "do you think you're doing?"

"He's staying," Robyn answered, unfastening John's quiver from the saddle. "I'm going with you."

"You're bloody not."

Robyn wasn't listening. Eyes still fastened upward and upon the hoary silhouette of All Hallows, he shook the wet from his hood. The spray of it caught Gamelyn's cheek and hung, tears of ice.

"I said, you're not going." Ire and trepidation were fighting for supremacy, slicking the back of his throat and rasping into his voice. Gamelyn gritted through it, "*John!*"

Neither was John paying heed, turning away to shoulder the quiver Robyn handed down. That rattling against the longbow already athwart his back, John started unlacing one of the near saddlebags.

Gamelyn tried again. "You promised your men you'd stay out of trouble. You promised *Marion.*"

"Well, and what am I to do, as trouble"—Robyn slid his eyes to meet Gamelyn's—"seems t' have a way of finding me. Of finding us both, aye?"

"And what about what you swore to me?" It was low, a growl. "I heed the oaths 'twixt us ever as constant as you, pet."

A glint of teeth beneath that hood finished the volley.

Gamelyn started to lob his own, was distracted as John gripped his leg, then Robyn's. It was not gentle. "T-take care." Soft, with a hint of the old youthful stutter about the edges—beneath surety, John was uneasy.

Smile fading, Robyn's eyes veiled themselves beneath fringe of forelock and lashes, black as sloe and glimmering silver in the damp half-light. "*You* take care, love." And there it was—a tiny quiver, hesitant telltale in the set of his shoulders.

John acknowledged it with a lean of his head against Robin's thigh, then turned to Gamelyn, pierced him with an unfathomable gaze.

Within was an echo: the Lady's voice.

Do you trust him?

In thisnow, Gamelyn wasn't sure what he could trust. John, leaving Robyn behind despite any promises to the contrary? Robyn, intent upon . . . *something,* so sudden-strange and wilful, a mien as remote as any with which Gamelyn ever cloaked himself.

What? Why? he asked of John, an open, naked silence. John merely smiled and, with a nod, turned away.

Robyn's black eyes rose, followed, and his lips moved. Silent, the whisper, but Gamelyn could . . . *feel* the power of it, a pressure behind his eyes and ears akin to diving into a deep ocean bay. It had other effects. As if summoned, a horned silhouette rose from earth and trees and shadows.

John flew towards it, unerringly as one of Robyn's loosed arrows.

Robyn sighed, shook his hood back, and adjusted his wet reins as he turned to Gamelyn. No longer absent within a deep cowl, the look was fond, heating with that reckless glint Gamelyn both adored and deplored.

"Well, then. 'Tis time for a proper mummer's play, aye?" And Robyn nudged the grey into a trot towards the slope.

Gamelyn could only watch him go, a thousand protests waging war for possession of his tongue.

So. Do you? Not the Lady's light voice, but a heated breath that steamed the rain into a gust to quiver his damp forelock.

Gamelyn turned in the saddle, prepared to shoot an angry-silent query towards that antlered silhouette. But the *Do I what?* faded into the black as he watched John's slight frame disappear; indeed, the light itself seemed to suck inward, glimmering then morphing into hundreds of black tendrils.

Tens of possibilities.

Aye, Oakbrother. Time to scry the bones you yourself have thrown. Do you trust your Winterlord?

Better than I trust you.

Aye, well, then. A laugh, low thunder. *And better than you trust yourself.*

Gamelyn deliberately turned his back, nudged Falcon. The stallion leapt into an eager gallop, and with a few strides, caught up to his grey companion. They angled forwards as the hill rose steep beneath, keeping the horses to a cautious walk when they would rather take an easier gallop.

"Where is everyone?" Robyn muttered. "This area's best for grazing goats, yet not so much as goat or goatherd about."

Aye, few signs of incursion. Yet they were there, did one know how to look—and Gamelyn did. The utter lack of people. Smoke drifting through the rain. The edges of the road left behind them, rutted from men and laden carts, and the hill surround grazed in lawns and roughs—not by sheep but horses. The sounds, faint, of voices carried on the breeze. And a sullen orange glow, carried on the upper mists: fires, refracting off castle walls.

They shouldn't have been able to come this far unchallenged.

Robyn stiffened in his saddle a scant breath before Gamelyn also realised they had been flanked—and so cunningly, they'd not seen the approach. Four riders circumnavigated the hill below, tailing in unhurried threat . . . ah. Two were clad in white.

Gamelyn turned to face them, flung his hood back, and put two fingers to his mouth in a piercing, thrice-toned whistle.

Immediate response. Two of the riders wheeled and cantered away, out of sight around the hill; the others put spur to their mounts and came charging up.

Robyn sucked in a quick breath and snatched at the bow athwart his back. He didn't complete the motion. The grey, mirroring his rider's undeniable agitation, dug its rump in, spun, and tried to vacate the premises. Robyn stayed with him, turned the flight into another spin—the grey protesting this with a bound and crowhop a hare would have been hard put to match. The rouncey's antics were plainly a welcome distraction. Robyn rode them out—barely—with a clear laugh and a playful slap at the horse's flea-bitten neck, finally bringing him to a halt beside Falcon.

Falcon was doing his own excited dance, minus the airs above the ground. He wanted to meet the charge head-on.

The white-clad Templar was grinning as he came up. As if in answer to Robyn's display of horsemanship, he sat down in his saddle and demonstrated as pretty a halt as could be ridden on muddy turf, with a spin in place at the end.

"Mm," Robyn quipped at Gamelyn. "Not bad."

"Brother Guy!" Still grinning, the Templar raised one fist into the air, success and salutation. "Well come, to you and your companion. We were told to expect you both!"

Robyn's glance was a darkling blow. "Did t' man just say *expect us both?*"

Gamelyn knew his cheeks were tinting just as dark. "I'll explain. Later."

"Aye," Robyn acknowledged. "You bloody will."

"If at least we were *there*," Arthur ventured.

"Aye," Will chimed in. "Stead of tailing the likes of these across the shire!"

Their voices were low, purposefully so. The laden cart rattled and creaked, the reins gave a light jingle against bit and keeper, the sumpter's hoofs mixed a rhythm of shod *clop* fore and bare *thup* hind. All of it, plus the low conversation of the villagers, should have interfered. But Marion's ears were keenly attuned to the sound of her own people's voices, so she heard more, surely, than the three outlaws flanking the cart intended she should.

"It means trouble," Arthur mourned. "Nowt but. We're allus better when we've each other's backs, and now our bonny lad's amidst all that!"

"Robyn loves trouble." David's tone was purposefully light. "And he sees it coming a mile distant!"

"Not when that bloody Templar's involved," Will muttered, and so soft Marion almost didn't hear it. Almost.

Likely better to let them grouse it out, chew it to gristle, else it fester sore. Arthur's concurrence was expected, but Marion wasn't prepared for David's quick agreement.

"Aye. 'Twas different, like, when the man was here and one of us." David overrode Will's protest. "And he did try, you've to give him that. But he en't of us, is he? Robyn loves him that hard for nowt, with the man's loyalties all muddled and mixed, and his choice made, aye? He's a Templar."

Marion didn't need to hear the answers to guess what they'd be. Nevertheless, the reality of it sank her heart.

Beside Marion, Aelwyn gave a groan. She was clearly rethinking her wish to ride in the cart. Every jolt and sway tugged unmercifully at that too-gravid belly.

"The point is, Robyn's still in the midst of it now, aye?" Arthur growled. "With heart and head on the block."

As if to distract herself, Aelwyn began to sing, soft. At least she'd a pleasant voice. But in the doing, Marion missed some of the conversation. She tilted her head back and forth, pretending a stretch of her neck.

Heard "—never in his right mind about this. Never has been, since the day he met that bloody nobleman . . ."

That's where you're wrong, Will. You're the one as never thinks straight on this.

The song was catching on. Others took up the chorus, some humming and some singing. Striding point of the little cavalcade, Much had some time ago relinquished his rouncey to the two elders, who'd changed their judgment from apprehensive to appreciative—the rouncey's smooth gait had convinced them riding wasn't so bad after all. Much took up the song in his pleasant, if unremarkable, tenor. And when the littlest girl once again lagged, midstride he bent down, catching and swinging wee Tibba upward without a break in his song. The child gave a shriek, fright melting into delighted laughter as Much swung her around a few times before propping her on one broad shoulder.

Marion couldn't help but smile. The sight was one to set her more along the road to being well besotted with the man. His good humour was infectious, and memory even more so: the tune was one as had accompanied many planting seasons at Loxley village. A fit and fair round could lighten the heaviest load, and put a spring in one's step to make the work go swifter, be it bent down the rows or walking down the road.

Unfortunately, singing made harder any listen-in towards Arthur, Will, and David. At that, mayhap she shouldn't.

But she resisted a hum of the tune, kept listening.

"—helping a lot of Christians, taking 'em back to their bloody *church!*"

"Now, Will," David chided. "Marion said th' preceptories en't much different than any manor, like. And if we didn't help these folk, we'd be no better than the ones who turned 'em out."

"Helping ones as belong to those would see us gone?" Arthur argued.

"Mayhap not all of these are convinced. That breeding lass, f instance. The wee ones, who'll never forget what they've seen—no devils, but men and women like to them. Mayhap we'll make more friends than enemies this day, like Robyn said last night."

"Robyn said too damn many things last night! He's taking too many chances, he is. Gettin' too full of himself—"

"He en't the only one, William." The words escaped, tart-sharp and over her shoulder, before Marion could halt them.

A curse from Will, bitten off. Marion started to turn, hesitated as beside her, Aelwyn's song warbled into a cry, just as sharp, of dismay. She tottered sideways and caught herself with a quick clutch at the seat.

Marion uttered a soft oath, had her suspicions confirmed as Aelwyn parted her knees, lifted her skirt, and also cursed.

Said, "Me water's broke, Mistress."

The rain had moved from shower to torrent. Beneath the shelter of a lean-to, Gamelyn and Robyn were relieved of their mounts by several young Templar squires, and reassured their saddlebags would promptly follow.

As they were ushered towards the inner courtyards by one of All Hallows' monks, Gamelyn kept surreptitious scrutiny upon Robyn—who, for a wonder, questioned none of it. From the squires, who merely treated him with the same unswerving courtesy they'd give any guest of a superior, to the monks' bland and unquestioning acceptance, Robyn seemed more inquisitive than anything. He actually trailed one hand across the old stones of the outer walls with an odd twitch and curl of fingers. The church nave received a searching frown, as well as a flare of nostrils, as they passed farther inward . . . on their way to the calefactory, the guiding Brother explained.

"The warming house," Gamelyn murmured in explanation as Robyn interrupted his ongoing scrutiny of All Hallows with an enquiring twist of brow.

"Aye, well, and a bit of warmth would be welcome, at that." Robyn gave a shudder. "I'm wet to me skin."

Welcome luxury, in fact, to shed the damp beneath a snug roof and by a substantial fire, the latter tended by one of All Hallows' elder monks. There was also the aroma of pottage being keeled in the attached refectory. Robyn gave a deep and appreciative snuff. He stiffened, however, hand falling to his knife, as several of All Hallows' holy brethren advanced upon him. In the next instant, his black eyes flickered across the fire and found comfort, of a kind: Gamelyn had already begun shrugging from his wet cloak with the aid of another brace of monks.

Robyn's grudging assent to being stripped down and his clothing hung to dry on ricks didn't extend to his weapons, Gamelyn noted. Longbow, quiver, and daggers were placed within easy reach. A pair of cloth-wielding monks made an attempt to scour him dry; Gamelyn fought a grin as Robyn snatched one of the cloths and danced away. He ended up crouched naked at the fire—not a full seat, Gamelyn approved—scrubbing at his hair with the weapons at his toes. He kept shifting, too, on those toes, back and forth, the motion tiny but telltale.

Utterly brave . . . or utterly foolhardy, for a wolfshead to accept a Templar's invitation to church. Or mayhap merely cantankerous.

Either way, Gamelyn was conversely sorry and grateful when dry clothing came, in the arms of a genial monk. Robyn was a lovely sight, lithe and graceful in both his wariness and that odd curiosity, wet curls tracing inky veins over skin glossed into marble by the warming fires . . . but this was no place to indulge anything beyond the barest of glances.

And stranger still, Robyn didn't notice Gamelyn's preoccupation, not even with so much as a cheeky *caught you looking* smirk. Instead he scrutinised every nook and corner of the church with a focus that went far beyond caginess. So much, in fact, he didn't notice the Templar Marshal who entered the calefactory until the man was upon them. Even then, after a jerk and start, Robyn merely eyed the newcomer and turned back to his inspection of the thick walls. As if . . . searching.

The Under-Marshal beckoned, and Gamelyn followed him over to the far wall. Robyn left off his preoccupation to graciously accept a bowl of pottage and a woollen mantle from one of the monks. Stranger still, he looked to be drawn into what seemed respectful conversation with an elder monk.

Hearth law, the Lady reminded, heavy and soft as an overcast night sky, *is never to be taken lightly in any house. This place is not as ancient as I. . . yet it is indeed old in the count of your kind. Can you not feel it?*

Aye. He could. Gamelyn placed a gentle palm against the rough-quarried stones as he halted beside the other Templar. The arched doorway shivered with the barest of tensions. Like Tess undulating beneath one's hand, seeking tactile comfort. Curious, indeed; this place slept, somehow—yet was waking.

Somehow.

"Confanonier." The Under-Marshal gave a respectful tip of his fair, close-cropped head, leaning one shoulder against the wall. He gave no signs of feeling anything save cool rock and mortar. "It is very good to see you. Our Commander will be heart-glad of your company—he has, indeed, missed you during your convalescence away. But he informed me there might be more than the one archer?" If he knew that archer's identity, the Under-Marshal gave no sign. Likely would not, no more than he let his curiosity dwell upon the circumstances of Gamelyn's "convalescence."

Templar discipline was a vast comfort; security beyond measure.

Gamelyn tendered likewise respect, obeisance, and address. "Under-Marshal, you honour me and my companion. I had to allocate the remaining archers to another trust. A displaced croft, which the Commander himself gave authority that I should see to." He displayed the signet upon his raised hand.

The Under-Marshal nodded comprehension. "A disappointment nevertheless. Our Commander let it be known they are, one and all, skilled with the longbow, and none of Pontefract's archers bend such a weapon. But then, not many do, save the Welsh and a few . . . eh . . . outcasts?" The Under-Marshal's sparse brows tilted; a tiny stretch of mouth suggested humour. "Baron de Lacy's bowmen are deadly skilled, aye, but the problem remains. A shortbow's range is not proving adequate to the task."

"The . . . task."

"The castle walls are crawling with crossbowmen. We cannot venture close save shielded, and even then the risk is unacceptably high. The Commander refuses to spend more men when other tools might serve. He mentioned how your archers might be of help. Even one might solve a problem . . . if he is goodly skilled."

Oh, he is. Gamelyn's gaze went to the hearth and the sloe-eyed man crouched beside it. *The best of the best.*

Do you trust him? Memory taunted, twisted into doubt all tight and small and serious. *Is not the result worth any risk?*

The old monk tossed another split onto the fire, poked at it, then settled back into his tattered old half seat, half sling cobbled together from wood, cord, and leather. Robyn asked a question, which the old one seemed pleased to answer. The others were dispersing to pre-Office duties, unheeding that a Pagan woodland god's avatar sat to sup with them, tendering respectful audience to an elder monk's fancies.

"My orders," the Under-Marshal continued, "are to see you fed and, if necessary, billeted with my men. But the day is still young enough, and the Commander would, of course, prefer you come soon as possible. I've sent word to the front lines that you and your companion will partake in a good meal and midday Observances before venturing forth. No doubt a lad will be detailed siege-edgeward for your arrival."

Gamelyn nodded.

"And our Master Procurator is expected to return any day as well."

"Master Wymarec isn't here?" The sense of reprieve was disturbing—but hardly surprising, upon consideration.

"Aye, he was gone when we arrived, albeit his presence lingered." The Under-Marshal's eyebrows tilted again—no question this time 'twas humour. "All Hallows was in quite a dither. Seems the Master Procurator was fiercely intent things be in proper order, and the monks had been, shall we say, a bit lax?"

Gamelyn allowed a tilt to claim his own lip. All Hallows served a wide parish, was nonetheless somewhat off the path. Just as quickly he sobered, considering. Wymarec de Birkin, Provincial Master, Preceptor and Procurator of England . . . he wasn't here. Mayhap wouldn't be here whilst Robyn was, and so the greatest worry Gamelyn possessed could well be unfounded.

The Under-Marshal bowed. "For now, *Confanonier,* we welcome you home. Be content, warm yourself, and enjoy a good meal ere you go. I will see you and your companion upon the next bell."

Gamelyn returned the courtesy and watched the Under-Marshal retreat through a side door, considered the likelihood of Robyn consenting to attend a holy office. Even one known as Sext.

I'm allus up for being "sext." The memory, mischief in its grin, stole in and snatched aplomb sideways. Gamelyn almost wanted to smile.

Almost.

Mulling it all over, he ambled back to the hearth. One of All Hallows' brethren impressed upon him a huge bowl of pottage and a hank of bread, as well as a cup, into which the monk poured small ale as Gamelyn took a seat across the hearth from Robyn.

Robyn still crouched, still shifted his weight from side to side, his borrowed homespun giving the motion a bell and sway all slight but palpable. An uninvited distraction at first, Gamelyn began to wonder if it was something else. The hall was large but confined. The prayer-laced stones that . . . purred—there was in truth no other word for it—beneath Gamelyn's own touch had not often proven so kind to Robyn.

Hazarding a keen glance, Gamelyn saw the rime of sweat on Robyn's cheek.

We are well enough, the Horned Lord whispered with Robyn's voice, which faded into Hers: *These stones know you, so they know Us. Summer waxes whilst Winter wanes. You will keep the Holly Lord safe.* Gamelyn hoped their confidence was justified.

"The old one says he once saw the Lady upon the nave altar," Robyn said, light as if discussing the weather.

Gamelyn eyed him briefly, engaged in the small juggle of bread, bowl, and cup. He set the latter upon the hard-packed earthen floor and turned his attention to the elder monk. The old one nodded, eyes meeting Gamelyn's with a surety belying the milky film 'crost them.

"'Twas the Holy Mother who took my sight," the monk said, his voice touched with the soft music of the Welsh upper coast. Like, yet unlike, the way Robyn's words would purl and sing, his mother's birth tongue strong counterpoint to the broader overlay of southern Yorkshire's rearing. "But to have such beauty the last of any seeing . . . The archer here says you are being of Hirst, where Our Lady is biding honoured as She deserves."

"I am *Confanonier* to Hirst Preceptory."

"The archer also says he has not been having the pleasure of seeing Her in all Her glory, but that you, young knight of God, are being blessed with that honour."

Gamelyn slid a frown Robyn's way, but Robyn was busy scraping his bowl with the remnants of his bread. His eyes were soft upon the old monk.

Aye, my Knight, you have. Will have, in ways inexplicable in these walls, at this time. The Voice was mild, but sent a frisson up and down Gamelyn's spine.

Taking a gulp of ale, he admitted, "Aye, Brother, I have."

The filmed eyes seemed to follow him, as if they saw much more than shadows. The old monk gave a beatific smile. His eyes closed, followed a few heartbeats later by a small snore.

"Aye, he's done that thrice already," Robyn offered around a mouthful of pottage. "I think he actually is asleep." Another bite of bread. "Brother Cadog's been quite free wit' information, bless his auld toes. Talked to me in me mam's tongue, off and on. Says himself the Provincial Master was here, settin' things all t' sixes and sevens. Also said they were expecting some wild Welsh archers, for aid of t' siege." This time the black eyes held a cunning satisfaction. "Mayhap I should be enough to go on with, aye, since a shortbow en't 'adequate to the task.'" Robyn's talent for mimicry often stung; this time was no less, considering what he said next. "So, what does your Master order now, milord Templar?"

And who would that be? followed, silent but nonetheless there.

"As you no doubt heard"—this just as stinging, with a lift of eyebrow—"I'm to report to him after Holy Offices." Gamelyn turned his attention to the pottage. Nigh to Marion's standards, it was.

"You mean *we* are." Robyn finished scraping his bowl of the remainders, scoffed the last of the bread, and licked his fingers. "According to your orders."

"You needn't attend Sext." It was deliberate, provocative.

Robyn didn't take the bait. He did take another bowl of pottage from an attentive brother. Gamelyn merely accepted a refill of ale. The brother bustled back to the kitchens, leaving Robyn and Gamelyn the only ones remaining in the calefactory—save the old monk, who shifted with a creak of cord and leather merely to snore louder.

"So, pet." Soft, but with a snap and crackle of temper that nigh put the fire to shame. "When were you going to tell me?"

"I figured I wouldn't have to." Gamelyn's reply was just as quiet—and as terse. "I never dreamed you'd be set on pushing it this far."

"And let you go in on your own. That's bloody likely."

"I'm not on my own. I never have been, not here—can't you get it through your head? *You're* the one . . . Damn it, Robyn, that's the point! You're the one at risk. I'm more in jeopardy amongst half your outlaws than ever I am here!"

That last hit well and truly home. "Through my head? According to you, *milord*, me head's thick as any peasan—"

"Especially when you refuse to think of the consequences."

"You're a right one to talk of consequences, seeing as how you're the stroppy Motherless pillock who refused to tell me I'd been given proper invitation t' siege!"

"Oh, there's a stroppy pillock here, all right—and it isn't me!" Gamelyn pointed out. "It's an arrogant sod of an outlaw who somehow thinks he's untouchable, walking into a castle that could well be a trap."

"Seems to me anything outside my Wode is likely a trap. Of some sort."

Gamelyn, preparing for more argument, found the breath seeping from his mouth and the words tangling upon his tongue.

Brother Cadog shifted, with another pop and creak, and kept snoring.

"Aye, old one, keep dreaming." Robyn's deep baritone turned from biting to soft as swan's down, almost pensive as he loaded another bite on the manchet. "These monks fix a proper tasty pottage, with some fair and fancy bread for their hearth-guests. Reckon I'll do 'em like courtesy and see what *they* consider Sext."

"Robyn, are you out of your sodding mind?" It was a hoarse whisper. "If you don't remember the last time you went into a church, I do!"

At Worksop Abbey, where the stones had wept, and screamed, and tried to gaol a Wode spirit's avatar with their despair.

Robyn's smile was grave. "Take care, pet. You'll give the singers more excuse for their ripe and silly tales. Like the one Alundel told us 'round the hearth when we were waiting out t' rain . . . about old King Henry's grandmam? Her as grew wings and flew t' escape a dunk in holy water?"

"Melusine." It was heavy.

"A fae name. Or"—the smile broadened—"just foreign. But this place . . . All Hallows. It bides proper quiet." The black eyes met Gamelyn's and held. "You've felt that much, aye?"

"Aye," Gamelyn answered, slowly.

"You need me. I can feel that much. I en't sure as to the whys and whatfors; no question but whats'mever plots you're hatching are too tight-bunged in that clever brain of yours. But you need me, pet."

This was harder. Gamelyn peered at the fire for long moments.

Then said, between his teeth, "Aye."

- IX -

They didn't attend Sext. Gamelyn insisted they leave before the bells rang, and Robyn wasn't unhappy with the reprieve. Particularly now.

The pent-up violence could nigh be smelt, even despite the green-wet patter of rain and the smoke wafting in thick hanks. The sward beneath their boots was another testament to it, shading from green to mud-dark, rendered by all manner of shod horses staked or hobbled, by hundreds of battle-worn boots.

The closer they came to the besieged castle, the madder it all seemed.

"I've seen beehives less deadly busy." Robyn couldn't help the murmur, nor the suspicion quivering muscle, bone, and nerve. He slunk, silent and hooded, a pace behind Gamelyn's tossed-back cloak and bared russet head.

Just like a proper villein.

Gamelyn seemed to pause—nay, likely not. Mayhap Robyn was indulging in wishful thinking. For Gamelyn kept walking, one hand resting atop his sword pommel—and whilst it wasn't the casual swagger of an *I've a bloody shunt of iron on my leg, of course I walk like this!* swordsman, it was nevertheless subtle and dangerous. Ready.

Whilst Robyn's own stride lagged further the closer they came. He was a . . . *an arrogant sod of an outlaw who somehow thinks he's untouchable, walking into a castle!* With every step his shoulders tried to hunch and shrug his hood farther forwards, hide his face. If hilltop scrutiny had given a rough shove, walking into the thick of it slapped Robyn in the face and went for the knees.

It was all over people. All over trampled earth. All over the clank of iron and equipment, the roar of forge and fire, the *thup* and creak of wood crying beneath axes or weighted down in a cart. Tents flew their lords' harsh-dyed colours, less gay than purposeful, and limp with the wet. The ready weapons were stark, with no artistry of display. It was close, impertinent. It reeked of too many bodies, rain, and smoke that hung in thick air made even denser with hundreds of voices and presences.

And beyond that, the undeniable centre: the tower keep squatting atop what the locals had long called *tica's hill*. Overlarge bailey surrounded by foetid moat and thick stone walls, fronted by a fortified maw of a gatehouse, it looked nothing like the proud, lively bastion a fifteen-year-old Robyn had first witnessed, with gates flung open, flags flying, trade stalls busy. Nor did it resemble the friend-foe shrouded in mists, a lurking giant from which they had rescued a queen. This time rain and fog seemed to close it up all the more—a sullen enemy, squatting obdurate and impenetrable. In thisnow it resembled a pus pocket, and one like to burst from all the intent pouring—*swelling*—upward.

That latter was the worst. Intention, aye, a thick skim at the back of Robyn's throat; persistent and hot, it wove back and forth amongst the preparations, a wing-charred wyvern waking, formed of fear and lust, doubt and appetite.

Not for the first time, Robyn wondered what he thought he was doing, insisting on this.

Ours, he reminded himself. *Ours, and they wain't have what's ours. Their like wain't take from me any more of what is mine. . . not any of it.*

Aye, Ours. Be with him, the Horned Lord whispered—and it was a mere whisper, His presence muted in this place, clinging within Robyn like flesh to bone. *Hold to your strength and right. They will know the place—beside Us and with Us—of the one they would claim.*

Gamelyn strode on as if he heard none of it, head high, eyes eager—and critical—upon the castle's ramparts.

See? A soft blast, heating Robyn's nape.

Aye. There's too much to see, he gritted back. Kept up. It was quite likely he'd lose Gamelyn in this . . . miasma.

Someone shouldered hard into him, nearly sending him sprawling. Quick as a ferret, Robyn recovered and danced sideways, hand to knife and a ready snarl upon his lips.

He faced a small brace of soldiers. The one who'd nearly ploughed him over hadn't so much as stopped, but his two companions recognised a threat when they saw it. Hands on sword hilts, one with yellow chevrons emblazoned on his tunic raised a mailed fist and a voice as tinged of the shire as Robyn's own.

"Gerrout, bloody fool!"

"Is there some problem?" Gamelyn appeared at Robyn's right,

voice soft, nearly too reasonable. Deceptive as always, were one not paying attention to the steel beneath the velvet—and most didn't. Robyn fingered his dagger into a better position.

These soldiers, however, eyed the red sigil upon Gamelyn's grey cloak. "Your pardon, Brother Templar," the one in yellow offered, with a conciliatory spread of hands. His companions muttered like apologies, ducking their heads: hounds threatened with the whip. One even crossed himself as they retreated.

Robyn watched them go rather stupidly, ears still heated, heart pounding. A hand snatched his sleeve and pulled him out of the main path, close by the roar and clang of a smith's furnace. For a half breath Robyn almost went for Gamelyn, too, stifled it just in time.

The flame was at forging heat, and they were closer than was comfortable; that and the *clang-ti-tink-clang* of the smith's hammer against iron and anvil struck Robyn back into his senses.

Both hands were gripping his arms, now, and hard enough to make him wince. Robyn tossed the forelock from his eyes and let a smile curve his mouth, jerking his chin at Gamelyn's tabard. "I keep forgettin' how handy yon sign bides in a tussle."

The disquiet knit upon those gilt brows melted. One arched, familiar vexation. "I can't take you *anywhere*, you daft pillock."

"And here I thought I were taking you."

"Hardly." Gamelyn gave Robyn a tiny shake, an unspoken *You're all right, then?* and at Robyn's shrug, released him. "We've too long been in the forest."

Nay, hardly long enough by my reckoning. But Robyn followed, gritted teeth and muscles against the beckon and lure of sensation. Gamelyn was right: what made up the purest of survival instincts in the forest could prove ruinous in this teeming, dangerous place. Even the silent, careful pace of a woodland dweller would be nowt to the likes of these but the cant of a hesitant villein . . . easy prey to the road-filthy men who were still arriving, marking territory with swagger and weaponry.

It was a lesson hard-learned in boyhood, long since shucked away in Robyn's own place. But thisnow, here?

Aye, here. What villeins bided in the camp were blending into the scenery, busy at the drudge work, not walking the muddy, main paths as broad-shouldered and accoutred—entitled—as the Knight Templar in whose wake Robyn ambled. No question Gamelyn had the way of it. Not just because of the cloak he wore, but the manner of his wearing it. People unconsciously gave way— and twisted a curious brow at the lanky fellow keeping pace with the Templar, a proper wild man dressed in furs and leathers with a monster of a longbow strapped to his back.

Why do you think Our Summerlord represents such a powerful weapon to Us? The Lady's whisper this time, spoken so soft as to barely twitch Gamelyn's shoulders, yet lying across Robyn's like a wet, heavy fur. One foot faltered and skittered sideways in a particularly wet patch. Robyn heaved his balance back and nearly ran into another soldier stinking of mud, blood, and balls.

Bloody damn, but it was a sad case when he couldn't even walk straight, and him proper sober!

"Robyn?" And bloody *damn* but Gamelyn was sounding as *Shall we wrap you in a wool basket, pet?* as Will Scathelock!

"Aye, but 'm fair enough to skelp you one, see if I wain't."

"Fine." Gamelyn's nose took a decided noble's tilt. "I'll just let the bastards knock you sideways next time, shall I?"

"You're saying that like I'm all up for *letting* 'em knock me sil-*ly!*" It rattled up into a yip as Gamelyn grabbed Robyn's arm— brutal, this time—and dragged him between two hobbled sumpters.

"I'm saying we've no room for pride!"

"Lessen it's yours, *milord?*"

"*Putain de. . .*" It was a barely stoppered growl between bared teeth, green eyes gone to gilt.

And bloody *sodding* damn but it stood every bit Robyn had to attention when Gamelyn transformed into a dangerous, knife-edge Templar. With the added mercy of blocking every other sensation, at that.

Abrupt exasperation filled Gamelyn's gaze.

Robyn's lip twitched sideways, and he leaned in, head cocked. "So that's the secret to doin' battle, then. Haver away t' noise by having a proper rod in your pouch and no way to ease it?"

Another Frank curse—and even fouler, Robyn would warrant, the way it burst from between curled lips and gritted teeth. "In case you've forgotten, you've a price on your head to make any man here wealthy."

"Ah, but your Master would see me safe."

"Safe." A snort. "That depends on which Master you mean, doesn't it?"

Robyn snorted back. "You and Marion both, thinkin' that bloody sorcerer more 'n he is."

"You seem to think that *you're* more than you are here. In *this* place."

"That sounds of a lord trying to put t' sodding peasant in his place, right enough."

Gamelyn sighed, shook his head. "Robyn—"

"I never forget what I am, even here. 'Tis you as en't believing in what you are." Robyn leaned closer, whispered, "What you can be. Here. Even against the likes of *him.*"

"What I can't be is *against* him."

"Your mouth keeps shaping that, but the rest of you en't so sure, aye?"

"Don't you see, I have to be sure! I'm not—"

"My lord *Confanonier?*"

Gamelyn lurched back as if he'd been caught with his hand down Robyn's breeks. No such luck, Robyn mourned, and angled his gaze upon the one who'd found them.

"Ah. Stephen." At that, Gamelyn had always been a right prince at masking any awkward situation with cool, prim arrogance.

The lad with the palm-sized crimson cross over his heart was not so fortunate. "They said you'd been seen, my lord, so the Commander sent me to find you." Young Stephen was fair-haired, flushed, and rather buggy-eyed at finding his superior surrounded by a pair of horse's arses.

And no doubt, given the look Gamelyn flicked his way, Robyn was being considered as a matched third of the pair.

Stephen's attention was fastened, not on Gamelyn, but Robyn. The lad tried to speak several times, then finally stammered out, "M-my lord, is that *him?*"

Gamelyn rolled his eyes, and Robyn started to laugh.

"He's your squire?"

"I'm afraid so." Gamelyn's mutter pitched like Robyn's own, inaudible to Stephen as the boy led them through the chaotic surround of siege.

"He's nowt on Much."

"He's young yet. He tries."

A snort. "Tries what? I mean"—this as Stephen shot a quick glance backwards—"the lad wain't stop eyeing me."

"I've noticed, believe me."

"Aw, pet. Jealous?"

Another eye roll.

"Your eyes'll pop away, you keep on like that."

The wide pavilion to which Stephen led them spread across the battered sward, unadorned save by a piebald banner with a splash of crimson, the latter set on a pole thrust deep into the soft earth. Set apart from more colourful pavilions, the bleached top and corners suggested it had endured much sunnier climes, yet the mossy tinge along its folds told of lengthy storage through several English winters. The entrance had been tied back akin to drapes on a rich man's bed, and shadowy figures moved within. Those figures held tension, aye, but also a sense of easiness, as if this small and transient redoubt was, somehow, hearth and home.

Home? More like a trap.

The boy motioned them to wait and ducked inward. The wind had risen—not much to stop it in this wide vale—and not only rattled the oiled tent fabric in its fastenings, but carried the smell of humid rot from the nearby fens. Robyn sucked the latter in, grateful for something that tasted more of Her earth than rusted iron or rancid sweat.

Stephen peeked back out, beckoned them in. Robyn dipped his head to Gamelyn, murmured, "After milord."

It was a sure sign Gamelyn was rattled when he didn't even bother to roll his eyes.

The pavilion was strangely roomy on the inside, as if Robyn had passed through some fae portal where time and space were not. His fingers reached for the sleek yew of his longbow, tracing an unthinking ward.

Proper subtle, though, and not about to give the warriors behind that large wooden table any sort of satisfaction. For they were that, no less than the man at his side: ten all told, five clad in a white that seemed to suck away what light there was, and Robyn's eyes already ill-adjusting to the dim. Another man, clearly no Templar with his rich tunic and fur-lined cape, was familiar . . . and nigh made of broad and brawn as Scathelock.

Robyn wished for Will at his back about now. No complications to him, just fierce defence.

"*Bon!* My prodigal returns!" Hubert came around the table, both hands outstretched, eyes blazing a fierce welcome as he grasped Gamelyn's arms. "You have come in good time, and brought a worthy guest!"

"I . . . brought no one, my lord, but he has come." Gamelyn's head bent, all respect, but his pleasure was undeniable.

The other Templars seemed pleased as well, even as they peered at Robyn. There was surprise, aye. Challenge, undoubtedly. But beneath that waited a startling apprehension, mixed with another odd factor which could, with some coaxing, be . . .

Respect? For sommat other than the nice purse to be gained by lopping off the Hood's head and turning it into the assizes?

Surely not.

Not that it mattered. Robyn had walked of his own accord into this dank and mouldy trap of white-clad shadows, but he wasn't ready for the noose yet. Wasn't weak. Was beside his lover, his Oakbrother, to see him safely home.

Robyn started a reach towards Gamelyn and belatedly remembered where they were. Instead he aborted the gesture into an aimless shift of his longbow.

That wasn't much better. Every armed man in the tent stiffened like a fighting cock. Robyn opened his hand and lowered it, altogether slow, kept the other also well within sight. He'd assumed Gamelyn an exception—and mayhap he was—yet these were no less creatures of war. No less predators.

For mayhap the tenth time, Robyn wondered what in the nine names of the otherworld he thought he was doing here.

Out of your element, aye, the Horned Lord soothed, surprisingly strong. *But Our Oak is well within his. Use that. Do you not remember Nottingham, My own?*

Remember dragging a wounded Gamelyn from castle walls? Remember standing down the Sheriff and riding the Wild Hunt upon Nottingham, where, as rumour would have it, spectres yet seethed in its corners and shadows? Remember the first time—and the last—they'd truly worked in trine, he and Marion and Gamelyn? How could he forget? *Is that what it takes, then? Knocking milord senseless so he wain't be blocking his own power?*

An amused snort, and the god faded as Hubert turned, eyeing Robyn.

Robyn tilted his head. "Milord Templar."

Hubert held out an arm, the greeting one of equals well met. "As freely as you came to this meeting, you will be allowed to leave it, should you choose. You have my word, Robyn Hode, and that of my men."

Robyn believed him, took the arm, and held it strong.

"I've no doubts that, beneath our differences, we've much to share with each other."

"And that would be?" another of the Templars voiced—and one of rank, from the way several deferred to him. "Though this . . . person is charitable when it suits him, is it not more likely he could turn and rend any handler? No more than a brigand, when all is said and done, the same sort against which we spent good men in the desert, and you, Hubert, would give an outlaw sanctuary? To what end?"

"The Commander of Temple Bruer," Gamelyn murmured to Robyn.

"En't he t' one as agreed to take in the villeins?"

"Aye."

Bruer, it seemed, was also charitable when it suited. Not that it eased the sudden tension one whit, in the gathering or Robyn's belly.

"We've archers a-plenty, as does the castellan of Tickhill," Bruer persisted. "Any who ventures nigh risks a crossbow bolt. What possible aid could a ragged wolfshead provide?"

"The longbow he carries might well be of use." This from the brawny lord not clothed in Templar garb.

Robyn's memory jolted, again recalling Nottingham. De Lacy of Pontefract. The Sheriff's brother.

De Lacy moved closer, slow but assured. "Aye, and from the looks of you, master archer, I'd wager you've more than a little Welsh blood. I know the breed. Wild, sneaky devils, the lot of them—and there's no besting them with those monster bows." Wry irritation started a tussle, then gave, commingling freely with a different sort of respect—begrudged, mayhap, but honest.

"Me mam was kin of t' Barrows." Between being kicked and kissed, Robyn didn't do what he wanted to: kick the Motherless sod right back. Instead he acknowledged de Lacy's words with a small nod. *Me mam, who* your *bitch-sister had murdered. Milord.*

Bruer wasn't convinced. "I prefer machines to jumped-up ruffians."

"Machines are costly to both sides, milord of Bruer. I surely understand your reluctance, but mayhap between wild Welsh cunning and *amour fraternel,* we can settle this matter all the quicker." De Lacy's eyes were flickering, all cool consideration, over Robyn; they moved to Gamelyn and warmed—this time esteem held unbegrudging. "A pleasure to see you again, Sir Guy."

Gamelyn's shoulders tightened, infinitesimal, at the name. Yet he gave no protest, as if it were a weight he'd determined to bear. "My lord of Pontefract does me grace."

So controlled, that voice. All the more to hide the burn beneath, Robyn knew. Or did he? This was, after all, Gisbourne's place.

"I suggest we more fully appraise our, ah, prodigal and his companion of the situation." Hubert moved to the table, where Robyn realised a small and cunning wooden replica of the castle had been erected. "As you may have guessed, Tickhill's castellan still refuses to yield."

"Aye," de Lacy put forth. "I've several times sent men to the gatehouse beneath a banner of truce. They were met by threats and once, crossbow bolts. Your brother"—a glance towards Gamelyn—"is proving how obstinacy can so easily swing into stupidity."

Hubert was nodding. "Better to decide how we wish to employ our . . . unlikely weapons before council fully convenes. Preferable, I should think, to convincing His Holiness the Bishop amidships."

Unlikely weapons. Robyn's brows quirked, and he tossed a glance Gamelyn's way, merely found a profile of ice and verdigris looking to—seeking—Hubert. Quirk sliding into frown, Robyn took in a troubled breath, held it, and let it go.

What choice did he have, after all?

"So," Hubert began, "with all my lords' atten—"

An upswell of noise from outside the tent interrupted, causing Hubert and all the rest beneath the pavilion to turn, curious. Moreover, the noise did not abate, escalating into a din of whistles, shouts, and stamps.

"The word has come via wings!" Announcing his entry with the cry, an old man burst into the pavilion, no less a gust than the wind rattling its oiled-wool corners. "Richard has landed at Sandwich, and all London is throwing flowers at his feet."

Another upswell of voices, boisterous as a tavern round, and this time from within the pavilion. Robyn had the impulse to dart out the still-open entry, only realised he'd started to obey it when Gamelyn's hand grabbed at the edge of his tunic. Robyn met Gamelyn's gaze, swift gratitude turning curious and concerned, found the latter mirrored in green eyes.

Said, to dispel it, "London must be a sight warmer than here, then. In proper country the flowers wait a wee longer. En't enough flowers to make a wreath hereabouts, let alone be tromped in t' mud."

Babies were curious things, Marion decided. They could bring an indifferent couple together, bespell a reluctant sire or dam, render an elder child into lifelong protector. They could bring untold and uncountable riches, further beggar a poor family, or render a wealthy family into jealous and tight-fisted factions.

Altogether powerful, their effect. And the one Marion felt, in thisnow, was an ache somewhere between her breasts and her belly. It mixed, oddly, both relief and a fatal, forlorn longing she finally recognised as envy.

"You," she told the squishy-faced and swaddled bundle in her arms, "have certainly winnowed the men from the boys, little one."

And most of the men had proven boys, from the time Marion had halted the horse and begun snapping the orders of any proper midwife. Once in the doing had it nigh proved Marion herself more bairn than woman, and that when she'd realised a brace of years had passed since she'd last helped her mam deliver a baby. And never by herself. But the other women stepped in—even Emma, whinging cast aside like a too-full piss pot. Emma had proven the grandest help of all, ordering the men—*boys!*—into some semblance of assistance. Camp had been set up in record time, and a fire started, with water bucketed from a nearby stream and hides propped on a lattice: a roof, to protect labouring Aelwyn from the rain.

Which was still coming down, tapping and roiling over the oiled hides.

Aelwyn slept to its music, washed and attired in a motley of fresh garments, warmed by the little ones tucked around her. No fault to her—it had been a long labour, but thankfully not a deadly one.

"Have some wine, love?"

Marion looked up and blinked. "Wine? You're fooling!"

"Nay. David's a right miracle." Smiling, Much handed her a steaming mug of what was, indeed, mulled wine.

Marion clutched it in her free hand, took a grateful and noisy gulp.

It had been Much and David who'd proved themselves proper men, not gone scattering like most of the others when they'd figured out the meaning of Aelwyn's drenched kirtles. Of course, Much had a baker's dozen of siblings, and David had been a father thrice. A good one, too, from the tender way he'd treated Aelwyn.

"We've some set aside for the lass." Much's lip twitched as he peered down at the sleeping babe. "Mayhap she'll call him Mushroom. Now, don't be sliding me that evil eye, woman, for the little lad resembles just that."

Well, all right, perhaps he did. Marion smirked, took another drink.

"You're going to give that 'un back to his mam, aye?" The tease was wry and just this side of serious.

"And what would I do with a bairn, y' silly man?" she retorted. "With t' life we lead . . . " She found her words tangling into each other as she peered at him. Lashes brushed his cheeks, hiding a suspicious glint in Much's blue eyes as he held out one thick finger and stroked the babe's palm. A slight grimace wrinkled his scarred forehead as tiny fingers clutched, altogether tight even in sleep.

Found herself wondering if, even should they, could they. She'd been careful lying with Much, balancing the whens and hows, but nevertheless hadn't once had to resort to the herbs every woman knew as a matter of course.

Found herself wondering what would come with the Maying, and the Summering. *With t' life we lead. . .*

Contemplated the consequences upon which no man ever had to dwell.

Bringin' life, her mam Eluned had said more than the once, *is the closest any woman comes to death. Every time we might consider tuppin' a man, the possibilities are there, twined in life and death. We're looking 'em both in the eye, to spit and dare 'em their worst. And all the while, 'tis being a challenge altogether easy to lose.*

Thisnow all the more—in the Shire Wode, outlawed, life already hanging on a parlous thread akin to what line lay between the birthing and the dying. Where the wild Hunter let the green boughs cover Him until it was uncertain what was Green and what was Man, where He let the god take Him even as His rival took Him, a passion play of life and death, where two became the one in an inevitable dare of challenge-heat.

Where the old ways had truly returned, and it was again the Lady's to call the cycles and claim Her consort. To dance from Maiden to Mother and one day to Crone, to bear—or not—the children of *tynged's* weaving.

Aelwyn's babe twitched, suckled in sleep.

Much smiled, freed his trapped finger, then used that finger to first stroke the babe's cheek, then Marion's. "All right, then?"

Marion nodded, watched him rise and pull his cowl over his brown head, meander out into the rain. Keeping watch, because it was necessary in the Shire Wode.

Aye, in the Wode, where time was both shifting and standing still, measured out to a clothyard of life-death-danger for those who lived outside the law and would never know the protections of those as lived within it.

What sort of life was that for a bairn?

The baby sought and nuzzled her empty breasts—strangely apropos, for what sort of life would *this* bairn have? Hard questions, and not so much as an answer in Marion's heart for *any* of them. From the moment his mam had lain with his da, the die was tossed: death and life, life and death. From the moment Aelwyn had squatted to drop her son into Marion's waiting hands, he was nobbut a serf, property owned by Church and Crown, his mother a drudge and his father dead from an ill-timed axe stroke whilst working another's land. His soft pate still bore the tang of his dam's birth blood, and he'd nowt ahead of him but the yoke and the cross.

The only freedom he'd never remember was thisnow, in an outlaw cunning-woman's arms.

- X -

"**S**ilence! Silence, I say!"

Any bids for control were futile. Durham's initial enthusiasm had proven contagious—their monarch on English soil once again, and every man stirred to fever-pitch. The small group of Templars waited quiet, habit and training adequate restraint, but the makeshift roof was filled to bursting with excited questions and eager answers, likely none of them sensible. The pavilion seemed to be shrinking; more people were filling the entry, wondering at what news would send a bishop scrambling. A few began inching towards the tent's exit. Robyn, too, looked as if he would rather flee—no doubt for differing reasons. Beneath cover of the tight-woven wall at their backs, Gamelyn took firm hold of dark green woolsey.

Robyn started at the tug to his tunic, eyed Gamelyn. Admitted, wry-soft, "I'm swimming wit' nervy sweat. En't been surrounded by this many soldiers since we took you from Nottingham."

Gamelyn risked a brief linger of hand to the small of Robyn's taut-muscled back, found reward in the crooked half smirk.

Durham pounded a fist on the head table, still trying to regain order—and still to no avail. Temple Bruer's Commander murmured an urgent aside to Hubert, also not best pleased with events. Hubert nodded, saying something in return as he looked up and found Gamelyn's notice. No words would cut the din; instead he slashed a motion of hand across lip. Gamelyn's mouth tilted; he nodded and complied.

The whistle shrilled through the tent. Robyn winced, hissed a curse to no one in particular as the ear-splitting blast gave a bounce off the low ceiling's contours. But it worked. Voices trailed off midthroat. Several turned, succumbed to mutters of outrage— a mere sergeant, calling them to heel? Breathing another curse, Robyn stiffened to the apex of his considerable height. Gamelyn gave another, chiding tug to his tunic

"Fear not. Whistling worth a good damn has never been amongst Hubert's talents."

Robyn's nervous edge turned upon another slight smirk.

Hubert could, however, take charge—and unlike Durham, had the voice for it, rich baritone rumbling into bass notes. Younger squires had been known to nigh wet themselves when they heard it dip, as it did now, into dry scorn.

"My lords, we are better than this. And if not, we should be. My lord Bishop?"

Durham, nodding his thanks, shouldered through the throng. Still panting, he leaned on the table where his siege commanders waited.

"I must apologise, myself. 'Twas no way to bring such news. But 'tis true," he continued, wielding the tiny scrap of parchment and scanning the faces turned to him, now settled. "King Richard is returned. He wants the matters of Tickhill and Nottingham settled"— a tiny tuck of mouth that could have been a smile—"without delay, as he intends a royal council at the latter within the se'nnight."

Mutters, many disbelieving.

"I fancy"—Robyn had turned, whispering it close to Gamelyn's ear—"things en't so easily done as said?"

"Your fancy is accurate," Gamelyn murmured back. "But this is the Crusader Lion of the Angevin, after all, who expects the wind to change when he beckons."

"And here you said he weren't no witch."

"Therefore, we must avail ourselves of every possibility to end this siege," Durham continued. "Neither castellan nor constable have offered to budge, even in the face of certain ruin beneath engines—one of which is nearing completion."

"One should be enough to take out that weak wall, my lords." One of the engineers, no doubt, to speak freely in such company.

"Of that I've every confidence. Yet time is all the more our enemy now." Durham scanned the room, falling upon the table where Hubert stood, arms crossed, a cast of serenity and patience. "Is the man here, my lord Commander?"

Hubert nodded.

Durham gestured for further explanation, gaining the table to stand beside de Lacy and the Earl of Conisbrough, de Warenne. One of Durham's attendants scurried behind, twitching at his lord's robes—hastily donned, from the look of them.

Robyn pretended a scratch at his beard. Well, at least he was making the effort to hide his smirk.

"One of my Templars might provide an answer to this siege." Hubert paused and motioned to Gamelyn. "This is Brother Guy, who wields the honour of *Confanonier* to Temple Hirst. Before he came to us, his family held the very castle we hold in siege. Moreover, the castellan presently holding the castle against us is his brother."

Brother Guy. The name was known—and not—from the way it floated amongst another rash of murmurs: satisfaction; hesitation; suspicion. Gamelyn himself felt all of them.

Tell me who I am, a small voice behind his eyes insisted, satisfied. The rest of him was not so pleased, yet it slunk away, unwilling to the challenge as the entire gathering turned his way.

A novel sensation, to be the centre of such exalted attention. Earls, bishops, commanders. Gamelyn found himself rising beneath it, lifting his chin. Ready for it.

Whilst beside him, Robyn's own readiness was more an instinct composed of alarm than acceptance. A soft breath escaped parted lips and sent Robyn sliding into shadow.

Gamelyn had seen Robyn all but disappear in the Wode; he had never thought it even remotely possible in a crowded tent.

Another low challenge had been issued, this from one of the younger and better-dressed lords. Durham was answering to it.

"Yes, yes, it could well prove of no use," Durham admitted, pettish. "But it is another chance."

"Chance of what?"

"My lord de Furnival." This from de Lacy. "Do you not agree that *any* chance, given our present situation, should be taken?"

Well, at least the name suggested why the lord turned upon de Lacy, antagonism barely restrained. De Furnival's new wife had once held the honour of Tickhill. He plainly wanted it back.

"I do not agree with foolish chances. There was talk of a cadre of Welsh archers, not one man."

"Talk!" Durham snorted. "There's been too much talk and not enough action!"

"There was nowt said of one archer, nor a Templar who happens to be related to the seneschal holding against us!" The careful and flat formality of de Furnival's speech was slipping about its edges; he was riled, sure enough.

"The man *you* supported," de Lacy reminded. "With his master, Count John."

"Even as many of us, uncertain of our King's predicament, did. Yourself included, Pontefract!"

Murmurs all around. De Lacy's cheek went dark.

"Points to me home turf and t' Hallamshire man," Robyn muttered from just behind Gamelyn's shoulder. "Here I thought I'd be bored juiceless."

A soft snort escaped Gamelyn. "Not with players the likes of this."

"Mm. 'Tis quite the game, here. And one you seem altogether willing t' be dealt back into."

"I've reasons." It was curt. All too easy, really, to slip back into the familiarity of Guy's cloak.

It was Robyn's turn to snort. "Enough for me to keep walkin' into stone traps?"

"If you recall, I didn't ask you to do so."

"Whats'mever. I en't about to let you do so without me." Robyn leaned slightly closer, breath stirring at Gamelyn's nape. It warmed, nigh banishing Guy like some evil spirit . . . and how apropos was that? "You're s'posed to be keeping tabs on the Shire Wode covenant, aye? By order of your Temple."

"Even if the Temple orders I bring you to them?"

"Seems they already did. Only you fancied you'd not tell me."

"I *fancied* you'd stay behind, so it wasn't important." Yet another snort, soft-wry. "And we've been over this already. Gnaw another bone, black wolf."

"If I were finding even the wee bit of marrow, I might leave off."

"Enough!" Durham thundered. The mutters subsided, and Robyn backed into the shadows once again. "Commander Hubert is correct, my lords. We *should* be better than this . . . this useless bickering!"

"With all due respect, my lord Bishop." Of an age with Gamelyn, de Furnival obviously had nerve enough to make up for it. "My questions are not mere bickering, but ones we all should ask. For mark my words, the castellan of Blyth believes our King perished—God forbid!—and therefore denies even reasonable counsel. He also"—his eyes flickered to Gamelyn—"believes his brothers dead: one battling some mercenary assassin complete with improbable tales of sorcery and mayhem, the other on Crusade. None have informed him otherwise, *including* the Temple that has, it seems, sheltered the latter."

"Do you doubt my word, my lord?" Almost a lazy drawl—almost. Gamelyn well knew the danger in Hubert's tone from witnessing its aftermath.

"Nay, my lord Commander. I merely wonder how this long-lost brother—this *one man*—suggests we inform Blyth of their errors? Count John's own archers are crawling the wall-walk! None of us can venture close enough to deliver any message or demand, and those damned crossbowmen are determined that none shall! I've lost five good men to their skills already, and I'm not the only one. I well know a Templar's prowess with war and siege, but my lord, do you honestly suggest we let this man of yours walk into target range and . . . and *whistle?*"

"Crossbowmen!" It was contemptuous. "Their like has no range, and sod-all skill!"

The collective gaze shifted from de Furnival's rant to the one standing at Gamelyn's left shoulder, lurking in the shadows with arms crossed over his chest.

Well, Robyn was visible now.

Yet he seemed to no longer care. A purl of anger layered thick atop his voice—and the reason for it blossomed absurd warmth in the pit of Gamelyn's belly.

"Assuming a lot of bloody amateur crossbowmen can even feign arse themselves to hit a target, I ent about to let the lot of you send this man where he'll end up nowt more 'n a target clout! Send me wit' your Brother Guy"—and Christ on the Cross, but was Gamelyn the only one to hear the rumble of sarcasm in that?—"and I warrant those crossbows wain't have so much as time to aim before I pick 'em off."

The gathering buzzed, this time to varying shades of outrage and disbelief.

"Who is this man?"

"Impossible to—"

"You bloody fool!" De Furnival rounded on him. "Those walls are nigh to thirty feet, and the moat besides! Do you carry a Welshman's bow, then? I mean, who do you think you are, that sodding outlaw Robyn Hood?"

Hubert's mouth quirked. De Lacy went from barely checked fury to the satisfaction of a cat who'd raided the cream pans. Gamelyn laughed. He couldn't help it, and immediately he choked it back, but . . .

It set the rest of their gathering on its collective heels. Confusion and affront strung itself, tight as Robyn's bowstring.

Inconceivable. Absurd. But none more so than Robyn, with a sudden step from the shadows. His horn-tipped longbow gleaming at his back and one hand at his breast, he shrugged the hood from his dark hair and dipped a mocking bow.

"I fancy I'm as much of t' Barrows as of Hallam- and Yorkshire. I also fancy, did you have a lot of real archers, as opposed to ham-fisted crossbowmen, you'd already have done with this siege.

"Until then, I s'pose milord Templar will have to make do with Robyn Hood."

"Hoy, the castle! I've a message for your lord!" A small volley of crossbow quarrels answered Gamelyn's bellow. He stepped back, more from reflex than need—he was out of range. Several crossbow bolts went into the moat. A few others landed some distance from their approach.

There wasn't a secondary volley.

Instead there was a shout—two of them, actually—as one soldier crumpled on the wall-walk and a second tumbled over it, an arrow in his throat. The latter hit the moat with a substantial splash. None of it drowned out the sounds of shocked surprise, the snap and bark of orders, or the curses. Particularly the curses.

"That set the Motherless sods back, aye?" Robyn grinned at Gamelyn and nocked another arrow to string. He'd a clutch of them in his right fist, and more knotted into the hair flung over his right shoulder. Those thick black curls also, by chance or design, obscured the tiny cross upon the dark brown tabard Hubert had insisted Robyn wear in camp. Cheeks flushed, eyes glittering, he was wild and careless—*dangerous*—as pole lightning in a flat meadow. And Gamelyn's own reaction to that, utterly outrageous. If it wasn't for the castle waiting, stolid and hunched, or the soldiers trying to perforate them, or the troops behind them, waiting for the *dénouement* of this little sortie . . .

Well. Gamelyn would throw Robyn to the ground—tabard, arrows, and all—and rut him until he begged mercy.

Another bolt sailed towards them from the wall-walk. In abortive reflex, nothing more, Gamelyn reached for the piebald shield thrust into the ground. Otherwise, he didn't move, eyes keeping scornful watch as the thick projectile wobbled, then sank itself into the dirt a good stone's throw from their boots.

Robyn too remained still, scanning the wall with arrow to string. The drawbridge, of course, remained snugged tight to the portcullis gate, and the gatehouse guarded over well. They'd not so much as approached it. Instead they'd ventured the crumbling northeast wall, already the site of obvious sorties. It bristled with soldiers—they knew their feeblest defence, true enough—further weakened by the lack of new-fangled arrow loops. Upthrust stone merlons and long wooden hoardings perched atop the battlements: adequate protection for Blyth's defenders, but little comfort against the unexpected danger of a longbow's range.

That was something Gamelyn intended to change, given the chance.

And all the while, he and Robyn stood well within the safe "no one's land" about a stone's throw out from the moat. Soot and dust puffed up, settling over their boots and upon the moat's edge, a stark, burnt-out ring Robyn had accurately reckoned as warning and reminder of the range of Blyth's crossbows.

Behind them stood the loose semicircle of siege troops. Weaponed, ready, and in their turn flanked by curious others, waiting well back. The ever-present din of anvils, hammers, and wood saws had stopped, left idle with this newest possibility of entertainment. Even the *petraria* engineer was lurking, though clearly dubious. He kept an acquisitive eye upon that crumbling wall.

"Too bad Alundel en't here." Robyn's gaze never left the stone merlon behind where the crossbowman had ducked. A smirk giving sudden chase across his lip, he gave another, almost-lazy push to his grandfather's longbow. One would never think the thing heavy enough a draw to make Gamelyn's own sword-hardened arm howl quits. "He'd make a story of this, right—" the smirk turned wolfish, and Robyn loosed "—enough."

Another unwary soldier crumpled behind the hoarding wall, howling and holding his arm.

"Bloody damn. The silly bugger ducked the wrong way."

Gamelyn waited, dandling another arrow in long, freckled fingers. It possessed the same goose-and-peacock fletching of the ones Robyn kept loosing—in fact, was one of Robyn's. But there were differences. The point was narrow, light bodkin instead of deadly broadhead. Just behind that point, spun tight about the shaft with the lightest of gut, was a thin scrap of parchment.

"An ultimatum fastened to an outlaw's arrow." Gamelyn held it up, musing. "No doubt our fair-haired trouvère would make of it a *billet-doux* and have us playing the heroes, here to rescue a fair maiden forced to wed the ancient, hunchback lord."

"Knew a hunchback once," Robyn said, eyeing up the wall-walk, then, satisfied he'd sent the crossbowmen for cover, plucked his bowstring. "Nice chap. Swept the tavern at Loxley and did the washing up. Could drink like a river trout—wain't tell how much I lost to 'im, betting he couldn't." Another pluck, his gaze sliding to take in Gamelyn. "What's a . . . *billaydoo*, then?"

Gamelyn smiled, but it held absolutely no humour. "A love letter."

"En't much love lost t' that letter."

"Mm."

"I just hope your brother hearkens to sense." Another light-ning-quick look, dark and amused and merciless. "He's no idea what he's up against."

A murmur from the crowd behind them made Gamelyn glance that way, then frown as a small group separated from the others, advancing with no little caution.

"Robyn."

"Aye, I see 't."

All the approaching figures held bows. The lead archer in particular looked familiar, and the bow even more so, of Turkish make, curved and lovely.

"Guy? Robyn?" The leader wore de Lacy's colours, head wrapped in a linen *kaffiyeh* with one end trailing and the other tucked beneath her chin, chaff-coloured contrast to brown skin.

Her. The dark eyes gained confidence as they landed upon the familiarity of Gamelyn's habit, crimson cross against stark ebon, then widened as Robyn also half turned.

"It is you!" Siham crowed in Norman French, then ran the last few steps lightly as a deer. She slowed, eyed Gamelyn's tabard, and instead changed trajectory, tackling Robyn in a full-body hug. Careful of both their bows, of course.

A mild huff of derision escaped her as a smallish deluge of crossbow bolts was loosed from the castle wall merely to patter across the burnt ground, haphazard and wasted. Two of Siham's archers plainly wanted to run forwards, answer the challenge; Gamelyn hissed them back. The shortbows had less range than Robyn's massive Welsh bow; anyone wielding them would have to venture within shooting distance of the crossbows to hit anything. No doubt the same had killed de Furnival's soldiers.

Nevertheless, the show of solidarity was comforting.

Robyn was laughing, returning Siham's hug with fierce glee. He pushed back to peer at her. "What are you . . . " Midexclamation he remembered she had no Anglic; instead, putting one hand to his breast, said, "*Salaam alah-kum, ghazaal.*"

Gamelyn was impressed; it was quite passable, actually. Save for the last word.

The Saracen woman blinked, pleasantly surprised—albeit with a burst of laughter at the end.

"What?" Robyn blurted, shooting a glance Gamelyn's way. "I said it as you've—"

"*Salaam aleikum. . . ghazaal,*" Siham answered, with a return of hand to heart plus a wicked grin as she added a further smattering of Arabic Gamelyn's way. "O Knight, tell your gazelle to tread very carefully. Another time I might decide to take him up on it!"

Another brace of crossbows twanged up on the wall-walk. Siham's five companions loosed their own small volley, harry and bluff, as the wall crossbows laid a hail of bolts across the ground.

"You *did* say it as I have said," Gamelyn reassured Robyn. "Somewhat. Though 'twas my foolishness in thinking you wouldn't listen to *all* of it." Voice lowering, he explained, "Though in such garb, Siham might resemble a very lovely boy, at that . . . *ghazaal* is not only a desert hart, but a word for a lover. A young *male* lover."

Robyn blinked. Then grinned. "I'm liking those desert people more and more."

"Mm. I thought you might. But Siham also just warned you that you call her that once more, she might take you up on it." *And that's one for the poncy ginger nobleman,* Gamelyn thought with a smirk as Robyn flushed dark.

"However has he come here? With you?" Siham's swift Arabic queries diverted Gamelyn. "Here, amidst all this?"

"Rather a long tale, that."

"And we've little time to spare at present. Later, then."

"Be sure to tell her," Robyn ventured, "she's to come share a meal with my people once all this is done and said. I'd like her to meet sommun."

Gamelyn was sure he knew who Robyn meant. "Gilbert?"

"Aye, that. And Marion."

Nodding, Gamelyn passed the invitation along. Siham smiled at Robyn. Her companions were gathering behind her, shooting curious gazes towards the huge longbow and its wielder. "What is our next move here, then, milord Templar?" one asked.

"Not much," another groused, albeit mild-tempered, "unless we can get closer."

"Give it another go," Robyn told Gamelyn and plucked at his bowstring. "If one so much as makes a motion, I'll have him." A grin to Siham and the others. "Save your arrows for now. Methinks you need learn t' longbow."

One of the archers—a tall blond fellow altogether reminiscent of Scathelock for Gamelyn to feel too tender towards—chuckled and translated for Siham. She grinned again and shrugged.

"I wish me lads were here about now." Robyn's mutter followed Gamelyn's own thoughts too close for comfort, but it was more to himself than anything. Gamelyn didn't bother answering, instead toed the charred edge of their safety and filled his lungs for another bellow.

"Hoy the castle! Will you persist in—"

The resultant rain of quarrels came sparse, unconvincing. Robyn nocked twice and loosed, sending his own message: *Take cover.* He'd not spoiled a shot yet, Gamelyn thought, satisfied as two more soldiers dropped, one describing an impressive parabola into the moat.

A small waft of breeze brought a rash of curses from above, then finally a bellow in return. "What do you want?"

"Daft tossers," Robyn muttered. "What do they *think* we're here for? Target practice?"

"I want you to cease this bloody nonsense and take a message to your lord!" Gamelyn bellowed, with a wave of the parchment-wrapped arrow. "Nothing more, nothing less!"

A brief conference. None of the soldiers were so much as sticking their helmets into Robyn's sights.

Gamelyn smiled.

Another fortuitous gust of wind lifted the next bellow over the wall and down. "Bring it to the gate, then!"

"Not bloody likely," Robyn muttered and extended his hand. "They'll be lucky if I don't sink it in some squint-eyed crossbowman."

Gamelyn twirled the arrow in his fingers, shrugged, and passed it over, crossing his arms once more.

One of the soldiers chose that moment to peek over the wooden hoarding. Robyn let fly. The message-arrow sped with the papery rattle and hum of a roused beehive and imbedded itself in the thick wooden beam a bare finger-length from the soldier's left temple.

He froze like a hind in torchlight; no doubt new. With those instincts he'd be dead before a fortnight's worth of battle.

"Take t' paper, man!" Robyn hollered. "I wain't be shooting again! Lessen"—Robyn turned to Gamelyn—"those daft gits decide to waste more arrows."

"And now?" Siham queried.

"Now?" Gamelyn replied, declining a translation. Robyn knew. "Now we wait."

- ENTR'ACTE -

He wasn't sure what to expect when the captain of the guard brought word of the strange tableau taking place—though he had been prepared for just about any trick imaginable. The bastards had even claimed to be accosting Count John's castle in the name of King Richard, despite that everyone knew Richard was dead, God rest him, and the country torn apart by petty feuds and beggared, in the end, for no purpose.

But this? It made little sense. Even amidst the vast array of rubbish Otho Boundys de Blyth had been forced, of late, to endure to keep both his honour and his royal orders intact.

"Merely two men, you say? A Templar sergeant and an archer, just waiting?"

"The men have tried, milord, truly they've tried to take them down! But all we had for 'twere more arrows!"

"More arrows. But surely those were little—"

"The archer shot the longest bow I've ever seen, milord! Every arrow killed or wounded one of our own archers. There's talk, milord, that it's the wolfshead Robyn Hood, him what bested the Sheriff of Nottingham? Only his like, only t' outlaws of Sherwood durst carry such a bow in the forest!"

A Templar. And a wolfshead.

It made *no* sense. Of course, life itself of late was nonsensical. Otho determined he should look into this latest ploy.

He was being laced into his mail shirt when his constable de la Mare brought the missive, curled tight about a peacock-fletched arrow.

Memory flashed, dark and volatile as the pitch stewing in the great cauldrons above Blyth's portcullis.

At least five summers previous, it had been. A muggy, sun-drenched season with grass aplenty to graze the goats and sheep, and corn growing early-ripe to fill the stores to bursting. A coven of Pagan filth had killed a guardsman attached to his cousin's abbey retinue. A chance murder—or so he'd thought at the time, reporting the incident to his father and family over supper.

Only the plenteous harvest had been followed by lean years, and that one random-seeming killing had led to the ruin of his family: his father dead from grief and shock; his youngest brother driven out of his mind and exiled to war; his eldest brother's demise only last autumn at the hands of some mercenary cutthroat; and his abbess cousin's death at the hands of what was rumoured to be another peacock-fletched witchery of an arrow.

When Count John had offered Otho the chance to reclaim his family's honour, he'd leapt at it. The Count was all but king, after all, though it involved more political machinations than Otho wanted to track. Count John had been persuasive—and correct in that Otho would have little chance to rebuild his family's fortunes beneath Pontefract's strict and jealous rule. What mattered was his father's fief, and how in holding it he could ensure the security of Alais and their two boys.

Otho shrugged away both memory and the unholy, peacock-fletched thing. Instead he demanded de la Mare unwrap the parchment and hand it over, then burn the arrow itself.

The constable did so, frowning. Otho started to uncurl the tiny parchment, hesitated and quickly crossed himself, then opened the missive and began to read.

Several heartbeats later, it dropped to the floor from lax, quivering fingers.

"My lord?" De la Mare was still frowning. The arrow flared, burning in the brazier behind him as he strode over and retrieved the dropped missive, furled tight at Otho's feet.

It was not so much the note. It was the impossible signature accompanying the note.

Otho shrugged off his squire's assistance, jerked his head for the lad to follow, and started for the stair. Grabbing up his master's helm and mail coif, the lad obeyed.

"My lord!" De la Mare began to follow.

"Give the missive to my lady Alais!" Otho ordered and dove down the stair. Two flights down to reach the main hall, and a race of steps to cross it, with a demand that the gates be opened. During that wait, the squire finished lacing the mail, threading the coif links over Otho's sandy head.

It was impossible. Inconceivable.

Otho crossed the ditch bridge in several bounds and marched

across the long, nigh-deserted bailey. The villages of the surrounding countryside had already been occupied; those who had made it to the castle for shelter were hiding in makeshift cots beyond the chapel. Only soldiers patrolled here and there, and most of those were manning the walls. The ones he passed acknowledged his presence, intent upon their duty. Capable men, all. More, Count John's backing had established enough soldiers and provisions to hold Blyth Castle until her royal lord returned.

Save for that weak wall. Otho glared at it as he passed. What with all the coin in tithe and ransom being bled from everyone, even a royal Count's backing hadn't been adequate to restore it. Enough soldiers squatted there to see through any normal combat, but the wall would never last against machines. Otho had done some sweating over the past few days upon seeing the *petraria* being built, knowing he had to hold. Somehow.

Inconceivable. The situation, the possibilities, all of it.

He was close to a run by the time he reached the gatehouse stair and mounted it. There was a great hall within the gatehouse's upper story, used often for high councils, courts, and receptions. It had three windows. The largest, high to catch the most light, was blocked up, of course. But the two on each end were narrow, mostly unblocked.

Stationed men nodded acknowledgment as Otho marched across the wooden floor. Their lord castellan's presence was frequent, of late. The reason spread out beyond them: the scorched earth of the final approach to the moat and the concentric, ragged gather of an army in siege.

Otho's eyes were keen. A small clutch of archers milled the bounds of the burnt expanse. Behind them the army spread; it seemed to expand more every day. He could see the flags and colours of too many of those who should be his neighbours: de Warenne of Conisbrough; de Furnival of Sheffield; the piebald banner of the Temple; and, of course, de Lacy and that damned interfering Bishop who thought he ruled Yorkshire all on his own.

Durham has turned on me! Count John had raged. *He and his Church and all the lickspittle lackeys who deal in my mother's dead hopes!*

And with that the rumours, insidious, of how the most holy Archbishop of York was approaching, due any day. Some said it was to break the siege; others said he would join it, and the wroth of God would follow, surely.

There. At the edge, near de Lacy's archers. Two men, standing on the very edge of the scorched no one's land as if daring Blyth's crossbows. One carried a bow as tall as himself—no small thing.

But the one standing beside him, not so tall and broader, with copper hair and a stance all too familiar . . . he was the one to make Otho's breath catch.

It was *impossible.*

He didn't know what to think. What to do.

"My lord?" It was de la Mare, out of breath and lurching into the gatehouse hall. "My lady Alais read the note, and bid I was to come at once to your side, tell you merely this." He halted, took a deep breath. "That she 'would not see her own husband and sons perpetuate the same sort of bellicose circumstance in which their sire and his brothers existed—for in the end, it did not make them stronger, but ruined them'."

It stilled him, thought and breath. De la Mare waited, panting.

"Neither," Otho finally said, "would I." He turned to his captain. "Fly the flag of truce. Tell them we will send two knights down to speak with these men."

As the soldiers hurried to do his bidding, Otho himself prepared to exit the sally port gate . . . with his fiercest captain, to be sure.

He was the only one who would know. Save Alais, mayhap. But Alais would stay safe, with their children, in the keep.

A sturdy lattice, kept for just such circumstance, was threaded across the moat. Otho could hear the stretch and lock of crossbows above, ready in case truce was not honoured.

The two men came forwards. The archer sauntered, actually, bow light in one hand and arrows in another, manner suggesting insult lay just beneath. He was indeed tall, a lath of a man who, save for that height, resembled more a wild black Welshman than any proper soldier. But the Templar . . .

He stalked like a lion on the hunt, one hand light upon the hilt of the curved sword at his side.

Did memory play so false that Otho could not reasonably confirm the man's identity? Surely he should know just by looking whether this was indeed a brother thought dead or merely a trick to do just what it had: draw him out, make him careless. Apprehensive. He didn't know this bearded, broad-shouldered man clad, not in the white habit of a Templar Knight, but the ebon-and-scarlet of their commonest warriors. Otho had been able to ascertain that the youngest of his brothers had indeed joined the Order, been belted and knighted as one of the elite, and had died at the Siege of Acre. Within the past five years had three altars been dedicated in the chapel of St. Nicholas: one for Otho's father; another for his eldest brother Johan; and the last for Gamelyn, youngest son of Sir Ian Boundys de Blyth.

A trick. It must be.

It was the eyes that parted the mists of memory. Flat, yes, lacking anything resembling emotion, yet . . . Green as grass, possessing not only the same hue, but the same shape and set as a long-dead mother's had. Even the copper fall of hair hearkened to memory, braided back from those familiar eyes.

"My lords." The archer spoke first, a sardonic acknowledgment that indeed sounded of the Welsh hills but, just as strongly, of the shire's peasantry. "'Tis nigh time you answered."

"Do I know you?" Directed to the archer, nonetheless Otho's eyes were on the Templar.

"Aye, my lord," the Templar answered. "You do."

That left no room for doubt. The voice was also familiar, a gentle, light tenor altogether ill-matched to the warrior standing before Otho.

"I am here to inform you that King Richard has returned."

Again, the voice rendered Otho unsure how to answer. How to react.

"King . . . Richard," he said, finally. "Is alive. Too."

"Aye. That I swear to you, upon Our Lady Herself." A small show of teeth . . . and Good Lord, but it was *Gamelyn's* smile, gamin and somewhat shy, yet with an edge frosting the least hint of affability.

"Count John has fled to France; therefore the King of England desires the return of his castle. Brother."

- XI -

"Y ou're not going to this council."

"Aye. I en't."

Gamelyn, prepared to pull out his most arrogant and cutting sentiments, was instead left with an open mouth and nothing issuing forth. He blinked, closed his mouth, and slid a wary glance Robyn's way.

"Never seen the like." Robyn was in profile to him, peering with no little scorn at the noblemen standing around their own bonfire, deep in conversations that bordered on arguments. "Twere entertaining for the while, but more of it? Nobbut a lot of *yap yap yap*, ever on."

Blyth's gates had been flung open and the drawbridge lowered. The heavy tunnel of the gatehouse gleamed, stark white, with roseate streaks from the sun sliding downward in the sky. A goodly complement of soldiers, including Siham and her archer companions, had already been detailed through that gatehouse. The ranking lords would undoubtedly follow, accept the offered hospitality against the night, and make more plans.

"You will attend," Hubert had informed Gamelyn and, with a hint of twinkle in the blue eyes, "as Bishop de Puiset has specifically requested your presence."

Even the memory of those words sent a frisson of warmth up his spine.

Pride, Gamelyn told himself, chiding. *Avarice. Expediency.* Guy, lurking on the edges.

Shaking it off, Gamelyn took refuge in sarcasm. "This from one who has to have a council if he's contemplating changing the draperies."

"Draperies!" Robyn snorted, but it was halfhearted. He seemed preoccupied. Again. "*My* councils en't a lot of lords deciding who next fetches a boot in t' arse. We listen to each other, most times. A decision as affects everyone should have everyone's say."

"A fair-sounding system, but one that assumes everyone has the intelligence God gave a goat."

"Mm. Goats are proper smart."

"Point taken, but what of people? Neither does it alter the fact that if you'd listened to *your* people, you wouldn't be here."

"I said *most times*. Bide careful, milord." Black eyes slid Gamelyn's way, glittering against the fire. "You'll have me thinking you don't want me here."

Gamelyn rolled his eyes. His brain was already stuffed to bursting with minutiae; he wasn't up for a battle of wits with the Shire Wode's prize *pwca*, not now. Instead he narrowed his focus to the surround where he had grown to young adulthood, taking in both familiar and estranged.

Fires were beginning to dot the encampment, to fend off the remaining damp as well as the night sky—clearing, and no doubt coming cold. Bowls from the great kettle at one of those fires were being passed, as well as conversation that had nothing to do with the nobles at their own circle. No doubt the ranks felt more relief than anything: the siege had been settled. Earlier a wave of peasantry had funnelled out from the castle's great gate, clutching their belongings, scattering to all points and, as Robyn had pointed out, likely praying their homes still remained.

"Your brother wain't shut it," Robyn ventured. "Even when the other dogs nip him." Surrounded by the ranking lords, Otho *was* talking overmuch. "He's good as prisoner, en't he seeing that?"

"It would seem justification is still a tune to which my brother dances."

Otho also kept glancing towards the large bonfire where *his* brother stood, beside "that uncanny archer." Robyn ignored it, twiddling cold fingers over the flames, whilst Gamelyn, arms crossed, flicked an occasional glance towards Hubert. The latter, on the fire's opposite side and flanked by attending Templars, exchanged quiet observances with Bruer's Commander. Bruer seemed grudging but satisfied, Hubert downright smug.

Neither had it escaped Gamelyn's notice: he and Robyn were being given a wide berth. He didn't imagine it was all from respect of Robyn's aim. Or of Templars. More like the strange juxtaposition of a wild man of the forest *with* those Templars.

"Where'll you be staying tonight?" Robyn was looking off into the trees, once more intent on . . . whatever it was. "After that council Master Hubert wants you to attend."

Gamelyn hesitated, knew it a mistake but didn't know how to correct it.

Robyn's gaze returned to his, gauging. "John's waiting for us."

"Robyn . . . " It warbled off, still awkward.

Robyn looked away.

Gamelyn tried again. "Hubert requested—"

At the same time, Robyn said, "I see."

Silence.

"Wellaway, I've a few things to tend, meself," Robyn ventured, stretching his arms skyward. All too casual, and it set off alarms in Gamelyn's skull, jangling harsh. "John and me'll be at our cavern, when you see fit t' join us."

"Robyn—"

"But if we en't seeing you come out of that bloody castle before long, we'll come drag your arse out into the light."

"*Robyn.* I have to—"

"Brother Templar?"

They both jerked, taken aback, and turned to see Otho just beyond the fire. His approach was as formal as had been the soft query; decorum was, nevertheless, marred by a puzzled frown.

"I don't mean to . . . intrude." Otho's gaze, skirting both suspicion and disquiet, kept flitting from archer to Templar and back again. "Might I speak with you for a moment?"

Robyn sidled away, holding his hands out to the fire once more. Gamelyn's eyes went to Hubert, who gave an imperceptible nod.

"My lord." Gamelyn tipped his head, equally formal, one hand coming to rest on his sword hilt.

Past Otho's shoulder, the remaining lords still spoke amongst themselves. Otho had either been dismissed or requested it.

"This is . . . all of it . . . astonishing." His gaze still refused to land anywhere. "We'd no idea you were . . . well. You're of the Templars now."

There was a finality to it, a . . . satisfaction. But what kind?

Robyn peered at Otho as though he thought him witless. Of course, when Robyn's own sibling had proven alive, he'd been overjoyed, not this . . . well. Whatever it was. And why Otho should feel so awkward, when Gamelyn himself felt nothing . . . or so he thought. Otho's next words scythed tiny ripples into flat-calm.

"Alais, she . . . my lady wife expressed a wish to see you. To see for herself if you were still alive. To . . . well, to give you welcome, and—a brief smile—"introduce you to our two boys."

Pride there, mayhap justifiable. Yet Gamelyn had his own, and it had absolutely nothing to do with a trick any male dog could perform.

"Kindly convey my respects to your lady, my lord, but I fear—"

"There need be no fear, *Confanonier.*" Master Hubert broke the awkward standoff by striding to Gamelyn's side. Abrupt, the claim, and sliding all too easily into the space Robyn had vacated. "Or hesitation. We will accept this invitation as a welcome part of your hospitality, Sir Otho."

More grounds for Gamelyn to attend a council intended for those of higher rank—and Hubert grasping it with both hands. Only . . .

Robyn hadn't gone far. Eyes half-mast, glittering beneath a thick fringe of ink lashes and unruly forelock, his gaze took in Hubert. Threat, and threatened.

For several long and ruinous heartbeats, Gamelyn wanted to reach out, haul him close, spill everything upon Robyn's nape—*everything!*—and *tell* him . . .

It will be all right. I'll make *it all right, just let me do this, see it done. . . just a while longer, a few more steps. I'll see to it, trust me.*

The last two words had the power to snuff any confession surely as a light between spat-upon fingertips.

"Kindly forgive the insistence, my lord," Hubert continued. "Our Rule is very plain as to such things. We rarely go anywhere unaccompanied. And it would be an honour to see where one of my finest Templars spent his boyhood."

Ah, yes. Pride. It reared up, ever the serpent, vibrating with pleasure at Hubert's words. Particularly as the bald compliment inspired upon Otho a rather stunned expression.

"Indeed" was all Otho said before he cleared his throat and furthered, "I would be pleased. Before council, then? My lady will be unhappy if we keep the boys awake overlong, and council is to convene at sunset."

Hubert inclined his head. "Of course, my lord."

"If you will excuse me, then, my lords *Chevalier*, to send word to my lady?" Otho gave Gamelyn one last, puzzled glance, but nevertheless seemed glad of any excuse to be gone. He whirled and headed for the castle with his steward following, belated but quick.

Hubert's hand landed upon Gamelyn's shoulder. "All will be well, anon."

Gamelyn took in a deep breath, started to reply. Hesitated.

For when his eyes sought the lean, dark-haired figure so recently at his side, Robyn was no longer anywhere to be seen.

He was of a mind to head back to John, and to the Christians' peculiar hell with anything that involved Church, Crown, or sodding Templars—*including* bloody ice-eyed Sir Guy of Gisbourne, rot him!

Not a man stayed him, though plenty watched as Robyn strode

from the siege camp, head down, longbow and quiver strapped
athwart his shoulders, one hand at the hilt of the quillion dagger.
It took two swathes of muddy ploughland to slow him. As he
reached the main road he stopped, panting.

Considered the mud caked on his boots, as well as the other
varied wages of being a proper fool.

Gasped and tottered as the Horned Lord fully slipped back into
his skin, a claiming that tasted all of the insistent fervour of a lover,
all of heat and warmth and welcome. For just a breath, its ever-
present conflict of loneliness and entrapment scattered him, then
settled in, grounding into thisnow. His heart, skewed and aching,
nestled back firm into his breast.

Robyn knew what he had to do. Had known since he glimpsed
the tall, misted silhouette of All Hallows and discerned what lay
there.

The realisation of who had to have placed it there had come
later, and the whys of *that* were varied, but no matter. There would
never be a better time.

The sound of approaching horses alerted Robyn. He crossed
the road and melted into a stand of trees.

The horses came at a spanking good trot, their riders no doubt
hoping to make Blyth before sundown. A small group of well-
dressed travellers, accompanied by only a few guards . . . nay,
those were Templars. No easy pickings there, even had he been
prepared. Instead Robyn drew close behind an elm and watched
the travellers continue down the road, all the while wishing them,
too, to their hell.

Turned and disappeared into the gloaming—not towards the
easterly caverns and John, but west.

He wasn't sure what he felt.

So Gamelyn chose to feel nothing. Habit was a compelling—
and satisfactory—fortification, one almost as impressive as the
eleven-sided tower keep surrounding him. The last emblem of his
father's might spread beneath his booted feet, with massive oaken
beams arching overhead to twice his own height.

He couldn't help an occasional, surreptitious touch to the wood-
and-stone pillar beside which he'd chosen to stand. It was the one
to which they had bound him, in the days following Loxley's
destruction. And Otho knew it.

Twice, now, he'd offered Gamelyn a place closer to the hearth
blazing in the middle of the hall, overtly fuelled now the siege had
ended. Each time Gamelyn had refused with a slight, if merciless,
tilt of lip.

Aye, indeed some unspent resentment.

Talk had been sparse since the mistress of Blyth welcomed her Templar visitors into the great hall where Gamelyn had taken part in many a gathering at his father's side. Keys jangling, proud-heavy, at her girdle, Alais chose to serve her guests with her own hands. She poured good red wine, as well as offered a repast of fresh bread, a well-aged round of cheese, and several smoked fish at the wide board. For siege victuals—and Lent, at that—it was prime hospitality.

Gamelyn's thoughts went, arrow-true, to Marion. The Maiden of the Shire Wode had as keep either a mean cavern or woodland glen. She'd wrested miracles of sustenance from a hard, lean winter, gathered her own herbs and simples. Her clothing and tapestries were mended, bartered, or stolen, the rush mats carpeting cavern or mossy floor woven with her own hands.

The sight of his brother's wife making light of a privation she'd never truly known rippled honest fury within Gamelyn.

"You seem . . . content," Alais ventured as she began to refill Gamelyn's cup.

No doubt my seeming content eases your conscience. Gamelyn held his tongue, stared coolly down at her.

"Alais," Otho warned and, cheeks pinking, she mumbled a quick apology and kept pouring.

"You seem to be beneath the misapprehension that my *Confanonier* is vowed to silence." Hubert spoke softly, but his rich baritone filled the hall.

"Misapprehension? Does not your Rule prohibit you from speaking to women?" Otho made answer into apology, clearly eager to avoid offending a Commander of the Temple.

Gamelyn had to admit to hoping that Commander would allow the error to stand. Vows of any Holy Order were meant as sacrifice and privation, but an outsider's reading of them—mistaken or no—often proved useful.

Particularly *here.*

"Our Rule is necessarily strict, yes, but we also realise there must be allowances when one ventures into the world. And we are, I'm afraid, forced to be a very worldly Brethren."

Mayhap sacrifice after all, for Gamelyn to keep any anger behind his teeth, to accept both sentiment and wine with a soft "My thanks, my lady." For Alais did indeed possess a conscience, one he could easily pierce did he choose. Even when Gamelyn had been gaoled in his chamber for being mad enough to dally with a peasant boy, or pronounced mad in earnest and tied to the pillar a mere stone's throw from the welcome board, Alais had always been kind to him. He owed her like kindness.

"You are most welcome," she replied, solemn with a curtsey, "my lord Templar."

"I can scarce believe it." It wasn't the first time Otho had muttered the like. He also kept avoiding Gamelyn's gaze. Otho had his own conscience—of a sort. But it was much more selective, unwilling to push against any bounds of personal comfort. "I never thought to see you again . . . and here you are. A Templar. None of us ever believed—"

"That when sent to war, your youngest brother would survive?" Hubert's comment would have scathed the fish dry, were it already not so. "Or even thrive?"

Otho started a hot retort, bit it back, and looked down.

It was Alais who bristled. "If you think either of us wished harm to Gamelyn, you are sore mistaken, my lord Templar!"

"Alais!" Otho hissed.

Her eyes flashed, but once again etiquette demanded she lower her head and murmur, "Forgive me, my lord Templar. I am inconsiderate." The look that lingered in Otho's direction, however, suggested her husband best speak for her on the subject.

Instead Otho spoke to his son. "Ian, lad, come away. Stop your staring."

The youngest was still a suckling babe, curled in the nursemaid's ample arms where she sat close to the hearth, but the eldest—a bold little thing, stout on his pins for all he couldn't have been more than three—had some time ago crept nigh. With two fingers in his mouth, the boy-child was pie-eyed over the grand strangers who'd entered his father's hall.

Ian. Mouth a-quirk, Gamelyn knelt down, addressed the child with no little gravity. "My father was named Ian."

Those eyes, green as Gamelyn's own, went impossibly wider. Emboldened by the stranger's manner, the child reached out and touched the mail of Gamelyn's sleeve. "Wasee? Wasee Shovalay, too?"

Gamelyn blinked, frowning. "What?"

"Shovalay," the child insisted. "Wasee?"

Well, and if he could decipher Robyn's attempts at *langue d'oc,* surely he could parse this. "Shove what?"

A deep chuckle, echoed into Hubert's wine goblet. "I believe your tiny nephew is trying to say '*Chevalier.*'"

Nephew. This was his nephew.

It doesn't matter. Guy shrugged.

I'm afraid it does, Gamelyn answered.

"Shovalay!" It was victorious.

Gamelyn exchanged a bemused glance with Hubert. "Aye, my father was a most gracious *chevalier,* Ian."

"Ian," Otho repeated, "come away, lad."

"No wannu," Ian retorted, then, as if emboldened by one defiance, snatched at the tantalising glint of Gamelyn's sword athwart his shoulder. The hilt was well out of reach, but Gamelyn was quicker, grasping the small, podgy fingers with his own.

The child blinked, then frowned. Gamelyn peered back in warning and, when the frown looked well on its way to a fit of temper, put two fingers to his lips. "Wait."

Young Ian looked as if that would not do either. His frown began to deepen.

Gamelyn loosed him, reached back and grasped the hilt of the *shamshir a'shekârger*, tugged it upward. The curved blade parted from its leather scabbard with a soft susurrus. A quirk teasing at his mouth, Gamelyn arced the sword through the air twice and thrice.

A small gasp from Otho—did he really expect Gamelyn to break hearth law and take out a child?

You killed children. Guy again, overly patient. *In Acre. But ah, they were infidels. Pagans.*

And hearth law is a Pagan rule, he snarled back.

In truth, the Biblical implications of Otho's response told more of *his* conscience—and concerns—than any amount of adroit questioning could glean. Gamelyn glanced at Hubert midmanoeuvre, willing him to see it, and whilst Hubert likely did, there was also the real and wry censure: *Pride, Confanonier.*

Mayhap Gamelyn was showing off just a little. But the light in the child's eyes was worth that and more, kindling bright as the blade that flashed in the hall's waning sunlight. With an agile twist, Gamelyn brought the sword to rest, light as wood on water, in his palm.

This time young Ian peered at Gamelyn, fingers twitching—itching, surely—but polite. Gamelyn nodded. Breath whistling from tiny white teeth, Ian stroked his hand down the blade, back and forth.

"Ian," his mother said, warning. It was a mistake, for the child's attention swerved, and his hand slipped.

The bloodcurdling scream that met this was surely out of place with reality; Gamelyn knew, for he'd seen the slip start to happen and knocked the little fingers away before the blade had sliced too deep. But there was blood, lots of it. Green eyes fastening to his own, Ian howled, and suddenly . . .

Time . . . slipped.

Green eyes peering upward. . . the sword's swing. . . a shower of blood and a child's cry cut into breathless gurgle. . . and a voice— Robyn's voice?—scaling upward into shrill, raw denial. . .

Gamelyn tottered and fell forwards, barely saved himself from an ungainly sprawl with a quick prop of one hand. The sword wasn't so lucky; it slipped, gave a discordant ring upon the paving stones.

Ian kept howling, even after his father snatched him away. His mother gathered him up, produced a linen handkerchief and, with the help of a servant, bound the child's hand . . .

Blood, dripping from the blade and soaking into the damp

stones. . . the screams choke away, the piercing ring of them fading into broken whispers. . . someone is pleading with him—for him?— murmuring his name like a charm, over and over into the dank and mouldy dark. . .

This time Gamelyn fell facefirst, stone barking his chin and smacking full against his nose. He sprawled there, for several mad heartbeats wondering if he would heave his guts.

"*Confanonier!*" Hubert's voice, then a strong, merciless hand upon his shoulder, the familiar grip its own brand of comfort. "*Guy!*"

Guy, not Gamelyn, and it shattered the strange sense of . . . of otherwhen. Gamelyn stilled, sucked in a long, shuddering breath, and opened his eyes. There was no blood, no darkness, no drip-drip upon mould and mud. Between his trembling fingers was only the clean-swept floor. Little Ian's cries had subsided. As Gamelyn heaved himself upward and slowly raised his head, the child was glaring at him, offended that the stranger's toy had attacked him.

"It isn't so bad," Alais chided whilst a maidservant finished bandaging the cut. "See, no more bleeding, even."

Beside her, Otho stared at Gamelyn with a look half blame and half fear. No doubt remembering that youth tied to a pillar only a matter of years previous, thought bespelled and mad . . . for only a madman would attack his elder brother with a pestle and try to brain him in revenge for a bunch of Pagan filth.

"What did you See?" Hubert whispered against Gamelyn's ear. "Are you all right?"

What did I. . . See? Even as he tried to grasp it, the sense of otherwhen swooped away like a reluctant haggard. Likely better so, at that. Gamelyn shook his head, let Hubert help him up. After a frown and tiny shake to ensure Gamelyn was steady, Hubert released him and retrieved the sword from the paving stones. Gamelyn sheathed it with hands still a-tremble.

All the while, Otho eyed him. Gamelyn eyed him right back. Said, bitter-soft, "One can never be too young to learn that steel can bite, eh? Even in the hands of family."

Otho's gaze widened, then narrowed.

Aye, remember this much, brother. You tied me in this very hall, stood by whilst Johan stripped me of everything that was mine. And now? You have all that I was denied. A hearth, a home, a simple and shining faith.

"My lord!" Otho's constable came racing in, merely to slow halfway. No doubt the tension in the room was enough to slice good bread.

Alais, with Ian still cradled on one hip, walked over and put a hand to her husband's arm. Otho broke the odd stare down and turned to the constable. "What is it?"

"'Tis time for council, my lord. They're waiting for you in the great hall."

"Excellent. We will follow you, then, my lord castellan?" Hubert gestured outward.

Otho shot Gamelyn another wary look, was diverted by a servant twitching at his overcloak and straightening his chain of office.

"Otho," Alais said, then again, "*Otho.*"

He shook his head.

Once again, her brown eyes flashed and she turned to the Templars. "You have honoured our home, my lords *Chevalier*," Alais said. "I would hope you will return as you can."

Gamelyn peered sideways. Hubert peered back, indicating by his silence who should answer.

"As your husband has said more than once"—Gamelyn's voice didn't want to work, hoarse and somewhat rough—"I am of the Templars, now."

A frown twitching at her brow beneath the matron's veil, Alais nevertheless curtseyed, graceful despite the child in her arms. Ian squirmed, injury forgotten, wanting down.

And as they left the hall behind, he let out another howl, insistent.

"Shovalay! Come back!"

Voices carried outward from All Hallows, a lovely harmony that rang like bronze bells. The sound filled the stones, however hesitant with the way outward.

The hillside played tricks with it, Robyn noted, and the mists more so. The latter would close wet fingers and mute it to a hoarse whisper, then release it to waft, sometimes thin and sometimes replete, into the last rays of sunlight. There was no question of its beauty. Any breath brought forth and spun into full-throated song had undeniable magic in the making. But this contained a rather cold naïveté, summoning younger gods whilst it teased forth echoes of ancient ones, touching upon other spells sunk deep into this place.

The earthly voices stopped. But the ancient ones wafted out, curling about Robyn's nape and down to the soles of his feet. Tendrils, seeking root in something familiar.

We have a secret, they said. *Come to us, Lord. Find us, release us. Take us home.*

A sprint across open turf, a sidle and slip around the outward jut of the closest transept, and Robyn melted into the shadow of a tall old rowan. As surely as carven stone rumbled comfort at Gamelyn's touch, this tree shivered with recognition and welcome.

Trailing his fingers along one smooth branch, Robyn wondered what the Christians truly had meant when they'd set one of the most protective and magical trees of the *dryw* to guard their northmost gate.

Something to ask Gamelyn . . . and Robyn's thoughts started on another inward spiral of doubt and worry, the "black wolf" gnawing, persistent, the driest of bones.

Outer silence—and thankfully morose fixation—broke itself against another mortal voice: a call, and others in answer, then the brothers' feet scuffing against stone, exiting the chapel.

Robyn scaled the rowan, quick and agile—people rarely looked up, after all—but there was no need. The same consideration that had prompted his approach from the north side proved well-founded. The monks' footsteps headed opposite, towards the warming house and cloister beyond, likely with chores or sleep in mind. Despite what Scathelock thought, there was sommat to be said for having a renegade nun and two Templars in one's midst. The main sommat being how enemy customs were within easy reach.

Robyn waited for the monks to disperse, lying wary and eager in the rowan's embrace. He missed Scathelock about now, wanted a romp with nowt in it but a light heart and old trusts. But more, Robyn missed Marion. He could use her insight here, amongst their adversaries. With Gamelyn . . .

Back to back, there is none to stand against you. The Lady, insistent and stern from the stone-velvet bounds of Her chapel within. Aye, and Her mien changed in proximity to these places. No blame for that; indeed, there was all the more respect and reverence. 'Twere for sure he himself'd be a drooling madman, were he bunged in stone as they'd done Her. Even the Horned Lord lay taciturn, deep-burrowed within Robyn.

"None to stand against you." But with Gamelyn shying from his power like some skittish colt, it seemed there was nowt to stand with but the yearning for what could be. Summer had died and been born upon Solstice, but instead of clean passion and power blossoming with spring's breath, there was more and more fear, sprouting tall as the rowan.

But unlike the rowan, that fear of Gamelyn's sprang from so many places, and most of those unacknowledged—*unknown*—to Robyn and likely to Gamelyn himself. At least the one admitted fear also gave admittance to the passion beneath, and the worry.

Church walls *were* uncomfortable for Robyn. Not for any daft and made-up Christian tales of demons faced with crosses, or witches sprouting bat-wings when forcibly baptised. The stones sought the magic—*knew* it, called to it—and there wasn't much of the earth's sacred magic left untrammelled in thisworld. Even if the screams for attention were nowt but feeble whimpers beneath occupation, Robyn heard them.

Yet All Hallows was . . . uncommon. No screams, muffled or otherwise. More a murmur, soft and coaxing. Not only the trees as guardians, but the stones of its walls bore witness. The rowan's feathery leaves brushed his cheek as Robyn contemplated the figures hiding here and there, carved into the chapel's north face. Little beasties, all of them, even to the font Robyn had passed when they'd first arrived. The Church's stale excuse for blessing water made a pallid mirror within the stone font; nevertheless, the latter sang of years past counting, decorated with sea elementals.

Nay, Gamelyn had no need to fear for Robyn's safety, not here. All Hallows wasn't the likes of Worksop Abbey. Wasn't ringed with the fervent prayers of an enemy Abbess who'd had Robyn's parents butchered like cattle, or drowning in the cries of stones ripped from their mother without leave or sacrifice.

Elder prayers bided here. Almost indifferent to time's passage, yet old seemed to support new like . . . well, like a big sister helping her baby brother take his first steps. Robyn smiled, extended a hand to touch a jut of stone beside the rowan. It buzzed against his palm, patient and hallowed, knowing a time longer than the birth of Gamelyn's desert father-god, or the North-man's god whose ways of war and blood-honour pulsed in Robyn from his own father. Beneath the ash of Norman, Saxon, and Roman lay the ruins of an even more ancient occupation and conquest: his mother's Barrow ancestors.

All Hallows *was* sacrifice. It knew its own.

Within, the church seemed more a sealed tomb, and dark as a moonless forest night. The sun had retreated to a faint stain of purple in the west—no aid there. The only expressions of outward hearing lay in the faint stirrings from the monks' quarters, or Robyn's own breath, quick and shallow. Inner manifestations held stronger voice here: the rich, amber-flower murk of incense; the never-dying protest contained in mortar and stone; the not-sound of the Lady pacing Her darkened east chapel . . . all of it, a persistent swathe behind Robyn's eyes.

Taking a deep breath, he padded down the aisle nave. The progress was careful, one literally by the nose as Robyn followed the honey-char linger of the snuffed candles. If he were to find anything in this bloody tomb without stumbling over whatever lay between, he'd need some light.

'Ware the steps, the Lady warned just before he banged his toes.

Robyn didn't question the uncommon assist, just breathed a kiss of grateful blessing across his fingertips. Knelt, and felt.

He crawled one step, then two . . . three . . . that one long, so he stood again, discomforted at kneeling before the god of his enemies even by chance. Several more shuffling steps. A thick plank nudged his thighs, halting him.

The altar, She supplied.

A bit of fumbling about earned him a handful of embroidered cloth then—ah!—two candles cupped in shallow bowls. Robyn snapped his dagger across a flint, using a bit of oiled chaff to catch light for the candles. The tallest he left in its cup on the altar; the stub one he took up and, with aid of a pewter plate, reflected illumination into the altar alcove. He scanned the walls, taking in then releasing a soft, lingering breath.

His magic lay thin in this place, and well he knew it. He would need all the help he could fetch and hold. Robyn loosed the breath over the back of his hand—blood and bone, gleaming by candle-light—and let the breath become a whisper. *"Datgelu'r eich hun."*

Reveal thyself, the Lady concurred, adding, *Thy Winterlord calls to thee.*

Their whispers rose in the dark and tangled, forming a nacreous circlet of ebon and silver.

How is it, my Hob-Robyn, that you and I only couple in this fashion?

"Aye, and t' monks would say 'tis better for all that," he whispered, smile widening. "A wild ride, my Lady?"

Her chuckle resounded into the nave even as the power beneath the altar—harnessed, yet never truly tamed—responded more than he'd dared hope. The votive flames sparked and flared upward, burning trails of blue-white smoke. A stirring, soft and almost not there. As if Robyn had wakened some wing-fouled and ancient creature from slumber that stretched and shifted, coiled tight then stretched again, attempting to shrug away the weight of newer, fervent prayers.

"Aye, one could smother beneath such things," Robyn murmured, timed with the susurrus of the Lady's raiment, pacing the confines of Her chapel in fetters of indigo velvet. Even the thought-weight behind his eyes and upon his brow—horn and holly and mistletoe—seemed of stone. Robyn spread his feet beneath it, sought the tendrils of darkness and light.

"Aye, that's it. *Dwych,* old ones. Come closer. Even sleeping, tha' heard the god's steps, whispered His name. Dost tha' remember? Tha' wert mine once and I? I have always been tha's."

The old spirit—a wyvern, shaped with Briton heart and prim-ordial fire—unfurled crimson pinions, crooning.

"Where is it?" Robyn coaxed. "Help me, *Ysgawen.*"

A purr, as if he stroked a cat. Recognition, primal-sweet, between spirit revenant and godling remnant. Elemental breath commingling, as the spun-*tynged* of their cast circle twined tighter, ready . . . then sprang upward, loosed and soaring. Freed. Robyn smiled at the wilding aerial display, asked again, considerate.

Help me, Old One? You know this place; it heeds me not.

The wyvern glided to a sudden, silent halt. A glitter pierced darkness, lids drawing back from eyes long slumbering, to illuminate a small, three-sided alcove over Robyn's left shoulder. A carven saint stood there, staring blank-eyed. Mayhap nothing . . . or mayhap a possibility? If so, 'twere well-hidden indeed.

Robyn started forwards, hesitated as something shuddered and rippled outward. The ancient spirit hovered, intent. Its translucent wings extended, shivering.

The Lady stepped past the gates of Her chapel gaol.

Another shiver, this tasting of hesitation. Then, sudden-sharp, fright.

The wyvern folded its wings and dove back inward. The Lady's footsteps, free and quick towards Her Winterlord . . . stopped. Akin to the hot scent of blood upon a breeze, the trespass gusted over Robyn. A hiss of breath, vibrating *tynged's* threads with the passing of some . . . some deadly *thing,* puffing large and rearing upward, swaying and seeking weakness. Before his brain kicked in, instinct demanded; Robyn spun about.

The plate fell to the floor. The candle guttered, wax-melt and wind—but then, he'd no need of it.

The pale figure at the nave's end held a torch.

- XII -

"So you've finally decided to visit us, master archer."

Robyn considered both his situation and his adversary's approach. Smiled.

Said, with faultless courtesy, "You extended the invitation after all, milord Templar."

The torch shuddered and spat, giving a fitful glimmer to an aquiline profile, turning iron-grey hair into wobbly electrum, lighting faint a swift return smile. Only then did Wymarec de Birkin breast the dark, his boots a nigh soundless tread up the aisle and towards the altar, his white cape following like too-heavy wings.

Angels, those villeins called Templars, and aye, but from what me mam told me of such creatures and their bloody-minded ways, you'd make a proper one, right enough.

"Indeed I did. In truth? I took a chance that, did you indeed accompany my Templar to Tickhill, you might snatch the bait before my arrival. Thankfully roads were good despite the rain, and my horses fast. One can't exactly up and abandon Temple London when England's King has returned, you know. Or"—the smile broadened—"likely you don't. Trust me, there are formalities to be observed. Ones no doubt beyond comprehension of your kind."

Trust you? I'd sooner kiss your Frank king. And trust to 't but I've had that "daft peasant" card played by ones as matter. Including "your Templar."

Robyn shifted his weight to one hip and said nothing.

De Birkin seemed determined to say it for them. "Either way we would have met, and soon rather than late. But alas!" A small *tsk*. De Birkin halted, one hand falling to his sword hilt. The torch betrayed, here and there, a mocking light in pale eyes. "I'd not expected that the notorious Robyn Hode should be a ragged, lanky boy no older than Hubert's lamentably divergent *Confanonier*."

Well, and the Master Procurator of Temple England seemed hardly remarkable himself at first glance. Middling height, and filled through the torso like many a man once middle age caught them up without killing them. That white tabard looked fresh for one recently on the road; even his boots were brushed fair clean. And when a bit of char landed on the gloved hand holding the torch aloft, de Birkin's pale gaze flickered upward, noted it, promised it due. Nor did the man give in to the impulse, not in the presence of an enemy.

Yet he'd snuck in without so much as that enemy hearing the torch spit. That this Templar sorcerer was dangerous, Robyn didn't doubt for a scant heart's beat.

The edge of his mouth quirked farther. Peering through his curly forelock, Robyn remained still. Silent.

Such regard didn't sit well. De Birkin obviously was no minor lord's third son, keen with the survival tactic of hiding what thoughts he needed to keep his own. Yet there was no pinning him by dialect, his voice flat—colourless—as the most pretentious nobleman.

"Have you found your . . . property, then? That remarkable, horrible Arrow?"

And why don't you know, if you were watching?

"Or do the stones . . . inhibit you so much?"

Now this he didn't fancy, how the man should read the like from just watching. Robyn's own mistake—and arrogance—in thinking himself alone.

Aye, he'd best be on his game. Despite the ancient intensity lodged beneath, All Hallows was now of the Church—and this man could bathe naked in such a power.

De Birkin stepped closer, albeit slightly. An uncanny rush of . . . *presence* flared upward from behind Robyn, wet-cool and sudden. De Birkin's torchlit face betrayed nothing; nevertheless, Robyn's muscles tautened, to whirl and face this new threat . . .

Nay, Brother Archer. She gripped his nape, stilled him. *I am with you, in this place.*

Marion's voice, yet not. Despite the chill of the grip, warmth pooled in Robyn's belly. From somewhere deep, the Horned Lord pawed the earth and tossed His tines, backing His Mate even within captured, prayer-laced stones. Robyn's own hackles rose, quivered.

De Birkin showed no reaction. He merely took another step closer.

At the hindmost of Sight, Robyn envisioned Her, a split of thought-forms and aspects *between:* the tall, ebon Mother of Gamelyn's dreams, haunting these stones dressed in the weight of indigo, midnight, and sorrow, holding a suckling babe to one milk-heavy breast. But more the Wodewose Maiden who grasped his nape and called him brother. She crouched on the altar with kirtle rucked up about her hips. Woad adorned her naked torso, rimmed ebony eyes, and streaked russet-black hair. Twin-pronged antlers graced that mane. She was dark as earth, and small, and *of him.*

He sees nothing. He scorns Me.

Well, then, Lady, if that wain't make him the biggest fool of any of his like.

More soft laughter; a breath stirring his curls, a flutter of wings filling the church alcoves.

And still, himself the Master Templar heard nowt. Neither did he stay silent long enough *to* hear; he'd a need to fill the silence, this one—or hear himself command it, more like. "I could scarcely credit it when I heard such a thing."

Heard? A tiny niggle within Robyn's skull. Alundel, mayhap? Or . . . Gamelyn?

"After all, tales like to the one about the King's devilish great-granddam often reflect no more than superstitious delusions. Or survive as warning; after all, the woman was prideful and deserves the price of history's judgment for being above herself. But *this!*" The *scrape-scuff* of a boot skating stone, and the tone turned from mocking to curious. "Do the Church stones actually drain what . . . abilities you possess, then? Does the forest spirit refuse to heed your command within Church grounds?"

The Wild Girl hissed at Robyn's shoulder, and he growled, "Nowt takes what's mine by right. Not you, not your Church. And those as thinks to 'command' *my* god? Well." A short bark of a laugh. "They'll learn."

"I would relish the learning opportunity." The man was fair serious. Never taking his eyes from Robyn, de Birkin paced to an empty iron stand and sank the torch in its holder. Sank his next statement no less, a barbed broadhead. "But still, what sort of teacher could you possibly prove? I fancy were you left here overlong, you would start to pace, mindless as any beast in a cage."

Right, then. "How is it your like thinks the worst you can call anyone is an animal? I like animals, meself. They've talents nearly every civilised man fears. And envies." Robyn's gaze touched Wymarec's and held, a skein of gilt chasing behind. "Aye? *Milord?*"

Control gave a tiny slip-halt, caught unawares, and exhaled long from between de Birkin's teeth. Robyn could see him better with the torch no longer between them. More, he could hear the man's breath, sense the heartbeat, slow and regular beneath the fabric of that blood-dark cross.

You really have no idea what you're dealing with, do you? Just like "your Templar" last Samhain. Gisbourne also thought a jumped-up peasant had usurped a power not his own.

"You're right about this much, milord Templar. No matter the expense to cover it with lime wash and ochre, I fancy a cage is allus a cage."

"A cage, you say," de Birkin ventured, measured-slow. "Yet you pace these stones arrogant as if you own them."

"Mayhap you en't paying attention. Us *animals*, well, we're allus chary."

"Truly?" Another two steps, one toe grazing the bottom tread of the altar mount. "You don't seem overly fearful of me."

Aye, coom by, you smug Motherless. . . "You don't seem sommun as I should be overly fearful of."

With a small chuckle, de Birkin advanced; a frown quirked his brow as he paused and turned. Robyn heard it, too—footsteps, echoing in the south transept—but they quickly faded.

De Birkin shrugged it away, returning to his original tack. "And here I'd been told you were reasonably intelligent. For a peasant. But then, mayhap you and Brother Guy don't share much, ah, conversation." Another chuckle. "His character has always been . . . tainted, shall we say? And by a peculiar taste for the dirty and dangerous."

Robyn's own smile broadened, twisted. Gamelyn would have no doubt dragged him out by his curly black hair before letting him act upon the sly insult, but his poncy ginger paramour wasn't here, was he? So Robyn lurched forwards, halted just before he trod on de Birkin's well-brushed boots, and leaned in. Speaking of poncy . . . those too-pale eyes went buggy, and the narrow nostrils flared with distaste. It was surely everything the man could summon within himself not to retreat.

Marks for Templar brass; he didn't. Not even a little. Not even with well over six feet of outlaw perched on that last step, looming.

Well, then, all right. Robyn backed off just enough. "I don't think you like me very much, Master Templar. Was it owt I did? Said?"

De Birkin remained silent, glaring up at him.

Remounting the steps, slow and ever watchful, Robyn returned to the altar and leaned one purposeful hip against it. "Or mayhap just what I am?" Felt the Wild Maid's mirth, and the Mother's breath heat his nape: amusement and, mayhap, a tiny reproof.

Tisn't disrespect, Lady, not when you invited me to sit with you.

Marion's not-voice answered. *Are you trying to annoy the Templar, Hob-Robyn?*

The Templar was indeed annoyed. Another flare of nostrils greeted Robyn's pose. "What *are* you, then? Other than a jumped-up *boy* who thinks he's of importance."

"You're one as lured this *boy* here!" Robyn shot back. "Who gave orders I should come. Here." *And Gamelyn was all set to tell me nowt, disobey those orders, come alone, leave me behind. All because of you.*

In truth Robyn worried over what that meant—as much as the stolen Arrow, and more than any spell this sorcerer cared to utter.

"Mayhap I share with Brother Guy a base curiosity."

"You guaranteed a wolfshead passage because you were *curious?*" Robyn didn't bother to hide his disbelief.

"Surely you must realise you're quite the conundrum."

C'nun-what? Robyn raised his eyebrows. At least it didn't sound insulting. Overmuch.

"An uncanny notoriety precedes you, and outrageous tales linger after. Remarkable accomplishments for a peasant, let alone a boy years before his prime." De Birkin crossed his arms. "Commander Hubert is quite taken with you. But Hubert cares for our sullen *Confanonier,* as father to the son he will never have, and so will accept any of the admittedly few things Brother Guy fixates upon. Even wolfsheads. Even women."

The way he phrased that last made Robyn's lip curl. The Maiden/Mother upon/beside the altar growled, low.

Still the gormless sod Saw nowt!

"Your Christ was born of woman, O *man.* Our Lady wain't bide with disrespect."

"Even the most holy of women? Are no more than that—wo-men—in the end." De Birkin shrugged off both sacrilege and Robyn's risen hackles with easy contempt.

We will rend him. Swaying back and forth like a hunting lioness, the Maiden's voice purled a promise that broke Robyn in nervy sweat. The Mother remained silent, but that eased him precious less.

Another *scuth* of footsteps from the inner corridors; once again, they passed by and faded.

"Well, master outlaw, whilst this is entertaining enough, time grows sadly short." De Birkin crossed his arms. "Compline rings soon. Shall we do business?"

Robyn blinked. "Business."

"Indeed." A smile. "I possess something you want."

"Sure of that, are you?"

The smile widened, not at all pleasant. "I could name several, in fact."

Robyn didn't need the naming; he knew.

The Arrow. His own precarious freedom. *Gamelyn.*

"Mm. I'd suggest you consider this, milord. Whats'mever you'd think to possess?" Robyn hissed the last, all mocking. "Mayhap you'll find nowt but ashes should you try holding to 't."

"Ah, but I make a practice of holding many things. So far my gloves are spotless. As you can see." Wymarec held up one hand—the one unmarked by the torch, Robyn noted—and waggled the fingers. "But since *you* seem so careless in your own grip of such a powerful weapon? Wait there, boy, whilst I fetch it for you."

Robyn lunged upward from the altar, ready to give the arrogant sod what-for. Instead a chill and otherworldly grip descended upon him: this time, a Mother's calm to stay him.

Give him nothing of what he seeks. Grant him his blind-foolish opinions. In the end he shall bring the Arrow to you. And you, O pwca, shall know what to do.

"Very good. Like any brute—any *animal*"—De Birkin was still *smiling*, the sod—"your first impulse is attack. Yet you do retain enough presence of mind to control it. Mayhap you'd do better to heed the prey's first instinct, boy. Take flight. Leave the thing to me."

"A fair proper assumption," Robyn snarled, "that I'm the prey."

"You walked into my trap, did you not?" Voice floating behind, de Birkin headed for the northmost aisle.

Did I, then? Robyn wondered how smug the Motherless monk'd be minus his head. An arrow through his gullet, then do the job proper with the man's own sword . . .

A familiar, dull tingle rippled through him, muting impulse with sudden apprehension.

Oh, but this was indeed one skilled Motherless sod of a monk. The Arrow had been hidden in plain sight, clad in the trappings of offering at the stone feet of the same blank-eyed saint and alcove where the wyvern spirit had paused. De Birkin had taken some care in wrapping it: thick wool swathed in a heavy shimmer of silk, garlanded with gilt, purple, and scarlet. And the complic-ated shadow-spell with which it was further bound—*smothered*—slicked the back of Robyn's throat, alien and sharp.

Willow sought maker, faint but thwarted by silk shroud and foreign conjuring. De Birkin took up and cradled the bundle like a swaddled babe, turned back to face Robyn. Eyes gleaming, he began to unwrap it. His lips moved, shaped inaudible whispers.

Robyn didn't need to hear. Still foreign, and complicated past any sense, the conjuring slithered up his spine, iron-hard chill lingering in its wake.

Numbing. Blinding.

Hob-Robyn, 'ware your—

And the Lady's warning smothered silent, beneath a rime of frost.

"Marion?"

She started, shuddered, and realised she'd been staring at the fire altogether long. Her eyes were skimmed dry, hazed with the smoke of incense and the damp-dark flickers of torchlight upon ancient stones . . .

A broad hand gripped her knee, hard, and the voice repeated, just as firm but leavened with concern, "*Marion.*"

The fire beckoned. Marion turned from it to Will. No reassurance there either; indeed, he drew back, albeit slight, and Marion saw the moon-bow of her own gaze reflected in amber.

Yet there was enough of *dryw* in him to frown, and query, soft, "What have you Seen, Maiden?"

"Seen," she repeated, just as soft.

"Is it Robyn?"

"Aye. Nay. I mean . . ." Marion shook her head and peered about, as if expecting things had changed, or somehow *time* had changed. Yet the surround was much as it had been before her spirit's drift. The Rufford villeins, given a focus and direction with the birth, helped David and Gilbert put the finishing touches to a temporary camp. Aelwyn was where Marion had settled her, nursing her bairn. The other youngsters stayed close, fascinated with their newest family member. Much was seeing to the horses' comforts. Arthur was away, no doubt still scouting the perimeters.

"Mari, is it sommat to do wit' Rob—"

"*I don't know!*" she shot back—albeit muted—but added on just as swift, "Nay, I do know. 'Tis that, sure enough, but—"

"Arthur and I can be there in a half day's trot." Will started to rise, staggered as Marion grabbed his tunic and stayed him. "Blast and bugger it, woman, we should've gone in the first place. We en't needed here, an—"

She put quieting fingers over his mouth, fisting his tunic snug when he thought to override her. "So you go, as half-nocked as you ever claim Robyn does?"

"If he needs help—"

"If." Her fist beat a halfhearted tattoo upon Will's chest. "There's no help you can be giving, not with this. Mayhap he knew, all along."

"Marion—"

"He's found the Arrow, Will."

Will sank farther into his haunches, blinked at her.

"And I'm thinking none of us wants in his way when he takes it back."

He'd been feeling distinctly unwell since they'd left the main hall behind. And no wonder, with the unsettling splash of Sight that had come to him. Yet distance was proving no succour.

Gamelyn gritted his teeth, gave a tiny shake of his head, and kept close beside Hubert, tailing Otho and his constable across Blyth's wide bailey. Yet another council to attend within the great hall alongside the gatehouse. Stones, whispering to him, closing about him.

You have returned to us, Lord.

His feet grew leaden, slow, as time . . .

Slips. . .

Stones and incense, heavy sweet. Frost to cover fire, and the piercing, sorrowful gaze of a darkling Mother, watching Her consort spun into a web of silence. . .

Gamelyn stumbled and went to his knees in the new-wet grass. In a trice Hubert was beside him, grasping his shoulder, shaking him. It was not gentle.

"Confanonier?"

Only a few strides ahead, Otho had stopped, plainly conflicted betwixt concern and caution. The constable was not so conflicted; he was murmuring in Otho's ear, a plain *Take care, my lord. Did you not warn me your brother had been driven mad?*

Madness . . .

Madness working, blind amidst the stones. A web of enchantment spun by a master to foil tynged's *weaving.*

Wymarec. The Arrow. *Robyn,* and Gamelyn had brought him here.

"Have to stop it," he husked. "Stop him."

A hand slipped beneath Gamelyn's elbow, a merciless vice intent upon punishment as well as support. "Control it!" Hubert snarled. "By Our Lady, but ever since the winter . . . *sacrée* tête, 'twould be best for all of us did you come back to Hirst and we force you to the initi—" The words weakened. The grip did not.

"It's Robyn," Gamelyn murmured, just as unthinking.

Hubert's grasp tightened, wrung a grunt from Gamelyn as his Master looked over his shoulder and said, light, "I should have insisted he broke his fast at your table. There are limits to even a Templar's endurance, after all. Pray continue. We shall follow anon."

Gamelyn's focus winnowed down and inward; he barely heard the retreating steps and murmurs, said again, "Robyn. And—"

"Our Master. At All Hallows," Hubert confirmed.

Something within Gamelyn quailed, wanted to question; necessity overrode even that. "Then you know I . . ." It trailed off as Hubert didn't move. "Commander, please. I must go."

"You must not." Hubert's murmur was soft but still unmoved. Gamelyn peered at him, entertained a bare heartbeat's worth of insubordination.

"By God, what are you, a puling boy or a man?" Hubert dragged him upward and shoved him to his feet. "Brother Guy! You are a Templar! *Control* it!"

The name slapped weakness across its soft face, grounding Gamelyn as he nearly fell again, opening a reservoir of cold and ruthless might.

Thank *God.*

Gamelyn tossed the hair from gleaming eyes, started to speak. Hubert's expression snared any challenge, mystic or moral, by the throat.

Hard as stone—

—as the stones, calling to him—

—yet also comprehending.

"*Non,* Brother Guy. It is not our place. In truth, I think it would be the height of foolishness for either of us to attempt standing between them."

A familiar, sororal quiver, outside any hope of help. Another—closer, angrier—stood down like a leashed and muzzled hound . . . "Ah," said de Birkin. "The bindings are stronger than I thought. But then, the girl is your sister, after all. My Templar has lain with you. Of course they would know." A shrug, and he pulled the last of the wrappings from the Arrow.

It . . . whimpered.

The stones answered, a softling stir beneath Robyn's numbed feet.

Yet none of it would stir him, not even the artefact of his own making: a willow wand with knapped flint tip, black with char and old blood, lying pinioned in white-gloved enemy hands.

The peacock feathers upon it wafted, glimmered. Robyn's eyes flitted there then away, as if blind.

"*Niis,*" de Birkin hissed. The ancient command resounded through the nave, blurred and thick. As if underwater.

Come.

Every step leaden, tentative, Robyn obeyed.

"You have no doubt led Brother Guy a merry chase, but we'll see what you're made of, yes?" The pale eyes were nigh black, their pupils dilated. "One way or another, you will tell me what I want to know."

"What . . ." Robyn's tongue lay unwieldy-thick, his mind lagging, thoughts longing to be other than his own. "What . . . *do* you . . . want?"

The gloved hands tightened, infinitesimally, on the Arrow. It cried out—

—and still he could do nothing—

—as the Templar Master's gaze sparked even paler. Robin's slurred, tiny query had kindled wildfire. "My ancestors were lords of this land when your people were beaten slaves squatting in hovels. Yet somehow a ragged *boy* has come to possess the penultimate secret. I scarce believed it when I gleaned his thoughts, but it was there, spinning white-hot like an untold tale, the way of your dying."

Gleaned his thoughts. It crept through senses iced, numbing frost upon a winter heath. *Gamelyn.*

"That tale, at least, is true. There is the unmistakable language of death upon this"—de Birkin lifted the Arrow—"*thing.* So crude, so uncultivated and violent and . . . and *beautiful,* damn you, for I cannot break its ways. Cannot decipher it. I, Wymarec of Birkin, Master of the Inner Temple of England! Son to an unbroken line of practitioners of *seidr,* whose magicks chained and tamed the Barrows! Noble descendant of Æthelfrith, lord of Bernicia and Deira—yet this last veil I cannot pierce! This most precious initiation eludes me. *Me!* Whilst a peasant son of peasant slaves has walked the halls of Death, been broken, died, and *returned,* to speak and conjure with a naked shaman's tongue such powers of oblivion upon an artefact scarcely more deserving than himself!" Just as soon as the rage had risen, it guttered and wavered silent.

Robyn peered at him, hazed in darkness, mute.

"Still." A smile crept over de Birkin's face, quivering at the corners, unpleasant. "Secrets can be learned. Will be learned. Come closer, boy."

Hesitation; feet scuffing the flagstones.

De Birkin rolled the Arrow between his gloved hands, wrung from it a resistant spark of magic that made Robyn totter. De Birkin noted this, smiled broader, and offered up more of the darkling tongue. "*Noan oco nanaeel.*"

The words morphed about him—

Thus you are become servant to my power—

—and the spell feinted, drew away then came even closer, shadows a-swirl to drag Robyn forwards. The fingerlings of domination found faultless purchase within the Church's thick stones, enveloping them, stroking them tense and ready, siege to thought and mind and will . . .

Save for those two delicate fissures of instinctive protest.

De Birkin's smile slid mocking. He extended the Arrow, balanced on spread fingertips. "They will be of no help to you here, wolfshead. The girl is nothing, and Brother Guy . . . " A soft chuckle. "Well. The lad does his best, doesn't he? But he is sadly out of his depth. A shame, truly. All the power he has. All of it blocked, useless. Hubert had hopes you would be the key to broach those considerable barriers yet, alas. Hubert is rarely proven the fool, but I fear he is indeed mistaken about this. About *you.*" A *tsk.*

One more step closer, the Arrow still balanced, mien assured. Arrogant.

"And whilst there are still many things we can learn from each other, young druid, I must confess to a certain disappointment. I fear the ease with which I've suborned your will merely proves you not quite the power Hubert imagines."

Robyn neither twitched nor thought. Quicker than either, he snatched the Arrow from de Birkin's outstretched hands and danced away a bare half breath before gloved hands closed on empty air.

Shrugged away the frigid stones, with a grateful reach towards those tiny, twinned fissures of coppery light to warm a soul's chill. Backed away with a one-sided smile, the Arrow twirling in his fingers. It whistled—nay, *sang*—his name, high and musical against the stones.

Hands outstretched, de Birkin seemed stunned.

"Oh, milord," Robyn chided, smile gone sober. "You're so keen on who you are, yet you en't arsing yourself t' proper ken your adversaries? You'd think to bespell *me* with the likes of dark and cold?" He put just that much more distance between them, the altar at his back where the Lady hovered, twinned and waiting. "I'm *dryw ardhu* of t' Shire Wode, t' Hob who strips the branches bare and makes pictures of ice upon 'em, who calls the winds through long, bitter nights, and feathers snow amidst the blood berries of holly and sacred mistletoe. I *am* Winter, you arrogant, Motherless sod, and 'twill be the coldest day of your hell before even the likes of you can use my own tools against me!"

The man's face had reassembled itself into stone; other than the primary reflex of trying to hold to the Arrow, he'd not moved.

The Mother drifted back into the shadows. The Maid angled forwards, crouched keen as a hawk upon a meadow.

Then de Birkin started to laugh.

Control it! his Master had demanded.

And so he had obeyed. It was not Gamelyn who attended the gathering held in his father's demesne, but Guy de Gisbourne the Templar assassin, machine and extension of his Master's will.

The council was joined in the great hall south of the gatehouse, where many such events had been staged and held. The castle might be in need of repairs, but the banners and tapestries were clean, if faded. Lime wash coated the walls stark white, and the painting on the north wall, commissioned by Sir Ian in honour of the saint to whom Blyth's chapel had been dedicated, smiled down with hands outstretched. St. Nicholas, protector of children. Patron of repentant thieves and archers.

Nay, sentiment would do him no service here. Any remem-

brance of a kindly-stern father, any concern towards the outlaws'
journey, any inklings of Robyn's plight; all were captured—gently,
mind, as if snatching birds midflight—and stowed in a snug cage
for later action. He couldn't do anything about it, not now. When
the stones of the great hall greeted him, thought to cozen him,
they were bidden silent, easy as that. When the black threads of
tynged and thwarted power gathered and tried to spin possibilities
behind his eyes, he closed his mind and turned away, immobile.

And when Gamelyn demanded he take notice, Guy merely
rolled green eyes and shoved him in the cage as well.

"Indeed, King Richard is likely nearing Nottingham as we
speak." De Puiset of Durham was mayhap enjoying this a little
more than a Christian bishop should. But Blyth—an undeniably
powerful if older bastion—had been a burr in his backside and a
drain on his resources for over several fortnights. "It would be . . .
politic, my lord Otho, were you to accompany us. With a satisfactory support staff."

"Satisfactory?"

"I should think seventy-five well-armed men would ease the
King's ire, my lord," Durham suggested.

"I . . . my lord Bishop, this is intolerable!" Otho was nigh splut-
tering. "I cannot leave Blyth with over half her forces depleted!"

"That is for the King to say, my lord."

"The castle shan't suffer or be left unguarded." This from de
Furnival, standing beside Otho. "My lord Bishop has everything
sorted, and you will ride with me to Nottingham."

"Sorted? I'm not sure what you mean."

"My lord of Hallamshire is eager to reassure you, as any friend
should." Durham gave said lord a quelling gaze. "But he is correct.
We have sorted things from mere necessity."

"My lord," Otho began, "hear me out—"

"Nay, 'tis you who must hear." With two fingers Durham tapped
the table and the parchment upon it, emblazoned with the royal
seal. "I have been given leave by our rightful King to settle these
matters. Considering Tickhill's status in the eyes of that King, I have
deemed it best for all concerned that the castle and demesne be
placed—temporarily, of course—in the hands of ones whose impartiality is renowned. The Templars shall oversee security. Hubert
has offered not only his best men, but also your kin as surety."

Otho seemed at a loss for words. Indeed, Guy's own hard-won
calm tried to displace itself, nearly freeing Gamelyn from his
inner cage.

He sought Hubert's gaze, mouthed, *Master?* A smirk ticced
Hubert's lip.

"Until, of course"—Durham shrugged—"our liege decides what
ultimately is to be done. My lord Commander?"

"Hirst is at your disposal in this, my lord Bishop." Hubert

bowed. "Twenty of my best Templars to hold the castle, including my *Confanonier* as Marshal."

It was surely an arrangement made to satisfy any lord, great or small: a *mesnie* of the best fighting men in Christendom, securing his holdings and protecting his family.

Otho still was not best pleased. "It is a . . . generous offer, my lord. But—"

"Surely you've no reasonable objections, man," de Lacy pointed out and added, harsh, "Neither do you have much choice. The impartiality of the Templars is legendary. They have performed such services for decades and will treat your family with all due courtesy. They've little stake in this."

Yet the latter was not entirely true, and de Lacy wasn't even bothering to hide it. Otho turned suspicious eyes upon the one who stood, silent guardian at his Commander's back, arms crossed over a scarlet and ebon tabard.

Guy de Gisbourne met those eyes with a regard akin to the stone wall at his back. *You can't touch me,* it said. *I'm not here.*

Otho tried to hold firm. Couldn't. Said, gruff, "I would charge you, Brother, to care for our father's house and my . . . *our* kin."

Guy acknowledged it with a tiny dip of head. "So my Order has commanded, and so I shall do."

"Marvellous. Bloody *marvellous.*"

Robyn cocked his head, backed a half step.

"But of course, you're a trickster, an outlaw, mayhap even the Fool. Robyn Hode." De Birkin pronounced the last flawlessly. But then, he would. He'd said it: *"Son to an unbroken line of practitioners of seidr."*

Seidr, the old Saxon magics, the iron hammer that had subjugated the Barrow People and driven their ways into otherworldly refuge. Robyn knew many of the Saxon traditions himself, from his father and the old *dryw* master Cernun—as impossible to avoid as the Mother-lore of his dam's fae blood. The magics of their land had become so mixed together, with *tynged* spun out like chilled honey on a dipper, its crystalline strands folded into England's great and fiery cauldron: a concoction of cultures stirred complex-sweet.

"I must tender Hubert an apology. He warned that I might be underestimating you; indeed, I have. Well done, master archer. You present a most interesting puzzle." The Master Templar wasn't far from being his own puzzle, at that. Robyn would have to be deaf and blind to not ken the man was furious; trap slipped and his own arrogance tendering valuable information to the "prey."

Yet still, he kept smiling.

"As I have my . . . *property*," Robyn ventured, "I'll be taking my leave, milord Templar."

"You could," de Birkin agreed. "And I could have a cadre of Templars after you in a heartbeat."

Robyn stiffened. Behind him, the Wild Girl hissed.

"You also seem to be forgetting the other . . . possession, which I hold and you would claim."

Take him, She whispered, tiny tens of fae lights clinging to Her hair, flitting about Her horns and darting outward to gild Robyn's curls. Fireflies, otherworld heralds, sentinels both light and dark. *He threatened you, Winterlord. He would think to bind the Oak. He dismisses Me. Lay him at Our feet.*

De Birkin gave a careless tug of first one glove, then the other.

"You're quite the thief, grant you, but I'd warrant filching *that* particular possession won't be easy as a cheap sleight of hand." The pale eyes moved to Robyn. "Mayhap we should conjure an agreement between us. *Dryw ardhu.*" The title held respect—but just barely. The pale eyes skimmed the chapel. All the while aware of Robyn, and oblivious of what else waited, furious.

He didn't ken *any* of it: Wild Maid horn-crowned on the altar, or Mother with a newborn Summering King in Her arms. Didn't sense with his considerable powers what ancient presence curled in shadows beneath the stones, unfurling wings and waking, to admit a Pagan avatar amidst the incense and artefacts of a Christian church.

It was Robyn's turn to laugh, slow and soft. "Mayhap," he said, and lifted the Arrow, "we should."

The pale eyes narrowed as Robyn let out a long, whispered breath to set the peacock fletchings dancing. "*Oddi y tywyllwch i mewn i. . . golleuni.*"

Out of darkness, light. . . and the same lights dancing about Her horns spilled into his hands, seeping through his fingers to spin about the ebon Arrow and set its blood runes afire.

"What would you have us agree upon, O Temple Magician? What could you possibly give me that I don't already have?"

Surprise, then satisfaction at the conjuring; Robyn saw both in de Birkin's eyes, albeit with a wry twist of thought nigh heard: *More tricks, then? I'd hoped for better. . .*

It trailed off as the light separated itself into tiny winged forms. Dancing, gathering, ghosting thisnow. Mayhap de Birkin was still blind to the Lady's presence, but the horned shadow cowling Robyn to backlight, hot, behind black eyes? That he did see.

Again, the strange satisfaction and exhilaration—and well, but that latter, at least, Robyn could understand.

Show me, then. It was a taunt.

Robyn didn't bother answering. The fireflies clustered, and like a loosed arrow, sped towards de Birkin's heart.

It sent him sprawling with eyes wide in disbelief. Robyn didn't wait, leapt after. Bow-hardened hand twisting the cross into shards of scarlet, he shoved the Templar Master flat back on the stones. Laid the Arrow's broadhead point against de Birkin's throat.

"I'll show you." It was a growl, shadowed by horns and gaze of ebon gilt. "*Trwy angof.*"

By way of oblivion, the Wild Girl crooned, and Her Consort juddered, responding to Her voice with a furious snort and lurch within. *Take him, Hob-Robyn. Bring him to Me.*

The thick vein beneath the broadhead leapt, erratic as a cornered coney; de Birkin was not foolish enough to respond likewise. "If you kill me"—a rasp, barely audible against Robyn's hand—"will *he* forgive you?"

The Arrow, quivering for the kill, jerked in Robyn's hand. De Birkin flinched as it nicked—shallow, painful—but persisted, his eyes seizing Robyn's.

"Will he?" A tiny blood trail began to creep downward from the flint point.

"More like Gamelyn'll sing his freedom from t' likes of you."

Aye, the Horned Lord purred, sunk so deep within Robyn that it was his own thoughts, his own need, his own Voice. *Kill him. Now.*

Give him to Me! the Wodewose implored. *His magicks have slain Our own!*

"And when"—a short laugh, albeit wheezy—"has our *Confanonier* ever begged for such a thing as *freedom?*"

Try as he might, Robyn's hand refused to heed entreaty from god or goddess.

Worse, the man knew he'd hit square. "But let's set Brother Guy—"

Gamelyn! the Wild Girl spat, defiant.

"—aside for the present. You kill me, and you'll have the entire Order after you. After him, for he will be considered complicit. After that mangy pack of outcasts you insist are family. After your sister."

"We're outlaws," Robyn gritted back. "D'you think we en't used to that?"

"Oh, my lad. Truly?" The grizzled eyebrows quirked—and aye, but the man'd more balls and brass than any monk should, with a blood-spelled flint shard at his jugular. "Trust me, you've had rank amateurs hunting you. Sheriffs and nuns are hardly a fair comparison to the entirety of England's Templars avenging the death of a fallen Master." A shrug, clamped still as Robyn pressed closer.

"Hardly a fair comparison," Robyn snarled, "thinking 'tis only death I fancy givin' you with *this.*" A breath, ever so slight, across the Arrow. It quivered, eager.

Fear at last, whitening pale eyes. Belief, sending de Birkin pressing back against the cold paving stones. "Ah." The admission, nevertheless, bided calm. "Then what if I were to tell you that, working together, we can indeed gain freedom for the one thing that has eluded us both?"

"What?" Robyn snarled.

"You know what I mean. Guy's abilities."

That one didn't just hit square—it went for the vitals and sliced, deep-slow.

De Birkin continued, quick and persuasive. "You know as well as I, he's of no use to either of us with these . . . denials with which he continually shackles himself."

"Neither do I consider him merely as sommat to 'use'."

"And so what binds you is not only of flesh, is it? He is your rival. You are last in a long line of *rex nemorensis*."

My priest, She crooned—and a good thing, for 'twas a name he'd never heard even whilst it laid claim. *My Son Sacred in his blood. My Wylding King. . .*

"And while you claim within you the spirit of the forest, he was born with the right to challenge you, a tale acted with the seasons' passing as primitive folk will do. Only this is not some game of wrestling for the right to rut some peasant whore!" De Birkin's voice wavered, tight and hurried as the Arrowhead nicked another slow trickle of blood. "This is an ancient rite, a tale given flesh! Do you truly think I've not studied your woodland cult? Do you think I don't admire what has come to you?" It slowed, went to a whisper. "The *beauséant!* The all made one! You fool, can you not understand why I sent Guy to you?"

I know why you think you sent him, you heart-blind, Motherless sod was the answer from within; then, even deeper, *And what if indeed this magician can help free what even We cannot touch?*

Robyn leaned closer. Whispered, "You're one as en't under-standing. Not a bit of it, but you still think t' control sommat as you don't ken."

"Mayhap. But mayhap it's your like that refuses to understand. After all, your rival seems altogether loath to play this role you would have—!" It broke into a harsh whistle of sucked-in air as the Arrow bit skin.

"That's where *your* like misses the toss. It en't about control. None of it is about control. 'Tis about *choice*."

The pale eyes sparked, and de Birkin lurched up. Tried to, at any rate. Robyn shoved him back down, hard, and purled a harsh breath across the Arrow. "*Caethiwo ti*."

Bind him to Us was Her whispered concord.

The breath gathered itself into a whirl of blue-white fireflies, drawn to the flint broadhead. Robyn's snarl twisted to a smile as he turned it, flat, and pressed it down.

To do the man credit, he didn't flinch. Even as the broadhead smoked and scorched, de Birkin didn't drop his eyes. Even when the sweat popped and runnelled down his temples, reeking of salt and fear and fury, he held Robyn's gaze.

Robyn met him, matched him, and trammelled him to the ground upon which he lay.

Then leaned closer, whispered, "I've marked you. For the Hunt, when your time comes. And come it will. But for now you'll bide here, bound until I'm away." Robyn started up, smiled as de Birkin tried to follow—and couldn't—again dropped, kneeling close. "Gamelyn en't *yours*. He will never be yours."

"Are you so willing to wager, *wolfshead*," de Birkin sneered, "that he's *yours?*"

The fireflies spun, guttered.

Robyn leapt up and vanished into the sudden darkness.

- ENTR'ACTE -

"*I think we're losing him, John. I think I'm losing him.*"
The last words Robyn had said this morn—and those unwilling, as if they'd burnt his tongue. As if that curst, Motherless sorcerer had a way to bind not only Arrow, but Robyn's spirit with 't. And when John had tried to go to him, hold him close, Robyn'd backed away, cheeks dark. Humiliated by what he'd said—but even more, out and spoken, by its power. Turned away, snatching up bow and quiver—wallet already over one shoulder—and started walking.

John didn't stay him. Where Robyn meant to go . . . it were important to see t' Arrow safe, and the day at least promised to be right lovely for a journey, at that.

But as Robyn disappeared into the sun-spackled mists, John turned on the fire and, with one vicious kick, sent it scattering into smoking coals.

Fell to his haunches and began chewing on a thumbnail.

Contemplated following despite Robyn earlier saying him nay— and while John knew he'd be all the less welcome now, he'd at least know Robyn were safe. 'Twere what he'd promised the others.

Nay, the tiny heart-Voice told him.

John snarled at it—no matter t' little Voice'd never hurled him south or sour—but wrapped his arms about his knees, and stayed.

Mayhap he should go to the caverns, then, better for t' wait. Or mayhap just leave this bloody damn nobleman's warren and go south, meet the rest of his family midjourney back from . . .

Nay, it said, firm.

With a longing look westward—Robyn's path—John lurched to his feet and began seeing to the damage he'd caused.

It took a while to gather the embers, longer still to make apology with careful fingers and dry kindling. The fire weren't all that keen on forgiveness; John ended up coaxing it with a breathy whisper of the magic and a gobbet of fat from his wallet.

After, he rocked on his haunches and hunched over an ache tender as if someone had given him a right proper thumping with a sturdy staff, angry at that bloody Voice for bidding him stay. But accepting. For now.

"We're losing him, John."

Chewing intent upon that misery, John didn't so much as hear the man approach until he walked into the little clearing . . . and how foolish were that?

Gamelyn, thank the Lady. Yet, somehow, it . . . weren't. John's nerves, already scraped raw, shivered and prickled like a threatened hedgehog.

Surely Gamelyn were here because he shared the same knowing as John did. No help for 't and despite all denial, Gamelyn were bound to Robyn both as like and unlike as John to Robyn since Loxley's burning and Rob's dying. The firelight, the mists, and the throwing of the bones on his Telling hide had shown to John the happenings of All Hallows: the ancient, undying power subjugated beneath, coiled and sleeping; Mother and Maid showing Herself, one more surprise amidst a proper lot of them—She'd never found a companion in Robyn, after all, as She had in Gamelyn.

The undeniable menace of the Master Templar, cloaked beneath pale courtesy. And the final bluff and feint that meant Robyn had won.

This round, 'tennyrate. John understood that, too.

Marion had Seen. Gamelyn too. Should still, in thisnow.

But. This man standing so straight-dark was Guy, nowt more nor less, eyes and heart all verdigris and iron.

John knew, now, what he'd been waiting for.

Slowly he rose, with a gaze as never left the Templar. Fingers tingling, hands open and ready. For whatever.

'Tweren't any surprise that Guy noted it, neither, and conceded necessity with a tiny dip of his coppery head.

Yet what words he said next? Were the right ones. "Where's Robyn?"

John took in a soft breath, held it. Used one hand to sign *Robyn's gone. Took the Arrow into the Wode, to see it safe and tucked away.*

And Gamelyn were . . . back, just like that. Warmth returned to those chill eyes: the heat of relief.

"Thank God," he said, and as his legs wobbled, let them take him to his knees, hands going to his face like a blessing-prayer.

John considered him, frowning, then knelt before him. And when Gamelyn didn't move, even so much as to look up, John reached out, gripped broad, freckled-scarred wrists, and pulled.

He had to see if Gamelyn were still there.

I think we're losing him, John.

Gamelyn didn't give him the chance, rising from his crouch. Though John kept hold of Gamelyn's wrists, pulled upward and with, it didn't help. Red-rimmed, those eyes, but elusive, peering off into the trees. "I have to return," he said.

John kept peering at him, slowly raised Gamelyn's hands to his face.

More, Gamelyn let him.

John kissed the heel of one hand, tried to speak but couldn't. He settled for nuzzling the sword-callused palm. Fingers twitched, then cupped his cheek and slid upward to snarl in brown curls. Lightly shook.

"I have to." Green eyes peered down at John, distant and cool despite those tangled fingers all giving-warm. "Now, more than ever. Please understand."

But there was no understanding owt of this, so John lipped the palm still cupping his cheek. Breathed against it, a mute, secretive charm that wove and wrapped its way upward, blue-white echo of the veins roping Gamelyn's arms and to the heart beating beneath the sigil of their enemy.

And Gamelyn let him, even as Guy looked away into the distance—back towards Blyth, and contemplated . . . What?

"We're losing him, John."

Nay. John's eyes narrowed, as if against the sun, watching his Summerlord like a hawk staring down a wren in the meadow. *Not if I can help for 't.*

- XIII -

To say the villeins were ecstatic at keeping the cart and sumpter was perhaps an understatement; not a one had realised they went to their new home with such riches.

The lay castellan, a friendly sort, was there directing and sorting with several others from Bruer's household. Much and Arthur were off to one side with one of those. The Templar on duty was a swart, stout Turcopole with whom Much was speaking in a smattering of Arabic and Anglic both. The latter was mostly for Arthur's benefit. With intuitive curiosity he'd been drawn to the half-Saracen Turcopole, who also was missing one arm.

The longhouse on the outskirts of the eastmost croft, while in need of repair, held more than enough room for the refugees.

"It'll fall down about our ears." Emma, of course.

Marion was ready to box *her* ears, despite all the help with birthing the new bairn.

"It's a roof, and we've more than what we started with." Agnes was curt. "All it needs is a bit o' work, so put yer back into it, woman, and shut your whinging face."

"A good thing, this," Will admitted, helping Marion unbuckle the sumpter from its traces. "Though"—he cut an uneasy look towards Temple Bruer, tall and stark-white against the ploughed heathlands—"I'd not be keen on the likes of yon tower breathing down me neck."

"Me either," Marion admitted. "But they'll do well enough here." She gave him a teasing nudge. "Did I actually hear you say Gamelyn did sommat right after all?"

Will grumbled something that might have been a reply, tossed the flaxen hair from his face, and led the sumpter to one end of the longhouse.

Farewells were said, quickly. None of the outlaws fancied staying despite either the approaching dusk or the lay brethren's seeming goodwill. Aelwyn in particular held to Marion's hand the longest—gratitude and other things best left unsaid.

Then Aelwyn did say something. "Take me with you."

Marion had started to pull away; she froze in place.

"I can't stay here." It was low, nigh whispered against the woollen wrap where the newborn slept snugged close. "They don't want me. You know they don't. I en't *of them!*"

"You'll be outlaw. You and your children—"

"Better outlaw!"

"Easy to say, lass, when—"

"Not easy to say, but easier than raising me bairns 'neath whip and cross!"

This time Marion stilled, body *and* tongue. There was nowt to say. Nowt she could say.

"Lady." Desperate. But also a reminder, keen as a slap, stinging all the harsher as Aelwyn brought Marion's hand to her cheek, kissed it. "*Maiden.* I beg you. Help us."

A glint of moonsilver wafted behind Marion's eyes, further reminder: Her presence, Her expectation, Her avatar's right . . . and rite. Aelwyn's breath gave a slip-halt and slow hiss outward as she turned pleading eyes up to Marion's . . . *saw.*

Went to her knees, still clutching to Marion's hand.

Several of the villeins started forward. One of the lay brethren—indeed, Will and Much as well—saw Aelwyn go down and made as if to come over, concerned. A look at Marion's eyes halted the outlaws in their tracks. It took a gesture and quick shake of head for the others, all the while Marion averting her gaze, hiding Her.

She knelt, snaking arms around Aelwyn, the bairn, and the little girl clinging close. "Shh. Be strong, aye? Be strong. I'll see what can be done."

Will's explosion had been expected, and Arthur siding with Will. But David's concurrence, vehement in their wake, and Gilbert's, had been as surprising as Much's refusal to take any side.

Much had put distance between himself and the outlaws, was fussing with one of the horses he had managed to gain, through the Turcopole, for the journey back. Horses were needed Blythward; it seemed the siege had come to a halt and was moving on to Nottingham to assist doings there.

Much was also running interference, more than the once. The villeins were busy setting their new domicile to rights. Aelwyn kept looking their way, wary. The Turcopole stood with Much; they'd already been speaking longer than good manners demanded.

"Marion." David's tone was soft, eminently reasonable . . . infuriating. "How are we supposed to take in a peasant lass?"

"I'm a peasant lass!"

"You're Robyn's sister," Gilbert added.

"And a freewoman," Arthur put in, gruff.

"I was bound to Worksop Abbey when Gamelyn and Much freed me! And if I weren't Robyn's sister . . . So you're sayin' the only way you'll allow a woman in your bloody band is on account of her standing with a man?"

"That en't . . . " Will chopped it off, and tried another tack. "And you en't two bairns at your skirts, neither!"

"And if I had?"

"What sort of question is tha—?"

"One needing an answer, Will. *Would* you dare deny a woman sanctuary for the Lady's grace of bearin' children?"

Arthur groaned and threw his remaining hand skyward, plain entreaty to that same grace. David frowned, giving an absent scratch to a snoozing Tess burrowed in his cowl. Gilbert, mouth tight, was peering at the ground and shaking his head. Will's arms were crossed, eyes narrowed and strafing her as if he entertained sudden—and unwelcome, from the tilt of his mouth—speculation.

Marion glared right back, daring.

"Are you addled, woman?" Will finally growled. "It en't the same and you know it! Asking us such a thing, and 'specting we'll agr—"

"I'm not expecting you to agree to anything!" Marion shot back, furious. "I'm *asking* nowt! And you've no call to say 'woman' at me in that tone of voice like I *were* nowt!"

"Marion," Gilbert said, serious-quiet. "Robyn has always allowed assent to any new member. It happened with me."

"And me," David added.

"I'm not Robyn. I'm your *Maiden*."

"Marion—"

She refused to relent, felt a different presence cloak her, wild and angry—the same Maid who had shown herself to Robyn amidst church stones. "Young Aelwyn has asked sanctuary for herself and her bairns. Of me. *In the Lady's name.* Are we Hers, in the end, or en't we?"

Silence. It remained for long moments, heavy as the Presence lingering behind her eyes, demanding acknowledgement.

Will was the first to give it, a dip of head and a whispered "Aye" that the others soon repeated.

"I told Brother Hamid how the lass and her bairns were kin to one of us." Much had padded over quiet-feral as Tess. "That her man were dead and his people unfriendly to 'er, so we mean to take her back home."

Marion turned, preparing to hug him so hard his eyes popped. Those blue eyes, however, refused hers, malleable as proved iron. It stayed her, made her inexplicably reticent.

"I gave him a few more coins to make ower any loss and sweeten t' Temple's pot." Much shrugged. "For what good, who can say? The Lady's will be done, but bein' outlaw's no good place for a bairn."

"And being bound to lord and church is?" Marion knew her cheeks were heating, didn't care.

"We're all bound, one way t'other," he answered, soft, still not meeting her eyes.

"Mayhap Hathersage would take 'em in," Will suggested, with a satisfied nod Much's way. "We could provide some game, a few pennies to sweeten *their* pot."

"And the lass and her little 'uns would go to a place as would cherish 'em." David smiled. "Would that suit, Marion?"

Would it suit? Of course it would. Hathersage was a proper Heathen village, followers and friend both to the covenant of the Shire Wode. It was the best of solutions in a hard place.

A fine solution, aye, if not the one for which We hoped. The Lady, still a silvery flame within. Her agreement seemed . . . resigned. *It has been long, Maiden, since the covenant has walked this path. 'Twill be a rough journey back.*

The men were, all, still looking to Marion. When she didn't answer right away, Will reached for her hand. "Maiden?" Soft, respectful . . . waiting.

She peered at him for one breath, spent the next eyeing the others. Then, slowly, she nodded.

"That's fine, then!" He squeezed her hand. "And that bloody siege over and done with—"

"The best of good news," Gilbert said.

"Is it?" David wondered.

"Aye." Gilbert nodded. "It means the remainders of Count John's army won't be after us."

"But there's still King Richard."

"No doubt *he'll* be away once he's pounded a few heads hereabouts." Much's laconic observation was inarguable, given the experience behind it.

"Well." David shrugged. "Likely we'll head back home after we meet up with the others, 'tennyrate."

"And no doubt Robyn'll be at the caverns, waiting." Will's smile broadened. He still held Marion's hand, tucked it firm into his elbow. "You're sure he's all right?"

Marion nodded. She could See her brother flitting through the

Wode like the spirit he so often was, ebon Arrow in his quiver and his purpose plain. He might be there when they arrived, or mightn't. Mayhap they'd find him along the road to Hathersage.

She watched the men resume making ready to leave, their tension dissolving as if into air. Then she turned away and beckoned to Aelwyn.

All the while, Marion kept her thoughts her own.

All Hallows lay empty, ghostlike with the coming dawn. Gamelyn's breath echoed, heavy-harsh, into the alcoves, and . . .

Nay. The nave was not empty.

She was there, seated cross-legged in a luminous cloud of indigo and stars upon the altar, absorbed in nursing Her Son. Gamelyn started to back away, but those great, grey eyes turned upward and pinned him in place.

Where have you been, My Knight?

Where had he not been? All over the bounds, speaking with the soldiers, gathering information worthy to guard a castle. No sleep; hadn't been able to do so, mind set upon its task, unwilling to so much as look beneath and, in the doing, mayhap break open another spiral of thought.

Templars. It was soft, chiding. *Too many of you, set upon a blindness to what you have. To what you* could *have, did you bother to See. Instead, you long for. . . what?*

Gamelyn knelt before the altar—before Her, in truth. He wasn't sure what else to do.

"Lady," he whispered, "I am not blind, not to you. I have always Seen you."

Aye, you have, even when you would rather not. It was satisfied. *Why else would I choose you? You are My consort even as the Maid is My avatar, and the* pwca *My son.*

The curl of unease in Gamelyn's gut fluttered tighter; after all, he knew what had become of Her Son. Nevertheless, he steeled himself to ask what he had not let cross into rational thought since . . .

"And what, then, of—"

The pwca? A smile within the Mother's cowl. *How strange, that he should be the one to free Me.*

Gamelyn frowned. "Free?"

His love for Me is. . . uncomplicated. His love for you, however. . . Her eyes flickered down to the babe, then upward again, piercing. *You are unkind, My Oak, and he fears it means you love him the less.*

Gamelyn started to protest, realised did he speak just the one thing—reassurance—then all the rest would come spilling out, like a lanced pus pocket.

Not wise, to babble to a goddess about what destiny one intended to thwart.

Then shut up. It was Guy, coldly reasonable. *You do remember how to keep your mouth shut and your thoughts your own, don't you?*

Gamelyn did.

But the Lady had no need. *You cannot hold* tynged *any more than water, love, and your leman's will runs wild and deep. All shall run its course, from stream to sea. With or without you.*

It threw him sideways, made him scrabble for control. *But. . . you said we would stand together.*

Yet your actions, My Knight, "say" otherwise. You are here, set upon something even I cannot fathom—

Guy gave a quick, inward smile.

—whilst the Maid chases a life once desired. Even the pwca *is. . . "to the green Wode gone," was it? Considering circumstance, you have been as set as your leman upon twisting* tynged's *tail.*

The babe lost the nipple, fussed. She tutted and stroked one downy cheek, helping the little one latch on again.

Gamelyn stared; he couldn't help it. It seemed so . . . well. Ungoddesslike?

Her eyes slid to his. She was still smiling. *In any world, babes must be taught. What of you, Gamelyn? What will you learn from this?*

Gamelyn bowed his head beneath the piercing gaze, unsure how to answer.

All Hallows' bells chimed, sudden into stillness. Gamelyn started, but remained where he was. When the monks came—for they would—they'd not question a praying Templar.

Our pwca *quite surprised that lamentably blind sorcerer who would secure Our Temple's otherworldly gates. He holds too many keys, that one. You would do much better with those in hand.*

Keys? Blind? Through a mire of confusion, Gamelyn thought to query, abstained, and bowed his head once more as several pairs of sandaled feet padded their way into the church. Candlelight was a further giveaway, flickering against the church walls and scattering across the altar: the monks of All Hallows, summoned by the ringing of Matins.

The warm glow of the approaching candles turned Her robes into a diaphanous glimmer. Gamelyn crossed himself, couldn't help one last query: *But Robyn is. . . well?*

No one who makes enemies is ever truly well, My own. But Our pwca *continually sets Fateful threads astir, aye? Even now.*

"She bides beautiful, does She not?"

Gamelyn turned, ready to rebuke one who would disturb another's meditations, but found his protest withering. The old blind monk to whom Robyn had taken such a shine—Brother Cadog, it was—had stopped just behind Gamelyn's kneeling form, peering up at the altar as if he could actually see it.

"I'm sorry, Brother Templar," the accompanying monk said as Gamelyn rose. "He cannot help it, he often makes no—"

"'I am being dark but lovely, o ye daughters of Jerusalem'," old Cadog quoted, still peering at the altar . . . nay, at the Lady, in truth, who was returning his adoring gaze with an affectionate smile. "'Like to the tents of Kedar, the curtains of Solomon'." He reached out, made a remarkably unerring grasp of Gamelyn's shoulder. "You are doing well with your homage, Templar. She is bestowing the brightest of blessings upon you: Her loveliness."

The other heaved an exasperated sigh and started to pull Cadog away. A frosty glare from Gamelyn stopped the younger monk in his tracks.

"She has indeed, Brother." Gamelyn reached upward and gave a gentle squeeze of the old monk's parchment-dry hand. "I thank you for sharing your place with me."

"Will you then be sharing Compline with us?"

"Alas, Brother. I fear our wandering *Confanonier* is not fit for Holy Communion at this time."

And good *God,* but the man's talent of slithering up unnoticed was not one that gave Gamelyn any comfort. They all turned as the voice filled the nave, even the blind monk. A spray of dawn outside the south door backlit the white-clad silhouette gliding inward.

"After confessional," de Birkin assured, with grave genuflection to the altar, "Brother Guy will be able to join your Offices with a clean heart."

It seemed de Birkin was blinder than the old monk. He showed no comprehension of the Mother's presence, turning to Gamelyn and resting a hand upon his forearm. At first all but imperceptible, the grip settled down and fixed, went heavy.

"Come, Templar." Neither did the voice bode any good. "We have much to discuss."

The Lady's gaze flickered across Gamelyn's, a warning. The monks began adorning the altar with more candles, banishing Her once again to shadow.

Robyn is to the green Wode gone. . .

The arrow loosed with a lovely, familiar twang. Piercing upward-flung cloth through the cross upon its plain brown breast, the tabard was pinned, quivering, to a great oak.

Rather childish, mayhap. But now Robyn could *breathe,* the morning mists soughing against layers of linen and skin as he left both oak and borrowed tabard behind.

Robyn is to the green Wode gone.

A half memory not his own, the words nevertheless within his senses like some quipped tune that Queen Eleanor's minstrel Alundel would sing.

Trouvère, Gamelyn's voice chided. Another memory, this sweet-fair, and his own.

Robyn smirked, told it *Whats'mever.*

Aye, well, rather to green Wode gone than spend one more night in the reeking, stale air of siege and greedy men. John would look after Gamelyn—none better, at present, including himself—and Robyn let the rue of that settle as well, into an ache he could do nowt about now.

Kept running, the Arrow humming a broken descant in his quiver.

He'd not be careless again, in fact had thought to consign it to the flame. But that were best done with Marion and Gamelyn at his side, to ground the power properly. It held their magic, as well, after all.

But not possible, not now.

Mayhap never. It snuck in, petulant. He rounded on it, throttled it until it slunk back into the shadows. Gamelyn would have been right proud of him . . . which just brassed Robyn off all the more.

"We'll have this out later, we will," he muttered, all the while realising it wasn't the first time he'd so sworn.

First, to tend to this. Take the Arrow and see it safe. A sacrifice to elder powers, beyond reach of the new.

Robyn knew exactly the proper place for such.

Aelwyn was able for the travel but not to sit a horse. The Turcopole and Much came to another agreement: they would transport some supplies to the siege, via a cart in which Aelwyn and the children could ride.

The rest of her family seemed numb rather than sorrowful. Mayhap it was relief. Mayhap such things were so common—families torn apart at a lord's whim—that they'd learned protest was fruitless.

Whatever it was, it seemed to convince the men of the rights of such a thing. They'd little family save each other; to let one of their own go without some sort of protest was, as Will growled beneath his breath, "Sodding unnatural."

A few hours of rest were managed in a stable north of Newark. Marion fell asleep the moment she lay down, woke to sunlight crawling through the eastern doors, the horses nickering as Gilbert fed them, Aelwyn and the little ones curled up on one side, and the hard-warm pillow of Much on the other.

And after? It was proper good to be riding across the dawn-misted fields, towards the prospect of a visit to Hathersage and the whole of spring and summer lying before them. All of them, all together.

⟨♪⟩

"Ignosce mihi, Pater, quia peccavi. . ." The rote, opening words of the confessional trailed away, distracted, as a soft infiltration of voices began to waft through the stones of All Hallows.

Even here, within the closed doors of the Chapter House, morning-tide prayers could be heard.

Gamelyn bathed in the distraction for a few soothing breaths. He knelt, cloak pooling like black water upon the well-swept flooring. Lit by only a few rushlights, the Chapter House was nigh dark and all but deserted—save for himself and the Master Procurator of England.

Seated in a wide-backed chair, de Birkin was only partially attentive. One gloved hand rose, on occasion, to linger near his throat. Gamelyn thought he saw a mark there, as if the blade had slipped whilst shaving. When de Birkin caught his notice and held it with a severe frown, Gamelyn dipped his head farther, finished the remainder of the prelude to confession. And when de Birkin made no response—again, that hand to his throat whilst he gazed into air—Gamelyn made soft protest.

"Master. It is my right to open confessional."

"Indeed it is." De Birkin's agreement seemed almost lazy. "However, I would wager there are . . . certain subjects, yes? Ones that cannot be addressed in common gathering. You have often confessed to Hubert alone; so he has told me."

And I want Hubert here now.

De Birkin guessed at the silent plea. "Pride, Templar. Hubert has other things to attend than you."

"Could not the same be said of you, Master?"

The laugh came soft, yet annoyance ran beneath, a chill stream pushing at top ice. "To risk inflating what pride you possess all the more, Templar . . . you have become one of my priorities."

Gamelyn blinked and peered upward, wary.

"There are things we must speak of, you and I, that neither of us would wish to become common knowledge. Not yet. And not"—a pause, another absent rub at his throat— "before those unprepared to see the Great Work."

The Great Work. A phrase not oft used in the presence of those unsworn to the Inner Temple. True, once Hubert had thought to make Gamelyn privy to the mysteries that hummed and shivered at the Temple's heart. Both of them had been disappointed with failure—the magicks had failed to seat themselves within what should have been a puissant host—but in Gamelyn, discontent had also contained a faint taste of relief.

And now he knew why. Better to never know his power than let it play out, turn into nightmare. Better to . . . *set upon twisting tynged's tail,* no matter a path strewn with obstacles.

De Birkin lurched forward in his chair, wroth with some intention. "Your defiance is of use to us, Templar. But have no doubt: there are things—*important* things—to consider." It turned coaxing. "You have been overlong away from us, prey to wild influences. Your soul is torn, troubled—do you think I do not see it? I understand you better than you would choose to believe, Guy."

My name is. . .

Gamelyn? Is it, really?

"So make your confession, here to me. Let loose of what we both know lingers there, and then"—a smile, no less fierce or furious—"we can speak openly, one adept to another, of many things."

Gamelyn. Yet 'twas Guy who sloughed a sideways gaze at his Master, chary. Considering.

One adept to another...?

"I confess," de Birkin prompted.

The first words were hesitant, slow in coming. Unwilling to speak to anything that would betray his time in the Wode. Yet Gamelyn needn't have worried; what came instead was of here and now.

Pride, of course. Anger. Envy. *Avarice.* All of it swelling upward, loosed in a language impressed upon him from boyhood's pious innocence: that of confessional.

All of it centred upon a wish he'd thought well buried, unreachable. The wish made itself plain. The fundamental reasonings, thank the God of his fathers, remained obscured akin to everything else pertaining of Robyn, Marion, and the Wode.

Why, he wasn't sure. He was merely grateful.

De Birkin was silent for some moments after. Never willing to meet any gaze after the rawness of confessional, Gamelyn slid a scant glance upward. Seemingly de Birkin had forgotten the strange mark upon his neck; his face was lifted towards the high window, where both monks' prayers and morning light flooded inward, but his eyes were closed and both hands clasped.

The mark looked more a burn, newly inflicted. It looked like an *arrowhead.*

"De Lacy said as much; that you had reclaimed your name and birthright upon the body of your brother, in holy combat. I have no doubt he told the Queen the same. Which explains much." The pale eyes opened. "You want what your brother has. That is evident . . . and not outside our purposes at present. But what of his woman? His children?"

Gamelyn frowned. "I have no wish to—"

De Birkin made a sharp, silencing gesture. "I didn't mean your brother's wife or children. I meant your own desires, ones you might not have so much as considered before now. Particularly since you have lived with Pagans these past months, who, no matter their other . . . abilities"— another twitch of hand towards that mark, quickly aborted—"have the morals of stoats. You must remember your role, here, and why we allow you to reach beneath yourself in this case. For instance, I know you've lain with the outlaw, yet you make no confession of lust."

He hadn't. It surprised Gamelyn, found him reaching inward for some sort of explanation.

Guy gave one: *Because he knows. He sanctioned it, for the purpose he would see wrought.*

Nay, not that.

Mayhap, then, you no longer believe in the sin. Mayhap there is nothing to confess.

The realisation spilled sudden heat behind Gamelyn's eyes. *I do not. Believe. It is. . . no. . . sin.*

"Is it truly lust," Gamelyn murmured, closing his eyes to hide the glimmer there, "when you have sanctioned it, my Master?"

Silence, de Birkin no doubt contemplating the sincerity of the statement. "And the woman?"

Gamelyn opened his eyes, frowning.

"The forest woman. I've no doubts that one, given the ways of her kind and sex, would gladly wrest your oaths from you."

This time the fury was not de Birkin's. And once again it was Guy, not Gamelyn, who sublimated it with practiced, nigh-cavalier ease. "Another role, Master, to be played. Marion is part of this as surely as her brother."

A huff. "Yes, well, she has some import to them, and so, therefore, in our game. Yet you must take care, *Templier,* that a role does not subsume what you *are.*"

And what—the Lady flickered into view beyond de Birkin's cloaked right shoulder, dark and dressed in stars—*are you, Gamelyn? Who are you?*

He gritted his teeth, would not meet her gaze.

"Brother Guy, heed me. You wear the black so as to not be hampered by the same strictures as those of us who wear the white, but mind this: should I offer the hand of the Inner Temple, and should you take it?" De Birkin leaned closer, their noses almost touching. "You will wear the white of purity, and take within yourself the *albedo* of the innermost Truths. There will be vows left in dust, but others unbreakable. Sacrifices you cannot yet imagine. So." He settled back in his chair. "Have you anything further to confess?"

Again, it was Guy who looked his Master in the eye and said, wooden, "I have not."

De Birkin considered him for several long breaths. Obviously he was satisfied with what he saw, for he made the sign of the cross between them. "You will go to the church after Matins and pray for Christ's compassion for one hour, prostrate upon the floor. For the next fortnight, you will do this, wherever you are—in penance for your sins and to remember your place. Your *place*, Templar. While worldly desires are useful in our work, this overwhelming . . . hunger that plagues you must be sublimated into our work. *Dominus noster Jesu Christus te absolvat. . ."*

Murmuring the rest of the phrase, once the final *Amen* was said between them, Gamelyn began to rise.

"You are not yet dismissed, Templar." It was curt. "Have you no curiosity about what I mentioned earlier?"

"I am but a servant to my Order." Gamelyn lowered his head. "I am allowed no curiosity; only the knowledge that when time is met, I will be told of . . ."

More laughter made him trail off and look up.

"Good Christ, man, but you are indeed formidable for one so young." De Birkin was still chuckling. Until he wasn't. He bent forward. "You don't, however, fool me. You keep many things close, yet I saw the flare of avarice in your eyes when I mentioned the Inner Temple. I won't forget it, believe me. And"—de Birkin stood—"neither will you. After all, what would you give? What would you do—what have you already done—for the *beauséant?*"

Beauséant. To be *whole.*

It burrowed a small fissure into Gamelyn's heart, left it seeping.

"When that time is, indeed, met, I will hold out my hand. I myself will lead you through the portals of the Inner Temple. Together we will break open the barriers that have kept you small, and fragile. We will make you . . . *whole.*"

"And what price," Gamelyn said, hoarse, "will you ask in return?"

"Merely one to which you have already agreed." De Birkin leaned forward. "You will bring me the forest cult, *Confanonier.*"

Gamelyn did not let himself react even with a quickening of breath.

"As things stand, you are its greatest weakness, are you not? This role you are destined to play, noble-born sorcerer against the forgotten magics of the druids? Grasp it. You shall not weaken. You will meet this outcome, never fear."

Every nerve Gamelyn possessed drew up, wary of exposure... but shivered calmer as de Birkin continued.

"Whatever you must do, we will cleanse you of it, bring you inward. My dear Brother, do you not see the dark humour in it? You *are* the future of this cult, more so than a peasant whose magic is strong but ungovernable. Destined, like his druidic forebears, to fade. To fail."

Even a double tongue can speak some *truths,* the Lady whispered. *The trine of all worlds must be made whole. So We say, but as you do not listen to Us, mayhap you will listen to him.*

Gamelyn had no chance to turn away. He was listening. O aye, and he was.

You must be what you are. She faded, but her Voice remained, piercing-soft. *You must be what this blind sorcerer cannot begin to imagine, and claim* all *of what you are.*

"Are you hearing me, Brother?"

Tongue between teeth—a small nip, just the reminder of where he was and before whom he knelt—and Gamelyn raised his gaze, met and matched de Birkin's. Said, level-soft, "I hear you."

"Then I charge you to obedience, Templar. You have had your little lark in Sherwood, and your slack rope, and your . . . time. Take heart in that I give you even more rope, albeit with curb and spurs. You will have"—a sour smirk, and de Birkin's hand made another inexplicable rise to his throat—"a choice."

Gamelyn did not drop his gaze or so much as twitch.

"Bring this powerful knowledge to us, however it must be done. Or I myself will charge you to see it destroyed."

- XIV -

The impulse to flee de Birkin's presence was the ultimate humiliation.

Gamelyn didn't give in to it. Each step was careful and measured as he walked out into the clear morn towards All Hallows' stable block. He eschewed two squires' assistance, saddled and bridled his horse with much the same precision, led him outward, and swung up into the saddle.

Flight impulse still raged as he rode from the grounds, threatening ruin and wreckage: damn them all, this time, turn Falcon's nose for the green Wode, and ride like hell.

You would scuttle away like a whipped cur, when the goal looms this close? Guy scoffed.

Falcon danced, every other stride a small *levade*. Gamelyn peered at his hands, taut and shaking upon the reins. Considered his seat, tense-hunched, with the muscles of his thighs sprung outward like iron bands.

Instead took a deep breath and spun the bay stallion on his haunches, heading for the white-and-umber carapace of Blyth Castle at a round gallop.

"*Neither* of 'em here," Much said, quiet, to Marion. "Nor together."

They'd arrived at the caverns earlier than they'd planned, after a night ride beneath the waxing moon to beat a rain-heavy bank of clouds, and despite giving a wide berth to the gathered troops around Blyth. The sun was rising over the treetops into a lovely, still midmorning.

Much had called her over as the others were settling in. His mount had taken a misstep over the creek not a mile distant, going more short the closer they'd come to camp. There was heat in the right tendon, and the oil with which Marion massaged gave some relief; the gelding was relaxed, nigh dozing. It soothed Marion as well, warming chill fingers and clearing her sinuses. Much, however, seemed distinctly on edge. It wasn't just for her wortwife skills that he had drawn her close. He was perfectly capable of seeing to the horse.

"I en't liking this," he further confirmed her suspicions. "Johnny's . . . well. Uneasy, en't he?"

Marion had to admit to that, though John was doing a good job of hiding it—mostly amidst a quickly cobbled challenge of thrown daggers involving three leather clouts, Will, and Gilbert. The others were egging them on, plainly unworried. Robyn was away at the god's behest, no explanations offered or needed. And their newest companion was, along with her two children, taking a nap towards the back of the caverns. Aelwyn was exhausted from the journey, and no wonder. Marion had dosed both mam and bairns—valerian warmed in cider—to ensure it.

Not that she was altogether worried about Robyn. Gamelyn, on the other hand . . .

"I think best I go on t' camp right away. On me own," Much clarified when Marion started to speak. "I know we were talking 'bout waiting 'til after we'd all had a bite, but that en't such a fine idea now. T' siege done, yet milord en't returned, and he would t' least sent word by John if he were ordered on. So I'll be off and find 'im, take the horses and supplies. The quicker I go, the quicker we know, aye?"

As much as she didn't like it, he was right. She liked her own constraints even less, but her knowledge of armed camps was nonexistent even did she attempt dressing as a lad. The latter in particular meant more supplies than she had access to at present, a plain risk when one was back to a healthy weight and blessed with an abundance of feminine attributes. A smirk twitched Marion's lip, almost immediately vanished. While Much certainly fancied the attributes, he wouldn't appreciate her taking the risk. That he realised the dangers to a woman in a siege camp, Marion didn't question for a heartbeat.

"This lad wain't be up for even t' cart tail's pace," she agreed, running a final hand up and down the gelding's leg; with a grateful sigh, the horse nuzzled at her curls. "I'll poultice him well and have one of the lads take him slow when he's able."

Much nodded and started to turn away.

She rose, halting him with a hand on his chest, then a kiss, and lingered at his ear to whisper, "Just find him."

"Aye." Much took her hand with his own, kissed it. "That I will."

"Milord?"

The voice was familiar. *Beloved,* some corner of his mind acknowledged. Of thisnow, thisworld.

He wasn't sure he wanted anything to do with it.

"Milord. Gamelyn. Please."

A light hand to the small of his back juddered him, warm and *real.*

"T' priest says you've been locked in chapel here since last bells . . . Faith, look t' you—you're like ice!"

Two hands, now, and grey light an assault against Gamelyn's eyes. It seemed the doors had been flung open, letting in sun and warmth whilst the chill of hard and musty earth seeped, lethargic, through clothes and skin and down to bone.

And he remembered. He'd come here, to the chapel Queen Eleanor had dowered and his father had seen finished, scarce knowing what he'd intended until he did it: first his legs wobbling to kneel, then falling forward on his hands, then sinking further, stretching out, to prostate himself upon the floor. His assigned penance, of course. To what? For what?

It had proven of little significance. All that mattered was the lapse of mind into a blank and blessed void. No tanglings of *tynged,* no steadily being herded, then backed and pinned against an unassailable wall made of blood and betrayal and impossible choices. No sense of time's passing, no alternative stumble and *slip* into some endless, treacherous otherworld.

Only silence, earthbound yet illimitable. Lovely, *lovely* distance . . . even from the aloof and predatory not-self lurking just behind his own eyes.

Gamelyn wished he could stay there. Instead he thought to put his palms beneath his shoulders and rise. It remained mere thought. He could scarce move.

Much hauled him upward and folded him into the solid, searing breadth of his own body. "What's this all about, now?" A chide, and a shake, and all Gamelyn could mumble in return was:

"God, but you're warm."

Much chuckled. "Well, my arse is feeling it—this floor's bloody ice, and you lying spatchcock on 't . . . " Unsaid was *You daft git;* Gamelyn heard it nonetheless. "How did ye contrive t' fall asleep, somehow, or were you away wit' . . . " Again, unfinished, Much unwilling to whisper even a hint of green Wode magics beneath the weight of stone church confines.

Instead he gave Gamelyn another shake, this one gentler. "Well, no more t' now. Commander Hubert, he were looking for you. I said I'd come and find you. Several of our Brothers said they'd seen you come in here; then the priest were going on about how there was some Templar sergeant in his nave, all prostrate and praying nonstop, like—"

"How long did you say?" It creaked, rusty and frost-rimed, and Gamelyn allowed Much to assist him upward to stand. It was necessary; he was stiff, his limbs uncooperative. Moreover, the light had faded from grey morning drifting through the windows to a golden slant of post noontide. *Did I linger so long?* A strange, panicky thought. *Was it the otherworld, after all? Is it . . . mayhap . . . kinder?*

We both know better than that, Guy drawled.

Gamelyn gave a shiver, shook his head to clear his thoughts. "How did you . . . when did you return? Did it go well, towards Bruer?"

Much didn't answer immediately, merely began half pushing, half dragging him towards the library . . . only, Gamelyn realised as they entered, it wasn't a library any longer. The shelves that once had cradled Brother Dolfin's immense and varied collection were all but empty, the eastmost one fashioned into a small, plain altar, and the south side replaced with a cot. A fire had been laid in a tiny, central hearth.

The priest, Much had said. His cell.

Much lowered Gamelyn to a bench beside the fire, shrugged from his own cloak and wound it, warm-snug, about Gamelyn's shoulders, then started the business of feeding the fire hotter.

"Aye, nowt but a few hitches, easily mended. Bruer sent me with provisions and extra horses . . . and 'twere a good thing, wit' everyone here all sixes and sevens, sayin' King Richard's on march for Nottingham . . . aye, and there you are, Father. How proper thoughtful of you."

Gamelyn looked up to see a black-clad priest brandishing a small and steaming pot. As if prodded by the reminder, his teeth started to chatter.

"Prayer and penance is all well and good," the priest chided, "but you're a distinct shade of blue, Brother Templar. Proper lucky, you are, to have an attentive paxman."

"I know it." Gamelyn flashed a smile at Much, transferred it to the priest as he accepted the drinking pot. "Thank you, Father."

"Aye, well. I'll be in t' vestry, should you've need." The priest gave him another stern look, then exited.

Mulled wine. Gamelyn inhaled the steam, warming his hands.

Much sat on the bench, scooted close, and threw an arm about him. Gamelyn leaned in; Much was warmer than the wine, even.

"You're back from Bruer. And Marion? John, and . . . Are the others all at the caverns, then? Is Robyn . . . ?" Gamelyn paused. The words came slow and his thoughts more so, as if his brain were only now thawing out. "Hubert asked for me." Gamelyn started to rise—well, attempted, anyway. His brain was quicker than his body; the latter refused to budge.

"Wup!" Much rescued the pot just before it wobbled from clumsy fingers. "Nay, you sit, y' hear? Drink that lot down and I'll go tell Commander Hubert where you are. Might be a short while. Like I said, everything's proper upskelled hereabouts, packing up. Making ready to move out."

It was more than a short while.

Gamelyn warmed himself by the priest's fire enough to please Much, and even accepted another cup of wine before rising to make his way back into the darkening chapel. The priest, though relieved to have his own place back, was touched by Gamelyn's very sincere thanks.

He was merely polite, however, when Gamelyn offered to find some content for those naked shelves. Likely couldn't read, Gamelyn realised as the connecting door to the chapel shut between them. Once again he thought longingly of the haven where his boyhood confessor had kept a hoard of precious handwritten manuscripts and books. Dolfin's collection had been one fit to inspire a young lad's longings of scholarship at Ely.

A foolish young lad, who dreamt of the unattainable. If all transpires, we will make our own library. Or request Brother Dolfin to ply his work here, if. . .

Nay, he'd no longer the luxury of *if.* There could be only *when.*

He turned away. The remainder of the chapel seemed made of shadows, only here and there pierced by shafts of sunlight. Lazy and uncountable motes drifted towards the altar, as if seeking absolution.

Don't we all? And crave penance to dispel the unsurety. Ah, but what would we would do without the lure and vigour of it?

Thankfully the voice wasn't Hers. The Lady wasn't here. Not that he could sense, anyway. He was afraid to wonder why.

Guy continued, more pragmatic. *Mayhap the hymns of All Hallows hold Her ransom. Well. Better silence than Her prying, wondering, sifting thoughts. If She finds out—in fact, if anyone knows— 'twill spoil everything. There is no doubt what must be done, yes?*

Yes. There was no longer any doubt of what must be done.

The while turned even longer. Gamelyn contemplated going to find Hubert himself, considered it was more likely they'd just miss each other. Hubert would make time as he could; 'twas Gamelyn's duty to wait.

There were but several flickers of light within the dark chapel, and those wafting small. The Lady's altar was bathed in a small brace of lit candles, their appeals left to gutter in wax-melt. Gamelyn ended up lighting a taper from one of Her guttering candles—with proper obeisance, of course—with which to fire several torches in their holders. Sparks and oily smoke trailed up into the roof. Soot had layered telltales of many such lightings, of course, but the light also spilled over clean walls and freshened scrollwork. For all that Blyth's walls were crumbling, the chapel's interior had been well kept. Particularly the three tombs beside his mother's altar against the north wall, all but one of their candles guttered . . .

Three?

Gamelyn frowned, padded over.

This is why you haven't come before. It does no good to look back.

Be silent, he told Guy.

His father's effigy was immediately recognisable: the straight, broad nose and brow, the sword that had accompanied him on an earlier Crusade placed in stone hands. Gamelyn reached out in the faint flicker of light to trace first the sword, then, tentative, his father's face.

The next cairn inspired none of that tenderness. Gamelyn crossed his arms, inspecting his eldest brother's visage with an expression more at home upon a viper that, having bitten, contemplated its prey's death throes. Oddly enough, Gamelyn had no satisfaction in knowing he himself had put Johan there—and in honourable combat. There was . . . nothing.

It left him ill prepared for the next one. He'd thought a tomb had been erected for their mother, or her remains moved from Huntingdon to lie here beside her husband. But there was no effigy of the tall, slender woman who'd bequeathed so much of her appearance to her youngest son.

This was merely of smooth stone, incised with the Templar cross.

Amidst the Latin words of benediction was carved the name *Gamelyn.*

He mouthed, then murmured it nigh silent. As if it were unfamiliar. Foreign.

Most believe Gamelyn Boundys never returned from the Holy Land.

I believe. A soft breath against his nape. *I believe he has.* So, She was here, albeit so faint.

"Mayhap," he whispered back, tracing the lines of the cross. "Mayhap not." His eyes flickered, then held to the figure gracing the Lady's alcove. So small. So pale, and demure.

So unlike the reality.

Reality? This with a roll of eyes upon which Robyn would have made some mention.

He should indeed contrive to have the dark Madonna freed

from Worksop and brought here, where she would be honoured, not chained.

And *God*, but he missed Robyn.

Not now. Chiding. Less than patient with such weakness.

Footsteps tapped upon the entry stones. A slight pause, an intake of breath; a sigh, almost, definitely a murmur.

Gamelyn turned, fully prepared to see Much, mayhap with Hubert.

It was Alais. "They said you were here."

"They." It was flat.

Meeting his eyes, she came forward. Her folded hands betrayed a tiny, insistent twist. Her voice, too, denied outward composure. "I must speak with you."

It somehow scraped at every remaining nerve Gamelyn possessed.

Thankfully, Guy was not so burdened. "My lady." Frosty, allowing no nonsense. "It is not seemly that we are here, alone."

"In a chapel?" she retorted and kept walking. "Our patron the revered and holy Nicholas watches over children, after all. What better place to see to the fate of mine?"

It required no answer, so he gave none, merely watched her come to stand before him.

His silence seemed to put her on the defence. "Or is a tenant not allowed to query her new overlord's intent? Mayhap my lord Templar has no time for a mere woman despite that she is his kin?"

A tiny smile begged for admittance and was refused. Aye, but Alais had always been stone beneath sleek-soft feathers.

"My time is limited, as I await my Commander's pleasure, my lady. And I must remind you, I've no kin save my Temple Brethren."

"Then surely I am no threat to you. Unless your conscience decrees otherwise."

"Ah." Guy was in rare form, thank God. "But it is claimed Templars have no conscience."

"I'm hoping you can prove those claims wrong." Her chin gave a telltale quiver.

Ever a woman's tactic. Guy sighed and, with a roll of eyes, started to turn away.

"Gamelyn, you must hear me out."

"That is not my name."

It is.

Nay, it isn't. In this place and time, it is a luxury we can no longer afford.

"It is the name your mother gave you!" Alais countered. "*There!*" She flung a hand over towards the three effigies.

"A name," he countered, almost gentle, "upon a cairn."

Hands going to her breast, Alais started to speak, then just as obviously couldn't. Her eyes glittered in the dim.

Say nothing, Guy counselled. *Turn away, now.*

Instead he spoke. "I would have solitude for my prayers, my lady. But I imagine you shan't give it to me until you say what it is you want."

Alais' eyes brimmed over, and she started to reach for his sleeve. Eyeing the cross upon his tabard, she aborted the gesture just in time and instead knelt, bringing her clasped hands to her chin.

"Show mercy, my lord Templar."

"Get up," he told her, and thought: *Mercy?*

She remained where she was. "I plead with you, not for myself, but my children. For my husb—"

"You've no need to plead anything. I have been ordered by my Commander to see to the welfare of Blyth and Tickhill, and so I sha—"

"I have come to ask this boon, as I am presently your vassal and my husband is a captive through no fault of his own!"

"You give me too much power, my lady. His fate is not mine to decide, but the King's."

"But you could speak to your superiors, plead with them for clemency."

"Could I, then?"

"They would listen to you. Your Commander holds you in respect. Even that bloody bishop—" Alais seemed to remember she was reviling a holy personage within church walls, and took hold of her temper. "Please. Surely they will listen to you. My lord Templar, I fear they will hang him as a traitor."

"Unlikely."

"But he is a prisoner."

"Yes."

"Then you must help him!"

"Must I?"

"He is your *brother!*" It rang into the chapel, hung, and echoed.

The door to the priest's cell swung open, and the priest started outward with a querying frown. Gamelyn merely turned and peered at him. The priest halted, closed his mouth, backed the way he'd come, and shut the door.

"So." Gamelyn turned the same gaze upon Alais. Not that it did a damned bit of good. "If, as you wish, claims of . . . *amor fraternel* should hold, then mayhap you should thank God and St. Nicholas I've no wish to exhibit the same as I was shown."

"Said," Alais countered, her eyes meeting his and scorn rippling her voice, "just like your eldest brother. May God save him—for none else would likely bother—but Johan had nothing in his heart but the anger of indictment, sated only by grasping what power he could and lashing out in some ridiculous settling of imaginary scores!"

"I am altogether aware," Gamelyn retorted, deathly quiet, "of Johan's deficiencies. But neither was Johan the one to bind me like a rabid dog in my own home. Or is that merely another . . . ah . . . *imaginary* grievance?"

"Otho did as Johan bade him—"

"Aye, always."

"—and you know why he did. Particularly then. He'd no choice, Gamelyn; you were bewitched!"

"I was in *pain!*" It burst from him and, when more threatened, 'twas Guy who quelled the spill of words, choking them into a hard, brutal knot that swelled midbreast and burned.

Shut up, you bloody fool—for Christ's sake, shut up!

And *God*, but this ache was welcome; a molten core stoked altogether suitable for forging iron.

Alais, thank the Lady, was too caught in her own conflict to so much as ken his. "Then you understand what I'm feeling. I *beg* you, my lord. Please. Speak for my husband, ask the King's grace." She looked up, tears spilling silver upon pale cheeks. "Gamelyn, you must believe me. Otho has only ever meant to do what's right. With you. With Blyth. With everything."

"Right," he repeated, soft. "So *many* things, done beneath a convenient concept. So many mistaken, ludicrous, cruel, and horrible things. What is right, after all? Or truth?"

She tried to hold his eyes, couldn't.

He reached down, with two fingers tipped her face back to meet his. Said, neither penitent nor triumphant, "Believe this truth at least, my lady. The young man you knew is no longer here. I can do nothing, as I will not be going to meet the King. Neither is it my place to suggest to my betters where their duty or consciences lie. Your husband certainly does not need *me* to aid him in what he always has excelled: seeing to the security of his own complacencies."

Alais started to protest. He shook his head, laid those two fingers across her mouth.

"My charge has been laid here, and I will do it. Just as you will do yours. I shall see the castle secured and the inhabitants held safe, upon the honour of my Order and oaths. You shall keep yourself and your children in your place, see to the householding with those keys at your belt, and have the wherewithal and grace to leave . . . me . . . *be.*"

He loosed her, straightened, and turned away.

Nothing, at first. A heavy rustle of skirts finally signalled her rising, but still she stood waiting. He didn't turn, kept silent.

Surely she wasn't obstinate enough to stay there forever.

Fortunate salvation came in a familiar tread upon the step. To this Gamelyn did turn, expectant.

"I've brought some food, milord, and found a place to eat along the wall. Himself the Comman . . . " Much indeed had a tray piled with victuals, but went silent as he espied Alais.

Hubert tailed him. His meander turned a bit more purposeful as he peered first at Gamelyn, then Alais.

She had already turned away, making a halfhearted curtsey. "My lords," she said and sped down the aisle—but not without a last glance towards Gamelyn that said *We aren't done with this.*

To which Guy merely sneered. *So certain, are you?*

Hubert slid around her departure like water. An overburdened Much gave hasty way, and Alais slipped through the doors, out of sight.

"What did the woman want?" Hubert drew closer, a concerned frown twitching at his brow.

"Nothing," Gamelyn said, "that I could give."

"There have been, ah, some changes to our plans."

Amidst scraping his bowl with a hunk of bread, Gamelyn paused.

Hubert motioned him to keep on, allowing an eager villein to top off his mug of ale.

True to Much's assurance, they'd been made welcome at one of several cotters' fires along the wall just south of the chapel. The woman had bustled her children to the next cot, while the man had promised more ale; proper stuff, he boasted, that his wife brewed herself. Of course, Hubert's statement encouraged Gamelyn to finish up and pass the bowl to Much, who in turn was relieved of it by the ale-brewing wife. The children seen to, she lingered in the back, making it her business to see the Templars properly cared for. The man also hovered, a small keg under one arm, with which he topped off everyone's drink as needed.

"Changes?" Gamelyn washed down the last of his bread with the admittedly excellent ale, and brushed foam from his moustache.

"Indeed. Word came to Durham around noontide, via messenger." Hubert drew a small roll of parchment from inside his tabard.

Gamelyn accepted the offering, opened it, and scanned the quick-penned Latin. He blinked, lowered the parchment to frown at Hubert, then read it again, this time much slower.

"As Much no doubt told you, we're making preparations to leave. Stephen is packing your things. It was preferable to station you here, with the castle, *non?* But one does not gainsay a queen." Hubert seemed unruffled. "In truth, we should have expected it."

Expectations. Gamelyn possessed those, no question, but had imagined any royal promise of reciprocity, if it came, to proceed through less . . . direct channels.

He gave one more silent perusal of the missive. Weighted at the bottom with the Archbishop of Canterbury's seal, it held several requests, actually, mostly regarding the dispensation of supplies and armed men towards Nottingham—but the paragraph before the last held his attention:

. . .those insubordinate in, and responsible for, stewardship of the honour of Tickhill are commanded brought to Nottingham, under guard, to plead their case upon the King's pleasure and be subjected to what justice He shall deem appropriate.

In particular, the Queen Mother has Herself demanded the attendance and presence of several personages, to wit: Guy de Gisbourne, Brother Confanonier *to Temple Hirst, as well as the persons known as Robyn Hode, and his sister, the maid Marion, both of Sherwood Forest, the latter two who are outlawed but shall be given leave to approach Nottingham without penalty, by the Queen's grace and beneath the protection of the Templar Order.*

As to the dispensation of. . .

Gamelyn stopped reading and again slid his eyes upward to meet Hubert's.

Hubert nodded. He seemed quite unperturbed.

With a frown, Gamelyn read the missive again. A shower of sparks nested ash over this third reading; one of the cottars was rather overzealously tending the fire.

"It is my understanding that we, ah, have a small setback," Hubert ventured, peering into the rising flames with a sip from his own pot. "The *dryw ardhu* reclaimed what was his, to our Master's consternation. And satisfaction, truth be known. Wild Robyn has proven his mettle, but in the doing has vanished. Back into his forest, one presumes." A sudden grin. "I do hope your paxman can be convinced to locate him for us, my *Confanonier.* After all"—the grin widened, including Much as well as the cottars—"the Queen Mother has demanded it!"

The lake was . . . *alive,* all dressed in moon and stars, with just a ruffle of breeze to send dancing the gleaming mirror of its surface.

Sacred to both Lord and Lady, this was nevertheless Her place. No matter the support She had granted him within the stones of All Hallows, Robyn knew Barrow Mere was not a place he should heedlessly tread.

So he laid his quiver and bow upon the bank, sent a breath of soft appeal into the night and across the clearing. Waited.

If it was not rejected, neither was it approved.

Well, all right, then. He'd offer more.

Sketching invocations with utmost care, Robyn made his case, following each ancient form with an unhurried gravity that would have wrung a grunt of approval from his mentor Cernun, long gone to the Lady's grace. He acknowledged each of the trees circling the Mere—from the birch and rowan guarding the trail in, to the towering holly that willingly relinquished a sharp-edged sprig, to the willow trailing spring green and ripples in the water's edge, and all the ones between. Thirteen had been planted here, by the *dryw* and for the Lady, and each one he gave their due.

Robyn came last to the oak. "Devil's Oak," those villeins had misnamed it, but the only devils in England were ones as the Church had dreamed up. 'Twas the Hunter's Oak, this, sacred to the Horned Lord and set apart as guardian to the Mere, the one place in this vale of Her magic that was unabashedly male. At that, the goddess's ivy twined all through the wide-sprung branches. Robyn caressed a vine of newly furled spring leaves, let his hand trail across thick, mossy bark, then bestowed a like touch to each of the skulls girdling the oak's trunk. Ancient or recent, he'd a blessing-breath for each: *coom by again, gentler the next.*

Another gesture twined the holly sprig amidst oak and ivy, and this breath more an asking than any Telling. Robyn stood there, hearing only the beat of his heart and the wish of his blood, letting the last of the breath out in a tiny, quavering sigh. Then he turned from the tree to face the Mere, drawing the Arrow from his quiver. Damp earth gave as he knelt. The broadhead that had so burnt that head-blind sorcerer nestled in his hand, cool and familiar. Robyn turned it on its edge, whispered another grave run of syllables and, just as deliberate, carved a thin line of crimson across the heel of his palm.

He had expected the backwash of magic a King's blood would raise in such a place. Unexpected, however, was the heavy swell of not-sound roaring upward, from heels to head and back again. It would have toppled him, had he not been kneeling. Robyn reeled, let it wash through him without surrendering what was his, rightful and earned.

It tested him, nonetheless. Tiny sparks lit the night—fireflies where there should be none, thisnow and time of year. The sound of weighted wings, and a long, quavering howl that could have been a wolf's . . . or might have been the *baen si* from the western shores . . . but was undoubtedly the presence of ancestors, blood and bone and soul long given to this Mere, protected and protection.

Amidst it all Robyn knelt, wondering yet undeniable. Soon the presences granted him what grace and right he held. They subsided, tens of great unwinking eyes and shadows beneath the holly across the Mere.

The Barrow Folk, ancestors, spirits, the vengeance of the Wild Hunt personified, denizens of the otherworlds banished from thisworld . . . all of it or not even close, there were many names for them. Robyn remembered the Wodewose Girl upon the altar of All Hallows, proof of their cunning-right more and more taking form in thisworld, and gave due power of what name he knew.

"Hail, O fae," he whispered, and raised the thrice-blooded Arrow into the night.

Wings stilled. Shadows hung, waiting. Eyes followed the gesture, rapt.

"M' magic is yours, as much as me own," he whispered to Them. "I have called you to ask this much: keep it safe until I return for 't."

A rustle, then a sough of breath rippling across the Mere. Longing. Acceptance.

Assent.

Robyn stood, his bow fitting to his right palm as he nocked Arrow to string. It tickled, traced the sharp-sweet scent of blood upon his left cheek as he drew.

Fireflies lit, sped after the broadhead as it loosed into the air. They clustered, setting the tip aflame as the Arrow arced, hovered, then sped downward, extinguished into the black depths of Barrow Mere.

Robyn wiped his blood-streaked palm at the oak's roots, then took up his bow and disappeared into the night.

-XV-

It was too sudden, all of it.

Marion was alone in camp, mending a set of hose as Much and John came through the Wode. She was glad of that solitude, particularly when Much explained what brought them and why.

"To Nottingham? I don't under . . . This wain't . . . I can't . . ." Realising she was babbling, Marion set the needle in-and-out of the woollen fabric, put it aside. Took a deep breath and tried again. "The lads are off hunting, and I've seen nowt of Robyn; who knows when he'll be back? You both left only this morn!"

"I know," Much apologised. "It's ever that, well, things move fast when an army goes t' march."

John crouched down beside the fire and, with the mugs always to hand, scooped helpings of pottage from the warming pot—one for himself, one for Much.

Marion snatched up three more mugs, went to the fallen tree beneath which several of David's mead casks were propped, and drew them all a good measure. She was glad of the distraction. It gave her time to think; gave the men time to have a bite. They'd brought enough news to warrant a lord's feast—or a whipping, depending on the lord. If said news wasn't exactly bad, neither was it good.

"I fear there's no bread." She came back to the fire, handed over the drinks. "David and Aelwyn took t' wee ones off to Dadsley, with a few pennies for a good baking's worth and mayhap a sweet for the little lass . . . aye, well." She rubbed her hands against her skirts. "Gamelyn's gone on, then. To Nottingham."

"Aye."

"Twould have been better had he come to tell us, tell *Rob—*"

"He couldn't, lass. He'd his orders."

"Orders! What about—?" Marion bit the words until they burned, hot, in her throat, and realised she was still scrubbing her hands at her skirts. "There's too much bound up in this, and now he wain't so much as . . . ?" John was peering at her with no little concern. Again Marion trailed away, took a deep breath and another tack. "What he's asking. I dassent agree or disagree with the others gone. Not with *Robyn* gone."

Much started to speak, frowned, and looked away.

John was still peering at her. *You're the Maiden.*

"Aye, and that went so well wit' Aelwyn's situation."

Much frowned harder; John merely looked puzzled. Marion realised he'd not been with them, said, "Later, pet. Suffice it to say she wain't be staying with us, but going on t' Hathersage."

"En't that likely for the best, lass?"

Well, and Much picked a proper sorry time to start in on *that.*

"Packing a woman off like she's diseased just because she has bairns? That's for the best?"

"I didn't mean owt—"

"And surely none of you'll mean owt should the time come to pack *me* off like some leper!" The moment Marion said it, she wished she could have bitten it back. John's eyes went saucer-wide. Much paled and nearly dropped his bowl, and she was feeling just that tender, she wondered if it were dread or concern. "I en't breeding, if that's what you're wondering, or dreading, or whats'm*ever—*"

"Marion," Much started, low.

"Neither does it matter, not now, only that . . . bloody damn, but this is a bad job all 'round! If I were about making a decision on sommat this serious, 'tis sure the bloody lads wain't take it so!"

I will.

She smiled, had to. "Aye, John, but you're more man than most."

A shy grin, and silence all around.

"Mayhap I en't the man John is," Much finally ventured. "But I take what you say and do as fair serious, lass. Those that wain't . . . well."

The earnest appeal broke anger and trepidation both. Marion reached out her hands, one to each of them.

"And believe me"—Much graced her knuckle with a swift kiss— "you've two here man enough to stand with you, help you knock some heads do they cross you."

It made her chuckle, albeit wry. "I might hold you to that, but it en't solving the problem, aye?" *Mayhap wain't solve it,* she told herself, laced with rue.

Come the Maying, the Lady was implacable, *they will hearken. Or fail.*

John's gaze considered, sombre. Much was curious, waiting. Their hands were warm and solid in hers.

Aye, they will be true, these guardians of the path.

What path?

The one We must take. What would you fain See, Maiden?

She shivered, and Much's hand twitched while John's curled up tensile and quivering as a bird. Loosed them, and with the trail of fingers, also let fly the *tynged* weaving hot-sharp behind her eyes.

Said, "Still. This is no small matter. It needs to be put to every-one, and fair-like. 'Twere one thing to come with Robyn here, to Blyth, but altogether sommat else, this. Even at Queen Eleanor's request . . . well. To expect everyone to agree we should just saunter into Nottingham Castle bold as brass and announce ourselves?" Shaking her head, she folded her legs and lowered herself back onto her mat. "I've no rights to speak for none but myself wit' likes of this. And without Robyn here, I wain't."

"Surely himself should be back soon, aye? Surely he'll agree?"

Marion started to reassure Much; glimpsing John's face, she wasn't so sure. Because *he* wasn't sure, not of this, and . . .

Why? John knew Robyn better than any save herself, mayhap better in some ways. Marion knew the boy her brother had been, was still learning the man. John was lover and confidant and fierce ally; he had been at Robyn's side after Loxley, unto death and back.

Or were the doubts more concerning Gamelyn?

"There's more." Much looked uncomfortable as Marion flicked a glance his way. "I've to leave no later than t' morrow, to fetch my horse and catch milord up. He needs me, aye?"

Marion nodded. She'd expected that, true enough.

"Johnny says he's going."

This was not expected. She found John's gaze—still unsure, but steady—upon her.

"He needs me," John said, "too."

"I don't under—"

"Robyn w-w-will." With a sigh he resorted to signs. *He told me. Told me to look after* him. *So I'm going back tonight. You must tell the others. Tell Robyn.*

Silence.

Much broke it, finally. "If you come, where can we meet you?" He smiled, reached for her hand. "There's t' auld witch's hut where I first took you to find your brother, after we fetched you from Nottingham's gaol. 'Member?"

A brief smile, but her mind was staggering through all this in forced march. "Papplewick . . . nay. What if they don't let *you* come out that far?"

"There's a fork on River Leen, where 'twas cut to make t' castle moat."

"That's right close for a pack of outlaws," she voiced, small.

"So's amidst a siege camp." It was on Much's tongue—she saw it—to tell her to stay behind, not follow, stay safe.

But nowhere was safe, really. *If you come.*

Yet here they were, making all these plans that mightn't even come to fruit. And if they didn't? What if Robyn . . . wouldn't?

What is a pardon worth?

"I still don't understand why Gamelyn didn't come to me with this!" she burst out. "To *Robyn*. And orders or no, he's sent you on a hard errand, expecting you . . . me . . . *us* to . . ."

Much still held her hand, but seemed unwilling to meet Marion's asking gaze. John was also watching Much, intent. Both gazes, steady and unyielding, seemed to decide something in Much; he spoke, soft and slow and thoroughly miserable.

"He's in a proper state, Mari." The pet name was one Robyn oft used—Much, rarely. It shivered down her spine, not in yearning, but abrupt disquiet. "Sommat's . . . changed. Like a fire's gone out . . . nay, not out. Like coals have been taken from a hearth to kindle a forge. He's that set on sommat. Drovin' hisself like I en't seen since we were both t' Outremer."

"'Tis Guy."

"You keep sayin' that, Johnny, but you're makin' no sense."

Ah, but Marion thought he was. Perfect—and ghastly—sense.

The only ones to return that evening were Aelwyn, with little Tom swaddled close, and David, carrying Tibba peck-a-back. The sun was waning into the west copse as they entered camp, adding several loaves of bread as excellent complement to the pottage, and a few cadged-away sweetmeats that David displayed with a flourish to Marion—with a quick peek first to ensure Tibba wasn't looking.

And news. Dadsley's market, it seemed, bided alternately disgruntled and overjoyed that the siege was over, since the resultant custom—and chaos—were moving south as well. The exodus to Nottingham had begun.

With Gamelyn, no doubt, amidst it. Without so much as coming by camp. Marion worried on it, intent as a dog with a marrow bone.

Over dinner Aelwyn proved nigh observant as David, adding small details here and there of what they'd seen. Much added what he knew, save for the Queen Mother's ultimatum.

To the latter, Marion also kept an unsure silence. What to say? How to say it?

Those questions were still rampaging through her mind as later, fire banked and Aelwyn set to first watch—after all, she was wakeful with the bairn—they all bedded down beneath a clear and star-pocked night. David was soon snoring; either that or he was putting up a polite attempt to cover the sounds that would, every now and then, escape the small and writhing tent of Marion's furs.

Well, and they both needed some relief. No sense letting Much ride off without a proper soldier's farewell.

After, with Much in the sotted sleep of a man who'd been thoroughly done to, Marion lay wakeful in the crook of his shoulder—clinging, really, though she didn't want to admit to it— and stroked the thick, damp ceriphs of fur on his chest. Overthinking . . . well, everything. She didn't know what to do.

Nay, she really did. And long overdue, at that.

Marion started to rise. Either Much had been feigning, or soldier's instincts never slept; he pulled her back down, held her tight, and traced his mouth from her hair to one cheekbone.

"Don't go." A thread of apprehension stitched itself through the request, as if he knew what she meant to do—not that there was any chance of that; she'd barely come to the knowing herself. Then he nuzzled her neck, whispered in her ear, "Let me come with you," and Marion realised he did know. Somehow.

She turned in his hold, braced both palms to his broad chest. The answer must have been plain upon her face, for Much gave one more soft protest.

"John watches after Robyn. And Robyn after John, when he's throwin' t' bones."

The demand was not for his own pride, but her well-being. It made refusal all the harder. Hesitation gave him room for one more protest.

"You know I'll be mindful. Respectful."

"Robyn will know if something goes awry." Or more likely Gamelyn, considering.

Only Gamelyn wasn't here. Hadn't so much as said fare tha' well.

"Robyn en't here. I am."

"Aye, but—"

Much interrupted her with a kiss, hard-sweet, one hand tangling in her curls and the other cupping the back of her thigh. It kneaded her closer, encouraging a straddle and rock against his pelvis, where *sated* was beginning to show how game it was for *one more, eh?* Tracing kisses along the cords of her neck and down, he nuzzled and lipped one nipple, rising against her undertunic and just as ready for another go.

"Now," she whispered against thick, brown hair, "you're just trying to distract me."

"Mm." A light nip, and a grin. "Is it workin', then?"

Working, aye and quite. Her eyes were nigh crossing, and her hips starting their own rhythm. A blessing it was, to be swiving a man who was as intent upon his partner's pleasure as his own.

But she had to do this. And likely would need all the strength she'd left to muster.

"Keep the thought. And *this*." She slid her hand down and gave his promising erection a good squeeze. "Once the thing's done and past me, I'll be back and tup you gormless. Again."

His smile was wry with a bit of pout, reminiscent of a young pup who really, *really* wanted a taste of that rabbit roasting on the fire. Instead, with another longing pat to her arse, Much released her.

Part and parcel of the fascination: he never tried to hold or claim her. He knew what she was, sometimes more than she herself wanted to.

Marion dressed warmly, took the dagger he handed her with a brief smile. While she gathered necessities—including her largest satchel—Much rose and paced quietly over to Aelwyn, who was nursing the bairn but watching, her eyes gleaming in the dim firelight. They exchanged soft murmurs as Much sat, but she didn't retreat to her own furs.

Instead, as Marion came closer, Aelwyn spoke. "Take care, Maiden."

"Aye," Much appended. "Take care."

Both her lover's smile and Aelwyn's steady gaze warmed Marion, followed her out of camp and past the black woodland edges.

ᛝ

Maiden, it whispered to Marion, swinging against her hip and nestled deep in bag and woollen felt wrappings. *Maiden's blessings, Mother's right. . . and rite.*

Too shallow—and too fine—to be anything other than what it was, though it had been black with smoke, tarnish, and grime when Robyn had brought it to her barely a se'nnight after she'd joined the outlaws. Said John had found it during his wanderings those first bleak seasons after Loxley's destruction, in the burnt-out ruins of their parents' cottage. It was a treasure beyond any price— and no less a survivor than the rest of them.

The basin had belonged to Marion's mam, her mam before her, and on back, Eluned had claimed, to the Barrow Folk themselves. Marion had spent more than a few winter fireside evenings scouring and buffing, working at the blackened surface to reveal its true nature. First the coppery tracings at its rim, then the bright white of purest silver winking and gleaming between her hands. Marion had breathed the richest blessing she knew and wrapped the basin away, put by for the right moment.

It seemed now that moment was upon them. Upon her. *The magic is turning in its sleep, dreaming awake.*

The memory of Robyn's words tickled down her spine like warm water; had done, really, since he'd spoken them. The magic indeed was waking, and she, the Lady's dreamer, had slept too long herself. More was needed in this game of survival, and—her mam had Told it, long ago—'twas the Maiden's to untangle the skeins, parse the weaving.

And now, when their Summerlord asked they follow him into the unknown—

What is a pardon worth? Not you, not Robyn, not our lives, not us...

Sod you, Gamelyn, what are you on about? Why?

—it was imperative she See what still lay between, keeping them—nay, say't as 'twere —keeping *Gamelyn* from *their* purpose.

Barrow Mere was the best place for such a Telling, but even as her feet started upon the path that would lead her there, Marion hesitated. There was not only the reality of a good jaunt south and west, mid-night with wandering predators both two- and four-legged, but the illusory unreality of the Mere's changing nature.

Robyn had acknowledged that too: *We've called, Mari. In intent* and *innocence. An' they're answering.*

But as to who... what... they had called? Marion thought she knew. But until she understood more, shaking further fruit from an enchanted tree was unwise.

A smile teased her lip, somewhat grim. 'Twere Eve as had learnt that. Unfortunately, in the new religion, such sacred knowledge had been twisted into vilification, not only of her, but every woman born 'neath the rule of man's Church.

Robyn Hood and his outlaws always made camp near running water—with as much prosaic as otherworldly reasons. The bag over one shoulder, bulging with the wrapped basin, nudged at Marion's haunch as she followed the riverlet upstream. As considerable a comfort as the reasonable defences she'd to hand: her knife; her bow; the quiver of arrows fletched with the cerulean shimmer of the goddess's eye.

The deeper she ventured, the more the thick woodland tangle closed about her. The moon, rising into gravid silver, was allowed only a fleeting scrim here and there. On the occasion it did gild Marion's shoulders, it was merely a touch, another precarious half shadow to obscure her path. The riverlet beside her was thankfully audible, a rush and burble, punctuated by the sink and *squelch* of her boots did she venture too close. And, more and more, the darker-upon-dark of the trees bounded and barricaded the sky's bowl, more adversary than benefactor this night: willows encroaching upon the banks with long locks trailing; wild grandfather oaks with branches spreading, selfish of the light; witchwood rowan as stolid portals into pitch.

It came to Marion that she could lose her way in the murk, fall through one of many little fissures, break a leg or her neck. She might slip, tumble into the river, and strike her temple against the sharp rocks. Once surfaced, doubt niggled insidious reminders of a time too long spent in an abbey, surrounded by man-pillaged stones, deaf, dumb, and blind to memory. It slowed her steps and questioned her right to pass. She would wander here forever, never allowed to remain, or return . . .

Mother's child being tainted by iron and bells, this Wode whispered. *No longer being of the forest, no more being* of us.

Her feet turned clumsy, hesitant. Another footfall, then another; the third sank her up to one ankle in wet weight. Marion heaved her way on, trapped foot giving from the mud with a slick, sucking sound. She staggered sideways, tripped on a root, barely kept upright. A low-hanging branch clawed at one cheek and drew blood; gasping, she flung up a hand to shield her face.

What light there might have been swallowed itself away, as if there were no longer stars or moon lingering above the trees.

We've called, Mari.

The memory came to her, sudden-stark, of Robyn and John caught in the Hunter's caverns for over a fortnight whilst inside, with them, the fire had burned for merely three days.

Intent and innocence.

Remembered speaking with Gamelyn beside the Barrow Mere, where nightfall had turned to dawn uncanny quick. Of the Barrow lines converging into the Mere's clear depths, singing with the season's change—*aware* of seasons, again—and opening into thisnow the otherworlds, their influence rippling upon time's smooth-deep pool . . .

Nay, no longer mere ripples but an upsurge. The knowledge, though it tasted of ashes and rust, that she and her two lords, Winter and Summer, were not yet *Ceugant.*

And this dark stretch of wylding Wode knew it.

They're answering.

Robyn understood. He'd longer wielded his godling-heart; his blood beat wild and angry, hotter than her own. Robyn would know what to do in this place. But she was not Robyn.

Her bow clattered to the ground. The knife slid from nerveless fingers to sheathe gleaming iron into sodden earth.

The latter reverberated, soundless but *there,* behind her eyes. Spread into the dark, accompanied by a panicked scurry of unspoken and undeniable presences fleeing the soundless puissance of naked iron. Broke uncertainty into a hundred friable pieces.

She was not Robyn. She was Marion, Maiden to the Shire Wode, Lady's Voice and avatar. She did not need to be Robyn. His path was not hers.

Marion raised clenched fists to her forehead, paused. A silent, quick breath, then she opened her hands and cupped them over her face, both waiting and asking. Eyes closed, heart open to all of it: faith and apprehension; self-possession and disquiet.

There was no use appealing to the Lady Huntress. She must *be* Her.

She did not speak the iron charm, did not further the power she had raised—albeit by chance—in the dropping of her dagger. Instead she whispered a firm query across her palms, breath misting into the murk.

"Anadlu gyda fi, cyfeillion."

Breathe with me, friends.

At first there was nothing. Then, slowly, a shiver came from within the black. Tiny pinpoints—they were *eyes*—irising open to glitter against some faint light.

Marion once more drew her hands over her face, breathed across her palms, and spoke. "I am your Lady."

Another shiver, a wordless negation in the dark that nevertheless made itself clear: *You are not being our Lady.*

Marion insisted, silent: *In thisworld, I am She.* And when there was no answer, no sign of consent, she loosed the hex-breath, strong and long:

"Bendith y mamau. Yn gwybod i mi."

Be knowing Me.

It swirled over the riverlet, Called a breeze to set the branches dancing. Amidst those trees, the glittering orbs blinked. Considered. One by one, went dark.

Slowly the surrounding black turned into soot, then mist, revealing a path of silvery moonlight

Bending down, Marion retrieved both bow and dagger and walked inward.

Time seemed to be passing around him, not through him. As if he bided separate from it in some fashion, or so a part of it, he didn't feel even its breath uttering his name.

Robyn wasn't comforted by the fact. So many places—pockets, really—where the worlds were shifting, nudging each other for rights of position like deer upon a narrow trail. And which world would stay?—for it was in his heart they'd not bide well, side by side.

And that made him think of Gamelyn. Again.

So he stopped in Rotherham to drown sudden gloom in a pot of cider, three or four. Well, that, and some reassurance he'd not lost more than a day and night. 'Twere a pleasant surprise to find his head agreeing with the counting of days a weathered shepherd asked the potkeeper for . . . and aye, well, sheepherders lost time as easily as outlaws. An elder Saxon at that, for the shepherd spoke more of the old tongue than the new, and the potkeeper answering his query in kind:

"Aye, 'tis nigh t' twenty-six *Hreðmonað*. How'd the ewes fare 'pon Oimelc?"

"*Gôd.* Only lost t' one."

The old shepherd conveyed his herd's success with a few more monosyllables as the potkeeper poured him a drink. A tiny bleat came from the bag at his hip, and a pied dog rose up on hind legs to touch noses with two newborn lambs cadged warm and safe there. No doubt results of the lost ewe. The shepherd fondled the dog's ruff, tendering a grimy coin for his drink. As he turned to the wall of benches and tables where Robyn had settled, the dog came creeping over to Robyn, wagging and grinning.

Robyn grinned back and scratched the dog's ears.

The shepherd whistled, frowned when the dog merely looked his way but stayed put. With a grumbling sigh, he started over, lips pursed either for a second whistle or speech. But as Robyn looked up, still smiling soft, the shepherd stilled and took a sharp breath, out then inward.

Said, "*Hyrned galdrsfaðir,*" and with a quick glance around, came closer, albeit hesitant. "*Hæsere Hunta.*"

The dog gave a tiny whine at the murmured words, and Robyn stilled. He kenned his father's Saxon tongue as well as his mother's Barrow-talk; he knew what the old man had, somehow in the midst of a somewhat squalid tavern, Seen in him: *Horned spell-father. Lord of the Hunt.*

Said, soft and still scratching the dog's ears, "*Bendith.*" Then changed it to the father-tongue, "*Blétsunge, ealdhierde.*"

And indeed the old herder took the blessing to his heart with one gnarled hand and a tiny bow. "What brings tha here, *hæsere?*"

"A drink, of course." Robyn lifted his pot and left off newer speech for elder—some privacy, true, but more as courtesy to an elder. "But I am no lord, old herder."

The shepherd smiled, answered in comfortable kind. "Mayhap not in thisnow. You seem more scruffy young man than trickster or spirit. Aye, but Scut here"—the dog's ears pricked at his name—"knows t' rights of it. Animals knows their father. I listens to beasts. And I keep close watch 'pon the eyes of men."

"Mirrors and giveaways, those," Robyn concurred softly, and kept stroking the dog's shaggy black ruff. "Yours bide clear and strong, and you honour the god. Will you drink with me, old herder?"

The shepherd cocked his head, gave a wary twist of grizzled eyebrow. "'Tis said little folk dance t' stanes, and t' Making rites returning 'pon Mam Tor."

"Aye, old herder."

"And thyself, as spell-father, will be the rites a-calling. But now, which shall I be sitting and drinking with?"

"With t' scruffy young man," Robyn clarified, a grin playing with his lip. "No trickster thisnow. But mayhap you've some information the spell-father would gladly hear."

Pale light stabbed her eyes, and the trees gave way.

The little glade was sanctuary amidst a darken Wode perched so close and *watchful*. Moss stretched beyond, an ever-present carpet thick as a sheep's winter pelt; it cradled her steps, sinking-soft, and clung to the rocks and trees, blurring outlines of limb and root. The river, too, had changed. Shallow and swift, it curved into a bow-shaped eyot, where it slowed, deeper along the little island's other side.

In her time, Marion had wandered these woods enough to feel some familiarity. Never had she encountered this place. No wonder it had tested her. It made a worthy sanctuary to craft any Telling.

She set down her bow and quiver, and this time laid her knife blade flat upon the moss. With a deep breath, she unfastened the cloak from her shoulders. Released that breath, and the belt from her waist.

Unlaced and shrugged from her bliaut.

Toed off her boots.

Began to unbraid her hair. Listened.

"Dreaming awake." Robyn's words sprouted memory into wings, flitting and echoing branch to branch, as if the trees had found a voice warm and honey-thick. *"The magic is turning in its sleep. Dreaming awake."*

Dreaming. . . Waking. . .

"I hear you." The appeal soft but steadfast. The scrying bowl gleamed, uncovered, upon the bank as she bent to untie the garter at her calf, then reached for the dropped quiver, felt for and plucked at an arrow's fletching. "I see you. I honour you. We all would honour you, dance and draw down the moon-magic, to sing our Wode living once again."

Promises. Desolation. Iron. Fire and ash.

The pain and rage bid her open her eyes, but another memory, more distant—more *human*—whispered warning:

Breathe the fire of your soul.

"*Anadlu y tân dy enaid,*" Marion murmured and straightened, gathering basin and her thin linen underkirtle in the curve of one elbow, with the fletching's cerulean glint cupped in the other hand. "We all must die, to be reborn."

Opening gleaming, moonsilver eyes upon the glade, she stepped into the shallows.

The water was cold, tugging at her ankles, then her calves, the rocks slick-rough upon the soles of her feet. Speaking. The trees answered in their own tongue: creak and groan, soughing upon a sudden breeze that shivered the curls about her cheeks.

The eyot had built itself, sand and rock upon the current, and the river's path had cut deep on its lee side. It was from that edge she filled her empty basin, the water gleaming like hoarfrost, and knelt upon the sand.

First to drink and swallow, the water so cold it burned up beneath her cheekbones and behind her eyes. Then the sip and spit, tiny swirls upon the clear liquid, to be smoothed with the peacock fletchings. She traced thrice widdershins, then skywise, left to right and round again, motion and breath rippling round the copper-runed rim.

Laid the feather beside the bowl, wet but still glimmering. Whispered the magic in the language of the Barrows. Waited, as the ripples spread to the edges and spun themselves into long, thin strands.

Dreaming awake.

We've called, Mari. In intent and *innocence. An' they're answering.*

The basin warmed, as if with her breath, *tynged* plaiting itself into blackness, then a rainbow of hues, rippling a preternaturally still mirror.

Then. . . Now. . . Here.

Memory winged closer, skipped the shallow, frail spot signalling her days in the abbey, slowed further and fouled: the bitter winter, and Gamelyn's doubt . . .

We've come back to the garden, haven't we? Only Eden is long gone. We've seen too much. We know too much. We've tasted every fruit of a deceptive tree. And we're fools to want that garden back. But still, we are. Fools.

The Fool is indeed powerful. Her mother's voice. *In ignorance and doubt can such a one stumble upon truths hidden.*

Or, Robyn warns, *pass by sweet water and instead quaff poison. . .*

Poison, Will growls, *nowt but poison, and none of you see it!*

*I think—*Much shrugs, as if this particular wound isn't the one he cannot staunch—*he en't sure who he is.*

Enough! Marion's, the voice, yet also Hers, tipping uncertainty into blackness. The basin began to hum, a mirror gleaming beneath the moon, and she breathed, sank in, Saw.

Was. Might be.

Is:

Upon the fire-burnished ridge of Mam Tor, dancing the ring with flowers in her hair. Drumbeats make the time, shouts and yips and songs rise upward to meet the moon rising huge over

Mam Tor. Glowing coppery-red as the biggest of the Bel-fires, it backlights into darkness the tall, horned figure who leaps the fire and lands at her feet . . .

He's gone. Soft, sad, yet also angry as the fires wane into dawn. *He wain't be coming. . .*

. . .*back?* Gamelyn has one foot planted on the stair below, looking up at her, slow fire kindling behind verdigris. *I don't know, but I do know this is one path you cannot follow.* Dawn filters in from an upper window, casting new-painted castle stones in rose and ash, tinting stark his white-and-scarlet habit . . .

Aye, Robyn answers from behind her, *for you never ken where any path will take you. Only, sometimes, where it leads. . .*

Yet when Marion turns, he is gone. Both of them, gone, and she is alone upon the stone stair, one-third of a broken Wheel. It tears at her, looses a wanting deep inside.

I think—a groan, both anticipation and dread—*I think it's time.*

And Much takes her hand, says, *We didn't exactly start this together, but we'll finish it together, allus finish. . .*

. . .*finished, d'you hear?* Gamelyn, furious as she has ever heard. *It's over! Your day is. . .*

I knew this day would come, Hubert says. *Even as I knew what I would have no choice but to do. . .*

. . .*and do what?* Robyn sneers. *Y' think you can take me, light as any tavern whore. Run me to ground and rip t' magic from me like it's nowt. . . like I'm nowt!*

Oh, I'm afraid you are nothing. . .

That voice sent a horrific shiver through Marion, almost pulled her from the Telling—

—and the Templar Master comes out of the murk, one gloved hand extending a long, black arrow that whispers a dark, broken descant . . . its maker's name, Robyn's name . . . as with the other he winds, slowly, a thin, shimmering thread about the rune-marked shaft.

Don't you know, fool, that magic belongs to those who bind it? Chain it? Tame it?

The thread glimmers, catches upon the Arrow's peacock fletchings, sends spinning the blue-green feather floating within the silver basin . . .

. . .*green as juniper needles, they are, even that hint of dark blue about,* Robyn purrs, and grabs Gamelyn's hair, pulls him closer still, whispers, *You'll be the death of me, see if you wain't,* and Gamelyn shoves him away with a curse, but Robyn holds on and kisses him, smiles and holds up one hand. In it, gripped oh so gentle, is the Arrow—nay, the quillion dagger, gold filigree and oak pommel, its blade twined with mistletoe and ivy, oak and holly . . .

Whilst you promise Hell at every turn! Every vision. Every dream!

To promise hell, one must sanction it. Low. Angry. *The only hell truly extant in thisnow, in my forest, is that which* you *bring, lordling.*

Is that so? It is in your *forest, Horned Lord, where I am destined to betray my own! Where at any time our Winterlord could be taken and his head exchanged for a handful of silver!*

A laugh. *They have to catch Us, first. As to the rest. . . so sure, you are, of your* tynged, *my lord.*

I'm sure of nothing, including my own heartbeat, in thisnow. Running the words together as the Heathen did, Gamelyn heard the Lady's resultant croon of satisfaction but did not let it sway him. Persisted, *If Blyth were mine—*

If! Contemptuous.

If Blyth were mine, Gamelyn insisted, fierce, *then our Archer could once again ride free. He could be that forester a brutal fate denied him. Our Maiden could fulfil the longing—I've seen it in her eyes even if you have not!—for her own home, her own hearth, her own people depending upon her skill, and the proof of it in the jangle of keys at her girdle.*

Sunrise, streaming into the glade, and Gamelyn bends over Robyn—who lies still, so still—to cup one pale cheek with a shaking hand. He kisses Robyn's forehead. The hand drops, curls about the hilt of the quillion dagger at Robyn's belt, and draws it. The dying sun flashes, copper-and-gold against the blade and nigh blinding—

Purpose. It is what you are meant to be, and do.

—or is it merely the glint of Gamelyn's hair as he flings it across the blade with a rip like heavy silk, as long, coppery strands spill across Robyn's bared chest, mixed with blood and hoarse breath and salt tears . . .

As Gamelyn puts the blade to Robyn's throat . . .

Marion screams his name, but he does not hear—neither of them hear—and she is blinded, *blind,* eyes covered with a milk-white scrim, a thick-wet heat running down her breast, and *pain,* cutting her scream into a breathless gurgle, as though the dagger has carved her throat as well as Robyn's . . .

And Marion lurched back into thisnow, the silver bowl upended over the breast of her linen shift, shards of copper light still piercing her sight, splayed on her back with her scream echoing across the eyot and into the Wode.

- XVI -

The first time Guy of Gisbourne had entered Nottingham, he had been contracted to kill a wolfshead.

The last time, it had been after that wolfshead had killed Guy.

Killed? Nay, just one head shorn from the serpent, to sprout back just as powerful. Like to Tiamat, upon whose bones were built the shrines of Babylon. It was satisfied. *Robyn wants me. Marion needs me. You are me, and you know it.*

"You are very quiet, *Confanonier.*" A bag from which issued a tantalising mix of honey, grain, and—aye, dried apricots!—waved beneath Gamelyn's nose as Hubert nudged his chestnut stallion closer to Falcon.

"Young Stephen says you didn't break your fast when we broke camp this morn, so eat."

"Thank you, my lord Commander." Gamelyn's acceptance of the bag was mechanical despite the temptation of the dried fruit. Hubert knew his weakness for apricots. The consideration stung, somehow.

"You ride apart from our Brothers. Remember, there is little not made easier by trusted companionship."

Hubert's mild words also stung, prompted Gamelyn to look up and notice; indeed, he had ridden some distance ahead, a solitary standard between the Templars and Durham's mounted retinue. Unconscious, the decision, guarded and guarding with sword unbuckled at his thigh and the piebald banner flying, blocked at his stirrup. Similar to so many campaigns and sorties in the wild deserts beyond Outremer.

Enemy territory.

Save they were riding from Thynghowe, where the march had rested for the night at Durham's insistence. He desired a fresh—and visible—arrival this morn. Thynghowe, where ancient Saxons had met and the Hood's outlaws had but recently sheltered. Where a dream had encompassed the last fortnights, and Gamelyn had lain with his lover . . .

And quarrelled, aye? Over not only dreams, but nightmares, Guy pointed out. *Enemy territory indeed. We can afford no weakness. Not of any kind.*

To such good sense, Gamelyn looped the rein over his pommel and ate. A bit stale, but he relished the mix of tart and honeyed-sweet. Between his knees, Falcon shook his mane at Hubert's chestnut. The elder stallion curled his nose in return.

"*Bon!* Trust has ever been hard-won with you, but you ever guard *our* trust well." Giving an affectionate slap to his mount's neck, Hubert eyed the banner, wafting light upon the blissfully warm breeze. "Your thoughts are bleak, *non?* Is it, ah, the matter of Blyth's reassignment that troubles you? You have lost no honour in the eyes of our Order."

Gamelyn shook his head. Hubert seemed loath to believe it and started to speak. Instead he was diverted by a shout from the front lines of the considerable sprawl of men and horses. Gamelyn alerted as first Pontefract's, then Hallamshire's, then the Bishop's banner gave notice.

"The way is blocked," Gamelyn read. He gave his own signal with the piebald banner. As one, the Templar contingent halted. "A disabled wagon. Shall I send someone, Commander?"

Hubert nodded, and Gamelyn gestured to a brace of Templar sergeants. They spurred their horses forward, up the road's edge.

Falcon sidled closer to the chestnut, ears pinned, and feinted a cheeky nip to one shoulder. The chestnut all but rolled his eyes, gave an expansive sigh, and cocked one hind leg, recognising the signs of a wait.

And indeed they waited, silent with the dust settling over feet and hoofs whilst the troublesome blockage was, presumably, shoved out of the way. Falcon spent the time plainly longing for a good spar with the chestnut and not quite daring more than a tease at it. Instead, frustrated, he gave an occasional paw at the earth. Smirking at the young stallion's antics, Gamelyn kept nibbling from Hubert's stash.

Finally, another dip and flare of the Bishop's banner—red and black, boldly emblazoned with St. Cuthbert. The army once again began to move on, spreading over nearly a quarter mile's worth of the North Road.

Once they were not so tightly bunched, Hubert began to speak again, his voice pitched only to Gamelyn. "There is no loss in your being summoned to Nottingham, only more the gain. And a better chance of fulfilling our Master Preceptor's plans."

Master Wymarec had plans, O, and aye. Gamelyn found he was no longer hungry. He returned the bag to Hubert—after palming two lumps of honey-clumped grain, which he fed to both Falcon and Hubert's chestnut.

"Mind this, my *Confanonier*: we pray for your success, of course, but it is imperative you make your own. Press your favour with the Queen, for I promise you that both de Lacy and de Furnival intend to press their resources upon the King. The latter has many powerful friends amongst the younger lords; the former has not only a canny mind, but funding to back whatever it is he plans. All of us realise Blyth is a powerful and well-placed bastion upon the road North. And it is one our Order has the resources to repair and hold fast."

Falcon licked his lips and nodded, all but boasting *My treat was bigger*, and braved another sideways nip. The chestnut kept that one nostril curled, phlegmatic and contemptuous.

Gamelyn tugged at Falcon's mane—*Settle down, you*—and frowned, curious. "Preparations?"

"I can tell you this much, for you know it already. It is not only the castle that is of interest to us, but the abstruse power contained within the hill."

All Hallows. The nape hairs of Gamelyn's neck shivered erect.

Hubert nodded. "Master Wymarec believes the wolf of Sherwood has stirred some ancient demon to wakefulness within the chapel's demesne, but there is more than that, eh?"

A pause, the blue gaze a-watch, intent.

Gamelyn couldn't hold to it, his own gaze escaping to the surrounding forest. A breath later he realised what he was doing, slowly returned Hubert's appraisal. Respectful. Careful. Impassive.

"I believe"—Hubert nodded—"you have made your own, ah, *connection* with what—who—bides there."

Gamelyn couldn't admit it—couldn't, somehow, as if the Lady Herself held his tongue. But neither could he deny, not to this man with whom he had shared fire and sword, blood oath and hearthside.

Hubert smiled. "And so. We have our own knowledge, you and I. *Non?*"

Falcon made another snatch at the chestnut. The chestnut raised his curl of nostril to pinned ears, as well as a shake and bow of neck that promised, plain: *Keep it up, lad, and I will end you.*

The equine back-and-forth coaxed a chuckle from Hubert, softened Gamelyn's expression into a grin.

The Templars want All Hallows, and thusly the honour of Tickhill and its castle. Guy, musing. *That could well aid our cause.*

The grin faded. *Until the orders come to bring Robyn to them.*

'Twas my impression those orders had already come.
Shut up!

"Ah," Hubert said, soft. "Your thoughts bide in Sherwood, then."

"Master." It burst from Gamelyn before any inner and ice-eyed knight could stop it. "Part of me hopes they will not come."

And wanted to bite his tongue until the blood ran as Hubert frowned.

Idiot! Guy sneered.

Hubert sighed, contemplated the ox and wagon they passed— sure enough, it had a broken wheel pin, with their two sergeants and a brace of Pontefract's men assisting the elderly carter in replacing the wheel on its axle.

The trees were beginning to thin, branches catching the distinct layer of smoke adrift.

Hubert snuffed it, grimaced. Idly adjusted the lay of his horse's mane.

Said something that made even the inner predator fall into sullen and flabbergasted silence.

"I know, lad. But we do not always have what we want in this life, eh?"

Falcon tried another nip. The chestnut had taken enough; he whirled, fastened his great yellow teeth on Falcon's crest, and nearly had him on his knees, all in a flash. Falcon squealed outrage—and submission. Just as swift, the chestnut released him, one eye rolling at Gamelyn as if to say *Sorry, Sir Knight, to disturb your seat, but the stroppy bastard wouldn't leave off!*

Hubert laughed this time, and Gamelyn had to join in.

A horn blared from the army's head. As if in answer, the Bishop's banner dipped and several cries rose to concur:

"Hoy, Nottingham ahead!"

Then another, crowing, "The King's armies are there! The King is besieging Nottingham!"

"Cheer up, lass; he'll coom by again." Will sat on the withy mat beside her. "And iffen he wain't, then you've a lot of fierce hunters to see you proper warm and fed."

Marion raised an eyebrow at the first, but had no argument with that last. Will, Gilbert, and Arthur had returned with not only enough meat to fill the kettle to brimming, but also to tithe a few villages and smoke for later.

Thank the Lady for Spring, and new grass, and deer waxing fat.

Arthur snorted, wielding his smallest axe upon the second deer's carcass. "I've seen our fair Maid shoot, Charming William, and I'm thinkin' she can damn well feed herself if the need arose!"

David laughed agreement, snugging up another small tarpaulin full of meat to carry over to Gilbert for slicing.

"Aye, but what about the warming?" Will waggled his eyebrows, then gave an "*Oof!*" as Marion elbowed him square in the chest. Rubbing at his breastbone, he protested, "I only said warming!"

"I know what you said." *I also know what you meant,* she thought, but couldn't help the smirk. One of Will's most annoying traits, tenacity, was nevertheless also his finest. "I'm well enough on me own. It's just we've this meat to see to, quickest's best."

"What's t' rush?" Will leaned over and snagged a slice of liver from the plank at Marion's knee.

Marion actually started to answer, and add to it how her glum mood wasn't about Much's absence but what she'd Seen at the eyot, and the situation that had prompted . . . well, everything about now. Just in time she bit it back, ducked her head, and shrugged.

"The little mum is quite deedy, aye?" Will continued, gesturing to where Aelwyn was working.

The "little mum" seemed set on making herself indispensable—not that Marion disapproved; she was finding sensible female company quite agreeable. Aelwyn was skewering Gilbert's thin slices with nimble-quick fingers, then hanging them over a shrouded fire just beginning to maintain a proper smoke. Wee Tom was swaddled snug at her torso with a length of linen, and Tibba had plumped down beside her mam with the nigh-boneless agility of a toddler, making messy if satisfied inroads on a bit of the same liver Will had snagged.

He swallowed, continued, "Funny, en't it, how the wee ones bide proper quiet."

"Not so funny," Marion mused. "Aelwyn's plenty of milk. Keep a bairn fed and close-swaddled, but let a little one run free and fed, and they're content as a sow scratching in a sandy wallow."

"And you?"

Marion blinked, slid a cautious gaze Will's direction. Sure enough, he'd that light in his eyes that meant *danger ahead,* though it'd been some time since she'd seen it trotted out. So she kept it teasing.

"Are you comparing me to a sow, William?"

"Nay!" He wasn't looking at her, fussing with the hunks of meat with which she was, one by one, feeding the cauldron. "I meant . . . are you happy?"

Well, and now she was fair scunnered.

Arthur started up a tuneless whistle, kept on breaking the carcass with his smaller axe.

"Well, I wouldn't mind a proper kitchen," she ventured, with an awkward fastening of attention upon the meat-laden cutting board between her knees, upon knife and fingers.

Her own home, her own hearth, her own people depending upon her skill, and the proof of it in the jangle of keys at her girdle.

The Telling memory stabbed, sharp as the knife she held, and she gasped, doubled over.

"*Marion!*" Sharp, and Will's hand firm upon her arm. "Are you all right?"

She nodded, forced herself straight, found this time they all were peering her way, expressions running the gamut from worried to puzzled. "I'm . . . all right. A cramp, nowt more."

"You sure 'tis nowt more?" Will's grip on her arm was beginning to sting, and the light in his amber eyes was just as fierce. "I mean . . . well."

Again it dawned upon her what he thought, and mayhap the others did as well. Aelwyn in particular had that air of *well, aye, of course* settling slow across her face.

"You're blethering over nowt," Marion chided, gruff, and fed a few more chunks of meat to the cauldron. "I en't breeding, if that's what you're about."

The others kept peering at her, and Will's eyebrows did a sceptical dance.

Marion sighed, stuck the knife into the wood, and swept a disgruntled gaze over them all. "I *en't.*"

If only she were. Then she would push the issue, and damned to all of them did they try to send *her* away.

If only. It echoed, empty against the Wode's presence. For she wasn't. Mayhap *couldn't,* despite lying with a man for several moons now—taking care, to be sure, but nowt was sure with this sort of thing. The wortwives always said if a maid was going to, she would, and nowt but the herbs to help or hinder.

The taste of this was nigh as bitter. Her brother had reconciled himself with their god and goddess, sworn as virgin Winterlord amongst a company of men, giving himself only to those men, his rival, and their forest.

Would there be such forgiveness of a barren Maiden?

You heed part of the Telling, but not all? the Lady chided, soft from the green trees.

Memory came again, this one warm-sweet: a swell of belly 'neath her kirtle, and a sword-hard hand lingering in pensive, gentle wonder.

Aye, and mayhap, she retorted, *'twere nowt more than wishful thinking.*

Do you really think any of what you Saw wishful?

The truth of that burrowed into her heart, left behind a smear and sludge of ice.

"Marion," Will insisted, but loosed her as she shrugged at his grip, growing from sting to dug-in throb. Said again, "Marion."

"I'm telling the truth! And that I swear t' all of you, by our Lady!"

It satisfied them—no light oath, this—and they returned to their tasks.

Save Will. "See 'ere, pet—"

"Don't 'pet' me, William."

He huffed a quick breath, in and out. "I mean nowt by 't, pe . . . Look. You just don't seem . . . happy about now."

I've a lot on me mind, Charming William, and you en't helping *about now.*

"I can't be happy every day, Will. Why should you expect me to?"

"That en't what I . . . Do *he* make you happy?"

Marion blinked.

"Do he make you happy even do he gad off after that bloody ginger-haired Templar?" The words were still soft but nonetheless rushing outward, as if Will had to say them or burst. "Because *that* one's making our Rob miserable, en't he? And if you're thinking I'll just stand aside while *both* of you bide heartsick after trouble? Aye, and I'll pound me some hard heads, first."

It made her smile, remember the lad she'd fancied, so long ago.

Will smiled too. He reached out and thumbed a bit of fresh blood from her cheek. "Lass. Rob's allus been one t' throw himself from the tree until he's bloody-ragged, but you . . . I know you fancy Much. Hellfire, but I like him too. More, *he's* our like, where some as en't . . . "

Wisely he left off as Marion shook her head and returned her attention to chopping meat and dropping it into the simmering cauldron. The fire popped and hissed as a bit of fat fell on the coals.

Silent for a few breaths, nonetheless Will, true to form, proceeded to wreck the bridge he'd just built. "Still. You need to take care, aye? If you . . . well, if you kindle before summering, then t' rite wain't take so strong."

"Cheeky," Marion warned. "'Tisn't your concern."

"I'm of covenant t' Shire Wode, of which neither that bloody Templar nor Much bide!" Still quiet, no reason for anyone to notice.

Though Aelwyn was watching, so steady-wary that Marion wanted to tell her to mind her fingers, she'd cut herself.

"I'm second only t' John in our covenant, and I knows what my da taught. What *your* ma and da taught!" Still quiet, and grim, and infuriatingly, undeniably, Will. "That *makes* it my concern, cheeky or nay, and I shouldn't have t' remind you of such things. *Maiden.*"

"That I am, and I shouldn't have t—"

"*Robyn!*" A delighted crow from Gilbert, followed by a few more and, sure enough, Marion looked up to find her brother striding into camp. Smiling.

So much for me brother's misery, Charming William. Tart, mayhap uncalled for, but she was still stinging from being called to account. As if she were Tibba!

Will was lurching up, grim turning to grin as he strode over and grabbed Robyn in a fierce embrace.

"Leave off, y' pillock—you're squashing me!" Robyn hugged

back, belying the words even as his black eyes gave a quick roam
of camp. They noticed everything, including Aelwyn and the
bairns, but settled on Marion, questioning.

Marion couldn't hold the gaze. Not now. Not yet.

He took due note of this but left off, let Will take his bow and
quiver. Grinned wider and teased, "So I'm just in time t' eat the
meal what sommun caught us. Fair enough, then, I'm famished."

Aye, better to let mundane things take necessary precedence.

They quickly finished breaking the hart, covered the meat to
smoke over alder and hickory, and settled down to a good pease
pottage of venison and greens, with plenty of fresh bread. Her
mam's way of sweetening unsteady news had always been to feed
sommun placid and add a few measures of mead besides. Eluned's
advice oft proved fine.

Marion kept things pleasant despite yearning, alternately, to skelp
Will or kiss him. The first for her own still-smarting feelings; the
last because Will was sitting beside Robyn, telling a lot of stories
he'd garnered from over to Dadsley, and had Robyn laughing so
hard, Marion was surprised he'd not yet snorted mead up his nose.

Marion laughed in all the right places—it wasn't that hard, truly;
the stories were bloody funny and her brother's mirth contagious.
She watched Arthur and Gilbert take turns flirting with Aelwyn,
who giggled so at Will's jokes that she snagged a case of hiccups.
Saw David, a thwarted father's yearning never far behind his eyes,
take Tibba into his lap and entertain her with a bit of string
wound about his fingers.

Let her own thoughts simmer and build.

The Horned Lord lingered nigh to His avatar, soul-caul to rival
the hood draping her brother's black curls. The Lady slipped
beneath Marion's own skin with fire and promise and, even more,
the cool otherworldly flash of past-futures garnered from a silver
basin.

A hesitancy, almost fear yet not so simple, shadowed her own
heart when she thought of speaking to any of it. And that was a
huge assumption, that she'd words to describe what the Telling
had dredged forth.

Mayhap better just to share what words Much had brought.

Tibba fell asleep in David's lap. Will ran out of jokes, finally,
one arm flung about Robyn, who leaned against him like an old
tree. He'd not once asked about John, Marion puzzled, then
remembered: *Robyn told me to watch ower him.*

Robyn was watching her, too.

Aelwyn retrieved Tibba and took her to their pallet, stretched out beside. Nursing Tom, she soon fell asleep. David rose to see to the used bowls. Gilbert also rose, to check the smoking meat— and give an appreciative snuff of the lovely odours wafting.

Marion stood, took the silver bowl from her bag and over to the casks. All eyes were upon her by the time she brought the brimming bowl to their circle and held it over the fire.

Robyn sat up, eyes gleaming. He'd long since tossed back his hood, yet it remained, visible in a shimmer of dark cowl and pale horn.

"I call upon t' Shire Wode covenant, one and all." Marion sipped from the bowl, then spat it onto the coals with a hiss and flare of flame.

"Listen well."

They heard her out, as the ritual of council demanded. The silence remained for some moments after she spoke, edged enough to cut.

Then Will spoke, slowly, as if the words tasted of bile or he couldn't believe he had to so much as speak them. "You're actually thinking about doing this. You *want* us to go along with this."

"It's not about what I want," Marion answered, curt. "It's about what Queen Eleanor—"

"Tell me, lass, which of us has ever done what some noble asked?"

"Queens and kings don't ask," Gilbert reminded. "They require."

"We're *outlaws*, aye?" Ripe with scorn, Will rounded on Gilbert. "No law aids us, so no laws can bind us!"

"Lessen they catch us." David, sombre.

"We also happen to be outlaws who helped the Queen," Gilbert pointed out.

"Which means we owe her *nowt*," Arthur retorted.

"She's one as owes us!" Will agreed.

"Have any of you considered that she might be trying to repay the debt?" Marion snapped.

"By asking us to turn ourselves in?"

"She didn't ask—"

"He's only ever saying as you have, lass." David's reply was pointed-soft. "You said Queen Eleanor has requested you and Robyn by name, and the rest of us by inference."

Will snorted. "Or so that bloody Templar said."

"Gamelyn has no reason to lie about this!" Marion growled. "Nor Much!"

"Much en't about to question *his master*, is he?" It was a snarl. "And *his master* has every reason to lie! The ginger-haired git wants that damned castle, doesn't he? So he can do all he's ever done: break hearts and take up wit' his own!"

Desperate, Marion sought Robyn where he sat, cross-legged

and silent, at the fire's other edge. It was darker there, yet she could see him well enough. He didn't seem to be listening, instead sketching almost idly in the sand with the slender quillion dagger.

The blade glinted coppery-gilt against the coals and sparked another, sinister memory behind her eyes: what river water had Told of that dagger. What it had been, had done, and *would*.

Only an uncertain oath lain upon that dagger's edge. Only her own desperate kiss—*fare tha' well, return to us*—searing a promise in Gamelyn's soul. Would it be enough, in the necessity of two worlds about to collide, for better or worse?

The Lady would have all from them, in the end. One way, or another. And the path was narrowing, growing more tangled.

Gilbert and Will were arguing Gamelyn's motives, with David and Arthur adding their own opinions: here and there, back and forth.

Robyn, she begged, silent. *I need you.*

Do you, then? Black eyes slid up beneath his brows, shone gilt beneath the ghosting of cowl and horns, and lowered once more.

"—want us sidin' with some noble's cause, Gilly? You turning back to your own, then?"

That was uncalled for. Marion began a protest.

Gilbert merely snatched a rough cuff at Will's head. "You *are* my own, you daft sod! Even when you're acting a proper horse's arse! All I'm doing is trying to understand what—"

"From the wrong side!" Will aimed a return blow.

Gilbert dodged it with swordsman reflexes. "The *reasonable* side, you stubborn pillock. 'Tis better than fighting amongst ourselves just because we're scared juiceless!"

Will opened his mouth for another comment. No sound emerged. He flushed, looked away.

"Aye." David's concurrence was muffled by Tess. She had burrowed, tight-wrapped about his neck, in nervous response to the row. "We're all we have."

Gilbert reached out and stroked the little ferret, his eyes steady upon first David, then Will, who returned to his original plaint, focused as a shepherd's dog.

"D'you think I don't know that, eh? And all the while, that bloody Templar has only ever been bent on taking what we *do* have!"

"*William*," Marion warned, and threw a beseeching look at Robyn.

She wasn't the only one. Will also tried a bid for their leader's attention, just as unsuccessful. Robyn was once more bent over the quillion dagger, tracing spirals in ash and sand.

"Lady grace the Queen, I've nowt against her. She was good to us," Arthur said. "But she's asking sommat impossible. How can we take her word as safety, amidst every enemy we've ever made, and them crawling over a place cursed by t' Wild Hunt?"

"Franks!" Will agreed. "Nobles and mercenary bastards who'd just as soon take our heads! And the Queen's son—"

"Our King," Gilbert reminded, mild.

"Our King' . . . pah! He's t' worst of 'em, off in foreign lands, murdering those as don't believe as him. Nowt but a bloody-minded *Christian* butcher! Wain't you see, Marion, you're askin' us t' join forces with the same ones as murdered our families!"

"Nay. Nay I en't." And it wasn't merely Marion's own voice, but Hers: a soft purl of power, a breath of cool wind setting a hive of bees to thrum and warm. "This en't about the Templars and whether they're the same sort of Christians as that wretched Abbess. This en't about fighting for some king who scorns the very lands he thinks he rules. This is about claiming our own! *Our* reign, and what rights we can!"

"Our own?" Arthur marvelled. "Rights? We've *no* rights outside t' Wode!"

"We're wolfshead, Mari," Will insisted. "Have y' forgotten?"

"None of it. Never." She met Will's eyes, saw them widen and reflect the silver crescent, shining-sudden, in her own. Saw the others display much the same as she sought their gazes, one by one. "From Arthur's arm to David's family, all taken. From Will's mam murdered by one of those Motherless soldiers, to my mam and da beheaded on Beltane nigh to our sacred stones—and by the same cursed woman who butchered everything I loved and kept me like some trophy or spoil of war, wit' no more mind left to me than a pet dog. And you think I've *forgotten?*"

None of them could meet her eyes. Will flushed and glanced, again, over at Robyn.

Again, Robyn kept at his tracings. A short silence fell, all of them uncertain in the face of Robyn's adamant—and uncharacter-istic—reticence.

"You're right, lass," Arthur finally said. "'Bout so many things. But this? Nay, it en't worth th' risk. It en't just our freedom, but everything else as goes with it, from possibly getting shot 'trying to escape' by some trigger-happy soldier, to the King telling his ma he's no intention of pardoning the most notorious outlaws in th' Shire Wode."

"Aye," Gilbert agreed. "There's a bloody *lot* of what-ifs."

Marion bent down, dipped her fingers into the silver scrying bowl, flicked another offering of mead into the fire. It gave a *whuff* and whisper; she straightened.

Whispered back, "*If.* What. If."

Then she rose, crossing her arms over her breasts. "'Tis a proper wager, but one thing's certain. *If* we don't play this game? We'll regret it the rest of our lives, however long those are."

"Marion—"

She cut Will off. "'Tis proper easy to bide, a pack of men

beholden to nowt but each t' other, and two fingers up t' all who'd think to stay you. It's become a game, aye?"

"And why not?" Arthur demanded. "Sure, there's more than just us, but there bides more wrongs than we can ever think to right."

"Only they're creeping in here, en't they? 'Twas just fine before, weren't it—your own lads' guild, and one thing's sure, if I weren't Robyn's sister, would you've packed me away too?"

"Marion!" Will, stung. "You're one of us!"

"Yet all of you, so soon to dismiss a mum and bairns without that same chance, eh? Bent on packing them ower t' Hathersage—despite that she asked *me* for Heathen hearth-right and sanctuary!"

"*Marion*—"

"—and in the meantime, all *surprised* by how pleasant it's been to have little ones around, amidst us. What kind of life is that?"

"That en't *fair.*"

"What en't fair," she retorted, "is the assumption that grasping at life is *weak!* Did a one of you ever think upon that mayhap Gamelyn's after just that? Trying for offered chances?"

"Ah, fer—"

"If you interrupt me to whinge about *the ginger-haired Templar* one more time, William, I'll do you proper! Aye, of *course* Gamelyn's the honour of Tickhill as his stake. But what about the stakes we were offered? By the Queen?" She eyed them all, one at time. "Have you all forgotten what she promised us for our aiding her, fetching her out of Blyth Castle and to a safe place so she could ransom her son? This proves she en't forgotten!"

Gilbert started to speak, fell silent, and looked aside. Will scowled. Arthur frowned, scratched a palm over his bald pate. David swallowed, hard. John's absence was a pang, part and parcel of the silence.

"Mayhap she en't." It was a growl from the other side of the fire. "Forgotten. But nowt matters. Nowt but that *if.*"

Silence. Little Tess made a soft, purry noise, as if in query, then took that silence to unwrap herself from David's throat. She undulated down his torso, leapt to the ground, then slid around the fire towards Robyn.

"If," he repeated, still sitting by the fire, still watching the tracings the quillion dagger's tip described between his crossed knees. "What. If."

The little ferret humped to a stop, beady eyes intent upon the dagger as it moved, glinted.

Marion tried to bid her brother *look at me.* He didn't. And his next words were . . . chancy, making her unsure whether they meant support or condemnation.

"What are promises? What is any of this"—his gaze flickered upward, though 'twere more a blow—"but the beginning of another end? No beginnings, after all, without sommat cast aside. Aye, Mari?"

Marion frowned. The others were plainly uneasy.

Will protested, "Robyn?"

Robyn's gaze dropped. All the while he kept tracing the tip of the quillion dagger in the soil.

Marion could see the shapes even from where she stood, across the fire . . . nay, See them, a chain of wards and runes all tied together.

What are you after, Hob-Robyn?

"Ends. Beginnings. And only one thing's certain." It dropped to nigh a bass rumble. "We're still free *here*. There en't a one of us, Maiden, Hunter, or Men, as should be bearing the power to lead anywhere or anyone upon a path of *what-ifs*, 'lessen it be singing in sommun's heart to follow."

"And you?" Will retorted, shaky-hot. "What's in *your* heart?"

The dagger's path wavered, stilled. Robyn hunched as if the words were a blow, and Marion wanted—really *wanted*—to pick up Will's staff and have a go at him with it.

Why is it always you, Will? Why wain't you just. . . trust him, for once?

Only the shaky timbre of Will's voice, and his expression—almost frantic, thwarted and apprehensive and a thousand other things Marion couldn't name—made the impulse collapse in on itself beneath a surge of sympathy.

And no more could Will stop pushing. "Robyn . . . *Rob.* In the name of what our parents died for, in the name of the god whose steps you walk, answer me this much. Are you after this . . . this change, whatever it may bring into our Wode? Are you set on followin' that ginger-haired noble's brat wher*ever* he goes, daft and blind as a buck in rut? Even if your own head's forfeit? Even if *we're* forfeit?"

The dagger began, once again, its motions, and Robyn considered it, cocking his head. While the gilt-glimmer still backlit his eyes, no longer did the shadowy horn-cowl crown him. Merely the tangle of hair, ringlets long and damp as if he'd passed through a quick rain, or ran himself into a sweat.

The god was there, quaking and quivering within. Yet what spoke was no godling Voice, merely her brother.

"Is that truly what you think of me, Charming William? As nowt but some dutiful wife-slave from the Christians' book, aye? '*Whither tha' goest, I will, forsaking all others. . .*" It swam mocking, sank deep with contempt. "Allus do their like make of affection as a levy due in fetters and chains. D'you now do the same?"

Will flushed—the dart had hit square. The others lingered silent, unwilling and uncertain. Over by the sleeping pallets, the bairn started to fuss, and Aelwyn's gentle shush made it plain she wasn't sleeping, but neither did she move.

"Robyn?" Marion husked out.

Those black eyes flickered over her—just a breath—and over his men. Over the shape of Aelwyn huddling with the wee ones, then roaming up to skim the treetops and the starry night beyond them.

Fell back to the dagger, still moving almost gentle as he spoke. "Any more, seems t' me as some things are bent upon dancing past our reaching hands. Like mists, nobbut t' wisp away, faithless and lost. You canna hold 'em. Canna change 'em. Canna *trust* 'em. What is there for our like, 'tennyrate?—but earth beneath our feet, Wode around us, and t' wind breathin' our *tynged*."

"*Robyn.*"

"Enough," he told her, and finally, *finally*, met her gaze. "It en't worth it, Mari." One hand spread, gestured to take in their camp, their people, the whole of the Wode surrounding them. "It en't worth *this*."

The misery in his voice made her heart lurch upward and shiver tens of tiny cracks. "Robyn, you don't understand."

"Do you, Mari? Understand?" It was plain, and almost plaintive. "None of this is about what's best for *us*, aye? D'you think the Templars truly want to help? Nay, they want power. Their Master's set on conniving the secrets of our Wode, and if he can't charm his way in, then believe me but he'll use anything to take it. The Queen might think she owes us, she might be set upon what she thinks might help us. Still, in her world women are nowt but property to be locked away. What can even a queen promise as will truly last? And Gamelyn . . . " It cracked, high in his throat; he cleared it and went on. "Damn me, pet, but he'd rather let the trap gnaw off his leg than admit it's even *there*. Whats'mever he's bent on throwing himself after—"

"Hob-Robyn, you haven't seen what I have."

"I'm seeing too much of late." Each word ripped breathless, a staccato nigh to running, complete with slip and stop. "We're losing him. I told John the same thing, asked him to stay with Gamelyn, watch over him . . . but what good can it do when he wain't face us?"

"He wain't go against his orders, Much said."

"Oh, I know he wain't. Orders. Oaths. No doubt 'tis a proper fine edge he's walking . . . only what about his oath to us? He keeps going *back*, aye? Back to the iron and the bells and that bloody, sodding *cross!*"

"Have you given up, then? Because that doesn't sound like my brother."

"Even this arsy outlaw knows when t' whip has flails 'stead of a plain lash. D'you honestly think any of this'll change a damned thing? Change . . . *him?*"

"Change is exactly what this *means*—"

"Our like en't *allowed* change! Whilst their like'll see us dead or destroyed. We are *occupied*, Mari! And the only place where we can stand up like free Heathen men and women is here, in *our Wode!*"

All the while, the dagger never lost its rhythm, sketching the spell with exquisite care. The others were starting to mutter agreement. She was losing them.

"You were the one as led us here, Hob-Robyn! You were the one as challenged the Horned Lord in the first place! You offered the game—that you take your rival as lover and honour your Maiden as sister, give Her—*me*—the choosing, as 'twere done in ancient times! All the way down this path, you've led all of us, because you were following your heart and that deep-strong Voice in your soul, and we knew it. *Knew* it. I en't so sure, now, what path you're walking."

"And you know what path *he's*—"

"But I do know you're listenin' to fear. Just like Gamelyn!"

Silence. He stared at her, eyes glittering. The others barely breathed.

"You were t' one, baby brother, as agreed to help the Queen. You were t' one as talked all of *us* into the possibility of her terms!"

"Mayhap I were wrong!"

"Mayhap you weren't! Do you not see what a pardon could mean for all of us? Even a chance of one?"

He didn't answer.

Marion whirled, addressed the others. "Do *any* of you see what this could mean?"

"Could," Will pointed out, wooden. "More maybes."

"Some maybes are worth the try!" she persisted. "Say *if*, then. If you were pardoned—any of you—what would you do?"

Another silence, just as heavy as the first, and longer.

David broke it, resolute. "I'd go openly to Matlock, was I pardoned. I'd be a real father to my boy, not some outlaw he can't acknowledge or see without risking his own neck. I'd do for my old gramma, more than poached game and stolen coin."

Robyn's brows drew together and quivered; the dagger's movement faltered. Will grumbled a sigh. Gilbert put a hand to David's shoulder, squeezed. David covered it with his own and peered over to where Arthur stood, just past Will.

"Arthur? You once said, were you able, you'd like nowt better than a real fireside, a wife and bairns."

"And what wife would have a maimed man, even pardoned?"

"Helena'd have you, and you know it, man," Gilbert said, soft. "All you'd have to do is go to Hathersage and ask her."

A flush crept over Arthur's neck and scalp. He leaned over and gave Gilbert a shove. Gilbert smirked, but Marion saw the wistful cant to it. Aye, for Gilbert had *chosen* this life, seemed nigh conflicted as Robyn, crouching over his rune-poems.

Will was silent, frowning—*thinking*—and all the while, peering at Arthur and David.

This is the path We need take. The Lady's voice, ringing solemn. *This change is one We must admit to the covenant. If We're to survive.*

The men, nigh as one, inched back, and only then did Marion realise she had spoken Her words aloud.

Robyn was staring at her, eyes still glittering—no more with god-sprung gilt, but a passion all too human.

The bairn started to cry, muffled beneath the blankets.

The men jumped, startled. Marion unclenched her fists.

Robyn didn't. Instead, with swift violence he rose, in the same motion thrusting the quillion's blade downward. Marion felt it—they all did, couldn't help but—as the tracings muttered and gleamed blue-white, spiralling then skimming upward over the dagger, which kept shuddering to and fro in its earthen sheath.

Finally it stilled. The sketched charms sparked, faded, and disappeared, as if they'd never been there.

"It seems there's no choice"—Robyn yanked up the dagger, rammed it home at his belt— "but t' make the try."

- XVII -

Robyn had never seen the likes of this. Surely he should have been prepared. He'd seen Blyth, after all. Saw and smelt the warnings as the outlaws approached Nottingham. Great hanks of smoke setting the sun to crimson, their sources blazing the landscape, controlled and not. Deserted outlying clearances and villages, people long gone, fleeing inward or out and leaving their tofts unworked despite a glorious sunny day. The river dulled akin to a dirty mark, all but unrecognisable from an uphill vantage.

'Twere common people as always paid for lords' whims.

And more were taking to the same road Robyn trod, intent upon the practicalities of destruction: some afoot, some with packhorses, some with wagons either empty or piled with supplies. And noise. With every step it rose from a murmur, to a roar, to a literal cacophony of shouts and squeals, fires crackling, the thunder of hoofs, the thick whine of crossbows and harsh clank of steel.

The trees thinned, and the siege revealed itself in a swath of dust and smoke at the feet of Nottingham's great fortress.

The outer bailey wall was burning, a dark line collapsing, here and there, into char and fallen timbers. Rising from the smoke were strange, uncanny . . . beasts. Limbs and joints angled together, they looked more that than any human invention. Akin to dried grasshopper carcasses overcome by a swarm of scavenger ants. But these weren't ants . . . and carcasses didn't belch fire into the sky. Stories couldn't prepare one for the sight of King Richard's army expressing his wrath with the great war-making machines.

The *creak-clank* and grind of one being wound carried even above the other noise. Robyn stopped, fascinated despite himself. Beside him, Marion halted as well, with a cringe as the thing loosed. A *sproing* and *scree* of fiery stone sailed into the air, trailing a plume of black smoke. Half a breath later came a massive *crack* of impact, wood splintering, sparks showering. Just after, as if in echo, the ground shuddered beneath their feet.

"Bloody hell!" Will said from behind them, nearly dropping his brace of coneys. Arthur did drop his, muttering something that could have been a prayer—or mayhap a curse.

"Have yer gawkin' elsewhere, noddy fool!" a man warned, coming the opposite way down the road with a trio of horses on a common tether.

Will made swift way, Arthur close behind, clutching his fumbled load. They both started back towards Robyn, but he halted them with a fierce-slight shake of head. It was welcome reminder of what they'd all agreed for this primary approach: stay within sight, but scattered.

Beneath the makeshift yoke she shared with Robyn, Marion twitched her shoulders and squirmed, slight, against the thick gambeson and tunic padding her torso. Robyn snatched a quick, fond tug at her battered hat. Smiling, she gave a game try at a calming breath. Unfortunately, the linen wrap beneath the gambeson that flattened her breasts also foiled any deep sigh. Muttering, she took several smaller ones, shifting her grasp on the basket swinging between them.

Nowt more than a boy and man shifting a load of tubers to the siege, hardly worth a notice.

"Whoa there, whoa, lad."

It was soft but carrying; Gilbert had stopped to assist a man whose packhorse was clearly unhappy with the machine's uncanny eruptions. The horse's antics were threatening to slip a load of full panniers. David moved in. Between the three of them, they settled the horse. All the while Gilbert kept a casual hand near the sword at his belt, a well-to-do mercenary. David patted the horse's white-blazed face, the very picture of calm, save for a furtive stroke to one of John's protective charms. Another sign of unease lay in Tess, burrowed nose to tail in David's cowl and tight-wrapped as the charm about his wrist.

Aye, the plan was a good one, though it had taken some sweet-talking to convince everyone of that. Aelwyn and the bairns—even more a liability in this situation than an entire band of outlaws walking into camp—had been left in Matlock with David's grandmother and son. Altogether too many chances, too many nerves just that raw and on edge. Give the Queen the ones she asked for, whilst the remainder stayed hidden, able to act if the gamble went wrong.

With a furtive glance to his band, Robyn kept walking. It wasn't long before they descended into the valley. Nigh hidden by foliage from their vantage, farther south it was plain: a shining ribbon tied at the foot of Nottingham's cliff face, the River Leen. One of its prongs headed northward and the other fed the wide moat circling Nottingham's lower bailey.

Marion stopped dead in the road. "Robyn. *Look.*"

He followed her gaze to a cleared, charred space just beyond the river's hedge. Upon a hasty, new-made gibbet, within plain view of Nottingham's walls, dangled a line of men.

They moved, as if they'd just been dropped and the nooses only now doing their work. Closer inspection proved that an illusion, aided by the dark flutters and dives of carrion birds. And . . .

Robyn felt a shiver tease at his nape, as if Arawn himself had opened the underworld's gates and breathed His kiss into the smoky air. The Wild Hunt, once ridden, left a mark both deep and lingering.

No man who occupies the high chair of Nottingham shall rule it 'ere long, rumbled the Horned Lord. *Less he heed the curse, and 'ware My wolves.*

Robyn tried to shudder it away; the Horned Lord's presence merely sank further inward, lingered. Marion's hand trailed along the basket yoke to his, skin against skin, gentling.

"I wonder if *they* were outlaws," David muttered from the other side of the road.

Doubt, a brass held to all of them, reflecting fit to quash longing towards any Hunt, or the thrill-chill of tweaking danger's whiskers. Robyn glanced at Marion. Her expression in particular sobered him, eased the god-Voice. She looked as if she'd been punched low in the gut. Wondering—and again, he could feel it like his own—whether her convictions had done nowt but fetch them all into a contest they'd no way of winning.

This, Lady told Lord, *is no game.*

En't it?

For they were here, and if they'd any chance to see the other side of this, the moment had to be played. Doubt had to be banished.

Lifting a hand to shield his eyes from the smoke-banded sun, Robyn squinted the short distance. He gave a derisive snort. "Nay, no chance those're outlaws. T' sods're dressed too well."

Gilbert whistled. David chuckled. Arthur barked a laugh, and Will threw a smirk over his shoulder at Robyn. Marion shot a forbidding look. Robyn raised his eyebrows and stroked her fingers, still against his.

They all started as another wrench of metal and wood exploded from the far side of the milling encampment, and another fiery projectile went screaming and smoking across the moat. It landed short of its mark but bounced, tearing up turf before careening against the gatehouse. There were more shouts as the wooden tower began to smoke, then screams as it whooshed into flames.

"Pitch," a man heading away from the siege with two empty sacks slung across his shoulders said to no one in particular. "Stubborn bastids've been pouring it over their own gatehouse!"

Well, as a deterrent, it seemed to be working: those who'd been anywhere near the thing were scattering. Smoke curled into the air, adding a thick greenish-black to the miasma hovering over the valley.

The fireball that had hit the gatehouse rolled drunkenly into the water, hissing, and sank.

"There he is, then." Marion's pace picked up.

Much was waiting at the fork of river and moat, beside a new bridge that had surely been cobbled together a se'nnight at most. The wood, roughly hewn, was that green; even the mud slopping at both ends hadn't yet darkened it. A brace of horsemen clattered over it, making their way downriver at a gallop. Everyone gave them a goodly berth, but none crowded Much . . . and no wonder. Dressed in a seemingly unremarkable brown cloak, it was thrown back to display a dark tabard with a scarlet cross, palm-sized and heart-high. Broad arms akimbo, sword plain at one hip, Much looked every bit a Templar's paxman.

Marion's steps slowed.

The other outlaws were watching Robyn. He gave the expected signal. The band's discipline held. Will and Arthur headed down a small easterly path with their coneys. David turned west, and Gilbert, with a courteous quip to the man he'd helped and a fond smack to the pannier-laden sumpter's rump, followed. All of them according to carefully made plans: a lingering scope of the surround, ending with a covert camp north of the siege. The Thorny was a perfect bolthole, thick with brambles and marsh.

Robyn just hoped they wouldn't need it.

Then, as he and Marion headed towards the bridge, the siege engines went still.

A battle camp: chaos with a thin veneer of control, and that slapped on, mayhap careless, atop liability. If command was broken, there would be consequences. If men chafed beneath that command, they likely wouldn't be here—or would be *in* command.

Or would keep their mouths shut and *do*, as Gamelyn had.

John, of course, *did* as well—and that particularly annoying. Upon their arrival at Nottingham—complete with the fanfare Durham had desired, including the King's own presence in greeting—Gamelyn had bent to his most pressing duties, riding to where the sergeants and paxmen had started setting up picket lines . . . and, well. John had appeared out of nowhere, taken Falcon's bridle, and given no answer save a shrug to Gamelyn's quick-hissed "What in God's name are you *doing* here?"

Instead, John aided Gamelyn in seeing to the horses under his charge, made especial arrangements for one of the Templar squires to clean Falcon's tack, and proceeded from then on to shadow Gamelyn, implacable as any peasant serf bound by dutiful pride to his overlord.

To question further would merely draw attention—and trouble, no doubt—to John, so Gamelyn acquiesced to the inevitable, if a bit less than gracefully.

Much, on the other hand, seemed pleased to have John around. *Sommun seein' to you when I'm away,* he'd said, just before he'd gone to the agreed-upon outlaw meeting place at the temporary bridge upon the river's fork.

Gamelyn couldn't help but hope those outlaws didn't come. *Disappoint all expectations.* He couldn't help the silent plea Robyn-ward. *No question I've done as much to you.*

He's part of the plan, Guy insisted. *Marion will see to any reluctance.* Or so he hoped. Didn't hope. Christ, whatever . . . *Whats'mever,* Robyn's voice taunted from memory. Gamelyn simply closed his eyes.

He ate, mechanical, the midday's repast. The other Templars stepped lightly about him, kenning the *come no nearer* mien with the instincts of comrades used to biding too close in uncomfort-able situations.

Even the Under-Marshal respected the *Confanonier's* distance, crouching across the fire and eating in silence. John was the only one dared come close, disregarding any frost-and-verdigris sideswipe of glare with mute intractability.

Then, chaos becalmed.

All the men hesitated in their doings, looking up. Listening. The roar and rock of the great mangonels had ceased. In its absence there was . . . well, not nothing. Quietude, aye, but one that hovered in its own odd and not-quite-silent hum. Those who knew, waited. Watched. It would come, any moment . . .

And so it did, breaking the heavy lull with the blare of a horn. Upon the heels of that came a riot of shouts and calls, all merging into the inevitable cry:

"To arms! To arms!"

The Under-Marshal leapt up, still eating amidst barking orders to his surrounding Templars. Abandoning bowl and mug by the fire, Gamelyn rose, snatching up his sword belts, mindlessly grate-ful for the excuse—any excuse—to stop thinking, to *do.*

A horse came cantering across, its rider picking a jagged, not-so-careful way over and between unpacked goods, hastily flung-up tents, and eating soldiers. He was shouting commands.

"Mount up, my lords! The King has called for cavalry! The outer bailey has been breached. The rebels are fleeing to the inner bailey!"

The camp burst into activity, swarming from welcome respite to disturbed beehive: orders barked; everyone gathering flung-aside accoutrements; squires heading for the horse pickets and snatching up equipment as they ran.

"The *stone* inner bailey," said one of the Templars beside Gamelyn, grabbing up his own kit as he tossed ale remainders into the fire. "And he wants horses?"

"Show." The Under-Marshal scraped the last of his bowl with his bread, shovelled it in his mouth, and tossed the bowl to a nearby squire. "Not only both the Archbishops, but the Templars and the lords of the shire, mounted and led by the Angevin Lion? King Richard no doubt means to flood the outer bailey with men and horse, and so lay claim before ever a run at the wall begins."

"Will the whoresons listen to reason?" another grunted. "Struth, we'll be the ones payin' hell breaching *that* gate."

"The rebels fired the outer gates!" a squire, running up, reported with eyes bright. "The King's happy about it! He ordered his own tent set up within, in plain sight of the rebels. So Master Hubert's ordered our pavilion and standard as well!"

Gamelyn nodded acknowledgment to the Under-Marshal's canny guess. No surprise, truly; the man was an experienced campaigner. The Under-Marshal nodded back; within it lay an implicit order: *The standard, then.*

On any march, the piebald banner never bided far from Gamelyn's grasp. After a quick finish to the buckles on his sword belt, he hefted the standard from its temporary brace.

"*Beauséant!*" the call resounded as the banner unfurled.

"We're in, at last!" a younger squire crowed.

"Not until we're gathered, we're not," the Under-Marshal said, terse. "*Templiers allez!*"

And there was no more talk, only obedience.

John was watching Gamelyn. When Gamelyn met his gaze, he shrugged and went to fetch Falcon.

"Go," Robyn said.

They had waited at the bridge for tense moments, Much swearing beneath his breath the entire time, while the outer bailey gate went up in flames and the centre of the river valley encampment came alive with men and horses.

"I were ordered to bring you, safe and—"

"Nowt safe in that mob!" Robyn retorted and, as Much eyed first him, then Marion, continued, "I might be after me pleasures as I can, but I en't daft!"

"I wain't *let* him do owt daft," Marion insisted, and Robyn wasn't sure whether he should be amused or huffy at Much's palpable relief. A tiny grin slid into the corner of Marion's mouth—and that surely told which *she* was. "Until you know where to bring us, we're better here, aye? Brother and me'll wait for your return."

Her resolve seemed to ease Much all the more. With a swift hand to chest, he dipped his head, spun on one heel, and sprinted over the bridge.

Marion's smile faded as she watched him disappear into the fray.

"If I knew how to proper fight—"

Robyn grabbed her arm and yanked her away from the bridge as another group of men a-horse came thundering up the path and leapt onto it with a clatter and slide of shod hoofs.

"Neither of us kens that kind of fighting," Robyn admitted, peering into the mêlée—and that's what it was, no question. "Though they might welcome a decent archer or four if their lot makes it to that upper bailey."

The sound of galloping hoofs; more riders towards the bridge, this time with men running behind. The formation pushed Robyn and Marion farther against the riverbank. Marion was still watching after Much, though he'd long disappeared from sight.

"You would, wouldn't you? At his side?" Fond admiration warmed Robyn's voice.

"Wouldn't you?"

He would. Would Gamelyn let him.

"The Hunt still lingers, aye? Mayhap the walls would let *us* in, brother-mine. Just a spell to run it, Wild again."

He played along; 'tweren't hard, as it put a gleam in her eye and a thick song in his own heart. "Aye, we'd sing the spells and charge in like our mam's people, women and men side by side, painted blue and winding t' god's horn."

"T' *carnyx*," Marion agreed, chin set, then slumped. "After I baste his head."

Robyn's brows quirked in a frown.

"He didn't tell me, Robyn."

Tell her . . . ? Ah. Much's tabard, and what it undoubtedly meant.

"That un's been hanging nigh to his master too long," Robyn growled and slung an arm about her. "C'mon, pet, there's a stand of trees. Close as we'll fetch to our own place hereabouts, more chance to see what's doing."

"And less chance," she rallied, "of being trampled by sods wit' more balls and brass than proper sense."

The massive, iron-and-oak gates had already been heaved shut by the time the Templars charged past the burning gatehouse and into the inner bailey. A sparse rain of crossbow bolts greeted them, buzzing through black smoke and red sunlight.

One quarrel smacked into Gamelyn's shield and another snagged in the banner. He let Falcon hop and dance his rage, hurled abuse against the stone wall, and waited for the inevitable call to regroup. It came quick enough: a blare of horn. Gamelyn twirled the banner twice, signalling their retreat. Luck was with them; only two men down with slight injuries, and that from carelessness.

They gathered just out of crossbow range, detailed a line of ivory, ebon, and crimson backed by the cross of Canterbury and the gathered colours of three shires. The King's bannerman let fly the golden Angevin lions, and a cry rose from a hundred throats, roaring through smoke and red sun to impact against the second bailey like a thunderclap.

Nottingham Castle, just beyond, lay eerily quiet.

"It is good to stand with you again, *Confanonier,*" Hubert said beside him, and Gamelyn smiled.

They kept standing, a visible and implacable honour guard, whilst the King's tent was set up beneath the red-and-gold banner with its trio of golden lions.

It was too close to crossbow range for Gamelyn's comfort. He expressed as much to Hubert, and his master shrugged.

"*Exactement,* and when the lords of Huntingdon and Canterbury ventured as much?" Hubert ran a hand up and down his stallion's crest. "Our liege merely said there should be no doubt who was here to reclaim what was his . . . ah. Your man has returned."

Gamelyn inclined his head to see Much indeed approaching. A frown twitched at his bearded face—no doubt for the crossbow quarrel still sticking out from Gamelyn's shield. But then, the frown had another reason, explained in a circumspect hand-sign: *They're here.*

Unsure of his own reception of the knowledge, Gamelyn busied himself with steadying the banner in its stirrup block, and leaned down as Much reached his side. "Where?"

"Waiting," Much assured, quiet. Still frowning, he began to tug at the embedded quarrel. "Just himself and herself, by t' bridge. No others."

Likely for the best. It didn't ease the sudden, strange lurch within Gamelyn's breast.

Don't be a fool, Guy censured.

"Didn't want to lead 'em in," Much continued, "til I knew 'twas secure enough."

Secure. In a siege camp surrounded by all the nobles of England— the important ones, anyway—and most of those humiliated by the Thief of Sherwood.

"Mayhap better to wait until this is finished," Gamelyn murmured. "Warn them back into the forest, and take John with you."

"Johnny wain't come." It took a few tries and a small grunt to free the bolt. Much scowled at it. "Y' know how he is."

Aye, Gamelyn knew. He could feel John's gaze upon him even now.

"Have your paxman take your horse, *Confanonier.*"

Gamelyn turned at Hubert's voice, found the blue-grey eyes steady upon him, the vein-roped, powerful hands throwing the chestnut stallion's rein.

"The King's pavilion is raised, and we are to disperse, albeit ready to move back in with a moment's notice. Bruer and I shall join the Master Preceptor for further orders, whilst the Under-Marshal sees to the raising of our own pavilion there." A gesture just shy of where, indeed, the royal scarlet-and-gilt was raised, and Hubert's nod towards the Under-Marshal, drawing nigh.

"Give the signal and take the banner—see to its proper situation, *non?* We will soon rejoin there."

"Aye, my lord Commander."

"It should not be long." Hubert's gaze roved the new front line: stone walls, bailey, torn-up grass and the gate, then back to Gamelyn.

They missed nothing.

"Furthermore, should we have any . . . ah . . . visitors? Your man should ensure they are well guarded, and brought to our pavilion for their own safety."

Odd, how relief—or whatever it was Gamelyn felt—could both soothe and sour one's belly. "Aye, Commander."

They'd waited as the sun crawled out from beneath smoke, here and there, to make its way towards the western horizon. The underlying tension was nigh driving Robyn mad. He'd been contemplating his own siege, albeit swift and silent with arrows at nock, to drag his Summerlord out of this mess by his lovely-sleek head of copper hair. And, all the while, Marion watched the siege flow back and forth, muttering beneath her breath things that made it plain she'd help. Much had shown up just in time.

Nottingham's siege camp proved a twisty, tattered, filthy mud pit. Much led Robyn and Marion past the still-burning carcass of that outer bailey wall, and made a prudent traverse across the same lower bailey Robyn and Marion had once escaped at arrow-nock with an injured Gamelyn flung across Robyn's shoulders like a sack of grain. They passed tens of smaller tents—surrounded by torn-up earth, men milling and lounging, eating and tending to gear—to end up here. The pavilion would have held three cotter's families, and it wasn't by far the fanciest of those surrounding it. Sparse on the ground and newly raised, from the still-soft ground and the earth raked up wet-new about the stakes, all the tents hunched altogether too close to the looming, tight-shut inner gatehouse of Nottingham.

These flimsy bits of cloth and sticks would prove little protection on what was essentially a front line. Particularly that crimson front pavilion . . . its owner was either a ballsy sod or not terribly bright. Odder still, that nowt was forthcoming from essentially waving one's bare arse cheeks at the castle walls. From crazed action to yet another prickly lull, all within the time it took to walk from riverfront to castle gate.

And here *he* stood, Robyn of t' Shire Wode, within the becalmed centre of yet another proper storm raging through Nottingham . . . and did that make him ballsy, or just plain daft? Only this storm weren't any sort of magic. Unless they'd wandered into fae, and that explained why time was, all to the sudden . . . Other.

Robyn murmured a quick charm against the mention. Not that there was any likelihood the Barrow Folk would durst come near all this, with the iron and despite the blood, but he touched the hilt of his dagger to seal the charm anyway.

Where in bloody damn are *you, Gamelyn?*

No answer, only a horse neighing from somewhere behind the Templar's pavilion, answered by another. No sign of John either. Robyn was no more pleased by that than how Gamelyn had just up and left without so much as a kiss blown Robyn's way. Mayhap John was keeping his keen eyes fixed 'pon Gamelyn, like Marion and Much had said he meant to do. Mayhap the Templars were all gathering for a cavalry charge. Robyn would like to see that, he would.

"You look proper fetching in those breeks." This from Much, behind Robyn and just inside the drawn-back pavilion entry.

"I wish I could say the same for you in that tabard." Marion had lingered with him.

Silence.

Then, "Why didn't you say anything?"

If the wretched tone in Marion's voice set a crack in Robyn's heart, Much's answer shivered it into anger.

"Marion, you knew it was temporary, me being banished, like."

"It must run in your bloody Order," Robyn growled, just loud enough and with a glare towards the pulled-back pavilion flap. "Bein' so reticent, like, with sommun as shares your bed."

Within the entry, Much had his mouth open, about to make some retort. He thought better of it and shut it with an audible *pop*.

Marion let out a curse that could have scorched the pavilion's fabric.

"You'd best start talking, man, and keep on," Robyn muttered, though to which Templar, he was uncertain.

Another silence, then more conversation—this low, unintelligible. Robyn grinned—no pleasant expression—and crept closer, ready to lob another volley should it be necessary.

He halted. Frowned. Cocked his head and snuffed the air, turned sharp eyes upon the drifting smoke; previously aimless, it sucked backwards, then curled forth.

The soldiers began to appear, then, silent and armed to the teeth, akin to phantoms in the wisps of murk and sun. Despite any impulse to duck back into the pavilion and hide, a dull fascination kept Robyn there, watching the men pass with ranks doubling, tripling, all parting like water around the surrounding pavilions, including that ballsy crimson one.

The odd lull receded and filled itself with a singular rhythm; Robyn realised it was the dull *tap. . . tap. . .* of sword against shield, timing the tread of heavy boots, the *clink* and *thap* of chainmail against leather, the heat and menace of determination.

Some of them were Templars.

They were converging upon the gatehouse. Just a stone's throw away, the army—and it was one, no question there—stopped.

Waited.

Much cursed, a low echo within the pavilion that was followed by Marion hissing his name, then nowt from there, either. Robyn wanted to turn to them but kept his own watch upon the gatehouse, wary. What was about to fetch up, literally, into their laps?

There was a grind and clank from the main gate. A small door revealed itself, creaking outward from the great one's leftmost corner. The waiting army angled forward—slight, but there—and a shaky voice issued from the three-sided gap. A rich baritone echoed in answer, bouncing off the gatehouse door.

Robyn knew that last voice. With a tiny skip and step forward, he was able to confirm said recognition: the tall, white-clad Commander of Hirst with—of course—his most trusted bodyguard. Both of them standing in the bloody *front* of the battle line. Hubert was speaking to the one who was hiding behind the little door, and Gamelyn stood beside him, holding the Templar's banner, with shoulders squared and russet-gold head bared beneath an abrupt shaft of the inconstant sun.

That same bit of sun spilled upon the gatehouse tower. It illuminated, through a tall and bloody narrow opening, a figure lurking behind the thick, curved wall. The odd combination of sun, smoke, and shadows betrayed a glint, here and there, wielded within. Likely a crossbow.

Eyes narrowing, Robyn kept his gaze upon the arrow loop, shrugged the longbow from its place athwart his shoulders, and fingered a flax string from its pouch at his belt.

Whatever Hubert was saying, the man at the door wasn't having it, not a bit. The sun making its play for Gamelyn's bright hair slid behind a bit of smoke, and the gatehouse went dark.

Robyn stepped his bow with a soft grunt of effort, slipping string over horn tip, and kept eyeing that arrow loop. The sun glinted back into view. One shaft of light in particular kept dancing, above and behind, to backlight the crossbowman in the upper gatehouse. Pulling a quintet of arrows from his quiver, Robyn set to knotting three in his hair.

"What is it?" Marion came up beside; he spared a swift glance. Much was nowhere in sight, and her eyes were swollen, but the look in those eyes dared Robyn to so much as mention it. And— he smiled—she carried her own bow, strung and ready.

"Hearken where our Summerlord bides."

Marion's eyes widened, and her pale eyebrows did a dance, one up and the other down. But all she said was "Aye, well, no wonder Much lit out like he were afire" and drew several arrows from the quiver at her hip.

Robyn loved his sister.

"Y' canna chain t' wind," he quipped. "Such wishes are for Christians and rich men."

She smirked.

"There's more'n one bloody crossbow sighting our lovely Templars. Two there on the hoarding, one . . . nay, two"—he could see another now, moving into position behind the second loop— "in t' loops, and . . . bloody *damn!*"

This as the smoke stalled upon a breeze and the gatehouse went into shadow.

With a breathy paean to the wind, Robyn drew several arrows from his quiver, slow and sure. "You've the lighter bow, Mari. Best cover the ones up top." He pushed, light and ready, into his grandda's longbow as she nocked and fisted her own arrows. "I've marked those buggers behind the loops; do they so much as twitch, I'll have 'em."

"Who let this . . . !" A cry rose from within the walls and garbled into more shouting. The man at the door whirled angrily, then lurched sideways with a yip and disappeared. Several of the front-line soldiers leapt after as the door was heaved shut—one ran into it with a curse.

More shouts, with one from behind the wall that left no doubt.

"Shoot!"

And everything went to hell.

Crossbows discharged. Lances flew. The ground troops dove left and right, wrenching their shields atop them like turtles ducking into their shells. The Templar banner alone remained upright, sprouting from a ceiling of shields as, from the wall-walk—and more, from those damned dark arrow loops—the bolts kept coming.

Marion loosed once, then again. With a shout, a man fell from the hoarding and crashed into a brace of the waiting shields, an arrow in his throat. Robyn danced sideways, watching another quarrel spring from the loop. He loosed a desperate shot, chance and trajectory alone. It slid between the narrow lintels as if greased, and there was a yelp. Had he hit? No way to tell; instead he took aim at the other loop. Whoever was stuck in up there—they weren't the normal dusted-off clot handed a crossbow—kept loosing bolts with unerring efficiency into the soldiers below.

And still no sign of Gamelyn, though the piebald banner flew, obdurate. The shields below it were beginning to resemble hedge-hogs.

Robyn's heart clenched to quivering in his breast, forced tight his breath.

Surely he'd know, if . . .

"L'arbalète!"

The throaty bellow made Robyn start; indeed, 'twould have brought the cows in from a hundred-acre field. Save that all the cattle here were English, and that was definitely Frankish talk.

More shouts resounded against the high bailey walls. A burly, bright-haired man fair exploded from the fancy crimson pavilion a stone's throw west, still spewing Frankish.

It was answered by a round of cries—*"Pour le roi!" "Du roi!"*— and a mass of crossbowmen poured from behind the pavilions, rushing the gatehouse.

Roi? That was their talk for a king.

Robyn fisted two more arrows, all the while eyeing the man who still bellowed like some Frank bull. King Richard? Nay, that was unlikely. His tent was big and fancy, but the man wasn't dressed to match. His fair hair bore no crown, was tied back all haphazard, its gingery cast picked out by a shaft of breakthrough sun. He'd an even ruddier complexion, with cheeks and nose that seemed more *too much wine* than *too much sun*, and a bit too much around the belly, as well, for some warrior king.

Still.

Something in him required pause, a pure vitality slapping at

Robyn's face like sand in a whirlwind. And the man's bellow would stir an army from sloth to ambition, at that.

Robyn shook it off with a curse, aimed another arrow for that far loop, and hissed the wind-breath from entreaty into desperate command. Marion too was waiting, arrow to string, for another of the topmost bowmen to show themselves.

Sun rippled over the gatehouse, backlight and satisfaction and, as if similarly conjured, a rush of crossbow- and pikemen converged from behind the crimson pavilion. One of them was yelling, in Anglic:

"Archers! We need more crossbows!"

Marion picked off the last of the wall crossbowmen.

But Robyn saw only the two forms, backlit behind those arrow loops. With a half-breathed snarl, he loosed—one, then immediately another.

And just like that, no more arrows came from the loops.

The shields were dragging themselves back, slow at first, then with more speed as the reinforcements took up the slack, crossbowmen covering their retreat. The piebald banner was still upright, but it was waving, almost frantic. Robyn craned his neck, stretching to the apex of his considerable height.

"D'you see them?" Marion too was trying to fetch a glimpse past the carapace of shields. "Can you see him?"

Robyn couldn't. What he did see, sudden and startling, was the Frank bull. Standing beside the huge pavilion, girt in a short chainmail tunic and dirty hose, he was no longer bellowing but staring at Robyn. Robyn couldn't help but stare back. The gaze was that compelling, that fierce . . .

That *admiring?*

An angry snort from within—the Horned Lord, hitherto quiet but now rising in challenge. With that, sudden and frantic strands of *tynged* roiled outward, gold and bright yet frayed, as if with some harsh wind.

Then, darkness.

Robyn's knees wanted to buckle; he held them straight.

But he couldn't look away.

Several crossbow bolts whizzed wide to embed themselves at the man's feet. He hopped back—only slight, to be sure—and made a gesture Robyn had never seen before. Yet of its meaning there was no doubt.

Arsy sod, this Frank bull. Robyn smirked.

Several more arrows—closer this time, but the man merely bellowed abuse at the gatehouse. Robyn laughed, unwitting and unwilling admiration, and as if he'd heard, the Frank bull turned to peer at Robyn again.

Another thick swarm of men surged from behind the tents,

cutting off any line of sight, running for the gatehouse and the downed men.

The force of the charge threatened to take them with it; instead Robyn shook himself back to thisnow, grabbed Marion, and ducked inward. He was glad he had. The din grew all the louder. The pavilion rattled about them, as if with some stampede of rut-mad bucks instead of soldiers. Shouts, and clang of steel, and something that might have been a horn answered—only it sounded more a wounded, squalling cat than any proper horn. Others resounded almost immediately, as if ashamed.

But even those couldn't drown out the voice of the Frank bull, barking his unintelligible orders. Exhorting the charge against the gatehouse and leaving, once again, a strange and displaced lull separate from the fierce shouts and clanking steel of action.

"I think," Robyn said, "that was the King."

"Of course he was the King." Marion pushed back from his chest, eyeing him. "Didn't you see the royal banner out front? The golden lions on the crimson background?"

"Mmm. Mayhap."

Marion snorted a laugh and hugged him. "You're a proper git. And I'm glad we're in here, not out there, only . . . " She frowned, and he caught the thought as if 'twere a lobbed ball.

"Aye. We should go, find 'em—"

"Make ready! The King has called for the machines!" Commander Hubert's voice rose just outside the tent, odd and strained. "Have the men ready to ride!"

"The entry!" Gamelyn's order snapped like a dried branch. The tent flaps were flung open, and a quintet of crimson-splashed tunics, white and dark, scurried in. They'd their Commander in their arms, one at each limb. The leg Gamelyn supported had a crossbow bolt angling out of the thigh.

"Clear t' board!" Marion blurted out.

Robyn leapt at the broad table, sweeping a long arm across. Cups and platters and parchments went flying. Marion snatched a blanket from two cots in the back, flung one side at Robyn as he finished, and they flipped it flat just as Hubert was lowered—carefully—onto it.

A short grunt escaped him as his leg came to rest against the table—it must have been painful, but he kept giving commands the entire time. "Group with Temple Bruer. Brother Tom"—this to the first white-clad, burly Knight—"go now and tell Bruer he'll be the one to lead any charge."

"We can't just leave you here!" Gamelyn protested.

Hubert shook his head. "*Go,* Tom!" It brooked no argument.

The burly Templar bowed and made a hasty retreat.

Mail clinked and scraped as Gamelyn half knelt on the table

and took Hubert's hand. The look on his face was as wretched as Robyn had seen in some time.

"Shall I fetch sommun?" Much asked from the entry—he was the one holding the tent flap aside.

"Fetch the Infirmarer!" the second Knight said, and Much started to obey.

"*Non!* The Infirmarer has others, worse, to tend," Hubert insisted. "You must go, make ready!"

Robyn had never understood the phenomenon of panic instilled by a leader's fall, even when his own had revealed it. But now it was there, raw: in Gamelyn's flushed and sweated face; in the elder sergeant's back-and-forth between orders; in the other Knights' stance. Fear, curling about the edges of brave men.

Hubert refused to let it seize the command rightfully his. "Brother Alfred. You will guard Master Wymarec's left flank, with one of Bruer's Knights to his right. And *Confanonier,* you will, of course, fly our banner just behind them."

"You need the Infirmarer," Gamelyn interrupted. "And we will wait until he comes."

"*Obedience,* Templar! Neither of you will—"

"There's no need for anyone to disobey owt." Marion's voice overrode them, calm and sure.

And Robyn thought, *Aye, of course.*

Gamelyn peered upward, as if only then he'd realised Marion was there.

"I'll see to your leg." Marion stepped up beside the table. "Much and Robyn'll help me."

"Who is this woman?" the other Knight protested.

"The same one who healed my back," Gamelyn murmured.

"Aye, milord," she acknowledged with a tilt of head.

And wasn't *that* irritating as a flea bite, how Marion could call him "milord" and fetch nobbut a calf-moony half smirk for 't?

The horns gave another blast.

Hubert fixed a stern gaze upon his Templars. "I'm in good hands. Go."

"Aye, Commander." The other two men wheeled and marched back outward without so much as a second breath.

Gamelyn followed, yet hesitated in the entry, his eyes flickering to where Robyn and Marion stood. Said, "You're the ones who shot those archers, aren't you?"

"Aye," Robyn answered, soft. "Protecting a few interests, like."

There was, mayhap, warmth underlying the chill in those juniper-green eyes. Otherwise there was no response. Indeed, Gamelyn started to turn away.

A sudden and brassed-off imp prompted Robyn to draw the quillion dagger from his belt and hold it up, dangling, from his fingers.

"Not to mention, milord," he drawled, "I'd a dagger to deliver."

"*Robyn!*" Marion hissed.

Gamelyn stopped, stiffened. He half turned and eyed the dagger, gleaming in the dull light.

Then, a cold half smile quirking at his lip, he strode forward and held out his hand.

Robyn shouldn't have been surprised—but he was. To ease the burning in his gut, he smacked the pommel in the mailed glove— bloody hard, too. Not that it mattered. Gamelyn received it with that blend of chill and heat . . . nay, no heat remaining; this was Guy, indeed. Fingers closing about the hilt, he drew it towards him.

Stopped, frowning, as Robyn didn't let loose. Too good, those reflexes. The blade had barely crossed Robyn's palm.

"Take it," Robyn said, and let a smile twitch his lip.

Confusion warmed cold verdigris, if only for a moment. It gave Robyn time to purl the protective spell upon his tongue, suck in air through his nostrils, then murmur, as the keen edge bit and slid across his palm, "*Gwarchodaeth.*"

Before the blade could go deep, he loosed it, slicked with his blood. His hand stung, seeping; he clenched it, let the spell-breath waft between them.

All three of them sensed it. Behind, Marion gasped. Gamelyn flicked a gaze to her, giving the tiniest of judders, but controlled it just in time, his eyes returning to the blade, then Robyn. They narrowed.

Did he remember another time, another impasse amongst the ruined stones of Mam Tor? Robyn had used the same hand, then. Guy of Gisbourne hadn't hesitated.

"Brother Guy!" Hubert broke the standoff with a stern—if somewhat wobbly—order. "*Allez.*"

"*Oui, le maître.*" Brother Guy—aye, 'twere him indeed—broke Robyn's gaze without a qualm, shoved the blood-rimed dagger into his belt, bowed to his superior, and helmed his russet head. Striding back to the door, he took the banner from Much, delivered a few quick instructions, and was gone.

Much was not so indifferent. He slid Marion a crestfallen gaze as he walked to Hubert's side, but scowled at Robyn.

"I hope," Hubert said—to Marion, but his eyes were upon Robyn, "your brother is somewhat more merciful when he helps you take the crossbow bolt from my leg."

Foolish, and angry and heedless . . . aye, to all of it. Robyn looked at his bloodied hand, already sealing itself, hoped it would do what Gamelyn wouldn't allow him, and cursed.

Assuming they got to the end of this, would there be anything left for them *but* the damned pardon?

- XVIII -

"Here it comes." De Birkin shifted in his saddle. His words were somewhat unnecessary, for the siege engine trundling up the hill was presaged by a massive collection of groans and creaks. "Are our Templars in position?"

"Aye, my lord Preceptor," Bruer's Commander assured. "De Lacy's archers are in readiness, and the King's crossbowmen."

Perhaps that too was unnecessary, as said archers were more than obvious, crouched just before and to the right flank of the mounted cohort of Templars. But it was a fundamental skill; armies travelled upon redundancies, the best way to defend one's arse.

Falcon was, finally, learning another fundamental skill: the art of resource conservation. Sometime in the past day he'd stopped fretting in the wait; indeed at present, one hip cocked, he dozed. Gamelyn wished he himself could do likewise. It was difficult to still his mind and focus solely on the task ahead, instead of chewing over what he'd left behind in the Templar's pavilion.

His wounded master. Marion tending him. And Robyn . . . another and altogether dissimilar sort of wound.

Gamelyn's fingers, of their own accord, slid to the blood-skimmed dagger at his side.

Stop mooning like a child, the inner predator sneered. *'Twill do you no good.*

Clenching fingers into a fist, instead Gamelyn watched the *petraria* roll into place.

It took four oxen to shoulder the thing, mainly because of the soft turf, describing sandy-fawn furrows in the machine's wake.

Men with ropes at all corners steadied it on its way, and men with large triangular shields protected them.

Not that the latter was necessary at present. What few crossbow bolts flew hadn't the range to do more than spatter ineffectually upon the turf. That two factions were quarrelling within Nottingham's walls was no mere conjecture. The small group of peacemakers who'd come to the gates and spoken with them had been foiled—who knew why? The realities of facing a prolonged siege meant more within would entertain the inevitability of surrender. Particularly with a mangonel rolling up the hill, monstrous in the lingering smoke.

Not that Gamelyn would regret handing out some retribution for the treacherous arrow that had downed Hubert. Even if the actual traitor had been dealt with. A tiny grin ticked the corner of his mouth as he remembered the faultless length of flight that only longbows—and well-schooled archers weaned on them—could achieve. He'd seen that much just before Hubert had fallen and he'd yanked the shields over him, protection from the relentless rain of more crossbow quarrels.

The quillion dagger, snug in its sheath at his right hip, seemed to warm, vibrate.

"One hopes the rebels will come to their senses. The amount of waste . . . " De Birkin sat just ahead and to Gamelyn's right, in the front row of mounted Templar Knights. His ice-blue eyes took in everything: the approaching *petraria;* the crumbling-charred outer walls; the hanging bodies quickly becoming little more than stringy meat upon bone. The hawklike gaze also swept over the mass multicoloured troops—with their Brethren like piebald chess pieces at one wing—and landed upon their King. Richard had girded himself in a short chainmail tunic and trews, with merely a filet upon his gold-maned head.

"He was at dinner with his companions when word came as to the *petraria* being brought," Bruer said, his gaze following de Birkin's. "I wish we could convince him to come away from the inner bastion. Or fully armour himself. He is a . . . visible target, he and the others." Several higher-ranking lords stood with Richard.

De Birkin's gaze turned from piercing hawk to flat serpent. "God will protect his own."

Gamelyn flicked a curious glance in his Master's direction; unfortunately, the cobra saw. That, and how Gamelyn's fingers of their own accord curled about the quillion dagger.

"A new blade, *Confanonier?*" Curious, at first, then considering. "It seems familiar."

"We would parley!" A shout from the top of the gatehouse, shrill with apprehension.

"As you did last time?" one of the commanders—Pontefract's, from his tabard—shouted back.

There were accompanying murmurs, ill-tempered, from the siege troops.

"It was a mistake! It will not happen again, if—"

"If?" Catcalls this time, and jeers from the men.

The Templars remained silent and unmoved, as did the lords beside the King's pavilion. The King himself had expression enough for them all, demanding a translation. One of the mailed lords—Huntingdon, it was—quickly provided one. The King gestured to one of his guardsmen.

The man stepped forward, made a harsh demand in Norman French. "Speak to your liege in a proper language!"

A delay, then a reply came back in the requested tongue; it was no less apprehensive. "How do we know you accompany our liege? How can we—"

"You *lie!*" Another shout from beside the first, and a fist waving above the battlements. "All of it, lies! The King, God rest his soul, is lost to us, and England beggared and gone to hell all for nothing, torn apart with *your* petty feuds!"

The King spat a round curse and started forward. One of his companions pre-empted the motion with his own body. Even against the King's breadth and height, this man was sizeable—and brave, to gainsay his liege even in defence.

"Ah, the King's tame mercenary. "Mercadier will, please God, constrain our liege to sense."" De Birkin's attention had riveted back to the major drama, thank the Lady

You thank me, Gamelyn, but you do not lis—

It was becoming easier to shunt aside any distractions. No less painful, however.

With an inward growl, Gamelyn instead considered Mercadier— more, remembered his reputation. Hardly tame, but utterly loyal and utterly feared. Mercadier had been the one set loose in Normandy to protect Angevin interests. Such had been prompted by the French king's decampment from Outremer and return to France, which in turn had been prompted, it was rumoured, by a fight between him and Richard. And so had boyhood comrade-ship ended, with a quarrel more apiece of spiteful lovers than kings.

Well. With Richard, anything was possible.

Or you? The inner predator scented blood, no question.

Mercadier must be making sense, for the King halted—not without a few angry gestures. Mercadier took those like a stubborn pit dog, giving not an inch. Eventually Archbishop Walter came forward as well, his raiment stark contrast to the mercenary's but his pleas much the same. The King finally gave way with ill grace, stalked back to his lordly cohort and, with an impatient and ill-tempered fold of beefy arms, set himself to watch.

Walter stayed. It was Mercadier who—with a small clutch of

soldiers and a bannerman bearing Canterbury's cross—escorted the Archbishop forward, all the while keeping him out of crossbow range. A half shouted back-and-forth discussion began with the men atop the wall.

De Birkin lifted his rein. The broad, blond rump of his stallion lurched as he began to inch backwards, halting only once his knee rested alongside Gamelyn's. He was peering, once more, at the dagger, which was . . . well, it was vibrating all the more, beginning to warm Gamelyn's hip.

Did de Birkin sense it as well? After all, he was the First of the English Inner Temple.

Why Robyn had decided to blood it, Gamelyn might not fully comprehend, but some deep-set part of him recognised, *responded*.

He could not afford that response. He would *not*.

"It is good you think of your Commander. Take heart. Hubert will be well. A painful wound, but one a long way from his heart and mind."

The compassion surprised Gamelyn. He met de Birkin's gaze. A small smile, then the pale eyes strayed, taking in the stone wall rising beyond. The dark head cocked, heeding the verbal engagement, oft indecipherable, taking place.

Nevertheless, Gamelyn sensed the attention upon him, wound and cocked like a crossbow at full nock.

Such suspicion is hardly apropos, Guy snapped. *He is our Master.*

Nay, 'twas altogether apropos. Gamelyn waited, silent, for de Birkin to touch the trigger.

"We will see him well. We all need him." A pause. "How fortunate those archers joined the fray when they did. Undoubtedly they saved more than Hubert's life and yours." Soft and altogether smooth, the words, but edged in every corner. "It is making its way all over camp, how two peasants with longbows preserved a morn's rout."

Gamelyn's fingers twitched upon the dagger. Thankfully it was imperceptible to de Birkin.

"I heard one of them loosed a nigh-impossible shot. Not just once, but several times in quick succession." De Birkin leaned closer, his lips nigh brushing Gamelyn's ear. Whispered, "Such a man must be in league with devils. Or have the luck of one. Who could he be?"

Gamelyn barely breathed, staring at the wall with eyes as flat as ever the cobra could sport.

"Master Preceptor?" Bruer prompted, and de Birkin straightened, turning towards the gatehouse.

The small inner door was, once again, opening. Two men, sweat-wet and pale as chalk, nevertheless walked through the door with dignity. No cowards.

Archbishop Walter watched them come, extended a calm,

expectant hand. The two men did careful homage, rose. There was more talk, low and urgent. One query carried, echoing off the battlements

"My lords wish proof, most holy lord of Canterbury. How do we know? How can we know who he is?"

"How can we ever know who anyone is?" de Birkin murmured, as if to himself, and so soft, only Gamelyn heard. "Who will take the crown? Who will lead us back to the old ways, lines, and leys, and renew their might? Not a lion, but neither a mangy wolf."

Mangy wolf. At Gamelyn's hip the quillion dagger quivered, as if in response.

The two men were following Walter and his entourage back to the King's pavilion. Brave men, indeed. Shoulders squared, they seemed resolute upon whatever the fates might next throw their way, fair or foul.

The best of a bad situation, Guy concurred. *With a shield or on it.*

King Richard allowed the men close, held out his arms as if to demonstrate *Here am I, your anointed King,* then spoke to them with a voice that carried across the field, stern but not unkind.

De Birkin too was watching. "This is good. No more waste."

"Other than the ones the King will undoubtedly hang, does the mood take him," Bruer murmured.

"Of course." With a nod, de Birkin once again angled closer to Gamelyn. "Continuing our former course, then, I am led to believe we have welcome—if somewhat notorious—visitors. Eh, Brother Guy?"

Gamelyn slid his gaze sideways to meet his Master's. Faultlessly courteous, emotionless, *not there.*

My name is. . . is. . .

What? Damn you, what?

He couldn't finish it. Wasn't *sure.*

"Well?" King Richard's faultless and resonant *langue d'oc* rose into the bailey. "What do you think? Am I here?"

The dagger was no longer merely warm, but nigh searing a heated line upon Gamelyn's hip. He gritted his teeth against the oddling scorch, reached, curled his fingers about it.

Thought, *Stop it.*

And just like that, the dagger cooled.

"We do indeed, Master," he acknowledged, soft.

De Birkin smiled. "Very well, then."

Hubert lay on the table, head raised upon a bolster and Much's cloak, injured leg raised on a well-padded chunk of firewood and swathed in clean linen.

Moreover, Nottingham had surrendered.

Not that Marion had paid much attention, busy removing the crossbow quarrel from Hubert's leg. A quick and clean accomplishment: no bone compromised; just muscle pierced through. The quarrel had been sawn and drawn with a good, sharp knife, a bottle of whisky, and two sets of strong arms to hold Hubert down, just in case.

But Robyn had employed another tactic—the magic. When Marion had questioned the wisdom of Robyn compromising his defences in enemy territory . . . well. He'd been insistent.

And the magic had held, strong and sure, with no hint of weakness in the conjuring or the making.

Marion knew the whys to that, too. Gamelyn's body was elsewhere, but the quillion was athwart his hip, blooded powerful with protection. Moreover, Gamelyn's heart remained with his wounded Master, fierce if unaware.

Much had insisted upon staying with Hubert—no doubt Gamelyn had ordered it so.

Still tender from the words exchanged earlier, Marion let him, washed the blood from her hands in a basin of fresh water, then padded over to where her brother stood, watching the surrender play out.

King Richard himself led his gathered armies through the second bailey gatehouse, this time mounted on a great ivory charger. Whether his presence, or the massed and varied powers—the cross of Canterbury, the cavalry of Templar Knights flanking their King, the varied colours of the most powerful noblemen in the land—or mayhap the undeniable and stark facts of the castle defences crumbling about them, the rebels had no more stomach for the fight.

Robyn watched it all, a rangy silhouette by the flung-open entry, leaning against a deepset tent pole. His gaze lingered upon one soldier in particular, who held the piebald banner aloft and sat easily his prancing bay stallion as he and his fellow Templars followed the King through the flung-open inner gates.

No fault there; Marion was worried over Gamelyn too.

"They let the first pair go back" was Robyn's quiet statement as Marion came up beside him. "Those ones, there—see? The handful kneeling before yon fair-haired Frank bull all fancy on his warhorse? They're for the yield."

Frank . . . bull? It sounded as approving as derisive.

"Mm. I'll warrant they're fair nervous." Marion leaned her head against Robyn's shoulder. "He could have their heads on a pike wit' a word."

"And we're here, mayhap waiting the same."

Marion started to give a tart answer but fell silent, unsure of what to say. It was, more likely than not, as true as the words with which she had talked them into this. Mayhap more.

Robyn gave a foul curse and slid an arm around her. "Bloody damn, but I canna seem to keep my tongue tucked behind me teeth this day. I'm sorry, Mari."

"I'm one as should be sorry," she murmured.

"Nay, pet, you were right t' push this. Life's all chances, en't it?"

"Like you shooting those archers." She snugged closer, changing the subject. "That was bloody brilliant, Hob-Robyn."

"No more than yours. You've eye *and* patience. For more things than I can count."

"Marion?" It was Much. "He's rousing."

"Already?" Marion frowned.

"Templars are tough," Robyn quipped, following her back into the pavilion.

"'Tis Shire Wode magic." Much's smile started with Marion but included Robyn. "You've both done more 'n you know."

"The charge? How goes the charge?" Hubert's baritone was skinned of much of its richness; he sounded old, almost frail. Nevertheless, he was trying to sit up.

Much had a firm grip on Hubert's shoulders, not about to let him. "'Twere no charge, milord Commander. The castle surrendered."

"The castle?" Hubert refused to submit. "Take me—"

"You're to be taken nowhere yet, milord." Marion put a firm hand to his chest. "You're staying right here."

Hubert muttered something rather profane. Marion tried to hide a grin, but Hubert saw it. Frowned. Said, a bit petulant, "I fear I'm drunk."

"A good thing, milord Templar," Robyn put in. "If you weren't, you'd be more than hurting."

"Remember the leg?" Marion prompted, and this seemed to sink in.

"At least let me sit up, not lie here like a corpse being dressed for the crypt."

"Nay, not just now. You don't want to start bleeding again."

This, too, seemed to penetrate. Grumbling, Hubert settled back against the board. Robyn robbed a few more cots of their blankets, gave him a bit more padding for his head.

"Tell me of the battle, then."

Marion set herself to checking the leg as she, Much, and Robyn all obliged with what they could.

"I think those shots you loosed were the tipping point for us," Hubert mused.

"Bollocks t' that!" Robyn snorted. His gaze once more roamed the tent—had done constantly; not that he was about to ease down, in enemy territory—then returned to Marion, who was seated beside the Templar.

She eyed him back with a teasing crinkle of her nose.

"Nay, truly. Upon such things can battle fortunes hinge," Hubert continued. "At the very least, you saved my life, and many of my men. It was treachery, to lure us close with talk of surrender. We need more men skilled with those monster longbows . . . aye, my *Confanonier* told me what he witnessed as we lay pinned. His pride was for you, justifiable."

Gamelyn proud of him? It curled warmth in Robyn's belly.

Typical, the Horned Lord sneered, though faint. *He kills Us with neglect and anger, but he is "proud of you."*

"Even one shot such as you made would be remarkable. Twice and more?" Hubert's lip twitched. "Well, there are those who will cry it witchcraft. Either way, the legend grows, eh?"

"The legend"—Marion reached and patted his hand—"is what'll protect us. Or"—she shrugged, and Robyn saw a bleak wistfulness cloud her gaze— "see us hanged."

"All too true, Maiden." Hubert's eyes closed, stayed so long enough that Robyn figured him asleep. Marion too, for she straightened and started to pull her hand away. But Hubert's hand gripped fierce, and his eyes flew open, seeking hers. "I was surprised to see you, lass." It was suddenly fond, more so than Robyn figured the man would ever allow. Likely the drink. "Men's clothing was a . . . wise choice."

"Well, and t' Queen's grace requested us both." Robyn crossed his arms, the reminder purling soft, but a growl nonetheless.

Queen Eleanor, and bloody Guy of Gisbourne. Gamelyn. Whoever the hell he is in thisnow.

Do not abandon him, Hob-Robyn. The Lady was obdurate.

And who's abandoned who, Lady?

Marion was frowning up at him, puzzled; Robyn shrugged it away.

Hubert shifted, grimaced, then ventured, "Of course. I myself saw the missive that requested you. Nevertheless, we shall be cautious, *non?* You both shall stay beneath the protection of our Order until necessary; certainly until the Queen's arrival."

Well, and the man was used to giving orders, but that last piece of news tweaked Robyn. "You mean she en't here? We came for nowt?"

"She is nigh, never fear, and no doubt will descend like the wrath of God now the castle is secured. As will others, I warn you."

"Like flies to a blown carcass," Much muttered from where he was keeping watch by the half-pulled door flap.

Hubert grinned. "*Tout à fait.* There are many who will not know, or care to know, why you are here. And there are others who have reasons quite unfathomable . . . de Lacy, for example."

That one Robyn didn't trust as far as he could throw him. And the Baron was no lightweight. Not to mention his brother . . .

Hubert's thoughts seemed to run in tandem. "And de Lacy's brother, de Lisle lord of Peveril, has, ah, several reasons to seek your downfall."

"Peveril's lord," Marion repeated. "The old Sheriff of Nottingham, Robyn."

"Aye. Sounds as if trouble'll be running thick on the ground. All these nobles gathering and waiting like May wrestlers for t' prize ring and ram."

"Trust no one," Hubert said, firm.

Including you, milord? Robyn didn't fancy how he wanted to believe in Hubert's integrity. Templars took their oaths in blood and with as much reverence as Robyn received his own into the Shire Wode covenant. Who knew where such vows might lead? Despite the promises Hubert had made to the *dryw ardhu* of the Shire Wode.

Gamelyn, too, has sworn to Us and the Wode.

Ah, but what promises has Guy *made, O Lady?*

Well, and Herself had little answer to that. Marion peered at Robyn, troubled. Of course, she would sense Her presence, even if for some reason she heard nowt.

That troubled him, too, and for no good reason, to be hearing what his sister didn't. What he normally couldn't.

"The Queen has asked for you," Hubert said, "and now the King has noticed you. I think it will not be overlong until you are sent for. Until then, in our ranks is the best place for the both of you." A smile. "After all, a Templar's first and best role is to protect pilgrims."

"Even with *your* Master." Robyn said it slow, more abstruse senses testing out the flavour of Hubert's response, undertow upon an icy river.

"Just so," Hubert acknowledged. "It is with his blessing you remain here."

"But we're free to come and go?" Marion asked, her eyes still upon Robyn. Aye, and she'd had her own little run-in with de Birkin.

One more I owe you, Robyn vowed. Not that he'd so much as lain eyes on His Mastership since arriving here—which was fine by him, when it came to it. Only . . .

Robyn wasn't sure whether he'd made a bitter enemy at All Hallows, or merely another—what was it?—*conundrum* for the sorcerer to solve.

"Of course. But hearken this: it is not you who will suffer, should you further chance Master Wymarec's displeasure."

Marion puffed up like a threatened goose. "So he wain't face us, but take it out on sommun as he's able? Are we that much of a threat?"

"Oh, Maiden." It chided, and warned. "All of you, still so young for all your strength. My Master will use, as must we all, what tools lie to hand. He knows as well as you what card he holds in our talented *Confanonier*. The same trump that you, *dryw ardhu*, would toss upon a rebel's fire, to change and mould the worlds."

"We love Gamelyn!" Marion protested, while Robyn peered at the Templar, solemn and steady.

The Templar merely replied, "Do you think we do not?"

A pause, and then she said, careful, "I think *you* do."

Hubert chuckled, but it held little humour.

Robyn closed his eyes, let the Sight come. Moreover, recognised the fateful strands coalescing before his not-vision, a tangle-twine of dark scarlet fading into the black. Counted the pulse in his temples, opened his eyes. Waited.

Hubert sighed. "Heed me, Maiden. Guy does not know love. He knows only survival." This time the naming was blunt, his attention turning upon Robyn, though the words seemed meant for both him and Marion. "In truth, you and your gods have as much to answer for that as any Templar born."

It was plain Marion wanted to answer; instead she fell silent, looking down.

Hubert kept watching Robyn. Robyn didn't drop his gaze; gave no more away than the colour of his eyes. All the while, *tynged* danced behind them, promise and threat and unknowable phenomenon, as sloe-black and just as impenetrable.

Hubert finally dozed. Marion fussed with his bandages for a few moments, then rose and retreated to the tent opening.

She'd forgotten her hat.

Much watched as she came to stand beside him, kept watching, gauging, then decided to chance it. He put an arm around her. Marion stiffened, thought to pull away; instead she gave a huge sigh and leaned in. Much snugged her close, his dark head angled to her cinnabar one.

Robyn snatched up the hat and came up behind them. Laying it atop his sister's head, he ran a hand down the curls just beginning to reach between her shoulder blades. Tugged, gently.

She smiled, shifted the hat closer down.

All of them stood, silent, considering the smoking near-ruin of what had been Nottingham's greatest redoubt.

"Mari?" Robyn suddenly asked. "What does 'conundrum' mean?"

$$\text{(I)}$$

"How is he?" It was snappish.

It was also nearing dark as Gamelyn strode into the tent, sending his helm spinning into the corner. A yip sounded; it was altogether familiar, but he'd only attention to spare for Hubert, splayed out senseless upon the wide board where they had, only that morning, planned a strategy gone awry by treachery.

They will pay, Guy promised, tugging away his gauntlets and letting them drop with a rustle and clink to the hard ground beneath the pavilion. *They deserve no mercy, and I doubt the King will disagree.*

Already Richard had ordered the rebels deemed responsible for the false parley thrown into Nottingham's oubliette.

"Quiet, you," Marion ordered, low.

It was sudden and stark, the reminder of her voice; Guy and Much had fished Marion out of that same oubliette only the previous autumn. The memory had been faint until she'd spoken . . . as if forgotten. As if he'd bided with his Brethren all along. As if winter had never happened, nor spring begun to blossom . . .

"He's had a draught." Marion was peering at Gamelyn, one brow quirked. "But he's only just gone to sleep."

It was relief to see Hubert indeed asleep and comfortable as possible, with even a hint of colour to his face.

"I didn't have to cut very deep," Marion reassured. "The head was nigh through the thigh, and then we'd only to remove the shaft and clean the hole. That was painful, I'm afraid, but he bore up well."

"She packed it with mushroom dust. En't seen t' like since me old auntie t' Auckley and her cunning ways." Much snatched up the discarded gloves, banging them together with a stiff clink and scrape.

"Well, not quite dust," Marion amended. "But aye, dried mushrooms fight rot. Add some spider's web and slather honey atop, and none better. 'Twere what I used on you, if you remember."

Gamelyn didn't, not all that well, but rose from Hubert's side with a lighter heart.

"Wit' some of the magic." Robyn limped from the back shadows of the tent, one hand at his shin and another gripping the tossed-aside helm. "For you, and him. He's in good hands, you know. Neither of us are likely t' smother him in his sleep."

Gamelyn stared, mute, at Robyn, feeling that strange displacement again. Fate—*tynged*—plucking the strands of another life. The quillion dagger vibrated again, warming Gamelyn's hip.

Robyn kept holding out the helm. Gamelyn walked forward and took it, but Robyn didn't let go. His gaze had fallen to the dagger, black lashes lowering but not covering a sudden, eldritch gloss. Gamelyn tugged at the helm. Robyn still didn't release; in fact, used it to pull them close.

Whispered, a breath upon Gamelyn's cheek to match the one at his nape, "Why are you doing this?"

It was humiliating how a small, belligerent voice rose up from his chest, whispered just as insistent: *Tell him.* "Why are you here?" he rasped back.

"We were summoned, aye? By the Queen. By you." Robyn leaned closer. Ever so slight, the motion, and Gamelyn surrounded, not only by the heat and horns at his nape, but the warmth of Robyn's breath and body, shivering defences from ice to melt. There might have been none else there: no Marion; no Much; no Hubert sleeping sound-warm on the board; no camp of gathered warriors. Only Robyn's voice as he continued, soft, "Have you changed your mind, then? You don't want me here?"

Of course we want him here. And if this is the best way to lure him off the trail. . .

Shut up. Oh God, shut up!

Those god-sparked ebon eyes were watching all the while, and Guy rebuked, *Take care. He is no fool, though you are acting like one.*

"See, 'tis never easy to tell with you, pet. You spend as much time with *leave off* as *come here*, but of late I en't sure which you truly mean." There was a quaver, ever so slight, in the last words.

Dangerous, what it told in Robyn. What it teased from Gamelyn himself.

"Dangerous," Gamelyn said, and realised he'd done so aloud as Robyn's mouth—so close he could turn and kiss it, bury his face in black hair—quirked. "I mean, it's dangerous. You being here."

"Aye. For both of us." Long fingers—graceful and hard as a strung bow—trailed down Gamelyn's arm and rested upon the dagger. "Tis why I blooded the dagger, milord."

Scarlet upon the dagger, turning the sky to blood. The meaning of it plain—*alarming*—turning heat and longing to ice.

Gamelyn jerked back. "Yet you came anyway. Into the danger, bringing Marion with you!"

Robyn peered at him, brows drawing together.

"Of course I had to send the note. What else was I to do? Only I hoped you wouldn't be arrogant enough to come."

Oh, but that's not altogether true, Guy pointed out.

"Arrogant." It was flat, as flat and inexplicably opaque as Robyn's eyes. "Pot, meet kettle, I should think."

"Well, if you listened to anything anyone ever told you instead of being bent on the sound of your own voice, or letting the Horned Lord's supposed will be your excuse for traipsing into trouble . . . ! Do you just stick your neck out in the *hopes* it'll be lopped off?"

"I think you're one as doesn't listen to anyone, be it lover, Lord, or Lady." A mutter, just loud enough to be heard. "Only a master as holds a whip."

"And that's all right as long as you or your god are the ones holding it?"

"I'm holding nowt!" Robyn snarled right back. "And if ever I have, it's only ever what you wanted to give! And now you've decided you regret the giving, have you? That you fancy burying that heart of yours so deep beneath that sodding cross that nowt of what we are can so much as breathe? Well, fair enough, I'm *done!* I didn't come here for you anyway, or even for me. I came here for my men. For my sister, who seems to think, between you and the Queen, we've a chance for sommat more. Only all I see is less than I've ever had, and you turning into one of *them!*"

Aye, Robyn still held a whip; one laced with metal, a razored flail to split any composure. Gamelyn knew he should do something. Reach out, speak, deny . . . *anything,* only . . . Only.

If he spoke now, it would all come tumbling out. Every plan, every necessity, every terrified thought and wish, doubt and possibility.

His brain seized into silence. Like the closing of a stone cairn, it seemed to echo into the tent and hang.

"Why are you *doing* this?" Robyn cried.

The desperation of it nearly broke Gamelyn.

Instead, he let it buckle him, and fled the tent like the Wild Hunt was upon his heels.

Something just as brutal halted him as he ducked around and behind the pavilion: the dagger, radiating an icy cold, twisting his thigh with a brutal cramp.

He stumbled. The cramp locked tighter, immobilising him long enough to hear Much curse from within and fling the tent entry open.

Coming after, only . . . thankfully, the wrong direction. Gamelyn bit back a grunt as the cramp locked tighter, sending him to one knee beside the tent.

From within, Marion's voice rose, frantic. "Robyn. Go after him."

"Nay, Mari. Not no more." It was flat, bleak. "We'll do this. We'll play this cursed game, fetch what we can for our people, and go home."

- ENTR'ACTE -

"An amazing sight! Never have I have seen the like of it. Through an *arrow loop,* easy as breathing, and I wager the English didn't even aim!"

The spoken tongue was the rough patois of the commonest Norman foot soldier. Not that it mattered to the trouvère seated on a cushion by the fire. Words were his trade and languages his bliss. He nodded, running an arpeggio down the neck of his lute, and winced as the ripple of sound twanged discordant against the stone walls. Did it again. Confirming that the instrument tilted sharp along the third string, he set himself to tune it.

"Not just the once, either, but thrice in quick succession—it was no mere luck!" The trouvère's lord and king marched to and fro; his strides, too long for the small chamber, nigh overflowed with the dynamism of victory.

The chamber was indeed mean lodging for a King and his attendants. The covey of guardsmen were piled upon the stair beyond—thankfully it was a wide stone thing with a landing, made for pomp and show—pouring into the main hall below. Richard's body servants had drawn lots to see what trio of them would do him duty this night, and even those were nigh running into each other as they put away their lord's battle garb and tried to make the chamber more habitable.

Alundel stayed out of their way and Richard's. Though he might be less than pleased with the lodgings, he approved of his lord's reasonings. The finest of the main tower's chambers was being aired and prepared for the Queen Mother's arrival.

"And the other—he'd a lighter bow. There should have been no chance for a killing shot at that distance. But, *zwit-zwit*"—a motion of hand to accompany the arrowlike sound—"it was done! If only such skilled archers had accompanied me on the road to Jerusalem—leave off, I pray you; I'm warm enough!" This to one of the servants, hovering with a fur cape. "I tell you, Saladin's horse archers would have found a prime surprise in wait for their treacherous attacks, had I such men!"

Alundel nodded, only half paying attention. That one string was recalcitrant, twanging up one step, then down two. He only needed the half step . . .

The rush of back-and-forth footsteps halted, and a broad shadow fell between Alundel and the well-stoked, newfangled wall hearth. "You aren't listening to me."

"I am indeed," Alundel protested. "You said Saladin's archers would have stood no chance against the"—he looked up, tilted a sudden smile—"King of Sherwood and *his* men."

"Blondel." The name was both growl and reminder; to spar with an Angevin when his blood was up remained altogether dangerous. And the King was in a frightful temper. Already he'd threatened to hang the hostages from Blyth, only put off when he'd discovered his brother John's seneschal lurking in the chambers the Queen would occupy. Richard had ordered the unfortunate dapifer questioned—which, considering Mercadier, likely meant he would end the night all but flayed alive.

Danger or no, Alundel knew he would be yet one more castoff did he back away from too many of these verbal sparring matches. "Blondel." A sigh, accompanied by a strum of fingers, with a purposeful pluck to the sharp string as emphasis. "And whatever would my lord King call me when he's annoyed, should I pour indigo and walnut over my so-fair head?"

"An ass?" Richard retorted, and stretched out fingers to smooth one long, fair lock hanging down Alundel's blue tunic. The seeming caress tangled, nipped harsh. "After I shaved your damned head?"

"But alas! I should be cold, and unable to easily sing—ow!"

One more yank, and Richard turned away. "Wear a hat, then. I tire of this game, Blondel. It's time to retire."

"I thought you wanted music, my liege." Another run; another grimace at the string. The damned thing was refusing to cooperate.

"Let the lute warm up a bit more." Inconstant as ever, Richard ambled back over, held out his goblet. A quick servant took it, filled it from a small cauldron just starting to steam, then sipped it and nudged it back into his liege's outstretched hand. "I'm not tired, anyway. I've a mind to finish that *lai* we started on the voyage to this sodden, dreary island, and we will need the lute for that."

"You've a full day come the morrow, lord King. If we start composing, we'll never sleep."

Amidst inhaling the warm mist of the wine, Richard gave Alundel a narrow look over the goblet's rim. "You aren't my mother . . . but God's legs, you're right. She'll be here." A shrug of powerful shoulders, and then Richard flung himself into a chair opposite Alundel, peered at him. "A story, then, before we're off to—"

"My lord King?" From the other side of the thick wooden door, the voice sounded as if its owner had swallowed pitch and gravel, but it was respectful, and punctuated by the meaty thud of a mailed fist.

"I didn't expect the man so soon," Richard marvelled.

More pounding, and "My liege, may I enter?"

"Better answer"—Alundel smiled, though the words held their fair share of scorn—"before your pet mercenary stoves it in, all unaware."

"Blondel." Warning, low, then Richard raised his voice. "In, Mercadier!"

The mercenary never simply walked anywhere; he rolled, bowlegged and stout as an oak. And about as subtle as a blow to the face, Alundel considered, glaring over the neck of his lute as the man came to a halt.

Mercadier returned the favour, upped it with a sneer. He was known to aid and abet his master's various amusements, but he had scant esteem for the amusements themselves. Especially if he hadn't procured them.

Alundel angled his lute onto its stand beside the fire's warmth and wished Mercadier afoul of some legendary Nordic raid where the men were blind and somewhat desperate. Or better yet the northern shires, where 'twas said men fancied rams instead of ewes.

"Have some wine, Mercadier," Richard urged. "Have you found him?"

"No, thank you, my liege." Mercadier used as a matter of course the same vulgar patois the King fancied. "You serve a powerful wine, and there is still the matter of the dapifer, you understand."

Alundel rolled his eyes. Brabançon savage.

"I don't imagine that one should cause you any trouble," Richard scoffed. "Give him to your men and have a good's night's sleep. Did you find the archer? You must have, else you'd not be here."

"Word is flying about the camp, my liege, about the longbow wielder of the bailey gatehouse, but I followed the rumours to their source. The archer is in custody of the Templars, my liege, and one of the squires says he is indeed the one of which you've been told."

"So Blondel was right." Richard turned a brilliant smile upon

Alundel, and that one joyful expression was worth all the slights, all the games.

Pathetic, Alundel told himself.

"Yes," Mercadier said, with a grimace that suggested he'd rather stab himself in the leg with a rusty dagger than admit anything wholesome towards a catamite. Even the King's noble-bred catamite. "Shall I fetch him for you?"

Alundel raised his brows, reached towards the lute, and plucked a tiny arpeggio . . . better; the heat was helping. Said, mild and pointed, "Through an army of Templars? That might be even beyond your skills, Captain."

"If the King orders, the Templars must obey."

"If only the thing was so simple." Richard pondered his goblet, then drained it. "I owe them much. They owe me very little. And only the Pope can claim their true loyalty. Worm that he is." He tossed the dregs on the fire with a taut, seething fury. Alundel knew it was for all the time rotting in Europe, passed about from enemy to enemy, and Rome turning a blind eye to the sacrilege of an anointed King and crusader gaoled like some common criminal.

Immediately, of course, Richard crossed himself and muttered a short prayer, penance for doubting God's mouthpiece. It didn't last long. Richard too was God's chosen—and, moreover, knew it.

"Our royal mother said this young outlaw was close with the Templars—one in particular. Childhood friend, she said. Another 'to whom We must show gratitude.'"

He scowled and held out the goblet again, suffered its refill and tasting. With a thick-fingered hand that betrayed a slight tremor, he retrieved it and breathed in the thick steam.

"Gratitude always has a price; mayhap We'll ask the Templars to broker it. Such things are to their taste, after all. And the English Master Preceptor has been most accommodating." The scowl deepened. "A pity, that Grand Master de Sablé died in the Holy Land. He was a true friend, one of whom I could be sure."

"It is always better to be sure of any trust," Alundel said, half singsong, with a longing glance towards his instrument.

Richard saw, and his frown broke into a chuckle. "We will leave it for tonight, Mercadier, and more thought. After, mayhap, my trouvère"—the grin widened, and he raised his goblet in a toast—"advises me further. Good night, my friend."

Mercadier slid another sour look Alundel's direction but bowed low to his King. "Good night, my liege."

The door shut behind him. Richard peered at it, thinking.

"Advise you?" Alundel half teased, watching Richard beneath shuttered eyes, uncertain where any of this was going. "Me?"

At first there was no answer. Then Richard snorted and turned about. "Indeed! You've entertained me with many a tale about this peasant archer who charms clothyard shafts into his enemies like one of the faery folk and, it seems, has claimed the rights to run riot. In *my* forest. You were prey to one of his famous robberies and ended up conniving with him to sneak my lady mother from that ivory tower she insists upon as gratitude's expensive tender." A toast with the goblet, whether to his lady mother or Alundel himself was uncertain. "So ply me another tale—mayhap that lengthy *geste* you've been working on, to settle my mind one way or the other."

"So." Alundel raised his eyebrows. "You're beginning to believe my outlaw tales contain more than romantic fancy?"

"Fancy? Come now, Blondel, you know exactly how romantic I can be!" Richard challenged, collapsing into the broad, upholstered chair with a creak of skin and pop of strings. "I believe in the love when eyes meet eyes and songs speak from the heart, in a fair cheek to stroke or strike, in God's purpose behind the sword I wield. I *believe* that in the wake of my brother's treacherous mismanagement, it is more than possible for a puffed-up, arrogant peasant to become a lodestone of discontent. It seems I must now even believe he is the most consummate of archers. But that a wild boy has the power to do all your stories would claim? Fantasy! Or blasphemy."

He held out his goblet; Alundel waved off the servant and rose to pour it himself. Richard accepted the due homage but peered into the fire, silent for so long that Alundel frowned, prompted:

"My liege?"

"God's legs, but it was like watching a falcon a-wing! Cruel and cunning, devoted to the flight." He fell silent again, one hand fingering his thick, ginger-grey beard.

Alundel frowned, exchanged a glance with the two servants at their lord's elbow, and reached for his lute. He started tuning again, and the instrument, warm from the fire, finally began to respond.

"I still haven't decided whether 'twould be best to hang the peasant bastard or conscript him and his archers for the upcoming Normandy campaign," Richard said, sudden against the beginning melody. "So, my heart, tell me more of this . . . how is it? . . . Robyn Hood."

- XIX -

Queen Eleanor arrived after the bells rang Terce the next morning, riding a milk-white palfrey, and flanked by the flag of the golden lions. It hung somewhat limp in the lack of breeze, but she really didn't need it. The scatterings of midmorning sun gleamed upon the jewels at her throat, picking out the shimmer of her silk wimple and barbette, the nap of sky blue in her velvet bliaut, the ermine fur of the capelet cloaking her shoulders. She'd an escort tens strong, a group of ladies a-horse and, only slightly less well-accoutred, a baggage train behind and soldiers trailing, a Bishop and retinue to one hand, and a straight-backed, greying lord with his own *mesnie* to the other.

England's Queen Mother knew how to make an entrance. Standing amongst his Brethren, Gamelyn grasped the piebald tail of the banner, allowing it a careful dip as they all knelt upon the sodden ground.

The Archbishop came forward—Canterbury, not York; there had been some set-to concerning rights and rank when the two had converged on Nottingham—and all around answered the Archbishop's final *Amen* with their own. With the sign of the cross, all rose.

And if Eleanor knew the rites of ingression . . . well, then, so did her son, albeit in a much different manner. The King came bursting onto the scene and halted a stone's throw away from the new arrivals, planting fists on hips. Proclaimed, with all the exasperation Norman French could command, "You're late!"

"And you're dirty," Eleanor answered in same, taking the rein in one hand and leaning on the saddle pommel. "Ah, but a mother's work is thankless and never done. Earl Marshal, see how I arrive in some state, merely to see to a decent bath for my son?"

"God's legs, Mother! I have been a bit busy, you know!"

The lord beside Eleanor smirked and, with a strength and grace belying years of acclaim, dismounted. Gamelyn had the distinct wish to goggle like a damp-eared squire. *Comte le Mareschal.* William Marshal looked no less a peerless knight afoot—save a slight trace of limp as he went to stand at his lady's stirrup. Gamelyn had never walked in such exalted circles as to lay eyes upon the knight he had, as a young boy, idolised. Marshal had also been a younger son forced to make his own way in life, and through a combination of luck, skill, and fierce loyalty had risen, with lands and honour accomplished, to ride beside queens and advise kings.

Whereas you—the Lady took advantage of his lapse in concentration—*who could be a King, instead hide your light beneath a stark banner and serve blind men.*

He shuddered, pulled away. With a last grasp of insistent and unseen fingers, the piebald banner fluttered, teasing at Gamelyn's hair despite the lack of breeze. Eleanor, amidst taking the Marshal's hand to dismount, noted the banner's anomalous motion—more, noted who carried it. No reaction, though—save, perhaps, a twitch of lip as she slid from her horse.

De Birkin eyed banner, then banner-wielder. It was Guy who let shudder become shrug, a placid statement upon nature's vagaries.

"I was beginning to worry after you." Richard loped over and grabbed his mother's hands. "As of yet, we haven't stamped out all the wildfires."

"But you have started a few of your own, I see." Eleanor was peering out and over Nottingham's smouldering outer wall, crashed-in gatehouse, and the pitted, blackened keep door. Her gaze flickered over the machines sitting idle, lingered upon the hanged corpses. A few more had been added to the previous ones.

Gamelyn entertained an odd and shaky relief that his brother wasn't amongst them. Guy, on the other hand, waxed more practical. *It just means more trouble, down the road.*

Mayhap the conflicting voices in his skull would proclaim open warfare. That would be all too apropos.

"Not wild, but well under control," Richard assured. "The whoresons were intransigent, Mother; you'd have done the same thing. They're damned lucky I haven't hung them all, after what John's little weasel told me once I . . . "

Gamelyn was watching, so he saw the clench of Eleanor's hands, and her frown—slight, but adequate to quell even a king. No doubt a reminder: before the entirety of England's nobility, such an open parade of family dysfunction should cease.

Her words, though, teased. "We haven't missed council, then?"

Richard snorted. "Would I dare plan such a thing without you? But this much is true: had you been any longer, I was ready to send men after you. And here I'd hopes to hunt this day."

"Mayhap this old woman enjoys a lie-in as she can," Eleanor chided. "And you still should. Hunt, that is. We all deserve some respite, and the details must be set in arrangement, as you know. Not to mention"—a grimace as Eleanor looked around once again—"the place is a mess."

Gamelyn had to admit it was, rather.

"Ah, but I knew you would be the one to organise it all—who else?"

"Which means I merely go from ordering a bath for my son to seeing the castle scrubbed clean."

Richard laughed, held out his hand. As if that were a signal—and Gamelyn knew it was, of a kind—two of Eleanor's ladies immediately dismounted to flank the Queen. "Come, let me show you your quarters. Then I'll go hunting. Mayhap see to Clipstone before my lord of Scotland arrives to parley. I've heard some fine tales of Father's most-beloved hunting lodge. Hopefully little brother hasn't managed to turn *that* into a sybarite's brothel."

"There is something to be said for comfort, my dear. At least John never comes to board in chainmail. But nay"—Eleanor declined as Richard started to lead her towards the inner keep—"I've greetings to see to, the line to progress."

"You needn't—"

"Of course I do." She had already turned towards the waiting importances. "It will set me up after riding all morning. My lord Earl?"

Richard acquiesced with a bow and a kiss, then handed his mother to the Marshal, who bowed in his turn to lady and liege both.

Eleanor took her time with the progress. It was quite a line up. Some of the most powerful men and women in England were gathered—and still gathering—to acknowledge their seat of puissance. Three earls—Huntingdon, de Ferrers, and Chester—had pride of place with Canterbury as the chief besiegers. Chester in particular gave not only a deep bow over Eleanor's hand, but a sly utterance, which prompted Eleanor to raise a sceptical eyebrow, then give a hearty laugh and a tiny dip of head—*well done, you*—in return.

Next to them Hubert Walter, Angevin man first and Archbishop of Canterbury a definite second, bowed to the Queen Mother and noticeably did not proffer his ring for her to kiss—likely she already had done in Canterbury's nave itself. Stubbornly beside was Geoffrey of York, denied his own Archbishopric standard and still holding a grudging scowl, which his stepmother's regard didn't appease. Beyond him stood the Bishop of Ely—the monastery college at which a young Gamelyn once swore he'd kill to study— alongside a cluster of lesser nobles, all greeting Eleanor with both artifice and eagerness. In particular Maud de Caux, whose distaff line had long held the rights as Keeper over Sherwood Forest, made much of welcoming Eleanor. Her face could have curdled milk as Eleanor merely gave a polite dip of head and turned away, ignoring further entreaty. Next was de Lacy and—Gamelyn narrowed his eyes, stored away the notice for later contemplation—Brian de Lisle. Nottingham's ex-Sheriff was grave, subdued, and had obviously decided he was done with making poor choices.

As Eleanor advanced upon the Templars, Gamelyn found himself indulging in surreptitious regard of William Marshal. A derisive snort echoed Guy's opinion: *Like a wet-nosed squire!*

Amidst staunch refusal to heed Lady and Her Consort, now he was reduced to arguing with himself! Truly, it was its own sort of madness.

There is no argument. Was none, until. . . until he *proved a distraction. There's no time for this. The prize is within our reach.*

"My lord Templar, to you and all of your men . . . but where is the Commander of Hirst this day?" Eleanor's concern was real and sudden. "Master Preceptor, kindly reassure?"

Wymarec did so. "Commander Hubert de Gisborough is well enough, if disgruntled at having to neglect this honour, my Queen. He took an arrow through the leg. It is being well tended, but all of us were keen to ensure it would not become worse."

"Mother of God, bless him." Eleanor traced a cross upon her breast. "Rest assured We shall keep him in Our prayers. And if he needs further care, We will have Our own physician come to him. Though We have seen what physicians are employed by both Temple and Hospital, so no doubt he's in goodly hands." She took a deep breath and furthered, most formal, "Please convey to him— indeed, all your men—that spoken thanks is not enough for what you have done for Us, not only in the matter of Nottingham, but over the past months. Rest assured Our regard shall be commensurate with that assistance."

"You are too kind, my Queen. Our Order exists to serve." De Birkin's bow was a study in controlled grace. Gamelyn wondered what exactly the Master Preceptor thought of his circumstance: after all, Eleanor was a woman, was she not?

Eleanor tilted her head and made as if to move on. Instead she hesitated, smiled, and met Gamelyn's gaze. "You in particular We have Our eye upon, my lord *Confanonier*. As well as several within your acquaintance."

Such open acknowledgment was beyond expectation; startling, in fact. Ingrained manners were all that saved him. Thankful for their distance and requirements, Gamelyn bowed, held Eleanor's gaze with grave respect, and murmured, "My Queen does me grace."

"Not as much as you and yours have done Us. Kindly tell the sister of your . . . ah . . . unlikely companion? Yes, if you would do the honour of requesting her attendance upon Us whilst We bide here? There was mention of chambers prepared in the tower proper, so if she could be brought . . . Master Preceptor?" Eleanor turned her full battery of charm upon de Birkin, who, beneath his own implacable mask, was unquestionably taken aback. "It would be a kindness beyond measure, should you allow your *Confanonier* to escort the maiden to the Queen's presence. We hear from reliable sources that there are . . . ah . . . unsavoury characters hereabouts."

Taken aback, but thoroughly routed, there was truly nothing de Birkin could do save bow and give assent.

Marion was speechless.

Robyn watched her, not liking what he saw in her face. More, what he didn't see.

He also didn't like that Sir Guy Himself had returned, unscalable as the cliffs of Nottingham's castle. Not that it mattered; do what they came for, the chance his men hoped for, and Marion . . .

Who was still speechless.

"It is an honour, make no mistake," Gamelyn offered, no doubt also flummoxed by the uncharacteristic silence.

"An honour!" Robyn snorted. "T' be bunged up in a tower at sommun's beck and call?"

"An *honour* to be asked to attend the Queen Mother of England."

Marion still didn't speak. She was seated upon the far cot of the little tent that had been set up for them. At the Master's order, no less, and Robyn sleeping but lightly the previous night, expecting a dagger in the dark, or some foreign, fatal spell.

Why are you doing this?

Robyn somehow couldn't stop the asking, though he'd despaired of the answering. Marion's grey eyes, wide in that set, pale face, flitted from him to Gamelyn, then back again.

It put Robyn all the more on her defence. "No doubt 'twas *honour* in attending Herself the Holy Abbess of Worksop too! Seem to me 'tis nobbut another word for bondage. And you've a lot of nerve, to ask this of her."

"It's not . . . I'm not the one asking, but the Queen—"

"And you're all ower a Queen's man, *Templar*—"

"The same Queen the Lady Herself named to wear the Crone's

face—or so *you* once claimed. Was that another of the Hob's ruses, then? Or do you even bother to listen when the Lady does speak to you?"

"Pot, meet kettle," Robyn shot back. "What about when She says *Stay together?* How about *Back to back, nowt will stand against you?* You're one with proper choosy hearing, is all I've to say!"

Gamelyn stilled. A tiny flicker of gilt turning juniper to verdigris, he sucked in one slow breath, started to exhale . . .

Instead whirled. In one blinding-fast motion, he'd toppled Robyn flat on his back against the chill earth with a knee to his chest and a hand at his throat.

No knife, though. Robyn was fair surprised. Not that Gamelyn needed one.

Instead, Gamelyn leaned close, eyes still filmed with rust and rain.

"Do you really want to do this?" His voice was soft, a draught of ice against Robyn's cheek. "Here? Now?"

Robyn let a smile twitch his lip. Purred, albeit nigh breathless, "Depends on what you're wanting. Milord."

A snarl as the fingers quivered, tightened. But just as inexplicably, they shook.

"Bloody *damn*, but if . . . !" Marion hoved into view and grabbed Gamelyn's arm. "That's enough, both of you!"

Both instinct and impulse went *click* within that gaze, muscles quivering throughout Gamelyn's body, wire-taut. Robyn went just as tense, prepared to whack some sense into the Mad Templar—somehow, for those hands upon him were like iron. Fortunately, instinct turned *that quick*. Gamelyn allowed Marion to take hold of him, even fling him back a few paces.

"Stand together?" Marion either didn't know or didn't care how she'd just escaped a predator's strike, and turned on Robyn just as angry-eager as he scrabbled up. "Is this how we *stand together?*"

"I en't the one—"

"*Shut* your daft yap!" Marion growled and, as Gamelyn started forward, turned and pinned him in place with an equal growl. "You're no better! What is wrong with you? Either of you?" was the amendment as Robyn started to second it, because he'd surely like to know.

And bloody *damn*, but when it came to wielded weapons, his sister didn't need any but her eyes.

"You en't starting it, mayhap, but you're set to finish in t' worst ways, any excuse to sink a barb in!" she snarled at Robyn, and as Gamelyn lifted his chin—*all self-satisfied, the poncy git*—Marion rounded on him too. "And *you!* Refusing to rise to anything 'til you're set on doing damage . . . sod *both* of you! As it stands now, the only reason I'd say nay to the Queen is I'd fear you two'd kill each other!"

"Well, and that wain't be a problem!" Robyn snapped. "Seein' as how Sir Guy's never about. He'd rather play servant to a Templar than arse himself with bloody *peasants.*"

He knew Marion would smack him for it, and she did, hard enough to make him see stars and wish he'd the hood upon his head—it would have padded the blow somewhat.

Yet worth it, in the end. A spark kindled—tiny, but there. If the only feeling he could wring out of Gamelyn was indignation . . . well. At least it was something. Meant *something*.

"You came. *Agreed* to this." It was a soft grate through Gamelyn's teeth. "Why do you insist on fighting every step?"

"Why do you think?"

Gamelyn stiffened, denied it with a deliberate fold of arms . . . ah, no doubt but Sir Guy was in rare form indeed. "Are you backing out? Do you fear to face the King's justice?"

"Try another hall, Templar; that one's empty. Of *course* I fear what yon sod of a Christian King can do. But all t' more I fear what it means for me sister, should she agree to put herself in their hands."

And you. I don't want to, but I do. I fear what all of this is doing to you. To us. Why wain't you see it?

"This isn't the King, but the Queen," Marion interjected. "I doubt she'll let any harm come to me, not when she's called me to attend her."

"*We* were t' ones as had to rescue the Queen from imprisonment, Mari. She's been locked up, one way or another, for most of our lives. So how much power does she truly have to keep you from harm?"

"King Richard was the one who set her free," Gamelyn pointed out.

"Which only proves me words, aye? He's the one as gives what should be hers by rights, including her freedom. 'Tis a man's whim, *milord,* and a noble-born one, what drives this bloody damned carthorse!"

Gamelyn looked away, mouth tightening.

"I agreed to come here, take the gamble, but 'tis nowt to do with Marion traipsing into Nottingham Castle alone!"

"She won't be alone."

"And hearken to you both, now!" Marion lifted her chin, grey eyes flaring like a summer storm. "Playing the man's game."

Now what was this in aid of? "Mari, pet—"

"Aye, and when you're all set to make up me mind for me, you start in on the 'pet'! This is my decision, brother-mine—*my own!*"

This was patently unfair. "I'm only ever looking out for you, just as you'd for me!"

Gamelyn had gone quiet, his expression pensive as he looked from sister to brother, then back again as Marion spoke.

"We agreed to play this game out to its end. I know the risks."

"And if you end up trapped in yon tower with the Queen?"

"Then mayhap I'll be the one as fetches us out!" she snapped. "I resided in that castle for well over a fortnight. Spent what time I could wandering the place . . . d'you remember, Gamelyn, 'tis where you first saw me, before Samhain, sneaking about on the wall-walk?"

"Before you had your memory." It was a murmur, still odd, pensive. "Before any of us knew . . . well, any of it."

Robyn abruptly wanted to reach out, tangle fingers in the ginger-gilt hair. Shake sense into him, kiss him stupid, rut him senseless . . . Something.

Aye, and like as not he'd lose those fingers, if he so much as made the try.

"I know Nottingham nigh as well as Gamelyn knows Blyth. And if I've the need, well, then." Marion's smile invited them to join in. "I know a few Templars, and me brother's Robyn Hood!"

Robyn had to smile. Because, well, his Mari would, wouldn't she?

Meanwhile, her words were also cozening Gamelyn, who was trying hard not to soften that stone face, yet failing just as certain.

"But," she continued, "that means we have to stand together. Even when we're miles apart."

Gamelyn sobered *that fast*. "If you think I'm not"—it wasn't Robyn's eyes he caught and held, but Marion's—"then neither of you are paying attention."

All I know is you're miles away, even as you're standing here. Robyn found himself leaning forward; Gamelyn's eyes glinted warning— but of what?

Instead, Robyn turned away, snatched his overtunic and hood from the pallet he and Marion had shared. "Well. 'Tis past time I should find my own, any road, let 'em know the lay of things." He slid his eyes to Marion. "You're sure about this, then?"

Marion nodded, came over, and curled an arm about his waist.

Robyn kissed the top of her head, reached a hand out to Gamelyn. "Be safe. I trust your like with nowt I treasure." Asking, wry; words meant for them both.

Gamelyn misconstrued, evading any touch with eyes glinting dangerous. "I won't let anything happen to her, I tell you! Sweet *Christ*, you trusted Gisbourne to fetch her from the Nottingham gaol, so surely . . . "

Robyn caught the slip even as Gamelyn trailed to silence.

"Sweet Lady!" Marion's timing was suspicious, but her horrified gaze downward at breeks and boots and blood-streaked tunic was real enough. "To the *Queen!* And I've nowt to wear!"

"Moving out," Gilbert told Robyn. "David and Will saw 'em, a whole lot of soldiers a-horse."

"Just the soldiers?"

"A few nobles in charge, as well," Will answered. "And some churchmen."

It had been no chore for Robyn to offer a swift retrieval of his sister's only good bliaut. She'd even told him where to fetch it. Gilbert had been waiting for Robyn at the woodland edge, just dropped out of the tree where he and John were perched. The latter stayed behind, keeping adamant watch over Nottingham from his willow roost whilst Gilbert had taken Robyn to their small, scratched-out camp.

'Twere also Gilbert as reminded Robyn he needed more than just the bliaut. Proper accoutrements, for instance.

"Where were this lot headed?" Robyn picked a few stray bits from the green woollen gown, gave up and rolled it into a tight parcel, then tucked it in a bag for good measure. The Queen had given Marion this, after all—it was faded but surely would do.

"North." Will was bending over the cauldron. The smell wafting from it made Robyn start salivating like an overheated hound.

"Damn it all, but we should have thought of better habiliments when you two first went in." Gilbert was also the one helping Robyn search—both of them proper careful towards anything resembling wortwife doings. Will had already declined any assistance, claiming Marion would have their guts for bowstrings, the havoc they'd chance making of her medicines. "What with every noble in England converging on Nottingham, we could have done some careful pilfering to provide the necessary." Gilbert slid Robyn a wolfish grin. "Goods aplenty hereabouts."

Unlike the past season in the Shire Wode. Reputation had its own problems. Pickings had been slim of late; not just game and food, but the silver marks, clothing, and gear that accompanied unwary travellers. Robyn considered a length of soft woollen he knew Marion fancied as head covering, then saw the stains upon it. He grimaced and flung it back in its basket.

"The soldiers left in Nottingham are movin' camp, coming farther out," Will added with a scowl.

"Too close for . . . Ah!" Gilbert held up a clean length of soft grey linen. "This should do the trick."

"I saw 'em too," Robyn agreed "Likely best to move camp deeper in, aye?"

"How about the hollows up the Leen?" Will suggested. "Not too far from here."

"See to't, then, once the lads return from wherever. Wain't she need some braided head thing—what's it called?—to keep 't in place?" Robyn added. "And what about a belt? Sommat fetching . . .

hoy, as I recollect, Will nicked a nice embroidered one from that bishop last spring."

"Um," Will mumbled, sheepish, around a mouthful of pottage just scooped up from the cauldron. "I gave it to that lass near Whitwell who did some baking for us ower winter."

Robyn smirked, kept looking. "She must've been fair good, to warrant a bishop's girdle."

"Aye, she was."

"The bread was fine, too," Gilbert quipped. He tossed Robyn a thin length of cord braided from cloth strips to keep the veil in place, then held up another length, this a wide leather belt decorated with bronze and amber. "'Tis a man's, but the best we seem to have."

"Good protection, this." Robyn approved the amber, tracing each stone with a careful fingertip and whisper of hex-breath to ensure it.

"I sent Arthur and David along after the riders." Will ventured another careful sip from his pottage.

Robyn's stomach gave a growl as he tucked all the necessary bits into the pouch. "Well, they'll find out what's what. Fetch me a bowl, aye?" This as his stomach growled again, louder.

"Feed the man!" Gilbert ordered, tucking a pair of embroidered, if somewhat worn, slippers into Robyn's pouch. "Else he'll faint on the way back and all our work'll be for naught!"

"Milord Templar. Mistress." The woman, plump and well-dressed, smiled as much with her eyes as her mouth, bowing a gracious welcome into the Queen's outer chamber. Marion, with Gamelyn playing Silent Templar just behind, had to pass between a brace of strapping soldiers wielding pikes and wearing the Angevin lions.

A much more pleasant gauntlet, in Marion's view, than the one waiting within. Well-dressed and -coifed, a covey of females lingered against the far wall of the solar. No doubt these were— what had the Queen termed them?—ah, the "would-do-well *pucelles*." Their expressions ranged from curious to contemptuous.

The latter was no doubt reserved for Marion. Though she'd endured a quick wash, dressed in her finest, and let Robyn braid her hair back and secure her veil, there was no doubt upon which rung of rank and class she stood.

Or the murmurs, some quite audible.

"That's her, isn't it?"

"The wolfshead's drab."

"So is she sister or dox?"

"Mayhap both."

A low and unpleasant rash of shocked giggles, then one of the elder ones, not laughing but hissing caution, "Fools, mind your tongue! They say she's a witch!"

Gamelyn's shoulders were stiffening; he was beginning to project Murderously Dangerous along with Silent. Not that this put the *pucelles* off. Quite the contrary—several eyed him, secure in their own imagined subtlety.

Marion's lip tilted, good humour restored. "Shame t' good Christian lasses, fancying a Templar!" It was just as purposefully "quiet" as the *pucelles'* whispers had been.

Several bristled like hedgehogs.

"They fancy safety, more like." Gamelyn's voice dripped scorn. Though *safe* wasn't the word Marion would have tagged to that glare.

Aye, well, summer's sun could wither as well as warm.

Heavy draperies stirred against the wall just past the ladies, then parted, betraying it was not, in fact, a wall but an entrance. A woman who, though garbed rich and sombre, looked to be no more than ten years Marion's elder, slid through and busied herself with tying up the drapery. A bare breath later, Queen Eleanor glided in, straight-backed and graceful as any swan . . . nay, more a pheasant; she'd the copper-bronze plumage of embroidery glinting upon scarlet hem and sleeves, with dark crème silk veiling hair and throat. Rings sparked in the mix of day- and lamplight as she extended one hand and spoke, courteously, the *langue d'oc* she knew her visitors understood.

"So you have brought her, Brother Templar! Even as We requested." This last was accompanied by a quelling look sideways.

The ladies quickly found something to do, be it twitch at a dress hem or study the whitewashed masonry, painted with curling vines of indigo and umber.

It was altogether easy to forget this formidable woman had seen nigh to seventy winters.

Marion was already bending the knee, her poise decisive against those scornful eyes. Gamelyn also knelt, swift and just as nimble. Placing his hand beneath Eleanor's, he lowered his forehead to her knuckles.

"Aye, my Queen. You honour us both."

"Ah, but the honour is Ours, my lord Templar. We accept your service gladly, and that of the maid, Marion. It is a distinct pleasure to see you again, my girl." The beringed hand came to rest, briefly, upon Marion's linen-coifed curls. "Rise and be welcome."

Marion did so, with a respectful lift of her gaze to Eleanor's.

With a smile and softening of that steely-grey countenance, Eleanor held out an expectant arm. "See me to my chair, girl. The sun has decided to make an appearance, and I want to have a better look at you."

Marion took the Queen's arm, sliding a glance over one shoulder towards Gamelyn. He hovered nigh to the door, looking oddly bereft.

Eleanor didn't let him hang there for long. "Thank you, Brother Templar. I'm sure you have many other duties claiming your attention. We'll take proper care of her. And of you"—again Eleanor slid a reproving gaze to the ladies as several giggled—"when the time comes."

If Robyn had been told a bare season ago that he'd be openly wandering a battle camp on a sunny day within the inner bailey of Nottingham Castle—moreover, that he'd be weaponed, unhindered, and in the company of Christian nobles? He'd have said *Aye, and pull the other one.*

Yet here he stood, bow and quiver athwart his back, good meat in one hand and a fragrant, nutty ale in the other, watching the Templars' blacksmith repair a dagger. He was making a proper job of it, too; a pretty bit of work as Robyn had ever seen. His assistant plied the bellows with his own gift: that of timing. The fire roared, stoked nigh white, with that particular shade of yellow about the edges the old smith from Loxley had always sworn by . . .

"Master archer?"

The voice was familiar, spoken low and just beside him to combat the noise of molten metal being shaped. Robyn turned, stopped chewing. Took a drink.

It was the Queen's trouvère, dressed more akin to a peacock than someone wandering a siege camp. Alundel's fair hair was half loose, half braided from his fresh-shaven face, and—of course—the lute lay 'crost his back.

The smith stopped hammering, contemplating the glowing length of the dagger. The forge still blew, but Alundel took the relative quiet as opportunity.

"I've been looking for you."

Robyn cocked his head, chewed and swallowed the bite of pork. "Have you, then?"

"Indeed. The King asked another, at first, to fetch Robyn Hood to him." As Robyn frowned, Alundel smiled and explained, light, "One of the foresters, who seemed unwilling to the request. It seems his like fears you."

Robyn's frown slid into a smirk. "Fancy that."

"The King did not. Fancy the answer, that is." With a tiny grin, Alundel continued, "He was put out, in fact, and had the forester escorted from his presence. I offered to come instead, and assured our liege I would enjoy a ride in the sweet greenwood without a train of hangers-on."

The smith gave a grunt, put the dagger back into the forge, and nodded to his apprentice. The forge howled all the more.

"A ride . . . " The smirk faded into puzzlement. "Here, what are you on about?"

"Walk with me?" Alundel queried, still smiling. "I have a request to share with you, and no doubt yon smith will be . . . "

Sure enough, the smith took the dagger from the flames and applied his hammer with a loud, rhythmic *clang-tek-clang*.

With a shrug, Robyn followed Alundel well away from the forge, nigh to the edge of camp and the inner bailey wall where— Robyn cocked his head, curious—a pair of tacked horses stood waiting. The two grey palfreys had been there a while, it seemed; both they and the man who held their reins were nigh dozing.

"Are we off somewhere?"

"I should think that was obvious." Alundel kept up his pace— and he'd a long one that, despite his shorter height, somehow matched Robyn's lanky reach of stride.

Over by the wall, the waiting man heaved himself straight and gave a tug at his tunic.

Robyn slowed. "Obvious or nay, I'm going nowhere 'lessen I know where I'll end up."

"That would truly be less than sensible" was the answer. "I told you already, Robyn Hood. The King requires your presence."

The King. Robyn halted.

Alundel kept going, took the horses from his man with a murmured "Thank you, Ralph."

The man bowed and departed, gave a tug of his forelock to Robyn, who watched, nonplussed, as Ralph disappeared around the nearest row of tents.

Only then did Robyn make himself meander over to the horses, a wary frown twitching at his brow. "Why did you come after me, then?"

Alundel shrugged and proffered the reins to the tallest of the palfreys. "I told you that as well."

"Aye, the forester's sure I'll turn him into a toad, all that. Doesn't truly answer, does it? And why *you?*"

Alundel put the rein in his hand. "Mount up. 'Tis a lovely day for a ride, and mayhap you'll have your answers on the way."

- XX -

" Ah, good day, my *Confanonier*. It is good to see you." Seated to the right of the tied-open flap, leg padded and propped on another bench, Hubert's Anglic was somewhat slurred. An elderly lay brother hovered, attentive, with a steaming cup of wine.

It was a good day indeed, to see Hubert sitting up, albeit well lubricated. After delivering Marion to the Queen's chambers, Gamelyn had for some time been consumed with other duties, unable to return and see to his Commander's comfort. The King, after ordering the majority of the armies to decamp outward, had ridden for Clipstone with just about every ranking noble in residence. Such an absence meant the work could be done without hindrance; not only overseeing the shift of camp to a decent spot just east of the outer bailey, but insuring billets for the injured, checking that the men and horses were settled, and countless other little tasks to set the camp to rights. Despite his own misgivings, Gamelyn knew Hubert would be well taken care of.

Yet when the curt summons had come from de Birkin himself, not even the suggestive and wary light in the squire's eyes had deterred Gamelyn. He'd made his excuses to Temple Bruer's *Confanonier* and headed straight for the Templar's main pavilion.

The squire had stayed behind, as had Much, to assist with the remaining duties. In a bit of short temper himself, Much was; it seemed Marion hadn't told him she'd been dispatched to the Queen's retinue.

And so, between regrets, risk, and tenacity, here they all were. Gamelyn refused to so much as allow himself a thought, much less a look, towards the guest tent, squatting—remarked upon but unremarkable—amidst the communal lodgings of his Brother Templars.

He obscured it with the very real gratification of seeing how well his master was being cared for. Not that he'd expected otherwise. Hubert was attended in some state, not only by the lay brother, but a small, select handful of white-clad Knights, and . . .

An apprehensive and expectant arpeggio thrilled up and down Gamelyn's spine as he fully considered the figure lingering in the pavilion's doorway. Why *was* Master Wymarec not at Clipstone?

"Good day, my lord Commander. Master Preceptor. Brothers." With a respectful dip of head to each, Gamelyn joined the small group lingering about the front of the pavilion, reaching chill fingers towards the well-stoked fire. "I have come as ordered. And," he added to Hubert, "glad for the opportunity to reassure myself as to your comfort."

"Be reassured then, and let Sayme see to yours." De Birkin, seemingly in no hurry to explain his summons, gestured to the lay brother. The man leapt to obey, ladling steaming wine from a cauldron nestled in the fire coals. "It's been a pleasant sunny day, but the wind has a nip to it. Our Brothers are well billeted, then? How do the horses?"

Well, and two could play at nonchalance. "We have eight wounded men. The Infirmarer is with them and promises to come see to you, Commander, before midday observances. Three of the horses have injuries from the set-to at the gatehouse—minor, all, but one is trying to colic. We gave him a drench and Much is walking him." Gamelyn peered at Hubert, knew he was fussing, and didn't care. "My thoughts have been with you, Commander. You are well?"

"I am indeed, and you can content yourself with a job well done. All of you have earned some quiet time with good comrades around a warm fire, eh?" Hubert tried to shift, grimaced, waved off several of their Brethren—including Gamelyn—as they angled forward to assist. "*Non,* I am truly well enough, if only I don't persist in moving the damned thing. It is always worse the first few days, eh?"

Sayme brought a pottery cup to Gamelyn, who took it with another nod, this one grateful.

"Take what respite as you can," de Birkin agreed. "The King is away for some recreation, but the next sen'night will be . . . chaotic."

"Indeed. He intends to hold court at Nottingham, reward the virtuous and punish the wicked, all that." Hubert was well into his cups.

Gamelyn smiled.

"But first, the King has expressed a desire to hunt in Sherwood."

De Birkin's gaze met Gamelyn's. "And the Queen's trouvère, no less, was here earlier, seeking to no avail. Mayhap your next task, Brother, shall be to ring that obstinate ram of yours."

One of the Templars chuckled, turned it into a cough as Wymarec slid a cool look his way. Hubert smirked.

Ram? What? "I beg your pardon, Master?"

"The King requires the wolfshead, yet he is nowhere to be found."

Ah. "I do not keep him in my pocket, Master, nor is he mine—"

Is he not, then? In winning one wager, will you lose another one? The one that matters?

"—and I thought him well guarded."

A *tsk,* and Wymarec shook his head. "See how your protégé attends me, Commander."

And good *God,* but Gamelyn's own tongue was playing fast and loose this night. The game was getting to him. Inhaling the spice of the wine's steam, he curled his hands about the warm pot and lowered his gaze.

"I merely speak the truth, Master."

"No doubt. But it does not change the reality. The king requires the wolfshead, who was last seen speaking with another of *your* unsuitable comrades nigh upon Sherwood's edge. Mayhap 'twill be necessary to send you wherever it is they're skulking, Brother Guy. And find him, upon the King's request."

A slight warning beneath the light words—Gamelyn heeded it close even as a tiny protest formed, nigh buried and immediately silenced.

My name is. . .

Not here, it isn't.

"Not only did a display of unusual prowess with an equally unusual bow catch the King's eye, but it seems both Queen and trouvère have regaled him with stories of the wolfshead's somewhat lamentable familiarity with Sherwood."

Shire Wode, Gamelyn insisted. Guy merely gave due deliberation upon how Wymarec kept refusing to call Robyn by name.

"Our liege has asked for you as well," Wymarec continued. "Your squire is preparing your horse as we speak."

This prompted a reaction: puzzlement. "Me, my lord?"

"I believe the King's exact words were 'Since your man knows this outlaw and can likely untangle his damned rustic Anglic!'" Hubert added. His grin slid sly, infectious. Tilting his wine cup to Gamelyn, he drank.

A responding smile ticced Gamelyn's lip, and the men shared a round of quiet laughter.

Wymarec, too, was chuckling. "Well, our liege did make the request with some humility. He knows our Rule does not allow us to make sport of hunting."

"Neither is it a sport to Robyn Hood's people, but survival." The mulled wine, sipped slow, began to warm Gamelyn all the way to his cold, booted toes.

"I would suggest you encourage this tame wolfshead of yours to ingratiate himself with the King." Wymarec gave a shrug. "Even in London were the tales making the rounds, making *geste* of a scruffy outlaw's doings." Another shrug, purposefully diffident, but the words told otherwise. Whatever had happened at All Hallows, Wymarec was still chewing over it.

The only thing that concerns you from All Hallows is that he gave an ultimatum, Guy reminded. *The question remains: will you heed your vows?*

"More important, Queen Eleanor has praised *your* virtues as varied and numerous. Therefore, the King has requested your presence at Clipstone, where he plans to gather a hunt . . . and also"—by damn, but the Master Preceptor was *pleased*—"that you should remain afterward. I shall join you upon the morrow, where you shall stand with me as witness to King Richard's conference with King Malcolm."

Malcolm: ruler of Scotland, brother to Huntingdon, and intractable thorn in the former King Henry's side. This was no light request, to observe to such a meeting; from the approving murmurs gathering 'round the fire, all present appreciated the fact.

There is a greater plan in this, Guy insisted, *and we are part of it. An important part.*

"So." Wymarec held his goblet out for the squire to refill. "You will fetch the wolfshead from wherever it is he has gone and escort him to Clipstone. Our liege is expecting you. You will bow to his will in this and other matters concerning the wolfshead."

"Aye, Master." Gamelyn stared at the fire, started as a hand tugged his sleeve. Sayme stood beside, holding a pitcher. After topping up Gamelyn's cup, the squire made the rounds, doing the same for all.

"Heed this, *Confanonier.*" Hubert's words cut through, soft and abruptly sober. "Those of us who well know the King also know his attention easily wanes, save with instruments he can use. With the Queen's help—"

"And that of your Masters," Wymarec inserted.

"—he has found one to use in you. The question is, what use will a Christian king find for a *dryw* priest?"

Gamelyn blinked at the open reference. Realised, with the exception of the lay brother, Sayme—who was deaf-mute, Gamelyn belatedly remembered—that all present were bound fast. Six of them, Knights wearing not only the white, but the plain signet ring of the Inner Temple.

Save himself, fingers bare, a resolute shadow of his Brothers in the ebon habit of the half-caste and half-sworn.

"Nay, my Brother." Hubert read any sudden misgivings. "Your penance has become your strength. *Beauséant.*"

This time it was Gamelyn, not Guy, who noticed that Hubert was no more using his name than Wymarec was Robyn's.

"Your Commander speaks the truth." Wymarec had slid to Gamelyn's side, silent as a serpent and still as deadly. As eerily perceptive. "You bide in their company as our offering to their gods. All you have done—will do—is sanctioned by the Grand Master himself. By Hubert. By *me*." It wavered off, murmur to whisper. "All you need remember, *Confanonier*, is the leash."

"The *dryw* are all but gone; we cannot let them—and their considerable knowledge—disappear from our soil." Hubert seemed unaware of Wymarec's last words, grimacing as he settled his leg into a more comfortable position. "Therefore, the more use we can coax the King to find for your comrades, the better for them."

"And us," Bruer acknowledged. "Thankfully, the Queen has her own purpose for the outlaw's sister. That in itself could have turned out much worse, were the King's brother in his place."

Gamelyn was beginning to feel as if he was running to catch up whilst everyone sprinted ahead. It wasn't something he was used to.

"Count John?"

"The Count"—Hubert eyed him, sober—"fancies women."

O

Give him honour, Hooded One.

Robyn twitched his shoulders, like to the horse ambling between his knees shuddering off a fly. Ahead of him Alundel rode easily, humming a fair, confident tune despite already taking a wrong turn. Robyn scowled and wondered what would happen did he whirl the palfrey on her round haunches and head for the Wode.

Nay, My own. Follow in.

With a piercing look into the green surround, Robyn spotted Him. Sure enough, no enclosure could hem in—or keep out—this stag. His huge rack of antlers glided through Clipstone's park unhindered, though the form that bore them was sometimes two-legged and sometimes four. Sometimes it paced them, well ahead of the trouvère and outlaw riding tandem upon the well-groomed path leading inward to the gates of the Lodge. Sometimes it lingered behind. But it persisted, presence and Voice: *Do honour to the lion. 'Twill cost you little, and gain all.*

The twitch went deeper. The palfrey slowed, hesitant. Robyn relaxed his seat, nudged with his calves, and answered, *He's of the Christ. You're saying I should honour Christians, now, in this daft mummer's play?*

Did not the Christ die for his land? Bleed for his people?

But this one is no Christ! None of his like are, are they, no matter they'd kill us in 'is name! This. . . king—it slid sarcastic—*would play at t' hunt and woodland ways, pretend at donning darken hood and silver sickle, but he's no Cunning, no green Wode in his veins. He bleeds for his own glory, for his damned* Church!—*not for his people. Let Gamelyn have t' sod, play his noble's games and welcome!*

Noble's games! While Gamelyn—the Oak, the light of Summer—this was his time!

Our Oak is a still pool running deep. There are places he will let none touch. The Horned Lord's huff came startlingly soft. *Not Me. Not even Her. Mayhap not even you.*

Yet our Oak, as y' so sweetly put it, would have us serve a Christian—one what takes our land for granted, sells us to the highest bidder, then shrugs off the debt. Because he thinks he can.

Yet he cannot. This was soft, merciless—and feminine. *All debts will come due, and what path you walk today is but the first steps of the changing.*

And if I don't want this. . . changing?

Come now, My own! Light, teasing. *By choosing to mount the Oak instead of Me, you spread your arms wide to change.*

That en't what—

But it is, Winterlord. The Horned Lord's smoky whisper was self-satisfied. *You chose in passion—and with uncanny instinct that none of us then foresaw. So your choices are no less true. This leonine Pretender's blood will buy what we need most. Time.*

"You're so sure I've that, are you?" Robyn murmured aloud.

When World and Time run apace, what is Time? The Lady's soft breath was nonetheless ominous. *'Twill be enough, Hob-Robyn.*

"What did you say?"

Beneath Robyn, the mare lurched to a halt. Blinking, for the time it took to breathe twice, Robyn saw only the gilt shimmer and heard the echoes of god-Voice behind his eyelids.

Alundel backed his gelding to stand beside Robyn's. "Did you say something to me?"

"Nay. Just nattering to meself, is all." It was true, after all, in its way.

The trouvère peered at him, unconvinced, but nudged his mount on.

Robyn followed. The Presences retreated—not far, never far—beneath the music of the palfreys' pace and the occasional vibration from the strings of Alundel's lute. As if the wind were playing it, soft and breathless . . .

"You need take care hereabouts. You, and the Templar."

Well, and the rush of the words told another soft tale: Alundel had been waiting overlong to say them. They were nearly to the Lodge.

Still, Robyn was caught unawares by the manner of it. "Are you about to make some matter of sense, singer?"

"I should think my advice sensible enough," Alundel answered, so unruffled that Robyn fought the urge to hasten his pace, lean over, and shove the man from his horse, just to damage that calm.

"Pardon my chary ways, milord, but I'm a bit out-armoured hereabouts. So you're now t' give me advice?"

It was Alundel's turn to slide Robyn a disgruntled glance.

"You've had a wide-wheeling eye on meself and Gamelyn since you first sat to sup with us in wintering Wode—aye, you weren't unnoticed, believe me—and yet nary a word have you spoken to lord or lady, though no doubt you've had the opportunity. Methinks if you had, we'd be hanging from the outer wall like the others, since your like puts men who fancy men only slightly above traitors and murderers."

"I have my reasons."

"Mayhap you fancy watching ower doing, then?" Robyn drawled it sharp, though he knew exactly what the trouvère refused to say. Not that there was altogether much to take care *with* of late.

"I fancy—"

"Then why should it matter to you what we do or don't, long as we answer your lieges' every beck 'n' call like proper hounds?"

Alundel's horse gave a slight stumble over a rut in the road, and the lute whispered. Alundel reached back, quieted it, and shook his head. "Surely you realise your innocent green Wode cannot shield you forever."

Robyn smiled, wry. "Which shows even well-travelled singers en't knowing the lot. There's nowt innocent about my Wode." He leaned upon the saddle pommel, eyeing Alundel all the closer. "It's brutal wet and cold starry nights. It's blood spilled on the quickening ground and bale-fires to dance, heat in your loins, and magic—"

"Magic!" Alundel crossed himself.

"Aye, *real* magic, slicked wild over your skin like sweat and rain, sending dreams—*nightmares*—to send you quaking. All that, yet there's shelter to save damned souls, warmth and breath to spin whole skeins of content. *Freedom.*"

"Said like a peasant with nothing to lose," Alundel pointed out. "Freedom is seldom free. I prefer living."

"D'you really think my like too stupid t' know the cost of what's denied us? You think I *en't* talking of life? Of living?"

"I think you and the Templar are heading straight for a very ugly and public dying, if you don't heed some common cautions."

With a roll of eyes fit to challenge said Templar's preferred expression of scorn, Robyn snorted. "Christians! For a folk so ready to insist on the virtues of your heaven, you're sure set on greetin' and wailin' even the prospect of venturing there." Nor could he mute the growl that followed. "You think I've nowt to lose? Man, have you even been paying attention?"

"More than you realise, *Robyn Hode*." The slight twist of ancient dialect nigh dripped with scorn, and the lute, through another chance of breeze or misstep, shivered sour. "You've made home, of a kind, untrammelled beyond the dreams of normal existence—but is it? Is it even yours?"

Robyn laughed, this time—he couldn't help it.

"You're the one who says it—*your forest*. I'd advise against saying that to King Richard, whose forest it truly is."

"Is it, then?" Robyn marvelled. "Fancy that. And fancy you thinking I hold my sweet Wode *for* me, 'stead of sommat older than all of us and your cheeky god combined . . . never you mind, lad." Robyn shook his head as Alundel started another retort. "Mayhap I should put it plain. Does your like dare come near my places or try to take me? Nay, they stay away, and cross themselves when they do venture inward. By any means *you'd* fancy, that makes the forest mine."

"You own *nothing*, wolfshead—not even the arrogant tongue in that head, should the King fancy it torn out!" Alundel was proper irritated for one who'd started down this path. And here Robyn had imagined a quiet trot towards the Lodge. "My liege dares what makes lesser men quake like fools. You and your people are here beneath his sufferance, and at the Queen's mercy."

"Yet fair milord Himself, wit' his soldiers and his flags and his lion's heart? He sends for a wolfshead to guide 'im." Robyn kept the smirk upon his face, though it had twisted fair cold. He wasn't keen on the reminder that Marion—indeed, Gamelyn—bided in enemy hands. "Who, I wonder, would guide him through *his* forest, did he string me up and break me like so much game?"

Alundel laughed, but it plucked and scratched at desperation.

"He'd find another. You're not as irreplaceable as you think yourself."

"I never said—"

"You need say nothing, wolfshead. And I *have* been paying attention. You're caught up in it; you've begun to believe your own reputation." The lute spoke again, no doubt on the breeze that slipped Robyn's forelock into his eyes. "King of Sherwood. Son of devils, walker with spirits, ghost in the green Wode no one can ensnare. Only you are snared, aren't you—as much as I in my own passion play—yet it's a Templar, not a king, who has snared a druid and delivered him to his downfall. Just as Vercingetorix, brought to Rome in chains, or as Viriatus, betrayed by his own in his own tent." Alundel cocked his head and, when Robyn began to reply, murmured, "Are you ready for the justice of Summer, O lord of the wintering Wode, crowned in holly and bound in mistletoe?"

It staggered Robyn back a few steps—not only the glimmers of truth beneath the spat-out words, but the strands of *tynged* weaving behind his eyes, fates' fingers quickening.

This will change. . . everything. The memory of Marion's voice, so soft and pensive and . . . resolute.

It was what Robyn hoped. What he dreaded.

Storytellers, the Lady whispered, *know more than any would wish to ken.*

How is it, O Lady, Robyn retorted, silent and shaken, *You never speak to me save in the most sinister of* tynged's *shadows?*

Her laugh rippled through the trees like wind-blown silk. *Come now, My love. Do not think to play the blindfolded Fool with Me.*

Alundel, meanwhile, had also regained control of himself. "I am neither your enemy nor your friend, Robyn Hode. Only one who knows what it means to see a crown contended. You might be willing to share yours, but King Richard is not. And, like you, he is ever dutiful to the God who crowned him."

Like you? Ah, but the man's insight has limitations after all. You, obedient?

You fancy a bit of a fight, you do was Robyn's quick retort. *'Tis why you fancy Gamelyn so.*

With another laugh—this one acknowledging the skilful parry—the Lady faded into mists.

Alundel was peering at him, half puzzlement and half annoyance. "I did not mean to start a quarrel, merely to warn you. Be humble, however difficult it may be. Do as your king requests—whatever that may be. Such men are not overly burdened with a conscience. You mightn't fear death or suffering, but there are others beholden to you."

If that wasn't a warning . . . and one that pricked Robyn in all his softest places. He met Alundel's gaze. "Again, singer. Why should you care?"

"My profession is mayhap my undoing. What man who crafts tales of the unlikely does not wish that unlikely into being? After one fashion or another?"

"Again, that's no answer."

"Mayhap you're the one not paying attention, then," Alundel said, curt. "He's waiting. We'd best quicken our pace."

The small guest tent was barren of any sign of habitation, and the only hint of Robyn's presence was from the few who'd seen him, brief and unremarkable, just before the bells had rung Nones.

"Find the man," Gamelyn muttered after walking all over camp. "Easier to take Jerusalem, I should think."

As he went to retrieve his mount, he found no squire, nor Much, but John holding the reins to the two grey mares Gamelyn had for such errands. Farasha and Anjum were of the Templar mounts that didn't tower over John; both made up for being small with the swift endurance of their desert-bred ancestors. And, like every horse seemingly born, they were utterly besotted with John, snuffling at his brown curls.

You needn't go to camp, John signed. *He's ridden away with the trouvère. To Clipstone. I've told the others. They're already on the way there.*

And *putain de merde,* but of course John knew. He knew bloody everything, didn't he? Well, not quite. He didn't ken the reasons for Gamelyn's careful distance. His lack of knowledge—and affront, particularly—prickled outward like hedgehog spines.

Nevertheless. "Why didn't he—"

If you tell him nowt, why expect him to? A shrug. *I'll ride with you. Much needs to stay close to Marion.*

Much normally would have asked . . . or at the very least, humbly pardoned the necessity. Not that Gamelyn blamed him, even if the lack twisted, a pain somewhere and somehow that couldn't be indulged.

The Queen has acknowledged us. The King has asked for us. Keep to the plan.

"Mount up, then," he said. "We're for Clipstone."

O

"Do not address the King unless he speaks to you. Kneel as he approaches—a bow is permissible if he is not approaching you directly— but once you do so, meet his eyes respectfully. And don't wear your hood! Unless he asks, of course," Alundel added, almost thoughtfully.

Aye, so far no different than toadying to any other noble.

They were approaching Clipstone's main gate, after a few more wrong turns that Alundel insisted were right, and an advance bevy of guardsmen who passed them through with no questions once they spotted the King's trouvère. Oh, and a raucous, tuneless groan that Robyn supposed to be a hunting horn. It sounded more a braying mule.

Alundel's wince was plain agreement, but he continued on as he had done since they'd passed the first round of guardsmen. "You may call him 'milord,' 'milord king,' or, if you can manage it, *'mon roi.'* It means—"

"My king."

Alundel seemed surprised.

"D'you honestly think I've spent time tuppin' a man who speaks such talk easy as he breathes and learnt nowt?" Robyn borrowed said tupping partner's favourite exasperated expression and rolled his eyes as he furthered, "Tis a marvel I survived in the Wode this long, being such a knob-headed peasant."

Alundel blinked. Then murmured, flat, "Well put. On the other hand, were I you, I should henceforth refrain from references of 'tupping' anything, particularly a Templar."

The wide oaken gates were flung open, and the courtyard beyond teemed with an excitement more suited to a market day— if Clipstone had a market. Robyn wondered yet again if he'd left his mind deep in the Wode, because surely if he'd it with him, he wouldn't be willingly marching into this mob of noblemen, most of whom he'd likely robbed, humiliated, or somehow brassed off.

Alundel reined his horse to a halt and dismounted, speaking to the gate's guardians, who were obviously expecting them. Robyn followed suit, stiffened as the guard bearing a pike started forward with a jerk of his head and a "'Ere, you!" to another villein lingering by the gate, slight with hat pulled low. "Take milord's horses!"

The villein scuttled forward.

And Robyn smiled, ever so slight, as his little John tipped up the hat, met his eyes, and took the horses.

The main guard was speaking to Alundel, polite but terse. "You're late, milord. Is this him, then?"

"Indeed. Pray tell, good fellow, where is the King?"

The other two guardsmen were staring at Robyn, eyes wide. John had no chance to do more than sign a few quick reassurances before he was off to the stables with horses in tow.

Robyn watched him go, digesting those few things. So, more than John had followed here. It was both reassuring and worrisome.

"Milord King is at the stables, seeing to matters with the rest of 'em. You heard the horn, no doubt?"

"As did we all, unfortunately," Alundel drawled, no longer the ill-tempered riding companion offering serious advice on how not to offend a Frank bull who happened to be King, but a charming storyteller snapping wit like a whip. The man had more masks than . . . well, than Gamelyn. "One can only hope the young man has other talents."

The head guard grinned, and the other laughed out loud.

"You'd best go on, milord. He's done the morn's business already."

"Of course." Motioning to Robyn, Alundel strode through the gate and straight into the throng of merrymakers. "We are late," he muttered as Robyn caught up. "I hope we've not been keeping him overlong."

"En't my fault." Robyn dodged a small cluster of servants

hurrying into the main hall, following as Alundel made his way towards what looked like a stable block. "I kept trying to give you proper directions."

"Fine!" Alundel seemed to have a talent for making a path where none had existed. People made way for the trouvère, with many a curious look at his scruffy companion. "Next time I'll listen to an outlaw."

"Mayhap you should, since this outlaw bloody well *knows*—" The horn chose that moment to bray again. As it ended with a high-pitched squawk, Robyn growled, "Better than listening t' that bloody horn!"

Alundel laughed, then slowed so abruptly, Robyn almost trod his heels.

"Hoy, what's—" Robyn's protest swallowed itself as they rounded the edge of what was, indeed, the stables. Beyond lay a wide green expanse festooned with coloured banners and milling people, dressed rich as the banners. Dogs were barking from behind the stable block, and horses were being led back and forth, some of them bearing coloured scraps of cloth upon their bridles. Several were objecting to the additions with fierce shakes of their heads; one reared up, front hoofs striking the air, twisted away from his handler, and galloped back to the stable. Laughter at such high spirits echoed around the walls.

A lovely, sunny market day, aye, but sans produce and goods with, instead and everywhere, the glitter-gold trio of the Angevin lions a-romp upon flags and tabards.

"This is more the thing." Alundel's tone was satisfied.

Aye, well, his like would take to such as this. Alundel reminded Robyn of his mam Eluned's favourite mouser—that cat had been quick and quiet on the hunt, but demanded a saucer of milk and a well-worn cushion by the fire as dues. No doubt plenty of cushions could be had in this place . . . even some milk, did one fancy. It was no austere warrior's camp, but made for comfort, and to impress.

As they came closer, another crimson pavilion became visible. More guards were in evidence, a loose ring of mailed menace Robyn wasn't keen to broach. But as he hesitated, Alundel took his sleeve and pulled him on, through the impassive guards and closer upon another periphery of personages. These lingered, standing and seated upon benches. Some held parchments and quills; others held items as varied as a jewelled goblet and a well-worn saddle.

A familiar, broad-shouldered form—clad in stark black and standing apart from the waiting horde by chance or design—was particularly treacherous to Robyn's composure.

The scarlet cross on Gamelyn's tabard clashed with that of the banners, the latter muting his hair despite a brilliant shaft of sunlight. His gaze was fixed, impassive, and bloodless, upon midair—an expression Robyn loathed.

Give me what paltry weapons I have, Robyn Hood.

The soft memory from winter snuck in and hamstrung Robyn. The reasons for it. Weapons. Defences. None of them gratuitous, here and now. Nay, understandable.

He didn't want to understand. *I'm tired of wanting, waiting, wondering if this time you'll choose t' poison ower me. I hate what you are here, what it means.*

But memory made the latter into lie, as well.

Way I see it, Mari? Gisbourne is the one as kept our Gamelyn alive.

Was this how loyalty's ropes were knotted, with memory and longing?

He had to stop looking at Gamelyn. Stop hoping and pay bloody attention in this vipers' den.

Beneath the expanse of crimson roof was an ornate chair, nigh a couch. That must be the throne which housed the Royal Backside, yet no kingly presence lounged anywhere nigh to it.

"Remain here." Alundel halted Robyn beside the motley group set to wait and strode away with a bold assurance that provoked a mutter, subdued but resentful, amidst said group. They turned their attention to Robyn, and another mutter echoed—whispers, really, flitting person to person.

Robyn ignored all of it. Instead he ambled towards Gamelyn, feigning indolence despite fancying he'd a target clout hanging between his shoulder blades. His approach bade the guards tense and, mayhap, flickered the tiniest warmth in Gamelyn's eyes.

"Good day, Brother Templar." Robyn knew better than to neglect any man's title in this noble company. As a peasant lad, he'd been whipped for less. As an outlaw—even one who had gained the King's notice and the Queen's sanction—he'd do well to mind every detail. That fancied target clout wasn't all that imaginary.

"And to you, master archer." Gamelyn's return courtesy was no less cautious. "I was told to find you. Imagine my surprise when a . . . mutual acquaintance informed me the Queen's trouvère had assumed my orders for me."

John, Robyn thought, and couldn't help the smile. "Orders?"

"I was sent to find you by the King." Gamelyn started to return Robyn's half smile; instead the expression closed tighter than any vault as a broad, loud laugh rose up over to one side of the pavilion.

Robyn glanced towards the sound, where a group milled back and forth, resembling more hens pecking at scattered grain than noblemen. A quick patter of Frankish followed the laugh; the scratching "hens" separated into distinct individuals, and the bearer of that voice came barrelling through with Alundel at his heels.

Robyn—with the sudden aid of Gamelyn's hand knotting and snatching the hem of his tunic—realised everyone save himself and the guardsmen had sunk into some semblance of a bow.

And here he'd been gawping like a serf fresh from the plough arms and, without meaning to, had broken the first of Alundel's rules.

This time he'd not the luxury of a quick and sideways dance of disappearance into a crowd of soldiers. This time the whirl-wind's gaze sought, found, then proceeded to bear down on him, leaving no doubts to a sheer presence cloaked in a rather unlikely form. Robyn bowed his head. At least he'd not broken the second rule. The sharp-slurred Frankish kept on, still nigh bellowed as if Richard's mam had never smacked his pate and told him *Enough o' your bawlin'!— what are you, lad, a weaner stirk?*

Though from what Robyn had seen of Queen Eleanor, he doubted that "never."

Another tug to his tunic. Harder, accompanied by a soft growl from Gamelyn, and Robyn realised he'd disregarded two more rules. Before they could be considered broken, he pressed one knee into the soft earth. Stretched fingertips down to touch and answer the tingle spreading upward through his frame—the magic, there even when a great sodding nobleman's tent was trying to smother it—and raised his gaze, slightly agleam, to meet that of England's King.

Those eyes widened as if surprised, going ash-grey in the sun. Like Eleanor's, they were, but 'twas there any resemblance trailed away. He was still the Frank bull, and a handsome one, no question. But closer scrutiny proved the first impression of excess: a ferment of wine and sun and choleric blood had sent fair magnificence south to sour. That foreign gaol in which he'd spent so much time was obviously the likes of which Robyn would never grace; whilst hard work had gone amiss, the meals had been steady, leaving thick muscles lax and a girth straining at embroidered woollens despite the cinch of a massive, gold-studded leather belt. The hands hitched upon that belt gave the occasional tremor, more akin to an elder worked too long at the plough than any liege lord in his prime. The thick curling beard was ginger-yellow and grey, yet the hair on his head was the colour of plumped wheat nigh to harvest. Slicked back beneath a gold filet, it hung past his shoulders, wavy-thick and leonine.

None of it lessened the raw vitality of the man; like a slap across the face, it was.

Robyn lifted his chin, ever so slight, into the possibility. Sure, and his da would have booted his arse for such presumption, but it had been a while since Robyn'd been able to claim the luxury of listening to his da. Mostly because this one's like had murdered him.

At Robyn's nape, another Lord growled softly, tangled tines in Robyn's curls, heated further the tiny gilded flame behind black eyes.

Quiet, you. Robyn didn't let the silent chide so much as tremor his frame. *You've picked a fine time t' blast challenge. His Kingship en't pissing on your boots.*

Yet, the Horned Lord rumbled, and it was all Robyn could do not to smirk.

The King blinked; puzzlement, not weakness. A frown tilting his sunburnt forehead—again, more curiosity than displeasure—he snapped something in Frankish talk.

Gamelyn rose with quick grace, clasping his hands behind his back.

And damned if Robyn hadn't almost broken another rule as the King motioned a second time, impatient and unmistakable: *Up, you!*

At the King's shoulder, Alundel uttered a bland "Our liege has given you permission to rise."

Robyn rose, just as lithe but not so quick. He also kept his hands in plain sight, used a momentary duck of head to sneak a glance sideways, first at the people gathering about this newest novelty, then to Gamelyn.

The latter was inaccessible. Gamelyn's mind was surely present—Robyn could all but see the wheels turning—but his body might have been wandering Outremer's deserts for all the expression he exhibited.

The King was rocking back and forth, thumbs still at his belt and gaze keen. First upon Robyn, then Gamelyn, then widening to include the people to one side and the other—a gathering Robyn dearly wanted to take to the trees over, for 'twouldn't take much to turn them into a mob. Just as swift, the King scanned the meadow and trees beyond.

Proper predator, this one. Robyn had to approve, though it made his teeth itch.

Still looking out into the forest, King Richard spoke. "*Vous êtes le frère Gui. Chevalier de l'ordre du Temple Hirst, non?*"

Alundel peered at Robyn, plainly asking. Robyn gave a tiny shrug. It wasn't so difficult to ken how Himself was asking if Gamelyn—well, Guy—was indeed Guy the Templar.

"*Oui, mon roi,*" Gamelyn answered, quiet.

A grunt. The King's gaze moved from the trees to Robyn, took him in. A tiny frown, and a murmured aside to Alundel, who answered it just as soft.

Again, the spark behind Robyn's eyes: the Horned Lord, spoiling for a row. Again, Robyn bade Him quiet.

And again, the King spoke to Alundel, a quick-clipped back-and-forth with those grey-blue eyes fixed upon Robyn the entire time. Robyn thought he caught the word "longbow"—strangely spoken, sure enough—before the King fell silent.

"The King says"—Alundel stepped closer to Robyn—"that he is pleased to finally come face to face with such a notorious longbowman, particularly since he made such an amazing shot, and not only the once from luck."

"*C'est le Gallois noir, pardi!*" the King put in. More than a few of the surrounding nobles laughed, and the King crossed his arms, chuckled.

Robyn's eyebrows quirked, and this time he did slide a look to Gamelyn. Himself the Templar didn't look best pleased.

Alundel inserted, blander still, "King Richard also imagines you've more than a little of the black Welsh in your blood."

Ah. Robyn held to the King's gaze. "No imagining t' be done, *mon roi*. I'm ower half owed t' me mam's blood, and proud of it."

That gaze shifted, ash to flint. The man mightn't have any Anglic, but no question he'd understood the tone of it. The surrounding murmurs trebled, overstated dismay. Well, the last of those rules broken, then—Robyn had spoken without leave.

He is in Our forest. You ask leave of none, here.

Not "mon roi" *in thisworld* was Robyn's silent counter. Aye, he knew the way out should he have need—always did, went nowhere openly without kenning four different methods of escape— but . . .

But. Gamelyn, here beside him. John, unseen but no doubt amidst the onlookers stamping about, noisy as cattle. Will, Arthur, David, and Gilbert lurking in the Wode. Marion, shadowed by an insistent Much and bunged in with the Queen. And in this place— this Christian, noble place—the Queen was nobbut a woman.

So small a number against this invasion, and all of them in the open, standing uncertain ground. Robyn wasn't used to this.

He had to . . . to *think* too much, here.

"*S'approprier!*" the King snorted, a sudden and unlikely smile twitching at his mouth. He took a step towards Robyn; it was all Robyn could do to stand down instinct, hold his ground. "Of you, I . . . eh . . . have understanding? Know?" The clip and slur of accent nigh made it unintelligible, but there was no mistaking the sudden jibe beneath the odd pattern of speech. "*Oui, bien,* of you I have knowing! *'Le roi de la forêt'! Robin des Bois.* Robyn . . . Hood."

Robyn didn't have to spare a glance for Gamelyn to feel him tense, ready for anything. As if they could do anything. Mayhap knock the Frank bull over—more feasible to take out a tree—and then hope a few of Robyn's lads were scoping the place with arrows ready. Any way it could be parcelled, Robyn would wager the King of England calling him what sounded like *king of the forest* wasn't good.

Yet Richard laughed, a short bark of questionable humour, and let out a spate of Frankish, first at Alundel, then several of the hangers-on. Orders, it would seem; a flurry of activity greeted them.

Gamelyn's taut body relaxed, ever so slight. Unfortunately, tension restrung itself almost immediately. The sodding horn sounded again.

And it was *close*. Robyn's shoulders hunched up nigh about his ears.

The King didn't seem overly pleased either. Alundel clapped his hands over his ears and made a heartfelt plea. In clear agreement, the King gestured to a lad at his heel, who dipped a bow, turned, and disappeared between two overdressed lords. Another tuneless blare and the King grimaced, shooting more Frankish talk at Alundel.

"Our liege says," Alundel translated, "that the lad giving instructions for the hunt is unfortunately new to his work. Of course, nothing is worth achieving that does not take much practice—often uncomfortable. He wants to know if the master archer likes music?"

"Aye, milord," Robyn said, and breathed a gusty sign of relief as the horn was cut off midthroat. "Which *that* en't."

The King's guffaw made it plain he understood. The crowd parted once more for the lad who'd so precipitously exited. In his hands was a crème-and-sepia beauty of a horn the likes Robyn hadn't seen since his da had kept one beside the hearth.

Jerking his head in dismissal to the lad, the King started to hang the well-polished horn at his belt. Instead he took note of Robyn's attention to it and spoke.

"A head forester's horn, this, gifted from one of the King's own at New Forest," Alundel translated.

"I know," Robyn answered and, when Alundel seemed surprised, supplied, "My da was head forester t' *his*, ower Peak and Barnsdale, and had one not unlike to 't."

Gamelyn's eyes slid towards Robyn. The King must have noticed, for this time he spoke to Gamelyn, whose brows arced upward—albeit slight, loath to any giveaway. He listened, nodded, and gave answer with soft and flawless courtesy.

"The Templar speaks of your father, says he knew and much admired him," Alundel murmured to Robyn.

King Richard seemed intrigued, peppering Gamelyn with more queries, pointed amidst Gamelyn's careful answers.

Alundel's smile was beginning to curdle as they continued on. He remained quiet for some time, at Robyn's puzzled look, relented. "He says I am"—a soft growl—"'No use with man's sport,' and perhaps since the Templar knows the wolfshead so well, he can best translate such things." Surely there was more, but the look upon Alundel's face stirred an unexpected pity in Robyn's breast, made him loath to ask. The trouvère continued, more a mutter. "Always it is so with him—yes, then no."

"*Va-t'en, mon cœur.*" This as the King came over to Alundel and put a hand on his shoulder, turned him, and shooed him off.

Alundel went—not without a long look at Robyn.

Robyn shot a *What t' bloody damn?* at Gamelyn, who seemed to be entertaining his own share of mystification. Even more startling, the surrounding cluster of men parted their ranks for the trouvère. There was absolutely no expression on their faces, which was fair unexpected from such a lot of opinionated busybodies.

In the odd stillness of Alundel's wake, a sudden bedlam of barks and whines resounded. There was a shout, then a dismayed yelp—human, not canine.

Then a lot of ginormous hounds burst through the crowd, straight for Robyn.

- XXI -

Gamelyn's first thought: they were dead, and the King had gotten Alundel—*mon cœur. . . my heart!*—out of the way and given covert orders to have hounds set on them to do it.

His second was to draw his sword. A dagger. Something.

His third was to deny that with a *Don't be bloody ridiculous!* as Richard stepped in front of the dogs, bellowing orders.

And his last thought, as the hounds poured around their master and went for Robyn, was *Well, and isn't that typical.*

Because the six brindled hounds indeed leapt upon Robyn, but wriggling and whining like puppies instead of ferocious hunting alaunts the size of small ponies. One had dived shoulder-down into Robyn's left foot to sprawl and display a pale grey belly; another was circling his knees, wagging its tail so hard that its hindquarters quaked back and forth; and the remaining four larked about, mincing like courtiers, darting to nip at Robyn's fingers and grinning all the while.

The King bellowed a few names, but the alaunts, cheerfully oblivious, were intent upon their job with one stark difference: taking their prey down with doggy affection.

The King said a few choice curses, then planted fists on hips, barked a laugh—albeit exasperated—and drawled in the finest Norman French, "In my experience, one so likable to dogs is either a very good man, or a very clever magician."

The surrounding men—and if those weren't a lot of toadies, arse-kissers, and bootlickers, Gamelyn would swallow his best shiv—seemed torn between concurring laughter and apprehension.

None of it eased Gamelyn's mind.

But he had to smirk as one of the hounds rose on his hind legs and plopped his forepaws on Robyn's shoulders—every bit as tall as Robyn, which was no mean feat. The smirk widened as Robyn nipped that with a gruff "Gerroff, you!" and a shove. The dog obeyed, merely to crouch down and start a playful gnaw at Robyn's boot toes.

"And there are my hounds, bred to hunt the wolf. Remind me, young wolf, never to hunt you with dogs should the need arise." King Richard's wry tone eased the surrounding tension; a few light laughs answered it, with some whispers back and forth from the arse-kissers in particular.

Robyn shot Gamelyn a puzzled look. Gamelyn quickly translated.

"I'll try to heed that, milord King." Robyn scratched at the largest hound's ears.

The kennel master came bursting through with several leashes in hand, black hair plastered to his skull with sweat, and swearing in Catalan. He'd plainly been expecting disaster, stopped, and blinked upon seeing his charges fawning over a peasant.

"Come round them up, Simó! Before they degenerate into complete uselessness!" the King ordered. In the next moment, he turned back to Gamelyn, brusque but good-humoured. "My lord Templar, kindly advise your unlikely companion why he is here. It is not to suborn Our hounds—sweet Jesú, catch the silly buggar, Simó! The finest houndsman north of Valencia, and he can't catch . . . Mercadier! Give him a hand, will you, man?"

With a smirk, Mercadier obeyed. A like smirk tilted Gamelyn's lip at how the assemblage made hasty room for the mercenary. King Richard didn't deign to notice this, but he did aim a lift of eyebrows at Gamelyn, who didn't wait to see if it signalled humour or affront.

"I would be honoured, my liege, to do so, yet would appreciate clarification of that reason."

"I told your Masters why I requested the man's company! Did they not tell you?"

"They mentioned a wish for the hunt, milord."

"Aye. And who better to lead my hunt than the *King of Sherwood?*" Drawled mocking, and the toadies in particular seemed to enjoy that, all satisfied murmurs and exchanges. Yet there was a definite twist of perplexity to Richard's brow as he watched Robyn bend down and give a playful tug to one of the alaunts' ears. Young Simó was in persistent chase of two others. Mercadier was truly no help, indulging more in watching and chuckling than catching. It was finally Robyn who, with a few well-placed growls and gestures, settled the dogs enough to be caught.

To which Richard gave a small huff beneath his breath.

"We shall see," he mused, "if this young and *ower aff* Welshman bred in English forests shall, indeed, prove more hound than wolf."

Gamelyn didn't fancy the sound to that, but pretended to a puzzled frown and a soft prompt. "My liege?"

And while Robyn seemed occupied with the dogs, Gamelyn knew him no less intent upon the quick back-and-forth between King and Templar. Even if he understood none of it.

"Tell him—wait." Richard's gaze flickered over the small assemblage, and his lip tilted. "Ask him. Ask if he will do me the honour of leading my hunt."

The gathering went still. Over the heads of those two over-dressed arse-kissers, Gamelyn saw Roger de Lacy and, next to him, his brother. De Lacy's expression was smooth, if somewhat perplexed, but Brian de Lisle's face was dark with barely contained rage. His eyes were fixed on Robyn.

Again the tickle of *This means something. This is important.*

Gamelyn bade it silent, said, "Robyn," and realised the mistake of familiarity the moment he'd made it. Eyebrows rose, including the King's, and Gamelyn answered them with chill diffidence, merely stated, "The King asks if you will do him the honour of leading his hunt."

Robyn straightened, frowning, and Gamelyn thought *Bugger.* Added to that thought a glare in Robyn's direction: *You're outlaw, remember? With one twitch of a finger, this man can have you hanged, and everyone around us helping him tie the noose!*

"I am very conscious of the great honour you do me, *mon roi*," Robyn started, precise and formal.

Gamelyn took in a slow, relieved breath, started to translate.

"But I fear you've asked the wrong man."

And Gamelyn wondered if *I can't take you anywhere, you stroppy daft peasant* was bleeding out his eyes. Keeping that glare on Robyn, his body tensing into readiness for—well, anything—he gave dutiful translation.

Both original and translated refusal was met with a steady and resounding silence. The bootlickers turned up their noses, the arse-kissers feigned horror, the toadies growled affront that one lower than they dared such a statement, whilst the remainder of the lords who didn't quite fall into any of those murmured to each other, uncertain and trying to figure the odds.

"The wrong man." Richard spun it out, gave a click of tongue to the last word. He flung one hand towards the dogs, still milling at Robyn's knees despite leashes and the pout upon Simó the kennel master's very pretty mouth. "Surely one as you can bewitch the deer to Our sights."

It was purposeful, daunting. The King chirruped to one of the hounds as Gamelyn translated. It ignored him save for a twitch of ears, gaze intent upon Robyn. Richard dug into his side-pouch for a strip of dried meat and chirruped again.

The pause at this lingered, heavy and expectant. Robyn was

plainly unsure of the best recourse—order the dog to the King and further prove a barbed point?—and Gamelyn could all but read the wish, naked behind those half-mast black eyes: *Aye, and I'd lief as face a mad boar headlong than all these poncy noblemen spoiling for t' fight, all balls and brass and not much sense.*

Gamelyn had his own fleeting wish, an honest one: that the blood of Robyn's father would run hotter at this moment. Adam Loxley had always been a cautious, careful sort, a fair and right-eous peacemaker, confident of men's inner virtues as seen from the security of his own.

Of course, the latter had, in the end, seen him killed.

"Mayhap"—this from one of the bootlickers, an unsubtle and purposeful knife in Anglic—"being such an . . . obvious villein, the outlaw does not know how to sit a horse."

"I'm no villein, but yeoman-bred." It was quick, with a hint of anger Robyn could not—would not—stifle.

"You're outlaw," another dismissed. Aye, once the sack was open, all the ill spirits wanted free. "You are, in truth, noth—"

"Enough!" Richard barked over Gamelyn's rapid translation. "You forget yourselves, my lords! This man has been invited to Our presence. We will not see Our guests abused."

Aye, none but Ourself can set barbs in the quarry, Gamelyn added, silent.

"Milord Templar," Robyn said, soft. "Does milord King wish me to speak plainly, or with the same double tongue as those around him?"

More murmurs.

If we fetch ourselves out of this, I just might have to torture you. Slowly. Instead Gamelyn ground his teeth and repeated the question word for word. If he mucked with it, the ones who understood would have all the more upon which to pounce.

The King frowned, and . . . sweet Christ, but was that another smirk Gamelyn saw tugging for admittance? Gnawing on the dried meat with which he'd attempted to coax his dogs, Richard waved one hand, gesture plain: *Get on with it, you cheeky sod.*

Gamelyn turned back to Robyn, against a tug and shift of his tabard hiding his own silent gesture, this one straight from John: *Don't be an ass.*

Robyn saw it but, for a mercy, didn't let any grin show—save a glint of eye. "Aye, well, I'm a fair horseman, milord King. My da were forester to yours, and he had me riding when I were nobbut a wean. But it en't my way, scaring up whatever moves and droving 'em into a draw to murder wit'out so much as a fair chance."

Well, Robyn had just insulted everyone within earshot. And Gamelyn's teeth were beginning to hurt from all the grinding. Nevertheless, he kept up a dutiful translation—and all the while kept his eyes open and his hands relaxed, ready for anything.

Particularly as the King's eyes lit—challenge or fury, Gamelyn was woefully uncertain.

"But should milord be after a proper stalk and shot, I'm all for that."

Gamelyn finished his translation into an utter, uncomfortable silence. Counted to three, then four . . .

The King threw back his head and roared with laughter. Gamelyn's knees nigh buckled with relief. Robyn started like a hawk-shadowed hare. The toadies joined in, thinly; the arse-kissers smiled, albeit sickly, and the bootlickers much the same.

The ex-Sheriff of Nottingham did not so much as pretend a smile.

Richard strode over, quick for his bulk, and gave Robyn a buffet across the shoulders. Robyn held his ground, not without a stagger, and gave a surreptitious rub to his outraged shoulder as the King turned back to Gamelyn.

"Tell the English he has given me a challenge I cannot resist!" Richard ordered, between chuckles. "To give one's rightful quarry a fighting chance is not in the nature of kings, I remind you all—but no matter, no matter! What and where does he suggest, then?" And as Gamelyn hesitated, prompted, "Tell him, Templar!"

Robyn was eyeing the King, baffled and wary. Gamelyn shrugged and complied—not without another hand sign disguised as a shift of tunic: *For pity's sake, play along!*

Dark brows describing several twisty arcs, Robyn did so. "Aye, well, then. Just a few of us should go, milord King—no more'n four, five. Quiet ones. You'll need a bow. Happens a crossbow's better than nowt; if you en't shot any other kind, you'll nobbut scare off a prime shot."

"Insolent—!" one of the bootlickers started, but it and the murmurings it inspired cut off, sharp, with Richard's raised hand.

"An honest call. I've certainly no affinity for a peasant's weapon. We remind, *again*"—a growl—"that We called this man to Our side exactly because of his, eh, rather-ill-gotten expertise." Marvel of marvels, the King seemed more fascinated than affronted. "What else?"

Robyn's frown turned thoughtful. "Is he serious?"

"Aye," Gamelyn said, "I think he truly is."

"Well. Mayhap a pike should he fancy some pork. And he's in no fit garb for such work. Best t' have a bath and change of clothes—nowt puts a buck off like the smell of rank sweat."

Upon translation, the King smirked at his surrounding nobles, made a show of shrugging the ornate mantle from his shoulder and smelling one armpit. He grimaced, shrugged. "I'd daresay you don't smell so sweet yourself, master outlaw."

Gamelyn was glad no one else could hear Robyn's mutter, "How can anyone smell of nowt but filth in a bloody crowded camp?"

He said, louder, "Aye, *mon roi*. With your permission, I'll have a bath meself 'fore we start. No sense starting this time of day, at that. We'll have better luck come gloaming-time."

"My King!" One of the arse-lickers, who'd drawn close to help Richard unfasten the heavy mantle, gave protest through a glower Robyn's way. "This . . . the wolfshead would see his liege crawl through a tangled wood in the dark? This is surely madness!"

"Not dark, man," Robyn drawled before Gamelyn even finished murmuring the Anglic. "Dusk. I'm knowin' the difference even if you en't. And happens I know my way through every inch of m . . . t' Wode."

"Every inch, eh?" Richard mused. "Indeed, why We sent for you. Yet should dark fall before we catch our dinner?"

"Then I'm like to go hungry, milord King."

Richard had shrugged from not only the mantle but his surcoat, was contemplating Robyn with arms crossed over his broad chest, one beringed finger tapping an erratic time against crumpled linen. Another laugh, short but just as booming. "And I won't, eh? Go hungry?"

Robyn shrugged concurrence as Gamelyn translated and, remarkably, held his tongue.

"But then, this is my forest. Those who trespass are breaking my law." Thank God Richard wasn't truly watching Robyn; a good thing, with Robyn's eyes glittering nigh unholy at the casual words *my forest*. Nay, the King was intent upon another hunt, ash-blue eyes flickering here and there amidst the surrounding nobles. "There are other ways to obtain a meal. If we fail at the hunt, not only Clipstone, but Nottingham should have stores with which to feed us. *If* our subjects have made suitable preparations, that is."

The whispers changed timbre, somewhat. The hangers-on were unsure as to where those barbed comments were supposed to land. Gamelyn saw de Lacy once again, hanging back and murmuring to Huntingdon; they seemed uneasy and, moreover, sympathetic to Gamelyn's own plight amidst a peculiar game of King and Wolfshead. Indeed, de Lacy gave Gamelyn a tiny shrug. De Lacy's brother, however, was inching forward, eyes gleaming with anti-cipation.

King Richard's attention returned to Gamelyn, waiting. Gamelyn gave a slow relay of the words and thought *Let it go, Robyn. Don't scuttle this, or I'll scuttle you.*

Black eyes still sparked, yet Robyn heard caution as well as threat. Again—and amazingly—he held his tongue.

The King seemed just as determined to provoke some sort of reaction. "As to you, man of the forest, *outlaw*, who breaks Our laws with impunity? I should think you rarely go hungry."

Robyn's carapace, never thick at the best of times, was broached with that. "This time of year, crops not yet in? Anyone'll go hungry if they miss t' mark. But aye, milord King, while an outlaw can only be hanged t' once, a peasant's like to go hungry all the more, wit' too much t' lose and no relief to so much as hunt and feed their family."

Gamelyn gritted his teeth as murmurs rippled around the crowd and back again—this time more aggressive.

The arse-licker, arms weighted with his king's garb, hawked and spat at Robyn. The King motioned him away, queried Gamelyn, sharp. "*Qu'a 'til dit?*"

With a glare Robyn's direction, Gamelyn took another breath and complied. Richard listened, eyebrows drawing together thunderously, eyes darting.

And de Lisle's black expression was not the only one tilting into a smirk, dark brass to the remainder of the crowd's anticipation: the certain halt of this stroppy outlaw's inexplicable rise.

It didn't come. Still frowning, Richard said, "Your father might have been yeoman and royal forester, but you have as little appreciation for facts as any villein."

Robyn bristled like a cornered badger. Gamelyn sent another silent set of signals, desperate reminder: *Don't forget where we are!*

Saw it dawn in the glossy eyes, gilt within black, affronted god and cornered avatar manoeuvring each for dominance . . .

More, Richard watched, from Robyn to Gamelyn then back to Robyn, his gaze dark as slate and just as transparent. Gamelyn had no idea what he was watching, but it left him uneasy, and even more so with the sensation.

Richard snorted a brusque dismissal. "How typical. Like most of your kind, you think Forest Law unjust." He gestured over the surroundings and crossed his arms. "What should happen to this great greenwood—*my forest*, within which you have seen fit to make your own tourney field!—should everyone be allowed to run riot? To cut the timber and hunt the animals without limits?"

Robyn protested, "Lord King, surely that wain't be likened to feeding a starving bairn!"

Richard shrugged. "This is a rich country—"

And well you'd know, having suckled it dry. Gamelyn heard it, an intrusion plain as if Robyn had spoken, and wondered if it had been Robyn or the Horned Lord. Or both.

"—and if its people go unfed, the solution is not to let them make havoc amidst Our hunting grounds and lay waste and ruin through lack of wit and insight." His tone changed; patronising, an admonishment. "When things are ordered in accordance with God's will, young archer, compensation runs naturally, like a mighty river. At the stream's foundation is God's chosen, Our royal selves, with dominion over the land. Better, through those laws, that We lease the lands to those who can pay, and better those who cannot pay do an honest day's work and pledge to their lords.

Best of all for those lords to, in return, honestly reward that service, not dam the stream or benefit from largesse unduly. If a lord's serfs are starving, it is from greed, or poor management."

Oh-ho, but *that* set a fox 'mongst pigeons; murmurs trailed into silence before Gamelyn finished the telling of them. The King slewed a fierce gaze through the crowd, gauging reactions as surely as Robyn himself testing the wind for a prime shot.

And when Robyn made as if to speak, Gamelyn finished his interpretation with a muttered, "Christ's blood, Robyn, hold your tongue!"

Robyn complied, watching Gamelyn watch the King, his long fingers twitching, impulses sparking gilt and quicksilver beneath that tangled ebon forelock.

Gamelyn's thoughts rushed just as headlong. What would come of this? What . . .

"Do him honour, the Horned Lord said," Robyn muttered, sudden and dark.

It startled Gamelyn. "What?"

Yet before Robyn could reply, Richard shot another quick spate of instructions to Gamelyn. With that he was done, turning away.

Gamelyn chewed over this latest. Not that there was any choice but say it; the vultures were still circling. Strafing outward a glare to which only a few thought to rise, he took the opportunity to move closer to Robyn. *Liberties of a translator, nothing more. Quit staring, you bloody bastards.*

"Our liege suggests you might know the best place hereabouts."

"Place?" No doubt to most, Robyn looked indifferent to the situation. Yet Gamelyn knew, from the unearthly glint sparking behind dark eyes and the tremor in the normally smooth baritone, he was not.

"To follow your suggestion and bathe for the evening's hunt."

"I didn't figure him the type to scorn hot water."

Robyn. Take care. The signed warning was not what he truly wanted to give, yet was, in this situation, all he could.

Robyn sidled closer, his words a bare whisper. "No worries there. That one's like? He'd burn our Wode down to fetch a day's hunting, did it suit him. And laugh."

A quick glance around to see if any lingered—and that those were out of hearing. "That doesn't sound like 'doing honour.'"

"Aye, well, honour 'mongst thieves, they say. And honour en't trust, last I heard."

"Aye, well." Drawled to match Robyn's, it quickened a welcome smirk, which in turn quickened Gamelyn's heart to thud just that much faster. He chided it and uttered, even softer, "Never put any trust in kings."

The black eyes slid to meet his. Narrowed. "So says the King of t' Summering."

"He does." The words escaped, unwitting, and Gamelyn's hand moved, just as instinctive, to the quillion dagger at his belt. Robyn followed it like a tracking wolf, blinked, then started to rise once more. Gamelyn turned away.

"Wait." Robyn's voice halted him. "You en't coming?"

The sudden scratch of uncertainty in it nailed Gamelyn as unerringly as one of Robyn's arrows. It made him hesitant and, conversely, furious. His voice didn't want to work, came out gruff.

"The King says he's no further need for translation this evening, and he knows my Order does not hunt. His dismissal was most courteous, mark you, but one nevertheless. Not to mention"—this time he did look at Robyn, warning—"I've no wish to swim in tandem with an outlaw, beneath the regard of King and country. Rather unwise, I should think. Considering."

"I understand King Richard has gone to Sherwood, to hunt with Robyn Hood."

The wooden chess pawn slipped from between Marion's fingers like a damp apple seed, bounced off the side of the table, and went skittering across the wooden flooring towards the ubiquitous covey of noblewomen attendants. They stood at the eastern window of the solar, gathered about an equally ubiquitous embroidery frame.

"I said hunt *with*, girl, not hunting *for*." Eleanor idly switched her peacock-feather fan. "Though I well understand your worries towards the latter."

Several mutters—too low to pick out, but their tone nevertheless obvious—came from the noblewomen. All but one of them were younger than Marion herself. All maintained blissful ignorance of the fact, stolidly superior to That Outlaw Wench in both comportment and dress. This despite years of novice discipline insuring some familiarity with the former, and the Queen providing Marion with a new and lovely example of the latter.

The bliaut and crème linen underkirtles were the most sumptuous things Marion had ever felt against her skin. Nowt against her warm green one, mind, but this was spun thin as gossamer, of a rich, woad-deep hue that turned her clear grey eyes nigh blue. She knew, for she'd checked in the Queen's silver mirror.

If only the lads could see her, polished like a pearl. If only she could see to the same for them, somehow.

The Queen, meanwhile, continued to toss words like stones into a still pool. "He is considering my request, it seems, by testing your brother's mettle."

"How thoroughly unexpected." There was a very real affection in the statement, however wry, from the woman watching the chess match.

"Joanna," Eleanor warned, and her youngest daughter smiled.

"*Maman,* you know what I mean." Joanna, former Queen of Sicily, obviously knew the regal realities of public expectations. In privacy, however, she chose comfort over stateliness, perched cross-legged on one of the trunks like a young lass. Her midnight-blue skirts, of a wool that gleamed like good health, were gathered and bunched to show one embroidered leather slipper.

"Indeed I do." The admonition lingered with a glance—just as fond, then Eleanor continued, "I have given my word, Marion, that your Templar Knight will regain his honours—"

Another mutter from the *pucelles,* this one plainer, no doubt directed towards the pronoun preceding "Templar Knight." The cheek of an outlaw slut to even think upon wooing a handsome Templar! Still, it was not vocal enough for Eleanor to take notice. So, Marion thought with a tiny smirk, even noblewomen resorted to the least of peasant devices.

"—and that your brother and his men shall gain a fair pardon. I have not forgotten any of it. Indeed, I've spoken to the King."

"Several times," Joanna put in helpfully.

"The King has many things to consider"—Eleanor threw another reproving glance in Joanna's direction—"over the next days, but I've no doubt he shall grant my requests."

No doubt. Marion smoothed callused fingers against her skirts, once again marvelling over not only the wool's silken nap, but the equally flawless weave of Eleanor's resolve.

"Marion, your tongue is altogether more silent than I remember. Lucia." Eleanor gave a wave of her fan towards the *pucelles.* "Kindly fetch the chess piece."

Lucia gave a twitch at her brocaded skirts and glided over. Still graceful, she ducked down and retrieved the pawn, brought it over, and extended it, not to Marion, but her Queen. To a demure dip of head and knee, Lucia added a sullen tuck of her rouged lips towards Marion's place of honour, as well as a smooth of her hair, unbound and sleek as a raven's wing.

Marion was yet again reminded she was nowt but a peasant—a redheaded one, at that, with said hair thick as a pony's mane, and kinky-fuzzy from an insistent combing out by one of the Queen's maidservants. This despite Marion's attempt to explain what she and her brother had long ago realised: dry brushing curly hair merely meant one ended up resembling a deranged milkweed puff. Marion had resorted to confining the worst of it back from her face in a fashion disaster born of desperation: braids *and* a head wrap, from which the ends of her hair poufed nigh wide as her shoulders. She felt like a dowdy peasant matron next to Eleanor's elegant veil and barbette, or Joanna's veil and long, lovely braids.

Or those equally well-coiffed, snooty maidens.

"I'm merely trying to keep up with your chess game, Madam."

Eleanor chuckled and waved Lucia back to her place, onto fresh game as she contemplated the pawn, turning it back and forth in long, beringed fingers. "So to the men." With a sudden snort, Eleanor inverted her hand and snapped the pawn onto the board with a loud *crack*. "Yet a woman needs more security in our world, *non?* I must think upon this. It's still your move."

Marion, perusing the board whilst awaiting the Queen's pleasure, moved her *chevalier* to block the Queen's *donjon*.

"You meant for me to take that pawn." Eleanor's mouth twisted sideways thoughtfully. "Merciful saints, but you are altogether too good at this little game. Nay"—she waved the fan as Marion started to speak—"no apologies. It is a relief to engage in a battle of wits with someone armed for 't. My daughter is the only other here to challenge me." A surreptitious roll of eyes towards the *pucelles,* and a smile for Joanna. The latter faded as Eleanor once again peered at Marion. "Hm. That dress will do. But the slippers are too small, I see."

Marion gave a self-conscious tuck of her bare toes beneath the embroidered hem of her skirts. The kicked-off slippers told their tale regardless. "I can't thank you enough, my Qu—"

"Lady Cecily has feet sizeable enough to match any barefoot peasant." Eleanor continued her impartial scourge of egos by shying a few more words-*cum*-stones to ripple and sink. "Cecily, my dear, can you contrive to loan our Marion a pair of reasonably handsome slippers until we find ones to fit?"

"Yes, Madam," Cecily vowed meekly enough. The sideswipe of glare Marion-ward, however, gave due cause to ensure said slippers didn't come with a dead rat—or a live snake—tucked within.

Was Eleanor *trying* to fetch Marion into trouble?

Or mayhap Eleanor considered Marion well up to the task. Marion let another barely perceptible smirk tic her lip, well-hidden by the pouf of overly brushed curls. She was taller than any of them, to be sure, and her arms overlain with archer's muscles. Robyn had always maintained she'd a fearful right cross. And did any of the whey-faced maidens fancy poison, Marion was skilled enough a wortwife to sniff it out. Well, most of them, anyway.

"And Joanna? Can you have that lovely girl with the clever fingers see to Marion's hair? It's"—another frown, and for Eleanor, remarkable tact—"*extraordinary.* However did you achieve such a . . . look?"

"A combing out at the hands of an overzealous maidservant, Madam." Marion tucked a random bit of fluff behind one ear—to no avail. "Nowt a proper bucket of water wain't cure."

Joanna was smiling—ah, she had a bit of curl to her hair. Marion could see it, escaping beneath her silk veil where it wasn't contained in those long, gorgeous, and golden braids.

Eleanor tapped one well-buffed fingernail upon the chessboard, used it to scoot a carved *donjon* along its path. "We will need to have you looking your best when you stand to serve me at the coming feast."

"At . . . the high table?" The ripples from those so-casual "stones" seemed set to swamp the chair Marion occupied, akin to a leaky boat. The irate whispers of the *pucelles* made it plain they would not so much as offer That Outlaw Wench a paddle.

"Indeed. The presence of your Templar and your brother—indeed, all his men—has been requested. That is, if my son remembers to tender the invitation amidst his excitement of killing God's creatures."

Marion recollected her wits, bowed her head. "I am pleased, my Queen, and grateful for such an honour."

"We'll see how grateful you are if His Eminence of Canterbury drinks too much and spills wine on that gown." Eleanor winked, grinning. "Not to mention, I should think you've earned the right to let someone else cook for those ruffians of yours for the once."

This time Marion didn't bother to halt her chuckle.

"Which brings me to another matter. Do you think your brother needs be reminded that he and his men should be well attired? I've no doubts they've stolen adequate clothing for such an occasion."

This time, Marion laughed. No doubts, indeed. "Gilbert will keep them on task, Madam." When Eleanor looked puzzled, she reminded, "The manor-bred archer; the one who procured the horses for us near Cadeby, seeing to your escape from Blyth."

"Ah, yes. That lad did seem to have an eye to his appearance. That's a relief. As it is, I'll likely have to persuade my eldest with a horsewhip to shuck his hunting clothes. Men are such babies, are they not?"

This time, every woman present was in open agreement. Agreeable silence fell as the Queen continued the game. The *pucelle* plying the needle started to sing in a pleasant-enough voice; several joined her whilst Joanna checked and refilled her mother's cup.

"Where is Blondel?" Lucia wanted to know. "I miss his playing."

"Likely pouting." Joanna shrugged. "His fair lion is off hunting new game."

"That"—Eleanor slid a quelling gaze—"will be enough of that. In fact, Joanna"—another wave of the fan—"why don't you take Marion into our bedchamber, find her something nice for her hair, some jewellery, a decent necklace. If she's to wait on me at Council, she'll need to look the part. Not to mention"—a severe scowl at the board—"she's trouncing me round, here. Both of you, be good girls and save my dignity. Later we'll have another game. I'll need a chance for revenge."

- XXII -

It was a winnowed-down party, in truth, that Robyn led to the nearest and clearest pool. Only a guard or two—though Robyn knew there were more lurking about. Four at least, that he could hear. And smell.

And the silent trio lurking outside any notice but his own: John, Gilbert, and Will. They weren't about to let Robyn wander alone in such company.

The King was no proper woodsman, striding though the brush as if he owned it. Well, then, Gamelyn would say he did, in deed if not in truth. Which made Robyn want to go back to the Lodge and clout him one, just because.

But neither was Richard stupid. After several furlongs of crashing through and making enough noise to scare the game for a mile broad—and after nearly running up Robyn's heels for a fifth time—he seemed to realise the quiet hesitation was not some put-upon jape just to annoy him. By the time they reached the stream-fed pond, he was taking note of Robyn's silent footfalls and gliding passage, of the darting gaze and ever-present tension Robyn could no more purge from his being than stop breathing—and wasn't about to, with a Frank at his back.

And said back kept itching, mind, not liking that it was turned towards sommat it considered *enemy*, nowt but.

Robyn gave it a scratch by turning, gesturing the King should go on ahead.

The King was watching him, eyes narrowed. Soon as Robyn turned, the odd, intent look was replaced by a charming grin.

With a Frankish shout to one of the guards following, King Richard muscled past Robyn, brash and subtle as a slap in the face, making Robyn wonder if he'd somehow imagined that earlier regard.

Wondered why he would, at that, and what it meant if he hadn't.

His shoulder blades gave another fierce itch. He must be mad, roaming the Wode with a Motherless lot who'd just as soon see him hang. Sodding noblemen . . .

Save for one ginger-haired Templar who Robyn really, *really* wished were nearby about now. Only Gamelyn was right not to be. Snit or no, swimming together almost always led to some sweaty fun for afters. In fact, the snit might make the fun all the better, at that.

Bloody damn, but just the contemplating was giving Robyn a proper unhealthy reaction to sprout in the company of Christians.

An owl gave a soft *hoo-hoo* from an oak an arrow's flight away— 'twere no owl, truly, but his little John asking *All well?* Robyn didn't glance upward, though he wanted to; instead he scratched at his head, brows quirking, then ran his hand down his face to further the thought: *Well enough, but what the hell?* Then a hand shielding his eyes, ostensibly peering after the King beneath a stray bit of sun, but with two fingers curled: *Keep watch.*

The visible brace of soldiers pushed past Robyn, following their liege lord and unaware of their outlaw guard dogs. Robyn smiled despite the shove he was damned sure the first one had meant. A few well-aimed arrows could take out the sod, did Robyn so much as twitch.

He paused, thought hard about twitching—a proper hex-breath might also solve a few problems, at that.

But the King was already shrugging from his clothes, with a curt motion indicating Robyn to do likewise. Whilst the careless superiority of it galled, it also meant trust, of a kind.

It wasn't on, to bewitch any animal to a snare.

So Robyn merely followed and, at least a stone's throw from his royal bathing partner, started to strip down. Hesitated, as the King's gaze moved to him, narrowed.

It was altogether . . . unsound, the hesitation.

Or not, the Horned Lord whispered behind his eyes. *Have you so soon forgotten lessons well learned in childhood? You chided the singer for fearing death, but neither should you needlessly court such. And you well could here, my own. Heed the Oak: take care.*

Robyn shivered beneath the heated presence—and he didn't particularly care for his reaction to that either, like some cur welcoming the snap of the leash. True enough, though: hesitation could save one's neck. Wariness could dodge a crippling blow. Keep your eyes down, head bowed, not even a suggestion of challenge . . . for sure as the breeze drifted with spring's coming, some arsy noble-man full of balls and piss would take it up just to prove a point.

Robyn blew the forelock from his eyes and shucked from his garb—save, of course, the skinning knife strapped to his calf. The quillion dagger still bided absent from his hip, its own type of phantom pain. All the while, he abided vigilant for something he didn't quite fathom. The chill water, bloody welcome, submerged vagrant thoughts and shuddered the blood to roaring within his veins. Robyn dove several times, otter-quick, and on the fourth heard, underwater, a huge splash from down the bank. The resultant shout meeting his ears as he surfaced was, surprisingly, a pleasurable one.

"*Quelle bonne idée, maître d'arcs!*" the King bellowed, exploding upward and shaking the water from his mane like a great yellow dog. "*Ce sont des vies!*" A grin, genuine and wide, flung Robyn's way.

Well, then, it seemed Himself approved. Robyn would keep his head for a bit at least. And watch his back the while.

"Aye, milord King. Whats'mever you said." Robyn waded into the shallows, grabbing at several clumps of grass. Soon he'd enough, and with a few quick twists and knots, he'd a wisp fit for scrubbing human or horse hide.

Meanwhile King Richard, with head cocked curiously waded closer. Robyn's fingers faltered, his gaze sliding sideways, wary. Richard babbled some more Frank, midspeech trailed off with a shrug and chagrined mutter, then pointed at the wisp of grass. Shook his head.

Mayhap kings didn't use such things. Robyn held it up to demonstrate, scrubbing at his armpit.

Richard frowned, then chuckled, shook his head, once again let out a bellow that would—aye and again—chase any game to the farthest reaches.

Robyn winced and put finger to lips, hissed for quiet. Instinctive, but likely not sommat one should tell a king.

This one blinked, stared at him. It was not pleasant.

Robyn reacted the only way he could. He pointed around at the forest, made several gestures with his fingers. Hunting signs between he and his men, but accurate mimicry of the animals' movements.

Richard's eyes turned from frosty to understanding, then amusement as he made quick imitation of the gestures. "*Je comprends. Lapin. Cerf. Effrayer!*" The last was with a flung-out hand.

Robyn nodded, hoping he wasn't agreeing to fling himself on some pike.

"*Mon roi!*" A shout from one of the guards, wielding a small bag like a flail.

Richard whirled and shushed the guard, a finger to his lips. Robyn couldn't help but chuckle.

The chastened guard dug in the bag and tossed a small round

to his liege; Richard caught it—a feat in itself, it proved, to catch soap with wet hands. Robyn grinned again, and when it was offered, shook his head.

"*Merci, mon roi.*" He knew that much, at least, even if Gamelyn always insisted the clip of Yorkshire mixed with Barrow lilt didn't sit terribly well with the bite of Frankish. Robyn reverted to hand signs: the deer, then a tap to his nose and a sniff, then a brandish of the sweetgrass wisp at one furry armpit.

Again, from the smell of that fancy soap, the deer wouldn't have to hear them coming.

"Ah," said Richard, and held out an imperious hand.

No help for it, then; Robyn would have to twist another, that was plain.

●

There had been a lot of what surely translated to *'Tisn't safe, milords* and *This is no goodly way to hunt, my lieges*, but the more protests were made, the more the King seemed set on this path. Indeed more Frank bull than any lion. Whatever hopes Robyn entertained of Richard abandoning the novelty of hunting *with* outlaws as opposed to merely hunting them were swiftly fading.

Robyn didn't want to be here. He wanted his own place and people and a meal. Wanted some head-clearing conversation with Marion, to kiss or punch Gamelyn—either'd do about now. Wanted to curl up beside John, swap affectionate insults with his lads . . . *Something.* Anything other than babying this butcher of a Frank bull through the forest for some unfathomable, pissed-up-proud reason.

Robyn supposed he should merely be thankful there was, after all, no need to wrap the King in wool batting. He didn't even have to wonder if the soldiers would trip over their armour—which soldiers inevitably did, in Robyn's experience—because the soldiers didn't come.

No wonder the Franks howled as if they were birthing a twin breech. Their liege insisted upon going hunting with a notorious wolfshead and only a few besides.

One of those few ended up being another outlaw. Despite Robyn's firm gestures of negation, John had materialised at the hunt's beginnings. Only the two foresters—a middle-aged man and his half-grown son—had noticed at first; aye, and his little John was that quiet. But it wasn't a few steps longer that the burly Frank mercenary upon whom Gamelyn had kept a wary eye—Mercadier, wasn't it?—also noticed the addition to their ranks. Some woodland craft to him, then, and a light stalk for all his bulk. His murmur to the king roused a glance and frown John's way, but nothing further than an accepting shrug. The forester settled in well enough, not enough brass in him to dare judge a king's company. The son was overeager, yet showed with every careful step how well he'd learned his father's craft. It gave Robyn a spare, aching thought for his own da, dead with Loxley.

The forester bore no such fond musings. He wore a sprig of rowan in his weathered cap—a charm, no doubt, against the Hood's evil magic. And he kept his son close, well away from the outlaws.

Not that they were needed, save as flank. Robyn was merely pleased they were competent. He kept the passage quiet and all followed suit, even if the mercenary's determined breath on his heels didn't reassure. Robyn'd rather have a vengeful tree spirit on his tail. And no doubt of the mercenary's intentions of staying there, despite warnings they'd have to split up. There were several too many for a proper stalk. Likely the foresters would be the ones to lie in wait once they'd found fresh sign. Unlikely the King would be willing to sit out any action.

Of course, if Himself did sit it out, mightn't the outlaws get nicked for taking Himself's deer?

A pretty predicament, whether to trust a Frank to keep to any implied word. Robyn shook the worry off like snow on sleeping furs, knowing his men tailed ready-close through their green Wode, silent insurance against treachery.

He took his charges even deeper, onto wilder paths. They found faint sign more than once, carrying sure telltales of spring. Robyn and John silently agreed to say nowt; does with fawns at heel deserved better than to feed a bunch of noblemen. Farther in, farther down; over moss matted thick as sheep's wool and roots big around as the mercenary's thighs, through thick stands of fallen, well-rotted trees nursing tender new growth. And down. The bottomlands squelched underfoot, overflow and seasonal tributary of the Trent, which burbled not far away. Mists hung in the hollows, obscuring the sun save for a golden scrim, here and there, fingering through.

Perfect. Like wild hawks a-fishing, deer preferred shadows to sun, mists to confound perceptions. Clear skies had warming rays, but also stark exposure.

The King slowed, muttered something that sounded like a prayer. When Robyn peeked, his face was full of wonder, not terror. The forester's expression showed more of the latter; he muttered a short prayer, fingering the rowan in his cap.

Some forester! John signed Robyn's way with a disgusted twist of mouth.

Better wary than daring trespass, Robyn signed and smirked, knowing he and his band were part and parcel of that wariness.

It was John who first spotted the cleft pressed sharp in a patch of damp earth. A heavy buck. Everyone went searching. Not long after, Robyn found several tufts of fur on a stand of bramble. One was a mottled agouti, the other red-gold as Gamelyn's forelock. More confirmation wafted on the rank odour coming off the moss: a brace of bucks, browsing the river bottoms.

Crouching on that moss, John hesitated with head cocked, brows twisting.

Aye, love?

It smells, John signed. *More than deer.*

Robyn dropped to his haunches, snuffed the lower level of mists, and . . . aye. There. Another scent, ranker still, wafting from the south. A boar laired somewhere about. He turned to gesture to their companions, was distracted by the forester's son. The lad had gone a ways, searching nigh to a small copse—*eager wanker,* Robyn thought, both fond and irritated as the lad began an excited dance, gesticulating wildly at his feet.

His reason proved true enough: a scattering of fresh dung. Robyn gave the lad a smile as he toed the droppings, eyes flickering all about for more sign.

Unfortunately, he found it. Just past that small gift of deer pellets, something gleamed wet-dark within a stand of gorse. The lad was still restive with his accomplishment; he gave a lurch sideways, looking further.

The gleam coalesced into a pair of beady eyes, following. Tracking.

Robyn darted a hand out, grabbed hold of the lad's woolsey tunic.

"Be still."

Mists wafted with the creature's inhale, then blasted outward.

The boy heard. Froze. Behind them, Mercadier cursed, and the King murmured a question. John made a questioning cluck with his tongue; Robyn answered it, but that was all the attention he paid to what was behind him.

It was no longer a question of if, but when the creature charged them.

So he didn't wait for it. With a shout that echoed into the tranquil bottomland, Robyn waved his arms and danced into the creature's sight line, gave the lad a quick shove sideways. The beady, scarlet-tinged eyes slid his way; Robyn didn't stop moving, slid two arrows from his hair, kept it up whilst nocking one to string.

Another blast, warning.

Robyn loosed the first arrow just as the boar burst from the undergrowth, all sharp tusks and heat and fury.

The ruse had worked, but scarce time to think about it or acknowledge the Frankish-hued shouts of dismay from behind him. One arrow wouldn't stop a boar. Robyn fired two more in quick succession—hoping to at least slow it down.

More than three arrows loosed. From behind him—John—and also seeming from nowhere, they came: a hail of humming, perfectly aimed missiles. The boar stumbled, flailed sideways, rolled.

Gained its feet and shook, looking for a target.

More Frank curses; the King's voice rose, insistent. As if he believed he could command nature, the daft . . .

The boar was still tracking Robyn. John waited a stone's throw behind, bow at nock. Robyn feinted to one side. It was enough. The boar charged. Robyn ran.

He took care over the hummocks and squelch of the ground, quick enough but not overly so. Just as he felt the creature's breath at his calves, Robyn flung himself sideways, against John. Bows close-held against their bodies, they stumbled towards an old birch, bounced off the tree's trunk and rolled about, ready; John pushing his bow as Robyn snatched another brace of arrows from his hair.

A cacophony of furious squeals and snorts were issuing from a bramble stand; the boar had charged straight into it. Too enraged to realise the arrows had killed it, once it fetched its arse from its nose, the beast would be back. The forester knew this too; recurve ready, he stepped in front of his son. To do the lad credit, he'd his own shortbow in hand.

King Richard strode towards the bush, gesturing and issuing orders. Mercadier tossed his liege a pike. All the while his gaze swept the surrounding trees. Robyn's lip tilted, sly. No doubt the man was wondering where those phantom arrows had come from.

Robyn didn't need to wonder. He'd recognised Will and Gilbert's shafts.

Richard let out another shout, banged his pike on the ground. No translation needed: *Come on, you sod!*

A vicious, angry squeal answered. In a burst of foliage and bloody vengeance, the boar exploded from the thicket, blind with rage . . . Nay.

Not *blind*.

There was an uncanny gleam in the tiny bloodshot eyes. It raced sudden chill up Robyn's spine to match the sudden-hot breath through his mind.

Accidents. . . happen, the Horned Lord purled. *What should a King do, after bleeding a land dry, if not bleed in return?*

A gasp from John—he had Seen.

But Robyn barely heard, swept away in the Seeing . . .

Blood.

Fear.

Fury.

Panic-pride-pain. . . intruder! *my place. . . myplace mypla-cemine. . .!*

"Robyn!" A hiss, and the sane jolt of John's hand snatching at the small of his back, grounding, wresting him from a Hunt not Wild but certainly maddened.

Not in this way, the Lady whispered, and drew cool fingers of reason through Robyn's mind.

Robyn raised his bow, drew.

"Nay!" Mercadier roared—in Anglic. "You'll hit the King!"

"I wain't unless I bloody well mean to!" Robyn snarled back. Nevertheless, he relaxed his push, uncertain of too many things, including his own convictions.

The boar charged straight for the King. No novice hunter, Richard dipped and swayed with the beast's charge. It stumbled, then all but ran onto the waiting pike. The momentum shoved Richard back, twin grooves in the soft earth for several ells and more. The boar was refusing to die.

The forester raised his bow, tentative. Robyn's uncertainty lay in another direction altogether, his rise slow and his push into his bow faltering. John followed suit, just as hesitant, as Mercadier started to move forward with pike ready.

Richard warned them off with a hoarse *"Non!"* Teeth bared, he set himself into the pike.

Slow but sure, the boar kept shoving the King backwards. If the boar managed to break the pike . . . or wriggle off it . . .

It seemed to take forever, a nigh-equal match of grunts, straining muscles, and growls. Finally, the boar gave a long, heavy shudder and went limp.

Mercadier pumped a fist in the air, let out a low smattering of congratulatory Frank as he strode over, not without a cautious toe to the downed boar.

Robyn lowered his bow as John came closer, nudged him with worried eyes. "M well enough," Robyn murmured. The hand he rested upon John's shoulder was nevertheless a-tremble. John covered it with his own, breathed soft comfort against Robyn's palm.

I will take him, soon enough. The Lady's breath also gentled. *But not thisnow. Not with this face.*

The forester was hugging his son close, with that mix of relief and fussing that was surely in every father's stockpile. The look he threw the two outlaws was even more complex: wonder; incredulity; naked gratitude.

It brought the balance of reality back to Robyn, sluice from a winter-chill stream. Did the man really think they would have just stood there whilst a boar took his son? Richard was nodding to his captain's comments, well pleased. There was that, at least.

"I fear we've chased off the deer, milord King," Robyn ventured, wry, with a pluck at his bowstring.

Looking up and over at Robyn, Richard was frowning.

Mercadier muttered what must have been a quick translation. The frown turned swiftly to a grin, then that booming laugh, surely putting paid to the chasing.

Still chuckling, Richard took the horn from his belt and put it to his lips. Robyn had, many a time, heard his father imitate the bucks in autumn with one of those horns; Richard employed it with no less finesse, but after another *look at me!* fashion. All brass and balls like any noble, calling to his own kind. Warning everything within miles to danger a-horse.

The forester, one arm still flung across his son's shoulders, also had an amused quirk of brow.

No doubt, though—the horn was exquisite, and made a lovely sound when sommun knew how to proper use it.

Occupied in a quick back-and-forth with Mercadier, Richard nevertheless noticed Robyn's attention, seemed to consider the horn inspiring it. Running sturdy fingers down the braided leather lanyard attached, he smiled.

Then, fingers still tangled in the lanyard, he strode over.

Robyn stilled any impulse to retreat, annoyed it was there, but having to acknowledge it as the King halted nigh toe-to-toe with him. A flicker of something—dismay? displeasure?—no doubt His Overlordship noting that he had to look up to meet Robyn's gaze. True, Richard was tall enough to be unaccustomed to the happenstance—yet wasn't it enough that in sheer bulk he could've made four of Robyn and likely pounded him into butter? He had to be taller as well?

"Baissez la—" Mercadier started, midsentence realised Robyn couldn't understand, and instead growled, "Outlaw, are you such a fool? Lower your head!"

Peasant's reflexes, rusty from disuse, creaked into motion. Robyn ducked his head. His knees quivered—again reflex, agreement to follow suit—but Robyn refused them.

Richard seemed well content with the former. Humming some small tune to himself, he threaded the lanyard over Robyn's head. Not only that, but took his own sweet time nestling it just so against Robyn's breastbone, fingers following the lanyard upward. An innocent motion, outwardly an effort to straighten the twist of leather. Yet the callused, thick fingers lingered at Robyn's nape. Trembled, then curled. Trailed, tiny, a caress.

Robyn started, couldn't help a glance upward. Thankfully the same unruly length of forelock to which Marion threatened a blunt knife on a regular basis covered that glance.

The fingers left his nape, slid around and down to the horn. Gave it a tap. The horn vibrated, hollow and rich, against Robyn's breast. The King met his eyes, nodded. Then he turned away, gesturing to the boar's carcass and addressing Mercadier in a rapid burst of Frankish.

Robyn let out the breath he only then realised he'd been holding and slid his gaze to John's.

John's brown eyes were wide as a Samhain moon.

Surely the brace of soldiers, summoned by the horn, would take with them not only the boar's carcass, but their liege lord. Go back to Clipstone's hall, their departure marking the end of Robyn's stint as royal hunting guide.

Not so. The soldiers took the slain boar back, sure enough. The two foresters were equally dispatched with a message, conveyed in purposeful if faulty Anglic by Mercadier: their liege was not to be bothered, was well accompanied, and might not return until the dawn.

Then Robyn and the King, flanked closely by John and Mercadier, set off to track the two bucks.

Miraculously, said bucks hadn't left the hundred. One evaded Richard's crossbow, but fell to Robyn's quick loose. As dark began to settle over the Wode, the King decided they would make camp and unmake the deer. He also insisted, through the scanty auspices of Mercadier, that Robyn play host "since you know Sherwood better than most, master archer!"

There was also further discussion, quite heated, after which the King clasped the small cross at his breast and murmured a few words whilst Mercadier rendered that his liege would be honoured should Robyn prepare from the valuable haunch an impromptu venison feast.

"It is Lent, of course"—the mercenary also crossed himself—"but the King says God will surely understand."

Lent. Like most Christian rituals, the seasonal fasting had been stolen from Heathen necessity—as Robyn had told Richard, springtide brought green and flowers, but short rations.

The unmaking ritual, though, was a proper mystery, more like pissing on boots than honouring one's kill, full of rules about who got what and how. Robyn knew some of the ways of a nobleman's hunt from his father, who had occasionally received the quarry's shoulder as his rights. Leaving the Franks to attend that duty, Robyn and John made a proper camp.

Later, the fire dying into coals and the night folding about them, dinner was more than welcome. For being so fond of a good bellow, Richard had lapsed into quietude, leaning back against a fallen tree stump and observing the murk-upon-pitch of the Shire Wode's night as if he'd never seen such stark, tenuous beauty.

Robyn's curiosity must have been apparent, for the mercenary offered him a refill of his mug and an answer, of a sort.

"He has always preferred the campsite and his men about him to any court. No doubt you, master archer, can understand such things." Mercadier's Anglic was faltering, and trimmed heavily with the nasal hum of Frank talk, but he spoke it well enough. Though he did seem to have more problems understanding Robyn than Robyn did him, and was much less patient than was mannerly.

You look like Gamelyn, John had even signed once, and to Robyn's puzzlement, explained. *All that eye-rolling.*

Robyn couldn't help it. Here he was, roasting a side of venison for the King of England. A *Frank* King, who'd raped and pillaged his way across more than one land he thought he'd rights to, and who Robyn would have earlier been willing to see gored by a wild pig. A man who, in truth, Robyn had long wanted to gut for what Gamelyn had endured under his command in the Holy Land, let alone every other blind and bloodthirsty ideal Richard damn-well represented.

Only it weren't so easy, were it, in thisnow?

"Nowt better than a clear night and a fire with t' Wode all 'round," Robyn replied, soft.

Mercadier paused in his application of wood splits below the roasting meat and frowned, parsing the words slowly. Richard, lounging with powerful arms crossed, spoke a soft patter of Frank to his captain, chuckled as he answered, spoke again.

It was Mercadier's, this time, to laugh. "He says his half brother the Archbishop of York is correct. England's northern shires do speak a language unintelligible to all but their own."

Says one who wain't arse himself to speak any *Anglic tongue,* Robyn thought but did not say. Instead he let his speech curl even more into those "northern shires." "M fair upskelled tha's nobles loosed milord King wi' nobbut ussen'."

Mercadier blinked. Frowned. Robyn hid a smirk beneath a scratch to his beard.

"Again?" Mercadier demanded—and well, but Robyn had to give him that much for tenacity. "Slow, *si'l vous plaît.*"

No sense of humour, these Franks. Robyn obliged—minus his grandda's way of speaking. "I'm surprised all t' nobles let milord King out on his own, like."

Mercadier brows twitched—mayhap he'd caught the joke, mayhap not—and shrugged. "He is the King. I am with him. And despite your archers hiding in the trees"—his eyes gleamed, and not only from the fire's light—"it would not be easy for you to take either of us."

"Mm. Nor you, us." Robyn tilted his head, tacit acknowledgement.

Not that he would start any fight, not here and now . . . but neither did he expect some Frank to comprehend why.

Granted, he'd given hearth-right courtesy to men he despised more. Could do no less, in fact, when asked to oversee both hearth and sup. Likely both mercenary and king bided ignorant of such ancient custom as Robyn was of their ways . . . still. It was done, the men guests at Robyn's fireside, and if that was deep in the Wode beneath a night sky? Well, and that was the most normal happenstance of the past se'nnight.

Even the Horned Lord's wrath had been winnowed calm beneath the power of a shared hearth. Lingering about the edges as if He'd not tried to lose Himself and Robyn to the madness of a near-Hunt, meek as if the Lady had Herself donned Summer's cloak and wrestled waxing Winter to a headlocked standstill.

Mayhap She had, after Her own fashion. Gamelyn surely wasn't about to enter any fray, save this one he was so set upon, silent and solitary.

Robyn let it go—'twas either that or chew until his mouth bled—and sought John, gaze and presence.

The second he received but not the first. John's knee touched his, close as they dared, but the brown eyes stayed fixed upon the King, a deceptive mildness Robyn well recognised for what it was: steely threat.

The King and his mercenary were oblivious. The latter kept up a regular scrutiny of the surrounding trees—no doubt seeking those outlaws he knew were there but couldn't find. Richard, on the other hand, was peering at Robyn, steady and gauging. There was an odd respect in it; odd, because 'twas a bloody king gracing it to a peasant. Even if that peasant wielded a monster longbow and had dead-dropped not just tonight's supper, but several trigger-happy tossers of guards through a Nottingham arrow loop with nowt more than favourable light, a wind test, and a cock of his black head.

There was sommat more, though. Sommat stretching *tynged* sideways, and no chance lay-by. Like the lingering touch of fingers at Robyn's nape, and upon the horn which Robyn had lain, chary, beside his bow. Like a breath across the bones' fall upon a worn, marked stag hide for the Telling: *This will matter, anon.*

Will you give me my Summerlord back? Is that why my god insists honour be done you?

Honour done, and unexpectedly returned, not with a great and merry disturbance upon the green sward as Robyn imagined a king to demand, but in this small and nigh intimate meal beside an outlaw's fire, in the wake of a companionable hunt, with a gift bestowed.

Honour, when the King had made it plain he considered peasants little more than gormless draught animals.

Honour, in the devout and single-minded prayer that traced the White Christ's cross over the meal a Heathen had provided, yet denying everything that gentle Jew had preached, off conquer-ing—nay, *butchering*—his darker-skinned brethren just because they called the same god by another name.

Honour, whilst he channelled his god's guilt into war and anger and, all the while, buggered his trouvère. Sin, and unnatural, his like called it, but he was a king and could do what he fancied, be it breaking fast days or tupping soft, flaxen-haired boy-men who were clever and wore a hundred masks, who were *no use with a man's sport*, who sang tender, biting songs of love and hate both, who desired the flame but circled, unwilling to the moth's certain fate, gaming by nature—or design.

Alundel was more like Robyn, mayhap, than Robyn fancied believing. Flying nigh to the flame, because the pain meant he was alive.

Well, mayhap not that alike; Robyn wasn't fair, or soft, or all that clever.

But his own lover was just as full of guilt and rage, haunted past bearing with equal measures of love and loathing, driven towards some unfathomable nobleman's dream.

- Entr'acte -

"I had the dream again, Hubert."

They were alone by their fire, with just Sayme in attendance. Nottingham lay in darkness, its only light a few fires dotting the bailey encampments and beyond. Quiet, as well; merely the sounds of horses in their pickets, or men snoring in their billets.

"The same one? Again?"

Wymarec nodded.

Hubert frowned, accepted another cup of wine from Sayme. Sleep was difficult at present. Better to sit up, enjoy the peace of stars in a clear night—the sound of rain on the roof if not—and have a little too much liquor to ensure a bit of slumber despite the leg. It itched and ached, which meant it was healing well, but also that it would be damned uncomfortable for at least another se'nnight.

"It has . . . changed." Wymarec was well into his cups—rare enough in itself. "It's this damned castle, seething with the *dryw's* power."

"The elder powers are growing," Hubert agreed, and thought, *Like All Hallows.*

"Aye, and we will harness them. One way or the other." Wymarec sipped at his wine. "Even the Count was subject to them. And he is careless, undisciplined. Blood has told, in him, with magick and temper both. The latter is . . . unfortunate."

"We may not need worry after his fate." Hubert shrugged and bent closer to the fire. "Considering."

"We need worry after all who show such raw talent. Such things cannot be allowed to root and sucker, wild."

Such as the young dryw. *And Gamelyn.* Again the thought came and went, random.

Hubert bowed his head, made a quick and silent paean to his Lady for guidance. Since he had lain at the gate of Nottingham, an arrow in the leg and his *Confanonier's* body as a shield, it seemed the stout foundation of his thoughts had become . . . unsound. Undermined.

It made little sense. This was not the first time he had cheated death and the devil, with or without the quick grace of a bodyguard. Mayhap it was merely that he was no longer young. It was the way of things as the years waned: sombre contemplations of twilight instead of the expansive salutation of a golden summer morn.

Not unexpected, but indeterminate, that his own affections should become so . . . precarious.

"You seem . . . out of sorts, my friend. The leg?"

Hubert shrugged.

"Take heart in your healing. It seems the Hood's witch sister indeed knows a wortwife's skills. Also take heart in that our main players remain in the game. Including"—Wymarec's gaze met Hubert's—"the Count."

"Indeed?" Hubert shook off his own musings and leaned forward, a curious frown drawing his brow. "Tell me."

A tread, booted-heavy, approached: one of their Templars on light patrol. He saluted his superiors, kept on.

Wymarec waited until the man had disappeared into the night. "The Count will return to this land. He loves it more than any of his family, in truth. For that he will swear fealty to his brother, and Richard will forgive him, take his oath. We all know that the Angevin squabble and reconcile like fickle lovers. Moreover, the Count is not stupid, and has come to realise his place in the Great Work. Unlike his brother, who scorns any art but the sword. 'I leave prophecies and alchemies to the priests and my mother,' he says."

"I doubt even the sorceries of Solomon could sway Richard. The myriad spiritual wonders of the Holy Land, his admiration for Saladin, the Pope's spineless inaction when he was in gaol— none of it could assail his convictions. Though he certainly is keen to boast of being spawned of the devil's brood when it suits him."

"He might be inconstant with many of his appetites, but aye, in matters of faith, he sees no other way but that of the Deception. I doubt he would have paid heed to even our late Grandmaster. De Sablé was his friend, and ours, yet not of the Inner Temple." Wymarec shook his head. "All our players have faults. Some of them fatal for our purpose."

"I had begun to wonder if the Count was suitable," Hubert admitted. "After the madness here, last autumn."

"Well, and we must credit the wolfshead with part of that—he called the spirits to lair in Nottingham, after all, and revealed to Count John what he had scorned. But more we have you to thank, Hubert, for convincing the Count how he overstepped himself with Brother Guy."

"Guy." Hubert contemplated his pot for long moments, then said, slow, "And how did, ah, *his* role play out in your dream?"

Wymarec nodded, and surely the sense of relief it gave Hubert was not wholly unfounded. "That has not changed. Our recalcitrant Brother shall be a sorcerer fit to guide a king of the ancient blood, and we shall stand with him." A shrug. "Not upon the morrow, of course. Our liege refuses to value the most ancient blood-claim of England. And Guy's abilities still lie useless to us—for all the druid's power, he has done little in aid of *that.*"

"And those abilities?"

"The futures, all save a few, show them freed."

Wymarec's insistence gratified. The vagaries of Sight had never been Hubert's true métier. And he might as well admit, here beneath the stars, how he worried after Gamelyn's state of being.

"Mayhap we must after all force him to the initiation. I've never thought it wise." Hubert contemplated his bandaged leg and thought of what had happened to Gamelyn at Blyth. "But now . . . "

"Yes. Now. One way or another, he will bring us the forest cult, yet . . . " A glower. "He is plainly out of his depth with them. With the young druid. Our Brother has let worldly yearnings interfere with his judgment."

But which ones? Hubert mused. *The love and honour that holds him to the Templars, or his passion for the* dryw *and the Maid? Which is his true purpose?*

He thought he knew. A strange pain, the knowledge. Both beautiful and forlorn . . . and dangerous.

Instead he cast such treasonous thoughts aside and ventured, quiet, "What happened between you and the *dryw?*"

Wymarec's hand went to his neck. It was obvious the Hood had marked him. Resentment simmered, as did renewed respect. The former might lie dangerous, yet the latter remained cause to be thankful. "It is said that Robyn Hood plays both Trickster and King Fool, but at All Hallows, he played me for a fool. You gave excellent advice regarding him, Hubert, and I did not heed. I was... impatient. I will not make such a mistake again. Neither shall I underestimate the druid. Again."

Hubert nodded. "Just so."

"For the Great Work, then. Our path is plain."

Another thought stole, vagrant, into Hubert's mind: *Is it so?*

Disobedience? Or truth? Unsure and loath to the feeling, he sipped at his cup and said nothing.

- XXIII -

K ing Richard left with the approaching dawn. He also left not only the deer carcass, still hanging in a tall wych elm, and the forester's horn, but several things to mull over with his parting words. Translated, of course, by Mercadier.

"Bring the stag to Nottingham's great hall on the morrow, master archer. You will dress in your finest and be guest at Our hearth, attend Our feast—you and those invisible archers as well, all of them! We have unmade the deer but not portioned it properly, and We shall see, within the feasting hall, that you are rewarded with a prime—and honourable— portion."

Anticipation tickled Robyn's belly. The King meant to welcome a band of outlaws into Nottingham as his honoured guests. It might not be the sacrament of hearth law, but by any law of the Franks, a public gift of venison was its own ritual.

Mayhap this was going to work out after all.

John, however, was in a temper as the King and his mercenary captain made their way outward. He used it to express his own opinion. *Good riddance.*

Bloody damn. Not only Gamelyn in a snit, but now John, too?

Robyn made noises of meek agreement, offering food as conciliation: slices of venison from the portion roasted the previous night and some dried apples from his pouch. Gilbert and Will made an appearance once their noble visitors were well and truly departed, and they all sat down to a fine—and much more relaxed—meal.

"The King slept all night," Gilbert marvelled. "Though I'm sure I saw the mercenary wake a time or two."

"Sleeping with one ear open," Robyn agreed.

"I wonder," Will ventured, reaching forward to slice more meat, "if t' man fears anything?"

"Everyone fears something." Gilbert shrugged. "If they don't, then—"

"They should," John snapped.

The burst of vocal ill humour rocked Will back on his heels to blink at Gilbert, who in turn peered at Robyn all wide-eyed. Robyn shrugged.

Don't ask. I don't know.

"So you've done the pretty with Himself," Gilbert continued, mild, after a small pause. "Enough that he's asked all of us to the feast."

"A good night's work, Rob." Will grinned around a hank of meat.

Robyn smiled, but it was thin. "Mayhap."

"Aw, Rob, no mayhap to 't!"

"Either way, I hope it en't ower long before they all leave us be. I'm proper tired of this game."

"En't no *game.*" John rose and stalked over to where the remaining portions of the deer's carcass had been hung, started working at the rope's knot.

"John?" Robyn started.

"I'll go help," Gilbert offered and rose, padded over.

Robyn watched for several indecisive heartbeats, then returned his gaze to the fire.

John was right. It wasn't a game. Not really. Not to his like. He'd best remember that, no matter what some man born on the right side of the blanket thought to offer.

A hand alighted upon his back. He started, relaxed as Will began to apply a steady pressure, up and down Robyn's spine.

"You're takin' a sight too much on yerself," Will chided. "As usual. No wonder John's a mad-on."

Robyn wasn't sure he cared, merely slumped gratefully into the back rub. He sensed rather than saw Will's smirk but definitely felt the effects: Will leaned in and started to massage in earnest.

Will soon began to fill the quiet with a nattering of inconsequentials; he had never been one for silence, after all. Many a time 'twere irritating; now, it strangely comforted. Robyn let the chatter flow over him, washing away the strange, unresolved tension as sure as Will's hands, beneath which Robyn's eyes were beginning to cross, blissful.

"Y' know, I think David's taken to Aelwyn and her bairns. I swear when we left her at Hathersage I heard him ask her if she would consider Matlock instead."

It tilted a smile to Robyn's lip.

"We're doing the right thing, Rob. I'm stubborn as damn, but even I can see that. Everything's changing, aye, but Marion's right. It's for the better."

Robyn couldn't help it; he tensed up again.

Will misconstrued it. "I know all this is proper grief to you, what's happening. But en't it for the best? To know, now, what that one truly wants?"

That's the trouble. I don't know what that one truly wants. All I know is I want him with me, want to feel his body against mine and his magic slicking my blood, want to place the horns at his feet and see him honour, not fear, what he's meant to hold.

"He can have his bloody castle," Will continued. "We'll have each other, and a pardon, and soon we'll be able to go home."

"Home," Robyn murmured. "Where's home? It's all changing . . . and aye, it should. If Marion can have a place to call her own, ply her skill like old Maud once did at Papplewick? If David can have his family, mayhap take in Aelwyn and her bairns wit'out the worry his own'll suffer, being tied to an outlaw? If Arthur can court widow Helena and have a proper home . . . aye, well then. 'Tis worth any of this."

Silence. Will prompted, soft, "But?"

Robyn scarcely wanted to voice it, afraid the ill luck of it might hex the good. But it escaped as he leaned back, sudden, against Will's chest. "*Home.* We wain't have each other, will we? Robyn and his merry band of thieves will no longer roam the Shire Wode . . . " A shudder, then eyes shut tight as Will put strong arms about Robyn, held him tight. "I want what's best for them, I'd give my heart for it . . . have done"—and blast and bugger, but his throat was beginning to close up—"but what am *I* to do wit' a pardon? Eh? T' only home I've ever truly known—"

My Wode, with my men, my Maid, and. . . and my Summering light.

"—the only one *left* to me is my Wode."

"King Richard gave you a forester's horn," Will protested, soft. "Mayhap 'tis what he means to do, make you forester t' Shire Wode." From the tilt of his voice, he fancied the notion.

Robyn wasn't so sure. "Dogs were once wolves, weren't they? But men figured the best way to tame 'em: feed 'em, make 'em all dependent, like, then slip t' collar on and set 'em to *proper* work, aye? King's forester!" The words burst forth, nigh a curse.

"But Rob, we could do. Like when we were boys, riding with our da—"

"And what has that ever meant? A snap of leash when we don't mind our betters, bein' trammelled by laws *we'd* have to uphold? The same laws as demanded my da turn yours ower t' rot in bloody Nottingham's gaol."

"Rob." The hands upon him had slowed, shaking.

But Robyn could no more stop the words than the memories

they brought. "Your da and mine, they were good men, initiates of t' most powerful covenant in three shires—but they let that collar noose 'em, tame and tight. *King's foresters,* aye, and nowt beneath the laws they themselves upheld! And you 'n' me? Their sons? We're less than nowt and outside the law, worth no more 'n the price of a wolf's head at the hundred court. But still, in t' Wode—*our* Wode—we're free, aye? We refuse their laws, for *here's"*—his gesture encompassed the entirety of Sherwood, and beyond—"where we can live and breathe like men, not dogs. Where we can practice our ways and watch the magic of the wheel turning, ever on. Where we help those as look to us. *Outside the law.* Bloody damn, the sodding *law* were what saw our parents *murdered!"*

Will was silent, breath troubled and halting upon Robyn's hair.

"That sod of a Frank bull? He said it t' my face! There's his sort, and my sort, and I've no wit and too much wanting, no more to it. But I en't cozened so dull I canna see what he's done, will do. Nowt is safe in such a world! 'All things should just flow downstream, natural,' he said, as if he even knows what natural means. I know what it means, and what it brings when t' nobles shit upstream! Those who live downhill have nowt but a good river made foul!"

"'Tis true enough," Will murmured, hoarse. "There's their sort, and our sort, and sure as rain there's nowt between to tie us. But what Marion said, Rob. The pardon. And we're so close to winning back from 'em what's ours."

"And what *was* ours? David wants his boy back, and his gramma, but 'tis the same existence as starved his wife. The same *law* what saw Arthur's arm hacked to a stump for darin' to feed himself. What Aelwyn wants to leave so her bairns wain't grow up 'neath a whip. And Marion . . . me sister is that clever, and that loving, and wants what's best for all of us, I know. But what happens to a cunning woman when our ways are all swept under theirs? What happened to old Maud at Papplewick? She was a powerful, wise old woman, and they drowned her as a witch in t' end!"

"We wain't let it happen," Will growled against Robyn's shoulder. "That's all there is to 't. We wain't just . . . knuckle under. We'll be freemen. Our *own* men, wit' our ways and rites to ourselves and none of *them,* no matter what the Motherless sod thinks to make of us."

"The King?" Robyn asked, somewhat hoarse.

"Aye, him too. Listen. You and me . . . hell, Johnny and Gilbert and Marion too, come to 't . . . You're right. The Wode's *our* only home." Will's arms were locked firm, but quivering. "So we're with you, no matter what happens. Pardon or nay. Like y' said. 'Whither tha goest, so shall I.'"

It niggled at Robyn that Will had chosen that particular phrase, but he shook his head, let it go. Burrowed in deeper, for right now it was all fraying—from *tynged* disappearing into scarlet and ebon, to the magic shuddering awake and wild as if to deny the iron and bells that would sing it quiet again, to Gamelyn's unfathomable purpose and Marion's acceptance of it, the former shadowed-cold and the latter brilliant, warm as a will-o'-wisp lighting a dark path . . .

All of it scattering to the winds, and who knew what would come of any of this?

So he just leaned hard against Will and let him make whatever claims he would.

Nottingham's main hall was splendid.

There really was no other word, Marion realised, that would do. One could scarcely credit how the castle had only recently been under siege with her gates burnt, her towers breached. A line of corpses still hung near what remained of the outer bailey wall. Nevertheless, the folk of the outlying villages had been galvanised into returning only the previous day—some to the kitchens, some sweeping the floors and laying patterns of fresh rushes, some still yanking crossbow bolts out of the main doors.

The influx of return had prompted another immigration, this of fish and game, produce stocks and table goods. Anything available was being carted and carried in from all over. The market stalls were setting up. Foresters were hunting—with the King's permission, of course—and gardeners were gathering the spring herbs for savour and bite. There would be plenty for the upcoming feast days. Not only for Saturday and after the Palm Sunday mass at St. Mary's, but also a special dispensation by Archbishop Walter himself: a banquet upon the morrow to herald the King's return, as well as his munificence in this holiest of seasons.

And all of it the doing of this woman of middling height and advanced age, whom Marion followed with a basket over one arm—and that containing not only nib, ink, and parchment, but the keys to the buttery, the undercroft, and the spice stores. Not that Marion needed to waste good parchment, instead committing to memory the last-minute details Eleanor rattled off as she inspected the hall.

The *pucelles* had been assigned other tasks, for which Marion breathed easier. The constant undertow of hostility was wearying. Marion would rather be back with her own kind—her lads—where nowt was allowed to simmer overlong lest it do harm, and matters were aired, sometimes with fisticuffs, then done.

But milady Joanna accompanied Eleanor, and her courteous manner towards Eleanor's odd and common protégé had not wavered. Mayhap 'twas no more than being a well-dowered woman who was sister to the King, daughter of the Queen Mother, and widow of a powerful foreign king. Joanna had nothing to prove. So it remained—despite their very different upbringing—that Joanna seemed friendly, helpful, and not all that dissimilar from the young women Marion remembered growing up in Loxley.

Seeming centuries, yet only a breath ago, those past summer afternoons. All spent not only in hard work, but also in gathering flowers towards the rites and fêtes, young lasses dreaming and conjuring homely charms upon what they would do as mistresses of their own hearths. Not all that unlike to Nottingham's renovation, save this was on a much grander scale, sommat as only rich and noble families could bring about.

"What about the dais?" Joanna asked her mother. "It looks small."

The dais did seem inadequate to seat the attending throng of highest-ranking nobles. Set apart not only by its height and separate placement, it had fewer benches than chairs, and also the ceremonial salt cellar, already in place if still empty. Below that cellar and throughout the rest of the great hall were lined row upon row of table boards set stout upon crossbeams, and benches beneath.

Marion smiled. So *many* details! Early spring flowers and greenery to see to and set just so, with enough candles throughout to buy and sell several villages. Curtains and tapestries brought in, beaten free of dust, and hung upon walls stripped bare by necessity, yet now warm and vibrant with colour. Kitchens scrubbed clean, and wagonloads of food being rendered upon wide boards and within huge cauldrons, with game being roasted upon spits—one of the pigs which, Eleanor had advised as they'd toured the kitchen hall, had been brought down with Robyn's assistance.

The smell of roasting meats and breads already wafted from the kitchens, a good arrow's flight away but no less potent.

It was, all of it, jolly good fun.

"The dais needs another several strides added," Eleanor agreed with her daughter's assessment. "On the east side, I should think, and more proper chairs. Benches will not do, even at the end."

Marion nodded, saw to it. All morning she had done much the same. Servants came when beckoned, gaped at the two queens, and were thankful to receive instructions—in Anglic, not Frankish— from one of their own. They had advised her, apologetic to be sure, as to the realities of supply, but tendered some welcome news about the state of progress as well. Even more welcome, upon dismissal several lingered, met her eyes, made the proper signs, and called her *Maiden.*

They knew her. She smiled and gave a discreet blessing in return. As if in response, a shiver and crackle of . . . something made itself heard up within the rafters. Not pigeons, either. It sent even the loyal ones scurrying, eyes purposefully downcast. One forked an evil eye towards the roof shadows, and Marion remembered, again.

The Wild Hunt.

Venturing a careful look upward, she could just make out what the servants had refused to: tiny flickers like witched candles perched in the heavily thatched gloom, and shadows flitting along the thick oak rafters.

Maiden. The acknowledgement wafted downward, a far cry from the belligerent challenge of the spirits at the crescent river.

Bendith y mamau, she breathed, a silent rise of heat into sudden chill. As one the shadow spirits settled on the topmost beam, gentled and watching. Waiting.

This was more than the lingering vibrations of what the Hooded One had called forth to subdue a castle and wrest a wounded lover from the otherworlds. This was surfacing—*advancing*—through those opened gates, artless and determined as a bairn taking its first steps across an earthen floor.

"We've called, Mari. They're answering."

No wonder Nottingham had been so intent upon keeping the chambers blazing with light, so much that they had begun to burn the table boards.

Marion sent another blessing-breath upward and turned away, sure of the spirits' acceptance but unsure what to make of it. Particularly here and now.

She approached the dais, thankful Eleanor and Joanna were intent upon other things. One being the soundness—and comfort, from Eleanor's frown—of the three centremost chairs.

"So she isn't coming?" Joanna's query was Frankish, of course, but audible to Marion. Particularly within the open hall and echoing down from the shadowed, fae-occupied rafters.

"'He didn't ask' was the gist of the letter."

"Richard never asks if he can help it. He expects."

"My son," Eleanor said, grim, "is more like his father than I should like at times."

"He also likely knows you have been true monarch of England these past months. The English know it as well. Who better to have at his side here?"

"I'm growing tired of the role!"

Joanna smirked. "Ah, *Maman,* I doubt that."

"I've earned the right to retire, for the love of Christ! The girl should step up and claim her place, not play at this passive—and stubborn—rectitude."

"Berengaria is a good woman."

"Good? Bah! She is supposed to be *Queen.* Instead she uses the excuse of neglect—"

"Well, she is neglected. Richard would rather court a pretty trouvère than pay heed to her."

"Ssst, girl! Richard would do his duty well enough were his wife more on her knees in the bedroom than in chapel! Instead Berengaria allows herself to be relegated to the sidelines, and in the doing leaves Richard with only a bastard made with some Limoges peasant maid! I thought to procure a falcon and gained a dove. So, Marion." Eleanor's gaze, wandering the hall, came to rest upon Marion's measured approach. "What do the good people of Nottingham say about furniture?"

"They are looking, Madam. It seems much was used as firewood, what with the castle's wood stocks being low, and the siege—"

"More foolery!" Eleanor snorted. "This is what comes of letting powerful bastions to those ill-equipped for the responsibility! Just because they had ready funds . . . How much coin do you have in your possession, Marion?"

Marion wasn't sure how—or what—to answer.

Joanna did, with a wink at Marion. "Legally gained or no, *Maman?*"

Eleanor waved it away, a graceful gesture with the ever-present peacock fan. "It scarcely matters. From what I've seen, Marion here could manage Nottingham's household a damned sight better than Murdac and his staff of incompetents. Letting the wood stocks run low, indeed! The siege didn't even last a fortnight."

Marion had to agree with that latter. She remembered how her mother had managed with a pittance of resources, and the women of Loxley village even less, for their husbands weren't foresters with accompanying privileges, however mean. For a castle there was no adequate—or easily explained—excuse.

Eleanor was still peering at her. Disconcerting, but Marion kept her chin tucked, her gaze respectful and steady.

"Royal Lady!" This from the doorway, from a short man dressed as fine as any lord with a seneschal's chain of office at his breast. "We have received word; King Richard is on his way from Clip-stone."

Joanna frowned. "I thought he was to meet there this morning with Scotland's king?"

"So. Either Malcolm has not yet arrived, or they did their business quickly." Eleanor had turned to witness the seneschal's hurried approach. "Richard has always gotten on better with the Scots than Henry ever did, and there are other matters to attend, after all. What, then, my lord, does the King command?"

The seneschal knelt—Archbishop Walter's man, if Marion remembered aright, and Walter's power second only to Eleanor's. According to the elderly maidservant within Eleanor's retinue, 'twas Walter who'd crafted Nottingham's surrender—and had urged the King to ransom instead of beheadings.

Aye, and what gossip occupied the *pucelles* did have its uses. Marion kept her eyes her own, and her ears open.

"My lord of Canterbury sent me to inform you, my Queen, that the King will have a meal with Madam, his royal sister, and his advisors, with council held immediately after, here in the great hall."

"I think not," Eleanor parried. "We are not going to allow our feast preparations to be put in disarray. Is the tower hall in good order?"

"My Queen, I do not know."

"'Tis in order, Madam," Marion spoke up. "So the servants informed me."

"I . . . see." Eleanor's expression shifted, annoyed into pleased. "My lord seneschal, kindly see word is sent to all the advisors, and tell your master the Archbishop in particular. We shall meet in the tower hall."

They were following her. Had been, since the nobles congregated the previous day in the hall atop Nottingham's great keep.

Moreover, they lingered above her, invisible save for an occasional shift of shadowy not-form, a random lamp of eye. Seeming nothing more than birds or bats nestled in the rafters.

Her mam would have forked an evil eye, not unlike what the serfs had done in the great hall, and captured them with a Barrow name fit to bind Their kind: *gwyllion*. Fae or otherworldly spirit, Marion wasn't sure, but she was sure of Their intent gaze. They seemed greatly curious as to why the Maiden should stand behind a hastily set up board in Nottingham's great hall, serving two noblewomen and watching an Angevin King sell shrievalties to the highest bidder.

The former, at least, was no novelty to Marion. Once and not very long ago, she had stood in much this same place, serving not a Queen but an Abbess. Gamelyn had been there as well—well, Guy de Gisbourne, then, brought here by the Sheriff, hired to hunt and slay the notorious Robyn Hood.

Gamelyn was still here, standing handsome and stark amongst his Templar Masters. His eyes often met hers—distant, to be sure, but attentive—and every now and then would wander upward, curious yet cool. No doubt he heard—mayhap also Saw—but refused to give way to acknowledgment.

Even when They—the *gwyllion*, Marion acknowledged—purred his name and begged his notice.

The man who had been Nottingham's Sheriff noticed them, even if he didn't know what or why. Standing alongside both his brothers—Roger de Lacy and Willem, Prior of St. Mary's—there was no doubt Brian de Lisle had come down in status. Peveril was a respectable holding, to be sure, but small in income and power when compared to the reeveship of three shires. There was talk he might lose that despite his brothers' influence. He slunk the hall more like a beaten dog than a once-powerful noble, eyes flickering upward every time the spirits moved.

Well. De Lisle had witnessed the Hunt's power firsthand. The *gwyllion* well marked him, too, fluttering and hissing.

Aye, so much change, and none of them what they had once been.

Save the Oakbrother, mayhap, the Lady whispered.

In response Marion sought Gamelyn's eyes. He would not hold to her gaze for more than a breath.

His mind is clouded. His heart of stone. This is Guy.

The words didn't ease Marion's heart, but the *gwyllion* quieted as She spoke. *What are they?* Marion asked.

My first children chafe at their bindings. Even as your consorts do, and do not.

Which was, mayhap, an answer. Or mayhap not.

Yesterday had been warm and long. Today promised the same— and with that rose the strange niggle of loneliness Gamelyn had entertained ever since he'd been summoned from Clipstone to Nottingham proper. Foolish, to hope for another chance to see Robyn, or speak with him. Robyn had, it seemed, again to green Wode gone. And John had taken up his place in the pickets, watching Gamelyn as if nothing had changed.

Come now, nothing has *changed. Or shall, until we're finished here.*

Yet still, they had spoken at Clipstone, more than snarled disagreement or duty of translation. Mayhap would again at Saturday's feast. As if everything were normal. Well, as normal as such things could be, two would-be lovers surrounded by ones who would fall upon them in an instant, with a hard choice between sodomy or sorcery for the hanging charges.

He looked up as the little . . . beasties—he could think of nothing else to adequately describe them—fluttered. It was habit, now, to harden his mind against their flirting. The iron sword at his belt was of help, at least, though they held an odd fascination for the quillion dagger.

Robyn's blood upon it, something in his mind acknowledged.

"The shrievalties are costing a pretty penny," Wymarec muttered to Bruer, so soft that only the closest Templars could hear.

Bruer nodded. "Hubert will be interested in how Geoffrey the bastard has bought Yorkshire. Though Geoffrey's fat isn't out of the fire just yet."

It seemed the Archbishops of Canterbury and York were still bickering. Richard had refused to hear any matters of perceived precedence until he'd dealt with the money side of things. To that latter, Gamelyn also took note that one of the noble siege commanders, de Ferrers, had received at a very fair price the reeveships of Nottingham and Derby, much to the disgruntlement of Brian de Lisle.

"Has he spoken to you about men for Normandy?" Bruer was asking, still quiet.

"There has been talk, aye. Hints and insinuations, but nothing concrete. He knows we are not obliged to answer a secular call to arms."

"But he hopes."

Wymarec smiled. "And I have barter for his hopes."

Hopes. Gamelyn's head was nigh to bursting with the tangle of too many hopes. Marion, at the Queen's side, every now and then catching his eye with that curious-clever smile; she was happy. The flutter in his belly wanted to answer that happiness with more hope, yet sank, morose, as thoughts of Robyn always followed. Robyn, who had hunted with the King, then vanished into the Wode. And always, the flinch of wondering: what would be bartered away next? It was inevitable, was it not?

The King was rising from his chair, signalling the end of this day's council. No doubt another would come with the dawn. But for now, thank God, mayhap Gamelyn could steal away. Find Much and let him know Marion was well.

At least that was going splendidly and to plan.

A tug at his sleeve stayed him from following his fellow Templars towards the doorway. Gamelyn turned to see the young nobleman who'd waited the King's pleasure at table.

All the others sitting and attending that table—including Marion—had already departed.

"My lord Templar." The attendant was flawlessly polite. "My lord King would speak with you. Alone," he added, still courteous but firm as Wymarec turned, frowning slightly towards Gamelyn's delay. "Please accept my liege's apology for the insistence upon breaking your custom, Master Preceptor, but it is the King's expressed wish that his audience with Sir Guy be private."

A breach of custom, indeed, for a Templar to be unaccompanied by a companion. But Master Wymarec didn't seem at all disapproving.

"Well, my lord Templar, for such an ordinary-seeming soldier, it would seem you possess extraordinary support. And such a wide range of it! From notorious wolfsheads to a court trouvère to barons and earls."

Gamelyn, kneeling upon the hard, wooden floor of the chamber, slid his eyes upward to meet those of his King.

"Even," Richard mused, "queens."

The best of the remaining chairs had been cushioned and made ready, but the King eschewed a seat, in fact had been pacing since Gamelyn had been ushered upstairs and past the two crimson-clad soldiers standing outside the curtained solar. He stopped his prowl long enough to allow his cup to be refilled, and by the same young nobleman who'd tweaked Gamelyn's sleeve and escorted him hence.

"God's legs, get up, man! I shall speak these matters informally and plain, but cannot do so to your scalp!" An impatient gesture, slopping wine within the cup. "I have many things demanding my attention, but this is also paramount: we must meet each other's eyes as we come to an understanding."

Eyes meeting eyes. Understanding. With a king.

Dutifully, Gamelyn rose and clasped his hands behind his back.

A snort. "Ever the soldier's ruse—ready but pretending ease. It is my understanding, Templar, that you were amongst my army in the Holy Land."

"Aye, my lord King." *Many things demanding his attention,* yet he made small talk? With a mere—if *unusual*—Templar Sergeant?

"No doubt you have heard of Philip's perfidy in my lands, even as you surely remember his betrayal in the Holy Land, and what it wrought for our cause." First bitter, Richard's voice slid genial. "It was in my mind to reward you, for the service you performed, with a lord's command in the upcoming assault in Normandy."

Normandy? The possibility scored a thin, painful line against Gamelyn's composure. He did not, of course, allow so much as an outward wince.

"Yet it is no secret I need trustworthy men to take firm hold in England. Ones born here, with some understanding of Anglic provincialisms and nonetheless loyal to the ideals of God and Our kingdom. Our lady mother insists you have these qualities and, furthermore, that you are due a more handsome reward than, and I quote, 'to be dragged away from kith and kin for another chance at the dubious pleasures of slaughter.'"

A charming smile, and shift of broad shoulders beneath the rich tunic of silk madder. Ash-blue eyes bored into Gamelyn's.

Since it was obvious some sort of reply was expected, Gamelyn obliged. "The Queen is very . . . kind."

"Nay, she often truly isn't, and if it weren't for that very fact, believe me, Sir Guy, you and I should not likely have known each other." Richard took a drink.

Gamelyn started to protest, was in the next heartbeat uncertain of what he'd meant to say. Until the King frowned. Said, "Or is your name Gamelyn?"

Still mired in some strange indecision, Gamelyn hesitated just that much too long.

"I'm sure I remember," Richard continued, musing, "that Huntingdon said so, and told me your father had been his sworn man, widower of a lady of his house before de Lacy acquired the honour of Tickhill and, therefore, the loyalty of its mesne lord."

"That is true, my liege."

"Huntingdon didn't need more of either property or power," Richard muttered, then, louder, "The matter of Tickhill is why we speak even now. I was not, at first, over-enamoured of my mother's request. Tickhill is a wealthy and influential honour, and its castle more so. I divided its power when I first left for the Holy Land." A sketch against his breast, mimicking the fine, filigreed cross that hung there: smallish, subtle, but of pure gold. "I woefully underestimated not only the cunning, but the avarice of those left behind. Too much power, unless ordained by God"— another touch to the gold cross, and a shake of the tawny head—"can give the wisest of men ideals above their station. And now I am loath to be advised, even by my lady mother and the Master Preceptor of England, to allot even more power to the Templars.

"So understand, *Templar*, why I asked to have our conversation private. And settle these things with no undue influence from either of our, ah, well-meaning overseers." Another grin, one cruel as charming.

Gamelyn wasn't quite sure if he could return it. "My King, pray forgive my confusion—"

Richard gestured again; this time the wine didn't slop quite so far, merely because he'd drunk much of it. "You will understand soon enough the need for circumspection. For now, heed my dilemma.

"My mother is correct; your aid of our cause leaves you well deserving the right to an honour your father once held. But 'deserve' in truth means little, no? Many deserve that do not acquire, and many acquire . . . well, you understand me, for 'twas your foolish brother who held Tickhill against me, and God was with you in the defeat of your eldest brother, toady to John that *he* was. Yes, I have heard tales of your exploits," Richard answered Gamelyn's puzzlement. "I do not lightly accord anything. Despite your youth, peers and masters all find you cunning, dangerous, and discreet; altogether worthy of esteem. Notwithstanding, as Master de Birkin tells, an 'unseemly regard for the more, ah, marginal of your companions.'" A snort of a laugh, then a quick touch of the cross at his pectoral. "The Master Preceptor is a holy man, if a prim one. I merely think you have found, as have I, that sometimes one can find the most remarkable things in the gutter, no?"

Gamelyn, unsure how to answer that as well, tipped a slight nod.

"Circumspect." It was approving. "Yes, I do believe you could prove a reliable guardian." Richard motioned to the attendant, gave permission to serve Gamelyn some wine. As if the interview were over.

And this time, strangely enough, 'twas Guy who wanted to howl victory.

Gamelyn knew better. None of this was worth the murky hazard of a private audience. Something else lay in wait. He took the proffered goblet and a polite sip both, his gaze an opaque glass that never left the King.

Aye, and Richard wasn't finished. Indeed, he returned Gamelyn's steady regard.

"Even now, circumspect. Though the gears are turning, are they not?" Again, that predator's smile, and Richard made a small toast. "Drink, I pray, and hold to that circumspection whilst I apprise you, man to man, of my difficulties in this situation."

Gamelyn took another sip and tasted nothing.

Richard collapsed into the chair, swinging a negligent leg over one broad, upholstered arm. "The Templars have a great deal of holdings in England, land that, by the Holy Father's decree, only God is allowed to use. Or tax. The latter concerns me, of course, in any country that I rule. Do not misconstrue my meaning, Templar: I am bound and willing to tithe God's true warriors. Your Order is a just and good manifestation of the one faith; it has aided me in my holy Crusade. Unlike that—!" The hands upon the cup shook even more than normal, Richard's face splotching with crimson as he leapt up from the chair, started pacing again. "That same treacherous milksop who abandoned us—you as well as me!—to such an ignominious and needless defeat!" The cup went flying, cracked the plaster against the far wall, and went rolling.

One of the guards peeked in. Eyes going wide, he turned about and yanked the curtain back in place. Gamelyn took his cue from that and also the young attendant, who remained stock-still, unwilling to attract the notorious fire of Angevin temper.

"Phillip of France ran like the coward he is, consorted with my enemies, sought to keep me prisoner, and even now invades my lands! Phillip will no doubt swarm over England if given the chance!" As sudden as the storm had risen, it subsided. Richard clenched his fists, growled a few more epithets, then closed his eyes and traced the cross upon his breast.

The attendant let out a soundless sigh and went to retrieve the thrown goblet.

"The priests tell me I must forgive him. I have foresworn communion, for I cannot. But that is another matter, personal." A shrug, and Richard held out a hand that quivered, expectant. The attendant was already there, the goblet refilled. As Richard took a long gulp of the wine, the silence drew itself longer.

Gamelyn had no impulse to fill it.

Nor did Richard hurry. Through several draughts of the wine and a swipe at his sweating face with one gilt-embroidered sleeve, his hands kept up their shake and did not abate as he spoke again, much calmer.

"This matter between us is equally personal but, moreover, a matter of pure logistics. Wars cost. As I told the wolfshead, England is a rich country and must produce the methods to preserve its shores. He could not understand, but then he is a peasant, and what wits he may possess beneath that lovely tangle of raven-black are necessarily limited. Whereas you, my lord"—a tilt of the goblet—"surely can understand."

Breath held, hot and tight within his chest, Gamelyn merely nodded.

Again, the charming smile—again, the dagger behind it, ready. "So, my lord-mayhap-of-Tickhill. What price would you pay? For the lands of your father?"

The breath still held tight. Gamelyn fought for it, knew he had to answer, even if it was shakily rote and, for the first time, somewhat bitter to taste. "My lord, I am but a poor knight of the Temple—"

A short bark of laughter cut Gamelyn off. "But of course. And if you were not?"

The breath clamped even tighter, allowing only a small query to escape. "My . . . lord King?"

"The Temple owns a quarter of England. Deservedly so, for it must supply God's holy army against the unbelievers. Your Masters would see you as castellan of another Templar holding. But I cannot simply hand them one of the most influential bastions guarding the main road north. It is beyond what even a King's exchequer can afford." Richard started another sip, grimaced to find merely dregs left, and gestured for a refill. As the young attendant hastily obliged, Richard slouched into the chair once again.

"I *can* afford, on the other hand, to have the honour of Tickhill and its castle productive, well held, and taxable. It seems to me no better way to ensure a man's loyalty to his land and crown than the promise of holding his father's honour as his own. Mayhap even with lands in fee simple for whatever descendants you choose?" He leaned forward in the chair, and this time the charming smile was conspiratorial. "Obviously you are a man of God; likely you have not fully considered the implications of worldly life. But there are suitable honours to be had. My lady mother says that matters of the heart are likely what keep you wearing the black of a common soldier and abstaining full vows. Of course, she does tend to the romantic, my mother."

Gamelyn scarcely heard any words after those three deceptively simple ones: *In fee simple.*

It meant his own land, earned and bought. Not leased. Not so easily confiscated upon a royal whim, or traded out from under one by a covetous neighbour.

"I will, of course, expect less recompense than I might in other circumstances. Due to your service, which, of course, I shall expect to continue and enrich the both of us. You alone must decide what that is worth to you."

It is worth everything! It is more than any hope, more than anything we have worked for, schemed for. Guy was, again, ecstatic.

Gamelyn wasn't sure he felt anything, not yet. Not now.

Aye, more than any hope. Eden, within his grasp. All it would cost was . . .

Everything.

No more a Templar. It was a keen of mourning, a silent, strangled howl behind his eyes. No more the existence that had given him purpose, mind and soul. No more the predatory, fouled, and fallen angel serving the arcane possibilities of the Inner Temple and its grace that had so far eluded him. Nor the trust and respect of battle-hard comrades.

No more to walk a treacherous line of head and heart. No more a predator set to hunt the wolf, to betray the covenant.

Robyn would claim his soul, Marion would claim his heart, the Lady would claim his future in the taking of his rights as Summerlord, but the predator was always lurking, always waiting. If it passed that he could not be one with them, at least he could give them this. As for himself . . .

He could make another Thwarting, this of *tynged,* twining him into an inevitability he refused to fathom. No rival, only lover. Robyn had done no less, facing down his god and demanding the same. No more death into the void, or blood on his hands. No more *nightmares.*

Only . . . Richard was watching him. He wasn't finished, not by a long shot. "I should think three hundred marks is a reasonable starting point. A bargain, actually. But we must consider my mother's wishes that you are suitably rewarded."

It might as well be three thousand. Gamelyn's stomach, roiling and churning, began to sink. "My liege, I have no resources. I don't even own my horse and armour. My Order forbids—"

"Of course, I understand. Times have been difficult for us all, even to those *not* constrained by vows of poverty. A pledge would do: so much down, and so much over time. Add in a few favours as thanks for your liege's generosity, and we could do some business." Richard was smiling. "You'd be surprised by what resources can be found when necessary. Mayhap it's time to call in some of your own favours, from those peers who think you worthy of such respect."

Peers. Who think you. . . worthy. Respect.
What is it worth? What price would you pay?

As if on cue, bells rang from Nottingham's chapel. The King rose.

"As you know, a feast day has been declared upon the morrow. In the few days after that I shall be hearing more cases of right and demesne. I give you until just past Nones this Saturday, when I shall call you forward to offer this again, before witnesses. Your decision shall be given to me then."

Gamelyn belatedly remembered to kneel, dropping his gaze to his hands as they clenched and folded upon one upthrust knee. They were shaking worse than the King's.

He didn't even try to still them.

"And, my lord?" The King's voice flattened, once again formal, almost diffident. "We would ask a preliminary favour. Earnest money, your Order would call it."

Gamelyn's thoughts charged full tilt, strong as a blood-maddened destrier; it was difficult to make himself answer, soft and neutral.

"Anything, my King."

"We would have you bring your archer companion to Us."

It seemed to come from nowhere, an arrow poorly shot and whistling past one ear. Gamelyn looked up, saw the King at the curtains, pausing in departure.

"My liege? You want to see—"

"Robyn Hood, yes." It was impatient. Richard was no longer looking at Gamelyn, but the curtain in one hand. The other was at his breast, clutched white-knuckled about the golden crucifix; it shook, noticeably so.

"Now?" And damn it, but Gamelyn found himself stammering. "Forgive me, my liege, but I don't know where he—"

"Nay, not now. Tomorrow evening will do." Gamelyn's confusion must have transferred, damnably, to his face, for the King explained, almost gently, "We invited him to Our feast, with his wild men of the forest. We shall reward him, too—this should please you, as you were children together, no? A reward for the service done Our royal mother, and after the feast We will further speak with him. You shall interpret Our wishes."

And, like hot wind upon desert pan, King Richard was gone, leaving the curtains shifting in his wake.

None shall notice you, cloaked and veiled. I've no doubts you have adequately learned the art of sneak-thievery from the best. Now is the time to prove your knowledge of the castle's lesser-known paths. Stay, hide yourself well, and, above all, listen.

Eleanor knew her favourite son all too well, it seemed.

So, my lord-mayhap-of-Tickhill, what price would you pay? What is it worth to you?

Deep in the shadows of the solar's adjoining alcove, Marion crept along the far wall, her breath held tight behind her teeth. A narrow closet was the first hurdle, then an even-narrower opening behind several musty cloaks, and she fled into the tunnel, led by the spastic flickerings of a torch lighting the next curve.

Stopped, her breath finally escaping, a painful quaver akin to a sob. Hoving hard against the wall, Marion laid her head back, fingers digging into the cold sandstone, and closed her eyes.

- XXIV -

Gamelyn wasn't sure where he meant to go: the chapel; the woodland depths; the pickets where he could sit at his horse's feet and bear no company other than animal silence and comfort.

Instead his feet marched him, straight and unforgiving, to the Templar's pavilion.

Hubert was still wakeful—awaiting, no doubt, his *Confanonier's* return from the King's presence—and attended only by Much and the deaf-mute lay brother, Sayme. Odd, that Wymarec was not also there, lying in wait. Gamelyn halted between the pair of torches illuminating the tied-open pavilion doorway and came no farther. The stark flicker no doubt limned his shoulders, yet would cast his face in shadows no inward lamp would pierce.

It seemed his survival instincts were still paramount. He refused—flawlessly polite—Hubert's invitation to sit with him, and shook his head when Much would come over. Instead Gamelyn uttered the barest, most wooden necessities of truth: the King had requested some specific business of him.

Hubert's smile, normally sought after, instead stabbed further ice into Gamelyn's heart.

We don't have a heart, Guy whispered. *Remember?*

"A promising request." Hubert was sitting up and only slightly potted, which to Gamelyn was even more promising. "How long will you need?"

A lifetime? "I'm not sure; through the morrow at least. But I shall return in the evening, see you to the feast."

"He—and you—shall have whatever time you need." It was satisfied. "A small price to pay, eh?"

What price will you pay? echoed, insidious reminder, and Gamelyn thought *The life and love, O my Master, that* you *gave me, in exchange for a life and love brutally lost. . . mayhap to be found again? If it isn't already too late.*

Sayme had drawn closer, a lamp in hand. The slight illumination must have revealed something in Gamelyn's face. Much, at Hubert's shoulder, was frowning. Uncertain.

Let him be uncertain. This is for his sake as well.

"Master Wymarec is meeting with Archbishop Walter," Hubert mused. "When he returns I shall inform him of this newest development. He should have no objections—"

Ah, but he will if all goes to plan.

"—and Much can go with you."

The torches spat and wafted. A sudden breeze guttered Sayme's lamp and, thankfully, cast Gamelyn's face once more into murk. "Nay, Commander, you've more need of him at present."

"Nonsense. I'm well enough, and Sayme can see this doddering old cripple to his bed if necessary."

"You're not—!" It escaped, too telling; Gamelyn modulated it. "You aren't any of those, my lord. Not to any of us. Not to me." This time, a waver; again, he denied it.

"I know, lad. Forgive me, it's the wine talking. And frustration, more than any wine."

"Much, you need to stay here." Tight, smooth, and boding no nonsense, for Much had started forward. "You need to stay here. Close to our Master. Close to *the castle.*"

The frown twitched deeper, and Much hesitated. Gamelyn had gauged that intervention perfectly, though it gave him little satisfaction.

"You worry overmuch," Hubert demurred. "The sergeant will soon return; he's merely been sent upon an errand for our Master Preceptor, complete with parchments and a gift of wine to Archbishop Walter. He and Master Wymarec remain deep in a night's worth of conversation. They have long known each other . . ." He trailed into silence, peering at Gamelyn.

All of them—even Sayme, who kenned body language as easily as the words he could neither speak nor hear—were peering at him. The torches flickered, again. With a small breath, Gamelyn bade the shadows curl closer about him. Instinct, nothing more. Subtle survival. And the shadows . . . obeyed.

"With your leave, my lord Commander?"

Hubert nodded, slow.

Gamelyn spun and started outward.

"Gamelyn. Are you all right?"

Hubert's soft voice halted him, nigh broke him. Yet he didn't turn. Couldn't.

You have been like to my own father, mayhap even more. We

should have known better, Hubert. I betrayed him, you see, and even now I begin to betray you. . .

But I haven't the strength to look at you and do it. Forgive me, but not now. Not yet.

Again, 'twas Guy who saved him. "Forgive me, my lord Commander. It's been a long day, and I'm very tired."

Silence. He counted the heartbeats, echoing in his ears: *lut-lub. . . lut-lub. . .*

"Very well. Take care, lad."

Gamelyn escaped into the night.

"What will you do?"

"Hard to say, love, when I en't sure what *he'll* do."

It was not a comfort. Of all of them, Marion would think Much to have a calm and knowing finger on the pulse of Gamelyn's thoughts.

Instead, it seemed he'd more a frantic thumb upon a spurting artery.

"No wonder." The words came slow, almost musing, and at Marion's curious look, Much answered, "Before you came t' find me, milord was there. At the pavilion."

A sleepless night, its tiny sliver of waning moon heading west and dawn approaching, from the bird-sounds gathering at the high, narrow windows. They were just off Nottingham's main hall, standing beside a brazier that let off some heat and light against the dark chill of the alcove. The guard had willingly given way and resumed his post at a discreet distance—with a knowing smile at the two of them before he'd turned his back.

To be sure, it was tempting. The alcove was quiet, the guard one of Much's compatriots. Unfortunately, they both had more on their minds than even a quick rut against the wall would ease. And . . .

"I have to return soon," Marion whispered. "She'll be waiting."

"She." Much wrapped his arms about her waist, shored up behind, and nuzzled her neck. "Why didn't you tell me before, that you were off to the Queen?"

"Why didn't you tell me you meant to don a Templar's tabard?"

"You've known all along I'd return to—"

"Aye, and I have. Just as you likely knew I'd be asked to the Queen's presence. But it's nice to be told, en't it?"

He huffed a sigh against her hair. "Aye, I s'pose so."

"We've never made promises. With our lives, 'tis foolish. I en't expecting such things, or more'n either of us can rightfully give. But I do want truth between us. And"—Marion snaked a hand upward, stroked the line of fur at his jaw—"whatever more we can grasp, as we can."

"Aye." Another huff. "There's others tied into this knot of ours, and likely allus will be. Whatever comes, we'll take what we can for each other."

It pooled an absurd warmth into Marion's belly. She twisted in his grasp and put her hands upon his chest, nestled her face into his neck.

"What d'you think Himself will do?"

That was just as hard to say. Robyn's face, as she'd told him, had been as cool as Gamelyn ever could display. He'd kissed her cheek, altogether absently, then disappeared into the trees and left her to walk back the way she'd come.

A daunting prospect. Beneath the castle and into the outlying crofts lay a veritable warren of tunnels, carved into the sandstone foundations. Not only leading to where Gamelyn had met with the King, but several others, many of which Marion had discovered upon her stay here last autumn with Worksop's Abbess. She had found the entrance to the King's solar—where she and her mistress had stayed—quite by accident. Exit was an entirely different matter. It lay within the Underkeep—the cavernous and notorious collection of brothels, taverns, and dives beneath Nottingham—which, post-siege, once again teemed with its normal allotment of questionable characters.

She had, for a breath, hoped to convince Robyn to walk back with her. Daunting, but also irritating. Marion was altogether used to walking boldly wherever she went. The simple and unwelcome truth remained: 'twere a different thing altogether to skulk the scattered remnants of siege whilst dressed in a wealthy woman's clothes, however shabby her cloak and circumspect her movements.

She ended up throwing that cloak back and, hand upon knife, marching into the Templar's camp. In the realm of thieves and pimps, her garb would be her undoing; amidst the noble's tents, it marked her as one of their own and, likely, belonging to someone. She'd found Much, and he'd insisted upon escorting her to the castle.

"Milord . . . Gamelyn . . . well, I know the Masters want him in charge of tica's hill," Much said, sudden. "I've listened, like, and they're all over not just t' castle and lands, but t' church. All Hallows." He shrugged. "No surprise there. Those of us born and bred thereabouts, we know stories of t' old howe at Hallows."

Marion nodded. She too knew what lay there; Robyn had told her.

"But now the King's shoved a hot pitchfork into dry straw. Small wonder milord was so . . . odd when he came to see Master Hubert. I'm glad you came to find me, tell me."

They stood there, silent, for some time. Then Marion sighed, patted her fingers against his chest. "I'd do well to return to the Queen's chamber. I've many things to tell her, and the feast to prepare for. But I needed to find Robyn first. Find you."

Much covered her hands with his own. "I'd best be off meself soon. Mayhap wander by the chapel. Case milord loses track of time on another damned cold floor."

"Losing time." It was a murmur as Marion raised her eyes to meet his. "Has he, then?"

"He allus has. More, of late." A shrug. He plainly didn't see the significance.

She did, however. "More, of late." Putting a hand to Much's breast, she traced the small, scarlet cross there. "Our Hob-Robyn Saw, to be sure. 'Tis an augury growing into sommat more, and . . . well. I weren't knowin' if Gamelyn . . . *knew*."

Much's brown eyes narrowed as he took in her words. "I'm not so sure he knows half of what happens when he's like this, only the task he's bent upon. You mean this sort of thing en't just him shutting things away? The like has happened to you? To Robyn?"

She nodded.

He gave a shake of his head, grumbling. "'Tis no better than what I deserve, bedding down with t' god's own." He raised one of her hands to his mouth, fond and reverent both. "Shall I see you back, then?"

"Nay. The *pucelles* will bare their fangs, should they see me daring to court *two* Templars."

"The pew . . . hoy, did you just call sommun a whore?"

"*Pucelle*, not *puterelle*." Marion grinned. "'Tis what the Queen calls her ladies."

"Ah. And with fangs, y' say? Sounds a proper snake pit. En't Herself being mindful of you?"

"Oh, the Queen and her daughter have been very kind. And the others truly don't qualify for the wisdom of serpents; they're more a lot of overblown, snotty heifers."

Another snort. "Aye, well. You can take 'em."

Full of certainty, it also filled her belly with more of that lovely, absurd warmth. She shrugged, leaned in, and kissed him.

He kissed her back, hard and deliciously thorough, then strode away.

Marion smiled, drew her cloak closer about her. Smile broadening for the considerate guard, she slipped through the hallway and started to mount the stairs leading to the Queen's chambers. Hesitated.

There was a figure halted halfway up, features obscured in shadow and blue cloak limned by the torchlights placed, here and there, in iron holders. Man or woman, at first she couldn't tell, but the figure saw her and leaned against the stones, as if waiting.

There was something . . . unchancy about it, and the stair narrow enough she'd have to pass closer than she'd fancy.

She was being foolish. All it would take would be one good scream. At that, David had shown her some proper tricks with the wrestling, and she'd two keen daggers to hand, one at her girdle and another in her boot.

Marion took the stair with a brisk, strong step, and kept every sense tuned, just in case.

It was a man. He didn't make any move, just said, as she passed, in a familiar, gruff voice, "Well, well, if it isn't the novice. *Ex*-novice, I mean."

Marion stiffened, couldn't help a half turn. The man had turned into the light, revealing the face of the Sheriff . . . nay, *ex*-Sheriff of Nottingham.

The chapel was silent. Dark. Cold.

Yet here had it all been set in motion. Forged from memories forgotten . . . nay, hacked off midreach and left dangling, unfinished. Through another beginning. Over the precipice and to another, inevitable ending.

Gamelyn had been falling all this time. Writhing against the inevitable end. 'Twasn't the fall that killed, after all, merely the impact, and he'd been so sure he'd not come through again. But here it was. And he was still walking, still breathing.

Surviving. Again.

He knelt before the altar, put his face in his hands. Tried to pray.

Oddly enough, this fall had begun barely two seasons ago, with Marion. With the reappearance of a beloved ghost into his solid, sterile existence. First upon the wall-walk, a chance encounter with memory, draped in the habit of a novice nun who had lost hers. Then here, in Nottingham's chapel, when the Lady had looked out from blank, bewildered grey eyes and spoken to him with Marion's voice: *Wake.*

Or likely not so odd. There was no longer any doubt in Gamelyn but the Lady had claimed him, first for the Church and then for the Wode. Likely from the moment he'd uttered his first cry and his mother her last sigh.

And then, another beloved spectre, shaking the foundations of his life with all the explosive finesse of Greek fire hurled by a mangonel:

Robyn.

It had all begun again. Waking. Falling. *Ending.*

Had Gamelyn known the nightmares it would divulge—and divine—would he have chosen to wake? Was there, in the end, no choice? Or mayhap one choice, and that merely which submission would be made, tied to *tynged's* snarled threads—which strand to pluck and hold on to for dear life?

"What price would you pay?"

Mayhap in truth the claiming had been sealed the winter after his own birth, when Her Hunter had been born into the world with love—but no fleshly longings—for any Maid. Or set in motion five winters before, when the Hunter's sister—Her avatar—had come from Mother's womb.

For Her. *Would you die for me, Gamelyn?*

For Marion. *You are my spirit, the face of our Lady, the lodestone of my conscience.*

For Hubert. *You are the father taken from me, the man I strive to be.*

For Much. *You too are the man I strive to be, the beloved brother I've never had.*

For Robyn . . .

O God, Robyn.

You are my heart, my soul. We will walk in the cool of the evening, beside our gods and each other, and. . .

I will not *be the one to kill you, not again.*

What price would he pay for *Eden?*

Whatever we must, the inner predator murmured, and Gamelyn wondered which self remained. Which link, in truth, was the weaker one.

Ending. It is but another ending, and you know what you must do. Her Voice curled around the corners of the chapel. She shimmered into form, indigo and stars alighting barefoot upon the altar. *Surrender. Fall.*

Teeth gritting, eyes squinched shut, he chanted to himself *Nay, it's not over yet. We aren't there yet. Don't let anyone in until we're sure. Until we're safe.*

Until it's done.

You can't touch me. I'm. . . not. . . here.

Her voice scattered into silence, and Her form into darkness. He was alone, the stones radiating a chill and gratifying numbness. But instead of Thwarting cold, his mind lay afire; the predator, scenting an ending to the long hunt, could not be restrained.

Gamelyn stumbled up and fled the chapel.

De Lisle flung his cloak over one shoulder and made as if to take a step forward.

"Stay where you are, my lord," Marion said, fingers touching the hilt of her girdle dagger. "We have no business with each other."

"You're sure of that?" Yet for some reason he obeyed, once again leaning against the stones. "Don't you remember . . . ah, but that was the problem, wasn't it? You were the novice without a memory. Didn't have the slightest idea you were a witch, bred in a hovel to other witches. But you remember now, don't you? I wonder, does the Queen Mother know that?"

"The Queen knows me well, my lord. I'm going back to her chamber now. Leave me be, or you'll be sorry."

"Sorry? You come here, prancing halls once mine, and think to threaten *me?* You wolfshead's *whore*—what more can you possibly do to me? Your band of scum killed my sister, gave Count John cause to disseise my reeveship, and now I'll be lucky if I can keep hold of Peveril, as my name was linked with traitors!" He started forward again; the light betrayed a hectic gleam to his gaze.

The latter made her stomach lurch. This was trouble, no mistake.

She'd bet herself against most attackers—there were advantages she'd gladly claim upon that epithet, *wolfshead's whore*—but de Lisle wasn't about to listen to any reason. She sidestepped, palming her knife.

He followed.

A soft hum and flutter resounded from the rafters of the tower beyond the stair, soft and almost coaxing. *Maiden,* it said. *We are here.*

It gave her courage. *Aye, and You are indeed.*

"I'm surprised *you're* here, my lord," Marion snarled back. "Within the halls where the Wild Hunt once rode, and cursed all who stayed within 't."

Words were power. Especially where spirits of Hunt and haunt indeed still lingered. As if her words had been a summons, They descended about her. Shadows snaked down the stones, seeming dust motes against the flickering torches. Their progress merged into a long, drawn-out hiss, became another, nigh-inaudible promise—*threat*—from tens of unearthly not-throats.

De Lisle recoiled, a shudder of violent instinct, with one hand covering his face. Just as sudden, he seemed to catch himself, regain control. He lunged for Marion.

She was too quick, dancing sideways and away, and fled up the staircase leading to the main solar. Didn't stop even as a howl—rage, anguish?—floated up the stairwell and was abruptly cut off.

Marion hauled the solid oak door open, slid within, and heaved it shut behind her. Leaned against it and closed her eyes, stood there panting for several long moments.

The outer alcove lay oddly peaceful. The elder maidservant was snoring with her feet against the centre hearth, upon which a pot of spiced wine still warmed. The *pucelles* slumbered in their well-rushed cots.

"Marion? Is that you, child?"

The maidservant stirred with a snort, eyed Marion sleepily, then shrugged and once more closed her eyes.

Marion padded to the chamber and peeked in. Eleanor sat in the corner chair, wrapped in a thick robe. Several rushlights darted and glanced off a steaming pewter goblet as she raised it, took a sip.

Marion started to speak, hesitated as she spied Joanna curled in the bed, curtains only partially drawn.

"No fear," Eleanor said. "My youngest girl would sleep through fire and siege. It's too warm to close the curtains all 'round." A sigh. "Methinks summer is finally coming."

It gave a tiny thrill in Marion's belly. "I do hope so, Madam."

"A lengthy winter, indeed." A sigh, and Eleanor gave a self-conscious brush at her silver hair, loose and gleaming upon the robe. "I dozed a while, but then you were longer, Marion, than I thought you'd be. Did you have any trouble?"

"'Tis somewhat trickier, Madam, to wander the castle dressed like a lady." Marion grinned as a quirk ticced Eleanor's lip. "But I managed. Even with milord de Lisle, just now. He tried to detain me."

A frown. "He dared interfere with one of my ladies?"

"I don't think he sees me as any sort of lady. He's angry, full of blame for his sister's death." *And rightfully so,* Marion added, silent, though she regretted nothing.

"Ah." Eleanor understood revenge—and the strange compassion of witnessing one beholden to it. "I shall, however, see it doesn't happen again. That one is lucky he's allowed to even approach Nottingham." She turned. "So. Was it, then, as I suspected?"

"Aye, Madam." Marion noted the solar's hearth had not been fed in a while, set herself to do so.

"I *knew* you'd prove your mettle!" Eleanor leaned forward in her chair. "Have a tot of wine, then, once you're finished with the fire, and tell me what terms my son has given your Templar suitor."

Of course, he would come here, in the end. Hadn't he always, one way or another?

The Wode at dawn had its own melody, thick with the rustle of spring leaves and vibrant with birdsong. A breeze, scented with myriad new-birthed flowers, teased his forelock from where it had been braided back, and sprayed russet across his eyes. Beneath his feet lay a soft carpet of loam and moss and, here and there, grassy tufts. Gamelyn knelt, as reverent as before any altar, then tumbled onto his back with a groan, relief and sorrow and discord, all in one.

Looked up into the tossing cover of new sunlight, old shadows, and spring green, wanted to sob and, instead, smiled. Closed his eyes.

Ah, my Summering love, but where have you been? The Voice was soft, but tensile as a garrotte slipped about his throat. *We have sore missed you.*

And where the chapel set him the power to erect walls and silence out of stone, here in the Wode all he could summon was a sharp breath and exhale. The walls held, but a treacherous, brittle admission escaped. "I have missed you."

"Have you, then?"

This voice echoed from above, strayed more shards of light across Gamelyn's face to blinding as his eyes snapped open. Before he could summon a single thought, he snatched the dagger from his belt, lurched up, whirled . . . Froze.

The quillion dagger slid from his fingers, bounced off the moss, and hit an upthrust root with a harsh, rattling cry.

Longbow in hand, Robyn merely leapt down from the elm. "You should really be more careful with your kit, man."

Approximately fifteen questions squabbled and bickered for importance in Gamelyn's skull; they were all insensate beneath what he had just done.

Beneath the dagger, lying innocent and deadly upon the green sward between them.

"Especially," Robyn sauntered over, eyes rising to meet Gamelyn's, "since I rather fancy that dagger."

All of those fifteen-odd questions were reasonable ones, some full of defensive sarcasm and the rest holding at least some sort of intelligence.

So it was past any belief that the only one rising to Gamelyn's lips should be "What are you *doing* here?"

"I live here, remember?"

Gamelyn couldn't help the scowl.

"Oh, you mean *here.* Nigh to bloody Nottingham, despite I'm proper tired of t' sodding place." A shrug of broad, bony shoulders. "You keep asking me that. Wellaway, but *I* keep asking me that."

Gamelyn's brain remained sodden and limp, leaving him, in result, mute.

Robyn kept coming. Just before nudging toe-to-toe with Gamelyn, he crouched down, bow a staff across his thighs, ebon gaze downward and considering the dagger. "So." It was soft, almost thoughtful. "Have you, then?"

"Have I what?" Confused, off-guard, yet still the habit of self-preservation lingered too strong to deny.

"Have you missed Her? Missed us?" Robyn's voice deepened, went soft as the fertile earth between his booted toes. "Missed . . . me?"

What do you think? and *What do I think?* and *You should know.* Instead the questions scratched outward, *again,* into "Why are you *here?*" It was close to panic as Gamelyn wanted to admit.

Robyn peered up at him, slow though his eyes refused stillness. Spanning every approach and every escape, glimmering more than even an abrupt shaft of sun could account for.

But 'twas no god presence, this. Merely the hint of tears.

"I was on my way back to Nottingham, saw you leave. Followed you. Here." A promise unwilling to keep or hold, the darkling gaze met Gamelyn's, then chased away. "Twere Marion as fetched me from the Wode."

"Marion?" Inconceivable.

"Sometimes I think she's the only thing holding us together, pet. Winter and Summer, eternally bound of Her. Coupled by love and hate."

Again the questions, and many of them protests, vying for utterance. Gamelyn eschewed them all. "I can believe the Horned Lord hates me." *Do you?* lingered beneath it, naked and, thank all the gods he could name, unspoken.

"Ah." The tears hadn't made good on their promise; this time Robyn's eyes flared white-gilt with the god. "But I'm Himself, and as to belief? Lately mine's been hard-pressed. I've been wondering exactly what it is you do want me to feel for you."

"I asked you to *trust* me . . . !" It choked off, kenning the feint even as it presented itself.

Robyn put his bow to one side and reached for the dagger, took it as gingerly as if it were a viper. "Nay, never you have, not the once. You've never trusted *me* enough to ask, aye?"

"It isn't *you* I don't trust, it's me, it's . . . oh God, why won't you understand?" Bursting outward, all of it pouring from Gamelyn like a boil left too long then lanced. "Why can't you just *See* it, damn you? You're the bloody avatar of a bloody *god*, but somehow you can't . . . won't . . . and thank the Lady for that because . . . " *Too much*, his mind babbled, trying to slap some sort of fierce plaister over that burst wound, *shut up, you fool, shut up!*

Robyn shifted his buttocks on his heels, uttered a short laugh that held absolutely no humour. "Tis only the Christian's god professes to know everything, pet. And I'd challenge the truth of that in a heartbeat."

"Then why. Are you. *Here?*"

One long-fingered hand curled about the dagger's hilt, snapped it into the air, end over end, and caught it. "Because Marion told me what she'd heard."

"And what"—Gamelyn couldn't stop the bite of the words, in truth didn't want to—"has Marion heard?"

"What the King offered you." The dagger once more went spinning. Then again. Robyn's eyes rose, met Gamelyn's. Held, this time. "And the price he asked for 't."

Surely Gamelyn had experienced more revelatory moments in his life, more blows, physical or otherwise, meant to fell him.

But this one tottered him, slow and breathless, to his knees. "She . . . Marion . . . heard?" *How?* wibbled on the back of his tongue, mute.

It seemed Robyn heard it, nevertheless. "Twere after council. The Queen asked Marion to follow you and *mon roi*"—sarcasm nigh dripped, venomous—"to eavesdrop on your little chinwag. Seems Herself didn't think it likely her son would go so far as to renege on a deal she'd made, but she'd no doubts he'd twist the terms to suit himself. Quite the horse trader, this King of yours."

Gamelyn couldn't stop staring, any more than he could rise from where he'd knelt or force his tongue to gather any semblance of coherent speech.

"As to why I'm here?" Robyn stuck the dagger point-down into the earth and shrugged his quiver over his head, letting the leather down between his knees. It seemed heavier than normal, gave a metallic rustle akin to chainmail . . . only not. Deliberately, Robyn pulled the arrows out two at a time, stopped to lick smooth the cerulean-and-grey fletching on one bent askew, then laid them beside his bow. He inserted his arm up to the elbow; this time he drew from the quiver a full pouch.

Tossed it. More reflex than reflection, Gamelyn caught it.

Heavy, collapsing over his hands with the dull roll and *chink* of good silver. Callused fingers snagging against the soft doeskin, giving beneath the weight, Gamelyn slid his eyes back upward. Met Robyn's.

"First payment," Robyn supplied. "None of 'em clipped or light. There's more where that came from, but you should never travel t' Shire Wode with three hundred marks about you. Not if you aim to keep 'em." A smirk chased over his face, but faded as Gamelyn kept staring, mute. "Three hundred were the price of Blyth and Tickhill, aye? 'Lessen Marion heard wrong."

"The price of . . ." A whisper, all he could summon. As Gamelyn fell back onto his heels, his hands, filled with coin, dropped limp between his knees with another *chink*.

"Aye, well." Robyn began replacing arrows into the quiver. "I thought it proper fitting that whatever damned *price* that bloody-minded Frank bull should demand, we should pay 't with what we stole from his Motherless lackeys."

Frank . . . bull? The uncanny—and appropriate—insolence of it made Gamelyn choke with something between a laugh and a sob. "Pay it. I can't . . . you can't possibly . . . I've no way to make good on this, even if I—"

"I'm sure we can work sommat, aye?" The cheeky grin flickered once more, and Robyn gained his feet, slid his quiver back over his shoulders. "I've me own beliefs, and I'm after believin' our Lady will make good on those marks, with some fair interest. Any road, pet, it en't about owing. It en't about controlling owt . . . though your Master Wymarec would have it that way. I told him bollocks to that."

With a shrug, as if he'd not thwarted the most powerful Master in England.

The same Master who might no longer have the power to order Hirst's *Confanonier* to bring Robyn Hood to the Temple, a prize of arcane war.

"This way"—Robyn toed the bag of coin nestled between Gamelyn's knees— "you can *choose*. Clean, like."

"But *this*. . . this is more than anyone should . . ." Gamelyn realised he was babbling, hoarse and thin. "I know how little marks have come your way through Sherwood of late. Winter was hard, and people have need—"

"Mayhap with this you can help those people, too. Mayhap Summer'll rise, warm and fruitful and . . . kind."

"But . . . " *After what has happened between us, after what could happen. . . Don't you see, I'm terrified to* move *because of what could lie ahead?* He took a shallow breath, tried again. "Robyn, I can't accept this."

"Bloody damn, but for all those thoughts tangling 'neath that thatch of ginger hair, you can be thick as a cob fence! There en't no *accepting* to 't!" Robyn once more dropped to his haunches, sudden, his nose a bare finger-length from Gamelyn's.

The wish for retreat was instinctive, but not as much as the impulse to lean in, glean some of Robyn's warmth. After all, he'd been so cold of late.

Instead, Gamelyn merely closed his eyes and lowered his head.

"Wain't you understand, you great poncy sod? What I have, 'tis yours. Heart, head, and aye, horns. It's allus been yours." All of it, a furious growl, yet Robyn leaned closer still. "There's no sodding *price*. All you have to do is just reach out and take it."

What price would you pay. . . to keep them safe? To keep him *safe?*

A damp touch against Gamelyn's forehead made him start. Still he couldn't react, even so much as to open his eyes. Time seemed to . . . stretch, now and here and *then*, as Robyn lingered, breath and lips ghosting a caress.

Then he rose, and padded away, and disappeared like a wraith into the Wode.

- XXV -

The arrow sped the length of Nottingham's great hall in an eye's winking, sent the upright willow wand vibrating, and let out an angry *spang* as it impaled the solid oak of the entry door beyond.

Not a half breath after, a longer arrow split the wand lengthwise and sank itself beside the first arrow with another *crack* and flutter of cerulean tufts amidst grey.

A shout went up, ringing the rafters and sending a lot of pigeons looking for escape. Marion yipped as well, past caring if the decorous row of *pucelles* looked down their scrubbed-clean noses at her. The first archer was fair skilled, holding her own, but Robyn's last shot had been just short of brilliant.

Eleanor was showing loud approval, the flat of her palm rhythmic against the board. Joanna, too. The lengthy row of high-ranked nobles seated with them were reacting in kind: amazement with a healthy dollop of chagrin.

"*Magnifique!*" the King bellowed, banging the pommel of his eating knife on the board.

Frank bull, indeed. Marion smirked.

The bull had been fair quiet when the outlaws first arrived; ominously so. Robyn had led them inward, a gorgeous forester's horn slung at one hip. It swung to and fro, emphasising the arrogant swagger that Marion, hands clenched behind her back and breath held tight, knew was sheer bluff. John and Will paced stubborn at his heels, David and Gilbert just behind, and the latter three shouldered a pole from which dangled a deer's head and hide. The latter had been filled with parcelled venison. John carried a smaller bundle, upon which rested the buck's spring antlers.

Indeed, the silence had spread to every corner of the hall, pressing down upon the new arrivals like crossbows at nock. Everyone looking to the King, waiting for him to so much as twitch.

But the King didn't. He merely watched the outlaws approach, a strange little smile twisting his lip. Had continued to watch as they stopped in the middle of the hall, unloaded their burden on the flagstones and, somewhat awkward and uncertain, knelt. Richard let them stew there for the barest of moments—letting the nobles stew more, in truth. It was all very theatrical.

And disconcerting to Marion. The hands folded behind her back twisted and wrung, tight.

Robyn possessed his own sense of theatre, but he didn't "stew" well. With a sudden smirk that nigh matched the King's own, he gained his feet—without permission, and if that wasn't enough to set the silent hall to whispers, what Robyn did next had it buzzing akin to a mad hive. He bent over the loot, hefted it, brought it single-handed to the dais, and plunked it down. Then the antlers, which he retrieved from John and lifted to his forehead—a blessing few in that hall understood. Gently this time, he also settled them before the King's seat.

"We of t' Shire Wode have brought your deer to you, milord King. As you requested."

King Richard sat there as if stunned, then exploded to his feet. The bellow as he did so was no demand that the arsy villeins be shot. Nay, it was laughter, accompanied by a lengthy story, pacing the while, as to how the deer had been hunted and taken. It culminated in a demand that His venison be taken to the kitchens for array, and His special guests shown to their table.

Marion wanted to nick Eleanor's gorgeous peacock fan and apply it beneath the heat and rush of relief.

More awkwardness came when the King had demanded an archery demonstration. Most of the nobles, unwilling to contradict their liege, nonetheless were underwhelmed. Allowing notorious outlaws to sit in their company and sup like equals was bad enough. Letting them loose with the weapon of their trade? Nay, my liege, surely not!

But they'd mellowed, Marion mused with a smile, when de Lacy rose from his place at the dais's end to offer up a wager: the Thief of Sherwood against his best Saracen archer. A trio of jugglers provided some entertainment whilst the butt was set up at the hall's end and de Lacy's archer sent for. Marion even had her own turn, along with John and Gilbert. Wagers flew thick and fast. But the flabbergasted applause her shots inspired—particularly once Robyn twined a peacock-fletched arrow in her curls as favour and prize—was nowt compared to how her lads' eyes had popped when Eleanor first requested she make those shots. She'd purposefully been sister and mam and often another brother since coming to the Wode; it was proper brilliant to be garbed all fancy with feminine banners a-fly, to see Robyn's eyes light up and Will drop the piece of bread he was slathering with pottage, to feel a tug on her overkirtle from David and a smirk from John, or Gilbert's admiring whistle and Arthur's awed grin. Even Gamelyn watched her with what Robyn would have called "calf-moony eyes"— though surreptitious amidst his Templar companions, to be sure.

Much was the best, though, his expression making some fine and carnal promises.

All of it, great fun.

But not as much as watching Siham and Robyn go at it now.

Small, dark, and slim, Siham seemed overfaced neither by her sex, nor the summons, nor a crowd. Granted she passed more boyish in her eastern-cut tunic, trous, and *kaffiyeh* than Marion ever could, but Siham also seemed more than willing for another chance to best England's most notorious archer.

And aye, Siham was indeed a fine shot, but she wasn't Robyn Hood. Indeed, at that last shot she conceded defeat with a beautiful smile. Robyn mimed her bow very prettily, hand to his heart. His grin was cheeky, unrepentant.

Many were avid upon the happenings at "the wolfshead's board"; of those many, the majority watched the Queen's newest project in a mild blend of curiosity and contempt. Some, however, radiated open fury and affront.

Richard made an abrupt lunge upward and over the table board, planting his fists upon it. "Master archer! Were one looking for prime foresters, one might consider buying the Saracen's service from the Baron de Lacy!"

The implications of such a statement set the room alive with mutters. De Lacy took it in with a mere narrowing of eyes. His brothers, both seated well below the salt cellar, were less careful. Particularly de Lisle. Beside the Prior of Newstead, de Lisle watched the proceedings—and Marion—with skin-crawling intensity.

Robyn, of course, didn't understand. Siham had both a slight frown and the obvious desire to translate; she'd no Anglic, Marion remembered. It was left to Gilbert, a bit flustered beside John and their strung bows, to oblige.

The run of emotions over Robyn's face made Marion pray he'd mind his tongue. Gamelyn, too, by the slight twitch of brow as he watched. Instead, Robyn bowed very low, kept his tongue *and* his eyes his own.

"We do not waste the talents of clever and capable men!" King Richard's voice was well suited to a noisy hall. A sharp gesture. "Bring the portion!"

"Good," Eleanor murmured in her seat at Marion's right hand. "Very good."

The prime haunch, normally reserved for the lord of any hunt, was brought in, displayed upon the hide. To each end the antlers, gleaming, lay.

"These former outlaws, assisted by the maiden who waits Our lady Mother at board, and led by the noble *Confanonier* to Temple Hirst, risked their lives to see the Queen Mother freed from treacherous detainment. In doing so they further enabled Our own deliverance from an imprisonment just as unlawful, just as treacherous. I know with whom, and how, these things were done. Those party to such deceit shall be dealt with, if they have not already."

It was a threat, no less. Marion held her breath. Again, Eleanor murmured approval—as did more of the nobles seated at the high dais.

"What better way to hunt wolves than with one of their own kind, eh, my lords?" Richard fell silent as the venison was delivered to the head of the table where the outlaws were seated. Gilbert was there, translating soft and quick as his companions listened, uncertain. Considering that last volley, Marion wasn't sure she blamed them. "Other rewards are forthcoming, believe Us. But for now? These men, once outlaws, are no longer that. They are free men, and Our guests. In fact, upon this very day have We sealed the documents to prove not only their place, but their pardon! They will serve Us from this day forward, as foresters to the same Sherwood over which they have held such lamentable—but *admirable*—control!"

Gilbert kept translating, unable to repress his broad smile. As he finished, Will let out a fierce whoop. Arthur pumped his one fist into the air. John's smile flashed, reserved but genuine. David's relief expressed itself in the filling of his hazel eyes, with Tess sneaking from her hiding-hole pouch to lick the overflow from his cheeks.

Much was grinning, standing in his place behind Gamelyn. The latter's eyes were upon Robyn, who was calm, almost diffident, save for an uncanny light to his gaze. As if to deny it, he once again faced the dais and bowed low to the King.

Richard recognised the obeisance, to be sure, but his attention was fixed upon the entire hall. Amidst refilling Eleanor and Joanna's jewelled goblets, Marion watched Richard peruse his attending nobles and realised the open display of pardoned outlaws for what it was. Those who openly sneered at a King's munificence were sneering at said King—and the Royal Gaze was honed as a good sword upon every instance and inference.

"Some music, my lords and ladies? Whilst the next course is served and the dancers gather?" Alundel strode forward with lute in hand. Well, Blondel, but Marion couldn't help but use the name he'd first given them the past winter. Indeed, he strummed a chord that vibrated into the hall, turned towards the dais, and did it again, fair hair flowing behind him,. "Such royal benevolence is more than just cause to bring out a tune or two." He bowed, graceful enough for a hired dancer, first to Richard then to Eleanor. "Aye, my lieges?"

"Your voice is my prop and stay, and definite boon to my aging digestion," Eleanor concurred, her eyes lit with good humour. Joanna covered her mother's hand upon the board.

The dais was alive with agreement: Archbishop Walter, in his place to the King's right, was pounding the table; Huntingdon, Chester, and de Ferrers were engaged in what looked like a cheerful wager.

"This gesture is ever Our Royal Mother's largesse as Our own!" The King's smile stretched broad and cheerful—but those eyes still scanned the hall.

"How about a tune of your own devising, my liege?" Alundel prompted. Marion grinned. Plain as plain, the trouvère bided as intent upon gaining Richard's notice as that one *pucelle* who kept sashaying by Gamelyn to "take some air" near the door.

Cheeky bint. Alundel, too, for he started playing and hopped onto the dais, leaning one buttock against the board next to his king.

"No prisoner even tells his story truthfully;
Rather, it is cloaked in sorrow—"

"Another song!" Broad hand once again slamming down, Richard's interruption sent Alundel fumbling into a discordant tangle of sounds.

The hall went quiet. Eleanor reached a hand to her son's sleeve—under the table. Only he and Marion, behind her, saw.

"Another song, Blondel," Richard repeated, quieter. "We look to the future, tonight—not the past."

"Se savoient mon tourment
Et auques de mon afaire
Cil qui demandent conment—"

"Bloody damn," Will complained, "but I can't understand a word the minstrel's singing."

"Trouvère," Arthur corrected. Robyn gave a faint grin and glanced Gamelyn-ward, found the juniper-hued eyes already upon him as Arthur went on, "But aye, I can't understand what *any* of them are saying, much less singing. Gilly needs to stop flirting with that lass and fetch hisself back ower here to translate."

Aye, and Gilbert needed to do that, right enough. Robyn saw what might be the lass's father, glowering. Even free men could still lose their bits, if they didn't mind where they wagged 'em.

"The tune's good, though." This from David, smiling up at Robyn.

Robyn smiled back and laid a hand on David's shoulder. Tess nibbled, gently, one finger.

"Aye, there's that at least." Will's drawl was pleased—and more than slightly squiffy. "King's foresters and a pardon! I told you so, David—"

"I can scarce take it in."

Alundel had regained his form after the forceful interruption, tossing his blond mane of hair over one shoulder and wandering the hall. Many had joined in the singing, the King loudest, of course. All that bellowing must set him up; his singing voice projected strong, yes, but also oddly sweet:

> *"Je puis tant de chançons*
> *Il diroient vraiement—"*

Hubert, seated beside Gamelyn, had hobbled in on a crutch and his *Confanonier's* arm. He ate sparingly but with a healthy man's appetite. Well done to him. Beside Hubert sat his Master, whose pale eyes would, on occasion, light upon Robyn. There was no telling what he was thinking, not at all.

Gamelyn was no less a cipher. His eyes kept flitting towards Robyn, though they revealed little. He was not singing, nor eating, but he was drinking more than he ought.

So, mon roi, are we already paying the price for this night's work? Robyn wondered, his gaze sliding to the King.

Who was also peering back. The well-groomed beard dipped towards his velvet-clad chest—a nod, at which Robyn frowned and belatedly repeated—then the King let his attention meander elsewhere. All of it made Robyn's nape itch like *damn.*

Alundel wasn't half-pleased that the King's eye seemed to be wandering from his performance; he stepped it up. Suspicion trickled through Robyn; what hunt was the Frank bull upon now?

"'Twill be right enough now! Eh, Robyn?" Will persisted with a tug to his tunic. A fine one, too, the tunic—a dark blue they'd stolen off some lord. The same one as Gamelyn had once claimed Robyn wouldn't wear long the time he had done, and true enough, Gamelyn'd had it off in the time it had taken the two of them to go to the stream for a bucket of fresh water . . .

"'Specially with that bit of marksmanship," Will added. "You've right impressed most of this lot."

Robyn nodded, giving a gentle touch to the horns gifted their table, and continued to eye the nobles. The King sang along with Alundel, coming to a rousing finish of the song they'd begun. Several were having a good-natured argument over, it seemed, one of the serving bowls. The Queen laughed at something the woman next to her was saying, and the woman past that one smiled and added a reply. Marion looked as relaxed and happy as Robyn's men—and all of them tipsy on good wine and promises—whilst his sister, puttered about behind the table of Importances. Obviously in charge of seeing to the head table, Marion were fine in her pretty feathers as a peacock, though he thought her just as lovely without.

Aye, more pleasant a notice than Richard's quasi-predatory eye, or Gamelyn's . . . whatever-it-was. Gamelyn might be reaching for the normal *see, damn you, I don't begin to even* think *of feeling anything* that could turn his copper-dusted face to an impervious idol, but the drink was diving him in headfirst and challenging it. Robyn could see—See—what lay beneath: scarlet strands drifting and fraying into the thick black of *tynged,* any number of futures tangling, uncertain as the rust-clouded verdigris of Gamelyn's eyes.

It didn't ease Robyn, not a bit.

Add to that the remnants of the Hunt, spiralling in to linger close. The *gwyllion,* Marion had called them—aye, and they were— at the same time she'd told him of the King's offer to Gamelyn and how the little spirits were following her about the castle. Robyn saw only a few trailing her now. He didn't blame them; the hall was proper crowded with men and their iron. He wouldn't mind escaping himself.

Protect her, he breathed, nigh silent. *Protect him.*

And the spirits answered, making promises. Lingering, asking a Maiden to sway and dance. Calling stone-magic for the Summer Knight. Woodland encroaching, spring boughs flowering and new-green sprouting wild upon castle walls. Attendant upon the Winterlord who'd first called them, ride and Rade, upon Nottingham.

"Another song!" Alundel suddenly crowed from across the hall. "A gift, and one devised in Anglic for our wild woodland guests, and"—a strum of the lute—"their . . . special friends."

> *The tales grow long and remain strong*
> *In seasons ever turning*
> *Of ritual 'twixt the battle trees*
> *A legend never-dying*
> *With cold and heat, dark and light*
> *A struggle ever-lasting. . ."*

The words tweaked Robyn's notice, as did the lute's voice: soft, almost melancholy, a noticeable change from the bright tune before. Alundel wandered over to the outlaws' table, gaze upon Robyn as he sang.

> *"Yet in the lands of Holy War*
> *A tree bides, never-fighting*

It bears the thorns of holly green
In heat and sun un-dying
And sheds the fruit of oaken might
From catkins all re-borning
A holly oak in spirit bound
To holt and home, ever-binding. . ."

He began strumming, soft, a lengthy bridge, peering at Robyn. "There en't such a tree," Robyn protested, soft.

"Ah, but there is," Alundel chided midchord. "Is it not so, *Confanonier?*"

Robyn turned to glimpse Gamelyn's face; drink had softened the chill, but 'twere the song as made it pensive. "There is. In the east."

"Hearken!
Can such a dryad's holt survive
In rain and mists, ever-falling
Does it not miss the sand and wind
Beneath a sun ever-shining?"

Marion was listening, rapt, eyes shining. Why, then, did Robyn feel so . . . lost? Why was Gamelyn's face so pale?

The chords changed, slightly.

"And aye, I say, when firmly plot'
Cherished, ever-thriving
Its battle-nature overcome
While undying
The holly oak will root anew
In honour and devotion. . .
Ever-lasting."

The lute wavered silent, and Alundel's voice drifted up into the rafters, where several lamps of eyes glittered, then went out.

The applause nearly lifted the roof.

"A lovely song, and a fitting gift, a song of trees for my foresters!" Richard's voice was a match for any applause. "But come now, 'tis time to dance, not be so serious!"

Others took up the cry. "A dance! Play for us, Blondel!"

With a bow to Robyn and a slight tilt of head to Gamelyn, Alundel sprang into action, gesturing towards several other musicians waiting on the sidelines. Soon a sprightly tune spread through the hall. People were beginning to gather in the cleared space, and several women were linking hands.

Thankfully, the others had begun to shake off the strange spell of the music. Robyn, however, found it difficult; he slid his gaze towards Gamelyn, found him downing another drink.

Aye, difficult.

"Well, if Siham won't have me, I might have to ask Marion," Gilbert claimed.

"Like *she'd* have you!" Arthur elbowed him, hard.

"She's allus been proper lovely." Will's claim was stout, renewing a proud grin to Robyn's face. "Even without bein' all tarted up!"

"Aye, I saw you looking!" David snorted. "We were all looking!"

"So was the King," Gilbert put in.

"At Marion?" Aye, Will'd drunk too much; hackles all a-rise.

"Nay, y'fool, at Robyn. All agog during the archery, and I'll wager should we look now—"

His Gilly-lad was speaking proper nonsense, but Robyn chanced it was bloody funny how they all looked, while pretending not to. Badly.

Thankfully, the King wasn't.

"Just your type, Robyn," Gilbert continued, "all muscular and fair-haired. Even a bit of ginger to it—*ow!* John, that *hurt!*" John had smacked the back of his head.

"Hardly!" Robyn snorted, wry. "More like that one'll be asking us t' beg and fetch, next!"

"Lookit!" David sang out. "Who's joining the circle!"

The woman who'd been sitting beside Eleanor was pulling a laughing Marion with her, towards the growing circle of dancing women.

Robyn smiled.

Marion was dancing.

All of the women had, bit by bit, joined the carol until it was less a circle and more a cramped oval between the shoved-aside boards and benches. Several servants were correcting this, darting in and out amongst the flow and ebb of the dancers.

Marion's ease and grace set her apart, made her blue skirts sway and twist out from her hips even when her torso was steady. The plain gold filet and barbette only just confined the riot of cinnabar curls hanging down her back, and she was laughing, hand in hand with Queen Joanna and another, younger maid dressed in Huntingdon's colours.

Marion was dancing, and Gamelyn was drinking too much, and it was suddenly all he could do to not get up and join her. Despite it was a woman's dance, despite the habit, stark and black, weighting his shoulders, despite his Brethren watching, more stern honour guard than revellers.

His ears pounded. Alundel's song echoed behind them.

Are you, the Horned Lord whispered, and he smelt of heat and sex, *finally listening to My song? Does it take a trouvère's voice, drugs, and drink to release the dreaming?*

Always, the Lady answered, wiser than Her mate.

A turn in the music, and all the women flung both arms

upward. Part of the dance, yet Marion looked more priestess than *pucelle*, invoking the spirits of the hall to come out, dance with her . . .

The spirits were there. Gamelyn could sense them. There was no denying the presences, the shadows against the stones, and something within him wondered what would happen if they, too, were roused by a priestess's call.

So, you would make a scene, the goddess purred at his nape, *and force them to expel you, if they would? A fine way to deny what choice you have been given, my lord.*

But a way, nonetheless, he answered, some less-drink-sodden, imperturbable part of his brain realising that, was the choice made, it wouldn't—couldn't—be like this.

So he watched, drunk as much upon the waft of desert roses as any wine; watched a black-haired shadow stroke the antlers a king had put upon his table, and a priestess dance.

The night deepened, food and drink fortifying more drink, music, and dance. The carol gave in to another, then another, then a lively *estampie*, with both men and women joining. Much begged leave to partner Marion. Not only because Will Scathelock was already heading that way, Gamelyn gave quick assent. Others joined, and the *estampie* turned a bit rowdy, with King Richard egging them on and, several times, joining in. Partners changed and changed again; no doubt there would be many clandestine couplings within the castle's alcoves this night . . .

As to you, my lord? What will you seek, thisnow?

With mindless precision, Gamelyn found Robyn. He wasn't dancing. Instead he observed, sloe eyes quick and sober, missing absolutely nothing. His gaze met Gamelyn's; Gamelyn returned it, roused and bewildered and seeking some sort of control . . . only the stones were whispering his name, and Marion was dancing light as one of the spirits skittering about the castle's corners, and Robyn had gilt in his eyes, mirroring a shadow standing beside a full-leafed holly oak tree, its catkins brushing the antlers that crowned his head . . .

"My lord Templar?"

Gamelyn started. Turned, slow, to blink at the same squire who'd taken him to King Richard's last . . . chinwag, had Robyn called it? Aye, indeed, and likely another one, for the lad stood there as if ready to wait all night, head courteously tilted.

"My lord Templar, King Richard requests the honour of your presence. And the archer's. I am to lead you both to him."

Gamelyn frowned and scanned the great hall, realising some time had passed. The revelry would no doubt continue well unto dawn, but Queen Eleanor had retired and the King, too, was nowhere to be found. Alundel was still playing, looking somewhat put out. Marion danced across from a tall, fair-haired man. The outlaws—nay, no longer that—were, some of them, still fit to meet any dawn and taking giddy advantage of the new camaraderie of drink and royal sanction.

"Confanonier?" This from Hubert, curious-stern. A short distance beyond him, Wymarec spoke with York's Archbishop and several other churchmen. A slight etch between his brows and a slide of eye betrayed he was aware of all that happened at the Templar board. Mayhap even his *Confanonier's* unusual state of drunken dreamings.

"If you will excuse me, Master?" Gamelyn paid close and careful attention to his words. "It seems the King requires an audience with Robyn Hood and wishes me to translate."

Wymarec heard, for his frown became a satisfied half smile. Gamelyn was just that much too tipsy, wanted to blurt, here and now, *I wouldn't be so damned smug-sure, were I you, O my Master.*

A soft chuckle wafted through his mind, tinged with roses. Thank his father's God, this time it prompted more panic than passion. He answered with a clench of teeth and silence.

"Of course," Hubert said, a tiny smile quirking his mouth. "Much, I know your master has bade you to my side, but kindly attend him . . . Ah, young man," this as the squire started to protest, "the paxman will not interfere, merely stand by, at the door. I insist."

The squire acquiesced. Wymarec already re-attended his discussion. Much seemed relieved, a willing shadow as Gamelyn rose, albeit careful—aye, most careful; the floor seemed set to trip him—and went to fetch Robyn.

It never failed to set Robyn sideways—or wobble his pins, at that— the sheer amount of chill restraint Gamelyn could summon, did he have the need.

Robyn had been keeping his own surveillance. The squire had come over, spoken. Gamelyn had been more than tipsy at first but, as the squire had begun to speak, then as they had approached Robyn—with Much in dogged tow—and then whilst Robyn let his band know what was what . . . well. More and more, Gamelyn was moulding himself into that damned coppery idol. By the time Robyn finished talking to John in particular—John didn't want him to go before the King, and Robyn wasn't too sure what that was about—Gamelyn had bunged away the slur to his voice to answer John's stern look with a tight-clipped "I'll watch after him, you've my word."

Watch after? Between John's pout and the rod obviously up Gamelyn's arse, Robyn was beginning to feel managed, and that he didn't fancy at all. So much, as they followed the King's squire up the stair and down a narrow hall to the chambers where the Frank bull had settled himself for the duration, that he'd hissed, "So what is this all about, then?"

It was Sir Guy who answered, bloodless. "Do you really think any one of us, biding here beneath a King's eye, has the where-withal to ask at this point?"

Well, and that was a mouthful for a drunken man. Robyn considered, then chose to not answer.

Strains of music echoed within the stones, punctuated with voices here and there. Robyn hoped this little meeting with the Frank bull would be quick, like. While Robyn hadn't possessed the heart to gainsay his lads celebrating what they'd gained this night, he didn't trust any nobleman's truce. Just as chancy as their treatment of their women, such things were liable to be broken on a whim.

Guards lingered at the stair entry, making Robyn's nape hairs stand on end, his steps falter, and senses cast instinctively outward.

No Voice responded, prop or warning. They were likely submerged too far within hewn stone for a woodland god's comfort. A few of Marion's *gwyllion* fluttered in the rafters above, and one even wafted down to nestle in Robyn's curls, akin to Tess. Here in the castle's deeps—even more than the great hall—the Hunt lingered, thrumming the barriers of thisnow like hoofs or a heartbeat.

Comfort, of a kind; fearsome to any save the Lord of that Hunt.

Gamelyn followed the squire—and that lad was a bit of work. Younger than either of them by a few years, but he'd a nigh-scary composure fit to match Guy the Templar. Only the Templar wasn't altogether himself, what with the drink and other circum-stance. He took the first steps up the stair with a rub to the back of his neck and a surreptitious glance upward.

The *gwyllion* in Robyn's hair crooned. The russet head gave a slight shake.

Much slid his eyes left and right, hearing something but unsure what it might be. He settled for forking an evil eye and staying on Gamelyn's heels.

The squire led them on, oblivious.

The King's chamber had more soldiers crawling all over it, including the mercenary guard dog, scowling all the while they approached. Nevertheless Mercadier tipped a respectful nod to both Gamelyn and Robyn. Snapping a mix of Frankish, he sauntered away into a dark side hall.

The remaining guards obeyed what must have been orders, moving a spear's throw away from the entry and granting unhindered passage. With a searching glance at Gamelyn, then a shrug to Robyn, Much meandered over to join them. The entire thing was too easy. Robyn hesitated, his nape hairs once again on end as the squire called inward, soft entreaty.

It was answered, curt. The squire turned to Robyn, expectant. Gamelyn too turned; some expectancy, but otherwise all but unreadable. Damn him, anyway.

"After you, milord," Robyn drawled.

Gamelyn had known all along he was drinking too much—past caring, at this point—but his instincts seemed to unhinge and become something . . . *other* when he did, so mayhap 'twas a good thing he was just this side of drunk.

Because those instincts were screaming.

The problem was, he didn't ken why. The King was waiting by the hearth, no longer accoutred in layers of gilt, scarlet, and samite. Sans crown—though the rings were still present—his distinctive gold mane no longer slicked back but falling loose upon a long, thick robe. And while the latter was simple, there was no doubt the fabric alone cost at least a quarter of the three hundred marks demanded of Gamelyn.

More, the Angevin lion seemed well content, not likely to lop off visitors' heads on a whim. His greeting was warm, almost effusive . . . and deliberate, meant to set them at ease. Which was a good thing for Robyn. He was as on edge as a hart in a sunlight-drenched meadow. Not that Gamelyn blamed him.

Richard seemed to sense Robyn's apprehension, peering at him as he spoke. "My lord Templar, kindly convey to the archer I mean him no harm." A gesture, and the squire came forward to offer wine, poured into rich goblets.

Robyn tipped the goblet in thanks and murmured, very soft, "Aye, well, what *does* his like mean with all this."

It really wasn't a question, and Gamelyn didn't possess an answer, at that. Instead he sipped at the wine, felt it sparkle and flare on his tongue to melt down his throat. He'd never had anything this splendid, even across the sea.

Still, his instincts flared even more. *"All this,"* Robyn had muttered and aye, *all this* was calculated to awe and impress . . . but why bother? Surely they'd both been made altogether aware of the King's puissance.

"So, my lord Templar." Richard tipped his cup, almost a toast. "I realise you have important decisions of your own to make; we shall not revisit those until their time, two days hence. Tonight's focus is upon your uneasy friend. Did you not reassure him?"

"My liege, I did. He is always tense within stone walls, prefers the woodlands and fields. It is his . . . nature, no?"

Cherished. . . its nature overcome. . . The holly oak will root anew. . . Gamelyn strangled it. Or Guy did. He wasn't sure anymore.

"I see." Richard nodded. "The young wolf does not easily consent to a taming hand."

Robyn threw Gamelyn a curious twist of brow and gulped down the rest of his cup.

"Go easy with that. The wine is good, better than either of us are accustomed." It slurred a bit more than Gamelyn cared for. Good wine, indeed.

"*I* en't drunk," Robyn muttered. "What does he want?"

"I think he's curious about you."

During the quick back-and-forth, Richard had taken the wine pitcher from the squire. Shooing him to a corner, Richard himself strode over and filled Robyn's empty goblet. Robyn heeded Gamelyn's advice—thank any god that would listen!—and with a soft "*Merci, mon roi*" merely sipped.

This seemed to amuse Richard. "Such a peasant in so many ways . . . and then not. How did such wildfire kindle in the crofts? Unless the tales Blondel tells me are true, and forest spirits speak to the man."

"With Robyn Hood, anything is possible." Gamelyn knew it a fool's mistake the moment it left his lips, for Richard's face darkened. He raised one hand to the small cross hanging at his throat.

"I spoke merely in jest. Surely a man of God such as yourself has no belief in such unholy foolishness."

Think. Fast. "My mother was Scot, mostly Saxon, and my father partly so." Gamelyn smoothed admittance into wry discomposure. "Some things are bred into us, bone-deep. Nigh inescapable."

It seemed to mollify Richard; he repeated, as if troubled, "Bred into us, yes. Inescapable, our sins, and those of our forebears. You are right, my lord Templar: we cannot escape our . . . nature. All we can do is pray for forgiveness."

"Yes, my liege."

Other than the mention of his name, Robyn had given up on the conversation, wandering over to finger one of the draperies. Curious, he lifted it to his face, sniffed it, then brushed it across his cheek with a slight smile.

It shivered Gamelyn like a lute string plucked and sounded. He'd overmuch wine, to be sure, but it had been too long since he'd touched Robyn. Too long, and too *cold.*

It is almost over. The inner predator was nigh purring, satisfied and roused. *A few more days, and it will be done.*

"O, were I that cloth." Soft, a nigh-echo of his own thoughts. Another shiver rendered Gamelyn head to toe as he turned to Richard and saw the sudden, predacious gloss in those ash-blue eyes as they followed Robyn.

Thought *Oh.*

Remembered, fleeting and supposedly inconsequential, *"One can find the most remarkable things in the gutter. . ."*

Robyn, meanwhile, was inspecting the room's finery with an uncommon—dangerous—oblivion. And how was it he didn't sense the undercurrent, didn't know? He was bloody Robyn Hode, the Horned Lord's Avatar . . .

Gamelyn could only listen, blinking stupidly, as Richard turned to him.

"Tell him I can be as smooth as the finest drapery, Sir Gamelyn, but also unyielding. Tell him I would . . . know him better."

This, somehow, tweaked Robyn's attention. "Did he just call you Gamelyn?"

"Tell him." It was no longer request, but command.

"He did indeed," Gamelyn said to Robyn, deliberate. "He also made it plain he wants to bed you."

- XXVI -

"Fuck me sodding stupid!" Not quite what Robyn would say in the presence of a Christian king, but then, he felt proper upskelled by just about everything this se'nnight, let alone *this*.

And bloody damn but if the copper idol didn't just raise those pale eyebrows and barely hesitate before he shrugged and answered, wry, "I do believe that's what he has in mind, yes."

"He's a Christian!"

"So am I."

Robyn just peered at him, one eyebrow crawling upward.

"Well, I am!" Gamelyn snapped. "Somewhat."

Meanwhile the King himself said something in Frankish—and in a much quieter tone than Robyn had yet heard. Gamelyn hesitated. The King frowned, spoke again. Still quiet, but with a sharpening edge.

"He says," Gamelyn relayed . . . nay, no matter the King's address, this was Guy at his courteous, frozen best, "that you are a very beautiful man."

How sodding lovely for the Motherless tyrant to have noticed. "I see. Does he like wallowing in the dirt, too? For 'tis no doubt a common, dirty, peasant sort of thing, my uncanny beauty."

He'd aimed purposeful, but oh, was the idol in full display, fully masked and soldiering on, "And he will be considerate, gentle—"

"Well, that'd be a difference, wouldn't it? Compared to other nobles I've bedded."

Proper nasty, that jab, but as the idol's upper lip gave a slight, snarly quiver, Robyn wasn't sorry. The *gwyllion* gave an uneasy croon against his ear, wrapping tighter in his curls. The remainder had retreated to the farthest rafters as if the small cross, peering now and again from the folds of Richard's sumptuous robe, had driven them hence. Over by the hearth, the squire's remarkable composure also was beginning to fray, making Robyn wonder if he knew some Anglic after all.

"Pray forgive me, but I was under the impression you fancied it rough in a noble's bed."

Well, and he likely deserved that, but *ow*. "I en't sure I fancy what you're asking."

"I'm not asking. We're in the King's presence, I'd remind you, and I'm merely interpreting."

Richard spoke again, stepping closer. His eyes narrowed, flicking from Gamelyn to Robyn to Gamelyn again, back and forth.

"He says he can be generous." Wooden, rote, yet more than a few cracks were splintering the mask, prey to drink and a startling discomposure. "To those who . . . please him."

"And have you been asked to please him, too?"

"Of *course* not."

"So I'm supposed to be flattered that the man who'd just as soon whip, burn, or butcher my kind has decided he'd rather, after all, tup me?"

"Now is not the time to debate whether we should have choices! The King, aye? He's the *King,* and we've too much at stake to do anything but shut up and take what we're given!"

Unsure whether it was what Gamelyn was saying, or how he was saying it, Robyn's anger was dissolving, pooling into a strange, silent lament. "Just . . . take it."

"What do you think *I've* been doing? And for God's sake, Robyn, how can you suddenly pretend you've *ever* been unwilling to a good, dirty fu—?"

"*Templier!*" The word cracked like a whip.

And Gamelyn—*Guy,* damn him—responded like a broken cart horse. Shoulders thrown into harness, head bent, ready for another lash. "*Oui, mon roi.*"

Silence. Richard was even closer, now—had come closer without so much as a creak of wooden flooring, and Robyn now twice caught unawares in the bloody stones of this bloody chamber. The hearth flickered behind Richard, indeed making him more lion than bull in thisnow, limning his bulk and the golden mane, casting his face in shadows even the wall sconces couldn't pierce. There was only the cross, winking its dull spell-threat.

The ashy eyes gleamed into view as Richard lifted his head. They fastened upon Gamelyn. "*Je comprends. Vous*"—a jerk of head towards Robyn— "*et lui. Non?*"

That made an impression. Gamelyn jerked his head up, eyes wide-white.

"*Va-t'en,*" Richard ordered, and when Gamelyn hesitated, pointed to the door and growled, "*Vite!*"

Again, the damned obedience moved Gamelyn's body; he bowed and turned away before his eyes so much as flickered with thought. Considering everything, Robyn wasn't sure whether he wanted to curse him or tell him, *Run, now!*

He decided to heed his own advice, follow, and give the Templar a good clout in the jaw once they were in the clear . . .

Instead a broad, beringed hand clamped his arm and yanked him back to face Richard, who was shaking his head. A quick smattering of Frankish had the squire lurching from his corner, ever as obedient as Gamelyn, who had made the door and turned, ever so slight.

No doubt just as sure the summons had been for them both. More fool, they.

The expectation in the green eyes slid to alarm, then panic, as the squire slammed the door in Gamelyn's face and shot the bolt home.

"Nay, thank you, you are very kind," Marion insisted.

The young nobleman was proper handsome, and his attentions flattering, but she'd no intention of things going any further. She might be an intriguing new face, but she was of peasantry and, moreover, the Queen's ward. This wasn't her Wode, or a croft festival where any partner was willing for the fires. To behave as anything other than a maiden—Marion smiled, thinking on how that description varied from church and castle to croft—meant to forfeit all the protections of the Queen's grace. Which in turn meant that sneaking into corners with pretty men would not be wise.

Her smile, however, let him assume encouragement. He began to insist, taking her hand and babbling, tongue loose with drink, as to the delights they could share.

"I think not."

The voice was rough, as was the hand that cupped her arm— and both were unfamiliar. Marion shot a glance towards her lads. All of them were wary-stiff as bucks scenting a challenger, staring at her.

Nay, at the man who'd taken her arm.

Brian de Lisle smiled, false pleasantry. "It seems another dance is offered. Will you join me?"

Will slowly rose to his feet, and Arthur. Gilbert caressed his sword hilt, glaring. John was creeping around the table, and the way his hand hovered at his waist suggested he'd a knife ready.

"I don't think they really want to do that." De Lisle's grip tightened on her arm, a promise of brutality. "Not with the King and Queen already retired for the night. They've only just been pardoned, after all, and things could become . . . ugly."

Marion shook her head, tight but firm, at the others.

Unwillingly they stood down, but only just.

The young noble started to protest; a glower from de Lisle halted it midthroat. Clearly outranked, the younger man bowed over Marion's hand and backed away.

"What do you want?" she asked.

"It's only a dance, after all." De Lisle's hand gripped firm her elbow. "Mayhap a few questions. Or are you afraid? To answer questions?"

Head high, Marion acquiesced. Better than admitting, yes, she was wary of this man. And much better than fetching the lads into some stupid brawl. Mayhap, with his *questions,* she could even find why he seemed to be . . .

The music started again, and de Lisle gave her a rough shove towards her place in the line.

"Have a care, my lord!" one of the men chided from his own place, giving Marion a warning glance. Like she needed one.

One of the *gwyllion* flitted into range, chittering not unlike Tess when perturbed.

De Lisle heard it—heard something—because he flinched. Shrugging it away just as swift, he scowled and extended a hand. It was quivering, yet went hard as iron as she laid hers atop it.

The dance was a simple carol, but one intended for the late evening; it involved more engagement with a single partner than most others. Close enough to murmur promises, to flirt or mayhap claim a chaste kiss.

Or spout bile.

"Which of you did it?"

"Did what, milord?"

"You know what I mean! Which of you killed my sister? I know one of you did it!"

"I swear to you, milord, none of Robyn Hood's men laid a hand upon her. Though," she rallied, remembering the Abbess and what she had wrought, "every one of them had cause!"

His hand twisted, clenched. She gritted her teeth, used the next circular step to yank away.

He, too, made the circle of steps then returned to her side—all within the bounds of the dance. "I saw how she died, mad with the nightmares of the damned."

No more than she deserved, with what she did to me and mine! But Marion held her tongue.

"Witchcraft and sorcery, all of it! It still lingers in this castle!" He shot a glance upward, then levelled it upon her. "They follow you, Maiden of the Shire Wode. They know you, and I do, too!"

The music cued a small spin; she took her time, thankful it hid the shock his words gave her. That he could see the nightmares lingering was no true surprise, but this? How did he know what to call her?

He'd a self-satisfied smirk touching his lip as she turned to him once more. His hand extended, waiting, and her hand lit upon his fist like a hawk—taloned, ready to rend or fly at any given opportunity.

"They're your nightmares, milord. The Lord of the Hunt cannot bestow upon you what is not already there."

His eyes glittered. "You pagan witch, I'll see you burnt—"

"So you've tried. But I'm still walking, aye?"

In answer he yanked her close—too close for any dance step—and kissed her.

She was so shocked that she let him, for a scattered set of heartbeats. It was no demonstration of affection; it was brutal, and invasive, meant only as humiliation.

Fury quivered through her muscles. She bared her teeth and bit his lip. As he lurched back with a curse, she rocked after him, grabbed his arm, booted the side of his knee, and sent him careening sideways before she could even think.

The hall lay strangely quiet, with a half-cleared circle about them. The music trailed away with several broken notes; Alundel staring, half approving and half stunned. Will, Arthur, and John, who had started over at the first sign of trouble, halted.

"A Marion!" This from David, who'd taught her that very move, and a rousing cheer from the rest of her lads in answer. A ripple of laughter answered from the onlookers, began to grow.

De Lisle started upward with a growl.

A hiss of "Marion!" and she turned to see a bow sailing her direction, tossed by Gilbert and still strung. Again, instinct bade her catch it and back for range; remembering the arrow Robyn had tucked in her hair, she tugged it free and nocked it. All of it one smooth motion, halting de Lisle in his tracks. De Lacy had grabbed his brother's arm; at one look from Marion, he held his hands up and began to inch backwards.

"Aye, that'd be wise, my lord of Pontefract," she said, clear in the silence. "If he so much as twitches I'll have him. And at this range, an arrow'll go through him like grass through a goose. Who knows who else 'twill hit?"

Silence again. The *gwyllion*, whispering and gathering. De Lisle covered his ears and cringed like a whipped dog; none else showed any signs of hearing. His brothers hovered in a discomfited mix of pity and distaste.

"Who knows who else 'twill the arrow, in truth strike?" Alundel suddenly sang. "Should a Maiden loose her bow, or a Queen discover who thought to importune her?"

"Or the Queen Mother be told."

The voice rang into the hall. Murmurs rose in its wake.

Marion relaxed her push on the bow, turned to see an elegant figure gliding towards her.

"Marion." Joanna held out a hand. "It is time to retire. Queen Eleanor has requested your assistance." Her gaze swept, haughty and prepossessed, over to where de Lacy was helping his brother to his feet—and from the look on his face, growling a reprimand all the while. "My lord of Pontefract, I would advise you to look to your kin. Has he not caused enough trouble?"

"Yes, royal lady. Rest assured I shall see to him."

"The kingdom is indeed in disarray," Joanna continued, eyes sweeping the remainder of the hall, "when one of the royal hand-maidens can be insulted in such a fashion." Her attention alighted upon the former outlaws, warm acknowledgement; next she turned to Marion. "You seem well guarded, however, and capable. Put the bow away for now, no?"

Marion realised she still held it, half-nocked at her hip. With a smile, she stuck the arrow back in her hair and tossed the bow to Will, who caught it with a grin.

"See that you treat the remainder of your liege's guests with more care, my lords and ladies."

And with that pronouncement, Joanna swept from the hall, taking Marion with her.

"*Je comprends.*" It was quiet. "*Vous devez comprendre.*"

Both were phrases Robyn recognised as he turned to face the King. *I understand. Now you must understand.*

"Aye, and more fool us, to tangle words as naked were we alone in the room. You didn't need Anglic to read us like parch-ment. Did he, lad?"

The squire started, marking Robyn's guess for truth. The lad had backed farther into the shadows, out of the way.

The King smacked two fingers over Robyn's mouth, leaned close. Smiled, then, "Shh."

It was so like the mimicry at the pool before the hunt that Robyn couldn't help the chuckle that emerged—full of rue and with a head-shake, to be sure.

A spate of conversation from beyond the door distracted him. Gamelyn's voice, with several others. Richard overrode it with his own, raised his free hand, and ran the back of it down Robyn's hair. The *gwyllion* hissed and scuttered out of the way—at the rings on that hand, at the cross glinting in the rich robes—no matter. Robyn was the only one left to perceive its presence.

He shook his head.

Richard growled something and the grip on Robyn's arm tightened, promising bruises later.

"He says you his now," the squire uttered from his hiding hole, the Anglic attempt faltering, but with its own music nevertheless. The next suggestion was his own, a tiny offering making its escape from the purposeful carapace. "You no fight him, you no hurt."

The beringed hand tightened in his hair, started to pull him close.

Robyn propped his free hand upon the broad chest. The cross tangled, ice-cold against his fingers, and he curled them, sliding sideways in retreat. Richard smiled, began to lean in. With a negligence of strength that years behind a bow had given, Robyn pushed back.

"*Mon roi.*" He locked gazes with Richard. "*Non.*"

Eyes sprung wide with disbelief, then narrowed, ash-laden glass. The uncompromising hold on Robyn's arm slackened. Robyn nodded, started to back away.

A smile flitted across Richard's face and slid into a sneer. It was the only warning Robyn received. First the blow, a meaty backhand slap. The hold on his arm tightened, twisted. Before Robyn could so much as draw breath, he was shoved and slammed facedown on the broad board of the table.

The *gwyllion*, shrieking, disappeared.

The board gave, sending Robyn nigh to his knees with the other end rocking ceiling-ward from their weight. The forester's horn, so boldly displayed on its strap, rolled into his armpit and jabbed sharp against his ribs. He bucked upward then sideways, mad as a horse who'd first felt the girths. Richard snapped a Frankish command, one hand scrabbling for purchase at Robyn's nape, twisting his arm. Through a haze of painful stars, Robyn watched in disbelief as the squire lurched from his corner and snatched at the board's swaying end. He hung from it, his weight tilting it back to rest in its supports, and lay on it to keep it there.

The board slammed into Robyn's hips, tossing him forwards. He took the opportunity to roll and drag his free arm beside his ribs. With a prop of his palm against the board, he shoved upward with a grunt. But even an archer's arm was no match for the Frank bull's fury. Richard slammed Robyn's head back into the board, then yanked his arm up nearly between his shoulder blades. Robyn yipped against the hard wood. More stars, and more blood to add to what already lay, metallic, upon his tongue; those rings had cut him. His arm felt as if it were nigh close to being torn off, and the breath knocked from him because the Motherless sod outweighed him twice over. Indeed, Richard was nigh atop him, growling something into his ear that was surely curse and threat, whilst the squire sat at the end of the table, watching with those composed, dead eyes.

How many times had the squire just . . . *taken it?*

The lad wasn't his people, but aye, he'd no choices. All of 'em, owned like cattle and valued for nowt but slaughter or use.

Like Gamelyn, bending his neck and following orders, bent on some mad quest; like Marion, dancing with Will in the winter because she didn't want to make a fuss; like Will's mam, who'd died with her son watching her *take it.* Like the scars on Robyn's own back, because he'd said nay to a soldier and *taken it,* all so the potkeeper's daughter at Loxley wouldn't find herself in the same position as Robyn was now.

Blood dripped from nose and lip, landing slow-thick upon the board. Robyn melted down against the hard, scarred wood, feigning capitulation even to sinew and muscle softening. *Just let me breathe. Let me take one breath, you miserable. . .*

As if in answer, the weight was taken from between his shoulders and his nape was loosed, letting a gasp feed starving lungs. "*Bon, jeune sauvage,*" the King murmured and trailed fingers down Robyn's rib cage. That hand shook, but it didn't promise clemency any more than the mumble of words; Richard was already hard, ready for the deed. Mayhap he merely meant to draw out the claiming. Mayhap he needed it. Mayhap he didn't want the fight so much as the surrender.

A skim within the blood staining the table, and a whisper against Robyn's hair; a lilt of gilt and song and the *gwyllion* regathering, with a promise: what Robyn couldn't siphon from wood and stone, Her people would give.

"Aye," Robyn murmured. "There's nowt good about this, you murdering rapist sod of a nobleman. For me *or* you."

Richard seemed to realise it wasn't poetry. His grip tightened and he gave a brutal upward yank of Robyn's tunic, muttering.

Robyn sucked in a breath and let it out, to mist the board and slow the galloping pace of his heart into a sluggish, thick lub. Purled, "*Rhyddhau i mi.*"

The hands upon him trembled. The mutter trailed away as Richard tried to remember what he'd meant to say, and do. The board shifted beneath Robyn, and the weight pressing down upon him began a retreat—again, confused.

The spirits buzzed just behind Robyn's consciousness, more distraction than aid. Otter-quick, Robyn twisted. The horn creaked, gave a sharp *crack* as the leather strap gave. He shrugged it away, meeting Richard's confused gaze with a growl.

"Bide you still, aye, for it's done."

But the bull was strong and Robyn challenged, within stone and away from his places. With a trembling-slow force, Richard tried to speak. His hand, inexorable, tried to rise, grasp the cross at his breast.

Belief against belief, is it? The Lady's voice sent the *gwyllion* darting and dancing; the sudden puissance of it sent shudders down Robyn's spine of both dread and yearning. *But I have chosen, by earth and water, air and fire. My guardian and Consort, My first children's King shall be a winter wolf crowned with mistletoe and holly, and thisworld's liege a Summerlord made of oak and iron—not a lion crowned glorious with empty prayers, who refuses to heed Me in all My power. You are* nothing, *O monarch.*

"Nothing." A whisper, a hiss. "Though you and your like shall suckle it dry and hound it to death, this land will never be yours." The *geas* came from Robyn unbidden, breathed and sparked about them, like the *gwyllion* drawing closer, like the Hunt ghosting through the stone halls, like the shadowy horn-crown weighting Robyn's head, granted right in this place by She who bore them all. "You would take, and take, and never give, so that not even your blood is worth spilling upon Her soil. You'll find no rest or solace upon the lands you've pillaged, and no heirs to sire upon your Queen to take *this* land from us. It's done, O *lion. Be tha stilled!"*

Hand midway to his breast, Richard shuddered and dropped like a stone.

"What have you done?"

It was a strangled moan, cutting off into a gasp as, still purling the hex-breath along his tongue, spinning the spell tighter, Robyn turned around.

The squire's composure had finally been breached.

"*Witch!*" A hiss culminating in a hiccup of breath, nigh a sob. "You . . . you cannot! He is the King! God's chosen!"

"So," Robyn said through his teeth, "am I."

The boy panicked. "*Au secours! Aidez-nous, le roi—!*"

Robyn leapt across the table and ploughed into the squire. The board seesawed, fell from its supports with a loud *bang* and sent them both rolling. Over and over, and on the third one Robyn straddled the lad, knees pinning those silk-clad arms and a hand clapping over his mouth.

Silence. Finally, after what seemed forever, a polite rap at the door.

The lad tried to struggle and scream again. The *gwyllion* flitted and darted like hummingbirds protecting a clutch.

Robyn merely bent closer, gave the sweated forehead a kiss, and breathed the sleeping spell. Midstruggle, the squire went limp. Lowering his head to the ground, gently, Robyn spared a glance over where Richard was lying, just as senseless.

Then he smiled and peered at the door. Rose, with the *gwyllion* flitting about him like fireflies, and upon his lips the Barrow tongue: "*Unlock.*"

Not even the discomposure of drunkenness could excuse the mistake. Nevertheless, Gamelyn realised the gravity of it—all of it—as the door shut in his face and the latch shot home.

He couldn't help a lurch forwards and a lift of his fist, as if to pound at the door. Barely begun, he checked the motion as its swiftness attracted the attention of one of the King's guards. And Much.

"Milord?"

Gamelyn throttled the pound into a small slap against the door, and a rueful shrug to the scarlet-clad guard who, thankfully, merely shrugged back and turned to his comrades. They had been brought a share of the feasting, were spreading it upon an upended barrel.

The King obviously wasn't worried overmuch about his chances.

Much had been invited to share the soldiers' loot; instead he walked over. Slow, careful. He knew something was wrong. "Milord?"

Gamelyn shook his head, stared at the door, and stewed. It was likely he could get back in. The guards weren't any more worried than their liege lord, and there were only four of them. He and Much could take them, burst in . . .

And ruin, utterly, every chance you've so carefully made. What did you tell Robyn? Not to wreck everything?

He'd been . . . sideswiped. Taken by surprise. Else he'd never . . .

It's worth any price. Any chance. Robyn can certainly take care of himself. He doesn't need a Templar bodyguard, and didn't you just make the point that he'd never been averse to swiving just about anything?

The predator's logic was impeccable; nevertheless, Gamelyn couldn't help a cock of head. Listening.

Fearful.

"Do we need to get in there?" Much's voice—calm, quiet, and ready to single-handedly take out the door and any guards who'd get in his way—broke the spin of sudden panic.

"I don't think we can."

It was too quiet, beyond. Of course, the door was thick, and . . .

"That singer's here," Much murmured, and almost at the same time, a light voice queried:

"My lord Templar?"

Alundel had just mounted the last stair, advancing with a caution that proved he, too, bided somewhat in his cups. Still he eyed up Gamelyn, Much, the guards eating and drinking, and the door. His last steps alighted almost wary, and his voice was dull. "Robyn's with the King."

Gamelyn didn't want to acknowledge how the spasm of his gut surely matched the sudden misery of the trouvère's expression. Would not.

Then a muffled clatter from behind the door, and a thud. Alundel started. It was everything Gamelyn could do to not start banging on the door.

Instead, the inner predator throttled the impulse as one of the guards slid a glance towards Gamelyn, as if questioning. Gamelyn nodded towards the trouvère and shrugged. It seemed to satisfy the guard, who returned to eating and drinking.

The next sound—a cry, cut off, then a huge scrape and thud and scramble—couldn't be ignored. Two of the guards turned, their obvious unwillingness to intrude upon their lord's recreation melting into alarm even as Alundel muttered, "God's robes, even Richard wouldn't . . . "

And a sudden, enervating . . . *pull,* was the only word Gamelyn could use upon it. It nigh hoisted him sideways, making him prop a supporting hand against the wall . . . and as if with that touch the air in the tower seemed to suck itself inward . . . and his wits with it. For surely otherwise it would have been himself and not Alundel who strode forwards to pound on the door.

"My liege?"

Silence. Two of the four guards were coming forwards, hands to sword hilts, confused.

Then another rush and pull of . . . *whatever,* and the door was unbolted.

Alundel pushed it open, cautious—and Gamelyn didn't blame him. He shoved away from the wall, managed to gather his wits enough to signal the guards: *wait.*

They were all too glad to obey. They'd obviously encountered this sort of thing before. Better that the Templar and the trouvère fetch trouble for interrupting the King at his chosen pursuits.

Much started, halted as Gamelyn shook his head, peered at him. This silent command was quite different from the one he'd given the guards; Much nodded and stepped in front of the door with arms crossed. He leaned against the lintel, a perfect, massive portrait of nonchalance.

With a flicker of a grin, Gamelyn slid behind him and around the heavy door. He nearly ran into Alundel, who'd halted just inside, staring.

The table was cocked half-on, half-off its far trestle, still rocking. The squire was flat on his back, limp. King Richard was sprawled across the floor, just as senseless.

And the cause stood amidst it, lit with tiny flecks of gilt, eyes aflame and a silhouette, faint, of a horn-crown shimmering atop tangled black curls.

The fireflies lit a bruising face, complete with a bloodied nose and lip. It made Gamelyn want to do sudden and brutal murder. Instead he closed the door.

And the predator's brain kicked in. "What in *hell* have you done?"

As if the snarl had banished them, the tiny fireflies . . . spirits . . . whatever they were . . . went dark.

"What *have* you done?" Alundel's voice was a cracked whisper. "If you have killed him, I will kill you both, here and now."

"I've killed nowt." No longer the spirit-clad avatar, Robyn was no less daunting. "And done? What should I have done?" His gaze strafed Gamelyn. "*Taken* it?"

Alundel fell to his knees beside Richard, and put a hand to his throat. The gentle hesitancy there was telling. Heartbreaking, did one *have* a heart that wasn't frosted with sudden fury. And fear.

"What do you think *I've* done all this time?" Gamelyn hissed.

"You keep saying that, but I've no idea what you've been doing, *my lord*. You en't told me owt!" This time the ebony gaze locked against Gamelyn's, a blow.

The inner predator met and matched it, eager. "Taken it? Of course I have! Every single blow and smiled through all of them, because there's too much at stake to turn aside now—"

"So letting the King have me like some tavern whore was part of some plan of yours?"

"Tavern *whore?* You can say that, when you'll rut anything most days!"

"'S long as it fetches us what we want, is that it? And I'm to have no say, no choice? Just *take it*. Bloody *damn*, but you think *just like them!*"

"I *am* them, or so your men keep saying! And now you've decided the same, but it remains, doesn't it? Because I can *think like them* means we'll be able to fetch from this what we want. Christ's *blood*, but if *you* bothered to think for a change, instead of ploughing through things like a mad buck—by God! Do you even realise what you've done?"

And Robyn smiled. *Smiled*, damn his black eyes. "Aye," he said, with a smug glance towards the fallen King that made Gamelyn want to shake the teeth from his head. "I do."

"Nay," Gamelyn snarled back, "you really don't. All this while, every step, twist, and turn, and all the while trying to . . . to . . . Then to have you just piss it away and take out the sodding King of England!"

"If I have, it's only what you've *already* pissed away! Mayhap my men are right, mayhap William has it right, and all you're after is your bloody *property*, because you're damn-well set on treating the rest of us as that, en't you?"

A deep nick, and one that started to bleed. But Gamelyn had survived worse wounds, after all, and for worse stakes. "Scathelock is a spiteful, jealous fool, and you're blind if you can't see it. I told you I knew what I was doing, that I had to see this through—"

"So I'm to trust your like more than me own? To trust sommun as wain't even do me the same courtesy, even as he says he loves me but keeps handing ower to my enemies all I hold dear? And you say I play t' game?—you play it fine as any whoremonger or pimp, sellin' us all! And for *what?* A bloody sodding keep of stone?"

"For a *future!* It burst from Gamelyn unwilling. "For a place to call our own, a . . . a *sanctuary*. . . our own! . . . one where we can all be *safe!* Where your people can live free. Where you won't be hunted like an animal, or Marion, and you can be that forester, she can have a wisewoman's prestige and hearth! Where you and I . . . where we can be *together,* with no fear of gods or judgment or . . . or a fate that would see us set against each other again . . . betrayer and betrayed . . . Oh *God!*' Finally, *finally* he choked it off, into a silence that burned.

Alundel stared at the both of them—had been staring for some time, Gamelyn belatedly realised, with hair hanging into his face and mouth slack, still crouched over Richard's prone form with that odd mix of solicitude and resentment.

And Robyn . . . O, but Robyn's eyes.

"All this time." It was hoarse. "All this time, and it were . . . were . . . All the while, you nigh killing me with your bloody hard heart, landing blows every time I'd try to so much as fetch myself close to you . . . even with the silver marks. Even with Marion . . . " Robyn's face drained of colour. "Bloody damn. *Marion.*"

"Robyn . . . " It was just as hoarse, uncertain, though Gamelyn tried to will it steady.

"We have to fetch her out of here!" From rage to remorse and now to as close to active panic as Gamelyn had ever seen him. "When yon great sod wakes, and she's the only one close t' hand . . . We have to fetch her out, Gamelyn, we have to—!"

Robyn would have fled straight into the hall—and into the soldiers' clutches on the other side of that shut door—the shortest path to Marion, to be sure, but, nay.

Gamelyn grabbed him, whirled him around when he thought to fight, and pulled him close, swift as an ambush victim whose neck he was about to break.

"You won't help her," he growled, "not like this!"

"We canna just *leave* her, we have to—"

"I know, I know! But if you run out that door now, you will set every dog the King has upon us, do you understand?"

"But—"

"Nay." Gamelyn clutched just that much tighter, felt Robyn's heart hammering against his forearm and his breath all ragged, and whispered against Robyn's hair, "Hold fast, just for a while longer. I have to think this through."

Realised, suddenly, it was the first time he'd held Robyn since . . . since . . .

Since he had been Gamelyn, and winter had turned into spring.

Continued softer than he thought himself capable, here and now, "*We* have to think, you and I. We have to figure out a way, make this work *for* us. Do you understand?"

Slowly, Robyn nodded, leaned back hard against Gamelyn. It hurt, somehow; a pain the predator was not prepared for. Like peeling away a deep-stitched scab, or hammering the last bolt of a dented helm still stuck on one's skull. Agony, almost. But with the sweet, foreign promise of *freedom*.

"What about *him?*" The lithe, hard frame shoring up against his own was quivering; another predator, scenting prey. Alundel.

Who seemed oddly unconcerned. "Leave me here." With one last, gentle touch to Richard's flung-aside mane of hair, Alundel rose. There was a cool and considering expression upon his face. Already youthful, this new mask was smooth as any pearl, yet held odd depth and candour. "None knows anything of what has happened here, save us. It need be nothing more than the King had a strange recurrence of the sickness that plagued him in Outremer, and in prison. More than once it has taken him without warning, like a fit."

"And if he remembers?" Gamelyn's fingers didn't want to release what they had once again found; Robyn also seemed loath to pull away.

"He saw nowt, though the lad saw more," Robyn muttered. "But 'tis the nature of sleep to take or muddle what memory as is bound to 't."

"I will take care of the boy. And tell my liege how he took a fit amidst his . . . diversion with the archer." Alundel peered at Robyn "Twould be best for you to stay away for the while, did you defy him. Which, from the marks upon you, I assume you did."

Gamelyn peered at the trouvère, eyes narrowing. "Why would you do this? And why should we *trust* you to do it?"

A *tsk*, and Alundel shook his head, fingers rippling upon the hem of his tunic as if playing his lute. "I once told wild Robyn why."

Robyn frowned.

"Or mayhap I long for another tale like my *geste*, or the holly oak, nothing more, with which to stoke the fires of inspiration." Another flick of fingers against the hem of his cloak. "Mayhap I, too, would believe in this *sanctuary* of yours, Templar. Though"—a shrug—"I think one great age of possibility and learning even now passes into a meaner, smaller one. None of us will see such a thing in our lifetime, I'm sure."

"Particularly wit' *his* like"—Robyn jerked his head towards Richard—"on England's throne."

Gamelyn's fingers nipped warning.

Alundel stiffened. "You don't understand."

Robyn pulled free and paced over to the table. With a grunt he righted it on its stands; next he bent, snatching something from beneath.

The forester's horn, Gamelyn realised.

Alundel frowned at Gamelyn, who shrugged, unsure himself as to what Robyn intended, or why.

"Robyn." It was sharp. "We have to go."

The horn's strap ends dangling from his hand—they'd broken and small wonder, considering—Robyn instead ambled over to Alundel, stood before him. His regard lingered, grave, for long moments. Then Robyn leaned forwards, took Alundel's chin in one hand and laid a gentle kiss to his cheek.

To Gamelyn's surprise the trouvère didn't move, didn't so much as pull away. Instead he closed his eyes, nostrils flaring as he took in a deep breath.

"Mayhap I understand better than you think," Robyn admitted. "Some of it, anyroad. You're no innocent, but all the same you're set on this like a silly lad in love for the first time. You let him have you—all of you—like you're hoping it'll turn from sour to sweet."

"He is the King. If I refuse . . . " A hard swallow, then silence.

"What?" Robyn prompted. "If you refuse, then what?"

Gamelyn realised he wanted to know, to hear. Advanced slow, despite the inner predator's derisive snort.

Alundel's expression ran a gamut of bewilderment and chagrin, then congealed into a condescending pity, his too-young face abruptly old. "Hearken to the boy outlaw who would set a forest afire to defy King and Church, whose sister claims the rights of a Heathen shieldmaiden, and whose leman dreams of a common sanctuary for Pagans, Gnostics, and sodomites. And you have the stones to say *I'm* naïve."

"That en't no answer. If you refuse to take it, then what?"

"Trust me, there can be no refusal."

"Only if you en't willing for t' price." Robyn leaned close again, whispered, "Alundel, we should never be afraid to die."

"There are things worse than death, Robyn Hode." Alundel's gaze moved from Robyn, to Gamelyn, then back again. "The Templar knows."

"So do I." Robyn turned away. "En't that what I just said?"

A rap at the door made them all jump, and the voice sent a chill down Gamelyn's spine.

"My liege, are you all right?"

Mercadier. The guards must have sent for him, unsure of what else to do.

"I am here as well, Captain!" Alundel sang out. "A moment of privacy, if you will?"

Sullen silence gave assent. "Help me get him to the bed!" Alundel hissed.

It took some doing—the King was no lightweight—but between the three of them they wrangled his limp form to the curtained bed in the corner. In the doing, they almost forgot the squire; as Alundel arranged Richard with some care beneath the bedclothes, Gamelyn and Robyn arranged the lad on his own pallet.

"My lord King!" It was muffled, but insistent.

Alundel slathered outrage onto his pale face, flounced over to the door, and opened it halfway, nigh dragging Mercadier inside before he slammed the door shut again. In two soldiers' faces. Gamelyn had seen them, waiting and ready for anything.

"What is the mean—?" Mercadier was ready to pound some heads, no question, but stuttered to a halt as he saw his liege bundled up in bed.

Like a threatened goose, Alundel pounced and pecked. "I had no wish to embarrass the King in his discomposure! Considering everything, it would not be well to have it become common knowledge that the fit has recurred!"

"The . . . fit?"

"The weakness and tremors caused by the miasmas of Outremer—which he still suffers, as you well know!"

Mercadier's gaze snapped, flint to steel, across the peaceful face of the King, the room, Gamelyn . . . then Robyn's bruised and bloodied face. Dubious and more, no question.

Gamelyn's muscles drew ready; he felt rather than saw Robyn likewise tense.

Then . . .

"I didn't know what else to do, Captain." Robyn stepped forwards, for all the world like a peasant lad caught stealing chickens. "He . . . well, he went all red, and shook, and dropped like a staggered ox. And, well, I'd made the mistake of telling him I'd rather not . . . well, you know, such things being a sin and all, and I didn't . . . well, I didn't think he'd get so proper brassed off, all red-faced and t' like, an' . . . well, milord, I didn't meant owt by—"

Mercadier was listening . . . well, trying to; he apparently didn't follow more than one word in ten. With a curt chop of one hand, he cut Robyn off and snapped a quick Frankish query in Alundel's direction that basically translated to *Damned rustic talk—what in hell did the man just say?*

Alundel complied, with embellishments, and Gamelyn had the unholy—and unhealthy—urge to laugh. Hard. He bit his tongue until one incisor scored blood.

And Robyn, damn his black eyes, *smirked* at him.

The smirk vanished as Mercadier turned back around, shot Robyn a narrow glance, then spoke, courteously, to Gamelyn.

"My lord Templar. I think it best you leave, and take the archer with you."

"Of course, Captain."

"And my lord . . . " The mercenary hesitated, a manner that didn't well suit him. "I would suggest nothing further be said about this, no? Express to the archer how he, too, should keep his mouth shut, stay out of sight for the while. It would be . . . safest, do you understand?"

"I do indeed," Gamelyn said, and meant it.

"We need t—"

Gamelyn gave a short hiss, aborting Robyn's protest as the door shut behind them. The guards were watching, blocking the safest retreat. Much's ready lean at the sill had tightened into an even-more-ready stance—he'd espied Robyn's bruised face.

"I'm to take this man back to my Order's keeping." Gamelyn kept the announcement mild, careless, even. "The King has finished with him."

The guards acknowledged this with several sidewise looks and mutters; unsure, aye, but more disdainful.

Prime opportunity to indulge his own tight-wound wrath. Gamelyn snapped, "So. You think yourselves capable of judging a king's requisites? Shall I inform him of your . . . opinions?"

Disdain evaporated beneath the threat, as did solidarity. "N-nay, milord," one managed to answer.

"Then I suggest you mind your post. And your tongues."

Gamelyn marched on. Instinctively the guards leapt out of his way—and his wake, including Robyn on his heels and Much as rear escort. They were well into the hall beyond, with only spare torches here and there to light the gloom, before Gamelyn started to breathe easier. His brain, however, kept spinning, a jumble of whys and what-fors desperately trying to catch up with what had just happened. What had been said, and done . . .

He slowed, and only then processed the murmurs behind him.

"I'll go." Much, soft but insistent. "Not you. If there's a smell of trouble, I can fetch her out, aye? As we arranged."

"Aye," Robyn answered between his teeth.

Much brushed past Gamelyn, paused, and took hold of one shoulder, halting him. "All right, then, milord?"

Gamelyn nodded. Much disappeared into the gloom.

"Aye, well, no doubt you're proper gorgeous when you're being a horse's arse. So Himself was finished with me, eh?"

The Horned Lord's prize *pwca* had his own gifts when it came to caustic wit.

Gamelyn inhaled deep, held it, and spun about.

Merely to find Robyn focused on retying the split strap ends of the forester's horn. "I think I'll keep this. A—how would y' call 't?" He threaded it over one shoulder and tossed a grin at Gamelyn, more wicked than pleasant. "A spoil of war, aye?"

Voices wafted from down the hall, silencing any reply had Gamelyn possessed one. As one, he and Robyn retreated deeper, slowing as they reached a curve darkened beneath a spent torch.

Gamelyn closed his eyes, forced himself to halt. To turn about. To say, "Robyn—"

Fingers tangled in his hair—cruelly tight. Gamelyn's eyes flew open to find an ebon blur: Robyn pulling him close, breath against Gamelyn's cheeks and curls tangling with his beard, nose scrunching his sideways, mouth taking his—taking, not asking. Gamelyn started to pull away—inner pedant yapping on about enemy territory and dangers—but that lithe-muscled frame didn't let him, shoved him hard against the stone wall. Gamelyn shuddered, closed his eyes once more, opened his mouth, and lost his mind.

Robyn didn't release Gamelyn until his knees threatened to give way—then, as if to further prove the point, Robyn stepped back. And no more could Gamelyn stop the stagger and sway after than he could fly through the upper window. He knew, because he tried.

Acknowledging it with a cock of head not unlike a cheeky raven, Robyn smirked.

And swung.

The blow took Gamelyn square in the jaw and pitched him, sprawling, against the wall. He hung there for long breaths—both of them, huffing like a smith's bellows—with Robyn staring at him, inky curls falling across his face and absolutely no hint of god-gilt alight in those shadowed eyes.

Gamelyn tested his jaw, back and forth. Shook his head, slight. It didn't stop his ears from ringing. For being such a lath of a fellow, Robyn possessed a left cross the devil himself would envy.

"Well." Raising fingers to his mouth, Gamelyn wiped and peered at the thick smear. "I believe I deserved that."

"Aye," Robyn said. "You did." Then, "Are we fetching ourselves out of here, or what?"

- XXVII -

"**I** think we must see to it you are granted Keepership of Sherwood Forest."

Another glorious, sunny dawn was edging its way over the shire.

Nottingham was stirring, albeit slow, from the night's feasting. Eleanor was more of a morning sort than even Robyn. Despite several days' lack of sleep, she rose more chipper than most of her retinue, including Marion, who suppressed a huge yawn as she paced back towards the chamber's board, bearing a sumptuous meal on an enormous tray.

The meal had been brought from the kitchens by a maidservant who'd curtseyed to Marion as if she were a proper noblewoman, explaining the consideration with a quick hand sign—*Bendith y mamau*—as she'd whispered, "Blessings of the morn, Lady."

"She's no lady!" one of the *pucelles* nigh to the entrance had scoffed. The *gwyllion*—just as awake and cheerful as Eleanor—had hissed at her.

Marion merely returned the maidservant's sign and let her heart warm with the knowledge—some from Nottingham would come to the Maying.

Even that, however, scattered to the four corners beneath what the Queen had just said. *Keeper of Sherwood?*

The little spirits were practically doing somersaults in the rafters. Marion stumbled and nearly lost her grip on the tray, lurched the rest of the way to the board, and landed it with a small clatter.

"Careful, girl," said the Queen, lightly. "Anne, kindly fetch my fan."

Mayhap Marion had misheard. Or Eleanor hadn't been speaking to her after all. She clenched her hands, forced some semblance of calm, and began transferring the meal from tray to board. Today's Lenten restrictions were welcome after an evening of indulgence; nevertheless, there was plenty of bread toasted over the fire, traced with honey, and leftover fish from the previous night's feast.

The fan, now in the royal hands, slapped down on the table—and blast and bugger if Marion didn't nearly drop the honey pot. "*Marion*, did you not hear me, child?"

Marion gripped the table with both hands. "I were proper sure Madam weren't speaking t' me."

"Well, Madam were. Speaking to you." Several of the *pucelles* tried a giggle, but stoppered it when Eleanor glared their way and continued, "I *said*. . ."

"*Maman*," Joanna said, quiet, "I think she heard you well enough."

"Good." Eleanor peered at Marion. "You seem surprised."

Surprised wasn't half of it. Marion kept eyeing her hands, white-knuckled upon the board. Her skirts—not the sumptuous bliaut fit for a banquet, but a sensible grey wool—quivered. Shaky knees. Likely she'd go down did she let loose of the table.

"Things are all coming into place," Eleanor continued, switching the peacock feathers at a persistent fly. "Your brother and his men have been pardoned and given proper situations. Your Templar Knight will regain the honour he deserves. Not without some sacrifices"—this with a frown and shrug—"yet I've no doubts he shall find men willing to aid his need. Nothing worth having is easily gained. Still, all this leaves you, Marion, without adequate provision."

And without adequate voice. She tried, really she did, but nothing would come out.

One of the *gwyllion* chirruped. Thank any god who would listen that none in the chamber but Marion heard. Or saw it flit down to cling to her braid.

"Therefore, a Keepership should suffice. My word, girl, but your freckles do stand out when you're surprised. I hope it is a good surprise?" Eleanor frowned, then snorted. "Of course it is; how not? Sit, child, before your knees give way on you. Put some honey on that bread, have a bite."

Marion sat, and obediently took the offered bread and honey. The latter filled her mouth with sweet and steadied, somehow, the erratic thud of her heart. It made it easier to speak.

"Madam, do you truly mean it? You would make *me* Keeper of the Shire W . . . of Sherwood?"

"Why not? It makes more sense than most honours bought or wrangled so far. You were a forester's daughter. You have experience with woodland ways to which most cannot aspire. Certainly more than the one who previously held the honour. She, too, is a woman." The smile grew once more malicious. "Ah, but Maud de Caux wagered upon the wrong horse, didn't she? Didn't heed the advice of one who helped ensure her possession in the first place, and so my lady Maud is left with no present means to wheedle her way back into favour. Richard's might be easily swayed by a purse full of coin, but she'll pay Hell before buying mine."

Not for the first time, Marion hoped she never fell into Queen Eleanor's bad graces. Difficult, since she'd no idea how she was in *good* ones.

An inexplicable rash of hot tears stung behind her eyes. She slid from the small stool and to her knees at the Queen's side, made an impulsive snatch at Eleanor's beringed hand, and drew it to her cheek. "My Queen, I . . . " She nearly choked on it, and somehow forced her tongue to work. "I truly don't know how to thank you. For . . . everything."

The fingers curled, gave her cheek a tiny pat. "As I said, you will eventually, my dear. Consider it all as *my* thanks. For many things."

Marion looked up, met Eleanor's eyes. The Queen gave a nod and brief smile, another pat to Marion's cheek.

"Get up, girl, and have another bite of bread. You can—"

"My Queen!"

All eyes turned to the door as a somewhat ruffled and breathless Alundel emerged from 'round it.

"Forgive the intrusion, my Queen, but I thought it best to warn you—"

"*Maman!*"

The bellow nigh filled the castle, even muffled. Eleanor frowned at Joanna, who had frozen amidst slathering honey upon bread.

Alundel skittered full into the solar. "By Holy Mary, I swear I tried to keep him in bed, but he's got it in his head, you see—"

"In his head? Blondel, what are you blathering a—?"

"*Maman!*" It shook the floors to the spacious main solar, was followed by a rash of Frankish curses.

Alundel rolled his eyes skyward, clearly imploring his Almighty to grant him patience . . . or at least stamina. The younger women were beginning to gather in a tight clot by the window. The elder maidservant, determined despite a trembling of lip, came to stand behind her lady liege.

"Saints preserve us . . . Go, all of you!" Joanna shooed at the attendants like a covey of partridges. "Lose yourselves, now!"

Just past the solar door, a mailed scuffle signalled guards were scattering to all points. The *pucelles* did likewise.

"Aye, and I can handle him better on my own." Eleanor loosed Marion's hand.

"I'm stayin', milady," the elder maidservant claimed.

"No, you're not. Take them both, Joanna. Blondel"—Eleanor's eyes went to him, one brow arching— "can stay.""

Joanna obeyed, taking the maidservant's hand and jerking her head at Marion. "Come. I certainly don't fancy being here if dear Richard's in a mood, and considering . . ."

"Considering?"

Joanna shot her a strange look. "Never mind. Come *on!*"

"Damn it, where . . . ?" Another scuffle, this of wood and metal rolling down the stair. "This damned place is a cursed *warren!*"

Marion followed Joanna and the maidservant towards the back solar. The rest of the women had disappeared. One must have made a bad choice of turn; there was a low oath and a small shriek as King and *pucelle* nigh collided on the upper landing.

Joanna rolled her eyes—but exasperation didn't cease her from reaching out to yank Marion farther into the dimly lit bedchamber.

"Get out of my *way*, woman!" A growl from Richard and a second, albeit tiny, shriek. Footsteps tapped a hasty retreat down the stair.

"By all the saints and martyrs! Richard, need you frighten all my ladies?" Eleanor demanded, with a creak of wood and leather as she leaned back in her chair. "I'm not so young anymore, and they are a help."

"You'll never grow old, never die." The bellow had softened, the words startlingly fond and open.

"I've evidence otherwise." Eleanor's riposte was wry. "Even you, milord King, don't always get what you want."

"In few things, mind. But those few . . . Jesus *wept!*" Richard's tone veered back towards fury—and so quickly, Marion angled forwards, worried after the Queen.

Joanna aborted the impulse with a snatch at Marion's arm, pulling her against the cool stones with a shake of her veiled head. Well, surely Eleanor's daughter would know her family better than most.

"Blondel." A growl. "How did you get up here? The man is quick as a damned stoat, Mother, and an overbearing nursemaid, at that!"

"I think only to keep you sound, my liege."

"So I'm unsound now, am I? Like a wind-broken horse?"

"You twist my meaning, lord King!"

"Your meaning, my lord de Nesle, is most suspect at present!"

"He wounds me, my Queen, most cruelly. And after all I've done, will do!"

"What have you done, indeed? What game are you playing this time, Blondel?"

"Good *God!*" Eleanor's voice was a whip-crack. "What in the name of Heaven are you two on about?"

Silence. Marion hardly dared to breathe.

Richard didn't wait overlong to fill that silence. "I've no idea what your trouvère is conspiring about, believe me—"

"Blondel is always *Mother's trouvère* when brother's displeased with him," Joanna hissed in Marion's ear.

"—greeting me this morn with some nonsense about how I took a fit last night amidst a . . . It isn't to be borne, I tell you! Insufferable!" Richard's voice made its inevitable climb, from growl of thunder in the distance to full-on storm overhead. The oaken floor creaked with the weight and stamp of boots, back and forth. "I show mercy, and I am repaid with arrogance! I show gratitude, merely to have it thrown in my face! More and more I agree with the infidels of the East—they would say gratitude is merely another word for resentment!"

"Yours," Eleanor drawled, "or the ones who have invited it? Have a seat, son."

A quick flash of teeth against the dim candlelit chamber as Joanna smirked and shook her head. Not chiding—admiring.

Another growl answered it, and a clunk, groan, and bang that could have only been a boot connecting with the bench, and the bench flung sideways.

Marion puffed up like a goose. King or no, if any man had stamped in like that and started abusing good furniture in her house? In fact, Robyn had once tried his temper on Eluned's table . . . but only the once.

This time Joanna's expression held warning. For Marion, not her mother.

"No one has insulted you, my lord. I would swear to—"

"Shut your damned mouth, Blondel."

"Richard!"

"He wasn't even there at the time! It doesn't matter what conspired afterward. And believe me, my squire has a thoroughly different tale than you, trouvère."

"Now he calls me a liar. On the word of a simple squire! My Queen, will you not—?"

"She will not."

"Richard."

Marion recognised it well—*Mother has had enough of you, little lamb*—and wouldn't like to be on the receiving end of that, true enough.

Neither, obviously, did Richard. "Tell him to get out, then. Or I swear I shall turn him over to Mercadier, and he'll have the truth from him!"

Joanna's eyes gleamed in the dim, wide as a good plate.

Silence. Then a rustle of clothing, footsteps retreating as Alundel exited the door and mounted the stair.

"I do not interfere with your . . . fallings-out with my trouvère, Richard. So I will not dignify your threat with a reply. But your explanation needs be phenomenally good."

"When I have one, you shall hear it!" Richard snapped back.

"Blondel said you had a fit? Another one? Shall I call a physician to attend you before the day grows—?"

"Blondel said!" Several coarse gutter snarls, the meaning of which Marion's grasp of Frankish couldn't begin to parse. "Blondel has it in him to say overmuch, and whatever he is hiding, I shall find, believe me. Yet this much remains, *Maman*. I should never have listened to you! You cannot treat with these people as if they are anything like to us!"

"I daresay that listening to me has fetched you from more than a few rough situations. Sit down, I say, and attempt to speak sense." Another scrape of the bench suggested Eleanor's suggestion was being heeded as she continued. "Whatever is possessing you? And like to us? Hardly, when you are King of England, Duke of Normandy and Aquitaine, Count of Anjou and what-all, and I, your mother. That does not mean 'these people,' whoever you mean, don't have their own qualities—"

"*Qualities?*" It was a roar.

"For pity's sake, even the horses in your stable have *some* sort of worth and right, Richard."

"A horse, aye! But this . . . *this*. . .!" Richard was incoherent with rage. Again, the bench raked the floor.

Joanna had inched up to peer around the curve of the lintel, careful and curious. Marion gave a cautious go at it herself; being a full head taller, she had the advantage of peeking past without Joanna noticing it overmuch.

Behind them, the maidservant had long abandoned any pretence of bravery; she cowered over by the bed with a shawl flung over her wimpled head.

Pacing, gesticulating with a long dagger as if it spoke better for him than any speech, the King was florid, his gold-ruddy mane flying in the stark morning sun. Marion had never before realised the Angevin Lion was only this short of red-haired himself.

"This whoreson! This *outlaw!* He *has* no rights save what I choose to give him, yet still he spits in my face! As if he were my *equal!*"

Joanna turned to peer at Marion, and Marion thought, with a shaky catch of breath, *Robyn, what have you done?*

"We have no outlaws remaining in this demesne, by my request and your decree. *Lord King."* It curled, sibilant, Eleanor not backing down one whit.

Neither did her son. He whirled and slammed both fists on the table. "The pardon I gave. The pardon that I can, like *that"*—a swift, cutting gesture—"take away!"

"And in the doing, send a message clear as water to all your English subjects."

"Aye, it would! Too many men have reached above themselves in my absence! Too many of these damned *English* have defied me! And I tell you, they will see how ready my vengeance lies!"

Marion clenched fists in her skirts, bit her lip. The *gwyllion*, buzzing just out of regular sight, were not hiding.

They seemed somehow rejuvenated. They seemed *angry*.

"The English will see their King reneges on agreements at a whim!"

"If I choose, yes! The scum humiliated me, and I want him dead!"

Marion shuddered, started to back away from the doorway. Joanna snatched at her skirts, further held her in place with a warning look.

"Tell me, O King," Eleanor drawled, "how this peasant who could be your son—aye, another bastard son, whilst your Queen has none from you—has *humiliated* you."

A pause.

Eleanor sat back in her chair, fanning herself; necessarily so, for her colour was high despite the languid pose. "As I thought."

Richard's florid cheeks went pale.

"He refused you, and that's what this is all about. You thought to rut him like some animal, with no more thought for his soul than *were* he a brute beast!"

"Soul? You think that one has a soul, when he called his devils down upon me, first to seduce me—"

"I thought to be a seducer, one had to be willing." Eleanor's voice might have been etched in acid. "Not refusing."

"I am his sovereign!"

"And were I you, I would thank God he had the courage and wherewithal to turn you from sin. Oh, I know you dally with your diversions as you see fit—girls, boys . . . even my trouvère, to his shame *and* yours. You always have and always will. But you will *not*," Eleanor said between clenched teeth, "abuse my word or promise merely because you want to sodomise some peasant lad."

Again, Richard's face paled. "Mother, you go too far."

"I go too far? I, who bore you and nine other children, all in keeping with my duty to Church and two crowned husbands? Whilst you *waste* your duty—"

"I am no sodomite! I keep to my own amusements—which are a King's prerogative, I am assured by that same Church as bids you mind your duty, as long as I act a man and not boy or *woman!*"

Marion ducked back and looked up into the dawn-filled solar, pressing her shoulders hard against the wall. It was either that or lunge from hiding and slap that broad, flushed face.

Eleanor clearly felt likewise. "Semantics, is it now? Try another path, and mind what *woman* taught you to speak those words you'd twist and turn."

Silence.

"Richard, you aren't thinking, that much is plain. You may care less for this island than your other territories, but here, you are

King. It is to *these people*—the commonest souls bred from England's earth—we owe your return. They willingly filled the coffers with your ransom, and cheered your arrival—you heard them! All of them, common and noble alike, welcoming the great warrior king, tall and broad and golden-haired. King Richard took up the cross and tendered unto Saladin several crushing defeats—"

"And lost Jerusalem to the cowardice of his allies."

"And overcame the treachery of those allies, who would have seen him kept prisoner," Eleanor pointed out. "So you, in the eyes of the English, have returned to right the wrongs their land has suffered. You are the gleaming symbol of all the treachery done them by corrupt overlords and officials. You yourself threw the pardon of Robyn Hood and his merry band like a gauntlet upon the stones, testing those same officials. That lad is a hero here in the North. We need heroes. We need the North." Her voice tightened. "Why am I explaining these things to you? You well know how it must work. You know better than to toss this victory aside over some . . . some . . . prideful tête-à-tête gone awry!"

"Even if, indeed, he is an enchanter?"

All Marion wanted to do was leave. Get away, somehow, find Robyn, and warn him it had all gone wrong, *run.*

But the only exit for this chamber lay past the danger.

"If? You did not see it?"

Richard hesitated, fuming, then growled, "The squire saw. Things."

"The same squire whose truth Blondel disputes?"

Another growl.

"Then you have a problem, lord King, of proof. Was another present? Because surely to entertain any of your subjects without adequate attendance is foolhardy at best . . . ah, that's right. Witnesses might be a problem in certain . . . circumstances, no?"

Richard was beginning to pace again. "Don't start this ag—the Templar was there."

Gamelyn. Marion didn't know how much more she could take without howling.

Joanna's fingers touched hers. The sympathy was palpable—and its own sanity. Marion gripped the offered hand.

"You attempted . . . to . . . to . . . !" Eleanor was clearly flabbergasted. "In front of a *Templar?*"

"He translated, nothing more!"

"By all the saints and martyrs, are you trying to tell me—?"

"I've no doubts as to that particular Templar's . . . inclinations." Richard's anger was foiling his wits at present. "No, he was not there. During."

"So, no undisputed proof, you saw nothing, and you've already admitted to the lad refusing your . . . offer. Foolish of him, mayhap, considering his circumstance, but hardly enchantment.

Even if the lad lives up to his reputation and has any tendency towards the old forest ways—*if*—then can you blame him for using them to defend himself?"

"There is no power but God's own, and no magic by pagan or infidel that God cannot vanquish. I would call that blasphemy!"

"I would call it stoppering one's ears," Eleanor replied, tart. "And singing fa-la-la all the while! I warned you there were old powers in these northern woodlands, ones to rival your Templars who study the rites of Solomon and Moses. More akin, mayhap, to the she-devil whose blood—and unholy *temper*—runs through the Angevin."

"Myth!"

"I've heard you claim kinship of the devil's brood often enough, and laugh! Myth! What is that but forgotten religion? Even the Holy Fathers knew better than to attempt the destruction of what powers have come before. Or obliterate what, with time, could be swept up into Christ's love and mercy."

"You listened to Uncle Raymond's blasphemies once too often, Mother."

"And you've forgotten everything you learned as a boy in the south of France. Too much of black and white, yes and no and little in between, too many years slaughtering those who might have, with the wisdom of Jerusalem's triumvirate kingdom, come to respect Christ and each other." Eleanor leaned forwards, her fingertips stroking the fan flat upon the board. "You need remember the power of forgiveness as well as war. You did, once."

Joanna was nodding beside Marion.

"You mean with John."

"Well, of course you will need to make peace with your brother and set him here to tame these English. He understands this land, loves it as you do not."

"Little wonder. He's an unholy bastard, as well."

"How telling, that most men's insults begin with shaming women!" was Eleanor's caustic reply. "But nay, I mean what has come to pass in this castle. You have a chance to make a commoner's hero into *your* champion. And, despite your attempts to weasel around the terms of reward—"

"I did not weasel anything, I made adequate and necessary terms!"

"You will need men such as the Templar beholden to you. And grateful for your mercy and forgiveness to his comrades, particularly with the brother of the woman he loves."

Marion had to smile; that was intended for her, no doubt. How correct it was, whilst just as thoroughly mistaken.

"Hold to your purpose here, son. The puissance of reclaiming your rightful fealty means to hand out forgiveness as well as blows. And pray to Christ for the same in your own heart, in this season of His Resurrection. You, too, have come from the darkness and into freedom, no?"

Joanna's hand quivered in Marion's. Richard stared at Eleanor for some time, then fell to his knees beside her and buried his head in her lap as if he were once again a young lad, longing for nothing more than a mother's touch.

Eleanor ran her fingers through his hair, and peered out into the sun.

Resurrection, Marion thought. *Indeed.*

(ᛋ)

John was waiting for Robyn at the edge of the Thorny, where it followed the river. They trailed it some way in before Robyn slowed, began shrugging off the horn, his cloak, and fancy clothing.

Wordless, the agreement: *I stink of that place, of stones and possession, of the dirt and dung of a fouled lair.*

They swam in the river, then rolled in the fresh new grass like young otters courting. It was more than play and pleasure; it was sloughing away another skim of worldly wreckage.

After, as they lay in the slats of new sunlight and green, sweat prickling skin and breath commingling, Robyn finally spoke. "I don't ever want to go back there. 'Cept," he amended, "to fetch Marion, if they don't let her out proper soon."

John snuggled closer, both giving reassurance and needing it, not with just touch but more caresses, and kisses, finally trailing a damp flame of breath and tongue all over Robyn's body until he twisted, and shuddered, and cried out.

Odd, to let the trees ring and echo with their pleasure. Sound could either travel or be smothered in thick green; outlaws couldn't afford the chance. This time the echoes were answered with more sun, and cooling breezes, and the cries of courting birds.

To lay here in the arms of a beloved, surrounded by his Wode . . .

"He'll come back," Robyn said, kenning the question before John so much as asked it, and traced kisses in brown curls. "I think . . . think he always meant to come back, but he had to go away for a while."

John shivered. It was plain his time in the camp had neither been kind nor comfortable.

"I don't know how they bide it. If he comes . . . nay, when. When he comes to us, well . . . we'll know. What happens next. Whether the King will keep his word." A sigh, in then outward, to chase the remaining sting. "I should have trusted him."

"*Trust goes both ways,*" John signed against Robyn's chest, and Robyn kissed the top of his brown head.

Said, soft, "Aye, love."

Then started to laugh as the brush rustled and a motley-clad group of men appeared from the underbrush, grinning.

"We heard you coming a mile away, man!" Gilbert teased. "Literally!"

Gamelyn heard a trio of birds begin to sing, opened his eyes, and found the chapel no longer dawn-grey but filmed rose-gold.

No doubt the hour would be struck at any time, yet here he was, on his knees. The hard, swept-clean stone of the chapel floor had long since crept chill into his legs. Hard to shrug off the habits of childhood. Of a lifetime.

He had learned through heartbreak and war to kneel before the altar of his father's God and spill neither bile nor begging. What had once been prayer now had a different taste to it, one more complex.

Sometimes he missed the simple ease of those former prayers. Yay and nay. Black and white. Good and evil.

Nay, not missed. Mourned.

Mourning, after all, had seen him take the first steps into battle, hoping for death. And when death had turned its face from him, denied him, he'd covered himself in the sackcloth of survival, to wrest a new life from the old and ravaged one.

Guy de Gisbourne, whose only allowance to that mourning had been penance—wearing the black and never taking a cutting edge to his hair after he'd survived Acre. Whose answer to life had been, when all was said and done, the simplest of things: obedience and service, freely given.

What I have, 'tis yours. Heart, head, and aye, horns. It's allus been yours.

The quillion dagger lay between his knees. Once a sword had signified the sign of the cross. How apropos that this dagger implied, even more, its deeper meaning: a relationship to sacrifice.

Another sacrificial offering—the pouch filled with coin and freely given, the price of putting aside mourning—was with Much. He'd come from the Queen's chambers with reassurances—all seemed well—and met Gamelyn as he'd trudged back inward, having seen Robyn safe through Nottingham's front gate.

"Mayhap you should go wit' him, milord? Just for a while?"

"I can't. Not until it's done."

And then Gamelyn had told Much what he intended to do.

"Aye, well, whatever you choose, whatever battle you mean to fight, I'll hold your back. Like I allus have, and allus will."

There's no sodding price to it. All you have to do is just reach out and take it. . .

He'd retired here, to Nottingham Castle's small chapel.

Through the high windows, the sky turned and shifted, slow. A bell tolled, muffled; not the chapel bell. Behind him, the door creaked open. Gamelyn stiffened, waiting. The bell rang clearer, but no nearer, then muffled once more as the door was pushed shut.

Several breaths, then a peculiar rhythm issued from the entry. A wooden click, then a *shuss*, as if a boot were being dragged across the paving stones.

Gamelyn turned, frowning.

Hubert was there, leaning on a crutch and holding a rushlight. "Pray, *Confanonier*, go on with your contemplations. We should have some peace this Hour at least. Today the Archbishop intends to hold High Mass at St. Mary's Abbey. I will"—a small grunt as he lowered himself to the nearest bench—"merely sit here and reflect. No doubt the Holy Mother will understand if I do not kneel."

Without a word, Gamelyn rose and went to his Master, knelt at the bench before him.

It wasn't easy. His legs were half-asleep, wobbly—and his knees were killing him. A growled internal reminder of Hubert's leg wound stopped such weakness and kicked it into the gutter where it belonged.

"Here, then," Hubert murmured, "what is this, lad?"

"You shouldn't be walking alone, so soon after—"

"Well, and you know I prefer a walk alone before midmorning prayer, but young Stephen insisted upon helping me. He's been quite obliging, as you know, and waits outside the door, no doubt having a quiet chat with Much."

Gamelyn hadn't realised Much had stayed . . . but of course he had.

"I didn't mean to interrupt your prayers, but I felt somewhat in need of my own. And when I saw Much, knew you were here. Forgive me, but I felt even more the need to see you. You seemed . . . troubled last even."

"I was. I am." And there would never be a better time, out of reach of other ears. While Gamelyn had no compunctions at presenting Wymarec with a *fait accompli*, he owed Hubert much more than that.

"Do you need confession, then?" It was matter-of-fact. "Tell Much and Stephen to hold the door for a bit, and if you will give me some moments to pray, I can make myself ready to—"

"Nay, my lord Commander. I mean . . . it is indeed a confession, but not of God. This is man's doing, entirely."

Hubert's eyes met his, steady, curious—and oddly accepting.

It had never been otherwise, no matter what Gamelyn had divulged—and in the pursuit of duty, there had been many things to declare, secular or otherwise. It would have also been easy to look down.

He didn't allow himself to do so.

"There are other . . . ties. Strong ones," Hubert suggested. "This I have known since the *dryw ardhu* and the Maid tossed down a gauntlet with your name upon it. Master Wymarec is well invested in those ties. As am I."

"It is that, but more." Gamelyn swallowed, held Hubert's gaze. "The King has made me an offer."

"And so we expected."

"This is past any expectation, my lord. The King has offered the honour of Tickhill to *me*. Not the Templar, not Sir Guy, *Confanonier* to Temple Hirst, but to Gamelyn Boundys."

"Hm." Hubert cocked his head, thinking. Said, soft, "I am sorry. I know you long for the heritage, the rights that were stolen from you. Unfortunately, it sounds as if the King has no intention you should have the castle and honour any more than should the Temple. There are several lords in line well able to purchase both. The King seeks to salve his mother's promise and have a way to justifiably renege."

"I told him as much."

Hubert's eyebrows rose.

"Well, I didn't quite phrase it so. But I did remind him I'd not even the price of a warhorse with which to stake any promises. That without the Temple, I am nothing."

"I wouldn't quite say that, lad."

"I *have* nothing, then. The King merely reminded me of what allies I do have, and suggested they would lend support."

"And own you thereafter, you must realise."

"I do. And if I am to be owned?" It rasped from Gamelyn's throat as he lowered his gaze. His next words held barely above a whisper. "Then let it be of my . . . choosing."

Silence, settling between them.

"There is more," Hubert said. "*Non?*"

"My lord, there is . . . " It warbled and creaked like a seldom-oiled hinge. "*Hubert.* If I have the means, I could take Blyth and Tickhill as my own. But I would no longer be a Templar."

"I see. And have you"—gentle, so gentle—"those means, somehow?"

Gamelyn nodded.

"The Queen? Huntingdon? Mayhap de Lacy?"

"Robyn." He swallowed. "O my Master, it is considerably more than the requisite thirty pieces."

Another silence. He hardly dared look, much less breathe.

Then, altogether quiet and rueful, a chuckle. Gamelyn glanced up, found Hubert looking towards the sunlight, shaking his head.

"But of course. I should have known." Hubert started to turn his head; Gamelyn ducked his own. "Ah, but the *dryw ardhu* and the Maid have played well, very well."

Gamelyn remained silent, hunched and waiting.

Something touched the top of his head; he nearly flinched away before he realised it was Hubert's hand. Fingers tangled in his forelock and tugged; when Gamelyn merely ducked his head further, the gentle fingers nipped harsher.

"Look at me, lad."

He did so, wary, but Hubert's expression was contemplative, not angry.

"Do you remember when we first came back to England? We stood upon deck in the rain and watched the approach unto a thoroughly drenched coastline. It was home, nevertheless, *non?*"

Home. For all his longing for the desert, the forest was that. Gamelyn nodded, felt a waft of warm breath at his nape, smelt roses as She whispered *Hariq aljini alshier al-ghaba. My fire-haired djinn of the forest.*

Hubert closed his eyes, nostrils flaring as if he, too, scented Her presence.

"It is clear to me that our Lady speaks to you. She has chosen you for a much greater purpose than being, ah, a *Templar's lackey.*"

"I have never felt—"

Hubert waved a hand. "I misspeak. The drink helps the pain, but it makes my tongue flap other than what it should. I have never"—the blue eyes pierced—"considered you anything but a Knight of the Temple, one possessed with more talent and, ah, entirely too many scruples to rise as he deserves."

"Scruples!" Gamelyn protested. "My lord—"

"Yes, I am still your lord at this moment, and I say you have many stubborn scruples. And fears, I know. It has not been easy, to balance upon the precipice. It never is." Hubert's fingers softened, feathered into a caress not unlike a father's benediction. "That day on board ship, I said I would release you from the Order, did you wish it."

"I remember."

"Do you, then, wish it?"

"My lord, I cannot wish it. But if this thing can be done with what I have . . . " Gamelyn tried to shrug, failed miserably. "I have to try. So I must ask it."

"Then I must, in blessing and respect, give it." The hand smoothed over Gamelyn's unbound hair and down to his shoulder. "I have my own wish, you see; one for you. It is what I would grant a son of my own body, had I one. I pray, Gamelyn, that you will find what peace has eluded you far too long."

Gamelyn grasped Hubert's hand, drew it to his cheek, and closed his eyes. It cupped his face, a caress, then patted, light.

"Retrieve your dagger from the altar. That *is* yours and you will need it, *non?*"

He nodded and rose, taking his time at the altar, kissing the hilt of the dagger before he sheathed it at his belt. Turning, he found Hubert listing sideways. He looked exhausted, but also satisfied.

"Help me up and to the door?"

"Of course."

"Mind you, after the thing is done, you will turn in the Order's belongings to the Draper and the Marshal. I will draft the papers myself." A pause. "I need not tell you Master Wymarec will be . . . displeased."

Nay, he needn't. "My lord—"

"Hubert. I shall soon be Hubert to you, Gamelyn." He leaned hard against Gamelyn. "Ah, I will miss your strength by my side. Yet you have my blessing, in whatever you must do. Mayhap you will be not only lord of Blyth, but truly what was meant from the beginning. Mayhap as *dryw alban,* you will come to treat with me, as has the dark one and his predecessor. *Beauséant.*"

"*Beauséant,*" Gamelyn repeated, soft.

- XXVIII -

"What you ask, my lord, is quite impossible."

"My liege, he begs if you will but see him, allow him the chance to explain—"

"I shall see him." Richard leaned back in his wide chair, curling his hands about the ends of the leather-clad armrests. "In London, with the rest of the traitors who held my castles in John's name. I will hear him then, in his own words and not yours, de Furnival. You are treading a very thin line, my lord. I would suggest you plead your own case rather than a misguided, if admirable, attempt to gain lenience for a foolish comrade. The man is no kin to you. If he were . . . We cannot choose our family. I know this well, as does Baron Pontefract—are you still here, my lord?"

"Indeed, my liege," Roger de Lacy answered, his expression suggesting Richard's shot had not gone wild.

"You see, my lord de Furnival? My lord de Lacy has also been forced to request clemency for similar . . . issues. But family is family, for good and ill. Most men are able to make wiser choices in their friends."

They were speaking of Otho, who was on his way to Winchester to meet sentencing, likely gaol or ransom. Otho, whose wife and children might wait a long time for his return.

All that remains is to deal with them, then, Guy said, but it was soft and readily silenced.

Standing towards the back of Nottingham's great hall, Gamelyn had waited his turn at petition for most of a long morning. Quite instructive, the wait. He was beginning to realise the "bargain" the

King had driven with him was indeed that. Particularly considering the amount of coin and taxes Richard was determined, yet again, to squeeze from the rest of his English landholders.

Robyn would be livid. Gamelyn himself wasn't all that happy—nor was he alone. None of the barons were foolish enough to exhibit any ill temper. Yet being forced to reinvest in lands they'd already put in hock to ransom the same King who now demanded not only soldiers for Normandy—or the scutage to replace them—but a new land tax as well?

No one was happy. No one had any choice but to accept it. The old danegeld had proven itself riddled with legal dispensations and loopholes, so a new method had been implemented—no doubt with Archbishop Walter's canny assistance.

"His Eminence the Archbishop could make tuppence shit a shilling," Gamelyn had heard a minor lord murmur, and not all that long ago. Order had been restored, and a firm hand set upon the rein. Nevertheless, the gathered nobles were . . . ruminative.

"No man should have to stand alone at court." A soft voice sounded at Gamelyn's elbow; turning, he was treated to a familiar, charming smile. Royal deal-making must have gone well enough for David, Earl of Huntingdon. "Even one who was a Templar."

"Thank you, my lord, for the courtesy. I will confess to feeling somewhat . . . naked at present." Gamelyn couldn't help a return smile, despite the reminder of another sacrifice: the right—and protection—of the Order's distinctive habit. In its place he'd a fine woollen tunic, breeks, and cloak suitable for a royal audience—as ill-gotten, of course, as the sword at his belt and the promissory silver he would no doubt turn over to the exchequer. Indeed, the Archbishop of Canterbury himself sat to the King's right and down, making precise notation of every promise, whilst beside him, a clerk made just as careful weight of every mark placed on the board.

More than a few gazes followed Huntingdon, curious and considering of the tall, copper-haired newcomer with whom the Earl was standing. Without the Templars, Gamelyn was recognisable only to a few.

Those few, however, were notable.

Marion, eyes shining and hair unbound like a maiden—and how apropos was that? She'd coif and kirtles fit for a woodland queen and stood, not as Eleanor's servant, but as a lady possessed of her own new status. Beside royalty, at that, for the lady Joanna had stood with her whilst she received the Keeper's post of Sherwood from the Queen's own hand.

The Queen herself, complacent that things were going to plan. And her son, with an expression upon his face that suggested puzzlement as he saw Gamelyn, present and in ordinary clothes, accepting the invitation that had been sent with the parchment agreement. King Richard no doubt wondered what deals had been made without his knowledge.

De Lacy, too, took careful note of Gamelyn's comportment and arrival, the gears turning all the while. He'd no doubt expected a Templar lackey to oversee Blyth, was instead encountering a fellow nobleman who might end up an equal.

And a small group of Templars. Amongst them, of course, were Wymarec and Hubert. The first looked as if he'd bitten into sour fruit; the second . . . dare Gamelyn think Hubert was pleased for him? He hoped so. The kiss Hubert had granted had been readily given, in tandem with the honourable release that burned, a parchment tight-rolled within the royal summons, both tucked into Gamelyn's tunic.

Mayhap 'twas pride that prompted the notion that Wymarec wasn't done, not yet. Mayhap he'd merely written off a turncloak officer.

Though Gamelyn didn't think so.

This newest champion was the most inexplicable, however. "The Templars' loss is the shire's gain, if I may say so. I hope you will find the exchange a fulfilling one." Said with the sincerity of inside information, Huntingdon nodded. "Just don't forget, lad, if you have need, feel free to call upon me. Family is, as the King said, family. And we could make good business with that as binding, you and I."

The smile was no less magnetic, but Gamelyn, conscious of all those eyes, merely nodded. "You do me honour, my lord."

Huntingdon peered at him for a moment. He seemed rather perplexed. "Family, indeed. You're very like your mother, young man. Her eyes oft expressed everything within her heart, then, just like that, they would say nothing." A nod. "You'll do well enough amongst us."

Us. Gamelyn started a reply. Instead, de Furnival silenced them both with a statement that made Gamelyn's nape hairs stand erect.

"If I may, lord King, bring up the unresolved matter of Tickhill?"

Eleanor, sitting in a cushioned chair to the King's left hand, also sat up with a lift of her veiled, crowned head.

"Ah," said Huntingdon. "Here we go."

Richard's look managed to combine boredom and warning both. "Pray, my lord, what of Tickhill is unresolved?"

De Furnival was as persistent a horse-trader as any nobleman born or bought. "The honour was granted as part of Hallamshire many years ago, my liege. My concern is for my wife's dowry, and my father's wish, to see his future grandsons well considered. He fought with you in the Holy Land, my lord King. I'd hopes that—"

"Hopes are for silly young men, my lord, so easily dashed," Eleanor ventured, leaning slightly forwards. "You are not silly, since your lord father trusts you to act in his illness despite your youth. You must mean you had *expectations.*"

"My Queen," de Furnival made hasty assurance, "we take nothing for granted. I merely bring the matter up, as is my right."

"It is that." Richard slid a fond, if chiding, look towards his mother, who shrugged and peered at her son in turn for a long moment before angling back in her chair, plying her fan. "However," Richard continued, "you and Pontefract once again have something in common. Why add to already sizeable holdings at such a time? You see how Our thoughts are for you, Our most noble lords, and why We have parcelled out many royal holdings to younger blood. It can only ease your carucage burden, no?"

De Furnival looked as if he'd bitten into a honeycomb only to find it still housed bees. "Of course, my liege. I understand."

"In fact, We might as well settle the matter of Tickhill ahead of time. You are not even the second man to mention the matter. My lord de Gisbourne, if you would approach Us?"

"Chin up, lad," Huntingdon murmured and, unfathomably, stayed several paces behind Gamelyn as he took a deep breath and strode forwards.

Again, such company was not unnoticed. Particularly by the King and his lady mother, the latter who smirked.

"A man who deserves respect, my lords, is one who gains the respect of powerful men. High"—Richard nodded at the Earl and sat back in his chair as Gamelyn halted before the dais and bowed—"and low. Eh, my lord de Gisbourne? You too have made unsavoury choices in *your* friends."

A mutter rippled across the hall; everyone knew exactly what—who—the King meant.

Gamelyn was merely glad of Robyn's absence. He didn't dare seek out Marion with so much as a glance.

"But We have returned to right all wrongs, no? We show favour to those who remained true, no matter how unfortunate their circumstance. Your friends, due to their loyalty, have received a royal pardon and commission in Our forests. Now"—Richard beckoned Gamelyn to rise and move closer to the dais—"We will treat fairly with you, in the open."

After seeding the deal in private, the inner predator felt the need to point out. Gamelyn wanted to smirk. Didn't.

"We should have bargained further with you, no? Considering how, eh, desirable this honour seems to be?" Richard's gaze strafed every man in the room as he, too, rose. "Yet some things even money cannot buy. Loyalty, for one.

"This man has served God; now, nobly discharged from his Templar Brethren, he has chosen to continue in his service of God's representative upon earth." His eyes flickered to Huntingdon, stayed. "Do you seek to stand as witness, my lord earl?"

"I do, my liege."

The soft acknowledgment runnelled a strange, precognitive shiver down Gamelyn's spine; nevertheless, he tucked his chin and met the King's expression, respect beneath a scrim of wary calm.

"Well enough. Are you willing to swear homage to Us, Sir Knight?" Richard held out his hands, spaced apart as if holding a ball that wasn't there.

Gamelyn took in a deep, silent breath, knelt, and placed his own hands, palm to palm, within the King's. He had rehearsed the words with some care; still they came out with a tremor about the edges. Never had he let himself believe he would utter them.

"I, Gamelyn, son of Ian Boundys, by royal mercy lord of Blyth and Tickhill, and the lady Marjory, noble lady of Huntingdon, so promise, upon my word and faith, even as I make homage with hands and mouth, that I shall henceforth be faithful in service to my lord the King of England and his successors. I shall observe my homage to him, in matters of life and limb and earthly honour, without deceit."

"And I, Richard, Duke of Normandy, Aquitaine, and Gascony, Count of Maine and Anjou, and by wrath of God, King of England, do promise to protect you and yours, to be a just and faithful lord. I commit to your loyalty, care, and lordship the honour of Tickhill with its castle, manors, and lands. I also concede to you, your heirs, and their successors, the rights to certain lands within the Peak and the eastern border of Wales as fee simple, and will receive both homage and fealty for those. Rise, Gamelyn Boundys de Blyth, Lord of Tickhill."

And with the kiss of peace, it was done.

"—Hope Valley and Hathersage moor, from the Stone Edge east to Peak's Arse to the northwest valley of Mam Tor, including the vills of Hope, Hathersage, and Edale . . . '" Marion left off midread to leap upon Gamelyn, hug him until his bones cracked, and kiss him just as soundly, not caring who in Nottingham's upper bailey saw.

It didn't matter, anyway. Not anymore. After a small and involuntary stiffen, Gamelyn realised it and snogged her back. Then let out a yell altogether close to her ear and swung her around, kirtles and one shoe flying.

That didn't matter, either. "He gave you *Mam Tor*," Marion insisted, and kissed his ear as he let her down.

"None else wanted it. Save de Birkin, and he'll have to find out from his brother or by listening to the clerk later, when the day's business is detailed."

Marion was glad he'd not been allowed in and said so as she retrieved her shoe.

Gamelyn nodded, made much of offering her his arm as more people exited the great hall. "Come with me. I want to find Robyn, tell him what his silver bought us. What *you've* bought us. Keeper of Sherwood, Marion . . . it's beyond any belief! All of it." He was smiling, a broad, unburdened expression she was sure she'd not seen since they were children together roaming Loxley Chase. And . . .

Us.

It brought a moist sting to Marion's eyes. She took his arm and laid her head against it. "I know. I can't believe it's actually—"

"Marion?"

She turned at the call, saw Joanna at the doorway of the hall, gesturing a bit wildly. The Queen herself emerged from the interior, blinking and raising a hand; the sun was that bright.

But she was that adamant, it seemed. Accompanied by Joanna—and two trailing *pucelles,* clearly unhappy to see That Outlaw Wench arm in arm with a handsome lord—Eleanor strode over to stand before them. The fan tapped against one shoulder as she crossed her arms. Expectant, that—as well as the gaze she levelled upon them both, a reminder that sent them both to kneeling.

"My Queen—?" Marion's query was hesitant; a sidelong glance to Gamelyn proved he was just as uncertain.

"We have not given you leave, girl." Eleanor's voice was stern. "Either to wander the bailey with a young man or to abandon your charge with Us."

It left her speechless for a half-breath; her try afterward wasn't much better. "My . . . my . . . Madam, I didn't know. I was . . . inconsiderate . . . "

"And no wonder." Still forged steel, Eleanor's voice, but there was what might have been a rime of humour slicking its edge. "Considering the day's events."

Marion dared a look up.

Eleanor's mien was stern. Yet beside her, Joanna—fair weather-vane to her mam's moods—had a smirk playing at her mouth.

"Get up, the pair of you," the Queen ordered with a tilt of her own lip. "Frankly, I'm pleased to witness a brace of fair and pleasant expressions after milking *that* lot of sour cows." Eleanor cast grey eyes back towards the hall, then down the bailey. "I've something for the both of you and . . . well, mayhap it's for the best he isn't present, but nevertheless, I would be grateful if you should carry something for me to the other edge to your unholy triumvirate."

"I assume, Madam, you mean Robyn?" Gamelyn asked as he rose and offered a hand to Marion, which she was glad to take.

The indigo bliaut was full-skirted and *heavy.*

"Indeed. No doubt he's lurking in the forest. Most politic of him, to make himself scarce. Considering." A grimace, tiny but unmistakable.

Marion dipped another bow, tiny but politic. "My brother is, occasionally, wise."

It was the right thing to say; Eleanor gave a snort. "Well, I wanted to thank him for saving my son from a poor decision. Again. Soon our King shall head south, away from any"—she shrugged—"temptation. I will, of course, accompany him, and I have my doubts as to whether he will return anytime soon." Her gaze, keen as any hawk's, swept over the sun-drenched bailey, then back to Marion's. "Mayhap it is better so. This land is a law unto itself, unkind to those who love it not. The both of you understand that, don't you? England is *in* your bones, and the darkness of the forest stirs the blood in your veins. Its mysteries speak to you, and to your Robyn Hood. I do not discount that." Eleanor paused, then nodded, as if to herself. "Give your brother this, if you would."

She extended a lined hand that held the peacock fan, her fingers dandling a jewelled ring. Marion dipped a curtsey and took the latter, only to find the former, also, placed in her outstretched palm. By accident, she was sure; but when she attempted to hand the fan back, Eleanor shook her head.

"A prop to help display your new status. There is a fair stipend associated with the Keeper's duties, of course, but I hear"—the Queen leaned in, conspiratorial—"that there have been outlaws of late in Sherwood. So may all those cerulean eyes help you in watching over your demesne, Lady Marion."

Lady Marion. It was both thrill and chill.

"Not to mention, I have eyes of my own. The peacock has long been sacred to the feminine, no? The mother of Christ would surely approve."

And there was nothing for Marion to do but vane the gorgeous, expensive fan and press it flat against her breast. "Thank you, my Queen."

"And so I release you to your new duties. Mayhap some chance magic shall bring us together again someday." Eleanor started to turn away, hesitated. "My lord, before we part . . . a word of personal advice, if I may?"

"Of course, my Queen."

"You would do well to cultivate this woman at your side. Trust me, she was born to manage an estate." Eleanor slid her gaze from Marion to hold Gamelyn's. She smiled. "And you're no longer a Templar, are you?"

"Proper bollocks!" Marion was blushing as the Queen walked away. *Blushing.* "Did she truly just give you permission to marry me?"

Gamelyn thought of Much, unable to attend the council but

no doubt waiting at the outer gates, and smiled. "To anyone of your choosing, aye."

"I don't think that's what she meant."

Now it was his turn to flush.

She smirked, threaded her arm through his. "Twill take some getting used to, these nobleman's—and I do mean *man's*—ways."

He shrugged, glad for the breeze upon his cheeks. "She's been making the assumption all along. Marriages have been made for lesser reasons, you know." It was soft. "And with less fondness between the consenting parties."

"I've no wish to marry anyone." Settling Robyn's gift onto one finger for safekeeping, Marion slid a sideways glance, nudged him. "And you're Lord of Blyth and Tickhill, now. Quite the catch, aye? You can wed anyone you fancy."

"Nay, I'm afraid I can't." Still soft, bitterness tinged the statement.

Marion's face fell. "I'm sorry. I didn't mean . . ."

He pulled her closer as they navigated around a small gathering of people, also enjoying the sun. The bailey was not overly busy; guards, of course, and horsemen coming back and forth with messages that never stopped, but most of the residents were focusing on a meal unencumbered by fasting before the bells of evening Mass.

"Let's go find our men, eh? Leave behind sorrow, on such an auspicious day and with what we've accomplished." He found himself believing it for the first time. No past or futures lurking, no culpability of living, only . . . *thisnow.*

So how apropos that his first action should be to set Marion's face alight once more. "Either way, the Queen is right about one thing: there's none I'd rather have managing our home."

"Our home!" She smiled again, the spring returning to her step. "Truly?"

"Truly. Why else should we have endured this, but for a home where we can choose our fate? The Queen just put that choice in our hands."

"*Your* hands, O man," Marion corrected, wry.

"This from the Keeper of Sherwood."

She laughed. "I am, aren't I? With a feather fan"—she waved it—"fit for a queen! Wait until we give this lovely ring to Robyn, and then tell him *I'm* ower even a Royal Forester!" Midstep she turned to face him, skipping sideways. "Tis a new world for all of . . ." She stopped, her face pale and voice wavering silent.

"Marion?"

"You'd best turn around."

Gamelyn heard it, then: more hoofbeats. He turned, saw two horses approaching, across the bailey side by side, and at a slow canter. They carried two Templars, one in white and one in brown.

Aye, and any foolish hopes he'd had of escaping into insignificance had obviously been just that. They hadn't even reached the burnt outer gate yet. It was too late to run, anyway. Even had he wanted to.

Instead Gamelyn met the Master Preceptor of England and his paxman, hand on sword hilt and voice carrying. "My lord. Did you have horses waiting at the entry to the great hall, just to chase me down?"

He wasn't sure what was better, the satisfaction of snapping the words, or the look on Wymarec's face.

The latter's recovery came annoyingly swift. "Your pride will be the death of you. Just as avarice and lust"—this as Wymarec shot a look of pure loathing over Gamelyn's shoulder, towards Marion—"have clouded any sense of judgement you might possess!" He swung down from the horse, tossing the rein to his man, and came on, meeting Gamelyn halfway. "You have even swayed Hubert with this . . . madness. It is madness, nothing but."

"No doubt my brother Otho would agree. Mayhap, my lord Preceptor, we're all mad."

"You cannot do this!"

"It would seem," Gamelyn pointed out, "I already have. It is my right, my lord, to seek—"

"You seek some foolish dream!" Wymarec shook his head. "You will not escape your fate, not this way. Neither will the *dryw*."

"You don't know Robyn's path. You never have. You wanted control over his power, over Marion's, over mine. You will no longer have it."

"Are you so sure, Sir Guy?"

"My name"—he couldn't help the way it grated, between his teeth like a snarl—"is *Gamelyn*."

"Your name is Fool!" Wymarec snapped back. "I see before me a boy, once Hubert's sharpest-edged weapon, shorn from the canny intelligence that would make of him something more!"

"More than your acolyte, you mean?"

"Oh, my dear." It was a laugh, soft but still harsh. "You never managed to *be* my acolyte. Just as merely rutting Pagans will never make you one of them."

"He *is* one of us." This from Marion, who had come up behind him, radiating fury like a badger with a den of kits.

"You'll have less than nothing, you stupid woman. He knows it. Your precious brother knows it!" The pale eyes flicked dismissal of her.

She just as plainly refused to be dismissed. "There are other ways to wield the magic—and those as *you'll* never know, or have."

"How unappetising," Wymarec said to Gamelyn. "You hide behind a woman's skirts yet cannot bridle her foul mouth?"

Gamelyn lurched forwards before he thought. Only Marion's

hard hand upon his arm—and the look upon Wymarec's face, suggesting he welcomed the possibility—halted him.

"Neither have you leashed that killer, have you? Well, amongst a lot of ignorant and brute beasts, it might serve you well, at that. But I thought better of you, boy, than you would break your oaths to bed some peasant *whore*."

Again, Gamelyn couldn't help angling towards him.

Marion was quicker.. A lunge, and swing, and her punch landed square across Wymarec's jaw.

He staggered back. The squire stepped in, set on doing damage to the woman who'd dare lay a hand upon his Master.

Gamelyn got in between, shoved Marion behind him, and glared at the squire. He knew the young man—and the young man, moreover, knew him. The charge petered into a halt, with an uncertain glance towards Wymarec.

Who was staring, furious, at the blood-spotted glove he'd dabbed against his cheek. The Queen's ring had cut him. "I could have you *whipped,* you bitch!"

"Nay," Gamelyn said, very soft. "I don't think so."

Several soldiers had turned to watch from the ruined outer gate. Several passersby had slowed, sensing drama.

Wymarec turned on them, growled, "What do you want?"

They found other things to do, rather quickly at that. The soldiers turned away.

Wymarec waved the squire back and advanced closer.

Gamelyn tensed, ready for anything.

Except, mayhap, what was said. "I know what you are." It was a hiss. "What that wilding boy is. All that power, yet still useless. To you, to anyone. Do you really think he will be able to loose your magic? And if he miraculously succeeds, mightn't that bring about what you so fear?"

Again, Marion gripped Gamelyn's arm. "Don't listen to him."

"Does the wolf-bitch fear the truth? Have you shared with her your blood-spattered and treacherous nightmares? Or have you somehow learnt the secrets I would have taught you, found the keys to break the Barrows and deny their hold upon the land, still lingering, still demanding their unholy teind?"

"He's talking rubbish." Marion's fingers dug into Gamelyn's arm. "Come away. It's done."

Still, charmed by the cobra, he listened.

"Blood calls for blood. The sacrifice is inevitable. You *know* this. The fight, the defeat, a King's blood upon the ground . . . The waste of it, boy. The *waste!*"

The words played out before Gamelyn, a visual that even closing his eyes would not terminate. "It will not happen." Wooden. "I will not let it."

"Let? As if you have a choice?" Wymarec laughed, low and

contemptuous and—somehow—so intimate. "You are indeed a Fool, and you've listened to a leman's folly! Even the *dryw ardhu* cannot deny his fate! You are the Oak 'gainst his Holly! The fanciful tree of which the Queen's trouvère so tenderly sang cannot thrive here, upon England's damp soil! This conflict, it is what you are meant to do, were born to do, within this little Dance in which we've found ourselves!"

Gamelyn froze, eyes wide upon Wymarec, the words shivering down his spine with icy fingers. Or was it Marion's hands upon him, trying to pull him away? Her murmurs to *leave it, leave it, coom away. . .*

But Gamelyn couldn't move. He'd never heard Wymarec say the words aloud. Only felt them, lingering on the edges of dreams.

"Leave the Temple now, but you will come back. I have Seen it. You will have no choice!" Spat, as if venomous. "The druid and his witch sister will never free you, only corrupt you. You will suffer, and you will return, with the forest's secrets, to wield the staff of Solomon at my side!"

Marion spat her own words, soft and full of the magic, as if lifting a curse, and yanked hard enough to dislodge Gamelyn, shake and shudder away the cobra's spell.

But he refused to retreat, or turn his back upon his enemy.

No longer Master, but enemy.

Wymarec bowed, mocking, then deliberately turned, mounted the horse the squire brought, and rode away without a backwards glance.

"Arrogant git," Marion murmured, one hand rubbing a firm circle upon Gamelyn's back. "It doesn't matter. It's done. You have us."

"I do." It was a growl. "Finally, I do."

Marion didn't chide him. She merely laid her head against his back, curled her arms about his ribs. And instead of flinching away—a mindless response drilled with rod and privation—Gamelyn found himself leaning in, grateful, allowing the comfort.

"Come on, pet," said Marion, muffled against his tunic. "Let's away from this place. Let's go home."

- Entr'acte -

"We have a problem, my lord. A crisis of faith, one might say. And so We have called you here, in the strictest of confidences, to address it."

The King was seated, with only Archbishop Walter at his side and Mercadier at his flank. No servants, with the only guards on the other side of the thick chamber door, through which Wymarec had been allowed to pass. Alone.

The King had apologised for that already. Still, the concession made Wymarec's teeth clench.

Only momentarily, as it shot agony along the left side of his jaw. That damned whore of a wolf-bitch had more powerful a right cross than any woman by rights should possess. Bloody *peasant.*

"I will speak plainly. When I told the Archbishop of my dilemma," Richard continued, "he agreed with my decision to come to the Templars. Walter is, after all, more attuned to matters of state than those of a more, eh, spiritual nature? Not a bad thing, considering my family's history with Canterbury."

Walter shrugged, while the King gave a charming smile.

As jokes of questionable taste about Thomas Becket went, mayhap it wasn't bad. Wymarec dipped his head in tacit acknowledgment of his liege's cleverness, wondering what in bloody hell Richard wanted.

"All those rumours, you see." The King leaned forwards. "Even as Moses and Solomon gave their holy art and alchemy to God, so, I've no doubts, have the Templars. De Sablé hinted at such."

Which was why de Sablé had never been allowed to do more than guess and hint. Well, that, and he'd been woefully less than talented. It was, lamentably, not the first time a politician had been elected instead of a true Grand Master.

"And if so? If I am correct and the Templars have ways mystical in the sight of God? They are, of course, much more powerful than any lad possessed of some English demon."

"My lord, are you asking me if I can rid you of this . . . lad? And his demon?"

Walter leaned closer, murmured something. Then Richard snapped something at Mercadier—some soldier's gutter patois, it must be, for Wymarec understood little of it. The mercenary answered, somewhat reluctantly.

"We hunted with the young man, as you know," Richard admitted. "We admire his skill. But he is insolent. He used Our admiration to humiliate Us." He sprang up from his chair, began to pace in front of it. "We also believe that, indeed, he beguiled Us with craven art. My trouvère denies it, and while I believe he has no reason to lie—"

Mercadier murmured something; Richard shook his head angrily.

"Blondel . . . he is entirely too susceptible to such things. The artistic temperament, you understand. I believe him bewitched as well. You heard what he played, in my hearing and my hall! Such acknowledgement, and for no more than a hedge-born *boy!*"

Aye, Wymarec had. Quite a bit of leverage, that ditty was proving, despite that Richard had misinterpreted the intent.

"One of my servants was with me." The pacing was increasing, commensurate with kingly ire. "He says the archer used foul magic against me. Yet the lad remembers little after the archer turned on me, so likely he was ensorcelled as well."

So, Wymarec pondered, *you tried to rut the druid, and he refused you. I'll wager good marks he left you paralyzed on the ground much as he did me.* His hand went to his neck, fingers brushing the scar there. He did not snarl, though he wanted to; instead, he let a smile twitch his lip.

He was about to receive the entirety of the forest cult on a royal platter. This was going to be beyond satisfying.

"The devil took Jerusalem," Richard stated. "But he won't take this island. That is why I have called for you. We need God's holy power to . . . " He frowned.

"Contain them," Wymarec supplied, soft. "Make them ours."

"Indeed!" Richard slapped his hands together. "I see we have an understanding, my lord Preceptor. I cannot afford to have the archer or his men killed or injured. Do you see my dilemma? Contained. Yes!"

"And the woman?" As Richard frowned, Wymarec explained, "The wolfshead's whore."

"Is she?" The frown deepened. "I thought this Gamelyn Boundys was smitten with her. Not that it matters. I thought Templars were above thinking such things, Master Preceptor." A rebuke. "And please, you must understand this—the archer is no longer wolfshead, but one of Our foresters. I pardoned him. I pardoned them, one and all, including the girl. Whatever you have against her"—the ash-blue eyes flickered across Wymarec's colourful jaw, as if the King knew from whence it had come—"she belongs to the Queen. Her own little project, if you will, and believe this, my lord, but your ire is nothing compared to Our lady Mother's. You will not touch the girl."

"Yes, my lord." Wymarec chastised himself for Pride with a bit of spite, focused upon the longer goal. "What, then, of my Templar, my lord?"

"If you mean my lord of Tickhill, he is, by his own choice and my allotment of seisin, no longer *your Templar.*"

Wymarec inhaled, slow, and broached, just as grave, "Even, my liege, if I believe he, too, is bewitched by the powers of this wolfs . . . archer?"

Again, the mercenary muttered; this time Richard nodded. "From what Mercadier tells me, the man who was your *Confanonier* was there, afterward. I'd asked him to translate my wishes before all of this. It wouldn't surprise me. I've no doubts that, despite the girl, Boundys and the archer have . . . known each other."

A grimace of distaste flitted across the Archbishop's face, just as swiftly smoothed away. Wise, when one's liege lord fancied boys as much as girls . . . likely more, considering.

"Contained. Yes. We want them contained, and their foul art under your Order's control, my lord Templar. Are we decided?"

"Yes, lord King," Wymarec dipped his head, heartbeat singing in his ears. "We are, indeed, decided."

-XXIX-

Mam Tor rose beneath them, aflame.

The moors were alive, with slats of sun falling molten, rippling ripened fawn and burgeoning celadon like breaths snatched upon breezes. The trees did likewise homage, a swaying half ring of dark green dressing the foot of the great hill.

Impervious to the short-term effects of any wind were the gilt-licked stones upon a flat promontory of Mam Tor's nor'west face. Most were broken, but some had been lifted erect; one in particular was centred amidst them, sprayed scarlet by the dying sunlight. And upon the air, heat-glimmers trailed from those stones, curving upon the lengthening shadows, stretching as if to meet an upward-flowing, irregular chain of flickering torches. Light from all quarters, breasting upward to the ridge.

And atop the ridge . . .

The largest of the need-fires had been kindled there, with wood stacked that morn wide as one could leap, supported by broad, flat stones hallowed and old when the Romans had broached the Tor. People were gathering, their number small as of yet, but talking and laughing as if on holiday.

Gamelyn trod upward, but didn't approach them, instead turning on a path to wind his way towards another, smaller blaze.

As surround upon every compass point, lesser fires had been

set. This one burnt near the southmost cliff edge, its flames still new, hungry. Reaching and darting, they leapt high as the man standing beside it—and he was tall, this man. Just that much too close to the blaze—and the cliff— he'd a mane of thick ebon curls tossing and fetching in the heat-shimmered breeze.

Robyn's arms were corded, brought up with wrists dangling from the bow propped 'crost his broad shoulders, and tanned with a fortnight's worth of lovely, sunny days, contrasting the paler sinews and muscle of his bare torso. There was a stark defiance to him, leaning into the wind, as if he'd just as soon clothe himself in a hawk's form and fly off the cliff.

Another Beltane, spreading from Tor to the river valley a horse's gallop east. A night where light and love dies, where songs become screams to hang in fire-glow treetops. . .

Gamelyn closed his eyes, clenched his teeth, and raised one hand to touch the worn amulet hanging about his neck. Thought of John's hands fashioning it, last autumn, to remembrance. Thought of what they had now, in the raw beginnings of protection and promise. A base of operations, his commanders would have called it.

Counted to three, slowly.

It is no time for fear, thisnight, the Lady chided. *Remember what you were, but more think upon what you are. What you have made, will make this night. What you can and will be, all of you together. Let it go, My Oak.*

Her voice was, like Robyn to the fire, just that much too close. Powerful enough to make Gamelyn take a false step on shale and slip sideways.

Robyn turned, frowning. "Have a care, now."

And just like that, She was gone. Gamelyn gave his head a tiny shake and moved closer to Robyn. There were only the two of them here; with that came relief. There'd been little enough chance for solitude this past moon. Preparing Blyth for its new lord and his retinue of former outcasts, preparing for this moment, all moving towards something more. Something Gamelyn really wanted to parse—but couldn't.

The remainder of the outlaws had scattered over the Tor, tending to various necessities—only nay, they were outlaws no longer, but respectable foresters and cotholders. Marion was nigh to the central needfire, overseeing the hospitality even though there was no need—she swas attended by a female cortege any queen would envy.

He and Robyn were alone, and of late that was its own form of Eden. Gamelyn took a page from the Book of Robyn, and seized the moment. "It's not that sheer a drop," Gamelyn ventured, light.

"Not along here, leastways." Robyn was still peering at him, steady. It left Gamelyn wondering, for at least the hundredth time, exactly what Robyn kenned—or Heard. "Lessen our lovely Mam decides to shudder us poor wee fleas from her pate. And did She . . . well, to die after seeing all this?"

Gamelyn followed Robyn's gesture out over the vast expanse of peaks and valleys unfolding before them, a cloak of fire and shadow. In the folds of that cloak, tiny specks of illumination spun upward. Lanterns and torches, held by tens of people gathering upon the old paths, all drawn to ancient, sacred fire.

Standing beside one such flame, Gamelyn knew why. He reached for Robyn, uncaring if his fingers burnt to bone.

"Words are . . . inadequate." *For too many things,* he added, asking and silent, pressing his palm against the warmth of Robyn's back.

"Mm. Me little John tells me that's why *his* words come so spare. Not just the stutter of a wee lad, but wandering ower these moors wit' nowt for company but great sky and heather and sage. I'd more say it gave rise to that lovely great heart of his. No words; he just *knows.*"

Gamelyn felt his own heart tug sideways. That, too, needed no words. Better—much better—to bask in the flames dancing beside them and the need-fire kindling behind Robyn's eyes.

"Even as"—those eyes turned to Gamelyn, golden flickers burning in the black—"your heart kens what *you* must do, thisnow."

"Robyn!" It was Gilbert, coming up the path from the west-nestled circle of stones. Seeing Gamelyn there as well, he flashed a quick smile.

"The hobby lanterns are all shielded, and John's laid the horns and the skulls from the old oak upon the altar stone. There's none yet come up that trail, just as you said."

"Aye, well, memories die hard."

Death, not life, shrouding the last Beltane held in this place. A lean, lone silhouette held at bay several miles east, loosing arrow after defiant and deadly arrow as a forest burns around him.

Another tug, another memory to loose into the wind. *"Start over,"* Robyn had said. *"'Tis past time."*

"Only t' good," Robyn continued. "John's still there?"

"Nay, he's having a wander. I'm for the cook fires. I'm surprised you aren't already there, slavering." Gilbert gave an appreciative snuff into the air, then grinned. "David's outdone himself with the venison. Despite the gaggle of old women hovering, all doubting a man can cook anything."

"I'll have mine soon enough." There was a tiny thread of . . . something beneath Robyn's voice, sombre-soft and almost undetectable beneath the cracklings of the bonfire.

Gilbert might affect to flippant, but the pause of his step and the small dent marring his brow told otherwise: he'd heard. "Anything else?"

"Nay, nobbut staying alert for the while. I doubt any'll dare try us, but—"

"It's been done," Gilbert agreed, with a sly grin Gamelyn's direction.

"Aye, and if a proper clever terror like Gisbourne could sneak in . . . " It was Robyn's turn to nudge at Gamelyn.

Gamelyn rolled his eyes, refusing the bait. Still grinning, Gilbert walked on by and down the eastern back slope, towards the cook fires. Voices were beginning to rise into the sky. Eagerness and hunger were conquering wariness of a hallowed—and oft-forbidden—place.

"Aye, well, then." The grave hue had left Robyn's quiet baritone, yet there were others, deeper still. "First t' play, then t' purpose. Hungry?"

Gamelyn shook his head, eyes roving over the countryside. Staying alert, to be sure. A small movement caught his eye to the west: Much, signalling the all clear.

"Have 'im be done."

And, between them, like thunder roiling back and between the hills: *We shall know, My Own, if the rites are despoiled.*

Again, just that much too close, and Gamelyn suppressed a shiver. *You didn't know then.*

And strangely, he knew the answer before it came, purling through his brain: *All of you slumbered, then. The magic lay waiting, to be waked with Sacrifice.*

Another shiver; Gamelyn shrugged it off with a signal for Much. *Two more rounds, then come in.*

Robyn leaned back against him. "You're proper quiet 'bout now."

"Not sure I've owt to say 'bout now." The mimicry was deliberate, light.

An unfathomable smile quirked Robyn's angular face as the black eyes slid to Gamelyn's own. Gauging. Unfooled. And just like that, within Gamelyn tens of insecure, gibbering idiots demanded voice. Things like *I don't know if I can do this* and *They're waiting, can't you see, waiting like wolves for me to slip up,* and *It's the last, finite step down a path we can no longer backtrack; I can't trust it* and, immediately after, *Why do you trust me so?*

Thank God the stranglehold upon his voice held.

Abruptly a hard hand curled at Gamelyn's nape. Robyn twisted, pulled in. The kiss was so unspeakably gentle, a chaste touch upon the forehead that brought an inexplicable and sudden sting of tears to Gamelyn's eyes.

"Buck up, pet," Robyn whispered, then, mercurial as ever, snatched the tie from Gamelyn's hair.

A sudden breeze tossed a spray of coppery forelock across Gamelyn's face, obscuring his vision for the moment it took for Robyn to sidle away. Pulling stray, persistent strands from mouth and beard, Gamelyn followed. With intent.

Telling him to *buck up,* indeed. Arsy peasant.

And the Horned Lord was chuckling.

But Robyn's smile had faded, his eyes keen to the south as he stepped towards the peak's edge—already onto fresh game. "Tell me again he can see us."

"The entire bloody *hundred* can see us, Hob-Robyn."

"Aye, but I'm wanting to hear of *that* sweet tower." Weaving Gamelyn's hair tie haphazardly through his fingers, Robyn leaned on his longbow, eyes fixed upon the stone redoubt across the valley. It was massive, etched all red from the waning sun, but nonetheless dwarfed by the rise of stone and earth beneath their feet.

"Oh, he sees us all right." Gamelyn raised a hand to Robyn's shoulder. "Brian de Lisle, once High Sheriff of Nottingham, York, and Derby, now has nothing remaining but his brother's favour and a king's inexplicable mercy."

"Nowt inexplicable there." Robyn snorted. "'Tis money."

"Well, Peveril Castle is all that's left to him. And he knows"— Gamelyn's fingers tangled in black—"who started his downfall."

"Count John?"

A tug, warning. It was not gentle, and Robyn gave a purr deep in his throat that set every nerve in Gamelyn's body to quivering attention.

"'Tis ours, tonight." Another purr, soft and dangerous as Robyn leaned against him, hard. "With none daring t' say us nay. *You* are lord of this place, and a Crone has set it so."

"The Queen," Gamelyn murmured, looking out over the sunset-spattered hills, all orange and deep magenta. *His lands. . .* Robyn was right.

"And thus"—a gesture out over those lands—"we claim our places back, light fires into the night, and dance the light back, make oath. Wander where we choose." Black eyes slid Gamelyn's way, and there was no doubt Robyn's smile could light the pyre, crackling hot beside them. "*Ours.*"

Yet such surety made resolve shudder cold, whimper, and scut from the light with tail tucked. Another whorl of wind tossed a blast of heat to nigh singe Gamelyn's cheeks; he tilted his face, welcomed it.

Said, wry, "You seem quite certain."

"Aye, well, if you'd stop thinkin' so damned much—"

"Someone in this bloody band needs to use what brains they were given."

"You're starting to sound like Sweet William." A smirk. "You scared, O mighty Templar?"

"Only a fool wouldn't be. Make no mistake, Hob-Robyn—we're backing a lion."

Robyn laughed, then, and hefted his bow. "Aye, well, that we've done already!" He took mocking aim for Peveril's stone tower, and let an imaginary arrow fly.

"And so Winter fell to sleep, deep in the embrace of Summer's coming, whilst from the Oak sprang new green and fat fruit, 'til in His turn He'd seek the laird sleepin' in the snow, untwine mistletoe from His tines, and kiss Him awake to greet the Lady in His turn."

The soft, homely voice trailed off into silence. Approving murmurs wafted on the breeze. The meal was well started, so all that remained about the cooking fires were a few boys turning the roasts, and several elders—with David overseeing—to give the occasional taste and stir.

The fires blazing bright, and most of their people gathered, the storytelling was in full swing.

Gunnora had the honour at present. She also had pride of place, not only as elder and headwoman of Hathersage, but across from a hallowed stone. It had been Gunnora who'd led Marion to sit upon the Maiden stone, hair unbound and garbed in the green of new leaves, with flowers strewn about her bare feet.

Another close-held companion sat to Marion's left hand: Aelwyn had been chosen Mother, and perfect for it, too, with Tibba at her skirts and little Tom wrapped against her breast. An unbroken curve from Maiden to Gunnora's Crone, Aelwyn's fingers nimbly plaited a crown of willow withies and ivy. Occasionally she'd reach out and pluck a flower from the scattered ones; more often Tibba insisted on lending a podgy wee hand.

Marion had spent the last fortnight and a half coming to grips with the unfamiliar territory of castle management, and she was still unsure she'd any grasp of it. But this? To be seated in the place her mother had, years ago, graced, to know she was setting into motion a revival of, not just the mummer's plays and japes acted into being, but powers possessing thisworld . . . ? It was a true and final homecoming, and one within which she felt capable. Only a few years ago—and Sweet Lady, but it seemed the longer—had she sat nigh to this stone and lessoned her reluctant little brother upon the many faces of love. Now that brother seemed much more her elder as he sauntered through the crowd, comforted and comfortable in his affections.

One of those trailed him. Gamelyn resembled more a man chary of a beating than a new-honoured lord who might have yet another tribute paid this night.

He is Our champion, the Lady said, satisfied, *though he scarce realises it yet.*

Gamelyn bent an elegant knee to the Maiden's stone.

Robyn merely collapsed sideways at his sister's feet and leaned his head against her skirts. "I'm famished! Is the supper ready yet? Can't a man have a bite? The dark comes upon us, and the dance."

Murmurs and whispers were darting around the gathering. They revered their Lady's avatar as the promise of good things, but that same love tweaked sideways towards the presence of the Horned Lord. All of them, over half fearful of His quicksilver nature: mild, now, but heedless as a summer storm were he riled.

Marion smirked. They'd obviously not marked the distinct whiny edge to her brother's voice.

Gunnora had, though. "Aye, we'd best feed our'n." With a low grunt, she rose to her feet. "Now, now," she chided as several children, too young and set upon Story to let even Robyn Hode sway them, set up a chorus of *awws* and *pleases*. "En't you lot hungry? I am, and 'tis sure bold Robyn is. Plenty time left for more stories after we've eaten." She winked at Marion and ambled towards the cookpots with a gaggle of children in tow.

Except for one little girl, standing before Robyn and Marion all agog. Marion's smile broadened and she started a reassurance.

The child, however, kept staring.

"Yeh!" she stammered. "I . . . uh . . . I know y . . . uh, yer purty hair an' freckles all ower . . . I *know yeh!*"

Freckles?

Not Robyn—anyroad, he'd the same apprehensive look as always when confronted with anything below the age of six. And not Marion herself, though aye, she'd freckles enough to be going on with. The child's gaze passed her by, tracking the one who rose from one knee and, until just now, had busied himself with replaiting the russet hair from his face. The cool diffidence that made up Gamelyn's typical expression in social constraints was nowhere to be found. His eyes sprang wide, his mouth fallen open.

With a speed seen only in the poorest of peasantry—primed to leap from harm's way at a twitch of a lord's eyebrow—the little girl sprang forwards. She nearly ploughed full-on into Robyn; equally swift, he squirmed out of reach. But then, she wasn't after Robyn.

An assortment of gasps and a scandalised feminine cry accompanied the child's leap. Gamelyn coiled like a spring ready to snap, at the very last instant forcibly stilling what surely was an instinctive reach for some sort of weaponry.

And the little girl smacked against him, climbed him like a favourite tree, wrapped skinny, bare arms and legs about him, and clung. "*Guy!*"

Reedy, and at the top of her lungs, the cry. Clearly delighted.

On the other hand, the surrounding folk had stilled.

"Oh, bloody hell." Much's voice, echoed, low, from the edge of sudden silence.

Gamelyn merely looked into the child's upturned, eager face. A sardonic quiver twitched his lip. "Hullo, Lizzie."

If he lived as long as Cernun had, Robyn would never ken how some notorious Templar assassin, with untold kills to his credit and scant patience for anything construed as weakness, was so bloody deedy with bairns. It just wasn't on.

Gamelyn, with Lizzie on his hip clinging adamant as mistletoe vine, stood by the fire chatting up Lizzie's mother. The woman's hands were wringing at her skirts.

Many hadn't noticed, after their own pursuits. But those who had heard the child's greeting—and what with the ginger hair and the rod-up-arse manner, and the poncy way of speaking—even the simplest of those paying heed would likely figure it. Were figuring it, with whispers and wary circuits about the scene. The moment wasn't over, yet.

This had been the one trick Robyn had been leery of the ways of turning. Not so bad to have a noble, disguised or no, attending the fête of Beltane—it had happened, after all, in Cernun's time and before. But what if someone recognised Guy of Gisbourne?

"Any so gentle with a maid-child?" Gunnora had come up next to Robyn. "Well, it bespeaks a gentle heart. 'Tis a good thing, what he's doin'." She paused. Sworn to the covenant by blood and ash, she'd had as personal an encounter with Gisbourne as little Lizzie. "Aye, well. I warrant his like's clever enow to knows 't, aye?"

Robyn smirked. While Gamelyn was comfortable with the child clinging to his hip—plainly so, in a way Robyn just as plainly couldn't be—there was no doubt Gunnora had pegged it.

"And herself's nowt but that clever," Gunnora furthered, with a tilt of her head to the green-clad woman who'd made her own move. Shadowing Gamelyn with one arm snugged in his all close, cinnabar hair wreathed with the withy-and-flower crown, Marion's presence lit another flame to ward any chill.

"I'd be nobbut an arsy archer without the clever ones, Gunna." Robyn shot a glint of grin sideways.

Gunnora returned it, nudging him with one work-broadened shoulder. "I knows yer type, Hob-Robyn, and yer cunning—play ass all you like."

He grinned and flung an arm about her, laying his head against hers. Both of them stood, watching Marion work the crowd whilst Gamelyn . . .

Bugger-all, but he was letting the girl-child feed him bites of bread!

"I know you love him. Our little John loves him. It's only . . . well." A shrug, then Gunnora continued, soft and formal, "Tha knows t' right of things, Hooded One."

Again the heat of the god, silent and waiting—*watching*—deep behind his eyes. Across the gathering, Gamelyn gave a tiny shudder and shake of head. It wasn't the first time.

Brother. Robyn combed the strands of thought and will smooth between them, set *tynged* quivering into the black. Asked again, *Wilt tha take tha's crown?*

"But he'll have more to prove," Gunnora continued. "Make 'is way, aye?"

Robyn didn't answer; didn't feel the need. It was part of why they were here.

"Does one as him even know what's to come?" Gunnora asked, insistent.

"Why should he?" Robyn's voice was not quite his own, and Gunnora heard it. Moreover, from her slight tremor, heard Him. "Do any of us?"

One could drown in stars, here.

Laughter, song, and the not-unpleasant discord of overenthusiastic pipes and drums had chased the sun into the western horizon, blood trails fading to indigo even as Gamelyn watched. Music skirled around the fire, unrepentant, and lifted up into a sky that was filling itself with starlight.

"What're seein?" Lizzie asked, with a tug to the hand she persisted on holding.

Gamelyn merely caught her eye, then looked up.

Brows bunching, Lizzie followed his prompt. Scepticism turned into wide-eyed awe, and the child fell into silent rapture, her hand going lax in his.

Which was a blessing, true enough. Gamelyn had begun to wonder if he'd see the morn still possessed of fingers.

And wondered why he let her. Mayhap it was the mead, free flowing since the sun had touched the far hills. He'd had more than a few despite trailing behind most of the others capering merry about the fires. Aye, it would have been altogether easy to growl the grubby little girl into retreat or scowl her silent. After all, he'd once threatened to toss her down a well, hadn't he? Lizzie's mother still remembered that fact, had been hovering, hands wringing her skirts, since Marion had left Gamelyn's side to join the women's dance . . .

Marion was a lovely dancer, and Gamelyn's absorption with that fact was no longer surreptitious, or undeniable. The restrained and humble maidservant allowed by sufferance to join the carol at Nottingham was, amongst her Heathen women, a landed queen. Nay, a wylding Wodewose *quean*, every bit and more. Barefoot and bare-legged, skirts tucked into her belt and a flower- and withy-crowned mass of cinnabar curls falling unbound down her back, her pale arms described sinuous shapes against the bonfire's light, her body twirling and leaping graceful as a roe deer in the dusk.

More, she knew he was watching. Her gaze kept meeting his,

mouth tilting in that curious, clever smile as she clasped hands with another woman and whirled on. There was, all about Gamelyn, the smell of roses: briar from the woodland edge, or blossoms fresh with desert rain.

Come. Dance with Us. It was a nip and tug at his spirit. *Why do you linger on the outside, Oakbrother?*

It's where I belong. This is. . . theirs. Their triumph. Their people. And yours.

Ours, the Horned Lord said, but it was Robyn's voice Gamelyn heard. Robyn, who hadn't yet danced but lurked about the edges of the firelight, nigh a spirit himself. Robyn, leaping through the central bonfire after they'd first kindled it with wood and bone. Robyn, standing upon the edge of Mam Tor, taking aim at Peveril Castle hunching in the distance, flickering with insistent torchlight that couldn't begin to challenge the bonfires of Mam Tor.

Not here.

If not here, where?

Long, strong fingers slid around his waist. A lean figure juddering him, nape to knees, and a soft, insistent breath against his ear. "Dance with me."

Robyn Hood had snuck up, after all, on Guy of Gisbourne.

My name—an interior growl—*is Gamelyn.*

"Dance with me," Robyn purred, with a nip and dart of tongue to the cords of Gamelyn's neck, arms tightening fierce. "Now."

"Watch the stars for me," Gamelyn told Lizzie, somewhat breathless. When she thought to protest, he bent down. "They dance, you know."

A frown, and a finger in her mouth. She saw Robyn then, a slender dark ghost behind, and her eyes widened. Her grip went lax.

Seizing the opportunity, Gamelyn untangled his fingers from hers. Robyn was chuckling against his shoulder, soft and bloody merciless.

"They do?" No question but Lizzie was a persistent little thing. "You promise?"

"If you watch long enough," Gamelyn answered as Robyn began to tug him away. "I promise."

A roar resounded across the Tor, thunderous as any battle cry from tens of throats, as a fair-haired, half-naked giant leapt through the flames and landed with a showering of sparks and a twirl of the oak staff that had propelled him nearly to the fire's edge.

Will hadn't waited for the blaze to be raked tame, witness the fierce whistles and stamps of appreciation from the watching revellers. But neither had he taken off his braies, which began to smoulder. He discovered this thanks to Arthur, who decided Will's bowing to his admirers was the best chance to douse his smoking arse with a full bucket.

Will let out a holler—the water was *cold!*—and the audience roared again, this time with laughter.

"And that," Marion called, all too sweetly from her place of honour upon the altar stone, "is why you don't wear your clothes jumping ower the Bel-fires! It's bloody dangerous!"

"Have to keep me goolies constrained somehow!" Will called right back, and Marion snorted her opinion of that.

Others were more impressed. "Are you proper big everywhere, William?" a woman called. Seated with her friends on a patch of grass nigh to Marion, they were laughing—and enjoying.

"I'll say he is!" a Hathersage lass put in with a waggle of eyebrows.

The first woman dissolved further in giggles, eyeing Will with renewed respect.

Which, being Will, made him preen all the more, slicking the leather tie from his mane of hair and letting it fly. Marion had to laugh.

Gunnora, seated on the edge of the altar stone, nearly spewed good mead with her own laughter. "Faith, but that young buck needs taking down a notch, eh?"

Beside her, Aelwyn gave a satisfied snicker. "I think I see just the one to do it, too."

Following her gaze, Marion had to agree.

"Sizeable, or just slack?" Much sauntered forwards, arms crossed over his bare chest and grinning for all he was worth. "Your arse is proper dampish, 'tennyroad. Why so shy? You fear the lasses'll see how t' shoots and roots en't matching t' leaves?"

Beneath that flaxen thatch, Will flushed bright crimson. "I don't see you or His Scarlet Lordship giving it a go! Maybe *you'd* rather wait until the fire's raked out for the bairns?" His gaze flicked over to where Gamelyn stood, a dark-clad statue a mere staff's length from Marion and her cortège. "Or play alongside t' women?"

Aelwyn snorted. "I'd jump ower that fire faster than you any day, man!"

This brought a rout of calls from the women.

"Go it, Mother!"

"Show t' cub how 'tis done!"

Much was unruffled. "En't playing wit' lasses all ower t' point of May Eve?"

At this everyone laughed and catcalled; Marion sent a wink in Much's direction, then put two fingers to her mouth and whistled encouragement. Half the fun of the fire dance was the brass and balls of male challenge.

Come on, now, she urged towards the copper-haired statue. *Step up.*

At least he was laughing. At least he'd let Robyn bring him into the dance, earlier. And the way he'd watched her would have, with any other, made a case for the wanting.

This one will need no blessing cup to make him able. If he proves himself worthy, the Lady whispered, entirely too smug. *There is still the challenge to come.*

"Anyone for another go?" Will strode around the fire, giving a nimble, lightning-quick twirl of his staff.

Much, next to Gamelyn, gave him a nudge.

"I wouldn't mind seein' our pretty Scarlet lord have a go," one of the women muttered, just loud enough for Gamelyn to hear.

And Gamelyn did. Marion hid a grin. It was proper fetching—and funny—how a notorious Templar assassin could still flush like a twelve-year-old lad.

But it was Much who began shucking his garb, to a round of encouraging shouts. Will grinned and tossed him the staff. Much caught then twirled it, back and forth between his hands, then overhead.

"You gonna use that staff or play wit' it?" Arthur called.

Another roar of laughter—Much's included—as he ran for the fire, stabbed the staff into the ground, and leapt, light as a buck. Another chorus of shouts as Will followed—minus the staff. Much came sailing back through, also minus any staff.

"The menfolk have all the fun!" Aelwyn groused.

"They don't have to!" Marion insisted. "Have a go!"

"You first then, Maiden."

Marion grinned, rose, and began shucking her kirtles. Aelwyn grinned and started to do likewise.

"I'm too old and creaky to jump, and too old for fires to bless wit' quickening," Gunnora demurred, albeit with a smirk. "I'll watch t' bairns."

The dusk chill upon her skin, Marion piled her hair atop her head with a twist of cloth, grabbed Aelwyn's hand, and ran for the fire.

To have Maid and Mother both go sailing over the need-fires threw down a proper gauntlet. Whoever had hung back now felt it a point of honour to join in. All manner of lads and lasses, with yips and shouts, roiled the game up in earnest.

Several elders, eschewing the leap, began a swaying step-to-gether-step on the merrymaking peripheries. One held a drum, on which he began pounding out a two-beat rhythm akin to a heartbeat. A woman, grey braid uncovered, raised her bare, work-muscled arms and began to sing; first low and slow, it quickly rose, blithe and ribald:

"Fill thou the cup and I the can

"Hast tha well drunken, man?"

"Who's the Fool?" another sang, was answered by the entire gathering, roaring up into the starry sky:

"Fie, man, fie!"

"I saw a hare chase a hound," another elder sang out. "Forty miles above the ground!"

"Hast tha well drunken, man?"

"I hath!"

"Fie, man, fie!"

The dancing was growing wilder. One lad let out a cry as he ran for the flames, was answered with admiration as he balanced at the top of his staff, nigh hovering over the fire. When he finally dropped to the other side, it was to lengthy and rowdy applause.

Marion tossed him a flower from her hair and gave a curtsey, quitting the field.

"I saw a flea heave a tree!" the lad sang, twining the bloom in his hair in triumph, "twenty miles out to sea!"

"Thou hast well drunken, man!" This from Gamelyn; he and Much tipped their mugs to Marion as she headed back to the altar stone. "Fill thou the cup and I the can!"

"Who's the Fool?" Much sang, throwing an arm across Gamelyn's shoulders and a bow to Marion. "Fie, man, fie!"

"I saw a Maid milk a bull!" Gunnora answered from the altar stone, "and ev'ry pull a bucket-full!"

"Tha' hast well drunken, dame!" Marion crowed back, gesturing to the fire. "But speaketh 'struth tonight!"

More yips and howls. One of the elders answered, "Fie t' any bloody Fool who'd refuse such a pull!"

The Maiden giving a favour had fired up the lads once again. The fire was stoked higher, the leaping rejoined in earnest. The balancing lad did his trick several more times.

"That un's sure to have his pick of partners when the moon rises," Gunnora chuckled as Marion gained her side, all damp and goose-pimpled, and began to shrug back into kirtles and cloak. "But what's Himself waitin' for? He's the right."

It was frustrating and accurate. Gamelyn was tipsy enough to join in song and applause, but not the game.

"He were eyein' *you*, to be sure," Gunnora confided, soft. Beside her, more children—not just Tom and Tibba—had gathered, playing on the grass and watching the fires with various expressions of delight.

Marion slid her gaze to find, once again, Gamelyn watching. Much was murmuring in his ear, offering up another drink. As Gamelyn took it, Much peered over his head at Marion and winked.

"Will t' Lord be coming soon?" A breathless Aelwyn bent down and offered to take Tom from Gunnora.

Marion looked about; her brother had indeed vanished. The rituals of the Maying were sweet memories untarnished by her absence these past years. She knew what had been, rite and ritual. But she also knew her Hob-Robyn's ways . . . or lack thereof.

"Mayhap."

Gunnora merely cuddled the sleeping bairn closer.

Aelwyn gave an obliging smile, which just as quickly melted away. "Sweet Lady, 'tis *Agnes!*"

Indeed it was, though surely Agnes hadn't come all this way unaccompanied. Aelwyn gave Marion a querying look, then smiled and ran to greet the elder woman.

Gamelyn was frowning across the gathering as well, though it could also be because the song had changed.

> *"Have any loved ye well down there*
> *Summers and winters through;*
> *Down there ye'll find her passing fair*
> *Summers and winters through. . ."*

No doubt Gamelyn recognised the source as well as Marion herself did. Queen Eleanor's poetess friend would be horrified to hear the bawdy use to which her lyrics had been bent . . . or mayhap not, Marion considered with a smile. After all, the Queen had said Marie de France was an uncommon woman, with a liking for the magic. And wasn't there some magic, after all, in words being passed down and remembered?

Or mayhap he'd seen something else. For the fire flared suddenly, hot and high and showering a thousand sparks against the glitter-dark night. There was a collective gasp. Then astonishment—fear and wonder and a gamut in between—as through the fire burst an enormous black stag. With eyes to rival the fire coals, he soared over the flames and landed onto the grass light as mist . . . and like mist, the creature wavered, darkened, dissipated.

Only the gilt eyes and antlers remained. The stag was no more; a man, lean and tall, with pale skin traced in blue pigment and black head crowned with gleaming horn and green, rose from crouch to stand.

The sparks seemed to hang about him, *were* hanging about him. Heralds of the otherworlds, of summer's coming, fireflies gathered and gave honour.

Another outcry, this more fear than wonder. Many of the gathered folk were retreating, slow and unsure. Many of them were not.

John was the first to kneel to the Horned Lord as He raised the staff in His hands. Will, Arthur, David, and Gilbert were on his heels.

The gathering followed suit, one and all. Gamelyn too paid homage, though his head was unbent, his gaze smouldering upon the god's presence. Marion was the only one left standing. In thisnow, Lady did not bow to Lord. Robyn's eyes moved to meet hers . . . yet they were not, quite, Robyn's. No more than Marion was all that walked towards him.

But neither did Marion miss the smattering of fireflies that drifted towards Gamelyn.

"Summers and winters through, aye." That mellifluous voice—Horned Lord's, Robyn's, *more*—seemed to shiver the earth beneath their feet, to still the wind and fill the glittering sky. He began to pace a circle about Marion, swinging the staff to and fro. It jingled, one end decorated with a brocket's antler, feathers, chain, and seed pods. "Our people are strong, dance long, and leap high. We'll see fruit aplenty from the fires tonight, maid and man, beast and field. All that remains is Her choice be made."

"You know my choice." Marion stopped his circuit by reaching out to take hold of the staff. Between them, hand in hand, she gave it a shake, set it to rattle and sing.

He went on one knee, still holding the staff, head bowed. In the surrounded silence, Marion took the horn-crown from his head, placing it upon the stone at her feet. She then twined her fingers into the black curls braided, here and there, with feathers, flint, and bone.

"Make him, Brother-Consort. Mark him."

He grinned up at her—all Hob-Robyn, this time—and Marion released the staff just in time. He sprang up, flinging the staff skyward, then down, pointing westward of the fire. The covenant, once of outlaws, stood there. Gilbert and John each held Gamelyn by one arm, as if he might turn and run from the oncoming antlered lance.

No fear there, Marion smirked; he'd seen worse.

Then she noted that Will wasn't there. Nor Much. Niggling strange, that—but her thoughts veered back to *now* as Robyn put the antlers to Gamelyn's bare collarbones, said something that made Gamelyn's lip twitch. Then the staff twisted, close and quick, and one sharp tine scored Gamelyn's chest, leaving a line of crimson.

The fire flared upward, sudden and hot. The people, leaning close in curiosity and awe, let out a nigh-united exclamation, skittered back. Various gestures, whispers . . . and then the fireflies reappeared, tiny lights of life, clustering and clinging . . . more proof. More whispers, more awe.

"He is marked, Lady," Robyn said with a grin in his voice. "But not yet made, I'd say."

Gamelyn flushed to match his hair—chagrin or annoyance, it was unclear.

Marion smiled. Answered, "Then let the challenge of My Consort be met. Who thinks to challenge?"

It echoed into the clearing, crept down the back of the Tor, and lingered, caught in the valley thicket.

Silence. The gathering waited, then started to look, sure there would be someone. Somewhere, somehow . . .

"Who, then?" Robyn turned, his voice gentle, asking. "Will none challenge?"

Still the quiet, almost eerie, with only the crackle of the bonfires in answer.

"So!" Robyn laughed and danced the circle, swinging the staff as he stalked around the need-fire. "Who has the *right* to challenge? Who seeks to dance the Eternal Return with sweat and firelight, blood and rebirth? Who will fight Our champion for the right to approach Our Lady?"

Silence.

Then a voice came from the edge of the clearing. "I will, All-Father."

And Much stepped from the gathering.

Marion supposed she should have been surprised. But she wasn't, not really.

Gamelyn was surprised. At first. But as he witnessed the look Marion gave Much—and the return glance, intimate as a kiss—he thought to understand.

"Once there was a darken King, who walked the long nights, waiting and watching as Winter ended . . ."

Gunnora sang the words, and as if in response, the fire leapt, sparks soaring into the night and wafting to the dark silhouette waiting behind Marion's seated, straight-backed form. They did homage to their Quean, then swirled about her brother to glint against ebon eyes, dancing like fireflies . . .

Nay, not like. Were. The tiny creatures darted with one intent, some landing upon Robyn's bared head. Some even glided across the cleared space and over to Gamelyn. As he extended a curious hand, they traced his palm all tickly-warm.

"That's an augury," Aelwyn whispered, and beside her, John smiled.

"He had honoured his Lady with the longest of nights, all furs and firelight, stars and ice across bare branches, dreaming time for tales and songs . . ."

It was extraordinary to have, not a paxman's, but a woman's assistance in shrugging away gear and garb. Aelwyn was competent, and what she didn't know, John did, but still. Unfamiliar. Even more so that Much waited on the other side of the ring stones, being oiled down and prepared even as Gamelyn was: the opponent.

This wrestling match had as prize no mere ram and ring. The antlered crown lay at the feet of the Maiden, upon the same altar stone where Robyn Hood and Guy de Gisbourne had engaged in another, different battle.

Was it so different? You blooded Winter upon the stones and took his name from him. . . and yours.

"No augury," Gamelyn said. "I'm not going to win this."

A disapproving hiss from John, but Aelwyn was the one to give him a hard smack between his bare shoulder blades. "Tis ill luck to speak of your chances!"

"There's no chance to it," Gamelyn insisted. "I'll fight him, but not to win. He's Marion's lover. He's—" Searching for words, he settled for the simplest and best "—my brother, in all but blood."

"Winter's lord was tired beneath his crown of mistletoe and holly. He longed to rest. But he could find neither champion nor worthy challenger . . . "

Aelwyn was smaller than John, but years of farm labour were behind the hand that grabbed Gamelyn's forelock, yanking his gaze to meet hers. "What else would he be? You know better, and if you don't, you should, 'lessen you're daft as bread. Our Lady en't kept in walls t' gaol and tame Her! She's no man's *property!* The Maying's upon us, and who's meant to hold Summer's crown will. The Lady and Lord will champion him. You've no call t' fight with owt less than your best."

"Much wain't profane the rite!" John added, with a frown that matched the vehement gestures.

"Until the sun came creeping, more and more, in the Eternal Return . . . "

Mayhap you are afraid—this from the Horned Lord, raising Gamelyn's hackles as nothing else—*to claim what is yours?*

Where is your pride now, Oakbrother? Thorns amidst desert blossoms. *Am I not worth the winning? Will you, like the Holly, see in Me only sister or mother? Moreover, do you so mean to scorn the Wode's magic, scorn the Eden all of you seek to raise in thisnow?*

John's fingers rose to the amulet at Gamelyn's throat—the one he'd made for Guy de Gisbourne, no longer enemy but working with the outlaws, to release their Maiden from Nottingham's gaol.

"Remember this. Remember who you are. Who you can be."

It shivered Gamelyn to bone. As did another memory. Robyn's voice:

"It's yours. It's allus been yours."

"For Summer comes, is born, and desires his time. It is his fate to challenge. His crown. His *right.*"

His right.

All you have to do is reach out and take it.

Much stepped forwards. The crowd edged closer as Gamelyn too paced towards the fire.

"Ooo, he really *is* red-haired," one of the women chortled, sudden.

"Aye, that he is."

The smug tone of Robyn's voice flitted a grin across Gamelyn's face, hearkening to recent memory: Much teasing Scathelock over leaves and mismatched shoots. No doubt he must also look a pale ghost next to Much, whose skin gleamed bronze beneath the oil. Much had always been more likely to pass for desert folk.

Mayhap it was not so different after all from the hours of practice in that desert, or bouts held beneath the lessonings of Temple Hirst's wrestling master.

Much dusted his hands together, put those hands upon his knees in a slight crouch, and grinned back. "Milord."

"Why, yes, I am," Gamelyn acknowledged, grin widening.

Much chuckled, tipped his head.

Gamelyn did likewise, adding a small bow.

Much ploughed full into him.

The crowd roared as they went rolling, parting the far row of onlookers, and roared even louder as Much wriggled free and leapt back up.

Gamelyn wasn't far behind. "You . . . *sod*," he managed, huffing his breath back.

"No rules, milord, in Her ring." The smile never left Much's face, his eyes, as ever, mild. "She'd have us do Her proud."

Indeed, that Lady was on her feet, shouting and cheering with the rest of the onlookers. And speaking of chaos embodied . . .

Robyn stood behind her, leaning on the antlered staff, eyes hot-bright with admiration.

The pwca *watches, for once,* She whispered. *'Tis yours, thisnow, to act.*

Or not, the Lord grumbled.

A snarl quivered at Gamelyn's lip.

This time as Much charged, Gamelyn was ready for him. He feinted to the right, then left and forwards. Much saw it too late, tried to change trajectory, and instead slid off Gamelyn's oil-slick skin to stagger headlong into a hollering mob of men.

"You know better!" Gamelyn called after him. "The sergeants would have you on bread and water for a mistake like that!"

Laughing, Much let the men prop him to his feet, suffering more than a few cuffs and backslaps amidst raucous encouragement to *flatten the sodding nobleman!*

He was sure he heard Scathelock's voice amidst it.

Much didn't plough back in, instead advanced light as a mousing cat, circling. They knew each other almost too well, the contest evenly matched and drawn by the intimate knowledge of comrades-in-arms. Each other's skills and failings had long been kenned, shared.

It wasn't going to be easy.

Several more silent feints and lunges. Sidestep and back, then advance. All of it, equidistant and measured. The Templar fighting master would have pissed himself with happiness.

The crowd was not pleased. They wanted action.

"Are you dancing or wrestling?" Arthur hollered, and more than a few took it up.

"Let's see some real scufflin', you two!"

"Or at least some name-calling!"

"Name-calling," Gamelyn growled back, "is for bloody amateurs."

"So's dancing like a tart at Misrule!"

Gamelyn eyed Much and shrugged, then lunged in.

Hold and twist, kick and heave and slide away. Dirt clung to their oily hides, but the slick addition of sweat meant even that was no guaranteed purchase. Much pinned and lost Gamelyn. Gamelyn spun and leapt, knocking Much flat, skidded sideways midgrip and went rolling. Much went with him, over and over towards the stones.

Gamelyn saw them coming, smiled as he realised Much, headfirst against his belly, couldn't. So he grabbed the back of Much's head—and damn, but that thick mat of new-grown hair provided a good handle, did he intend to get arsy and yank him around by it . . .

He didn't. Instead he spread his fingers, hand cupping the back of Much's head. With a final grunt and twist, Gamelyn flung Much onto his back at Marion's bare feet. The stone barked Gamelyn's knuckles and no doubt scraped a length of skin from Much's back, but the move had saved him the nasty head knock, at least. It didn't stop the air from exploding outward with a huge "*Huh!*" as Much hit the altar edge, arms flinging outward.

Gamelyn propped the momentum to a halt and straddled Much's chest, sliding both knees atop those thoughtfully-flung-out arms, then loosed his pate with a hard rub.

The audience was hollering fit to raise the toppled stones. Marion, at first startled by the offering flung literally at her feet, was succumbing to the same mirth as her surrounding women.

"Now and if that en't a fair and fancy gift, Maiden!"

"Shame you can't take 'em both!"

"I would, were it meself!"

"Struth!"—this from Much as he gained enough air—"but I've missed a good row, milord." His eyes were watering, but he hadn't stopped smiling the whole while.

"Give 'im a kiss, Scarlet!" one of the onlookers crowed.

Grinning, Gamelyn bent down and bussed Much's cheek. This prompted more laughter and shouts, which swerved into quiet as Robyn hefted his staff, shook it.

"Do you yield?" Marion's query to Much dipped soft, fair-sweet; still Gamelyn wondered if there weren't a hint of rue there, after all.

Still thinking like one of the Christians. Like a monk, the Horned Lord growled.

Not for long, She answered.

As if in further proof, Marion extended one bare foot and traced it, teasing, along Much's bicep. He grasped it, kissed it.

Then she did it to Gamelyn. Toes trailing down his ribs, then back upward, and he sucked in a breath, juddering like . . . well, like bloody damn.

"Do you yield?"

"Best take care, sister." Robyn, damn his black eyes, had leaned to rest his chin upon Marion's shoulder. "You might have *both* of 'em yieldin', do you keep that up."

"Nay." Much was *still* grinning, spreading his hands in surrender. "This ride's too wild for me! I yield for my Lady. And milord. If milord'll gi' off me, that is."

Gamelyn leapt up, extended an arm. Much took it, pulled himself up as Marion, too, stood. Untangling a pair of blossoms from her hair, she handed one to Much, then Gamelyn: the first was a twinned daisy gold and white, the second a wild brier rose nearly the hue of the cinnabar curls that frizzed and twisted over her shoulders.

With a slow bow, Gamelyn took the rose and twined it into the braid hanging between his shoulders.

The drums started up again, and the pipe followed like a tipsy dancer, skipping along the downbeats and twirling with the rest. The crowd moved in, bore Much away, dancing a line about the fires. Several lasses in particular seemed eager to console his loss.

"Time to catch your breath, aye?" Aelwyn snugged an arm in Gamelyn's, drew him aside. "Before any others would challenge."

He didn't need it, not really. Not that it mattered.

John waited, smiling as if he kenned Gamelyn's thoughts, a soft hide split in one hand. He leaned against Gamelyn's shoulder with a kiss and a trace of fingers over the amulet, then began wiping away the wet and greasy sand. It scraped and stung, like the salt rubs in the Eastern baths, but 'twas welcome. A scourge, albeit mild. Its own purification.

Apropos.

Before, there'd been no awareness of their tending; now he felt every touch, every ministration. John's hands were altogether conversant with Gamelyn, a lover's familiarity and ease. His reaction to Aelwyn's touch, however, was unanticipated, particularly after spending most of his life subjugating such things. Gamelyn found himself leaning into her oily hands and nigh purring.

But of course, his goddess purred right back. *She is Me.*

Aelwyn smiled, kept working. "A lucky Maiden, to climb yon pretty scarlet tower this night."

All right, one bit in particular was rearing like an edgy destrier, but how many euphemisms could they come up with?

"If"—she slid oily fingers across his lower belly, a-purpose, he was sure—"you prove worthy of Her." A low chuckle. "No question but part of you surely is."

And *putain de merde,* but there was no chance to hide the least of a flush at present.

John grinned.

Gamelyn focused on the people. *Their* people, singing and dancing . . . *free.*

Unfortunately the main one he sought wasn't among them—he loved watching Robyn move, lithe and perfect—but Robyn had once again disappeared into the shadows. The others had rejoined the merriment. Arthur, finishing his pot of mead, chatted exuberantly with a tall woman in a matron's veil. Gilbert was squiring two happy lasses. Much was determined to best him there, partnering three. David stood beside his grandmother where she sat, watched his son dance with a group his own age—choosing his first partner for the fires, no doubt. The grandmother beat one of the drums, and Tess played with the hem of her skirts.

Robyn slid into their midst and stood, silhouetted by the fire, the antlered staff raised.

It didn't take very long at all for it to spread, a warm, comforting blanket of quiet. Robyn started to go round, slow, staff clearing an area growing larger with every circuit.

"Hast tha more?" he asked, voice soft but carrying across the hilltop. "Or"—the staff halted, upright, like a bow aimed at Gamelyn's heart—"will he challenge *me?*" Silence.

The Horned Lord growled warning.

Then a soft, fierce claim. "Nay, Lord. He's no rights to challenge you. Ever."

And Will Scathelock stepped from the gathered people and into the firelight.

- Entr'acte -

"Is everything in place, then?"

"Yes. The serf from Bruer came yester's even, your introductory missive in one grimy hand. You must be desperate, Templar; the woman's old enough to be my grandmother."

"The woman," Wymarec replied, terse, "is nothing. Other than her confession to her priest, regarding her invitation to *that*." A wave of gloved hand towards the great hall's outlook. Unshuttered in the unseasonable warmth, the west-facing window framed a sight guaranteed to keep good Christian folk inside with doors latched.

Brian de Lisle didn't acknowledge the gesture. His eyes were fixed, nigh unblinking, upon Mam Tor. It was a beautiful, if blood-chilling, sight: her foothills lay misted, tens of smaller bonfires illuminating not only those but the surrounding moors. Yet it was the crest—aglow with the hugest of those fires, dotted with capering figures—that had kept him there, unmoving, since the sun had dwindled into the west. Wymarec knew this for a fact, as he'd been admitted to Peveril's tower just before sundown.

The seneschal had, at least, offered him dinner for the wait.

"*Look* at them," de Lisle growled. "Misbegotten filth. Avoiding the damned place like plague when I held it, and now? I'll see them all—"

"Let it go, man," Wymarec chided. "Eyes set upon vengeance have no clarity."

"Is that some Templar proverb?"

Not for the first time, Wymarec wondered if this particular

tool needed be broken for good. Or merely replaced, and preferably by someone with less wit and more respect. But nay; as long as the man was here, with a bird's view of the sacred folly . . .

At least he was motivated.

"And what are proverbs but mere common sense, my lord of Peveril? You're no good to either of us if you march onto another lord's lands and commit an act that could be construed as war."

"We don't live amongst the barbaric northern tribes! My family would—"

"Your brother de Lacy has already made some pointed choices by lending soldiers to shore up Tickhill's need, however temporary. As to your other brother? He's set up an altar within his priory to pray for your wretched soul! They've already deemed your fixation a luxury they cannot afford."

A short silence. Unaccountably de Lisle laughed, harsh as a stooping hawk. "Well. That's family for you."

"In which case I'm sure you don't desire I should make a choice to step aside and leave you to your own vengeance. It would also leave you to your own . . . resources."

The threat, idly tossed, nonetheless hit its mark. De Lisle's shoulders twitched, and one hand went to his nape, fingers clutching.

"Your . . . skills have been of some help, aye."

"Then be patient, my lord, and continue to enjoy your sleep. Such things as we plan must be done with consideration and due care. We need specifics before we can make any sort of move, whatever I choose that to be. Information, which we shall have from the old woman."

"If she has the wit to do as she's told."

Wymarec shrugged. "If she doesn't, her family might well deem *her* an unaffordable luxury."

- XXX -

R obyn seemed . . . surprised.

Marion stiffened, as if she wanted to feel her brother's disbelief yet couldn't. A smile finally tipped her mouth, grim.

Gamelyn was sure it matched his own. He wasn't the least bit surprised.

Nor was he exactly disappointed.

Truth be told, neither were the watchers. They'd no stake save the promise of more action. Shouts of encouragement grew louder as Will was taken over to the challenger's place. Like most of the fire leapers, he'd already stripped down. Gunnora raked back his hair and braided it into a tail as another woman oiled him for the wrestling.

John was sober as he checked Gamelyn over. The others—particularly Gilbert and David—were more resigned than anything. Arthur looked satisfied.

Aelwyn had been around long enough to ken the undercurrents. She peered at Gamelyn. "Are you rested enough?"

He nodded, bent over, and kissed her forehead. She blinked, then smiled and stepped back.

Robyn had taken his place behind Marion once again. What mirth he'd displayed during the first bout had fled.

Aye, for that alone Charming William was about to have his arse handed to him.

Gamelyn folded his arms and waited. Will wasn't the waiting type. A calm opponent flustered him. Before Gunnora could tie off her finished braid, he was striding into the cleared space beside the bonfire. A return of self-assurance was aided by overloud support; the same throng of folk who'd hoped Much would pound the bloody nobleman to a pulp were keen as to second chances.

Will even swapped friendly insults with a few as he ambled over to the altar stones. "You coming, then?" he shot at Gamelyn. "Or are you after a wee bit more rest?"

Gamelyn demurred.

"He's had his rest, William." Marion rose as he approached. "And his blessing. Methinks you're one as needs the latter, aye?"

The well-aimed tease roused the watchers to howl support and catcalls both. Will laughed with the rest, bent the knee to Marion, kissed her hand as she offered it, and rose, still holding it. He said something, low, to Robyn. Robyn shrugged and smiled.

Was Gamelyn the only one who saw it quiver in the corners?

Nay, he couldn't think on it. He couldn't look at Robyn, not now.

Marion, on the other hand, looked proper set to give Will a thrashing if Gamelyn didn't attend to it for her. So he gave a tiny nod, a promise, was somewhat satisfied as her grey eyes lit. He moved towards the fire, kept watching Will, kept waiting.

He didn't have to wait overlong. Will strode over, rubbing his hands together. "Well, here we are. Aye?"

Gamelyn tilted his head, kept a good distance, and said nothing. Remembering. Considering.

Scathelock's style was more the knife-fighter, akin to Robyn; though he wasn't that agile, he was agile enough, with the bunched-broad muscles of a blacksmith. Gamelyn had his own share of brawn, and more reach. But did Scathelock get him down, likely he could hold him there, and then . . .

No rules.

"I've sommat to confess, ere we start."

Well, of course he did. Gamelyn couldn't help a roll of eyes, did submit to a tiny smirk as Will saw it and frowned.

"I never believed you could take on the lackey." Whereas Much's smile had been full of mischief, Will's twisted mocking. "We en't fighting all pretty with swords and posing, here. I truly figured I'd be fighting your man, man. But aye, and isn't this all the better?"

"Better?" Gamelyn drawled. "Only if you can shut your mouth long enough *to* fight."

Another round of laughter from the ones close-gathered. Others were creeping closer, avid.

Aye, this was going to be quite satisfactory.

As long as he didn't look at Robyn.

He should have seen it coming. Should have known what Will was up to.

It only made Robyn realise how far apart they'd been walking, mayhap from the beginning.

"It's his right, to challenge." Marion's words were fierce, as if she were trying to convince herself as well as him. There was no doubt she was angry, though she kept her voice soft, carrying only to him. "Damn him, but he's been planning this all along."

That hurt, more than any of the rest.

Gamelyn had muscles and height; nevertheless, he was several stones lighter than Will, whose advantage of breadth had won many a dirty hand-to-hand. Will took that advantage right away, slamming against Gamelyn, fetching the first blow and following up with two more, brutal-quick, the last a round punch that sent Gamelyn sailing back to land on his arse in the dirt. But as Will sprang after, Gamelyn wasn't there. He leapt up and, darting sideways, twisted and hammered both fists between Will's shoulder blades, dropping him.

Marion muttered, "Does Will really think he can beat a trained assassin?"

"I almost did," Robyn answered.

"Almost."

"Aye, and 'twere only my pretty face as fetched me free of it. Charming William's never been short of pride, pet."

"Neither," Marion said, grim, "has Gamelyn."

Will hit rolling. The kick Gamelyn intended whistled through empty air. Sidling backwards as Will charged him again, Gamelyn spun at the last moment, kicked out again. This time it landed, booting Will's arse and sending him to his face in the dirt. But any intentions of keeping him there were foiled as Will made a swift roll sideways and up.

Made a rude gesture and a sneer: *Is that it?*

The gathering adored him for it. But Robyn's hands were clenching upon the staff. *You really en't wanting to ask him that.*

Will and Gamelyn had tangled once before. They'd tried to hide it, but Robyn had found out. Will had come away the better in that winter bout, and never fully realised why.

There was no debilitating injury to hamper Gamelyn today.

"Why is he holding back?" Marion muttered. "Lessen he's saving t' honour of killing William for us."

Not that Gamelyn was sparing so much as a glance towards them, Robyn noted. Which was mayhap a good thing; Will was getting the better of him.

Marion added her voice to the shouts echoing across the Tor.

The wind had quickened, blowing Will's forelock from its hasty confinement and into his eyes; he slicked it back with oiled hands. He kept trying to close in, grab hold. Gamelyn was having none of it, dancing away at the last moment, taking any blows as collateral for escape.

A pause, both men eyeing each other. Will's breathing came

heavy. Gamelyn seemed well set for air, though the flush to his face would claim otherwise. Both were dripping, this close to the blazing bonfire, sweat runnelling amidst sand and oil. Will said something, sneered, and tossed his forelock. The fire hissed.

He sprinted forward and made a snatch for the ruddy braid at Gamelyn's nape. Gamelyn ducked, but Will came away with the blossom Marion had twined there. Will tucked it into his own braid, hasty and now half-unravelled, and forked an archer's salute.

"Well, then," he taunted. "A man as wants sommat needs to be able to keep it, aye?"

Gamelyn was silent, shifting from foot to foot. A fool might mistake it for nerves.

But then, Will had always proven a right fool about this. "Aye, dance away, lad. Your game's up. You might think you can take what you want, but I've been on your tail, see? Watching. Waiting."

Gamelyn kept up his sway, merely peered at him. His face might have been carved in stone, except . . .

Was it a smile Robyn saw flicker across Gamelyn's mouth?

Just as quickly, it was gone; nowt but a mistake of light, mayhap. The bonfires lit the hilltop to nigh day in spots, but flickered with any breeze . . . and it had quickened, as if conjured by confrontation's breath.

Will charged. Gamelyn again slid sideways, but Will anticipated it, leapt after, and this time grabbed fierce hold of the russet-gilt braid. Yanked, hard. Gamelyn staggered back, and Will slammed against his shoulders. Crooking his arms under Gamelyn's, Will pulled even closer, snaring hard hands at his opponent's nape.

They struggled, fierce and silent.

The onlookers shouted for blood. The Lady's challenger looked to be going down.

Once more that flicker appeared; it was a smile, and one fit to grace Guy of Gisbourne's lip all cruel-quick.

Robyn held his breath.

Gamelyn went down, but not in any way Will intended—or anticipated. With a sudden drop, then a jerking twist, Gamelyn bent his neck and thrust sword-agile arms forwards, then back, threading through the hold. Oiled or nay, Will would as likely hold to a wet otter, and the swiftness of it jerked him off balance. The latter merely aided and abetted the mule kick Gamelyn delivered. With a loud *thwap* it impacted square into Will's hip and sent him flying towards the fire.

Marion rocked back, echoing the gasps of dismay that rose to meet this. They quickly turned to applause as Will turned his momentum into a dive and leap. Better over the fire than atop it. With a showering of sparks, he disappeared from view.

Shadows flickered beyond. A surge of people surrounded Will, egging him on.

Gamelyn spat in one palm, rubbed it into the sand before regaining his feet. He took his time, all the while seemed to be considering his prey . . . and that's what it was; Robyn could see it. A change abrupt and purposeful, like striking light from dry tinder: eyes flaring, chin lifting, moving on greased joints and muscles, low and expectant . . .

Bloody damn, but it wasn't the first time tonight Robyn wanted to shag his lover voiceless.

Laughter, soft and musical . . . the Lady? Aye, yet nay. Marion watched Robyn, shaking her head and grinning.

"If you don't close your jaw, your tongue'll fall out, pet." Then, lower, "I'm just glad there's no steel."

That sobered Robyn, and quick. *Aye. Will would be dead already.*

A howl ripped across the hilltop, and to shouts of encouragement from the watching throng, Will came charging back over the flames.

Too showy, Gamelyn thought, and sure enough, as Will landed, it was with an inevitable stumble. Gamelyn lunged. Another gasp ripped through the crowd. Before Will could so much as steady, Gamelyn had closed behind and returned the previous favour, tangling hard fingers in the flaxen-coloured hair all straggly from its untied braid. A vicious yank sealed the bargain, had Will staggering back. He flailed, both arms swinging, desperate. One hand slapped Gamelyn's temple. He didn't so much as flinch. Instead he took the blow and the opportunity it gave, seizing Will's other wrist with the sanded palm.

"Bastard!" Will spat, to the accompaniment of several ill-aimed kicks.

The marks of desperation, true enough. The predator crept in, somnolent and insidious. Gamelyn acknowledged its frosty nip with a tiny, welcoming smirk.

Passion had no place in this instant of the play. Let Will spend all his, and find how high its price could be.

With another nigh-boneless twist and arc, Gamelyn hoisted Will's arm behind him and skyward. A knee to the small of Will's back finished the swift combination. With a heavy grunt, Will landed with his face a hand's breadth from the bonfire's coals.

Gamelyn slapped a bare foot between his shoulder blades. Will tried to scrabble sideways, instead barely avoided having his nose shoved in the fire. He let out another grunt as Gamelyn twisted his arm, hard. Kept him there.

Encouragement trailed off into astonished murmurs, everyone gobsmacked by the swift and efficient brutality of it.

Gamelyn looked up, sought the lean-dark figure standing rigid beside the altar stone.

Fool, said the predator.

Be still, he hissed back.

He needed the shock of Robyn's gaze, so he didn't break Will's arrogant neck.

Because Will wasn't helping. Every word burst forth all snarled and foul and keen as a good blade. He managed to rear back a few inches from sheer strength, but no more. The heat was merciless, but Gamelyn didn't truly feel it. He leaned closer in and, almost careless, plucked with his free hand at Will's nape. Fair hair blew, loose, in the breeze. Gamelyn held up the rose and smiled triumph.

One man crowed, "You're supposed to deflower the Maid, lad!"

This, of course, was met with laughter, and that with rowdy shouts and suggestions. Will struggled, red-faced. Gamelyn lifted the bedraggled flower; saluting first the altar stone, then all round, and tucked it back into his own hair.

"Let me go, you soddin—uhn!"

"You're in no position to make demands, Scathelock," Gamelyn murmured.

Scathelock, true to form, answered with another string of curses—again, true to form, regarding his opponent's breeding, background, and sexual preferences.

Gamelyn merely gave a chiding *tsk* and leaned into his foot, cranked harder on Will's arm.

Will let out another harsh grunt and dove forwards. Just before he pitched headfirst into the flames, he arched backwards. Gamelyn let him, waited.

"He has you, lad! Yield!" one of the women beside Marion shouted, and it began to murmur throughout the gathering: *Yield. 'Tis time.*

Will didn't. Eyes wheeling wide-white, he growled, "Fuck you bloody, you Motherle—!"

Gamelyn shrugged, gave another crank. A hint of scorch shivered his nostrils; Will's flaxen hair had fallen too close to the fire.

Still, he hunched, sullen. Silent.

"Bloody . . . what is he doing?" Gamelyn heard Marion's voice as if she were beside him, saw her rise from her stone couch. Aelwyn and Gunnora, each to opposite sides of the circle, were peering at her, anxious.

"I think it's about what he *en't* going t' do," Robyn answered. Surely it was mere habit, how he gathered his men by eye; Gamelyn's gaze swiftly followed, noted their stunned confusion.

Yield. Yield! The plea was becoming demand, rising into the sky.

Will tried to lurch upward; Gamelyn shoved him back down. "It's finished, man."

"Nay! Wain't ever be . . . You can't own this! Not this *too!*"

"I don't"—through gritted teeth—"Own. *Anything.* And neither do you."

Robyn started forwards. Marion laid a quelling hand on his arm and stepped down onto the trodden sere of grass.

Aye, My Own, the Lady said, *this is Ours.*

Gamelyn's eyes rose and locked with hers, a gleaming connection. For a stutter of breath he Saw—*felt*—what Marion did: the backlit shimmer of antlers, milt-white with a heat-dust of copper, as if they'd grown from pale, freckled skin.

Felt Robyn See, smile, through tears burning black eyes at the cost, and the mourning. *Will.*

"Yield." Marion's plea rose above the echoes of itself as she came to stand with them, champion and challenger.

"You heard." A growl from Gamelyn, soft and holding absolutely no mercy. "It's hers to say, man. It's done."

And the soft chant: *Yield. Yield.*

"I wain't! Not to *you!*"

"Will." This from Arthur upon the sidelines. "You've lost, man, and you know it. Let it go."

"*They* lose if I let . . ."

Marion dropped to one knee beside them. Gamelyn wanted to reach out, stay her; she met his gaze, grave, and it halted him. The heat of the fire, altogether close, wafted stray, fuzzed filaments about her cheeks as she leaned close to Will, whispered in his ear. Whatever she said, it seemed to penetrate. Will slumped.

A few more breaths, tense and waiting. Robyn had stopped a length away, eyeing the three of them. Marion rose, both hands covering Gamelyn's grip upon Will's wrist. Grey eyes probed Gamelyn's. It was plain what she wanted, through it went against every instinct he possessed.

"It's done," she told him, sensing it.

Gamelyn released Will, stepped back.

Shoving up on his good arm, Will rose, stood. His head was dipped low—he clearly didn't want to meet anyone's eyes, though Robyn surely tried. Instead Will made a shallow dip of head to Marion, slid a glare Gamelyn's way. Turned away.

The crowd erupted in cheers—it had been a match worthy of any rite.

Will took the accolades calmly enough, then, Arthur on his heels, disappeared into the crowd.

"What did you say to him?" Gamelyn murmured.

Marion looked up at him, lips vibrating as if she were about to speak. Instead the forester's horn filled the space, long and belled sweet; as if it were a signal, she instead plucked two more briar roses from her withy crown and threaded them into his braid, snugging close the one Will had taken. "You've other things to think about," she murmured, brushing a kiss to his ear. "A crown to take, a stag to break."

A stag to. . .?

The others gathered close. Much was plainly angry and beside him, Gilbert looked nearly as irate. David was stricken. John wasn't there and—Gamelyn looked around—Robyn, too, had disappeared.

The breeze shifted, slow, into a light wind; it lifted Marion's unbound hair and rippled the robe she wore as she walked, slowly, towards her people—and aye, they were hers. All of them, giving way even as they approached; all of them murmuring, expectant. The gusts tickled and shivered Gamelyn's bare back and haunches, sweat drying, sand clinging. Some things he'd expected, some he'd been told, but more often than not, he was walking blind, following instinct . . .

Even as your heart kens what you must do, thisnow.

And if you don't, the Horned Lord snorted, *small loss.*

It stiffened Gamelyn's spine, drove him to pace Marion, beside and behind, his stance unconscious, instinctive. Guardian.

"Hast tha more?" Marion called into the night. "Hast t' right been proven thus?"

The murmurs stilled. Silence stretched across the ridge, leaving only the wind to utter its scattered sighs. In its space, one of the women advanced, slowly, holding out a torch topped with chaff and pitch. Marion took it, pointed it towards the altar stone, raised it to her chin, and breathed several soft syllables across the base. A circle, then skyward, and then she took it to the fire. Thrust into the heat, it sparked and simmered, then blazed as she held it aloft.

"The right must be proven, the light t' take the darkness." And as the gathering started to shift and murmur excitement, she arced the torch into a circle, shouted, "Pay heed! He comes!"

Gamelyn heard the horn again, winded from far down the valley, or so it seemed. Another fire, down the ridge and east, blazed where a tiny guide fire had previously stood. Again the revellers voiced their approval—this with awe—but it died to murmurs as another sound rose: a drum. Seeming to fill the night from all points, it was rhythmic, slow as a heartbeat in slumber. It vibrated deep into Gamelyn's chest, shivering the charm upon his breastbone.

The crowd sensed it and began to shift, parting not for the drummer, but Aelwyn and Gunnora. Robed dark, they slowly paced inward. Aelwyn carried a silver bowl.

Marion met them halfway, gave the torch to Gunnora as she knelt, reached out, and lifted, one at a time, the hem of each woman's robe to her lips. Gunnora placed a brief hand upon Marion's head. Aelwyn offered the bowl.

Rising, Marion turned and, with a drifting, smooth gait, brought the bowl to Gamelyn. She halted before him, expectant.

Gamelyn belatedly realised all the others had knelt, and swiftly did likewise.

Marion held out the basin, and Gamelyn took it, closing warm fingers about chill, sweating silver. Framed by the gleaming rim, a sweated and dishevelled shadow rippled within, tinted gold from the liquid filling the basin to nearly brimming. More mead.

The reflection also had sand on its nose, mimicked the gesture as Gamelyn ducked his face against his shoulder to merely encounter more oil and sand.

Marion's lips quirked, then steadied. "Drink."

He tipped the bowl to his lips.

"Half," she chided as he drank—and it was a goodly caution, parched as he was from his fireside exertions. "No more, no less."

The mead stung his lips and set his tongue abuzz. A different taste, bitter as well as sweet—but he swallowed, felt it lap thick down his throat to lay a fierce and fiery trail. Not an unwelcome sensation, at that; he drank more, welcomed the way it crept into his extremities.

Marion started to draw the bowl away; his fingers clenched upon it, wanting more. Another smile, this of wry understanding as she made soft promise. "Anon. Rise up."

He did, blinking as his knees gave a tiny wobble beneath him. More surprise—Aelwyn had come to stand at his right elbow, steadying him. She was humming something, wordless and musical.

Gunnora too was there, with an answer that lay an octave lower. She held the torch as Marion placed the basin at her feet.

Then Marion and Aelwyn began, with hands and willow scrapers, to scrub Gamelyn's hide. The mix of sand, sweat, and oil scraped his skin, another sting shivering just this side of pain . . . and God, but it was *lovely*. The stoic combatant suffering the preparations of battle was curling and withering beneath the drug's heat . . . or the sear of the hands upon him . . . it didn't matter, somehow.

A drug in the mead, some lucid portion of his mind reasoned: the inner predator, always on lookout. He found himself laughing at it, a clear, uninhibited thing. Gunnora answered, and Aelwyn patted his cheek, and Marion smiled . . .

She was wiping his bicep with her hair, for all the World like the Magdalene anointing Christ.

He juddered again as she met his eyes—another promise of imbibition, and again not-quite his fill. Having scoured most of the sand, they began oiling him down again . . . for what he didn't understand, but did it matter? It felt so *good* was what mattered, in thisnow, despite that somewhere, somehow, someone in his mind was nattering alarm.

Poor, poor Guy, desperate for control however he can claim it, he sneered back. *Better this!*

Marion was singing a lullaby. The watchers were also, song

rising into stars. The drum kept pounding, throbbing an untamed beat deep into his bones.

Aye, better Eden now and the promise of any Hell lived through or imagined than walk cold and alone without him—without them—*for the rest of my days.*

Marion's hands left him, and he swayed towards them. Aelwyn held him, uttered a soft "Anon." Gamelyn had no need to disobey; Marion hadn't left, stood before him with the basin gleaming in the crook of one arm. After taking a sip, she dipped two fingers in and knelt, her robe pooling about her knees. The sight made Gamelyn shiver again, inexplicable hope for . . . well, *whats'mever.* He couldn't help a smirk, and wasn't all that disappointed when she laid first her wet fingers, then a kiss along one instep, then the other. She peered upward, eyes tracing his body and giving him entirely too much hope—his back arched of its own accord. Alas, she regained her feet, mouth softened in the clever-curious smile that forever had meant *Marion.*

Aelwyn again murmured "Anon," then leaned a bit closer, whispered in his ear, "I like both lads and lasses too."

Not so simple, he thought, and again a memory of Robyn's voice chided, *Nowt simple wit' you, pet.*

Marion continued the blessing, tracing mead and breath and a light kiss. First upon his forehead, then his lower lip—lingered there for longer than was proper, for Gunnora chuckled and Marion retreated and Gamelyn had to settle for tonguing the mead from his lip. Another tap of her fingertips atop the mead, libation, lips, and breath brushing each nipple—hard as bloody pebbles, and no surprise—then trail, light, from navel and down, close but not near close enough to another point of his anatomy straining just as eager-hard and more than ready.

"Anon." This from Gunnora, with a fond chuckle.

Marion sipped the mead again, then stiffened, turned. Gamelyn realised the drum resounded even closer. She sped over to Gunnora, traded basin for torch with like speed. With it, she traced a sign in the air, called out what was surely a challenge. Aelwyn, too, had drawn closer, as if protective.

And the people, who had been closing in, intent upon his sacring, began to part once more.

It was so tense, Gamelyn began to count his own heartbeats, which had ramped up in response.

Yet no danger walked the aisle cleared inward. Merely John, with drum in hand and a withy wreath on his brown curls. His eyes met Gamelyn's, as full of heated promise as Marion's, gleaming against the scampering illumination like old honey. His skin was streaked with woad, spilling indigo over sunburnt cheeks and across pale shoulders, writhing down his arms to brown and agile hands, which never let up their slow caress of the drum hide.

He knelt beside the fire, seeming a feral and lovely boy, mayhap a faun from the tales of ancient invaders.

Then, in the faun's wake, came danger's face. A lean wraith, gliding tall and silent and self-possessed. No question he too had been sung over and anointed, consecrated to thisnow; a woodland spirit's avatar clad only in oil, woad, a braided long tail of black hair and, once again, the antlered crown.

Nay, he'd a garment, of a kind: a familiar quillion dagger, sheathed and laced to the muscle of his right thigh.

The breath hiccupped, held within Gamelyn's chest. Not only longing and need, not only lust that fired his loins and weakened his knees, nor only every inchoate nightmare dreamt by devout child or conflicted man and come to sudden, stark life. It was all of those things—more, it ignited a sudden and primal aggression that should have frightened him . . . but didn't.

This was his lover, aye. But it was also the Horned Lord.

Antagonist. Trickster. Tormentor. *Rival.*

"Pick a feeling, O Scarlet Knight," Aelwyn whispered.

He couldn't answer.

Marion stood between them, Horned Lord and Knight, brandishing the torch. "Winter must bow to Summer."

"And Summer in His turn, to Winter" came low, throaty answer.

"It is time to give way, my Consort. The land must soften, the ploughing must be made, the seed must be planted."

"If he can, aye."

Their words carried across the stilled people: Lord defiant; Lady insistent, protective.

Gunnora paced over to the antlered figure with bowl in hand, and he drank it down.

John's gaze flickered in the firelight between them. His lips were moving, soundless breath and life to the drum's steady heartbeat. Much had knelt beside him, was watching and nodding. The others of the Covenant had faded into the surrounding folk who waited, spelled to the drama. Save Tess, curled upon John's knee, despite—or perhaps because of—the drum's proximity.

Pick a feeling.

John's charm hummed, warm as the mead, but it was the god's words that kept rising: *If he can, aye.* The drum throbbed it hot behind Gamelyn's eyes, curled it into deep-set mnemonic: *Gadelyng.*

He would use a boyhood taunt. Gamelyn snarled, and gilt-laced ebon eyes flashed his way.

They seemed . . . scornful.

"Coom by, Brother," the Hob-Robyn said, soft and almost sung. "Hast tha' need for a crown, Summerlord?"

Summerlord.

Another feeling, fit for the picking: Robyn, loose-limbed and flushed, the mead having its way with him, his full lower lip damp and begging to be bruised with kisses.

A smirk; he knew it, the sod. "Anon." He echoed that damned word, holding out a hand.

Gamelyn nearly reached for it.

Marion came between them, brandishing the torch.

And the Hob-Robyn knelt, allowed Gunnora to take the horn-crown from his dark head.

"The Light must return," Marion told him as he rose.

"Then have him bring it to me, sister." He turned away, with one negligent hand catching the staff Gilbert tossed to him.

Much advanced with another staff, thickened upon each end, and extended it with a bow. It had pitch upon the ends and, as Gamelyn watched, Marion lit each end. Much then handed it to Gamelyn and, with a second dip of knee, backed away,

The gathering, their voices ranging from excited to anxious, gave way.

Robyn flipped his own staff into the air, whipped it into a blur over his head, then stabbed it into the ground. Leaned on it, smirking.

Gamelyn smirked right back, then lunged for him.

Robyn ducked, whirled swift as thought. Wood cracked together with a shower of sparks.

More excitement, a drawn-out *oooh* that rose into gasps as Gamelyn pressed the engagement. He knew he had to—he was no peasant, born to this weapon.

Losing was not an option, somehow.

Another thrust and turn, side-step and parry. Robyn whirled away, tossed one end of his staff to thwack Gamelyn's arse. And *laughed*, the cheeky sod.

The inner predator lurched upward, furious in the wake of mead and mockery; Gamelyn converted that fury into his own laugh and planned revenge. Lunged in another blur of wood and sparks. Was glad for the protection of the oil as one flaming end hissed and skittered off Robyn's arm too quick to burn. It guttered.

The crowd groaned.

Marion hollered, "*Take* him!"

Gamelyn dove in. Their staffs clapped together. Slid.

Held.

Both of them straining, shoved hard against, shuddering and slowly, ever so slowly, travelling overhead.

Robyn ducked inward and kissed Gamelyn hard on the mouth. Combativeness wibbled into a lust that didn't know where to turn. A roar of surrounding laughter greeted this newest jape; Robyn broke the kiss and joined the laugh, darting backwards. Gamelyn stumbled in his wake, confusion flaming back into aggravation.

You tricky. . . sod.

Aye, pet. Robyn's eyes gleamed, and he said, quite serious, "Pick a feeling."

It made Gamelyn hesitate, frown.

"'Tis time you did, after all. Aye?"

Still, the laughter, accompanied by hearty shouts. More and more they were picking sides. *His* side.

"Take 'im, Scarlet!"

"A Summer! A Summer!"

"Baste his head, Hob-Robyn!"

The words finally came, slow-thick and uncertain. "There are too many."

"The light has to return. 'Tis past time." Robyn glided sideways, nodding. "It's yours, aye? *Yours.* All you have to do is reach out and take it."

Yours.

And Gamelyn's body took over, swift assassin's instincts and Templar training disallowing defeat, or quivering-tired muscles, or fear.

Much caught the lit stave as Gamelyn tossed it—he'd his own instincts. Another quick exchange passed between them, grin for grin, as Gamelyn feinted to Robyn's left.

Robyn followed it with a mighty swing. Gamelyn twisted at the last moment and dove headfirst for Robyn. A grunt and a clatter—the staff, falling to the foot-packed earth—and another, harsher grunt as Robyn hit and every scrap of air escaped his lungs.

No need for any tricky holds; Gamelyn straddled him, didn't so much as let him catch his breath before he bent down and kissed him back. Hard.

The audience was roaring with appreciation; Gamelyn could hear Marion's delighted laugh most of all. He bent close again. "So, Hob-Robyn. I've come for my crown."

"Then take it," Robyn told him, still somewhat breathless.

Gamelyn frowned as the black eyes flickered down past his left knee; as he followed that gaze, he saw it, gleaming electrum against the fire:

The quillion dagger, still strapped to Robyn's thigh.

"Take it!" Robyn snapped, as Gamelyn hesitated.

"Take it" murmured through the gathering like a benediction. "Take it . . ."

Trust him, the Lady whispered but it was with Marion's voice. *Do you trust him?*

It left no choice but to reach for the dagger with a shaking hand, draw it. Gamelyn rocked back, staring at the naked blade. A thousand futures frayed and broke upon the gleam of it, charring in the firelight . . .

"I trust you." Robyn's whisper shook Gamelyn back into thisnow. A long-fingered, strong hand wrapped about the shining blade, shattering the horrified enthrallment those futures held. Robyn clenched his fingers, nodded, and hissed, "Make it quick, aye? Make it *matter.*"

Gamelyn started back—another, more primal instinct—but Robyn's other hand shot to his nape and stayed him, tangling harsh in russet. "Nay, take it. It's yours, Oakbrother. It's allus been yours."

How can you keep letting him put a knife to your throat?

Make it quick.

Take it.

Trust him.

I trust you.

Robyn had snaked one arm about Gamelyn, a strength of both seeking and tendering comfort. Gamelyn pulled the dagger from its sheath of fingers, saw the new blood staining it. Through a haze of sudden terror, he *understood.*

He stopped thinking, had to. Instead relied upon that easy assassin's skill to steady his hand, whip the blade to Robyn's throat and, at the last instant, twist it.

The flat of the blade slid across the pale, firelit throat. It left a slick of blood, but hadn't so much as nicked a pimple.

It had been easier to wade knee-deep in bloody Acre.

"Wind the horn," Robyn whispered, then wilted, head lolling over Gamelyn's arm, black curls falling over the fresh-raked earth. As if dead.

As if mimicking hundreds of never-ending nightmares.

As if *real.*

And it was, thisnow and this place. So real, he was blinded by tears . . .

"Nay," Gamelyn couldn't help but say, just as he couldn't help but pull the limp figure desperately close, spend ragged breaths into the sweat-damp hair, against the open mouth.

A gasp rose from the watchers.

A keen, raw and hoarse—Marion, collapsing to her knees upon the altar stone, her grief no less tangible than his own and echoed, no less ragged, from the women who clustered around her, bore her back up. The burn of the amulet at Gamelyn's neck: a warning of John's approach, with the Head Forester's horn in his hands and his eyes glittering like a brand. The others—once outlaws and now again a freeman's covenant—all gathered in a tight bunch.

Gamelyn closed his eyes against all of it, took in a deep, steadying breath, and let it exhaust over Robyn's cheeks and into the night.

Was. . . is. . . this it? Is this all it ever was?

There was no answer. No more questions. No Voices. Only a presence, sinking within.

Gamelyn *knew*.

A gasp escaped, half laugh, half sob. He lowered Robyn to the ground—gently, ever so gently—and lay the dagger upon his breastbone. Looked up to meet John's large, tear-filled eyes, and the outstretched hands holding the horn.

With fingers still shaking, Gamelyn took the High Forester's horn and put it to his lips.

Spoil of war, Robyn had called it, but it sounded a stag's bell, clear and low and pure, and echoed against the moon's rise over the Tor.

In the time it took for the echoes to die away, the covenant had answered the summons. Gunnora folding Robyn's hands over the dagger upon his breast; John kissing his mouth; Gilbert, David, Arthur, and Much lifting him and bearing him away.

Will was nowhere to be seen, some part of Gamelyn's brain warned, but any wariness skittered sideways, refocused upon the figure gliding towards him.

Wariness? Surely not.

But Marion was flanked by Aelwyn and an honour guard of women, and she held the horn-crown in her hands.

It was easy to kneel; his legs were shaky. The crown—*yours, allus yours*—somehow lay lighter upon his head than it should. Marion's fingers trailed across his face, tipped his chin up. He evaded the sudden intimacy—*eyes meeting eyes*—more from habit than inclination, cupped her hand with his, and nestled his cheek against her palm. Closed his eyes and thought of roses, dusky and opening into the morn.

Another impossible moment fit for dreamings—its own nightmare, really. Robyn hadn't known enough, obviously; thisnow Gamelyn had no idea what to do.

"Still?" Marion said, all too gentle.

"It's only that I've never . . . " He stopped, cheeks heating.

She knelt, skirts pooling over his thighs. "No vows or hearts remain to break, love. Save one given in a Summering Wode, long ago. And if you mean to break that, why are you here?"

He started to speak, found words tangling upon his tongue. Marion misconstrued, made quick reassurance. "He's with John, you know. Even as Much is biding happy with another tonight. 'Tis our way, you know that. Your way now, and no need to worry."

"It isn't that. It's only . . . he didn't *tell* me." Gamelyn's eyes held upon the sky, his voice all a-quaver. "About what it all would come to. The . . . dagger."

Marion leaned forwards, kissed his cheek. "He wanted to tell you. I asked him not to."

Gamelyn blinked, eyes narrowing upon her. "You . . . asked. . .?"

"You know the ways well enough, even if this was your first Bel-fire. And it was the first in so long where Oak and Holly made the magic together. But 'tis also true that no one knows how the rite will play out—save, of course, the dying Lord. The Lady writes the play, but 'tis His, to decide the manner of His ending. D'you understand?"

"I'm . . . not sure I do."

"Hob-Robyn was ready to set aside the custom, you see, and tell you. He knows you have . . . fears, but not how deep they lay. I knew more, and how it might leave you unable to give yourself to the rite."

"You knew—?" He started up, the fingers playing with his hair snarled, tugged him back down.

"I Saw it, in the scrying bowl. The dagger to his throat—your dagger. In the middle of it, I was . . . well." She rested her forehead against his. "I was terrified. But after, I knew what it was . . . what it *had* to be. It couldn't be anything else."

His eyes flitted sideways. "You sound so . . . certain."

"Do I?"

"After all, fate would have us rivals. Even the stories, told of Robyn Hood and his greatest of enemies, Guy de Gisbourne—"

"And what is your name?"

"What does that—?"

"*What is your name?*"

"Gamelyn." Unthinking-quick, and somehow a relief as he turned to her and buried his face into her cinnabar hair. "Oh God, I know now. But it's so easy to forget. To . . . fall."

Her arms curled about him, seeking and giving reassurance.

"Marion, you have to tell me. Keep telling me. *Claim* me, tell me who I am, over and over so I don't forget again . . . "

"Gamelyn," she murmured against his ear. "Once Gamelyn was dead, but now? He's alive. We're *all* alive. Together." Looking into the grey eyes, he had to smile. "Make the song, my Oak. You are my Lord, and Summer's King."

He rose to his feet, one hand still entwined with hers, and put the horn to his mouth, winded it.

A roar answered him from every throat, and he thrust the horn aloft, sang into the night, "Once I was dead, and now . . . now I'm . . . *alive. . .*" His voice choked, failed him.

"Blessed be the Lady, who did ye revive!" It was Robyn's voice, coming from a hooded figure standing on the altar stones, surrounded by fireflies.

Marion leapt to her feet, twirling Gamelyn around.

"To the Hunt!" she called. "Dance! Life is no more and less than this!"

- Entr'acte -

Challenge has been made and done upon the Tor, beneath the moon and between the fires; all now is frivolity and merriment, ribald jokes and merry japes.

And dancing.

The Maying-pole, erected on the east ridge, stands wrapped with garlands of every hue imaginable: first free and flippant in the wind, then a multicoloured weave bursting from the hands of those dancing and singing around, then a tower tall and evocative, wrapped potent in rainbows. Music sends echoes across the valley, measured in hands clapping and feet tapping, accompanied by leaves rustling in the breeze.

And amongst them the players: Mother dances with her bairns; Crone smiles and nods and claps; Maiden Ivy shrieks with laughter, swung up and over in Oak Knight's arms as he, too, laughs, a new-made and lovely ripple of breath.

In the maypole's shadow, tangled in rainbows and Fool's embrace, Holly watches out of Winter-black eyes.

He has waited forever, it seems, for this.

Power, runnelling off broad shoulders and into ground, relief and release. Shouts, rising from a hundred throats. Night finger-lings nestling 'round lantern's light. Well-dried wood crackles hot upon the need-fires, sending sparks and vapor into a cloudless, star-pocked sky.

And They dance. Maiden leads, and Knight, to spiral and join ranks, circling, in blessings begged from fecund fire. Hands join, refuse to release even as the music leads them faster, until they are followed by several trains of wild steps, tossing hair and nimble feet, each a link in a wandering chain, gathering as they go. The dancers group into one circle, then two, then three and more, each following its own path sunwise, the spiral of it tightening, then retreating, over and over again. Giving way, while upon the wind a whisper wings:

Take it. Aye, love, 'tis all of you and yours.

Indeed, the world seems hanging still between Ivy and Oak, Lady and Lord. Heat waves rise, shimmer them into coppery ghosts with fire-kissed cheeks.

Oak passes a cup to his Maiden fair, through the waves of heat and sparks. She takes it, drinks it, and when she lowers the cup, the mead has kissed her lips all wet.

His wonder is plain: shall the mead taste different, taken from those lips?

She smiles at him, soft and knowing, fingers rising to unwind the ivy from her withy crown.

The fire flares. Dancing has not slowed, the sense of mirth unabated. Two worlds, the circle within quiet and waiting, the circles without joyous and abandoned.

Two worlds, in thisnow. To make three . . .

Take 'im, lass! comes a call, then, *Make her work for him!* another joshes, then a small patter of good-natured laughter as another says, *She wain't be unwrapping that fine young Maypole lessen it's wrapped first!*

Mother laughs, coming to take the length of green from Ivy's hands as Crone takes hold of their wrists, first Maid, then Knight. Mother lattices the green vine around and through, then, with a kiss to Oak's freckled cheek that raises another series of teasing calls, steps back. *He's ready for you, fair Maid.* Mother's eyes sparkle, look down. *In more ways than the one.*

Laughter once again rings out, comments shouted and sung, some ribald enough to set Oak's ears humming with heat, whilst his Maid is smirking, unabashed, bound to him all gilded fire and copper-dusted skin, hair hanging down her back with several lovelocks falling over her breasts.

He wants nothing more than to touch that fire, brush it from her cheek, just *touch.* . .

The vine frustrates, stays him, and where in love-tangles he has found startling pleasure in the binding, here he is unnerved. Green eyes meet grey; the plea in them is plain.

Maiden bends, breathes a kiss upon his wrist. *Anon.*

Frightening, the feeling.

Exhilarating.

Instead Oak leans forwards, breathes her in; she smells of woodsmoke, grass, salt-sweat, bark and earth and . . . desert roses. Another shudder, a brush of lips across her hair. Maidenly breath quickens, cheeks risen to flush; she's anxious, too. This is ritual: performance, and art, and even a blessing cup cannot provide wisdom never known. They have never lain together.

She's a *woman.*

Surely it can't be *so* different.

A smile tucking into one dimpled cheek, she leads him in the sunwise dance of Maying.

The fire has muted to coals and heat. About it they dance, Knight and Maiden, slow and slower still. Sparks leap and float between them. Spry tune grows solemn-soft, a dove's call into the night; singing and clapping mutes to bare rhythm, drum and heart voiced with pipe and varied tongues, tread of feet.

Tiny lights appear, flit, and twirl. Fireflies, doing homage to rite and dance.

The magic of it slides music into silence. Watchers gape, voices petering to mere breath. Still, Oak and Ivy move 'round the fire, bound palm to palm, eye to eye, step to step.

It is then Holly steps from the shadows, with him Fool and Crone as well. She carries a tilling hoe. They come beside where Oak and Ivy dance, all alone, and stop.

There is work to be done.

Holly draws the blooded dagger, thrusts it into the ground. Crone brandishes the hoe, and Earth willingly gives way to Plough's blunt gleam. A sigh goes through the watchers. First one, then another, suddenly there are many advancing, all with spades, rakes, hoes, and even fingers, making rows to take the seed.

So they prepare a bower.

Green and sedge give quickly way to sandy tilth, need-fire glowing at one end, a small toft lined sunup to sundown, ready and waiting.

Maiden takes Knight by the hand, leads him to kneel with her face-to-face, row and row, Moon and Star and Bel-fire to limn them.

Moments stretch. Thighs shiver, belly muscles quiver.

Earth new-furrowed beneath their knees.

Cool light, Moon crowning them.

Heat, as eyes meet eyes, in love and longing.

Breath, as Holly kisses them both, his Maid and his Knight, passes the cup once more, wraps mistletoe vine about their joined hands. Breathes the blessings. Backs away, and leaves in his wake the messengers, sparks of quickening light.

Sighs ripple as all retreat, witness to the Ploughing.

Fireflies. . . Oak swallows hard, says, *Yet I've not heard Her. Or Him. All night.*

They don't talk when They're here, she answers, touching her throat, with another glint of clever smile. *He's with you. She's in me. Deep as* you'll *be, milord, anon.*

Anon. But . . . *Is it so different, with a lass?*

Aye, and nay. Doubled honey in her words; he shivers, smiles, goose pimples rising as she bends down, unwraps the green from wrist and wrist, then leans and breathes moist fire down his breastbone. *I'll see to you, love. I know enough to get on with, mind. Like how you'll probably like this.*

Fingers reach down, cup firm, encircle, stroke.

His own hands are bolder than he; curious, anxious to touch, they cup full breasts, slide thumb over one ruched nipple. It rises further to his caress and he smiles, enchanted.

Aye, it *is* different, in the sensing. But in the heart . . . ?

How a maid can milk a bull! A teasing, admiring whisper, and more appreciation with several slow strokes, to pull from him both purl of sound and slick-wept quiver. He lurches forwards and takes her mouth, tongues her lip, her neck, hands once more taking sweet measure. Not only does he want to touch, but *taste.* She knows it, wants it, tangles a hand in his hair, pulls down to settle his cheek into a soft, plump valley. He nuzzles, runs his tongue from valley to crest, casts to one side, curls his tongue about one erect nipple. She sighs, hand fisting, pulls steady-slow back, then forth.

He groans, suckles, nips. One hand reaches down, trails knee to hip, across her belly and down. She judders again, opens her thighs, rocks against seeking fingers.

Makin' me ready for the plough? she murmurs against his temple, reaches down, takes his hand. Shows him where, and how— warmth folds about his fingers; he slides back and forth, matching her hand's rhythm curled upon him. First slow circles, then quickening, *slickening. . .* her fist pulls/pushes and he thrusts into it; his fingertips circle, then stroke, drawing wet warmth across a tiny, firm rise. She moans, rolls her hips, tightens fist and stroke; he gasps/grunts/shivers.

Guide me? he asks, and *Oh, aye,* she answers, lying back. No longer green-clad Ivy but russet and cream against rich-dark earth, cinnabar hair flung up like winnowed wheat, copper fur curling between her thighs. He bends, tongues soft belly, breathes her in, dips fingers once more into that slick-warm cleft to make her arch and whimper. She pulls him closer, says something about stars nestling in his hair and shining in his eyes, reaches between them and grasps him, guides him.

He hesitates, but she sighs his name, is still as slick-warm-ready, so he pushes through her palm, slow. Pressure greets him but not so fierce, almost not enough; as if she knows it, she tightens, raises knees to grip his ribs, arches up to meet him . . . then it is enough, wet ease different, lovely, making up for softer sheathing. Too slow, wanting more; he snaps hips, thrusts harder. Lightning bolts of new sensation blaze; he growls, starts the rhythm. Beneath him, she groans, knees clasping tight.

About them more sighs, rising through trees: soft, heavy substantiation. Others giving way, minding the Making, then turning to their own cleaving for heart, hearth, home. They will feel Earth beneath skin, Sky lighting the way, Water to nourish, and Fire to tease the senses hot.

Few will lie solitary this night—yet those few are touched, regardless.

Here, a lass sits rocking, holding the cloak of one she lost but last month, cleansing sorrow with tears and memory, and while Winter kisses her crown as he passes, it cannot bring her husband back, cannot . . .

And there, a young blacksmith's son, awkward and shy in the dancing, alone until chill fingers stroke his cheek and draw him away, into the magic, and it's the one he longed for, surely it cannot be . . .

Or there, an old blind man singing to himself, seeing starlight for the first time though it is impossible, he surely cannot . . .

Or where the first of the Wode's covenant watches, tears of rage and wanting, and upon his lips the whisper wants to say *Not yours. Never yours.* But the whisper will not voice; *dryw* knows the power even as man wants to rend it to ribbons. He cannot. Cannot . . .

'Twill be well, by and by, whispers another, holding friend close, shunning Maying bower to ease another beloved's pain, but he cannot. Cannot . . .

Or how, not far away, a stranger skirts wide-eyed and wondrous. Once a child had seen the Rite, now that child is Crone herself and never thought she would witness such a thing. *Sin,* the priests say, and *evil,* and *witchcraft,* but when the old one would cross herself and think to fear, all she sees is Light . . .

And then Holy Mother steps gently before her and holds out a hand, says *Come with me, then. Come with me. . .* and it is better, is it not, to see the magic and take Her holy hand, rather than leave this magical place and tell what She, in truth, should not, cannot?

For what cannot be any other night, this night/thisnow *is.* And Spirit dances and sparks like fireflies, making the Marriage Sacred upon the eve of Beltane.

Maiden writhes and whimpers, shudders as Knight strokes against her, ploughs deeper, harder; he throws his head back and cries to Stars and spills into Earth, falls into soft loam and soft flesh.

Feels them, one and all and same, feeding triune fires of *Ceugant.*

- XXXI -

"**R**obyn?"
Insistent, the voice, but also soft. Mayhap a dream. So with a growl, Robyn shrugged it away. Burrowed deeper into his furs, and John, sprawled half atop him, and that lovely lad from Hathersage, the smith's son who'd found out exactly what he was about last night . . .

"Robyn!" Still nigh a whisper, but then something landed on his arm—

"That's a lass," Aelwyn encouraged, "wake him."

—and with tickly-sharp bits began to lurch up his arm. About the time it reached his shoulder, Robyn had opened bleary eyes to meet a whiskery, pointed nose and a beady gaze peering at him.

"Aw, fer t' love of . . . " he mumbled. "Tess, what're—?"

John stirred, fingers fumbling at Robyn's mouth: *Quiet, you, I'm sleeping.*

"Robyn!"

Tess began nudging his neck with her very cold nose. Robyn groaned. It must be serious, to shift a fellow predawn after a Rite.

Sure enough, David was there, and Aelwyn, and both of their expressions were drawn, worried. Robyn was wakeful, just like that, and sliding out from beneath John—not without a fond caress to John's naked haunch and a bemused smile for the blacksmith lad, who was snoring in plain content.

Aye, well, Blessing cups did tend to make even an excellent rut into something mind-scunnering.

"We've a problem," David said.

"It's Agnes." Aelwyn's face was blotched with old tears.

And that finished the job of waking. "Who?" Robyn peeled Tess from where she'd clung to his shoulder and started a quick search for his braies. "What?"

"The old woman from Bruer? Her as we helped . . . " David started, then shrugged a bit miserably. "Aye, well, you'd best see for yourself."

Giving up on his search—he didn't remember where he'd flung his clothing last night anyway—Robyn followed David.

The morn promised beautiful, with the sun still hiding beneath the hills towards Hathersage, the sky all rose-grey and calm. The Maying-pole stood proud, and about it a black flutter-dance of birds were beginning to send their song over the Tor. David, Aelwyn, and Robyn picked their way carefully along the ridge; it was an obstacle course of the sleeping and the sated, all curled up next to the night's choice—or choices, depending. Likely a few would be sore, head or pride, come the waking. The Church's ideas of guilt and chattels were treacherous, but Robyn would see his people happy despite that, he would.

And it was no longer just *he* who would. He slowed, fond smile slipping broad as they came nigh to the stones and the still-smoking remnants of the huge bonfire.

Sweet Lady, but it was the loveliest sight he'd had in some time, his Knight and his Maid all wrapped up slumbering and new-forged, joined in sacred heat and Making.

"'Twas a good Marriage." His voice dipped even softer, deeper with emotions fierce enough to bring the heat-fill to his eyes.

David's answering smile was soft agreement, and Aelwyn nodded, said, "Aye."

Then it sobered, and she gave him a nudge. "Let 'em sleep a while longer. We can deal with this."

"She reached out to me, then she just . . . fell over."

No question, the old woman—Agnes, Robyn reminded himself—was dead. And no question she'd welcomed death; she had gone cold and stiff, but her face was peaceful, almost smiling.

With a tiny sniffle, Aelwyn threaded her arm through his and leaned her head against his arm. "I think it was her heart. I don't know what she was doing here, alone."

"I do," David said, grim, and handed over a folded-up missive. "This was in her pocket, Robyn."

David couldn't read—likely Agnes couldn't have, either—but that hadn't kept anyone from deciphering the seal at the bottom: two knights astride a single horse. Templars. Robyn scanned it, brows drawing together; he'd always read slower than his sister, but their mam's training had taken. Anyroad, the message was short and to the point.

"She was sent with this, from Bruer to the Sheriff—the ex-Sheriff," Robyn corrected. "That bastard de Birkin sent her as a spy."

"Well, she wain't by spying no more."

"David!"

"Well, it's true, Aelwyn-lass. We invited her and her people here, and this is how—"

"Likely she'd no choice! Maybe they threatened her people!"

"Leave off, now, don't sour Blessing morn. Likely Aelwyn's right." Robyn kissed the top of her head, soothing, and handed the missive back to David. "Give that t' fire, and not a word to anyone. We'll see her buried proper, and likely Will should welcome a short trip to clear his head; he can go to Bruer, tell her kin . . ." Robyn trailed off as David's face twitched. "David? What is it?"

"Aye, and that's the other thing." His voice quivered: pain, deepset with sorrow. "Will's gone, Robyn. Nowhere to be found. And Arthur too."

Blyth/Tickhill Castle, Yorkshire
New moon waxing to Winter Solstice, 1194 CE

"I had the strangest dream, once."

"Aye, and did you, then?"

Gamelyn rolled over, flung the coverlets away, and listened. A pair of pigeons squabbled at the window of the adjoining solar, making free in the rafters. Down in the bailey, a young cockerel warbled a reedy echo of the elder's crow, warning and notice: people were beginning to stir along their territory. The scrape of doors being opened, the slide of heavy drapes being hoisted aside. The *chock* and tumble of logs, unloaded by the main hearth below. The creak of boards; footsteps from another chamber.

And a feast for the eyes, as well. The drapes, flung back, let hints of grey and rose into the lord's bedchamber. The burgeoning light dusted indigo over black, tangled hair, defined angles and contours upon the naked-pale back and buttocks of the man sprawled beside him.

Robyn angled—just barely—from a facedown and blissful worship of the bedclothes. Ebon eyes slid Gamelyn's way. "Do we *have* to get up now?"

Not that Gamelyn wanted to rise . . . well, all right, then, mayhap part of him. And Robyn knew it. A smirk tipped that full lower lip, gaze lazy, meandering.

Unfortunately . . . "I suppose *you* don't. But I've a full day ahead even without hallmote, and I'd prefer a good meal beforehand to set me up."

Ah, and *that* brightened Robyn's sleep-fuzzed expression. Even convinced him to stir and stretch—which was just bloody dangerous to anyone's heart. Gamelyn considered himself to have a fair amount of self-command; nevertheless, he couldn't help but reach out for a stroke of that well-muscled haunch.

Robyn's purr didn't help, either.

Gamelyn's throat tightened, so sudden as to choke any voice. Which was probably just as well, for something would have come tumbling out akin to: *Oh God, you're so bloody beautiful, a half-dozen jongleurs would skin themselves to write a poem about you. . .*

Aye. Very good that he couldn't speak.

Instead, Gamelyn hauled himself from the bed and padded over to contemplate the ruin of clothing piled against the far wall. The tapestry hanging there was slightly askew, as well. A quirk tipped his lip. When Robyn had shown up last night, they'd barely shut the solar doors, and then not made it to the bed. The first time, anyway. A fortnight's separation seemed absurdly intolerable these days.

"I still en't resigned meself to seeing those hips so naked. Wit'out the measure, I mean."

"You're the one who said it would be safer hidden away. Considering." Gamelyn felt more than naked without the cord about his hips. But it was a Templar measure, filled with Templar magic—and likely a weakness did he, as Robyn put it, "have brass and stones enough to keep on wearin' your measure when the bloody-minded Master Preceptor of England wants you and me on a platter."

"Aye, true enough." Robyn grinned. "Your naked arse is nowt but pleasure, anyroad."

With an answering grin, Gamelyn began fishing—or trying to—for his garb. It was harder than it should be, even with predawn turning the solar from pitch to grey. Even if his own clothes were considerably less whiffy than those of a forester who'd been living rough in the Peak for several se'nnights.

"You're lord, en't you?" Robyn insisted. "Surely you can have a lie-in if you fancy one."

"Only a lazy peasant would think so."

"Peasant, aye, but t'other?" Another cheeky grin. "Come back to bed, milord. I'll show you how lazy I am."

The laugh bubbled up from Gamelyn's chest, fit to fill the solar.

"Damn, but I've missed that laugh." Robyn propped himself somewhat more upright. "We've a few years of it to catch up on, aye? So what's this about a dream?"

"Dream." A shudder travelled up Gamelyn's bare spine; he gave up on the tangled pile of clothing and went to the press for fresh ones. Still a-shiver, he made quick work of donning undertunic and braies before continuing. "Nightmare, more like. The same nightmare I've had for . . . well, forever. I keep waking and expecting it to be there, lurking."

"Any other dreams? Better ones?"

A shrug as Gamelyn stepped into woollen leggings. It was a tender subject, truth be known. Wymarec's predictions remained dismally true: however promising and potent a Making, and the resultant bountiful harvest, Gamelyn's own magic had once again dived deep, a latent and locked cipher.

Instead, of late he'd thrown himself into what he *could* do, thisnow. Blyth was coming 'round.

"'Tis yours, dreams or no," Robyn said, firm. "I've been holding t' horns ower long." There was a feral, faint gloss behind the ink-black gaze, betraying the undying presence.

The one serpent in Eden, refusing to confer wisdom even when the Lady had bequeathed both rite and right. Even when His avatar lay naked in their bed, offering . . . well, everything.

Another shrug, making light. The morn—and aye, the night spent waking—were too lovely to dwell on Eden's price.

"You're quite the temptation, believe me. But the light is too short-lived this time of year, and I've overmuch to do. I'll wager Marion's already out and about." Still tying the laces of his breeks, Gamelyn walked into the main solar and looked out the window. The sun was just beginning to limn the bare eastern trees and, sure enough, a familiar, green-clad figure was on prowl about the bailey's household commons. Shawl wrapping her shoulders, cinnabar curls veiled in more warm wool, Marion moved slowly and with the telltale jangle of the household mistress, keys at her girdle and basket over one arm. Her breath tailed her, more mist, in another morn promising clear.

Gamelyn watched her for long moments, then shook his head and chuckled, fond. "You'd think of late she'd at least have the lie-in."

"Well, me sister allus has been one to rise wit' chickens." Finally sitting upright, lean, hairy legs dangling over the bedside, Robyn scrubbed at his face with both palms. "I could do with a bath and fresh clothes."

"I'll say. You're lucky I didn't kick you out of bed for a wash."

"It was late. Dark. I sponged off the bits that *mattered*."

"Aye, tell that to my nose. It didn't care."

"Neither did your knob." Robyn smirked. "You were begging, milord."

Gamelyn couldn't deny it. Didn't really want to. Instead, another grin whispering across his mouth, he rummaged in one corner of the press and flung a fresh tunic and braies Robyn's direction.

"Hoy! En't we finding ourselves all dainty in our fine castle and soft bedding!" Robyn flopped back down. "Mind you, I'm saying nowt against the bedding. A bath would be nice, at that. And food. And a rut after."

"In the bedding," Gamelyn agreed. "All of this is possible. Bed will have to wait until the evening, though."

"Bugger."

"As you wish."

It was Robyn's turn to laugh. He kept chuckling as two servants were allowed in and listened to their lord's instructions. Not without a wary glance to their lord's black-haired visitor. "Robyn Hood," one whispered as they left, and the other nodded.

"Those two looked new," Robyn ventured as Gamelyn came back into the bedchamber. "And you look less worried."

"Worried?"

"For the servants to see you havin' a man in your bedchamber. Even one named Robyn Hood."

"The latter likely helps. They fear you'll curse their tongues should they wag them unwisely."

"Well, and 'tis a lord's privilege, to fill his bed with whatever he fancies. I heard tell of Hallamshire's first lord and a fine sheep—"

"Are you saying I people my bed with livestock?"

"Wouldn't be people that way."

"*You're* going to quibble semantics with *me?*"

"Mayhap"—Robyn waggled his eyebrows—"I'm merely sayin' what a fine ram you are, milord."

Gamelyn tried to frown; instead it came out a chuckle.

"And mad to boot, taking in a wild man of the Wode."

"I'm sure most already know their lords are mad. Or so *you* told me, once."

Robyn shrugged, writhing in the bedding not unlike a young otter scratching his belly in river shallows.

Gamelyn smiled and forced himself to look out the window. It was either that or make a complete hames of a busy morning. Snugging the belt about his hips, he espied Marion once more, making her way to the Underkeep. "You know, 'twas the Queen who advised me to cultivate Marion. 'The girl was born to manage an estate,' she said."

"My mam taught us well."

"Aye, but what happened to you?"

Robyn's answer was to point his first two fingers skyward.

"I'm serious, Robyn. Marion has turned this place upside down and shaken it sensible. People, beasts, rooms . . . and she sees to it our people are either good Heathens, or better Christians than the Church deserves. So it falls that the only care I need take is not against them, but *for* them, as it should be."

"Doesn't surprise me. I know me sister. Though our mam and

da would be fair scunnered to see her possessed of such a dowry and, as rumour'd have it, wived to a lord."

"Rumour can have its own protections. And you?"

"Me?"

"Would you surprise them?"

A snort. "Well, they knew all along I'd be nowt but trouble and keep after tupping that ginger noble's son." Unwilling, mayhap, but Robyn had finally moved to sitting up. "So. Are we, then?"

"Eh?"

"Mad?"

"We're here, aren't we? Still alive, and together. Mostly"—Gamelyn eyed Robyn—"dressed."

"'M waiting for that bath you promised. Hot water!" It was a croon.

"I spoil you. Downstairs, by the hearth. Kindly put something on in order to make your way there."

Robyn sauntered over, began gathering tunic and braies. Gamelyn started for the door. Robyn's next query made him hesitate.

"And that dream of yours?"

Gamelyn considered the question, then smiled.

"The dream? I don't have it anymore."

"What is this I hear about you leaving again?" Marion censured. "I thought you and the lads were to stay for the while?"

For the while, indeed; and not a long one from the way Marion waddled over to him. She'd that telltale, joint-loose and tottery roll in her hips and thighs that suggested, aye, Robyn had planned his return just in time.

"Well, neither did I 'spect that belly of yours to nigh double in size over a fortnight!" he marvelled—and ducked.

Good thing too; he'd neglected to notice she'd a wooden paddle in one hand. Well, they were down in the buttery, after all; her checking the wort in the brewing vats, with plenty of firkins and butts lined up against the far wall. It was cool and nigh deserted, belying the heat and bustle of the kitchen above. Thank the Lady's grace Gamelyn had sent breakfast with the bath—otherwise Robyn'd never have made it past that pork roast.

"Cheeky bugger," Marion told him as he swept her up in a hard—albeit awkward—hug. Her gravid belly really did seem to have grown twofold.

"You carrying twins?"

"You carrying a death wish?" Again, she hoisted the paddle.

In a mix of self-defence and pure affection, Robyn snuggled

closer. Marion managed a small whack to his arse, but tilted her head against his as he cupped a hand over her belly. A tiny shiver of silver-gilt gravitated to Robyn's fingers, warming them, and he smiled, traced a sigil there: protection and welcome.

"Nay, no twins. But mark me words, this 'un has the magic spades-full."

"Aye, and what else would she have?" Marion kissed his cheek. "Red hair?"

A snort. "When did you and the lads arrive?"

"Late. T' moonbow's waxing nigh-dark, but she lit our path and didn't set 'til we reached the gates. You were deep asleep, pet, and only your man to let us in."

She smiled, fond. "Much takes his duties seriously—and he knows I'm fair useless about now when the sun sets. Lets me wallow the whole bed and takes what relief he needs elsewhere."

"Well, and me sister's allus kicked like a jenny ass in bed . . . Put that paddle down, woman!"

"Then stop giving me reason to heft it, man." Marion sniffed his hair and nodded approval. "You've had a bath and change of clothes. I saw Gilly heading towards t' stables—is John hiding out there, then? I figured he'd be bedded down wit' you and Gamelyn."

"Nay, he knew I was pining for milord"—he shot her a sly grin— "and bides no less considerate than your strapping soldier man. He's waiting for me in t' Wode. I've duty to Tor still."

Her face fell. "See, I thought you were staying 'til me time comes."

"We are. This wain't take long, and we'll be back to stay with the morrow's sun. That's a promise." He kissed her hair. "I wanted a night with me lover, and a meal with me sister. Who, as the Keeper of *Sherwood*"—he slurred it all proper-normal—"is owed a tally and report from her head forester."

Her grin held genuine delight. "I should think you've had the first, since Gamelyn was late down stair this morn. So the second's all to remain, and that you'll have, baby brother. Fixed with me own hands whilst you give me that tally."

With the morning's opening of the castle gates came the master stonemason, a month later than expected. Gamelyn accepted the man's gracious apologies, discussed preliminaries, and had David show the mason and his apprentice to suitable quarters. David was shaping into a fine steward. The same scrounger's instincts that had kept the Wode covenant supplied were more than adequate for Tickhill's needs. And his gramma and son were well into making their own useful places.

Standing in the courtyard and watching the masons follow

David to the west dwellings, Gamelyn realised if he scorned luncheon, he could likely make the stables before Robyn rode out.

And ended up propped and squirming, thoroughly being done to against a secluded stable wall by an insistent, kneeling forester.

He loosened the hard fingers tangled in Robyn's curls and slid down, panting, into Robyn's arms.

"Ride with us?" Robyn asked, working his way back upward to nuzzle Gamelyn's neck. It wasn't exactly a fair question. Robyn still had one hand down his braies. "John wants you, too. It's only away tonight for dark moon blessings and then back tomorrow at first light. I promised Marion it'd be quick, and . . . Sweet *Lady*"—this with damp fingers teasing at belly hair—"but I've missed you. Come with us."

Mayhap he could. Gamelyn ticked off all the things he could possibly delegate and found too many he couldn't. "I've still hallmote. And the master stonemasons have arrived . . . for the west wall? I have to see the work started."

Robyn pouted, and Gamelyn wanted to join him. Instead he wrapped hard arms about Robyn and breathed him in. Said, "It's only until tomorrow, aye?"

"Aye, well," Robyn concurred and kissed him, hard. "I might even coom crawlin' into your bed again mid-night, milord."

"You keep calling me that and you'll be sleeping on the floor."

"Aye, well," Robyn repeated, with a smirk. "Our like's used to that." He kissed Gamelyn again, got to his feet.

Looked down, a lithe and lovely shadow with hay-strewn black curls. "I'll be back before you know it, pet."

Robyn stood amidst the stones of the Tor, and watched the setting sun lick fire and shadows over the hills.

He had done—from the year-and-day after that long-ago Beltane and the Church's butchery of his parents and their people—without fail, to honour his dead. Yet ever since this year's Beltane fires, Mam Tor had been . . .

Serene. Cleansed. It was the only way he could describe the sensations that had greeted him these past moons.

He was alone, as always. John had stayed below. The *geas* upon the Tor was—had been—unforgiving. The Lady had laid a pall of mourning over Mam Tor, disallowing any to trespass upon moon-dark save those few who had borne witness. Just over a year ago, Robyn had thought he was the only survivor of the brutal slaughter that had nigh destroyed the *Ceugant* with it. Archer, Maiden, and Knight, all left for dead or dispossessed.

But now, it seemed, in the aftermath of a ritual left fallow for five years . . .

The spirits were quiet, no longer angry, blessed and blessing. The *Ceugant* was together—*back to back*—and Mam Tor had been reconsecrated by the Great Marriage.

He ran down the Tor, met John, hugged and swung him 'round until they were both dizzy, and told him.

That night they camped in the Hunter's caverns, and refreshed all the runes and spells that honoured the ancient place. Protections holding firm, nevertheless they traded off slumber.

Neither had forgotten the previous winter, when time had stilled in the cavern's magical depths. So much that when Robyn mentioned, over breakfast, he fancied a trip to Mere, John treated him to a mighty frown.

"Nay, there's no *reason*, other I just feel we should," Robyn defended. "Tor's changed, and t' caves; mayhap also Barrow Mere needs acknowledgement. You're starting to sound like Gamelyn, worryin' things to marrow rather than just *doing*. Marion's been several times—"

"Not alone," John signed.

Well, and of course not. Aelwyn had borne her company, with Much as fierce boundary guard. Robyn approved more and more of that man; a proper Heathen, respectful of the old ways. No noble or Christian would be so serene about his woman swelling with another's bairn—and weren't *that* like most of their kind, listening to corrupt priests instead of their own holy book. Christ's mam had carried a god's child, after all. No proper man had the rights to claim any woman as chattel—and no earthly man had the rights to claim a Beltane-gotten child.

Unlike Scathelock, who'd tried to lay claim to what couldn't be owned.

Robyn reached out and stroked John's cheek, persisted, "Neither am I alone, love."

John was just as persistent. *You'll have to be, sommat, if we go. It en't my place to wander in there.*

Well, and he'd more rights than most, but Robyn had long ago given up on trying to convince him of it.

"Look. Marion wants to have the bairn there if t' weather holds, just as Mam did with us. Mayhap I just want to make sure it's as cleansed as Tor. For her sake." Robyn leaned forwards, laid a gentle kiss to John's forehead, murmured, "I feel like I need to go."

John closed his eyes, huffed a sigh, and nodded.

The road between Hathersage and Sheffield was one they well

knew. Out of habit, they took smaller paths, trod light, and left nothing to mark their passing save the press of worn boot soles upon the damp, sandy ground, or mayhap the oil of fingertips brushing upon sandstone or gorse. The morn was passing fair, with an unseasonable warmth in the air that smelled, almost, of spring.

A relief, after last winter.

The moors were little cover any time of year, but they kept to the evergreen brush and weathered rocks, slow and careful any time they came close to the road . . .

Robyn halted and laughed out loud. "Would you look at us? Old habits hard press, aye, little John?"

John's face lit with mirth and rue.

They didn't have to hide. They were no longer wolfshead but royal foresters, with leave to travel any road they chose. And as to outlaws . . . Well, there weren't many as roamed the Peak or the Shire Wode. Robyn Hood's reputation still had its uses.

They took the road the rest of the way.

"Sometimes I hope we'll run across Will and Arthur in our wanderings . . . " Robyn's voice choked into silence.

I don't. John's jaw rippled and set.

"I should have known."

"He," John said, halting, "should have."

Well, and Robyn knew that. But it still ached, fierce at times. Like the phantom pains of Arthur's hacked-off hand.

They walked in silence. The heather and sage moors dipped into trees, then into thicker woodland as they came to the river and forded the shallows. Beyond, the road branched; both of them knew this place well, John as a neighbouring croft, and Robyn as vital core of a child's existence.

Or mayhap not. Loxley village had been home and family to him, but he had always belonged, heart and soul, to the forest. To his Wode, closing about him heady as good mead, and the spirits within it . . .

And how long as it been, My Own, since Robyn Hode has ventured to Loxley, or waded the waters of the Mere?

With the coming of Summer Solstice had the Horned Lord returned, biding not merely beside Robyn as he had during the Summering season, but within him. Almost as if He were . . . relieved, to have a place to settle in and embody. Gamelyn had never faltered beneath the weight of the horn-crown upon his head, but a . . . resistance remained, unwilling—nay, *unable*—to fully submit to the possession of a wild god's heated, potent breath.

Unless it was Robyn doing the claiming.

The Oak who scarce knows how to hold to power without his mates beside him.

He has his own power, Robyn reminded. *The Lady said he'd a peculiar, solitary strength.*

Peculiar indeed. If only he'd use it! The Horned Lord snorted. *Mam Tor was cleansed by your blood, let by your rival's blade. The gwyllion stir in tree and brook. The Ceugant walks thisnow, albeit faulty—another growl towards the gaoled magic in Gamelyn's breast— and the Wode is alive again, so alive, My Hob-Robyn, and for the first in far too long. It breathes your name—can you not hear it?*

He could, and 'twere proper lovely. "I've always heard it." A whisper, aloud.

John reached out, took Robyn's hand. He always kenned when the god was speaking and, through Robyn's reactions, of what.

Aye, Hob-Robyn. You are the last of Us.

It was pensive, the Voice, filling Robyn with a strange melancholy. He gripped John's hand, pulled him close, and kept on.

The trees began to thin, the path widening out—and up. Robyn was able to straighten—too tall to tread the deer paths other than angled forwards as any hunting wolf—and the branches no longer tugged at his hair. John, of course, had no such problems.

They were close.

Sound came before sight; the runnel of water over rocks. A small path meandering into green: the way to what had been Loxley village, now a tangle of bracken and broom and new trees.

It was our home. I was born there.

Nay, the Horned Lord reminded, *you were born here.*

Here.

Barrow Mere opened out before them, shimmering black and silver.

He descended alone into the hollow, breathed the blessings, asked the right, and heard Her voice:

Not in any croft or bound by wicket and wall, but where your mother's Barrow kin cast their power and their fortune, made the water's magic sing. You, my beloved Son, were born in this wylding Wode, by the mirror of Barrow Mere. Your first cries were damped by green and mist carrying across still waters. Your first cradle was of green fallen boughs. The blood of your birth nourished moss and loam. Your offerings have been hallowed here, accepted.

Here was where he had first lain with his Summerlord; here was where he'd offered the Arrow's magic for safekeeping; here was where Marion wished to birth her own child. By this Mere, with thirteen trees grown old in guardianship of her, one of them proud beside him. The oak extended outward and upward, branches draped with green vine. One broad leaf clung, stubborn amidst vines; Robyn reached up and cupped it, asking. It fell into his hand as if drawn there, complete with strangling mistletoe and an equally resilient acorn. With a muttered invocation and a light exhale of asking breath, Robyn laid claim. The milk-bitter berries of the mistletoe frosted with his breath, warmed in his fingers. A quick draw and cut of his quillion dagger and green was wreathing his palm, the brittle leaf leaving coppery dust on his fingertips.

He contemplated the leaf, then extended his other hand and caressed the oak's bark as gentle as if his fingers were trailing down Gamelyn's naked back. Something fond and altogether vulnerable teased Robyn's lips into a smile.

I see. You come to this place merely to mope and sigh for your scarlet leman. Go home to him, then! It was derisive, an old hart's snort of dismissal for a bud-horn's impetuous challenge.

"Anon," Robyn admitted, needing no god's voice to tell him he was being pathetic. Still, the leaf held faded remembrance of gilt-copper hair, the mistletoe green as his lover's eyes. His smile turned fond again. What, after all, was life without the bleeding?

Mortal men do foolish things in the name of loneliness. Again, a snort: the god was Displeased.

Robyn let out a small chuckle, misted frost into the morn, and leaned against the oak, hard. Aye, he wanted his lover at his side.

The Mere quivered, as if a breath had stirred it—yet no wind touched Robyn's hair. He tensed and cocked his head, wary.

But no presences, no whispers, no glitter of eyes betrayed the watchers he knew must be there.

Marion had said the same, that Barrow Mere had been quiet upon her few recent visits. As if waiting. Or eased. Mayhap it was as simple as that: the magic had been openly acknowledged in thisnow, blessed upon a sacred site. Mayhap the Mere, like Mam Tor, was fulfilled.

Gamelyn Oakbrother's scars leave him restless. As do yours, My Own. Winterking and Summerlord are not intended to bide together, forevergreen.

The Horned Lord also seemed quiet. Rambling, almost. Nevertheless, his words made Robyn think of Alundel's song-gift: the story of the tree from Outremer, the outland holly oak.

Idly braiding the oak and mistletoe into his curls, he paced through the grove and to the edge of the still, dark pool.

Why have We come here? 'Tis not Samhain thisnow. Remembrance overmuch is not the province of pwca-*kind.* The Horned Lord seemed . . . puzzled? *You would do well to turn aside from your path now. Looking back is treacherous, Hob-Robyn.*

"It is." A breath into the soft air. "'Tis time to wash it away, aye? For all of us."

Aye, My Hob-Robyn. The Lady, again, Her presence so strong, it weakened his knees. *Let it go. Time matters not, here. You must lead the way.*

Robyn smiled, tapped his fingers upon the surface of the water, then rose and stripped down.

Threading the forester's horn over his head, then his tunic, he laid them on the bank beside his leather breeks. Hesitated, naked but for the quillion dagger bound at his calf.

The god-Voice had burrowed silent, but Her words drifted through his mind again. They'd a sudden, familiar-strange cadence. *You must be leading the way. Be letting go of the ways of iron.*

Soothing, the rhythm of it, like the memories of his mam's voice. Robyn nodded to himself and left the dagger on the bank.

Barrow Mere took him in as he dove deep. Accepting.

He was hers; akin, yet not, to how he belonged to his forest—another vast-dark She that held him, bound, in soft, sweet fetters. The Mere did not speak to him as she did to Marion—or as to Gamelyn, more 'neath the Lady's claim—but she nestled close and stroked him. Their language was intimate, sensual, a silent innocence more soul- than body-hunger; recognition and reverence. Kindred, from the beginnings of time . . .

The water was bloody *cold.*

Robyn blew and surfaced and shivered, ducked and dived and swam until he was panting, sweat slicking his skin beneath the water's touch. Then he lay, floating on his back and gleaming-wet as an otter in the shadows, to stare up at the sky. Blue and brilliant, it was obscured only by the occasional wispy cloud that seemed to snag upon the branches, both bare and evergreen, of the sleeping grove.

So lovely, and *quiet.* Only the hiss and hum of his submerged ears, sealed by the Mere's echoes, and the burble, hollow and insistent, of the stream that fed the deep pool. Only the flick and scoop of fish darting beneath him—some coming so close as to give hopeful nibbles at his hair, wafting for the surface like tangled ebony eelgrass, and the green still braided there, acorn and white berries. Only the sound of his heart, a steady and swift drum's echo, and the tickly, crackling feeling of the hair on his chest drying and spiking upward in the chill air, merely to flatten as he exhaled and water crept over his breastbone once again.

Sometimes Robyn wished he were an otter, biding weightless, content and cradled in this place to sleep and float, hunt and eat and play with his lover . . . aye, 'twould be a fine thing to be an otter. But alas, he'd not enough of sleek fur nor rich fat to keep him warm and buoyant. He was more like to turn a distinct shade of blue, healthy shivers turning into shudders and his teeth beginning to chatter.

With another sideways toss of his hair in the water, Robyn turned onto his breast, and stroked towards the bank. He reached downward, found the bottom, and stood. Arching backwards, he dunked his head to slick the curls back from his face, belly muscles bunching as he started to hoist upward, to stand and wade out . . .

Instead something tangled with his hair, halted and felled him backwards, underwater. Robyn gave an ungainly windmill of his arms, splashed and heaved and tried to lurch upwards.

To no avail. Whatever it was had tangled at his nape—hard—and was pulling his head down and back. He flailed again, hit something hard with his right hand, forced his left through the thick weight of the water to the thing tangled in his hair. Felt the claws of a tree branch . . . Nay. Fingers.

Air escaped him, a silent-panicked yip of bubbles bursting into blackness. Robyn twisted, broke the surface, struck out.

Felt skin, and a hard slender hand in his . . . *John?*

Tried to hold merely to have it ripped from him as he sank, this time deeper. He fought, resurfaced, heard a scream . . .

"Marion!" He coughed, and sucked in air. "*Gam—!*"

Hands seized his ankles, a hard nip and yank sideways. Then more on his arms, fingers in his hair like stone and twice as heavy. Robyn had time for another hoarse gasp of air before the water closed over his face, and the hands dragged him downward, into the black.

"As you know, my lord brother, the King's mercy allows me a Christmas visit with my husband at Winchester. As the weather has held so fair, I thought to bring the winter's tithing early and make the best of an uncomplicated journey south."

Alais peered at him across the writing table, serene and direct. Well, she had never been anything if not practical. Not for the first time, Gamelyn was grateful for Marion's insistence upon finding a place for his brother's wife and sons. The fee was more than suitable for a disgraced knight's family—*his* family, in truth—one not overclose but not too far, either. Being wife to a man gaoled as hostage to treason, however unwitting, meant Alais was unlikely to any better berth. She had accepted her lot, and it had proven an equitable solution for everyone. Particularly since, over the past season, Alais had wrangled the demesne of Stainton into something approaching solvency. She would see her man ransomed and pay her owings.

Hallmote was thankfully uncomplicated this time out. The coming of Christ's Mass—and the Solstice—meant people either bided more charitable, or that they'd less light and outside work, so fewer arguments made in the doing. In addition to Alais's unexpected hearing, there had been the expected Yule tithes, a few boundary disputes, a fine levied to reprimand an alewife who was shorting custom at Dadsley's tavern, and a day in the stocks for the miller who'd scraped one too many measures of flour from his lord of Tickhill's millstones and sold them on the side.

"You have my thanks, my lady sister, and the blessings of the season. Is your escort adequate?"

"It is. The extra men were quite . . . helpful. Pray tender my lady's foresters my appreciation in their help with those brigands."

Alais wasn't quite sure what to make of the notorious outlaws who now bided tame at the court of her husband's youngest brother—but she was grateful for their abilities at routing what she no doubt still thought of as their own kind.

What is your kind, then, Oakbrother? This woman who both resents and respects you? These supplicants? Or Me?

The Horned Lord's presence slipped within, strong and unrelenting. Gamelyn had started to reply to Alais; midthroat it turned into a small choke.

Not now, he told Him, just as insistent. *Later.*

Another wave, battering at him. Like a bird against a brass, seeking in itself a futile mate—or rival. He lurched sideways in his chair, hands clenching at first the armrests, then the broad board of the table.

You should have gone with him. The pwca *is ever the creature of time, and trickery, and the otherworlds.*

"My lord?" Alais was frowning. "Are you all right?"

"I'm . . . well. I had no chance for luncheon, no more."

No more? Nay, but even as you sit here, deaf to anything but thisnow's voices, tynged *unravels, and She slips time's leash.*

Something lay beneath the looming presence, almost an entreaty. Which made no sense. The Horned Lord never begged; He only issued ultimatums.

Our tynged *slips the leash of Time, as a rift is slipped between the Worlds, even as Winter gives into Summer.*

This time a wave of nausea rushed over Gamelyn. He tottered upward, was forced to plant both hands on the board lest he fall. It rocked beneath his weight.

"My lord!" Alais, voice tight, no doubt remembering long ago madness . . . though it had not been madness, but grief.

Was this, then, grief? For tears rose and inexplicably spilled down his own cheeks. Something was . . . askew. *Wrong.*

The massive board had collapsed beneath him. He was on hands and knees beside his chair, shuddering-sick. People were shouting, and someone was speaking his name, laying hands upon him. He was sick, and filled with a well never drying of tears . . . tears falling on the backs of his hands, tiny rivulets to glimmer on the floor stones, glimmering with darkness and light . . .

They have taken him. Taken him, and left a rift in our World. What has been opened must be filled. You will find the way. Find it, fill it. You must!

"I . . . must?" he murmured. "They? Who are . . . ?"

"Milord?" It was fuzzy and faraway, but he knew Much's voice

like a mother's. Better, for Gamelyn had never known his mother
once he'd passed from her body and out into light and air.
"Milord . . . *Gamelyn*. Can you stand?"

"I don't know what happened, he just . . . " Alais, again. "Is it
another fit?"

"*Another* fit?" And thank God, but Much was helping him to
stand. "Begging your pardon, milady, but you're not understanding."

He had to stand *up*.

"There's a . . . rift in thisworld," Gamelyn managed to mutter,
just before he pitched headlong to the stones.

There was a rift in thisworld. A rent in the *Ceugant* that would
never repair, never ease, never . . .

She wanted to fall to the floor, screaming and beating at the
cold stones they had all begun to feel as sanctuary. Instead she
hurled abuse into the black, full of tears she would shed later. *You
took him! 'Twas not his time, but you took him! Where have you taken
him?*

I did not take him, Maiden. The Horned Lord's presence was
faint, alarmingly so. *Would not have. The Oak wears My crown
remarkably well, but the Winterlord is Me.*

Marion realised she was on hands and knees in the undercroft,
and it was still ringing with a cheated shriek: her own.

They have taken him, the Horned Lord told her. *They have taken
him from thisworld, to Her.*

"They? *Her?*" Marion reached inward, tried to find the Voice,
the connection always there.

The Horned Lord crooned her name. But the Lady remained
dark, and silent.

- Entr'acte -

Aye, and Much kept trying to tell Gamelyn, from the moment he'd lurched up from the hall floor and back into his right mind—if it were his right mind, at that . . .

But his lord weren't listening. Much had followed, midstride grabbing a lad to fetch David. David could soothe a broody hen; he'd be well able for navigating the bloody hames of an uproar left of hallmote after their lord had stormed out.

"Milord. *Gamelyn!*" And Sweet Lady, but the man was charging down the corridors like a destrier blood-mad. "Where are you going? What is—?"

Gamelyn whirled on him, and it was all Much could do to not lurch backwards, the god was that strong in his gaze, all gilt-shiny amidst thick green. "Do you not understand, Much? He's . . . gone. Somehow."

"Who's—?"

"Robyn!" It was a snarl wanting to be a scream.

Much couldn't speak. Didn't know what to say, other than how did Gamelyn know . . . but that was rubbish, of course he'd know. But where? How?

Gamelyn whirled again and ran for the back stair. Much could only watch for a half breath, and then lurched after. Glad for 't, too, as his lord took the stair three at a time; likely he'd break his neck 'fore he reached the bottom.

He didn't. Instead he shouted for his fastest horse to be saddled, paced a furrow as it was done, and didn't notice that Much had also ordered another horse. Much knew better than to suggest—

open, like— that his lord mayhap shouldn't be going anywhere in this state, but it didn't mean he couldn't act.

Then Marion had shown up, wrapped for travel despite being weighted by that gravid belly, and Much knew the world had tilted and gone proper mad.

He started to protest; Gamelyn did it for him. Or tried to, anyway.

"You can't ride."

"I can."

"You're pregnant, Marion, you can't—"

"I was riding only two days ago, to—"

"This is different! *Putain de merde,* woman, I won't lose you too!"

"Or I, you! He was at *Barrow Mere.*"

Silence.

"I don't know what happened, but he was there, and now he's *gone,* and She's gone silent, and . . . " A huge, hiccupped sob lurched her breast.

Much took her arm, pulled her close. Made his own try. "Mari, love, please. Stay. We'll go, find him—"

She yanked away, and faith, but her face was that pale, that set. "You wain't stop me! He's my brother! 'Tis my right! I can, and I *will!'*

There was an audible grit of teeth. Gamelyn turned to Much and said, between those teeth and wooden, "The black mare, the rouncey."

Well, and if this madness was bound to happen, Much had planned on that—the black was fast, and the smoothest gaited in all of tica's hill.

"I'll fetch her," Marion said, and disappeared into the stable gloom.

Much started after, but Gamelyn grasped his arm. Murmured, "I'll be faster if I ride ahead. Stay with her, see to her."

"You don't have to tell me such a thing, milord." It was soft, chiding.

And it broke him. Shivered and cracked and revealed sommat scared and tender beneath. Gamelyn closed his eyes, raised his hand to Much's nape, pulled him close to lay a kiss upon his forehead.

Said, "I'm sorry. I know."

- XXXII -

It made a scene from the worst of his nightmares. The dark-haired figure lying, wet and wilted; the Mere pulling, strangely gentle, at limp legs.

Only it wasn't Robyn.

Oh God, no, not both *of them. . .*

Gamelyn vaulted from the mare midgallop. Well-trained, she slid to a stop even as he kept going, a half run, half stumble down into the hollow, past its grove of trees and towards . . .

"John!"

But John was cold when he got there, limp as Gamelyn fell to his knees, unresponsive as Gamelyn grabbed him, shook him, screamed his name.

Still, nothing.

Gamelyn gathered him up and started, gentle, to rock him.

Marion shortened her stirrups and rode fast—faster than Much wanted, she knew, but it didn't matter. What mattered was that they reach the Mere, find Robyn, ensure Gamelyn didn't walk into the same trap. And John . . . where was John?

She found out as they arrived, saw Gamelyn crouched upon the bank and holding a limp, slender form. Some hard, hysterical inner knowledge said *Of course.*

John wouldn't leave Robyn. John would go after, even if it . . .

"Nay," Much whimpered. "Oh nay, *Johnny.*"

It was an effort to sling her leg over the black's neck, and as she slid down, both legs were like willow branches, whip-wobbly and tingling-strange after the ride. They didn't seem to want to work. Marion grabbed at the black mane and hung on, feeling sick. Tried to lurch into a walk.

Much grabbed her up without a word and carried her the rest of the way.

As they came closer, Gamelyn looked up and O Sweet Lady, his *eyes. . .*

"He's gone. Both of them, gone." Starting out a murmur, Gamelyn's voice was gaining strength: anger, betrayal.

Marion felt it too, but from muted distance. As if it happened outside of her, and she were wrapped in some thin cocoon of a strange and scratchy fibre. "What happened? Where is he, what happened, why would Robyn leave John? Why would John . . . *Why?*"

Her legs went wobbly again, and a peculiar, rippling discomfort stitched up one leg, across her belly, and against her back. Marion sank to her knees on the mossy, damp ground. Wanting to touch Gamelyn . . . daring not . . . she touched John's still face, fingers a-tremble over his lips. Froze.

If John had gone after, then why was he *here?*

And the scratchy muteness of the cocoon was pulled apart somewhat as, against her fingers, John's chill lips twitched.

"By all the . . . Let him go, Gamelyn. Put him down, on his—"

"Marion, he's *gone,* he's—"

"He en't! But he will be if you don't do as I say. Right *now!*" She lurched forwards and grabbed John, tugging him free. "On his side! If he's swallowed water, mayhap he'll puke it up . . . Damn you, do as I say, Gamelyn! His lips *moved* when I touched him!"

The shout, delivered up in Gamelyn's face, did the trick. The soldier kicked in, obeying orders, had John in place before she could breathe twice.

And her breath came hard at the moment, no question. "I need me—"

"Here's your bag, love." It swung into view, dangling from one of Much's broad hands. "I strapped it on t' mare, thought we might need it. Though from the looks of him, we'll need the magic along with—"

"We'll use what we have to!" Marion snapped, rummaging in the pouch with a heedless clink and rattle of contents, search-ing . . . there.

Mind the dosage, lass. Her mam's reminders were never far; and in this place of spirits, seemed to brush her ear. *Foxglove can stop a heart as well as steady it to beating.*

"Mam," she whispered. "If you're here, wit' your people? Help us."

Just a few drops at a time. It seemed to take forever, Gamelyn holding John and shaking like dried leaves in a breeze. Her hands were just as quavery. For several of the doses, John just lay there as if in some . . . stasis, unresponsive, breath faint.

Then he twitched, groaned. Rolled over.

Gamelyn caught him, pulling him even closer. Marion didn't object, this time; John was shivering with cold.

But no water coming up, not even a rasp of it in his chest. It made no sense. He was drenched, had to have been in the water . . .

"I don't understand!" Gamelyn said, a low growl. "The Horned Lord said . . . Who took him from us? Who did this to John? *How. . .?"* As his voice choked off, she could see the wheels turning, making sense of what he had been raised from birth to deny as evil. Or impossible.

John's fingers were moving, though his eyes didn't open. As if he didn't want to wake but knew he had to tell someone. *They've. . . been after us. After Robyn. All along. Time. . . slipping. . .*

Gamelyn was rocking, again, comfort but also compulsion. John burrowed against his chest like a wounded animal seeking warmth.

I tried. They wouldn't. . . Even his finger-signs were weak, defeated. *I saw them. Take him. Tried to go after. . . almost made it. Found them. They put a cowl over my face, threw me back. . .*

"A cowl?" Gamelyn was staring into space. "Was he dreaming?"

"Dreaming awake, more like," Marion answered. Another dart of sensation, almost pain, rippled through her haunches and up to her shoulder blades.

"Milord." Much had been scouring up and down the banks of the Mere—another soldier, finding solace in figuring and fixing. "He must've gone for a swim." He'd already cast aside a pile of clothing, but he rose from his crouch and ambled over. He'd Robin's horn over one shoulder, his longbow in one hand. In the other was the quillion dagger.

Iron is murder to the fae. Aye, and Robyn had said it, time and again.

"Once I lay injured in the forest," Gamelyn found himself murmuring against John's sodden hair. "I heard strange voices. More than once, I've heard them. Thought they were dreams . . . sometimes they were. Dreams. But that time, they said . . . " His eyes met Marion's. "Said I was of the iron and the bells."

With that same horrible and gentle control, he let John down. As if the act were a trigger upon a crossbow, or fingers loosing a bowstring, he exploded upward and stalked over towards Much.

Much slapped the dagger into his outstretched palm and got out of his way.

"Gamelyn?" Marion started upward but her legs, once again, failed her.

"They might have taken him, but They won't keep him," Gamelyn growled, stalking to the edge of the Mere. "We'll have him back if I have to scour the bottom of this lake inch by inch, or"—and this as from across the pool, one by one, flickers of gilt started to peer from the dark foliage—"gouge out every last one of their glittering eyes."

Those eyes dimmed, several winking out as he held aloft the quillion dagger, pommel upward like a cross.

"Iron," Gamelyn purred, "is murder to the fae, after all."

It seemed impossible, but the wind answered him, gusting upon his rage and through the hollow, rippling the Mere's too-calm surface and tossing the evergreens. The dagger reflected behind his eyes, pulled from him what it always had: a symbol of love and longing, brutal loss and betrayal and undying heart-oath . . .

And the Horned Lord came to him, tenuous-strong, trying to inhabit, if not his soul, his rage. Slipping into it like an ill-fitting glove, nonetheless one in the demand:

Give him back. He is not yours. Give him back to Me!

Marion slipped into the faltering, silk-spun connection, strong and cunning mortar to hold a crumbling wall. For the last and irreplaceable third of the *Ceugant* still bided here, in the spirit rising from the dark, dank trees, antlers sculpted against the dying sun.

And a cry, from Lord and Knight and Maiden. *Lady! They have taken Your Son!*

The water began to boil, swirl, as if something long sunken into the depths was stirring.

John still lay upon the bank, half-aware and shivering; Marion refused to leave his side, but her spirit curled about Gamelyn's, fierce and unwavering. Much was praying, in several tongues and to whatever gods might listen. But he didn't retreat a single step, sword drawn and holding Gamelyn's back like he led a regiment. None of them quailed.

Even as the Pagan thing rose, black and sinuous from Barrow Mere, its breath like fire and eyes that shimmered, great lamps of Time.

It had a great iron chain about its neck.

Free me, Lord, it said.

The quillion dagger trembled in his fingers, heating as if held to a forge-flame. Gamelyn didn't so much as drop his eyes, gritted his teeth, and snarled with the Horned Lord's voice, "Free *my* lord."

It echoed through the clearing. The man-stag shadowed amidst the trees tossed His tines in challenge. The great wyvern stilled, seemed to consider this.

It did not speak again. Instead She spoke.

There is nothing to be done for it. It purled thought the windy hollow, a terrible-soft aspect that chilled Gamelyn to marrow. Even the hair flitting about his face stung, cold. *You are unweaponed, my Lord, whilst your avatar would ill hold the iron-spell against My first children.*

Still beside John, Marion kept chanting . . . something.

See, you do not even recognise the biddance your Maiden utters! What keys you might have held, you've let slip through your fingers! You are crippled, weak! *Small wonder you cannot hold what once was yours.*

"The Winterlord is of me," Gamelyn snarled. "Of us, heart and bone and breath! You yourself said, O Lady, that *back to back, nothing can stand against us!*

I see no Winterlord in thisnow. It was immovable. *You and the Maiden are incomplete. Merely two of three parts. You refused your magic, and now you have lost his.*

"You cannot do this!" Marion lurched upward, staggered. "We have spun the Making, he and I! We are One, you and I!"

In thisnow, this place, you are not the only one to wear My face, Maiden. Suddenly, it softened. *I am. . . regretful.*

Swift as it had risen, the wind calmed. The great ebon wyvern seemed to diminish. It gave a long, wavering cry, then slipped, soundless, back into the depths.

Gamelyn lurched forwards. "*No!*" Kept going, to his knees, then his thighs in the Mere. "I won't let you . . . You can't . . . ! I . . . !"

Much had lunged after and grabbed Gamelyn's shoulders, but he'd already stopped. Futile, to even try; Marion's knowledge lingered within, telling him what he didn't know.

What he didn't know—and knew, now, for a certainty. The Mere was a door he had no way of opening. Even the dagger consecrated with his lover's blood couldn't open that door without the magic behind it. He *was* unweaponed, without knowledge of the Temple's foreign spells, or even the Saxon prayers of his ancestors to bind the fae or bar them.

It took pain to rive him from the misery, pain that, at first, he thought was Much's hand digging into his arm. But it wasn't his arm. It wasn't his pain. Nevertheless, it thrust a jagged sword through his vitals, then, just as inexplicable, vanished.

He turned, slowly, to peer at Marion.

She'd fallen to her knees. John had risen, holding to her, eyes wide and fully awake . . . and frightened.

"By t—" Much lurched from the water and ran over to her, Gamelyn on his heels.

They'd no time to fetch anyone; the birth was quick and inexorable, hour instead of day, screaming-brutal as the flash of a sword in firelight.

Beauty amidst ruin. A sacred fire delivered by sacrifice, from the light of a dying sun.

Marion fell back against Much, shivering and wet with sweat. John covered her with Robyn's cloak.

Gamelyn couldn't move for long moments, staring at the tiny being that lay on the sodden, bloody moss between Marion's thighs. It made a creaky sound. Of their own accord, his hands reached, picked it up.

It was slippery in his hands, fiercely—and oddly—warm. It smelt of blood and, faint, of warm-risen yeast. Squirming, it gave a lusty squall.

"Give her to me," Marion said.

A girl-child . . . *his* girl-child, with hair plastered to her skull . . . not gilt, or even copper. It was fine as silk and black as sloe.

Like Robyn's.

The tears came, then.

Tickhill, Yorkshire
Waning of Winter Solstice, 1195 CE

Yuletide had been quiet, a mix of mourning and rapture.

Robyn was gone as if he'd never been there—in some otherworld, Marion knew, not dead. She'd know if he were dead, surely? There would have been some hint of his presence, more than the defeat that slumped John's shoulders, or the strangled, eerie calm that drove Gamelyn's every motion.

At least they seemed to find some solace in each other; John slept every night at Gamelyn's side, and abandoned forester duties for stable work, familiar and unexacting.

Gilbert took charge of the forestry duties, promoted a few loyal Heathens to ride with him, and roamed the Wode as if he would find Robyn single-handed, and woe to any outlaw who got in his way. David took over as much of Gamelyn's duties as he could. Aelwyn lingered close, catering to Marion's slightest request or whim.

Much just held her, firm as he held the castle gates, and coaxed the cooks into making outrageous delicacies. Like Aelwyn, he was convinced she wasn't getting her strength back as she should.

None of them wondered why—it was obvious. Marion kept expecting to look up, mayhap even today, and see her brother's smile, hear him tell a tale as to how he tricked the otherworlds into letting him go.

She had to get better. They had to find him. Even if they didn't know how.

The latter had put the verdigris ghosts back within Gamelyn's gaze. Plainly, he thought of little else. Paced the castle at night and rode the bounds during the day, with nowt to ease his thoughts . . .

Save, at times, the wee girl-child. They all loved her, the one light illuminating winter's long nights. Only yesterday had Gamelyn held her, walking her as she'd fussed, wakeful over some incomprehensible matter only wee bairns could comprehend, and mams and das could only try to ease with cuddling and nonsensical songs.

She knew he'd not meant to be overheard, but still, Marion had heard him tell the little one, as if an oath:

"You will know your uncle, if it's the last thing I do."

There had been no Twelfth Night feasting. Snow and ice had blown in on the heels of Marion's unexpected birth, giving them even more of an excuse to hunker down. The roads were passable—sort of—but word was nevertheless sent out to all comers: Tickhill's lady had gone into belated confinement with an early birth: a healthy daughter, praise God, and there was still the matter of waiting for Marion to be churched . . .

Tickhill's lord received condolences for the sex, with tacked-on wishes for the bairn's well-being, and in reality Marion wandered the upper rooms of the many-sided tower keep as she pleased. She was not the least displeased with her daughter; none of them were. They clung together with their mix of sorrow and bliss; she, Much, and John rarely left Gamelyn's side, and the few servants allowed were ones who would not question their Lord or Lady.

Indeed, tonight they all sat in the warm main solar, with a supper of goose, cheese, and fresh bread baked with Aelwyn's own hands. The wind raced outside, and Tibba and wee Tom were having their own race—albeit toddle in the latter's case—up and down the adjoining hall. They'd long grown bored of the newest girl-child, too little to really play as of yet, all scrunched up and swaddled on a warm pallet by the hearth.

Gamelyn was leaning over her, murmuring all sorts of nonsense. It was lovely, really, how he had taken to her. When Robyn saw her, he'd no doubt run like . . .

Marion clenched her jaw, sighed.

Blinking those indigo-dark eyes, the bairn reached out. Gamelyn ducked, but not fast enough, and the bairn made a rusty almost-mewl: triumph, a fist pulling a long strand of coppery hair to her mouth . . . and a smile, soft and *there*, on Gamelyn's face.

Much chuckled around a bite of bread. "It never fails, how t' wee one can squirm out t' swaddlings. I've seen jongleurs less agile . . . y' wain't get free that way, milord, trust to 't."

Smiling, Marion leaned in for the rescue, taking the keys from her belt and jangling them. There was no bairn born to resist such a temptation and, sure enough, this one was no exception.

"Have you decided what to name her yet?" Aelwyn wondered from over by the hearth. A frown quirked her brow—Tom and Tibba had gone ominously silent.

"I was thinking Aderyn," Marion answered, keeping the keys just out of reach of the tiny, grasping fingers.

"That's Welsh, en't it?"

"It means *bird*," Gamelyn answered, and peered up at Marion, a pensive smile flickering through his mussed forelock.

"I like it." Much nodded.

A crash sounded from the outer hall. Aelwyn gave a small yelp, ran out. John rolled his eyes; it was the only comment, spoken or signed.

He hadn't, unless it was given to Gamelyn in bed, uttered a word since . . . since . . .

There has to be a way, Marion thought, and kept jangling the keys.

The Lady had retreated within, and the Lord's voice changed, within stones that nevertheless spoke to Gamelyn.

With the speed of a snake's strike, Gamelyn grabbed her hand. The keys gave one last *clunk* and dug into her palm. "Ow!" As his grip merely tightened and he pulled her closer, hand first, Marion protested, "Gamelyn, you're hurting me!"

Immediately, he loosed her. His eyes flickered to hers, held there, burning.

"Keys," he whispered. "He holds . . . the *keys. . .*"

Then he lurched up. "I know what I have to do."

"Gamelyn, what are you—?"

"Milord, what is—?"

He didn't seem to hear either of them, heading towards the door with John a shadow upon his heels.

Marion peered at Much, then scrambled up.

"*Gamelyn!*"

Her cry halted him as he reached the door with a lurch and stumble, barely saved with a hand to the lintel. He stood there—*hung* there—heavy, both hands clutching the stones. Then more, forehead against his hands, and those splaying against the stones, as if drawing strength.

And the stones answered, humming and whispering.

His lips moved—whispering back, Marion knew, could feel it like soft fingers tickling up and down her spine.

John watched; his eyes, so numb this past fortnight, went ablaze. He reached out and touched Gamelyn's shoulder. Gamelyn nodded. John hesitated, then looked back at Marion and Much. He brought his hands to his face, then blew across them.

A blessing, whispered. "*Bendith y mamau.*"

Then he turned away, slid through the doorway, and dissolved into the shadows of the hall.

Towards the stables, Marion kenned. John was leaving them. *Gamelyn* was leaving them.

Aderyn started to cry. Marion turned and scooped her up, cuddled her close.

Much rose, slow, beside her, put a hand upon her shoulder; buoying, steadfast. "Milord." It was rough, brooking no argument. Much didn't need the frayed threads of the *Ceugant* to tell him upon what edge his master was teetering—his knowledge was of thisworld, and all the surer for that.

Silence. Much's hand slipped, quivering, but held fast, as if he would release her and go after, but couldn't.

"It's done, Much. The debt paid, thrice over more—"

"My *lord!*"

"Aye, I will always be that. But I shan't ask this of you, shan't ask that great heart of yours to be torn. Not anymore. I *will* not. John will go to the caves after we travel this next road together, and you will stay here, guard what is ours." Gamelyn pushed from the lintel, half turned. There was a gilt madness in those eyes, and a shadow of leaf and horn ghosting the russet head. "I'm not sure even Hob-Robyn has ridden a Hunt this Wild."

Marion couldn't help it—a lurch forwards, still clutching the bairn close, with Much a bare half step behind this time. They both halted beside Gamelyn. All three merely stood there, peering at each other for long moments.

Between them the bairn squirmed, let out a creaky half cry.

As sudden as he'd earlier moved, Gamelyn bent close to her, stroked her forehead, said, "Shh."

And Aderyn listened, peering at him with large, indigo eyes.

"Where are you going?" And bloody damn, but Marion's voice didn't want to work. Instead she put a hand to his face.

He took that hand and went to his knees. "Maiden. *Mother.* I know what I must do. For the first in too long, I know what has to be done. The keys. He has the keys to the Barrows, so he said. And the Lady told me long ago, I had to take keys in hand . . . " His eyes slid upward and sought hers, a verdigris glimmer shadowed beneath that russet forelock, with the quick gleam of teeth. "I've left it overlong as it is, don't you think?"

Marion didn't know what to think. Couldn't think. All she knew was those strands so severed and fraying thisworld nigh to breaking—her heart nigh to breaking—were tangling tight, plaiting another set of futures. Wild, yes. Dangerous. Yet gleaming like polished Barrow-gold.

"I'm going to find him, Marion. I'm going to fetch Robyn back to us. Whatever it takes."

And the Lady's presence, a sudden swell from the silence within Marion, broad and fierce and . . .

Approving.

Before Marion could even start to classify her own emotions, she nodded. Pulled him upward, said calm and firm, "Find him, then. Bring him home."

As Gamelyn gained his feet, that smile broadened, heedless and reckless as Robyn at his worst. He raised one hand to his lips, kissed two fingers. Shared the kiss, callused fingers pressing gentle against Marion's mouth, then down to trail across Aderyn's cheek—a feather-touch, pensive wonder, just as quickly withdrawn. The signet ring upon that hand—the one that had not been removed since he had come to Tickhill as its lord—sparked, then guttered as he cupped his other hand over it. With a twist he removed it, regarded it almost musing, then placed it on his palm and extended it to her.

"My lady." It purled through the solar, Gamelyn's words soft and ritualistic as any blessing breathed across the need-fires. "Maiden. You'll find my measure with Robyn's. Hold them safe. Bind them with yours. Let the rumours stand as what truth they need be, and *are:* you're my wife, your children our heirs. Hold our forest and our lands, hold our honour and our keep."

Marion reached out, slow as if in a dream, and took the ring. Placed it upon her finger.

"Let Aderyn see it." It cracked, ever so slight. "Let her hold it, and sing to her. Tell her . . . Summer shall return.

"*Confanonier.*" It changed; just as soft, but underlain with steel.

Marion felt more than saw Much draw up beside her, straight and sturdy beneath the charge of it.

"Milord." Laconic, dry, accepting; were Much asked to fling himself from the tower stair, there was no doubt he'd do it . . . and for a smattering of breath, Marion wanted to grab his hand, prevent it.

"*Y' canna chain t' wind,*" Robyn's memory teased her. "*Such wishes are for Christians and rich men.*"

Robyn, she whispered back, *why have you been taken? And to where? Where will he have to go, to find you? Lady,* where?

Still, She was silent. But Her presence, satisfaction and victory, remained, cowling Marion's shoulders.

"Hold my gates and our lands." Gamelyn held out his arm, hand reaching. "Care for our Lady. Fly the banner, and do not let it drop."

Eyes glimmering, Much clasped that arm, so tight as if to never let go.

But finally he did. And in a whirl of burgundy and indigo, Gamelyn was gone.

– Postlude –

"Three. Four. Five."

Blood runnelled down the broad, muscled back, streaking pinkish over pale skin as it commingled with sweat. More than there should be, but then, most of it was from where a stray flick had raised another angry, scarlet stripe across the recently shaven skull.

"Six." The counter's voice made calm tally.

Head wounds always did bleed profusely, Wymarec considered. It had been an unfortunate miscalculation; an improper angle of whip and hand, nothing more, and no fault of the one bearing the ordered penance.

No fault, but the Penitent was bearing up too well, in fact. Still on his feet—albeit hanging by the ropes binding his arms outstretched to either side—he couldn't help but lunge as the whip whistled warning, and only cried out as those blows did land. No in-between whimpers or sobs . . . none audible, at any rate. And the blows were fierce; the first few had proven they had to be. Not unheard of in their Order, the thrill that could be gained from a proper application of pain. But this . . . obstinacy?

Wymarec gave a small *tsk*. Pride. Still.

They would break that pride, and without breaking the man's spirit. The latter would do no good.

Signalling the counter to leave off, he glared for silence when the attending Commander angled forwards. Small, yet telling, the protest.

But abortive. Obedience held.

It was entirely too soon to display any mercy.

Wymarec adjusted his trajectory. His next two quick strokes were lazy, almost light. Then, off any expected timing, he delivered two brutal strokes, forehand and back.

A hoarse shout, and the man finally—*finally!*—tottered to his knees, hands sawing for purchase on the ropes about his wrists.

With care and flawless aim, a humourless smile ticcing one side of his mouth, Wymarec finished it. Three more strokes, steady and swift. One could almost feel the frayed control being regained, sense an oddling relief at expectations being fulfilled, hear the tiny moans of breath trying to suck in strength between the strike and resultant cry. Wymarec nodded to himself, let the whip coil at his feet, and counted a slow, erratic five. Let a*9+nticipation shake and shudder those freckled, blooded shoulders. Let the Penitent think he'd miscounted, that it was over.

The next blows sent him sprawling, staggered and writhing and drawing his knees to his belly, with a cry that would have woken the damned in Hell.

Wymarec waited.

Still, no plea. Disappointing.

Tempting, to draw it out a bit longer.

Commander Hubert stepped up, meeting his eye. Said, firm and carrying, "The agreed-upon punishment has been meted."

Hubert was right, of course. To go any further would speak to personal desires, not that of the Order. And there were other ways.

The Penitent must have heard; his frame sprawled further upon the stones, shoulders bunched and distorted against the ropes' tug, ribs heaving and breath exhausting in tiny, hoarse catches.

Wymarec let the whip drop from his fingers, turned to the gathered Templars. "Indeed, the penance has been met. Do we then agree upon the application of this man's request for reinstatement? Has this satisfied our judgment, our place, and our Rule?"

The murmur that followed was made of many things: regrets, satisfaction, gratification ranging from smug to stirrings of carnal pleasure—but the most common emotion quavered through Hubert's voice.

Remorse. And beneath that, the patient necessity of sacrifice. "I bear witness to our Preceptory's wishes. It is done. Let him be welcomed back. Let him be bathed, and consecrated, clad in the white, and oath renewed to Temple Hirst in fullest measure."

Amidst the murmurs of agreement, Wymarec stepped back into the circle. With a jerk of head and hand, he indicated the ropes were to be loosened. Two dark-clad sergeants obeyed—with such alacrity that the Penitent lurched forwards and fell against the earthen floor with a limp, bone-jarring thud.

Hubert started over.

Wymarec held up a hand. Knelt, gloved hands upon his knee. Said, almost conversationally, "It is over. Welcome back, Sir Guy."

No answer for a moment, and Wymarec felt a stain of disquiet. Had he been too assiduous in carrying out this particular duty? There had been, granted, more pleasure than there should have in the humiliating of this one.

"My name"—it quavered, slurred on a tongue weakened by pain—"O my Master, is *Gamelyn*."

Wymarec knew he should be furious. Instead laughter bubbled up, soft and rueful triumph.

- END BOOK FOUR -

KINDLY TURN THE PAGE FOR
-- A PREVIEW OF BOOK FIVE --

The Green Man is lost to Sherwood Forest.
Yet the Horned Lord roams there still, and the legend grows.

Robyn Hood has vanished, and the mystic trine of the Old Religion—Archer, Maiden & Knight—has been broken . . .

Or has it?

Rumours abound as to a hooded man wandering the Shire Wode. Marion holds both the Wode's magical influence and the castle of Tickhill with shield, sword, and wit—not only for love of her covenant and her children, but as a weapon to bring her brother Robyn back. And Robyn's lover, Gamelyn, plays a dangerous game with his Templar masters. They believe he has delivered the Wode's Pagan rites to their use, all the while unaware that Gamelyn has sworn an even deeper oath: he will realise his own power and find Robyn, whatever the sacrifice.

For it is Robyn's to wield the deepest magic of all—he is the Sacrifice, and Undying King of the

A tug at his sleeve—*come away, it's done.*

Only for now—he'll see to that, he will—but aye, for now it is done. Over. He should retreat, 'twere merely sensible. Of course, his best friend—only friend left, truly—often made sense.

But 'tis as impossible to leave as to, in the end, stay away. He'd held out, he had, for a brace of years. Loath to return. Unwilling to believe.

Drowned in the black of Barrow Mere, it was said... or, more likely, poisoned by the Templars... or ta'en awa', as Arthur would say, to the fae and the otherworlds... Aye, the rumours were rife the further south they'd returned, telltales to one ill wind: the Hooded Green Man was lost to the Shire Wode.

Why, Rob? I told you. Told you the treacherous sod would be t' death of you. O, Rob...

He'd burned his own nest to give those warnings, was reduced to crouching a stone's throw away from the Maiden stones, nursing bruised ribs and a bitter heart.

"He'll come." Firm, the Maiden's words; her eyes gleaming gold against the flames, her chin held high despite a troubled swallow.

"But if—"

Those gleaming eyes slid sideways, quelling. Beside her, the younger lass bit her lip and lowered her head. To the Maid's other side, an elder woman muttered a sigh. Silence lingered and crept across the stones where they sat: a masked and honoured--if troubled--triumvirate.

And that was why he'd challenged, truth be told. Because sommat needed to be upheld. Especially since one who should protest just stood there, supposedly guardian to the women with hand to sword hilt but not acting... noble's lackey! Whilst their leader who'd have stood up to any noble who thought to take their forest--save the one, damn him to his Hell...

It was over. Rob was gone.

Drowned in the black of Barrow Mere... poisoned by the Templars... taken away to the otherworlds by the fae...

Yet May Day still blazed with light—somehow, and the Horned Lord's power all about them—somehow, pricking even the most dulled and unused senses. The flames licked high and into the starless night with that power, reflecting against heavy clouds to shimmer the sand and scrub about them, flinging dancing shadows across the hilltop. The gatherers, nearly fifty strong, circled, capering, singing... and if 'twere more shouting, really, it held its own merriment and music, and wasn't that the proper way of things during the feast of Beltane?

That, and the challenge to the god.

None had known him as he'd challenged the cocksure noble bastard. Thank t' Mother none had recognised who'd slunk away in defeat.

"Will." Once more, Arthur tugged at his sleeve. "Come away."

Instead Will glared through his greasy forelock at the victor, who stalked the hilltop like he owned it. A lord, right enough. Not the man Will had expected to find—hoped to find, take down, defeat, *humiliate*—but this one just as foul, a newcomer wearing a greenman's face that sprouted tiny goat's horns. Stripped down for the wrestling, hair skimmed crimson in the firelight, anointed as champion and challenger for the god's right—the cheeky bastard'd neither height nor heft on his side, but he was deceptively strong, and more treacherous-quick with the staff than Will'd believed any of his like could boast.

Noble-bred bastard.

He wouldn't've taken Will, if...

"I know. He'd not've taken you if you weren't drunk." Arthur's hand landed firm on his shoulder, proof that Will'd spoken the last aloud. "Faith, lad, you've been drunk one way or another since... since... Well, it's done. No use staying. I've no stomach for rites like t' these. Letting such folk in... the lass has turned away from our Lady's true face—"

"Marion did nowt!" Angry, clipped harsh. "I waint believe that from her or any our folk! 'Twere that ginger bastard, letting his kind run ower our places like vermin! Taking, allus taking, just as he took Rob!"

"*Bendith*, friends."

Drunk and slow Will might be, and Arthur soft from keeping a tavern by day and a wife by night... nevertheless both of them whipped around, hands to weapons, as quick as it took the speaker to finish the blessing.

A cool customer, he was. A blink of pale eyes beneath a grey cowl, and a slight tilt back of head, but his gloved hands stayed steady where they were, resting at his belt.

"It is blessing time, friend," the stranger repeated, stressing the last with a smile curving his lip. An old Saxon tilt coloured his speech--it even coaxed a fond smile from Arthur as he fingered the old axe hanging burnished at his belt. Yet Will could dredge up no like affection even for an elder tongue; the stranger's clothes, though of plain woollen, lay with a fine sheen no peasant hereabouts could afford.

And of course, he'd an opinion. "Tha fought well, but sadly, tha also fought as one with too high a stake—and too much drink in the belly."

"What's it to you?" Will snarled.

"I'm... drawn to lost souls." A shrug of the grey-cloaked shoulders. "One might say it's my profession."

"Your what?"

"He's a bloody priest!" Arthur spat. "It ent enough that nobles can take up the god's horns, now Herself's letting their like in here?"

"The Church can lay no claim to me or mine." Saxon warmth went flat and cold. "Why else would I be here, but to witness the elder powers? Refute the Great Lie?"

The man was raving. Great Lie? Will started to speak, scoff.

Instead a bellow from the fire reclaimed everyone's attention. "Come now! Are there none who dare challenge?"

'Twere the champion in his bold greenman's mask, crowing like a bloody cockerel and brandishing his stave. The silence hanging from the trio seated in state upon the Maiden's stone trickled outward, damping the gathering's songs to whispers, shouts to murmurs. Bare and booted feet scraped and shifted. The fire became the only sound, still crackling high but hissing as, from the heavy clouds, droplets began to fall.

The champion smiled, broad and entitled. Cruel.

Will wanted to wipe it from his face and break the mask over his head.

O, Rob, better you be dead than see this...

"You're Scathelock, aren't you?"

This time they did draw daggers, whipping about toward the stranger.

Who merely cocked his head and continued, still a murmur, "And this fellow must be Arthur, the famed one-armed axeman." A tsk as the daggers inched closer. "The time of a Great Rite, and you would profane it with unconsecrated blood? My, but you have wandered far from the Hood's people."

"How do you know who—?" A sharp jab from Arthur stiffened Will's drink-supple tongue, twisted it in another direction. "What gives you t' rights, judgin' us?"

"I make no judgements. I merely observe. And you seem overly edgy for one no longer wolfshead. Or are you so again?"

"I'm freeman, so is he," Arthur growled. "We're respectable folk, makin' our way."

"And here to defend something dear to you. So, good fellow, am I." A bow, graceful. "It so happens I represent a cohort of, ah, *respectable* men, both common and otherwise."

Will rolled his eyes.

"It is our desire to return to older ways. To re-open paths many would prefer eradicated."

"Rad-ih..." Will shook his head, growled, "'Twere better when you were speaking the old Saxon."

"Well enough," the stranger answered, in that tongue. "Dost tha miss wild Robyn? There are rumours of his return—"

"Robyn's dead!" Arthur hissed. "Else he'd be here, protectin' what's his!"

*Find this and the rest of the series (paper, ebook, & audio)
at your favourite retailer & Forest Path Books
https://forestpathbooks.com*

~ ~ ~

*Stay informed on Forest Path Books' releases and news!
Join the newsletter group at:
https://forestpathbooks.com/into-the-forest/*

Interested readers can catch up on the

latest news and releases by joining

J Tullos Hennig's Reader Group at:

https://subscribe.jtulloshennig.net

and/or by visiting

https://www.jtulloshennig.net

You can even nab yourself a free story or two!

- About the Author -

J TULLOS HENNIG

has always possessed inveterate fascination in the myths and histories of other worlds and times. Despite having maintained a few professions in *this* world—equestrian, dancer, teacher, artist—she has never managed to not be a storyteller. Ever.

Given a heritage of forest-dwelling peoples—Choctaw, Chickasaw, and Scots-Irish—the decision to make a home base in NW Washington State with the Amazing Spouse was a no-brainer. They live alongside an equine 'pasture potato' on a retirement pension, a wolfhound who alternates between leaping over the sofa and snoozing on it, and a press gang of invisible 'friends' Who Will Not Be Silenced.

Active in conventions and genre literature in the 70s/80s/90s, Jeanine returned to the authorial fold with the publication of an award-winning series of historical fantasy novels She is a member of the Author's Guild, the Historical Novel Society, and SFWA. In 2018 she was presented with the Speculative Literature Foundation's juried Older Writers Grant.

Her historical series *The Books of the Wode* presents a truly innovative re-imagining of the Robin Hood legends, giving emphasis and reality to both pagan and queer perspectives.

http://www.jtulloshennig.net